Merehr

Merehr

Shytei Corellian

iUniverse, Inc.
New York Bloomington

iUniverse books may be ordered through booksellers or by contacting:

iUniverse
1663 Liberty Drive
Bloomington, IN 47403
www.iuniverse.com
1-800-Authors (1-800-288-4677)

Because of the dynamic nature of the Internet, any Web addresses or links contained in this book may have changed since publication and may no longer be valid. The views expressed in this work are solely those of the author and do not necessarily reflect the views of the publisher, and the publisher hereby disclaims any responsibility for them.

ISBN: 978-1-4401-8808-4 (sc)
ISBN: 978-1-4401-8810-7 (dj)
ISBN: 978-1-4401-8809-1 (ebook)

Printed in the United States of America

iUniverse rev. date:01/15/10

Dedicated to Wing and Nien. Your story is a remarkable one. Thank you.

"A human being is part of a whole, called by us the 'Universe,' a part limited in time and space. He experiences himself, his thoughts and feelings, as something separated from the rest—a kind of optical delusion of his consciousness. This delusion is a kind of prison for us, restricting us to our personal desires and to affection for a few persons nearest us. Our task must be to free ourselves from this prison by widening our circles of compassion to embrace all living creatures and the whole of nature in its beauty."
— Albert Einstein

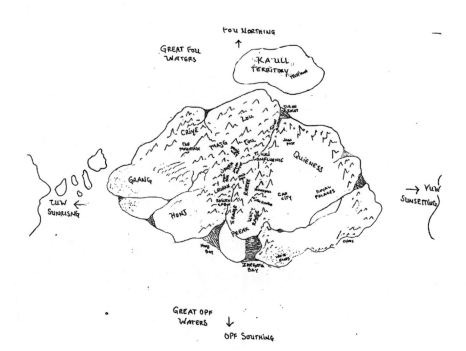

INTRODUCTION

Who He Was Before Me

With the gripping faith of a child, Rhegal looked up into his father's face and said, "I'll meet him someday, Fa."

Smoothing the rough edges of his doubt, G'dant felt the cool leather surface of the book beneath his fingertips and tried to sound optimistic as he said, "It is a nice thought."

"Do you wish you could see him? Meet him?"

"Yes, I guess I do."

Rhegal's eyes glinted in the firelight. "I've already imagined it. He comes up to me. I look up at him and I ask if he'll tell me everything."

G'dant swallowed reflexively. "Does he?"

Rhegal's small red eyebrows drew together. "Not yet. So far he just asks me my name."

"Well, that's a good start," G'dant said and went to set the book down. But Rhegal stopped him. "Read just a little more, all right? At least the next verse."

"One more and that's it. It's way past both our bedtimes."

Firelight from the room's wood stove burned brightly, casting lines of gold and orange across the pages of the book G'dant held in his hands.

Rhegal listened to his father read as a burning log split and cracked, sending tiny glowing sparks across the metal grating.

" 'He fled. Darker than night were the shapes and shadows that followed him. In cavernous trees he slept. There was death in his dreams. Before him, the void. Behind him, ruin. I saw a green valley mirrored in his mind. And then, nothing. When day came, I looked out across a foreign land and found him again. Though the passing of time was hidden from me, I knew in my heart that this was the Leader of Legend the prophets before me had spoken of.' "

1

Only a little over eight revolutions, Rhegal mouthed these words as his father read them. He knew them by heart—every Rieevan child did.

" 'And it seemed a sun was born in the heart of a cold star. And in his hands I saw a book and knew it contained the words I now write. Merehr would be that sun; he would be the blood of a new generation. I do not know if the length of my life will show me this, but into my long night has come a new hope.' "

"Do you believe it?" Rhegal asked.

Looking over the edge of the book, G'dant found Rhegal smiling up at him. His son's blue eyes shone from beneath his bright red bangs. As a father, G'dant did not often take notice of his son's atypical Rieevan features, but at this moment he did. Such unique attributes could only bring great trouble to a son born in Rieeve.

It was with an intermingling of adoration and worry that G'dant replied, "Perhaps you can teach your Fa a thing or two about faith. Now, off to bed with both of us."

CHAPTER 1

Wing and Nien

He had long black hair and eyes the colour of the sea. He was inter-twined with the land like the roots of a giant tree. Of its soil, he ate. Of its green, he breathed. He drank of the sky and jagged rise of majestic mountain. Ever-present in a world only he could see, his feeling was calm and centered, sourced from the core of the planet. This extra-sense helped him store up strength against the night, nights like this one, nights deep enough to pull him from the world of the living into a place no one could follow—

Except Nien.

Nien's skin was the colour of moonlight on black water. His hazel-brown eyes were flaked with gold. He matched his brother in height. He was kind. Not of a considered politeness, but kind of nature, kind of char-acter, a kind of character adored and admired. He challenged his adopted world and yet they could not help but want him near. And right now was the middle of the night, and his brother, Wing, had woken him.

From across the room, Wing's breath spoke a language without need of a tongue—with every clipped utterance Nien felt his fear, desperation, pain.

Nien slid out of bed. He stepped to Wing's bed just the other side of the room, just below the small window. Reaching out, he placed his hands upon Wing's shoulders and said his brother's name.

But Wing did not feel his brother's hands, nor did he hear him call his name for he was lost, carried, consumed by the night that twisted his mind, daring him to decipher which was real: the world of home and fam-ily or the one that held him bound.

He cried out: *Nien!*

But there was no answer.

3

He's here, Wing reassured himself. *He has to be. Nien would never leave me alone in this place—*

This place.

Where am I?

Hell. It was certainly hell. But it looked so much like home.

How could that be?

The cabin air around him was still, silent—an oppressive, heavy silence that carried the signature of demons.

Why can't I speak?

He was awake, but trapped—somewhere.

—Wait.

He knew where he was. He'd been here before.

The veil between what-was and what-might-be had been torn away and he lay naked between them.

Again.

In the deep silence of his brain he begged off what-might-be: *This isn't real. It hasn't happened yet. I can stop it.*

But the phantoms of what-might-be laughed and laid hold of him.

He writhed beneath their bony grip.

"Wing?"

Bright and beautiful, terrible and dark, Wing twisted inside the covers, the struggle layering his olive skin in a heavy sweat.

Behind the phantoms, light spun through a deluge of grey that blurred their malformed images into a maw of black.

Stop this, Wing begged. *Please…*

More painful than the black, a light brilliant as a sun flashed behind Wing's eyes. The light drove back the phantoms, but the heat left his flesh a smoking ruin.

He felt his life ebb.

So this is what it feels like to die…

A hand touched his arm.

Nien?

The flash of burning sun pushed up through Wing and coalesced into a pinpoint above him. Standing stark against a black deeper than the darkness of the room, Wing's eyes no sooner fixed upon the tiny glow-point than from it burst a single ray of blinding white. The white—knife-sharp and infinitely beautiful—raced a hole back through him.

Wing grabbed at his chest.

"Wing!"

Hands clamped down on his shoulders.

Wing thrashed and cried out. His cry stung the darkness and what-might-be collapsed into the present dragging the phantoms that tore at him through the closing gap.

From somewhere close, he heard, "Brother, I'm here."

That voice...

Wing blinked and opened his eyes to the world of the living. Bending over him, his brother's black, iridescent skin glimmered in the wash of incandescent moonlight coming in through their bedroom window.

The relief that flooded Wing was so intense he managed to mutter a withering "Nien," before consciousness fled. But this time as darkness came in to claim him, he felt Nien following him under, coming to stand between him and the Void.

Woven into a single braid, Wing's long black hair thumped against his back in a rhythmic pattern that matched the gait of his horse. Thankfully, morning had come and he, his brother Nien, and their father, Joash, were on their way into the Village.

Spinning retrograde, Wing watched as their planet's sun rose in the west, cresting over the rugged peaks of the Ti mountain range and mighty Llow Peak. The surface of the planet itself lay out in three massive continental plates and two great oceans. Rumour had it that some few ships sailed between these continents, but rare was it for any of their wayfarers to set foot beyond the sandy borders of the Len'ta Continent, for Len'ta was vastly non-negotiable for the ill-prepared, its mountain ranges so indomitable and lengthy that over the centuries its inner valleys had become ethnically, politically, and theologically distinguished.

In no valley was this condition more absolute than in the high mountain valley of Rieeve.

Small and perfect, teardrop-shaped as if fallen from a God grieved to have given it up, Rieeve glimmered like an emerald in its cradle between the Ti and Uki alpine ranges. Fields of waist-high grasses formed a lush green carpet that covered the valley from end to end.

Ahead, at the northingmost edge of the valley, Wing could see Melant, simply referred to as the Village. Beneath the watchful eye of one ancient castle lay carefully planned rows of older daub cottages and newer log homes, meticulously tended gardens and polished cobblestone streets all within which his people had formed a communal life of anchoritic isolation.

Wholly separate from their world, Wing regretted that his race had so long ago refused all outsiders. Effectively discouraged, even the independent tradesmen and caravans that once traveled through Rieeve no longer risked the route, for without rest and provisions the trek out of Rieeve over the Uki mountain range would prove disastrous for beast and man alike.

Astride the family's young silver mare, Wing's attention caught only fragments of the conversation between his brother and father. As the only family to live at the opposite end of the Valley, any work or social life among their people meant they had to make the trip into the Village, something they had down to a science—they knew exactly how long it took on foot, horseback, together or solo, through the tall grasses of Kive, shucks of Kojko, or snows of Ime.

With his eyes fixed upon the green blur of valley grass moving beneath his horse's feet, Wing shook his head and tried to escape the lingering ache in his chest. Last night had been the third time the vision had come to claim his life. At first, he'd longed to tell Nien about it for the demons that attended the vision seemed to be growing longer claws with each visit. But there never seemed to be a good time and so the days, turns, and seasons plodded on and just when the demon-claw lacerations had begun to heal the vision would come again, reopening and enlarging the tears until the resulting scar tissue had risen like a bulwark, shutting off Wing's sensitivity to it and finally even his longing to speak of it.

Beside Wing, Nien and Joash continued their conversation. "As affluent as Leeal-Branc purports to be," Joash was saying, "how much of her home is built with Mesko wood depends on the trees, not her social status."

"That's a good thing," Nien said.

"That's a very good thing," Joash agreed.

"So, no cutting this revolution?"

"No, there will be. There are three saplings with good chances."

Nien knew what that meant: One of the Ancients had to go.

"Do you know which one it will be?"

"Me'lont or I'ont. My next visit will tell me."

Nien nodded, a little disheartened. It was difficult to say goodbye to any of the Ancients, but the next generation of Mesko trees depended upon it, and as the Mesko Tender the sacred role of their preservation was up to his father.

Light skinned, dusty-haired, and hazel-eyed, Joash alone of the threesome carried the familiar genetic traits of their race.

"Don't fall asleep, son," he said to Wing.

With bright green eyes, Wing looked over at his father. "Just leave me be if I fall off," he replied tiredly.

"Sorry, can't. We've already got more than two men can do in the time we have left."

Wing offered a sigh of acknowledgement before glancing over his shoulder at Nien. "Meeting with Commander Lant this morning?"

"Yes. We've got in some new recruits. He'll probably want me to run them through drills."

Wing closed his eyes again.

As the three fell into a comfortable silence covered by the wind and the swish of their horses' tails through the tall grasses, Nien took a quick appraisal of his brother. Seeing Wing now—the very sight of him so comforting and real—he could almost forget how terrible and dark he had looked last night.

The memory of it made Nien shiver. He did not know what horrifying thing came to battle with Wing in those moments, but he could see the toll it was taking on him. Wing had never been one for much social contact, but in the past few revolutions he'd become even more reclusive than he'd been when they were young. Still more telling was the darkness Nien had noticed spinning behind Wing's eyes when he thought no one was looking.

But there could be a lot of reasons for that, Nien mused. *Not just a bad dream.*

Consumed with prophecy and anxious with fear, their people had singled Wing out as the answer-to and fulfillment-of the binding thread of their society.

Wing had been eleven revolutions old at the time.

Instinctively, and as it suited his nature just as well, Wing had gone into hiding. With the exception of the seasonal festivals, now, over twenty revolutions later, he went into the Village only at the behest of their father and sometimes for Carly.

Nien had once suggested to Wing that his distancing himself from their people only caused their curiosity to grow—

He now regretted having said as much, for the very sight of Wing in the Village aroused such an intense sense of the supernatural that even with his own moon-shadowed skin Nien had an easier time going unnoticed amongst an entire race of light-skinned people than Wing did.

Really, Nien thought, *I should have known. Nothing can be hidden or kept secret in Rieeve—except the truth.*

Looking up, Nien directed his gaze to the left and saw a familiar hut sitting at the edge of a large field, its tall grasses laid flat by Rieeve's small fighting force, the Cant, who used the area as their training ground.

"I'll see you two tonight," Nien said.

Wing opened his eyes again. "Good luck."

"And to you."

Nien was about to rein his horse aside, parting with Wing and Joash as he always did on the outskirts of the Village, when he noticed a large gathering of men coming towards them across the fields.

CHAPTER 2

Wing

On the outskirts of the Village the gathering of men neared the three men on horseback.

At the head of the gathering came Grek Occoju, the Spokesman of the Rieevan Council. The rest of the Council was with him as well as a surprising number of villagers.

What was going on? Nien wondered as the familiar surge of adrenaline he experienced during drills with the Cant set his limbs on fire. He caught his hand sliding toward the sword lashed to the saddle beneath his left knee and drew it back quickly, shocked at the inclination. The Council was annoying, persistent, but never violent.

The two parties stood face to face. It was Grek Occoju that spoke first.

"Father-Cawutt—Mesko Tender and honorary member of this Council," he said to Joash. "Sons Wing and Nien."

Joash, Wing, and Nien inclined their heads.

"We're lucky to have met you before you'd gotten into your day's work," Grek said.

Luck had nothing to do with it, Nien growled at them silently. *It's a point of Rieevan etiquette to know everything about us.*

"What is it, Gentlemen?" Joash asked.

"We came to talk to Wing," Grek said.

As if on cue, Joash's horse threw its head and snorted. "About what?"

"Lant has news."

Cant Commander, Lant, was also a member of the Rieevan Council and the only Rieevan that had any contact with the world outside of Rieeve's mountainous borders. As much as the Council resented, and for tens of revolutions had ignored Lant's extrinsic communications they, nevertheless, only had his word to confirm their worst fears: that a race from another continent had made an inroad upon their own; that this was the time the Ancient Writings had said would come.

"What is it?" Joash asked.

"Councilman Lant has received word that the northing Valley of Lou has fallen into the hands of the Ka'ull."

Every head in the group turned to Wing.

"What have you seen, Son-Cawutt?" one of the younger Council members near the front asked. "Will we be protected?"

Seen? Nien wondered. There were Wing's nightmares, but—

"Seen?" Wing asked.

"What have you been shown?" another Council member said.

There was a holding of the collective breath.

Aware that Joash was watching the throng of men, Nien kept his own eyes on Wing.

After an unendurable time, Wing said, "Nothing."

Nien had not thought it possible to experience a silence more awkward than that which already played between his family and the Council—

He was wrong.

"*Nothing?*" came the bewildered reply from one of the villagers.

"You need not hide your visions from us," Grek Occoju said carefully.

Wing looked at the Council Spokesman. "You would trust a vision I *might* have had over word from Lant?"

"We would," came the unequivocal answer.

"We know there may be trouble," Joash said, interceding. "That's why the Council approved the formation of the Cant."

Grek Occoju nodded. "Yes, but we all agree it will take more than that." Again, Grek's head turned to Wing. Again, the gathering drew into silence, waiting for Wing to speak.

It seemed to take a very long time for Wing to say: "Trust what Lant tells you."

Nien thought that would have been enough. There was in Wing's voice something of relief as well as sanction. But neither the Council nor the villagers could understand such nuances in his brother's tone—they took it as Wing rejecting them.

Again.

Through the crowd, a few voices broke here and there. From behind Grek, one yelled: "Why won't *you* tell us? Are we not worthy of it? Are you testing us? *Humiliating* us?"

The pulse of tension from the large crowd had the Cawutt horses nervous; Wing, Nien, and Joash had to work very hard to keep their mounts in check.

"Please tell us," one of the villagers said.

"There is nothing to tell," Wing replied. "Listen to Lant."

A new rumbling began to seethe through the gathering.

The heat in Nien's blood burned in the back of his eyes. He almost reached for his sword again. Was Joash not such a confident figure, Nien would have thrust himself between the throng of men and Wing.

From the back, a villager shouted: "You would rather have the Ka'ull take Rieeve, too? See our people die at their hands?"

There was a brief moment of shock, and then everything unraveled. Five men turned on the one who had shouted. Others pressed in to back the livid, frightened villager. Someone was shoved, a punch was thrown. The gathering heaved, pushing up against the Council members at the front. Grek raised a hand, but the gesture went ignored. Something flew in Wing and Joash's direction. Wing's mount reared. Blood appeared on Wing's face.

Someone shouted: "You've drawn Merehr's blood!"

Startled stares and still angrier cries followed.

We've got to get Wing out of here, Nien thought, trying to maneuver his horse around Joash to get to him, but the space between them and the gathering was too close, someone was going to get hurt...

Wing's horse snorted and swung her butt around. A villager reached for her bridle and she snapped her heels. There was a loud crack! and a cry. The villager fell back into the crowd, holding an arm. Wing's white shirt flashed crimson. Red appeared on the shoulder of the mare.

And then Joash did exactly what Nien had wanted to: yanking the head of his horse about and unhooking his toe from the stirrup, he thrust out with his foot and kicked Wing's horse in the flank.

The mare went wild. Pivoting on her heels, she nearly dismounted Wing before he reined her in—

But the containment was short lived.

She bolted and, this time, Nien was grateful to see that Wing was with her, leaning into her neck, his body long across her back, letting her carry him as far away as she would.

As Joash and Nien had hoped, the sight of Wing being raced off by his spooked horse punched a hole in the climaxing desperation of the crowd. One by one, the heated gathering drew into silence as Wing vanished into the endless length of fields before them.

Embarrassment rose uncomfortably hot; however, Nien noticed something far worse from the crowd—despair. A despair that seemed to set itself into the earth beneath them like the living roots of a pestilential ecosystem.

In the Ancient Writings were endless references to Merehr, but Nien knew there was only one on everyone's minds just now: "He that draws Merehr's blood shall unseal the gates of destruction."

Without words, the villagers collected themselves. More had been hurt than Nien had suspected. Some helped the villager with the arm broken from the kick delivered by Wing's mare. Others were holding hands to their faces and heads, or cradling broken knuckles and wrists from punches blocked or thrown.

There was a look from Grek Occoju to Joash, a lingering pause, and then Grek turned, motioned the gathering to disperse, and in a strange collection of moments Joash and Nien were left alone at the edge of the Village.

"I should go find Wing," Nien said. "It looked like he got hurt."

Joash shook his head. "Give him some time, son. Reean is at the house. We'll see him tonight."

"I hate this," Nien said.

Joash's voice was deep and heavy as he replied, "Me, too."

Together, Nien and Joash gathered up all the gear and tools that had been thrown from their horses during the scuffle.

Resecuring straps and saddlebags, as they mounted up and parted once again, Nien felt that something terrible had just happened—far beyond broken arms and bruised knuckles.

An ache followed his eyes into the distant fields.

A few times over their lives together, Nien had glimpsed, even experienced Wing's world. It was impossibly beautiful—it was also absolutely terrifying. Last night had been a dose of the terrifying....

And now, this morning.

I can hardly bear the weight of my own expectations, Nien thought. *How does he bear those of our entire people?*

Wing slid from his horse's back and fell into the dirt.

His mount had not stopped until reaching their family's fields at the far end of the valley.

As the winded mare stood by, Wing bowed and pushed his face into the dirt. A shuddering breath shook him, he inhaled the soil, coughed, breathed again.

Long beats passed.

He sat back. The dirt where he'd buried his face was stained with his blood.

The blood had come from being knocked in the face by the mare when she'd thrown her head. He wasn't sure if it had happened during the first scuffle or when Joash had kicked her in the flank, either way, he had not been able to staunch the flow. The white sleeve of his shirt was scarlet and the smell of it obviously unsettling to the mare.

Rubbing dirt over his mouth and chin and sleeve, he coughed, spit out the blood running down his throat from the back of his nose, and once again pressed his shirtsleeve to his face.

Finally, the blood began to ebb. Pain radiated between his eyes and he gingerly touched his nose.

When he finally climbed back to his feet, the crisp, cold cut of Kive air soothed the heat in his chest. About his feet the tall lengths of grass waved, caressing his boots with a fondness perhaps only he would have noticed. He inhaled deeply and raised his face to the sun.

The sky at this early time of revolution was clean, clear, almost translucent—a vastness of pale lavender fading to a silvery-blue on the horizon. In the air was the scent of fresh black soil, herbs, and young green plants.

As the revolution drew on the sky would grow deeper and richer into the season of Kojko. This second season saw the savory hues of sky and earth and the crunch of ripe challak leaves. By its end the sky dripped with colour so heavy it looked as if the sun had melted.

Wing could taste Kojko sunsets in his mouth.

And then there were the high deep nights of snowy Ime, when beneath the glistening sheen of stars the fields would glow, transporting Wing to times and places far beyond their glittery bent.

But no matter the season, there was always a preternatural calm that accompanied him in the fields, soothing away clamouring emotions and unsolvable thoughts.

Here, in the fields, he could let himself go, let himself be, without strain, without regret. At peace.

Bending down, he pushed his hand into a recently plowed furrow, turned it beneath the surface, and brought the dirt up slowly. Lowering his head, he sniffed. Normally, in scent and flavour, the soil spoke to him. There were the higher notes: footprints of animals or birds that had landed or nestled there. Deeper, he could find the story of the soil itself, the health of its mineral content, its strength for the next season of growing. Beneath that, he'd always been able to feel the heartbeat of the land, its slow, patient history. He listened to the valley as his father listened to the great trees in the Mesko forest.

But today, he only smelled blood. It seemed apropos.

Brushing the dirt from his hand, his thoughts passed to his father. As peculiar as Wing was as a Rieevan, a love of the land, of planting and harvesting and tending, was one thing he'd inherited in blood from Joash.

The two of them loved their time in the fields, but as the fever over Wing had continued to grow in the Village, Joash had taken up the majority of the construction projects and Wing had assumed primary responsibility for the crop.

Wing felt bad for this, and he knew Nien felt even worse.

Since the origination of the Cant, Nien had been torn between his duties there and the help the family needed. And there was something else brewing with Nien that Wing sensed but hadn't yet asked about.

Nien, Wing thought. *He saved me again last night. Were it not for the prophecy, perhaps the people could see Nien truly and see me for what I am—someone more lost and confused than any of them.*

Wing glanced over at the mare as she raised her head and looked at him.

"Curious?" Wing asked.

The horse looked back at him with large, familiar eyes.

"This section is ready," Wing said. He didn't need to be able to smell the soil today—he'd been in the fields every spare minute since the snows had begun to melt. "It's had a good rest. Here, we'll plant teeana this revolution." The horse put her head down to graze some more, but Wing cut her off. "That's it, etribias," he said, using a byname commonly used with house pets. "Let's get you back to the barn."

Wing led the mare across the fields back to the house where he cleaned up both of them with water from the trough.

Haltering the plow team, he led them out of the barn and headed back to the fields. All the land to the south-sunrise of the house and barn comprised their family's fields. It was a grand and beautiful stretch.

The team followed Wing to the farthest edge where he took up the reins and guided them around to what would be their starting point for their unplanned day, but no sooner had he done so than a fingerless touch pricked his back between his shoulder blades.

"You, too?" he muttered under his breath. "As if there hasn't been enough for one day." It was not the first time he'd experienced such a sensation while in the fields, as if someone were watching him.

He snuck a quick glance up at the sunrising tree line. With keen eyes, he searched the shadows, boring into the black beyond the valley's tree-lined edge.

In front of him, one of the team snorted and shook his head at a pestering fly, interrupting Wing's visual pursuit.

Gratefully, he let it go. Searching the dark was pointless, anyway. He'd tried before.

Adjusting his long fingers around the worn leather-wrapped handles, fitted perfectly by sweat and countless sunsteps to his grip, Wing flicked the reins and the team started out.

As the plow settled in, Wing could not help but wonder at all the subtle workings of plants, trees, and people.

So many currents, he thought, *flowing into and out of that world above and beneath our feet; so much happening just beyond our senses. What is the length of their reach? What powerful sway do they have over all that might be?*

Can they, he wondered, *help me know what to do before this all goes too far?*

"Lou," he whispered to himself. "Lou has fallen. All those people..."

Wing stopped his thought there.

Beneath his hands the plow jerked ahead and the dirt turned over.

"Son? What happened?" Reean asked as Wing and Joash came in that night.

Bruising was developing over Wing's nose, reaching out toward his eyes.

"He didn't tell you?" Joash asked.

"I haven't seen him," she answered, glancing from husband to son.

"I went straight out to the fields," Wing said.

"The, uh, Council met us on the way into the Village today," Joash said. "And there's other news."

"What?"

Joash guided Reean to the far side of the kitchen near the sunsetting window where he explained what had happened that morning.

Wing continued into the room at the back that he shared with Nien and Jake, set his gear atop his bed, then returned to the large main room where he lay down upon the chaise lounge, throwing one arm up over his eyes.

Reean turned from talking with Joash and passed across the room to Wing's side. Wing moved his arm away from his face as she sat on the edge of the lounge. Reaching up, she steadied his jaw in her palm, examining his swollen nose and bruised chin. "Is your nose broken?" she asked.

Wing shook his head. "I don't think so."

"How did that happen?"

Wing shrugged. "Maybe when fa kicked Faintsly in the flank."

Reean touched it carefully. Wing winced. She pulled her hand away. "Well, if it is, there's not much we can do about it. I'm so sorry."

"It's not your fault, mother."

"You boys always say that, as if saying it somehow invalidates the fact that I'm your mother." Reean placed her hand upon his shoulder and stood. "Rest a bit. We'll eat as soon as Nien gets here."

Wing was about to close his eyes again when his baby sister came over to him and placing one hand upon his, patted his face with the other as if she were soothing a wounded bird.

"Come on up," Wing said, scooting back.

Fey crawled up next to him, curling into the circle of his arm. Closing his eyes, Wing let the familiar sounds of home and Fey's downy scent fill his senses.

"Does anyone know when Nien might grace us with his presence?" Reean asked, glancing over the preparations for the evening meal.

Without opening his eyes, Wing said, "He's been with the Cant all day. I believe Lant is having him run the men through drills."

CHAPTER 3

Nien

The sword came down heavily, the arms that wielded it, tired. Nien blocked the sword and knocked it out of his assailant's hands.

"Surrender!" Nien cried raising his sword over his head, hilt high, blade angled down toward the man's chest.

Greal'e looked up at him and his brow furrowed.

Nien began to laugh.

Greal'e rolled his eyes and crawled to his feet. "I'm thoroughly done," he moaned.

"Me, too," Nien agreed, letting the point of his sword slide into the soft earth at his feet. His black, blue-hued skin stood in stark contrast to the sea of white men surrounding him. It was not a point often noted by Nien, or anyone else, for Nien had grown up in Rieeve and was now, at thirty-one revolutions, a respected leader in the Cant.

Passing his eyes across the stretch of land before him, he took in the mock battlefield and the seven thousand-member fighting force that was the Cant. The Cant as an organization was only seven revolutions old and was the first military force Rieeve had known in over two hundred revolutions. Nien himself had been at the vanguard of the Cant's progression and was a personal friend of Cant Commander, Lant. It was rumored among the men that it would not be long before Lant would officially put him in charge of all the regular troops he now drilled.

"Down swords!" Nien called.

Over the Cantfield, swords were lowered, some of the Cant members collapsing tiredly to rest in the torn-up grass.

Nien was about to dismiss them for the day when he spotted the Commander coming across the fields.

"Leave your gear! To the Mound."

Quickly pulling off loose bits of armour or climbing back to their feet, the Cant began to gather, organizing itself by rank before a short green mound where the Cantfields met the valley's treelined edge.

Nien stepped into his place amongst the others.

Lant took the mound.

The Commander usually got right down to business...

Not this time.

Watching him curiously, Nien's eyes strayed to the sun's setting rays as they glistened across the silver strips of grey-white hair at the Commander's temples.

"Seven thousand of us," Lant said at last.

Though Nien could see a new gravity in Lant's eyes, his voice carried across the expanse of field in the same calm tone they all knew.

"The Cant is unparalleled in our time," Lant continued. "We have come far in the past revolutions. Your trust in each other and in me has made this possible."

Lant stood tall, ever a pillar of fortitude and strength, a giant Mesko in a mountain storm. Upon his face wrinkles of age followed lines of serious reflection and in his eyes glinted a wisdom who's origin remained as enigmatic as the man himself. Though very little about Lant's past was known, all anyone knew for certain was that he had done the unheard of: he had left Rieeve as a young man, most thought, never to return. As the majority of the Cant Members had not yet been born at the time, tales of his unprecedented departure were gathered in bits from those few who would actually speak of it. When, to the shock of all their people, Lant returned to Rieeve, he was virtually ostracized for nearly seven revolutions by everyone, the main exceptions to this being his own father and a young Joash Cawutt.

As time went on, however, the people had begun to acknowledge him, speak to him, and finally accept him again as one of them. Now, as he was Commander of the Cant and a member of the Council, the tales of Lant's early life seemed almost unimaginable to the young members of the Cant.

Looking up at Lant, Nien felt the direction of the Commander's address begin to shift.

"As I'm sure you've all heard by now, I have received news from Master Monteray of Legran—it is true, the Ka'ull have made an inroad of our continent. Last revolution, I received word from the Empress of Quieness that some of her merchant ships had gone missing. There were also the reports from Master Monteray of other sightings in the lochs, inlets, and boundaries of our northingmost valleys and waterways. The tempest was stirring. Now, it is here. The valley of Lou did not fall, it was taken."

There was movement amongst the Cant members. Even Nien was shocked. Lant had never spoken openly of Master Monteray, SiQQiy of Quieness, or of Ka'ull sightings in the Northing.

Once, Lant had told Nien that the truth could not be thrust into another's face like a knife. That was the reason, Nien figured, why Lant had never been so forward.

Until today.

"When you return to your homes tonight," Lant continued, "be steady and patient with your families. Some may be anxious or angry with worry. Many may never have heard of the valley of Lou until today. Let them know that their support of the Cant is the best thing they can do right now."

Lant passed his eyes over the large gathering of Cant members, his eyes finally coming to rest on Nien. Nien knew the look, it meant: Come to the hut.

Lant bowed his head once and left the mound.

Nien turned. "Well done, everyone. We'll see you next turn."

Returning back over the Cantfields, Nien located his gear amongst the piles of packs, swords, and various odd bits of thick leather armour the Cant members wore for mock-battle sessions. Anxious to meet with Lant, he dropped to a knee and quickly set to removing his armour.

Those nearest Nien nodded their respect as they gathered their gear and began to leave the field.

Removing his waist girth, Nien was struggling with a long boot lace when he felt a hand light upon his shoulder.

Glancing up, he said, "E'te, Carly. How'd it go?"

One of only three women who had joined the Cant since its inception, Carly was the classic Rieevan, her light hazel eyes always happy, her pretty, round face smiling—

Except for today.

She didn't answer his question, saying instead, "Well, that was new."

"E'te," Nien agreed. "Lant is full of surprises."

"How's Wing?"

"I don't *know* how he is. I came straight here after it happened." Nien realized his reply was a little sharper than he'd intended—he'd been worried about Wing all day, wondering if he'd been right to take Joash's advice to not ride out after him.

"Now that we're done here, maybe I should..." Carly started to say.

"I'm heading home after I check in with Lant. I can let you know tomorrow."

Reluctantly, Carly nodded. "Well, Wing and I were already planning on meeting up tomorrow. Guess I can wait…" she paused. "Ugh. We have the leadership meeting in the early afternoon, don't we?"

Nien nodded.

Carly shook her head in annoyance. "I haven't seen Wing for so long he's probably gotten married and made two babies."

"I doubt that. Other than you, women have about as much luck getting Wing to see things their way as the Council does." Nien's fingers paused in the removal of his leg armour as he glanced back across the valley toward the far side where he imagined his brother working in the fields. "I haven't seen Wing much either. He's setting in some new rows of teeana and fa's got him busy any spare time with the Vanc home." He sighed.

"What is it?" Carly asked.

"They're so busy; they could use my help. But I just can't. I can't spare the time from the Cant"—*especially now, with the news we received today,* he thought. "And I'm trying to work out the possibility of the school."

"What?" Carly asked.

"Nothing," Nien said quickly, thankful his last sentence had missed Carly's hearing. "Never mind."

"Listen," she said. "We're coming up on taking a few days off for the change of season. Who knows, Lant may disappear on one of his secret missions. You could take the time from extra Cant duties to help your father and Wing with the Vanc home—and so will I. I'm sure there's something I can do."

Nien chuckled. "I guess you got it all worked out." But a twinkle lit Carly's eye. "Uh oh," Nien said—he knew the look.

"I want to take one of those days to play."

"That's what the festivals are for." Nien hoped that would appease her.

"Too long till Kive fest. I want to do something soon."

Nien furrowed his brow at her in question. "Like what?"

"I want a day like we used to have when we were kids. Do some exploring. You know, something fun like" —she lowered her voice to a whisper— "watching Wing fall into a labyrinth of ancient caves."

Nien glanced around quickly and finding them to be alone allowed himself a short smile. "You count that as fun? No wonder you joined the Cant." He returned to his unlacing. "I didn't suspect we would ever try and go there again."

"Don't you miss the things we used to do? Bleekla, finding an unfamiliar insect was fun back then."

"We're adults now—having fun takes a lot of work." Nien pulled the last of the leather laces from one of his shin guards and got to his feet. "Perhaps Lant wouldn't be adverse to a little get-together at his house."

But as they looked at one another they both understood it was not a good idea—

"Wing," they said in unison.

"Well, we'll think of something," Nien said.

Carly removed the training guards from her sword and slid the muddied blade back into the leather sheath at her side. "Right now, I'm going to go get some sleep. I'll see you tomorrow."

"Tomorrow."

Carly walked away, her tawny hair thick and playful about her shoulders.

Nien shouldered his sheath and gear and started for the small hut that sat at the edge of the Cantfields.

"Nien, come on in."

Nien stepped through the thin fabric flap that served as the door to Commander Lant's hut. The Commander's large home was not far in the distance—the hut served as an immediate area for Cant meetings and administration.

"How did it go?" the Commander asked, his regal features and wise hazel eyes looking up at Nien.

"Fine. A little off, actually, though not bad, considering..."

"I apologize for not letting you know I'd wanted to speak with the Cant today, but I'd just come from an unscheduled Council meeting."

The two men exchanged a look.

"You might as well sit down," Lant said.

Nien sat down, watching the Commander whose eyes were focused not on the mess of parchment and Mesko paper covering his desk but upon the thoughts in his head.

"I'm sorry I was not there this morning," Lant finally said.

"I don't know what you could have done," Nien replied.

"I may be on the Council, but they still do not tell me everything."

"I understand. When did you hear about Lou?"

"A couple turns ago. Master Monteray came himself. He stayed only a night. He'd already sent a messenger downriver through Preak and on to Quieness and Empress SiQQiy." There was a heavy weight to Lant's pause before he said, "It's only going to get worse."

"What do you mean?" Nien asked guardedly. It suddenly felt as if the bottom was falling out of their world.

"For Wing—now that the people know Lou has been taken."

"He doesn't talk about it, but I know what it's doing to him. I don't know how much more he can take."

"I considered, Nien, not telling the Council. But I have coddled them too long."

"For us," Nien said quietly.

Though Nien knew it was true, Lant said, "Not only for you. At first we needed to take it slowly with the Council and with the people. This last news from Master Monteray, however, has pushed us past that point." Nien could tell it pained Lant to say his next words. "Should I try talking with Wing again? If he were in the Cant it might at least give him, and your family, a reprieve. And give us leverage with the Council."

Nien appreciated Lant's impossible situation. The Commander was walking very fine lines, his loyalties, his devotion tested on all sides as he was forced to balance his love for Nien and Wing in the midst of the Council's constant needling regarding them. And then there was his tenuous position of being on the Council and yet Commander of the Cant.

"He won't," Nien said, referring to Wing. "Beleaguering him will only drive him further away."

Continually failing with Wing directly, the Rieevan Council's latest efforts were focused on pressuring Lant, hoping the Commander could persuade Wing to join the Cant on the premise that the Leader spoken of in the Ancient Writings was a man of strength not just spiritually, but physically.

Merehr would be a deliverer and Wing looked the part, if only they could convince his mind.

"How long do we keep obliging them?" Nien said. "Are they immune to their own hypocrisy? For generations the Council was set against a military force of any kind—because of the ancient prophesies. And now they want the one they perceive as the fulfillment of those prophesies to *join* the Cant?" Nien drew an exasperated breath. "I know Wing's silence on the matter hasn't helped. I know it's given the people license to impose their will and I doubt he's ignorant of that fact. Nevertheless, and no matter how much they think they care, they are not his family."

"It's been well over twenty revolutions since Rhegal disappeared."

Nien clenched his jaw in frustration. "It shouldn't be about how long it's been. It shouldn't be that if Merehr has not come, has not revealed himself by a certain time, that the people take it upon themselves to choose him."

Lant nodded empathetically. "I understand your frustration, my friend, and so much the worse when the object of the people's desires is your own brother." Lant paused. "This is not easy for any of us, and selfishly, I feel it has challenged my friendship with Wing."

Nien could see that Lant resented having his friendship with Wing held hostage by the Council. "Wing loves and respects you; he always has."

With a brief sigh—whether of acceptance or resignation Nien could not tell—Lant said, "I won't call for him again."

Nien met the Commander's eyes. "Thank you. And the Council?"

"They will do what they will do."

Nien swallowed. He was afraid of that.

As the two men sat in a brief, encumbered silence, another rap came upon the hut door.

"Fa?"

"Pree K. Come in."

Nien turned back to see the Cant's Premier Messenger duck in through the hut flap. In his twenty third revolution, thin and wiry of body with light brown hair bleached blond by the sun, Pree K was Lant's adopted son. His position as Premier Messenger had nothing to do with his father being the Commander but rather a set of remarkable gifts all his own: exact memory and legs seemingly able to ride the wind. His gifts were all but wasted in Rieeve, however, other than those rare times Lant asked him to deliver a message to Nien's family at the far end of the valley.

Like Nien, Pree K was not Rieevan but had been raised as one of them. Most figured it was because of Pree K that Lant had returned to Rieeve after his long absence. The Commander's only explanation was that the child had been abandoned in a foreign valley.

"Nien. Fa," Pree K said in greeting, but upon taking in the severe mood in the hut said to Lant, "I, uh, can see you back at the house."

"No, it's all right. There's been enough talking for one day." Lant shoved the paper and parchment on his desk into a slightly more organized clump and the three walked out into the twilight.

"I'll see you tomorrow?" Lant said to Nien.

"Yes. I'll be in before the meeting with the other Leaders."

"Good. Night then."

"Night."

Nien watched the Commander and Pree K walk off together—

His mind turned to his own family. To Wing.

Shouldering his gear, he headed to retrieve his horse. The trip home now would not be a quick one as it was too dangerous to run the horse in the dark. That meant he'd have lots of time to do the last thing he wanted to do: think.

CHAPTER 4
The Caves

The creak of the short-rimmed saddle helped ease some of the agitation from Nien's shoulders as he rode towards home, the setting sun reflecting splashes of colour across his eyes.

Watching the clouds, Nien's thoughts turned to the one place he would rather have kept them from: "Merehr." He said the word in a whisper, as if he were afraid to say it aloud.

Shaking his head, he tried to escape the encompassing gloom the subject invariably brought—

The attempt lasted mere moments.

Growing up there had been long seasons of reprieve where the people left Wing and their family alone, but those reprieves had grown shorter and shorter.

He and Wing had been children when the people thought they'd found the Leader in a man by the name of Rhegal. But this man disappeared one day as another had before him. So, the search began anew to find the Leader they were certain was to be born among them, as a Rieevan.

Wing had only been a youth at the time, but even then he seemed to fit the words of the prophecies precisely: " 'Of good height, great spirit and blessed colouring. He will be like no other...' "

Raising his face into the night sky, Nien drew a deep breath. Leer's First Moon had appeared over the Uki. At full, Second Moon was merely a gentle blue glow in the great distance—which was about the only time it could be seen at all.

Nien studied First Moon for a moment, remembering the conversation he'd had with Carly upon leaving the training fields. She wanted to spend some time together as they once had, just the three of them. He couldn't blame her, he missed those times as well, before everything had gotten all complicated, when every day was an adventure and trouble meant they'd forgotten to lock the barn door.

Nien closed his eyes and faded back over the revolutions. Their little three-member gang had been on many small journeys together, not the least significant being the last one.

In his mind, Nien retraced the memory to a place high on the northing edge of the Mesko forest and a very steep ledge...

"Wait, Nien. Hold on a moment."

Nien looked back at his brother. "What is it?" he asked, his voice tense. He didn't like pausing for a chat on this rocky ledge.

"Did you hear that?" Wing said.

"Hear what?" Carly asked, her eyes widening.

"Shh, listen."

They listened, not one of them hearing anything louder than the pounding of their own hearts. And then, as if in answer to some unspoken cue, the three of them looked up at once. On an outcropping of rock above them crouched a large cat. The black depth of its coat stood in stark contrast to the red rock and green foliage of the mountain behind it. The curve and line of powerful muscles could clearly be seen beneath the glossy coat. And from beneath its upper lip peeked two sharp points of white.

A shy'teh.

With jaws dropping slowly and fists tightening around thin branches of scraggly brush, the threesome gazed up at it—and the shy'teh gazed right back at them. Its eyes were bright, a brilliant green, and they shone as if lit from somewhere inside its large head.

For over two hundred revolutions the legend of the shy'teh had been told to Rieevan children. It was the only story outside of those in the Ancient Writings the adults weren't entirely averse to imparting. The story went that a small number of their people had gone into the mountains to seek refuge. Why they'd done so was a part of the legend so varied and confused that no one really seemed to know the truth of it, but once in the mountains the refugees had become lost in a perilous network of caves they'd entered in hopes of finding protection. In the end, they had survived only by the guidance and sustenance of a female shy'teh who not only led them out of the caves, but also sustained them with the kills she had made for herself and a single cub. Being so young, the cub perished from starvation. Reverence for this sacrifice had grown into a commonly held belief that the spirit of that cub lived on, never dying, forever choosing a single living shy'teh for its mortal abode.

But as it is with legends how much of it was true could never be known, and at this moment Nien and Carly could not have cared either way—they just wanted off the ledge and away from the big cat.

Lips parted, Nien and Carly breathed shallowly, watching in awe and horror as the cat narrowed its eyes, drew in the huge muscles between its shoulders, extended its claws from within the furry black of its paws, and pressed its ears flat against its head.

"Don't move," Nien said, his voice faint.

"Trust me, I'm not," Carly whispered back.

Described as a solitary and timid creature, that it was behaving as if cornered rather than moving to extricate itself from the situation was life-threateningly alarming.

And then Wing said, "Look away."

Startled and confused by Wing's tone and direction, Nien and Carly nevertheless lowered heads. With their eyes glued to the path beneath their feet, they waited, aching to see what Wing was doing.

The moments passed interminably long before Nien snuck a glance.

Wing hadn't moved. In fact, he was perfectly still until Nien noticed him slowly raise his eyes. Heart pounding in the nervous reaches of his throat, Nien watched as the cat's eyes shifted to meet Wing's.

Emerald eyes met emerald eyes.

Though he was unsure how, Nien knew that Wing and the shy'teh were conversing. Wonder mingled with the dread in his belly. He was about to divert his gaze again when the shy'teh's narrowed eyes rounded, its ears came forward, and its lips slid down over its silvery-white fangs.

Yeckthe'tey, Nien thought. *Alright, Wing, just hurry it along. You may be fine, but I feel like me and Carly are about to become dinner.*

"Go ahead," Wing said.

Startled as much at Wing's having read his mind as their predicament, Nien said, "Just uh, let us by then."

Wing had already taken a step forward, his eyes never leaving the shy'teh.

"Are you sure…?"

"Yes," Wing replied.

For Nien and Carly many sunsteps could have passed by the time they reached the other end of the rock-strewn ridge.

Upon more sure-footed ground, they stopped and glanced back at the short outcropping of rock.

It was empty.

With a chill coursing up his back, Nien shook his body, throwing off nervous energy like an animal would water from its coat. "Bleekla, that was so close."

Wing moved up the path and joined them as if nothing unusual had happened.

"That was…" Carly started to say. "That was unbelievable."

Which part? Nien wondered.

Wing glanced at him.

"Do you know how few Rieevans have ever seen a shy'teh?" Carly said excitedly, unaware of Wing and Nien's silent communication. "I'll wager no one, except for maybe Lant, and if he has he'd never talk about it anyway."

"I'm just glad we're alive," Nien said, and then with mock airs looked Wing and Carly over as if they were half his age. "It's pretty risky bringing you two up here. If either of you got killed, I'd never hear the end of it."

Carly threw him a castigating look.

Wing laughed. "Convenient that you're forgetting the time we brought Jake along…"

Nien pointed at himself. "Was that me?"

Wing's lips curled into a half grin.

Nien shook his head and started to walk away. "That was only once, and I must have been possessed."

Playfully aghast, Carly said, "If the Village only knew."

"No one in the Village knows," Nien said. "Not about that. Not about all the times we've been up here."

Wing grunted. "They'll find out eventually."

"You two live so far out, word would never make it into the Village," Carly said. "And my parents couldn't care less what I do."

"If you went back with a broken leg or a limb half torn away by a shy'teh, they'd care," Nien quipped.

The idea of such a thing happening to Carly clearly discomforted Wing, but Carly merely shrugged. "Either way, it's kind of a sign, don't you think?"

The three exchanged long glances—neither Wing nor Nien replied.

"Well, come on," Nien said, needing to break the looming silence. "You lead, Weed Farmer."

"I thought you were the leader here, Deviant; Carly and I the liabilities."

"Just go," Nien replied.

Carly rolled her eyes at their pet names as Wing took the lead only to have the ground beneath him simply disappear and he along with it.

"Wing!" Nien and Carly cried in unison.

Nien rushed ahead and dropped to his knees. He could see through the ground layer of dried leaves and fallen branches a small opening that had been entirely invisible a moment before.

"Wing!" Nien called down into the hole. "Wing, can you hear me?"

Silence answered. Nien could almost feel the wild hammering of Carly's heart behind him.

And then, from the black depth of the hole— "Ouch."

Nien gasped with relief. "Wing! Are you hurt?"

"No, but wow—it's dark in here. I can't even see my hand."

On her hands and knees behind Nien, Carly asked, "Is he hurt?"

"He's there. He says he's not hurt."

"About how far down do you think he is?"

"He doesn't sound too far away," Nien said, staring down into the blackness of the opening. "Wing, are you stuck?"

"No."

"Can you feel the sides of the hole?"

"Yes."

"Good, just stay put. We're going to clear away some debris and see if we can open up the entrance here."

Nien and Carly worked quickly to clear away the dirt, rock, branches, and reaching-vine.

Though a bit bony and not yet his full height, Wing was already tall, his shoulders broad—that he had slipped by so rapidly told them the hole was bigger than what they could see. By the time they'd dug away all the debris the hole was nearly four steps across. As the light shone down into the pit, Nien and Carly peered into the blackness, feeling the coolness of the mountain's interior waving up into their faces and glimpsing the whites of Wing's eyes smiling back at them.

"Hello," Wing said.

Nien threw him a nod. "Let's get you out of there."

"Great," Wing replied, and then, "E'te—wait."

"Wing?"

"Hold on," Wing called back up.

Carly and Nien watched as Wing disappeared from their view, apparently walking into the mountain and out of the spot of sunlight at the bottom of the hole. Nien and Carly exchanged a look: What was Wing doing—or more importantly, how?

"Wing? Wing! What's he doing?" Carly asked.

No reply.

Nien sighed, but a moment later Wing reappeared at the bottom of the hole.

"You're not going to believe this," he said, "but this pit has another opening."

"Well," Nien said, "here goes nothing."

"What?"

"I'm going down."

"So that I'll have two men to rescue?" Carly said.

"Nah, I'll use these vines."

"Vines?"

"They're sturdy enough," Nien said, thinking, *I hope.*

"Wing? I'm coming down."

"What?"

"Catch me if I fall, right?"

Wing backed away. "Not a chance."

Testing a handful of vine with a quick jerk and a short lean, Nien headed over the edge. Walking his way down into the dark with his feet against the dirt wall, he descended until he felt Wing's hands on his legs. "Are you reaching?"

"Yes," Wing replied. "Your butt's just above my head."

Good, Nien thought—he had just over six steps to drop. Releasing the vines, he landed on his hands and feet next to Wing.

Wing helped him up, flashing a smile. "Welcome."

Nien smiled back at him.

Carly looked down over the ledge.

"Come on down," Nien called. Above him he saw Carly turn around, yank on another handful of vines, and mutter, "This is crazy," as she started down.

Wing took her in his arms at the bottom, setting her feet to the floor of the pit.

Together, the three of them turned into the mountain and the black hole that yawned before them.

"We need a torch of some sort," Nien said.

"I swear, we're allergic to making any intelligent decisions around here," Cary sighed beside him.

Nevertheless, Wing disappeared again into the hole. "This isn't dirt," he called back at them.

Nien squinted after him. "What isn't dirt?"

"The walls in here." The pause that followed felt long and ominous. "It's rock."

Rock.

"The Shy'tehn Caves," Nien and Carly said together.

Nien dove into the dark after Wing. Not far along, he ran into Wing's back. Wing felt for his hand and, taking it, pressed it to the wall beside them. "Feel, here," Wing said. Nien let Wing guide his hand over a set of worn indentations.

"Think there might be a pattern in it?" Nien asked.

"I wondered," Wing said. "Not that it matters, in this darkness it'd be impossible to make out the vaguest outline." He was silent a beat. "E'te, I'm sufficiently spooked. Let's try and get out of here."

But Nien moved past him, saying, "I know, but hold on, I wonder what's—"

"Around that corner?" Wing said. "More darkness. My curiosity faded with the light."

"Did you notice the walls in here? They're getting colder. Wet, too."

"I noticed," Wing replied.

Nien went on a bit farther, practically able to feel Wing's nervousness behind him.

He's thinking my "insatiable" curiosity will keep us down in these caves all night, probably getting us lost or killed, Nien thought; nevertheless, he continued to probe into the darkness ahead mentally and visually, as if by sheer force of will he could illuminate what lay ahead.

Finally, he spoke to Wing from the deep, "Well, we need light, and it's getting late. Soon we'll be losing sunlight topside." He heard an audible sigh of relief from Wing.

Feeling for the wall beside him, he was about to turn about when he thought he saw a faint gleam of light.

"Uh, e'te, Wing!" he called back down the tunnel.

Behind him, he heard Wing start toward him slowly, feeling his way along the wall.

"I'm right here," Nien said. Wing came up beside him. "Do you see what I think I'm seeing?"

Taking a few more steps together, the pale gleam focused into a slender stream of light shining through at an angle toward the ground level of another tunnel.

In a few fortuitous moments the brothers had emerged into daylight.

"Carly!" Nien called. "Carly, we're up here."

Carly appeared at the bottom of the hole Wing had fallen into and looked up.

Kneeling at the top, Wing and Nien smiled down at her.

"We found an easier way." Nien held his hand up. "Wait, we'll come back for you."

Up a little from the cave-in where Wing had fallen and almost entirely hidden from the outside was an entrance between two thin, jagged outcroppings of rock. The slit between the outcroppings seemed innocuous enough at first glance, but just beneath the surface the break opened wide to the path that Wing and Nien had followed out, a path that rose easily to the break in the rocks from the larger tunnel below.

Squeezing through the fissure, Wing and Nien made their way back down the path and into the tunnel, appearing out of the darkness and into the light at the bottom of the hole where Carly waited.

"E'te," Nien said. "You'll like this way better."

The three returned together and crawled one by one through the break in the rocks into the fading light of day.

"Well, that was easier," Carly said with a grin.

The threesome hiked quickly off the mountain. The sun had long set by the time they crept from the tree line, entering the valley just southing of the Cantfields.

Kissing Wing, Carly said goodbye to Nien and Wing and headed for her home in the Village.

Continuing off across the fields, Nien said, "E'te, that was *something*."

The fields stretched out before the brothers beneath a brilliant blanket of stars. Wing walked along in silence.

"Well?" Nien prodded. "What do you think?"

"Think?" Wing asked.

"The caves."

Wing glanced up at the sky. "I don't know what to think."

"You must be thinking something."

Wing breathed deeply, enjoying the clean air, the cool edge of night. "Probably the same thing you are."

Obviously, Wing wasn't going to help him delve into the mystery.

"Well, whether they're the shy'tehn caves or not, I wonder if the legend is the real reason our people don't venture into the mountains?" A familiar anger tightened Nien's gut. "I'm tired of the excuses, Wing, for why our people won't travel, won't visit other valleys, or welcome outsiders. Do you think they really believe exclusion is the only way to keep our way of life consistent with the Ancient Writings?"

"I think some believe that, yes. Others—I have my doubts."

"Really?" Nien asked, curious.

"I think even the most devout villager has doubts. But once out of the ground love and fear get all tangled up, and so a choice once made in fear easily wears the face of love. The purest minds can conjure such rationalization."

"The lie is purity, the truth is we're afraid of having our beliefs challenged."

"Or losing them altogether," Wing replied quietly.

Nien ground his teeth. He wanted to claw out, scream, fight! Break
through the lies, hold them up to their people so they could see and
change their minds—change their minds about everything—about learning, about influence, about travel, about acceptance, about...

He clamped down on the thought; every time he went there it drove
him mad. No one could be made to see, and that meant there was no way
to change anything. No way out.

As they continued to walk, he wondered if Wing struggled as he did.

"In some ways more," Wing said. "In others less." Nien stopped. Wing
looked back. "—What?"

"You heard that?"

Wing's brow furrowed quizzically. "You were wondering how hard this
is on me."

"That's what I was *thinking*."

"Oh."

Nien shook his head, incredulous.

Wing shrugged. "—Well?"

Before replying, Nien monitored Wing out of the corner of his eye as he
thought, *You can be really creepy.*

This time Wing laughed.

"Just checking," Nien said.

As they began walking again, Nien found that Wing's trip into his mind
had lightened his mood. They'd been able to do it with each other a lot
as children, but like so many other things, it seemed they'd grown out of
it. Nien was pleased to see it was still possible, it made him believe that
as long as they were together, anything was possible. As long as there was
Wing, he wouldn't go crazy, wouldn't despair from having no one who
understood.

"For being so repressed," Nien said with a wink in his zealous tone, "we
still managed quite a day. Saw a shy'teh. Fell, literally, into a labyrinth of
caves—"

"*I* fell," Wing corrected. "You came down nice and gentle like on your
vine-rope."

"*You* fell, and though I would have taken it for you, I'm glad one of us
did. What a discovery! Not exactly your average Rieevan day. Too bad we
can't tell anyone."

Wing remained silent beside him and this time Nien knew what *Wing*
was thinking. "You've no appetite for it, anyway," he said.

Chagrined over not wanting to disappoint Nien, Wing admitted, "I really don't."

"However," Nien couldn't help snorting with a small dose of self-satisfaction, "you seemed curious enough once Carly and I shed a little light into that hole of yours."

Wing rolled his eyes. "Just don't get the idea that you have to push me into impossible situations before I'll generate a pulse of interest."

"Because that would be true."

Wing had never shared Nien's fierce sense of adventure. As a youth, Wing had been more willing to accommodate Nien in all of his exploits. But they were getting older, and Nien was aware that Wing's company on such excursions was coming to an end.

"So—you and Carly?" Nien asked, changing the subject.

"Yes?"

Nien smiled at him.

"What?"

"Are you *ever* going to make anything official? Or do you just think you're so grand she'll never look at another man?"

Wing guffawed. "There is that, but between my work and hers, nothing official seems likely anytime soon."

"I suppose a baby might affect Carly's sword play."

The brothers smiled at the image of Carly, pregnant, out on the Cantfield pounding another Cant member into submission.

"Not that we mind the practice," Wing said, "but I think a house might be nice first."

"Do you think Fa would give you the southing fields for that?"

"Possibly, though he may not know that a fair bit of ground's already been cleared in that area."

Nien snorted.

"Kojko furrows are the nicest, the rows of dirt are warm, soft, and curved just right."

Nien shook his head.

"As for a home?" Wing added. "I'm sure it'd be great for that, too."

"I thought we were talking about sword practice."

"You might have been."

Nien slapped Wing on the back and the two walked on, enjoying the night as they made their way toward the bright orange glow of the lantern shining through the back window of their home.

Opening his eyes, Nien returned to the present. The scene that lay before him now was the same as it had been that night over seven revolutions past when he and Wing had returned from their accidental discovery of the caves. Back then there had been a glimmer in Wing's eyes, evidence of the tenderness and courage that so often accompany the innocent and naïve. But so much had happened since that time, not the least being their people's interest in Wing which had intensified two-fold, that the glimmer had slowly faded and now Wing's eye contact was seldom with almost everyone. Only in rare moments could there be seen a flash of something intense and real, sometimes beautiful, sometimes filled with an unmistakable yet indescribable pain.

Nien's eyes fixed upon the sweet image of his home, luminous in the deep dark of the southing end of the valley, the only light against mountain and sky. Through the small window on the lower level glowed the light from the kitchen lantern, the one by which Joash and Wing read the Ancient Writings, Jake and Fey played, and Reean knitted. Its flickering flame shining out across the star-lit fields had always guided not only the way of his footsteps but of his heart as well.

Looking ahead, Nien saw that he was coming up on the large cleared area of grass leading up to the house.

"Let's go," Nien said, and kicking his heels into his mount, closed the distance between himself and home.

CHAPTER 5

It's About Home

The Cawutt home was a grand structure of Mesko wood. Two storied and beautiful, Joash had started to build it for himself, completing it not long after marrying Reean. The back of the home faced the long empty distance toward the Village. On the lower level it had one door that might have been part of the wall for no one ever used it, and a companion window which was used all the time by Wing who could be found standing next to it each evening, gazing out into the distant dark. Upstairs was Reean and Joash's bedroom and opposite it a small room nicknamed the Cove, which had been taken over as Fey's personal pout space, it being too small for any adult to stand up in. The front of the house faced the fields, the barn, and the peeiopi coop. It had a beautifully grained door and a large window through which Reean would often watch her husband and sons as they came in from the fields.

"Son," Reean said as Nien came in through the door. "How are you? How is Commander Lant?"

Obviously, she'd heard about what happened in the Village. The news had probably come from Joash since Nien couldn't imagine Wing having been forthcoming.

"As well as can be expected," Nien answered as he proceeded into the bedroom at the back that he shared with Wing and their little brother, Jake.

Reean stepped into the room behind him.

"The Commander talked with the Cant," Nien said, tossing his gear down at the foot of his bed and pulling off his boots. Wriggling out of his sweaty shirt and looking around for a new one, he glanced at his mother, knowing that what she really wanted to ask was: How is this going to affect Wing? But with Wing in the other room such a conversation would only throw a giant vat of discomfort on the night, so Nien climbed into another shirt and returned behind Reean into the large main room—an impressive space. Just left of the solid artistry that was the main staircase leading upstairs, sat a large stone fireplace with a carved wooden mantle. Gathered around the fireplace were various wooden stools and soft covered chairs sitting upon an array of hand-woven rugs. At the opposite side of the room sat the large wood-burning stove for cooking and heating the home, as well as a water pump Joash had invented and installed over a wash basin.

Moving through the main room toward the washbasin, Nien glanced at Wing where he lay, stretched across the chaise lounge. A moment later, Joash came in, stomping his feet and slapping dirt from his coat. Nien caught his father's eye and nodded his head toward Wing with the silent question: *How is he?*

Joash shrugged his, *I don't know.*

Behind Nien, Reean said, "Nien, find Jake, will you? It's time to eat."

Nien shook the water from his hands, dried them on his pants and went to find Jake.

The rest of the family was gathering around the table as Nien came back with Jake on his heels.

"I'm starving," Jake announced, reaching for a handful of bread.

Joash glanced at his youngest son. "So am I. And lucky for me, you now get to say the prayer."

Sheepishly, Jake redirected his hand and the prayer was said.

"I spoke with Carly before I left today," Nien said, passing the first plate of food.

Wing nodded. "Uh huh?"

"She suggested we get together during the season break. Maybe plan a return trip to the caves or something."

Talking about their old capers seemed like it could have been a nice diversion from the distressing events of the day, but it just made things worse. The conversation Reean and Joash were having between them collapsed and a tangible chill set itself upon the room.

Unthwarted by the awkward moment, Jake barked, "I want to go!"

Joash and Reean exchanged glances as Jake looked hopefully to Wing and Nien.

"Don't get your hopes up," Wing said to his little brother.

"Indeed," Reean said. "If they do go, you will not be accompanying them."

"Mom!" Jake protested.

"We're not getting in trouble for taking you with us again," Nien said.

"I was too little then. You wouldn't get in trouble if I went along now."

"Yes they would," Reean said. "And so would you."

Nien took a bowl from Wing. "Carly was teasing, Jake. We're not really going."

Jake's expression fell.

"Sorry, little brother. I shouldn't have brought it up. Besides, you and your friends are old enough now to go up on your own."

"None of my friends' parents would ever let them," Jake replied. "Not that it matters anyway. Without you two, I'd never find them."

"That's why it's called exploring," Nien said. "How many times did we have to go before we finally found them?" he asked Wing.

"Quite a few," Wing replied. Though this was not exactly true, the older brothers had no intention of encouraging Jake by saying otherwise.

Jake mumbled something under his breath.

"Ah," Nien said in a casual tone, "the chances of finding the caves again are next to nothing, anyway. That *we* found them was pure accident." He swallowed a mouthful of food. "That we escaped from them was miraculous..." Nien held Jake's gaze for a long moment. "We were lucky we returned at all."

Jake's expression grew serious until Nien surprised him with a quick finger jab to the ribs.

"Hey!"

"Nien, don't frighten him," Reean scolded.

"I'm not afraid," Jake lied.

"Well I am," Nien said. "I'm not going again." He cast a glance at his mother. "There's no need to worry. Our days of getting on your bad side are over."

Reean tried to smile, but it was obvious she was unsure about that.

"Where's the, uh, rest?" Joash asked, interrupting the conversation as he looked over the food on the table.

"Sitting over there," Reean pointed. "I'll let you guess why." She swept her eyes dramatically over the old, crowded family table.

"We just haven't had time to make a new one," Joash said, sorry he'd asked.

"I'm well aware, but this one isn't to going to grow larger on its own, or magically tighten its own legs."

"We'll get to it as soon as we can," Joash said, and the whole family knew what "as-soon-as-we-can" meant. The busy season of planting would turn into the busy season of harvest which would turn into the busy season of tending and in two revolutions from now they would still be eating at the same table. Wing, Nien, and Joash could build a house faster.

As the meal finished and Reean and Jake began to clear up after it, Joash took his seat near the family door to sharpen his tools, wondering, in light of this morning's event, whether the familiar nightly exchange would pass between his two oldest sons or not.

It didn't.

Normally, Nien would bother Wing to practice the Fultershier language with him or listen to recent musings over a new finding in one of his unorthodox books.

Tonight, Nien sat in silence with a favourite book on his lap, thumbing through it absent-mindedly, as Wing, obviously pleased to be let alone, worked on his own personal transcription of the Ancient Writings from the large family copy.

Other than the Ancient Writings and perhaps a book of letters or notes written by family members and grandparents, an official ban had never been placed on owning other written works simply because none existed, at least for those who were not inclined to great resourcefulness. But curiosity was a character staple for Nien—resourcefulness a natural ally. He had been only a youth when he'd come home with the first book, dug up in one of the many caverns beneath Castle Viyer. No one besides their family, Carly, and Lant knew Nien was in possession of them. Joash suspected that the Council may have an inkling on the matter but, like about a thousand other things, it was a massively disconcerting topic and therefore left in the ever-growing silence that lived with all of them like a disaffected spirit.

Well, since Nien's leaving him alone for once, Joash thought. *I guess it's up to me to ruin his moment.*

Putting his sharpening tools away, Joash walked across the room and slid the Ancient Writings out from under Wing's nose.

Wing, momentarily distracted by Fey, bowed his head back over the book only to find it missing. Glancing up, he saw Joash seating himself beside the fire with it in his hands.

Wing dropped his forehead to the floor in annoyance.

Picking up where they'd left off the night before, Joash began to read from the prophet poet, Eneefa, knowing the family would gather soon enough: " 'I saw a universe of worlds, spread out against infinity—the way of never-ending. And me, sadly aware of sunsteps and days, in this one moment was I gifted. I saw the circle come together and the Distant Star came into its center, illuminating all that had long ago fallen into darkness...' "

"Was that Rhegal?" Jake interrupted.

Joash looked up. "What?"

"What you just read. Is that referring to someone called Rhegal?"

Joash tried but failed to cover his grim reaction. "Where did you hear about him?"

"Well, after what uh, happened in the Village today, I heard some of the kids talking about him. Some were saying that Wing came along because this man, Rhegal, failed our people. Others were saying that he wasn't supposed to be the Leader anyway, they just didn't know that until Wing came along."

Joash let the book rest on his knees. "Jake, Rhegal was a good man. He may not have been the man the people wanted him to be, but he was a good man."

"But,"—Jake paused again.

"Go ahead," Joash replied, afraid where this was going.

"Well, it didn't used to bother me so bad, the talk about, you know, Wing being like the shy'teh and all. But now they've started calling him Merehr."

A profound silence filled the room.

Joash released his breath very slowly. "Jake," he said, "we don't know who the Leader is or when he will come. We don't, in fact, even know if he will be Rieevan. He may be of a completely different valley or race. The people are guessing, son."

"Well, if...if Rhegal hadn't messed up, if he hadn't run off, then he'd be here, he'd be Merehr and the people would leave us alone."

Something flickered then, and Joash understood. "What happened today?"

Jake glanced across the room at Wing. It was a shy glance, a strange one between the brothers. "My friends they're...well, some of them really believe you're the one, you know? The others are, well, they're angry." Jake's expression grew hard. "They're taking it out on me."

Wing slowly met his little brother's eyes. Silence filled the space between them like an ache.

"I," Wing stammered. He stopped. "I'm sorry." Getting to his feet, he walked across the room, paused briefly at the door, then stepped out into the night.

"I knew I shouldn't have said anything." Bitterness filled Jake's otherwise boyish voice. "*Everybody* except us will talk about it. Everybody else *is* talking about it. Especially after what happened this morning. Why'd Wing just ride off?"

He didn't exactly ride off, Joash thought as he said, "It's a little more personal here, Jake."

"No doubt," Jake muttered.

Joash noticed Nien's eyes stray to the door.

Dejectedly, acidly, Jake said, "Is he or not? I've got to say *something* to my friends."

Joash glanced up at Reean. Instantly, he knew Jake had caught him looking to her for reinforcement.

Through clenched teeth, Jake snarled: "Stop being delicate with me!"

A raw sadness spun out into the room.

The quiet against his shout was worse than any other reaction could have been.

With resignation, Jake lowered his head. "Just tell me what to say and I'll let it drop—forever."

"I don't know if he is or not, Jake." Joash had never said it aloud; he'd never even framed it as a cohesive sentence in his mind. "The people *think* he is, but they have thought so about other men, like Rhegal, and been wrong." Joash shut the Ancient Writings. The book felt unbearably heavy on his lap and he set it back atop the mantelpiece. "Is their belief in Wing enough for you? What do *you* think?"

Clearly, Jake was blindsided by the question. "I," Jake said slowly, "I don't know." Confusion and sadness played across his face. "I guess, I really don't know who they mean, either," he admitted. "Wing's my brother. He's a little weird, but he's still..."

"Your brother?" Joash said.

"E'te," Jake conceded.

Joash felt a touch of relief. "I know not having a real, definitive answer isn't easy. There are times, I wish for one myself." It was honest. Almost a confession. "All we can do is be a family."

After a few quiet beats, Jake said, "I understand."

Joash nodded, only then noticing that Fey had gone off to play alone, that Nien's eyes were now fixed on the door, and Reean was staring a hole into the floor.

"Right," Joash said, more to himself than to anyone else. Picking the lantern up off the mantelpiece, he said, "Why don't we all turn in?"

As the family solemnly prepared for bed, Nien pulled on a hooded cloak and draped another over his arm before stepping out the door into the night. In the distance, he spotted Wing's dark silhouette.

"Here," Nien said quietly, coming up beside him.

Wing looked over his shoulder and accepted the hooded cloak, swinging it around his shoulders.

"It feels good out here," Nien said. "Cool air."

"Yes it does," Wing replied.

"Want to walk?" Nien asked.

For a time, the brothers walked together in silence.

"Sorry," Nien said.

Wing said nothing.

"You and father going into the Village tomorrow?"

With resignation, Wing glanced up at the clear night sky. "The Vancs are getting itchy to be in their new home by the time the cold comes—so I guess I'll be going."

"I wish I could help, but what with the early Cant meeting tomorrow—"

"It can't be like the old times."

"Well, Jake's getting bigger all the time. It won't be long before he can take your place."

Wing was silent and it seemed the idea pained him.

"Don't worry about that. Jake's eager for it—it's more Fa's worry than Jake's ability."

Wing still said nothing.

Nien let it go, unable to decipher what else Wing might be thinking.

As they walked on, Nien's mind tugged all the day's disconcerting events together, drawing them in like a single thread gathering up a giant quilt. Things were building, or spiraling down more like, and Nien had no idea how to stop it—how to cut the thread that drew the rest in upon them.

The Ancient Writings were fairly clear in stating that the Leader would *be* like no other—they did not say the Leader would *look* like no other. Nien knew that if Wing could he'd change his silken black hair, naturally smooth face, tall stature, and olive coloured skin to look more like the creamy-skinned, medium statured, and thick brown-haired people of his race.

But that was only one problem. The shy'teh was another.

Nien thought back to his ride home earlier that evening and the recollection of his, Wing's, and Carly's last adventure together. It had not been until they were all standing on that ledge looking up at the big cat that Nien had understood how freakishly shy'tehn Wing was not only in appearance, but also in the way he moved through their world—silently, smoothly, disturbing silence in a group or between people no more than he disturbed the grasses in the fields or fallen leaves in the Mesko forest. Deeper still, was the less obvious but no less real matter of Wing, on the ledge that day, in some kind of silent communication with the big cat.

But even had Wing not looked the part of the man described in the Ancient Writings nor held any similarities to the shy'teh, there was still something about him, an almost tangible spiritual essence that covered him like sunlight on a cloudless day.

I wish it were just his quiet disposition, Nien thought. *I wish there was nothing more going on in Wing's head than work, food, and sex. Simple,* Nien mused, *and nothing wrong with it.*

Problem was, there *was* a great deal going on in Wing's head, and even though Nien himself was not sure what all of it was, taken together, it overrode the glaring fact that Wing, the one whom the Ancient Writings spoke of as being one of their sacred, solitary race, was a solid throwback to a heritage not Rieevan but to a paternal ancestor on their mother's side by the name of Lyrik, a man shrouded in as much mystery as Wing himself.

Nien glanced down at his own hands, shiny black in the star-lit night.

Like Wing, he looked nothing like a Rieevan should. Dark skin that shone an iridescent blue, and short, jetty hair, were characteristics of the people of Preak. It was only Nien's gilded brown eyes that set him apart from his race— "Must be a little something other than Preak in you" —or so Lant had told him since no one else in Rieeve, including Nien himself, had ever seen a Preak.

Situated just below Rieeve, Preak was a much larger valley than Rieeve. It stood with its face to the great Southing waters and its back pressed against the birth and split of the Ti-Uki mountain ranges.

But the fact that he was of a completely different race had never played long in Nien's mind, for he had grown up with Wing, as a Rieevan, the two having fallen into a familial bond from the moment Joash had come home with Nien in his arms.

It had been at the end of a beautiful Kojko day when Joash had found Nien at the edge of the family fields. The only evidence of his origin had been in a tightly rolled scroll tucked inside his tiny, worn jacket. Written in Preak, Lant alone had been of help in deciphering the short message; it read: "No more than life could I give him. I will forever be his darkness, he will forever be my light."

Poetic, Joash had noted at the time. But not very helpful.

Reean and Joash figured Nien had been little more than five revolutions when they found him, and Nien could recall only faint images and feelings of his life before.

Speaking from his reminiscing, Nien said, "Do you ever tire of the fact that we don't do anything normal?"

"Normal?"

"Yes, normal. Like living in the Village instead of being the only family to live not on the outskirts but cleeear," he said, dragging the word out, "at the opposite end of the valley? And what about actually going to tabernacle? Trading wares on a regular basis? Perhaps even—Council forbid—looking like Rieevans?"

"That would be far too much to ask," Wing said.

Nien chuckled.

"I don't know," Wing said in an uncommon show of recognition for the situation, "I think it would be bad anyway. Maybe worse. I'm glad we live out here. I love my life. I love our lives as a family."

"Well," Nien snorted, "without me you'd stick out like an eight-legged horse."

"Thanks for that," Wing replied, before adding in a quiet, out-of-the-blue tone, "Your body may be Preak, but your heart is Rieevan."

"And my mind," Nien asked, pleased with Wing's assessment, "I wonder where it resides."

"In your books, I imagine."

"They were my only salvation before the Cant came along."

"How is Commander Lant?"

Nien was surprised. Ever since the Council had started pressuring Lant to convince Wing to join the Cant, the subject of the Commander had become uncomfortable and therefore avoided.

"He's good. Busy. He's been working with Saam in the making of swords and short blades." Nien hesitated. He knew it was risky, but as Wing was being so...open, he decided to say what he'd wanted to say for nearly a season. "The two of you used to talk a lot. I know he misses that."

They walked on in silence and just as Nien was sure Wing wasn't going to reply, Wing said, "I miss talking with him as well."

Wing's words lifted Nien's gloomy mood. It had been far too long since Wing had been so forthcoming with his thoughts; nevertheless, Nien didn't press the subject, but moved on. "That reminds me," he said. "I've wanted to thank you for helping Lant and me pay Saam for his blacksmith work. It was great watching the sword design and first construction. Who ever would have thought we'd see weapons in Rieeve? And that we'd be the first?"

To this, Wing was back to his normal taciturnity—he only nodded his head.

"Anyway, I'm really grateful. I'll make it pay off one day. I promise."

"I know," Wing said.

"Thanks, Weed Farmer."

"Anything for the Deviant."

Nien was about to ask Wing if he was ready to head back to the house when a familiar sensation suddenly touched off between them. Falling into silence, the two slowed to an unspoken stop as the sensation stretched out like an expanding web to encompass them in a very familiar place.

They called it their Place. Impossible to determine when or how it would happen, when they were in it the world outside dissolved into one entirely indescribable to the former.

The first time it happened had been the day after Joash had found Nien abandoned in the fields. Little boys, the two had been playing together in the back room when Reean came in to get them. She'd spoken to them, asked them to pick up the toys and come and eat, but they would not respond to her words or her touch. It took only moments for Reean to realize that they were not ignoring her; rather, they were simply not aware she was there at all. That evening, Joash had managed no better luck. And so they were let be until the following morning when Reean came in again to check on them. This time, Nien looked up at her, as did Wing, and it seemed the spell was broken.

In the revolutions that followed the occurrence seemed to grow less acute, but as parents, Joash and Reean knew it to be the source of the magnetism felt whenever the two were together. Often, they'd watched the change that came over a room when Wing and Nien were present— how the most mundane of events could take on an expressive quality that hinted at a world full of possibility.

It had been some time since they'd experienced it. Part of the fallout of everything that had been going on in recent revolutions, Nien figured. He'd almost forgotten how big it was, how impossible to describe, how distressing to break.

When, at last, it started to fade Nien glanced over at Wing. They did not hold each other's eyes long, but there was in Wing's face a lightening and a longing, something Nien was feeling himself.

As one, they circled their walk, and headed back toward the house.

Entering and quietly closing the door behind them, they noticed their mother sitting in the dark at the dining table, a cup in her hands. Across from her sat two other cups.

"You're supposed to be asleep," Nien whispered.

"I'm not the only one," Reean replied.

Tossing their cloaks aside, Nien and Wing stepped to the table and sat down before the cups of tea.

"Thanks," Wing said, taking a sip. "This hits the warmth just right."

"I thought it might." She smiled. "How are you?"

"We're fine," Wing quickly said.

"It was good to have some time to talk," Nien added.

"So that's the secret."

The brothers looked at their mother.

"If I want to say more than 'dinner's ready' to either of you, I need to keep owl hours."

"No more sleep for any of us, then," Nien said, raising his cup as if to toast the idea. "Hot teeana doesn't hurt either."

She looked at them for a time, her expression something of love and wonder. "The two of you," she said. "Even when you were little you'd stay up all hours of the night talking or playing. Every time your father or I would try to get you up for early-morning chores you'd be back to sleep before we left the room."

"We were so rested after the nightly reading of the Ancient Writings that it seemed natural to do something active afterwards." Nien's eyes flashed to his mother; he winked.

Reean shook her head. "You're bad."

"It's a good thing we live so far out here," Wing said to Nien with a chuckle. "The Council would have you hung."

"They would have chased us out of the valley long ago if they knew even half of what we've done."

"I guess it's a good thing we never followed through with our plan to rob the Council treasury and use it to buy livestock," Wing said.

"At least that would have been profitable," Nien replied.

Reean laughed.

"And still a far less crime than making excursions into the mountains," Wing said, taking another sip from his earthenware cup.

"It's a good thing I hadn't found out beforehand that you two took Jake with you beyond the Mesko forest," Reean said.

"He begged to go," Wing offered to their defense.

"Of course he begged to go. He worships the ground the two of you walk on."

Nien snorted. "That will change as he gets older. He'll come to see the light."

Reean was quiet for a moment before shaking her head thoughtfully. "Not if he's anything like his mother."

The brothers looked across the table at her. They had never been bad boys, but as much as their family lived on the outside of Rieevan norms, Nien habitually pushed even the Cawutt standards to the edge, and often Wing had gone along with him.

The only reason they lived apart from their people was because of Joash's calling as the Mesko Tender. Though never an official election, the role of Mesko Tender was revered as a silent matter between the Tender and the Trees, so when Reean had fallen in love with Joash her family had let her go to live with him, leaving them, the Village, and their people—it was almost as if she'd died. Nien knew that his grandfa had nursed a quiet resentment over it up until his death.

"We're sorry if we've ever embarrassed you," Wing said.

"You two are many things. Embarrassing has never been one of them."

"Just know if we blunder," —Nien grinned— "or fail miserably, it won't be your fault."

Reean looked at them in the dim cabin light. "I hope we have not done you a disservice by living so far apart from our people."

"It suits us," Nien replied. "We would have it no other way."

The three sat in the silent stillness of their home before Reean said quietly, "Are you going to bed now or starting the day early?"

Nien downed the last of his cup's contents. "I don't think I'd be able to get back to sleep now. Besides, it won't hurt to have an early start into the Village."

"I'd just as soon stay up myself," Wing said, his voice subdued as he took back up his cloak. "I'll go fetch some eggs."

As the door closed behind Wing, Reean looked at Nien and asked, "Is he going to be fine?"

"I think so," Nien replied, his eyes and expression saying what he could not. "We haven't been able to talk for a long time. I miss it."

"I know," Reean said, her voice sad. "It's hard when things change."

Nien nodded, a hint of regret passing over his features.

"I'd swear you two are twins. How you got separated before birth, I'll never know."

Nien met his mother's eyes and even though he didn't say anything, knew as well he didn't need to.

CHAPTER 6

Quieness Acts

"Lead Netalf has arrived, Empress."

SiQQiy, Empress of Quieness, the largest valley on the Len'ta continent, looked up from her desk and saw Netalf, the commander of her personal bodyguard and a full-born Quienan, step into the room. Behind him came four other men. Three, she did not recognize but knew by their uniforms that they were from a small regiment of regular troops stationed near Quieness' northing border at Jada post. The fourth was a messenger—from Master Monteray of Legran. To him, SiQQiy turned first. "Messenger from Legran. Welcome."

He inclined his head. "Empress."

"What is your word from Master Monteray?"

"One of our spies, sent out by Master Monteray, returned with word that the Ka'ull have seized and secured the valley of Lou."

The first Empress of Preak and Quienan blood, SiQQiy's eyes, veiled by long black lashes, glinted against the perfect silvery-dark smoothness of her face as she took in the information.

"When?"

"At least a half cycle now, Empress."

SiQQiy turned to the men from Jada Post.

"Report," she said.

"No word, Empress," one of the Jada Post marshals replied.

"You came all this way to tell me that?"

"We were unsure whether to send another galley to look for them."

SiQQiy pressed her palms against the maps and old record transcripts spread across her desk. "How many galleys are now at Jada Post?"

"Thirteen, Empress."

"Thirteen battle galleys," she said to herself. "We still do not know what has happened to our merchant ships. We have no word from the galleys

47

sent to look for them." She raised her eyes and looked at Netalf. "All these cycles, the rumours of Ka'ull movement. No proof. Now, we know they've taken Lou."

"They are emboldened, Empress," he said, speaking SiQQiy's very thought.

The two old friends studied one another's eyes.

"Send out three more galleys—one up, two back," SiQQiy said to the men from the Post knowing there was not sufficient berth on the Tu'Lon River for more than three warships at a time. "But this time I want the ships tracked by land. I want only a small unit—no more than ten men—to follow the ships up river toward the Inlet. This unit is not to engage, only observe." She turned again to Netalf. "Lead Netalf, I want you to hand-pick these men. Choose wisely, for they will need to travel light and quickly. They must have good eyesight and experience in the high country. Above all, they must see without being seen, observe without being observed." Her head sunk then as she fought some inner battle.

The men remained quiet, still as the marble statues standing outside the doors to this, the Empress' tactical room.

"I'm tired of guesswork," SiQQiy said quietly, so quietly that the men barely heard her. When she lifted her face there was metal in her dark gaze as she said, "I want to know what's happened to those ships. I want to know *where they are*."

The men nodded quickly and left—except for Netalf.

As the doors shut, SiQQiy's thin hands clenched into fists and her eyes shifted to her Lead Guard. "Have the special unit ready to leave with the men from Jada Post."

"We will find out, Empress."

SiQQiy's eyes softened. "You want to go with them, don't you?"

"I do."

SiQQiy's chest rose and fell with a deep sigh. "You ask a hard thing."

"Only because *you* have asked a hard thing." Netalf smiled just a little. "You trust me to choose wisely—"

"I had hoped you'd think it wise to bear in mind the needs of the Empress of whose personal Guard you are the head." SiQQiy raised her eyebrows at him briefly. "But," she continued, "the greater wisdom lies in the good of Quieness and of our people." She held his familiar gaze. "You may go."

Netalf acknowledged her with a bow and turned to leave.

"Netalf," SiQQiy said as he stepped through the door. "You may not, in all your wisdom, choose Leit for this assignment."

Netalf turned back. He understood why SiQQiy would not allow Leit to be chosen for the special unit—he was Netalf's younger brother and a junior member of SiQQiy's Guard. For many revolutions SiQQiy had personally looked after and loved Netalf's family. She would not risk robbing it of both its sons.

Meaningfully, Netalf nodded to her.

"You know how he hates to be babysat," SiQQiy said. "So return as soon as you can."

Netalf's comely features grinned. "Certainly."

SiQQiy's mouth tipped in an uneasy smile. "Be careful."

As Netalf left the room and the door shut behind him, SiQQiy turned back to her large table covered in maps, books, and notes written in the delicate swoops and curls of her own hand. She suddenly missed her father so much she wondered if her female attendants noticed the shake in her hand. She pressed her palm to the table to steady it.

Her father was gone. She remembered his passing and how long it had been down to the position of the setting sun upon a sculpture in his room and the mingled smell of dysentery and incense. Both imputations she had tried to eradicate from her senses but could still smell at that same time of night when she was in his room—no matter that she had forbid the burning of that particular incense in her palaces ever again.

SiQQiy had spent more time in his room in the past four cycles than she ever had since his death. She'd never had the opportunity to miss her mother, she having passed on so early in SiQQiy's life, but her father she missed horribly, and more so, without even a brother or sister to share the burden of ruling the greatest and largest valley on the continent.

Thankfully, Netalf and his family helped fill the positions of family. *Surely,* she thought, *I would be lost without them.*

Nevertheless, they were not familiar with the Ka'ull, with the psychology of the Ka'ull people and their warriors.

And that's what I need right now, SiQQiy thought, vaguely aware of the anxious tension bleeding off her young attendants.

"Please," SiQQiy said, "refresh the water pitcher would you?"

Swiftly, the girls left, happy to have some task, as SiQQiy was happy to be let alone for a moment in order to continue...

Brooding, she thought, though she hated the word and rarely tolerated it in herself. *But this*—she hunted for the right definition—*this is...*

The words came to her in a quote from a book her father had loved: "Here we stand, on this edge, planning for devastation in the dark."

This is what that meant, SiQQiy thought. *This is planning for devastation in the dark.*

Receiving a messenger from Master Monteray was a blessing, a touch of sunlight though the news was terrible. But she needed more than word from him, she needed the man. She needed his wisdom and insight, needed to look in his eyes and feel his steady, clear presence. Her surrogate father since the passing of her own, she used to visit Monteray once a full cycle—it had now been the turning of two.

Monteray and his friend, Lant Ce'Mandu had come to the palace shortly after the death of her mother. Like angels in rough traveling clothes the two men had become her one mother. Eventually, Lant had moved into Cao City, but Monteray had stayed on at the Palaces, remaining for some time even after Lant had returned to his home valley of Rieeve.

It had now been many full cycles since both men had gone back to live in the valleys of their birth. She'd never seen Lant again, but she received news of him through messengers and her own visits to Master Monteray in Legran.

Just then, her attendants begged entrance into the room. SiQQiy called for them to come in. One set a polished silver pitcher down upon the edge of the table, the other a slender silver cup, then both stepped back to stand near a tall, thin-legged table with a bowled depression at its center. From the center of the depression grew an exquisite little plant with the brightest leaves of green SiQQiy had ever seen. It had been a gift—from Monteray. It had traveled far to reach her and survived, a thing one might not have thought possible in something so delicate and so beautiful.

As perhaps Monteray had meant, SiQQiy had seen herself in the plant: beautiful yes, rare yes, but also surprisingly strong.

She raised her eyes to it in question as she often did, drawing courage from both its fragility and liveliness. Aware of her own sincerity, SiQQiy almost laughed. *Think anyone would lose faith in me as a ruler if they knew I consulted a plant?*

But, as if Monteray had magically instilled his wisdom in the little green being before sending it, into SiQQiy's mind formed the thought: *The next best thing is, even now, in your house.*

"Very right," she said softly.

Straightening her back, she left the room, her attendants falling into silent step behind her. The three moved like liquid ghosts down the long hall, across a courtyard gleaming with sunlight through raindrops on plant leaves, and into her private palace where the messenger from Legran waited in her personal dining room before a table laden with food.

The messenger stood as SiQQiy entered the room.

"Please," SiQQiy said, waving at the table. "You must be famished."

The messenger sat down again and dug in. SiQQiy nibbled politely but held no real hunger other than for more information from Master Monteray.

Seeming to understood this, the messenger shared with her all he knew in between bites of food.

"And you delivered this message to Lant Ce'Mandu in Rieeve? Have things changed there? Are they now open to messengers?"

"No, Empress, I went around. Master Monteray, himself, delivered the message to Commander Lant."

SiQQiy took the disappointing news in silence. That Monteray entered Rieeve at all was, she imagined, on the precipice of compromising the strides Lant was trying to make with his reclusive, paranoid people.

But it would be so much easier, so much more efficient, if we could send our messengers through Rieeve, SiQQiy thought for the thousandth time.

Timely intelligence on Ka'ull movement from both sides could mean hundreds of thousands of lives.

Whatever news Lead Netalf and his team brought back to her would have to find its way to Master Monteray via messenger the long way around, and that would cost more waning of the moons in waiting, wondering—

Planning, she thought, *for devastation in the dark.*

CHAPTER 7

Stirrings in Legran

"You're going to get yourself killed."

Monteray glanced down at his wife where she stood twenty steps below him.

"And that thing," she said. "That contraption. Are you sure it won't slip or break or something?"

"It hasn't yet," Monteray replied, bouncing up and down on the balls of his feet. The large wooden ladder creaked beneath the weight.

Kate gasped.

Monteray laughed. "It's fine, dear."

Kate grumbled. "I don't understand why you started to undertake this now when the house isn't yet finished."

"The house *is* finished," Monteray said. "I'll get back to the addition once I've finished up with the Mietan here."

Revolutions past when they'd first purchased the land whereon their "unfinished" home now sat, Monteray had quickly thrown up a small cabin near the riverbank. The property was a fair stretch of fertile, grassy land flanking the Lennata River where the sunsetting end of the small Valley of Legran met the rising slopes of the Anrak-Ti mountain range. Their daughter, Tei, spent her baby revolutions in the cabin by the river while Monteray began to build the home of their dreams and Kate, wisely, taught Tei how to swim. The small family moved out of the cabin and into the house just before Tei's sixth birthday. Tei was now nearly twenty, and Monteray had taken a break from their home's addition to work on the Mietan—a special project he'd had in mind from the beginning.

Kate looked up as Monteray looked down at her and sighed. "It's close, Kate, and then I'll get back to the house."

She looked unconvinced.

"I've always wanted one—you know that. And, well, I feel now is the time."

Pushing her dark brown hair away from her face, Kate studied her husband's handsome face. He had always been given to premonitions. It had been nearly twenty revolutions since he had returned to Legran from an extended period of travel. It had been the night of his return that Kate first met him at a dinner hosted by his sister. They had left the home of his sister's that night together and were married two short turns later. Kate eventually came to learn that it was indeed a premonition that had brought Monteray back to Legran from his long absence. And then there was the hunch he'd had that their first and only child would be a girl—

His hunch, however, had not hinted at how precocious nor how stubborn she was going to be.

"Then you should at least have some help," Kate persisted.

"I will. Jason is coming out."

"Well, that's something. I'll make enough lunch for four."

"Very good," Monteray replied, turning back to his work.

Kate had barely disappeared into the house when another voice called up to Monteray, "You're the best architect in the valley."

Monteray glanced down to see his sister's oldest son, Jason, standing at the foot of the ladder. "I am the *only* architect in the valley."

The young man laughed, his thick dark brown hair waving over his face.

Monteray grinned at his oldest nephew before noticing a willowy shadow standing behind him. "Call? How are you?" Monteray said, spotting Jason's younger brother.

"Uncle."

Not nearly so handsome as his brother, Call's clear blue eyes revealed a ready intellect that belied the ungainliness of his body.

"You both ready to do some work?" Monteray asked.

"Absolutely," Jason replied. "Just tell me where to start."

Monteray eyed the two. He knew he'd ask Jason to come to the top, but Call...

Jason had always been a very athletic, physically capable individual, whereas the only coordinated muscle in his little brother's body was the large grey one between his ears, and even that worked a little...oddly.

"Jason, I'll need you up here."

Call looked up through a stray lock of blond hair, awaiting his own assignment.

Monteray considered him, then said, "I tire of retreating down this ladder to retrieve the tools I need—would you kindly?"

"Sure."

"Use this to send them up to me," Monteray said, indicating a bucket on a rope, rigged with a pulley.

Call nodded as Jason made his way quickly up the ladder and proceeded across the roof. Uncle and nephew conversed for a moment before Monteray's greying head appeared over the edge of the roof asking Call for a new set of fasteners.

Call glanced around at the seemingly endless array of tools, some lying in chests, others on the ground. "Uh," he stammered. "What?"

Monteray squinted, trying to find the box he'd placed the fasteners in. "That one," he said, pointing.

Fumbling around through two large chests, Call finally came up with the right box. Placing it in the bucket, he pulled hand over hand and sent it up.

Monteray took it, and returned across the roof to Jason.

"Uncle, you have any water up here?" Jason asked.

"Oh, yes. I brought some out, must have left them..." Turning back, Monteray was about to ask Call if he could see a couple bota bags of water lying around anywhere, only to find his young nephew missing. He looked back at Jason. "Where'd he disappear to?"

Jason shrugged. "He does that all the time. Mother usually sends me into town to find him."

"You think he took off, just now, for town?"

"That's where I always find him. Hanging around the bars and merchant shops."

"Why does he do that?"

Jason shrugged. "He's, uh, interested, I guess."

"Interested?"

"In the people." Jason paused, wondering if he could articulate the strangeness of his little brother to his larger-than-life uncle. "He watches them and he writes down what he thinks—about them, about Legran, about life." Jason shrugged. "I doubt that's where he's gone now, though."

Monteray's brow frowned. "Well, it looks like back down the ladder I go."

No sooner had Monteray set a foot to the green grass than Call appeared at his side, book in hand, saying, "Now, we can get to work."

Monteray recognized the book—a 'how-to' on carpentry. The cover was worn, the binding half torn; it was the first book he had ever perused on the subject.

Without asking, Monteray simply raised an eyebrow at his nephew.

"I don't know these tools," Call explained. "This way you tell me the name of the one you want and I will find it here" —he raised the book— "and then find it somewhere there," he said, waving his hand across the dismaying tangle of implements.

Monteray laughed and shook his head. "That will do," he replied, and slinging the bota bags of water over his shoulder, was about to proceed back up the ladder when Call stopped him.

"Uncle? Have you heard anything from SiQQiy?"

Monteray stopped. "Not yet. But I don't imagine the messenger I sent out would have arrived in Quieness more than a day or two ago."

Call continued to look up at him and Monteray wondered what else his youngest nephew might be wanting to know. "Anything else?" he asked.

"The townspeople are talking. A trader came through—he said another trader said that an old partner of his was up around the Inlet and saw *a lot* of Ka'ull ships. More than he thought the Ka'ull had the resources to build."

"We're looking into it, Call," Monteray replied.

Call nodded, but still didn't look away.

"Yes?" Monteray asked, feeling his patience thinning.

"The messenger you sent to Quieness—he, uh, wasn't that much older than me, was he?"

Monteray's brow furrowed, wondering why it mattered. "He was about Jason's age, I guess."

Call's eyes shifted nervously, then he looked away. "I'll get to know these tools," he said.

"Thank you," Monteray replied, and more confused about his youngest nephew than he'd ever been, continued up the ladder.

He'd been receiving reports of rumours circulating in town—rumours of rumours of rumours. It was frustrating. Annoying. But Lou had actually been taken. That much was confirmed.

Monteray reached the roof and glanced up at the sky.

Somewhere up there, he saw a circling doom.

CHAPTER 8

The Mesko Table

B usy turns had passed before Wing found himself standing beside his father at the base of an immense Mesko tree. A quandary of bio- logical contradictions, the Mesko grew only in a small section of the Ti Range on the entire continent: Rieeve's sunrising border. And it wasn't only the massive size of the trees or the peculiarity of the climate, but that within their giant cones were held not hundreds, but only one seed each, one seed of smaller size than those of the teeana that Wing planted in the family's fields.

Over four hundred and fifty revolutions past the forest had all but died out. For many revolutions Rieevans studied the forest, attempting to dis- cover the cause. From fire to the delicate balance of soil, desiccation and moisture levels, availability of wind dissemination, to insect predation and creature dispersal, it seemed they'd run out of ideas. In the end, however, they found the simplest answer proved to be the right one: Only saplings receiving direct sunlight survived.

Like most trees, the Mesko competed for sunlight, growing on a north- ing sunset-facing ridge of the Ti Range. At this aspect moisture levels and sunlight were perfect for them; nevertheless, beneath the great canopy of the adults, very few saplings could survive and more of the great trees died every revolution than were able to make it into adolescence.

For a time their people had tried replanting the saplings, but none sur- vived the relocation. So they'd set to cutting down a few of the giants.

The revolutions had proved the efficacy of this method, and now, though still small, the forest was flourishing once again.

Briefly, Joash laid his hand against the trunk of the great tree beneath which they stood and spoke its name: "Me'lont."

Me'lont was an ancient in the forest. Wing and Nien had spent many an afternoon beneath the shady reaches of its vast width and ever-reaching

56

branches, waiting for Joash to complete his rounds. Exactly what went on in their father's mind on these rounds, Nien and Wing never fully understood. They knew it had something to do with the saplings and the old ones, but how Joash knew which of the old ones were willing to go on to be something else and which saplings had the best chance to achieve adulthood were nuances that neither Nien nor Wing had ever picked up on, thus affirming Joash's special gift and why he was the Mesko Tender.

"So you've decided," Wing said.

"Me'lont has decided," Joash corrected, assessing the tree he, Nien, and Wing would be taking down.

Looking up at its massive branches, Wing turned a tight circle. Me'lont's great arms had birthed numerous saplings, but those same arms had also spelled death for all of them.

Joash walked slowly about the great tree. Beneath its addition to the Mesko canopy were three saplings. One was already beyond saving, but two were proving strong enough to live in two pale streams of light that reached them by the grace of a fallen limb from a neighboring tree.

Though it saddened Joash to fell a tree he had come to know as a friend (and as the Mesko Tender he knew every tree in the Mesko forest as a friend), the Rieevans had the preservation and working of the Mesko down to a fine art. Almost as indispensable as Rieevan crops and flocks, the Mesko provided wood for homes and furniture, the bark was used in thatching the roofs of poorer homes, barns, stables and local business shops as well as padding for floors and the making of rope. Most importantly, the Mesko was used to make paper for transcriptions of the Ancient Writings.

Joash smiled to himself as he gazed upwards. "Me'lont long ago passed from grandfather to ancient." The lines in his face deepened. "But he has agreed. He is ready to go on to be something else; give these youngsters a chance."

Wing had never found it strange to hear his father talk this way as he looked up at the giant branches ranging over their heads.

Joash walked around it carefully, avoiding the two struggling saplings. "Many of its roots have died. He is already passing." Joash glanced around. "We'll need to watch the fall. There's a break here in the saplings," he said pointing. "And we'll have to cut those large branches beforehand."

Wing nodded—he'd be doing the climbing to cut those branches.

"Me'lont," Joash said, gazing up through the great tree's wooden arms. "You alone will keep us busy halfway through next Kojko."

"Maybe even a new dining table for mother," Wing said.

"Fine idea," Joash replied. "It would be good to have a part of him at home."

"Mother will be surprised," Wing said. "I want to do it."

"Good enough, it's all yours."

The Rieevans took great pride in their carpentry skills, and truly, few were better. Work with the wood of the Mesko took a special skill all its own. Having been taught the art from his father, it was known in the Village that Nien and Wing had learned from one of the best carpenters and builders Rieeve had ever known.

Three turns spun quickly by. Between work in the fields and on the Vanc home, Wing still managed to construct a new table for Reean from Me'lont. On the day of the last pitching of the Vanc home, Wing left Joash and Nien to finish up in order to get back to the house and put the final touches on the table before Reean returned from her own errands in the Village.

Enlisting Jake's help, the two managed to get the table inside the house before Reean got back.

Walking into the house with her arms full of sundries, Reean stopped up short. In place of the old, splintering table there sat a tall, sturdy table of Mesko wood. Polished, the wood grain and colour shone impeccably, invitingly. Much larger than the old one, it was magnificent in its place, standing boldly, manly, its presence alone evoking a certain esteem.

Beaming with pride, Reean set her packages down on a chair as Wing stepped out of the back room.

"It's beautiful," Reean said, her voice tight with emotion. "Thank you."

"And we didn't even have to take the roof off to get it in here," Wing said.

Though its creation had afforded Wing his own joy, the look in his mother's eye was worth all the late night work he'd put into it after long days of construction and fieldwork.

Watching her walk slowly around the table, running her fingers across its smooth surface, Wing said, "It's little enough payment."

"Payment?"

"If I am anything good, it is because of you and fa."

Reean rounded the table and touched his face. Wing looked down into her eyes. "That you *are*," she said, "will forever be payment enough."

"Only a mother could say that."

"Perhaps."

Wing said, "I'm glad you like the table."

CHAPTER 9

Unprecedented

"I want to start a school, father," Nien said the following day as he met up with Joash at the edge of the Cantfields for the trip home.

"A school?" Joash said, as if he hadn't heard right. "I've suspected that you've had more on your mind lately than the Cant."

"I've been thinking about it for a while now."

"I'll ask the obvious question," Joash said. "Why?"

"Because I can't get Wing to listen to me."

"I've noticed. Any other reason?"

"Well, I think anything that can help us look beyond, look out *there*, would be a good thing."

"There's a reason there are no schools, Nien. Parents alone have taught their children for generations. As a people, we have gotten along quite well as we are."

"I know," Nien uttered, "but there's so much more to know. What of all the great works of art and sculpture? All the great things that have been written on philosophy, math, science?"

"And what of all those could be more important than reading the words of the prophets?"

Nien persisted. "If Eosha truly is the source of all truth, all knowledge, then what if what we know as the Ancient Writings is only what the Prophet-Writer or Poet had time to write? That doesn't mean that everything they *didn't* write isn't worth knowing."

"Yes, but maybe they only wrote what they did because they perceived those words to be of greatest importance."

Nien nodded his head in annoyance. "I know, I just..."

"I'm not meaning to frustrate you, son, but these are the type of arguments you'll hear from the people. If you intend on making this succeed, you'd better know exactly what you're after." Joash flashed Nien a short smile. "As for myself, it sounds like a worthy goal."

Relieved that Joash had been helping and not disparaging him, Nien said, "Thanks. You had me worried there."

Joash clapped him on the shoulder as Nien sank into thought. His father was right, of course. He'd need to have a better argument for his defense than the one he had now. Lifting his gaze to the mountainous horizon, he took a deep breath. There were still a couple turns before Kive festival where he was hoping to drum up support, as well as students. Between now and then he would think on it. Perhaps the right words would come.

"I hope sales will be good," Joash commented as the family made their way across the valley for Rieeve's Kive festival, one of three seasonal festivals held at the height of each season every revolution. "I don't want to have to pack all this stuff home again."

"Besides whatever you manage to lose in one of your little contests," Reean said, casting a look of feigned indignation at Joash, "I'm sure we'll be able to unload most everything—especially if we get some converts to your cream churner."

"It'll work," Joash said, striding along beside Nien as they led two of the family's horses burdened with gear. Behind them Wing was carrying Fey on his shoulders.

"I'm going to look for a few converts of my own," Nien put in.

"For the Cant?" Wing asked.

"No, for my school. I've been talking with Cant families the past couple turns and even some of them are holding back—because of the Council, I think. If I could persuade even one Council member to let his child attend the school, then the rest will probably follow."

"Much good fortune," Wing wished him under his breath.

Nien grunted. "Thanks."

The family arrived late in the afternoon at the great spread of field fronting Castle Viyer. All over the field colorful camps of tents and booths were popping up. After a brief setup of their own, Nien was the first to vanish from the Cawutt campsite, not wanting to waste a precious moment of recruitment time for the school. Jake took off with friends soon after, followed shortly by Joash who headed straight for the gaming field. Finally, even Wing disappeared, looking for Carly.

Near the Village side of the festival grounds, Carly saw Wing walking alone in her direction. Even from a distance, she could taste his nervousness, feel his unease.

It was the first festival since the day they'd all received the news of the valley of Lou and the Council's ill-fated accosting of Wing outside the Village. Other than the brief sightings of Wing quickly coming or going to the Vanc home construction site, no one had seen him lingering in the Village since that time—neither to shop, visit, nor pick up sundries for Reean.

Wing came up to Carly's family camp like a shy colt, greeting them with his eyes askance, his body angled as if to deflect a volley of some sort.

"Pull up a blanket," Carly's father, Hoath, offered.

But Carly jumped to her feet. "We're going to walk."

Though his voice was amiable enough, Carly could tell Wing was relieved by her intervention. "I guess we're off," he said.

Saying nothing about his obvious discomfort, Carly walked along beside Wing, letting him feel her touch, offering as much wordless support as she could, hoping the noise and excitement of the festival would allow them to go unmolested.

Walking close, their fingers entwined, they nodded politely to a family heading into the festival. Further up the street, a young woman was speeding along, obviously late for some festival event, her arms full, her concentration steadfast on the hurry in her head.

Carly noticed her before she'd seen them and watched as the young woman glanced up and saw Wing. Trying not to laugh, Carly saw the jolt that hit the young woman, saw her heel slip off the back of her sandal, and watched her fight to retrieve the sandal with her toes. But the cobblestoned street was not cooperating and one of the large, awkward packages tipped forward and fell out of her arms. By then Wing had seen her trouble.

"Son-Cawutt Wing, Daughter-Carly," she said quickly as Wing bent to retrieve not only the fallen package but her sandal as well. It was then the young woman noticed that the package had managed to snag the edge of her shirt and pulled it clean off her shoulder and left breast. She gasped, grabbed at her shirt, and dropped all the rest of the packages.

Wing set about picking up the parcels once more.

Obviously humiliated, the young woman let him pile them on top of each other and clutching them to her chest, took the shoe from his hand, mumbled thanks, and hobbled off down the street with the offending sandal dangling from her finger.

Continuing on their way, Carly couldn't quell her laughter anymore.

"What?" Wing said.

"Very gallant of you."

Wing smirked. "And nice of her."

Carly slugged him in the shoulder—not that she'd doubted his having seen the woman's breast.

Still, Carly thought, *nice of him for the woman's sake to have pretended that he hadn't.*

At best, the women of the Village were apprehensive of Wing, his looks as much a deterrent as an attraction. However, it had more to do with *how* they saw him, which was through the eyes of their people as some fragile and honoured thing rarely spoken to beyond the most dignified of terms and never to be looked upon as an object of sexual desire, than any true point of character in Wing himself. It had been Carly's religious indifference to villager fanaticism coupled with an abundance of energy for being just one of the boys that had saved her from the idea that Wing Cawutt was untouchable. Their relationship seemed to exist in a kind of magical place, a place Carly had rarely taken for granted, fully aware that she would not know Wing or be free to love him as she did without it.

As they continued their walk, Carly delved into the silence, recalling the first time she'd seen him. It hadn't been far from the street they now walked, and she had been a young girl.

Like Wing and Nien, Carly was the oldest child in her family by a large gap, so she'd grown up with a neighbor boy by the name of Mien'k. Mien'k ran with a group of same-aged boys who took Carly in as one of them.

It had been at one of the festivals when the gang of friends finally worked up the courage to approach not Wing, but the adopted son of the Cawutt family. Though there seemed to be some kind of fuss among the elders of the Village over Wing, no one really ever saw him, so it had been Nien the gang had spotted—it was impossible *not* to, what with that crazy blue-black skin of his.

Nevertheless, none of them had yet managed to approach him…

"You've got to talk to him," Carly said, elbowing Mien'k in the side.

Mien'k hesitated—he liked to think a thing through before jumping into it.

"Oh, you two," Teru growled. "I'll do it." Planting his feet and squaring his shoulders, he called out, "E'te, you! What's your name?"

The moon-skinned boy turned and saw them, all standing together a little way off, looking at him.

He walked right over.

"Hello," he said as he approached. "I'm Nien."

Carly smiled broadly. She liked his voice, his smile. "I'm Carly. And this is Mien'k, Shiela, Teru, and Bredo."

Nien had run with them from that day on for nearly a revolution until, one day in the Village, he stopped them in order to hail two people in the distance. One of the two—the younger—turned and raised a hand in their direction. Carly bumped into Teru and stopped, her eyes fixed. He had long black hair, and his skin was dark as a Mesko branch and smooth as a polished stone.

"This is Joash, my fa," Nien said, introducing the older of the two.

The gang was peripherally familiar with the Mesko Tender though none of them had ever spoken with him. They inclined their heads to him.

"And that's my brother, Wing."

Wing. So, the friends seemed to think in unison, *that's the one the villagers are all worked-up over.*

As the rest exchanged polite greetings with Joash, Carly's eyes remained locked on Wing.

Wing, too, had noted her out of the group. Unlike the other young women in the Village who would quickly look away at his glance, she met his gaze and smiled—a genuine smile, neither provocative nor shy.

When the gang welcomed Wing into their little community, it was because of Carly that he accepted. Nevertheless, the time he actually spent with them was small and after a few turns Carly found herself spending more time with the two Cawutt brothers than with her circle of friends. The three talked and took long walks together, dined over at each other's homes, and discovered trouble and enchantment in a friendship that outshone every other childhood activity.

"The old gang misses you," Carly said, coming back to the present. Part of her could hardly believe she and Wing had been together for so long. It wasn't often she considered it with such perspective.

Beside her, she could feel Wing's silent ambivalence.

"We're going to try and get together at Lant's," Carly continued. "Just a few of us. Mien'k, Shiela, Teru, Bredo, me, Nien, and you—if you'll come."

Wing was silent and Carly had her answer: none of his old friends would be seeing him any more than the villagers did.

Though saddened, Carly wrapped both her hands around his as they circled their walk and wandered up along the northing edge of the Village toward Castle Viyer. No matter how withdrawn he was, Carly was grateful for the small wonder of his presence, the feel of his hand, the quality and tone of his voice when she made him laugh. There was not a moment with him she regretted. Even in silence she felt seen by him, felt him more present with her, than anyone she'd ever known.

Yes, she thought. *More than anything in my life, he's worth it.*

Carly and Wing spent that night as well as the following day, unmolested. It seemed the festival might actually pass uneventfully until, on the third day at the Cawutt family booth, Reean looked up to see Councilman Fu Breeal's wife coming toward her.

*Great...*Reean groaned to herself.

Wishing she could magically disappear, Reean bought herself a few more seconds by ducking behind the booth on the pretense of looking for something.

"Mother-Cawutt, where's your son?"

"Which son would that be, Leeal?" Reean said, poking her head over the top of the booth. "I have three."

"Why, Son-Cawutt Wing, of course."

Of course, Reean thought, barely managing not to say it. "His whereabouts are important to you, why?"

"Not for me, I would never." Flushing with embarrassment, she cut her message short. "Certain members of the Council were wondering."

Reean's eyes blazed. "You tell them to leave him alone—it's the Festival."

Leeal's back stiffened. "Perhaps you should tell them, then."

"Perhaps they should have come and asked me themselves."

Leeal looked like she was trying to find some kind of reply, but the *Go Away* look in Reean's eyes decided her. She turned and left. Reean was about to plant a fist in one of the pies she'd made to sell when Joash walked up.

"I lost one of your pies," he announced and flopped into a chair. "Sorry." When Reean didn't reply he looked up at her. "What's wrong?"

"Leeal. She...she's so pressing."

"What'd she do?"

"She had the nerve to ask where Wing was."

"How dare she," Joash said lightly.

"I'm not being funny," Reean snapped. "She said the Council is looking for him."

Joash's eyes sunk to the tops of his boots. "Do you know where he is?"

"No. He's still off with Carly. Do you think we should warn him?"

"We can try. I don't know if he'll hear it."

Reean sighed. "Well, perhaps if we told Carly, she could direct him away, discretely..."

"I have a good idea where Nien is. He can find them." Joash pushed himself back out of the chair.

"Why can't they leave him alone?"

Joash met her eyes briefly. "Tradition." Soothingly, he laid a big hand on her shoulder and said, "I'll be back," before striding off, navigating the crowded festival grounds, heading for the familiar spot near the castle where Nien and the other members often lounged about during the festivals. He hadn't gotten far, however, before mutually spotting two Council members moving across the lawn toward him. It took only an instant for Joash to make up his mind. Deciding not to find Nien, he went to meet the Council members himself.

"Father-Joash Cawutt," the two Council members said, greeting him.

Joash nodded to them. "I've heard you are looking for my son." He didn't feel the need to say which one—both parties already knew.

"We were," the Council members answered in unison, one more timidly than the other.

"I'd like to talk to the Council myself, if you don't mind. Are they gathered then?"

"Informally, yes, it being during the festival and all."

Joash tried not to show his irritation. *Might as well get on with it,* he thought.

The three walked in awkward silence across the festival grounds and through the abandoned Village streets to the Council chamber.

Inside the door, they were greeted by Councilman Ne'taan, the Council's youngest member, who motioned for them to go on in.

"Father-Cawutt," Grek Occoju said, inclining his head from where he stood at the head of a large Mesko wood table—a table Joash had fashioned with his own hand when he'd been quite young. "It has been some time since you've joined us here."

"It has," Joash agreed.

"It is an honour."

Joash nodded politely.

"Will Son-Cawutt Wing be joining us?"

"No," Joash said shortly. There was a pause of discomfort felt by everyone in the room.

Grek was the first to adjust his composure and taking his seat, offered one to Joash.

Joash declined, briefly meeting the eyes of Commander Lant.

"We are sorry," Grek said, "about the unfortunate circumstance and result of our meeting on the outskirts of the Village last season."

"I appreciate the admission," Joash said.

"Did Son-Cawutt Wing come with you to the festival?"

"He did," Joash said. And then he shrugged. "I haven't seen him myself since about a moment after we arrived."

"We *have* seen Son-Cawutt Nien, however."

Here it comes, Joash thought.

"There is word circulating that he wishes to open a school of sorts."

Joash nodded.

"He has your approval in this?" Grek Occoju asked.

"He has my blessing."

"No matter how misguided?"

"I do not find his desire misguided."

"Perhaps that is where the problem lies—with both your oldest sons."

Joash's hazel eyes flicked to Cuiku. "*Problem,* gentleman, is a point of view."

Cuiku began to speak again, but Grek cut him off. "We were wondering if Son-Cawutt Wing has come to a decision regarding the Cant?"

"I know my son's heart—as well as any father can know the heart of their child—and he has no intention of joining the Cant."

"Can you tell us why he is so reluctant? Does he disapprove of it?"

Joash knew that the slightest hint of Wing disagreeing with the Cant would see the force dismantled by the end of the turn. He shook his head. "It's not something he's against, it is simply not part of what he is."

"Perhaps it is only a part of himself he has yet to discover."

Joash looked to Councilman Tael Ruke. "As you know, one of my sons is already a member of the Cant."

"Yes," Cuiku said, jumping in again, "and we were hoping he might be of some help in encouraging Son-Cawutt Wing to join."

Like a rash, Joash felt a familiar discomfort flush his skin.

"We are well aware, Father-Cawutt, that Nien is a high member of the Cant, but he is not pure Rieevan—as Son-Cawutt Wing is," Councilman Breeal said.

"Wing? Have you *seen* him?" Joash said. "If it's purity you're after, if it's the perfect Rieevan you want, you won't find it in him. On his mother's side his blood reveals the influence of a people from a far distant valley. Doesn't that make all of this...misapplied?"

"No," Breeal said plainly. "It is your lineage the code takes into greatest account, and yours is a Rieevan line as far back as we have record."

Joash's breath fell like metal shards in his chest.

"If you will not talk to him, then *we* will request to talk with him," Breeal said.

"You have spoken with him before," Joash replied. "His mind nor yours has changed in the time that has passed between."

"We shall see," Breeal said.

Grek Occoju leaned forward in his chair. "Apologies," he said to Joash, turning his steady gaze upon Breeal. No matter the current situation and concern, Breeal's lack of respect toward the Mesko Tender and honorary member of the Council was an affront to all of them. Turning back to Joash, Grek concluded the meeting. "Thank you for coming, Father-Cawutt. We hope you enjoy the rest of the festival."

Joash nodded to Grek and went to leave. Near the door, however, he stopped.

The Council members, beginning to talk amongst themselves, didn't notice that the Mesko Tender was still in the room until his deep voice filled the chamber. "You," he said. "All of you."

The Council members paused in their chatter and looked up to see the Mesko Tender's sinewy frame filling the doorway.

Secured of their attention, Joash said, "My son has never expressed an interest in either a prophetic calling or the Cant. I will not have his life destroyed as those who came before him." There was an unmistakable edge of warning in Joash's voice. "I will not have him cajoled, nor will I succumb to threatening him myself, especially when I'm not sure he is..." Joash paused as every nerve, every impulse in his body suddenly roared with a timeless ache.

His history in Rieeve was a long one. His influence quiet and profound with the great trees, with Commander Lant, with the older members of the Council itself, and even with the terrible circumstances leading up to Rhegal's disappearance. Taken together, his warning words had not only his but every heart in the room hammering out a dreaded rhythm.

Nevertheless, even with all his experience, intimate knowledge and influential power, he was helpless, helpless in the face of the prophecy. The prophecy that tore his valley apart, tore his friends apart, and now, was ripping at his own family, his own son.

Joash drew a breath—unsteady on the inhale, smooth on the exhale. "I," he said, "withdraw my honorary membership from the Council."

Around the Council table, a mouth or two gaped.

"In parting, I would ask only one thing of you: leave my sons alone. Wing and Nien have their own paths, it is not up to us to decide them."

In silence, the Council members watched as the Mesko Tender turned and left the chamber as one of them for the last time.

Back at the Cawutt family camp, Reean felt an unnatural severity rolling off her husband even before she could clearly see his face.

"We're leaving," Joash said, entering the camp and grabbing up the saddlebags from beneath the booth.

"What happened?" Reean asked carefully.

"I'll tell you on the way. Where's Nien and Jake?"

"Jake's with Fey over at the Yiete's booth picking out whistles. I think Nien's with a few of the other Cant members."

"I'll go get Jake and Fey."

Worried, Reean watched Joash walk away.

Nien came into camp just then, looking a little rough from a drinking contest amongst the other leaders of the Cant the night before. Nevertheless, it didn't take his hungover senses long to cognate the tense look in Reean's eyes. Without a word, he began to help her break camp. Nien was retrieving their horses by the time Joash returned with Jake and Fey. Quickly disassembling the last of the booth, they secured the packhorses and the four of them mounted up and rode out.

A few of the families watched them go, wondering at their early and prompt exit.

"So?" Reean ventured to say after a bit of space had been put between them and the grounds of the festival.

Joash replied through a tight jaw, "I spoke my mind to the Council."

"Did what?" Nien said.

"I told them to leave you and Wing alone."

"Me, too?" Nien said. And then he understood: the school. "Wow. Way to go! It's about time someone stood up to them."

Nien could think of no more than one or two villagers who would have done what his fa had just done.

"I'm not condoning it, son."

"Of course not," Nien replied, unable to restrain the smile that wrinkled the corners of his eyes.

"And don't tell Wing," Joash said. He turned his gaze on Jake. "You either."

Jake was quick to acknowledge that he wouldn't.

"Well, what did they say?"

"Not much." Joash hesitated. "They were pretty quiet after I withdrew my membership."

Reean, Jake, and Nien exchanged the same gape-mouthed looks the Council had.

"Really?" Jake said.

Reean was quiet.

Nien's triumphant mood flatlined. If Joash would make such a decision, if the Council would *accept* it...

Nien glanced at the ground beneath his feet and was neither shocked nor surprised to see that it was spiraling; spiraling down.

CHAPTER 10
Choice

An obscure section of field outside of the Village was chosen as the school ground. Nien watched anxiously as, in a short trail leading between the log homes and cottages of the Village, thirty children appeared.

Nien forced a smile, surprised at his own nervousness. At their first session there had been only eight. All were from Cant Member families, but this was only their fifth meeting and Nien was shocked at how fast it had grown in the eight turns since Kive fest.

"Jhock, how are you?" Nien asked the young man in the lead.

"Good, thanks." Jhock was the oldest of those in attendance. He had tender eyes, dark hair, and a curiosity Nien recognized as akin to his own.

"Where's your friend?"

"E'nt?"

Nien nodded.

"His fa won't let him come. His little brother or sisters either."

En't was Jhock's best friend. He was also Council Spokesman Grek Occoju's oldest son.

"We'll work on it," Nien said with a glint in his eye, but behind the glint there was a coiling weight hovering.

Jhock took a seat in the grass; the other students came and sat by him. The time went well, but as he headed home that evening Nien could not shake the looming weight he knew he'd have to deal with if he wanted the school to be viable—the Council.

After Cant practice the following day, Nien packed his gear with tremulous hands. He'd lain awake most the night working up the courage and counterargument to approach Councilman Grek Occoju.

Council Spokesman Grek Occoju and his wife had four children. Their family was one of less than a hundred families in Rieeve who would not allow any of their children to join the Cant, or as it followed, attend Nien's school. En't, Grek's oldest son, had wanted to do both and had been denied them by his father. Therefore, Grek and his family were first on a long list of Village families Nien intended to visit. If he could get Grek to allow *his* children to attend the school, the rest would follow.

Slinging his gear over his shoulder, Nien left the near-empty Cantfield and headed into the Village. The Occoju family lived on the other side of the Village from the Cantfields, near the festival grounds in the second to the valley-side row of homes.

Approaching the large metal-framed door, Nien released a deep breath to steady his nerves, rapped, and waited.

From the other side of the door, Nien heard heavy footfalls—not Grek's wife or one of his children. Suddenly remembering that he still had his gear over his shoulder, Nien quickly sloughed it to the ground as Grek appeared on the other side of the opening door.

"Father-Occoju, it's good to see you," Nien said quickly.

"Son-Cawutt. What a surprise. How is the season with you?"

"Well. Excellent, actually."

"Your parents?"

"Also well...and busy."

"I'm sure of it. With so much land, it is a wonder there is still time for construction."

Nien nodded.

"And you," Grek asked. "You have time for the Cant with all the work?"

The intended guilt spilt over Nien. This was not beginning in a very helpful manner.

"I do keep very busy," he replied. "But father's almost done with the Vanc home and Wing's in the fields all day and most nights, so..." The last was an exaggeration he'd hoped the Council Spokesman would enjoy, but such a reaction was not apparent on the aging man's face. Nien's smile faded.

"He's a good boy," Grek replied, speaking of Wing. Nien nodded, though he knew they were agreeing for entirely different reasons. "Well, you came here for something?" Grek said.

Nien looked him in the eye. "I did—if you have a moment."

Grek stepped outside, shutting the door behind him. Nien noted the affront but said nothing. Grek kept his children very sheltered and perhaps did not want them hearing what it was this lead member of the Cant wished to speak to their father about.

"I'm not sure if you're aware, but I have begun a school."

"I've heard."

"We meet in a field for now, outside of town. I'm attempting to procure a smaller edifice within the Village for the same purpose."

"What do you teach?"

"We'll be studying a variety of subjects," Nien said, then continued, probably too quickly, "I came here to ask if you would consider allowing your children to join the others that are already attending."

"What do you teach?" Grek repeated.

"We start by asking questions and go from there."

"And what source material do you use for answering their questions? Are you so old, so versed, that you feel you may give them adequate answers? Answers that we as their parents cannot provide?"

It was difficult, but Nien managed to keep his eyes from glancing away. "I think truth may be found in many places. I think living a tradition simply because it's a tradition should be...questioned."

"And you know the difference, Son-Cawutt? Do you trust in the validity of your distinction? Do you trust it surely enough that you may, without reservation, accept that in your words impressionable minds might believe?"

"I..." Nien stammered. He'd been prepared for Grek's first question; this one, however...

Feeling suddenly very foolish, Nien wondered, *Am I sure?* And then he felt something worse than foolish, he felt shame. Shame at appearing arrogant. He was a seeker and only hoped to share ideas, not facts that would be taken as binding truths by which to live one's life—that much Rieevan children already had. Of course he'd hoped to find such marks of illumination in time, but what about the children? Even though he knew he'd stepped right into Grek Occoju's questions like a trap, the Council Spokesman was right. The children may take what he taught them as axiom. Was he prepared for such a thing?

"I'm sorry," Nien uttered, and being unable to find anything else to say, added, "thank you for your time," as he started to walk away.

"Son-Cawutt, wait."

Nien stopped and turned back.

Grek rubbed his jaw. "Here's the thing, Son-Cawutt. Without the support of the Council, your school will not...continue, anyway."

Nien felt an uncomfortable knot beginning to form in his belly. He raised his eyes to Grek's face, trying to decipher why it was not enough for the Council Spokesman to have humiliated him.

"You will never have the Council's official *permission,* but it is possible for us to..." Nien could tell Grek was choosing his words carefully, "look the other way. Perhaps, even, allow those of our children who'd like, to attend."

There it was, the prize. The irresistible bait. And Nien knew: *He wants something from me.*

The only question was, where was Grek going with it?

But even as Nien asked himself the question, comprehension landed upon him with both feet: there was only one thing the Council wanted more than anything else—

"If you could help us by...talking with your brother."

There it was, the price.

"He listens to you as he does no one else. We are running out of ways to reach him."

At least in that, Nien saw Grek's honesty, his...*desperation?*

Nien's guts turned into twists of metal—it was the school or Wing. If he didn't try to convince Wing, the Council would close his school. It was bad enough that they were already not allowing their children to attend.

Embarrassed that his internal struggle must have been so evident in the length of his pause, Nien said, "There's no point. He...he doesn't talk to me, either. Not like he used to." The truth of it rode up in Nien's heart.

But Grek shook his head as if that were either untrue or a mere triviality. "Only you can do it, Son-Cawutt. It's that, or your school does not outlast the season."

The school did not outlast its next session.

Across the fields, Nien saw Jhock making his way out to him. Nien had spoken with Grek Occoju just before the turn-long season break. Today was to be the school's first time back after the break—their first class in the season of Kojko. Nien noted that Jhock's hands were stuffed in his pockets and that his eyes did not leave the path immediately in front of his boots.

Before Jhock said anything, before he'd even approached Nien, Nien knew.

"Jhock," Nien said as the young man stopped in front of him. Reaching out, Nien placed a hand on his shoulder. "It's all right."

Jhock raised his hazel-green eyes. "I'm sorry, we tried. We all told our parents we still wanted to come, but they wouldn't hear it. Council members even stopped by each of our houses." Jhock's face twisted a little.

"They wouldn't let me in the room when they came, but I overheard my fa talking with my mother last night. He said it wasn't worth losing his best employee over my attending."

Part of Nien couldn't quite believe the Council would go so far. Another part, however, believed it perfectly. The Council, the villagers, were frightened. And frightened people could do anything. They could do much worse, he felt, than threaten schools and jobs.

"Really, it's all right, Jhock. I appreciate your coming to tell me. I appreciate your courage in attending in the first place." Nien glanced up to see a couple villagers reclining not-so-idly on the outer row of cottages and homes. "You'd better go," Nien said.

Jhock nodded. "Pretty soon I'll be old enough to join the Cant as something other than a scrivener. Once I get my sword, you'll be my teacher again and none of them will have any control over whether my questions are about swordplay or books."

Nien forced a smile and urged him to go.

Jhock did so and Nien stood for a time, alone, in the middle of the empty field.

Turning away at last for home, Nien's mind spun as a feral band of emotions set upon him. He was angry with himself for not having been able to say something to the Council Spokesman—even if it had been to tell him to go away and die. Rage swallowed him in a gulp and every venomous thought he'd ever had about his people, about Rieeve, about his *life* swarmed to the surface. His fists clenched. He wished he had his sword with him—he would have used it to pummel every blade of grass to mulch between himself and home.

But it didn't take doubt long to claw its way to the surface.

Am I really that arrogant, that mistaken? he asked himself. *Because I long for knowledge doesn't mean others do. Who am I to change anything in this place—or think I can?*

Doubt and desire crawled around inside his brain like ravenous insects, munching his hopes into dust, crushing him between their incorrigible wills.

Just as he thought he might turn around, head straight back to Grek Occoju's and say the words he'd been dying to say for revolutions, into his mind something whispered: *"Wing."*

The rage in Nien's heart vanished.

Grek actually thought he could test my loyalties, Nien thought.

Raising his head, Nien stopped walking and, closing his eyes, pressed his face into the sunshine. "Show me a way," he said to the radiant orb.

"Show me a way through this before I tear everyone and everything I love apart."

Nien entered the house to the usual busy sounds and wonderful smells that accompanied nearly every evening in the Cawutt household. Wing was in the kitchen with Reean and Nien could hear Jake pestering Fey in the back room.

Reean and Wing looked up when he came in. Wing was about to say something but stopped, saying instead, "What happened?"

"They closed the school," he said.

"Closed the school?" Reean said. "Why?"

"Because it's going so well."

Wing and Reean were quiet. Jake stepped out from the back room with Fey dragging along behind him, latched onto one of his ankles.

Nien splashed his face and moved over to the table where he leaned upon the back of one of the dining room chairs.

"Did they tell you why?" Reean asked.

"It was exactly what I knew it'd be—'children should only be taught from the Ancient Writings under the protection of their parents'." He jerked his head toward the door. "There's more depth in the puddle outside that door than in the entire Council membership. If the next generation of Rieevans turns out as infantile as this one it won't be my fault."

Wing and Reean stood in silence, searching for something to say, some kind of resolution.

"Nien, I'm so sorry. I..." Reean paused. "There must be something we can do."

"There's nothing." Nien's knuckles turned white. "They won't listen. Even if they did, they're immune to reason. They're immune to **anything** that's not in that sech'nya book over there!" His eyes lit upon the suddenly despicable book where it sat atop the mantelpiece. The next instant, he found himself lifting the chair into the air...

"Whoa!"

Coming down from upstairs, Joash jumped to the other side of the staircase and ducked, but Nien managed to maintain one hand on the chair and brought it back to ground.

"Uh, something happen?" Joash asked, obviously grateful to have avoided a broken head.

"The Council closed Nien's school," Reean said.

"Ah," Joash said. Taking a breath, he came down the rest of the stairs and walked over to Nien. "I could try and talk to them, son."

Though Joash had withdrawn his honorary membership from the Council, he was still the Mesko Tender and that carried weight.

But Nien shook his head. "It won't work, Fa. For them, it's the way it's always been and no other way at all. I'm alone in this." He sat down in the chair he had been about to throw.

"Nien," Wing said quietly. "I'll go into the Village with you—talk to them."

Nien couldn't believe his ears. For a flash, he actually found himself tempted. Even though he'd already decided he'd never ask it of Wing, now that Wing was offering...

The next instant, he threw off the idea.

Wing was offering as a favour, one that would cost him, probably greatly. No matter how much the school meant to him, Nien knew he could not accept Wing's offer any more than he had Grek's.

"No, Wing," he finally said. "But thanks."

From the other side of the table, Joash said, "It's not their school to close."

"Still," Nien said, "they kept their children from coming and they're, well, kind of the point."

"Perhaps then, you should invite the children's parents to sit in on the classes as well, that way, if they disagree with anything you're teaching, they can let you know."

It was a good idea, but too late, and Nien couldn't tell Joash that the school would be closed, regardless, unless Wing stepped up as Merehr.

"It'll be all right," Nien said, almost choking on the words. "I'll be able to focus more on the Cant, help you and Wing out more around here and with the Vanc home."

His words helped no one in the room, the feeling of gloom impossibly dour.

"Come," Joash said at last. "Let's eat."

As the family gathered around the table, Nien thought that, even though he'd lost the school, he should feel some sort of relief over having stayed true to himself and to Wing.

However, rather than relief, a strange dread filled his mind. He couldn't pinpoint it exactly, but he knew it stretched into something beyond the closing of the school.

Maybe it'll just take time, he told himself as he sat down with the family. *Be patient.*

But it didn't feel like time would make it better. It felt like the end of a belief.

It felt like the end of an era.

CHAPTER 11

Impetus

"Nien," Lant said as Nien ducked into the small Cant hut the following day.

Nien didn't look well. Obviously, he'd lain awake all night, alone with his brain; it was a bad combination. The look of dejection on his face told Lant that Nien had moved through waves of rage, self-pity, and hopelessness until finally landing on the notion that there was no one to blame but himself.

Lant turned and, grabbing up a port from a short shelf behind his desk, poured Nien a cup and shoved it across the desk at him.

"I look that bad?" Nien asked.

"Yes."

Nien took a drink.

"I heard," Lant said. "I know what they asked you to do; I've tried to talk with them."

Nien took another drink. "Thanks for trying." He set the cup down. "The thing is, Commander..." Nien paused. "The problem is me. As angry as I am at everyone, at the whole mess, I can't blame Wing. I can't even blame the sech'nya prophecy or the Council. Grek Occoju said it. He was right. Even if they'd let the school be, who am I to teach...anyone?"

Lant could not remember seeing Nien so dejected.

"The truth is," Nien continued, "I don't know enough and I don't have access to the materials to learn—all I have are those few volumes I've salvaged from Castle Viyer. It's probably best I was forced to give it up now, before the children got really attached."

Lant caught himself smiling.

"What?" Nien said.

"You."

"Me?"

"You. Your fearlessness."

"Huh?"

"A great many treasures lay hidden in Castle Viyer, and yet you are the first in two hundred revolutions to look for them."

"I appreciate your saying so, Lant," Nien said. "But I think I've run that particular riverbed dry."

"I know."

"I want to learn about the geography of the land and Leer's peoples. I want to study the stars. I want to see works of art and read poetry. I could be considered a physical geographer by Rieevan standards and I can only put to scale Rieeve, Legran, and Preak. It's...ridiculous."

Lant looked on him for a time. Even when Nien had been a youth, the villagers had recognized some indefinable quality in him that would come across in a smile, a laugh, or simply a glance.

But Lant had seen beyond Nien's irresistible good-naturedness. He'd seen in him a noble sense of self and an innate curiosity that kept him into new things and ideas. Their friendship had formed early on when Nien was a little over twelve revolutions. Lant had been the only one who would not shun Nien's questions about the world outside of Rieeve—the one no one else in Rieeve would speak of.

"Answers far more important than these are inside you, Nien. They're inside all of us. Sometimes we only need pointers, clues to unlock their memory."

Nien's earnestness made his gaze hard. "Give me a pointer then."

Lant decided it would do no good to point out Nien's obvious attributes. He acquiesced. "All right, to the practicalities, then." Pulling a large sheet of Mesko paper from the shelf behind his chair, he laid it across the table.

"Here we have us, right?" Lant drew a small oblong circle in the center of the page.

Nien nodded.

"And here we have Legran, and here, Preak." Lant drew out the other valleys.

"Yes." Nien nodded, no longer slouched in his chair.

"Good then." Lant drew one more circle. "And this is Quieness—the largest of all the valleys in our hemisphere. It could encompass every other valley in our corner of the world and still have space to spare."

"I knew it was big, but..."

"Now, look at it in comparison to the bodies of water at Leer's poles: Opf, Fou." Lant sectioned off the top and bottom of the paper with large half circles. "From the edges of the great bodies of water at both poles rise three continents," Lant said, continuing to draw as he explained. "Each connected by a small series of islands forming one large ring of land circling the planet." Lant briefly appraised his work. "As you already know, our continent's countries, our races, are separated and distinguished by our mountain ranges. They form our boundaries on every side." A glint in Lant's eye bordered on impish. "That's helpful in one sense, I suppose: as a continent we know nothing of border disputes. But for the adventurous the mountains are endless regions where anyone may go and live. We Rieevans stay because going into the mountains means going into the unknown. Fear is our border."

Nien studied the map and the big circle to the right of Rieeve. "Tell me about Quieness," he said.

Lant closed his eyes as if relaxing into a warm bath. "It is a valley so large one side can be seen from the other only on the clearest of days, and even then the massive peaks to the south-sunset are small, almost insignificant. And it's beautiful—dirty, but beautiful. Being from an architectural family as yours is, you can appreciate what I tell you. There are buildings, palaces, of such unique and elegant construction it staggers the senses. And libraries."

A light flashed in Nien's eyes. "Libraries?"

Lant grinned mischievously, knowing what this next bit of information would do to Nien. "There is a library in Cao with books filling shelves over seventy steps high. To reach many of these shelves, you will climb ladders that are higher than the ones your father uses to access rooftops."

Nien's eyes went wide. His lips parted.

"Ahh, and the monarchal palace...I could never describe it justly. Great domed buildings, gardens filled with vine and fruit and every kind of tropical plant—no small feat, as Quieness is predominantly arid."

"I swear, is there anywhere you haven't been? Anything you haven't seen?"

Lant chuckled. "Adventure is in the heart, Nien. Just because the scenery changes doesn't mean the traveler will."

"I know, but..."

"I understand," Lant said with a knowing smile. "And I have visited much of our own hemisphere, yes. Of the others I have seen very little."

"So...?" Nien urged.

"That would take all night," Lant said.

"Anything," Nien said.

Lant sat back in his chair. "Though I didn't realize it at the time," he said, "the place my heart was in was more important than where my feet stood." He circled a finger absent-mindedly upon the rough map he'd just sketched out for Nien. "From the bellies of merchant ships so dark you could smell the night, to beaches of golden sand that stretched beyond the eye. From slave's quarters to palace halls, the campfire of a friend to the hovel of a stranger, I found only what I had brought with me—and that was this place." Lant's face seemed to take on a transparent glow, the nearly white blazes of hair at his temples glimmering in the fading light shining through the thin fabric that served as the door to the hut. Reaching out, he folded the map and pushed it toward Nien to take. "Home," he said softly, "is a very big word."

CHAPTER 12

Hell Arrives

The heavens had collapsed and hell itself unleashed from the depths of earth and water. Smoke and fire competed against shrieks and wails for breathable air.

A man lay beneath a heavy wooden desk—it was the only item in the structure still standing.

Struggling for breath, Tedahn began to crawl on his belly like a half-gutted snake. He'd thought the ships were from Quieness; they'd had the right markings, they'd had the right schedule. But there had been no merchants aboard, no foodstuffs or clothing, and the only livestock on board had been horses, heavily armoured horses a good three hands taller than any horse his Valley of Tou had ever seen. Explosions had rocked the bay. All their ships had been destroyed. Ships that had been under his charge—

None of that mattered now.

Crawling through a canyon of debris, Tedahn fought every step as if it were a furlong. His wife and son lived only a few blocks away. Tears spilled from his eyes washing out the dirt and smoky film as his mind fixated on the image of the small cottage that sat just at the end of the docks…

They would still be there—his wife and baby son would be all right.

Glancing up, he spotted a pale stream of sunlight.

A way out.

Climbing to his feet, Tedahn fought through the wreckage of the dock house, his big shoulders pressing up against fallen beams, his fists hammering at the rubble, blood running down his arms and legs and into his boots.

Tedahn exploded from the devastation and fell out onto the surface. Staggering to his feet he turned in the direction of his home…

But he had clawed his way up into another world.

Nothing was recognizable. His brain could not even comprehend what he saw.

In acrid fumes smoke billowed into the sky. Even the sun at the height of its ascent was dimmed and grey. Bodies lay about in the ruins: some hacked, some burned, some crying for help while others pleaded for death. To his left he saw a long line of his people. They were tied together with cords of thick, twisted rope and led by dark-robed men on horseback.

Tedahn gasped and gagged, finally scrambling off the ruin that used to be home away from home for generations of his family. As he moved down into the streets, his eyes focused on the near distance where a long row of similar cottages sat—all damaged, but some still standing. He did not hear the sound of galloping hooves behind him until it was too late.

Clad in a dark robe, the hood pulled low, the rider was upon Tedahn before he could react. A blow to his head sent him to the ground in a heap. Briefly, Tedahn heard the sound of the charger's hooves upon the rock-strewn street as the rider wheeled the horse about. By the time Tedahn's hands were bound behind him all had faded to black.

CHAPTER 13

What He Sees

His back against the chaise lounge in the large main room, Nien continued to read by the light of the last lantern as the rest of the family slept. They'd all long since retired, and strangely, Wing the earliest of them all.

The lantern flickered and its light dimmed another step. Nien glanced up at the oil, estimating the time he had left to either refuel it or blow it out and go to bed when the dance of flame caught his eye. He stared at it for a moment, delving trancelike into the blue at the flame's heart—

Wing.

It wasn't the first time he'd heard Wing's name whispered to his mind.

Setting his book aside, Nien got to his feet and went into the back room. His own bed sat empty to the left of the door. Stepping to Wing's bed near the small back window, he cracked the shutter for light and located the side of his brother's face beneath the quilt.

Wing looked to be quietly sleeping.

I must be crazy, Nien thought; nevertheless, he could not take his eyes away.

And then Wing convulsed, suddenly pitching about like a man suffocating to death.

"Wing, oh—*yosha*." Nien grabbed Wing's face hoping to wake him or see if he were choking on something. "Wing, breathe!"

But Wing was neither choking nor asleep.

Having set the Ancient Writings down after dinner, he'd retired to the back room. Pulling off his shirt, Wing had climbed face first into bed and curled his fingers into his pillow—small protection to keep himself from clawing his eyes out of his skull.

Not that it would have helped.

There was no escaping the vision that had suddenly attended his nightly reading of the Ancient Writings, blinding his eyes and enveloping his senses in the actualization of the words, showing to him with perfect clarity what they meant to flesh and blood, to living, breathing beings.

For moments that seemed to stretch into moonsteps, Wing had tried to fight it off: the black curling smoke, the long lines of human beings in chains of rope, great ships heaving about in a small bay like so many drowning parts of dismembered giants. But the vision gave no ground, finally rising up and swallowing him like a slippery-black snake, coiling its length around him, closing its grip tighter and tighter.

Holding Wing's head between his hands, Nien said his brother's name.

Twisting, struggling to breathe, Wing's mouth opened, but only silence followed by a miserable gulping sound issued out into the dark of the room.

Nien swallowed a surge of panic, took Wing by the armpits, and hefted his shoulders up against the short wooden headboard.

"Wing," he said again, and this time his voice was firm, powerful. Calling Wing back.

Wing sat up straight. He gasped, coughed, shuddered and slumped back to the headboard.

Nien knelt on the bed with a knee. Beneath his hands, Wing's shoulders were cold, wet with sweat. His breathing was terrible and there was a wild look in his eyes that told Nien he was unsure where he was.

Once more, Nien said his name.

This time, Wing's eyes focused. He looked at Nien as if seeing him for the first time.

"Nien."

"Bleekla, are you all right?" Nien asked.

"No."

"You were having a nightmare or something," Nien said.

Wing coughed again. "Or something."

"Want some water?"

"Yes."

CHAPTER 14

River Omen

The special unit of ten men from Quieness, led by Netalf of the Empress's personal Guard, moved steadily along a rocky incline at the edge of a large canyon that dropped down to the Tu'Lon River and the great bay that flanked the Valley of Tou on the other side. The lead ship that had been sent out from Jada Post—a well-armed galley by the name of Tregal—still moved steadily up the river far below them.

Netalf glanced up at the sky, then scanned the trail ahead. They never traveled beyond the length they had scouted beforehand, avoiding open areas and meadows as often as possible. Soon, Netalf knew, they would be able to see Tou Bay. He also knew that they would be able to see the bay before the galleys could.

Breathing heavily, the members of the unit neared the summit of a sloping ridge at the top of the canyon.

Netalf ordered the men to halt and wait—he would ascend alone and take the first look at the bay.

Moving carefully, Netalf dropped to his belly and spider-crawled to the crest.

The sight that met his eyes locked the breath in his body.

More than twenty Ka'ull warships were berthed in the bay. All were active, some docked, most waiting for entrance into or exit out of the bay. Netalf glanced down at the river. The three ships from Jada Post were making headway, with the Tregal a few furlongs in the lead.

Turning, Netalf scrambled off the crest of the ridge before pushing himself to his feet and running back to the waiting unit of men.

"The bay is full of Ka'ull war vessels," Netalf announced.

The men froze, some of their mouths gaping. Netalf began throwing off his travel gear. "I'm going to try and warn our ships on the river."

"We were not to engage!"—this from one of the Jada Post men.

"I know," Netalf said. "That's why only I will go. The rest of you continue to observe until you are sure of…the outcome. Word must reach SiQQiy."

"I'll go with you," said Jerra, one of the men from the Quienan Seventh Granj.

Netalf met his eyes. "I do not know if we will be able to reach the Tregal in time."

"We shall try."

Together, Netalf and Jerra turned and headed over the ridge. Time was against them. The canyon was the most direct route, but the descent would be treacherous.

The rest of the unit regrouped and, with the second highest-ranking officer now in command, made a general reconnaissance of the area. On the other side of the canyon lay a high plateau strewn with a field of massive boulders.

Making their way behind the ridge, they crossed the top in a low covering of trees, and then emerged onto the plateau. The boulders provided excellent cover, and with the rapid slope of the canyon away from the plateau, their view of the river and the bay was nearly complete.

Netalf and Jerra made their descent of the canyon toward the river. Only the urgency of their endeavor made such a feat possible. Had they given it any time for thought, reason would have talked them out of it.

Legs atremble, their bodies bruised beneath their clothing, their exposed arms cut and bleeding the two men were within sight of the river when the canyon rocked with the explosion of cannon fire.

Netalf and Jerra felt the concussion in their chests. It stopped them cold.

Up on the high plateau the small unit of men looked down. Far below them, they saw splinters of wood and ordnance shoot out the side of the Tregal as if by catapult. In freakish motion the debris floated up into the sky, hung there for a moment, and then tumbled back into the river. In a concussive wave, water bled back up over the deck of the Tregal, causing it to shudder and quake like a stone on the surface of a seaside volcano.

Netalf and Jerra began to move again, scrambling the remaining distance to a small cove where streams from the canyon flowed into the bay.

Hidden inside the trees, Netalf and Jerra watched helplessly as the Tregal engaged a heavy Ka'ull galleon. The other two ships from Jada Post were arriving within reach, but the Tregal and the galleon were already exchanging blows.

The trees beside the cove shook as the Tregal fired. The Ka'ull galleon took two short bursts to port. The great ship heaved, stalling in its course.

Netalf and Jerra could hear men aboard the Tregal shouting at one another; they were not shouts of confusion, but orders: clean and direct. Slowly, the Tregal began to turn about in the river—a precarious operation even were they not under fire.

The Tregal's flanking ships began maneuvers as well, turning about and bringing their gunports at stern to bear.

Netalf looked out into the bay. Other Ka'ull warships were beginning maneuvers, slowly helming their bows toward the southing inlet of the bay where the Tregal and its flanking ships from Jada Post were attempting retreat.

In terrible silence, Netalf and Jerra watched the behemoths in their laborious revolutions. Cannons screamed, and wood and iron buckled. Netalf's eyes flicked from the bay to the Tregal and back again, knowing he and Jerra were both asking the same questions: Upon whose back would the wind blow? Beneath whose feet would the current prove swiftest?

From above on the plateau the small unit of men also watched. They felt sick, the burden of the witness upon them, unable, per their orders, to do anything more than watch. But their warrior hearts still throbbed with feelings of helplessness—their brothers on those ships were fighting for their lives. And then there were the two in the canyon.

Had Netalf and Jerra even survived the descent?

Down in the cove, hope sprung inside Netalf and Jerra's hearts. The Tregal's flanking ships had come about and by staggering themselves along the river's edge had enabled the wounded Tregal to move between them. With stern cannons having beaten the Ka'ull galleon from bow to port, the helm of the Ka'ull vessel was ruined. The ship sat at the mouth of the inlet, like a great beached whale, blocking the path into the river from all the other Ka'ull warships—effectively trapping any pursuers in the bay.

From high above the river, on the great ridge of sunsetting mountains, the small reconnaissance unit glanced from one to the other.

"Let's go," their new leader said. "We have a report to deliver to the Empress."

None of the men argued. It was their directive. Their duty. Though they did not know the fate of their brothers in the canyon, they knew the Tregal was safely limping home with its flanking ships on course behind, and that the only way out of the bay after them was blocked by the sinking Ka'ull galleon.

At the bottom of the canyon, at the southing edge of the cove, Netalf and Jerra exchanged sighs of relief.

"Well, let's make our way out of here," Jerra said, but as he turned, Netalf said, "Wait."

Jerra turned back.

"What is that," —Netalf pointed— "there in the water?"

Jerra's eyes scanned the surface of the glimmering bay. "There's so much debris washed up here..."

"No, *that*—" And after a careful surveillance of the opposite shore and the men aboard the capsizing Ka'ull vessel, Netalf moved down to the water's edge and, wading in carefully, removed the item that had caught his attention. Slipping quickly back into the trees, he pushed the item into his pants' pocket and he and Jerra began to make a new way out, one they hoped would lead them back to Jada Port where they could procure fresh horses for their return to the palace city and their Empress.

CHAPTER 15

Imaginary Friend

H e sat up in the darkness of the camp. The whites of his eyes
gleamed in the pale moonlight. Trees lay thick and heavy across
the river to his left, and to his right the smoking ruin of what used
to be a thriving port town of Tou.

Their incursion forces had sufficiently subdued the local population
turns before. His regiment had arrived only a couple of days ago, and he
knew they were not meant to stay any longer than it took to resupply the
battalions that would be remaining.

Glancing around at the night-encased shadows of sleeping men, he rose
quietly and, stepping around the blanketed figures, crept down to the river's
edge. Upon the liquid blackness of the water, moonlight rippled mirrored edges against the bank as he stared down into the glistening depth.

For some inexplicable reason the river's glassy face reflected an image
of his childhood bedroom back in Tech Kon. It had been a small, square
room, adorned only with straw on the floor and a simple bed packed with
old fish netting. The only notable item in the room had been the bed's
four spindly wooden legs—something of a boon to his family as wood
was a rarity, the majority of it in his homeland coming from the occasional
washed-up shipwreck. What wood could be found was saved for con-
structing Ka'ull shipping and warring vessels, and stiff penalties would fall
upon anyone found with anything more of a tree than a rotting old bit of
wreckage.

The bed had been a gift his mother insisted he take. "It's all there is,
Tem'a," she'd said. He'd refused. She'd persisted—the bed with the wooden
legs was something precious.

Closing his eyes against the memory of his mother's sad face (he could
not envision it otherwise), the watery black mirage vanished. And so
Tem'a reconstructed the final details of the room in his mind. The thin

grey blanket—the holes in it that he'd stuck his fingers through, making shapes upon the far wall at night when the moonlight was big enough to make shadow. And the tiny window with the shabby curtain, the one by which he'd stood, his elbows upon its edge, his invisible friend by his side, both staring out into the night, night after night, dreaming, imagining, wondering, hoping.

My invisible friend, Tem'a thought. *Tchs'ya. That's been a long time ago.*

As it had been only he and his mother at the end, and as his mother had never talked much, in his sorry little room it had been to his invisible friend that Tem'a had spoken. He'd poured his heart out to that invisible friend, asked all his questions, divulged his fears and often his friend had answered in a voice Tem'a could even now recall in his mind, a voice as instantly recognizable as those belonging to the corporeal friends of his adulthood.

Tem'a poked his finger into the water. Reminiscing, even of a child-hood of such devout poverty, somehow helped. It was possible no one else might find comfort in the memories of a fishnet-filled-mattress, a depressed mother, worn blanket, four splintery wooden legs, and a friend no one else could see, but to Tem'a it had been a space he'd had all to himself, one he didn't have to share with a thousand other tired, sweaty, armour-clad men.

For the first time since he'd left his childhood home in Tech Kon, Tem'a spoke to his long-lost friend—

We were invincible together, remember? We could capture any idea, any dream I could conceive of. I was the desire, you were the wings. A bit too sweet, maybe, but it felt like we really flew...

Something caught his eye and Tem'a looked up, his gaze coming to rest on the ghostly behemoth choking the throat into the bay. The galleon had been sunk by a ship from Quieness just before Tem'a's supply regiment had arrived. Its shredded sails moved freakishly in the stiff night air. As he watched, the moonlight caught the grey-white sails and caused them to shine as if lit by the glowing spirits of the dead. Tem'a shivered a little, entranced by its beauty and chilled by the tricks it played upon his imagination.

I believed you, you know, he thought to his invisible friend, *when you said there were possibilities for the future I'd not yet dreamed of.*

The memory suddenly made Tem'a feel sick.

I hope this *is not what you meant. Because I never could have imagined such things as I've seen since leaving our land.*

Tem'a squeezed his eyes shut. Imagining what revenants and elementals might be playing upon the land and waters after such devastation struck terror inside him.

Don't ask me, he sent to his friend, *what I'm thinking right now. Better wait 'til morning."*

Morning.

Though he was with supply, he was pretty sure his regiment would be part of the cleanup detail come sunrise since they couldn't move their ships on down the Tu'Lon to their final destination until the wreck was cleared away.

There would be the rowing out and tearing down of the dead ship, and pulling bodies from the rubble, too.

Taking a weary breath, he glanced back over the rows of men to his empty bedroll.

Guess I should get some sleep, he thought, knowing just as well that he'd get none.

CHAPTER 16

The Lengths He'll Go

"Empress," a guard announced, opening the door to SiQQiy's tactical quarters within the military administrations palace.

SiQQiy turned and stepped forward as a young man, a pageboy in the private palace, hurried into the room nearly knocking over the tall thin-legged table holding SiQQiy's delicate green plant.

"Three members of the special unit have returned!"

Behind the pageboy, Lead Netalf stepped into the room—and stumbled. SiQQiy caught him as he sank to his knees.

SiQQiy turned to the pageboy. "Go get Rella, now."

The boy spun out of the room to retrieve the palace healer.

"Netalf," SiQQiy said, her voice pressed thin as the center page of a Quienan history book. "What's happened?"

Netalf fought briefly for air. "I'm not hurt," he muttered; nevertheless, SiQQiy began to look him over for injury, holding his shoulders and head in her arms as he spoke. "Twelve days past the lead galley we sent out— the Tregal—was attacked. The ship was badly damaged, but the crew and the flanking ships won the battle. They limped back to Jada Port." Netalf paused and allowed his breath to stabilize before continuing. "From a ridge high above Tou, we saw, in the docks and bay, a great wreckage of docking houses and ships. Leaving the unit atop the canyon, I and a member of the seventh Granj, descended the ridge and came as close to the bay from the other side of the river as we dared." Netalf struggled to reach for something shoved deep into the pocket of his torn pants. From it he pulled a thin piece of wood—on it was a golden bit of lettering. SiQQiy squinted at it for only a moment before recognizing it: It was the golden emblem of the Ketan, one of their long missing merchant ships.

"You have traveled so far in only twelve days?" she said incredulously. "An impossible journey. You came to the edge, Lead Netalf, of killing yourselves as well as your horses."

He nodded, swallowing against the sinister dryness in his mouth.

SiQQiy rested his shoulders to the floor and, stepping across the room, retrieved her slender silver metal cup. Supporting his head, SiQQiy tipped the cup for him to drink.

Helped as much by SiQQiy's hand as the water, Netalf sat up.

"We did not see any other ships in pursuit, though we did not stay long after the battle was over."

"Was it the Ka'ull? Did you recognize their ships?"

Netalf raised his eyes to meet hers. "Indeed, Empress, it was the Ka'ull."

SiQQiy's head bowed briefly into her chest. It did not take her long, however, to collect her emotions.

Touching Netalf's shoulder, she said, "You need rest now, and food. I will arrange for the latter if you will do the former."

Netalf nodded heartily. "I will gladly comply."

SiQQiy turned to her attendants. "Fetch a messenger for me."

"What destination, Empress?"

"Legran."

CHAPTER 17

He's Leaving

N ien bounded in through the family door, the exhilaration in his face lighting the room.

Reean looked over. "Why so happy?" she asked.

"I've made a decision."

"What?"

Throwing his cloak across a chair, he stepped into the center of the room. "I'm going to Quieness."

Silence fell like a hammer.

Reean nearly dropped the plate of food in her hand. Jake's eyes went wide.

Happily searching the faces of his family, Nien found only stunned expressions. Wing would not even look at him. Glancing back over his shoulder, Nien looked to the steady pillar that was his father. Joash sat quietly, sharpening his work knife.

"Father?" Nien asked hopefully.

Joash swallowed and, after a moment, set the sharpening stone aside. Upon his gentle face a genuine look of sadness and concern had settled. "Only two, maybe three people in our history have done what you just said you're going to do."

"Exactly! And one of them is alive right now—Lant. And what about Wing? Though not personally, Wing is proof that *someone* in our own family's past left Rieeve."

Wing looked at the floor.

"And there's me," Nien continued. "I'm Preak. Just because the people choose to ignore that little fact doesn't change the colour of my skin."

Reean was rooted on her feet. It was not the first time she had felt the repercussions of the decision she and Joash had made in placing their family on the edge, rather than in the middle, of their society.

Getting to his feet, Joash stepped toward Nien. "Changes are coming—it's obvious you will be a part of those changes, as you have been with the Cant. I am concerned, however, about you being received by the people when you return." Joash paused. "You *do* plan on returning?"

"Of course," Nien said with more urgency than he'd intended. "I'm not going to Quieness to get away from Rieeve, I'm going to Quieness to bring something *back* to Rieeve." His fists clenched in frustration. "There are no books, no information, no reference materials here." He looked over the family. They still seemed unconvinced. "Quieness is full of buildings filled with books. Libraries the size of Viyer!"

Reean swiped a tear from her cheek. Wing was still staring a hole in the floor.

Why is my good news always bad news for my family? Nien thought.

"Mother, I didn't mean to...I hoped..."

You all might understand, he thought, but could not say.

Reean looked at him.

Nien watched her expression shift from deep grief to a melancholy acceptance.

"I've known for a long time that we could not hold you—that Rieeve could not."

Nien raised his eyebrows, as if to confirm the permission in her words. Reean nodded. Nien laughed with relief and grabbed her, swinging her feet off the floor.

"I love you," she said. "I'm going to miss you."

Slowly, three more pairs of feet crossed the hardwood floor as Jake, Fey, and Joash joined Reean, each wrapping their arms about him.

At the center of the circle Nien stood, his heart almost breaking...

And then his eyes strayed to the door through which Wing had disappeared.

CHAPTER 18

Fracture

Wing had not come back before Nien and the family had gone to bed and by the time Nien got up in the morning Wing's bed was already empty.

Dressing and gathering his gear for the trip into the Village, Nien left it by the door and went to find Wing in the fields.

"E'te," he called from a short distance. Wing looked up. Nien could not quite tell what Wing's expression meant, but it felt like rain on a day that called for sun.

"What are you doing clear out here?" Wing asked, continuing to gather stocks of challak. The harvest had been a large one and villagers and Cant members had been out the better part of the turn to help Wing take down a load meant for the Village.

"Where's Fa?" Nien replied, glancing around.

"He went into the Village first light with the last of the challak. He'll probably be back in the southing fields later."

"Well?" Nien said.

"Well what?"

"You haven't said anything yet—what you think about my going to Quieness."

Wing made a couple more strokes with the scythe. "I think it's something that's important to you."

"You disagree."

"I didn't say that."

"You really don't have to." It was obvious by Wing's tone how he felt.

"You're breaking the mold, like you always do."

"You used to find that endearing."

Wing was quiet.

Nien ground his teeth. "Don't."

96

"Don't?"

"Don't go Mesko on me. Tell me what you're thinking."

It was an old saying of Nien's. As the Mesko grew in only one small section of the Ti mountain range on the entire continent and required such great care to preserve because of their fragile inability to adapt, "Going Mesko" was Nien's way of referring to something as narrow, confined to the point of strangling itself on inexperience.

"Don't go Mesko?" Wing said, his tone almost a snarl. "Because I don't want to travel? Because I want to live and die, right here, in Rieeve?"

For once, Nien's silence was *his* reply.

"E'te," Wing acquiesced. "I'll tell you what I think. I think you're running away."

"Running away," Nien mouthed, as much to himself as to Wing. "Coming from you, that's hilarious. You don't have to go anywhere and yet I've never seen anyone who can disappear in the middle of a crowd like you."

Wing's reaction to the insult was obvious but silent.

Nien ground his jaw—more in frustration than anger. "I have to go."

Wing was quiet another beat. "When will it ever be enough? The books. The excursions. You had many students from the members of the Cant, but you had to press it, had to have Grek Occoju's children, too."

Embarrassment wrapped a cold hand around Nien's heart. For a time he couldn't even speak. "I don't know," he said, his voice gutted. "Maybe never. But I can't just hang around here. Not now that they closed the school, the Cant's on Ime break, and—" He stopped himself.

"What?"

"You don't want to hear it, Wing. You never do."

Wing raised his face and looked at him. Rather than the protective distance Nien had become accustomed to in Wing of late, there was a close sadness, a sort of surrender in his eyes. "Just say it, Nien. You've needed to for a long time."

Nien felt like one of the great trees was about to fall in the Mesko forest, but this time it wasn't their people or the prophecy that held the felling axe, it was just him and Wing. "It's falling apart, Wing. We all know it is. But you won't talk about it. You won't say anything."

"I can't," Wing said.

"Yes, you *can*. Just tell them it's not you. Give them a sound reason why you're not."

"I'd think my refusal, all my obvious...flaws, would be reason enough."

"The only thing that's obvious to them is that you're the Leader. That's all they see. And your silence just makes everything worse."

"What do you want me to do, Nien?"

"*Say* something! Say anything! Yosha! Fa, me, Jake, mother. We can't keep covering for you. Did you know fa withdrew his membership from the Council last season? —threatened the Council to leave us alone. Jake, he's lost friends. Mother—she's just like you, won't say a thing. But have you heard her crying when she thinks she's alone in the house? —probably not, because you're always out here, *not* running away. And the school, they..." Nien nearly bit off his own tongue to keep from saying it.

But Wing's attention hit him with the gravity of physical weight. *"What?"*

Don't say it, Nien thought.

But the thought was too late, he was already saying— "Grek Occoju said if I'd help them convince you, they'd look the other way about the school."

Wing looked like he'd been punched. "Nien, I'm..."

"Don't." Nien waved him off. "I'm just tired, Wing. I'm tired of trying to make everything better when you won't do anything to help yourself."

The brothers' eyes locked on one another. The silence between them was deathly. There had never been one like it.

"Go to Quieness," Wing said quietly.

Nien went to speak again, but the look on Wing's face stopped him.

There was a single, long, painful moment.

Nien turned and walked away across the fields.

As the sound of Nien's pant legs brushing through the drying grasses of the fields began to fade, Wing looked up. His eyes found Nien and he watched as his brother grew smaller and smaller against the horizon. Eventually, his gaze had nowhere to go but up. The setting sun struck a path through a group of voluminous clouds and a single ray shone down upon the heart of the Uki mountain range, illuminating a solitary meadow in its light.

Drawn like a hand to a lover's tear, Wing reached out toward the shining meadow, almost able to feel the meadow's velvety softness beneath his fingertips. But as his hand neared, the clouds passed across the light and the brilliant ray scattered and disappeared.

As Wing's hand dropped, his knees buckled.

It was a long time before he climbed back to his feet.

CHAPTER 19
The Big Valley

*Q*uieness.

The immensity of what Nien looked upon struck an awe so deep and great in him that he nearly forgot to breathe. Never, even in his wildest imagination, had he been able to picture the sheer vastness of the valley that stretched out below him.

In Rieeve the mountains were so close they stood like a door to a house. However, on this side, the mountains opposite him were purple with distance, along their peaks and meadows clouds lay like sleeping women in long white gowns.

But as incredible as the landscape was, it was the civilization within it that lit a flame in Nien's heart: an endless tangle of streets crawling with carts, carriages, and wagons; buildings that stood up against the sky; and more people than he'd seen in a lifetime, all tiny ants, moving about busily in some unseen but well-orchestrated plan.

This is it, Nien thought. *Bleekla.*

The trip across the Uki had been a long one. Rather, it had *felt* like a long one. Wing had not even come back to the house to sleep the night before he left. Nien had felt so hollowed out after he and Wing's fall out that all he'd wanted to do was leave—as soon as possible. There was absolutely nothing keeping him in Rieeve. Not the rest of the family, not the Cant. By the time he'd left, even those things had felt empty.

Now, he was here; standing above, looking down on Quieness.

Hoping movement would steady his shaking hands, Nien began the last descent of his journey.

Though the way down the mountain was easy with swaths of domesticated herd trails—unlike the haphazard and narrow game trails he'd had to travel on the way up out of Rieeve—by the time Nien reached the outskirts of Cao his legs had the density of wet rags, and his head swam with a levity that threatened to peel his feet off the dirt.

Entering the streets of Cao, the people and carts that had looked so small and informidable from above came into sharp focus in an overwhelming kaleidoscope of intersections, shouting shop owners, rushing carts, foul-mouthed transients, and frustrated buyers. People belonging to every race Nien had ever heard of (and he supposed many more that he'd not), moved up and down the walled streets in opposing directions like great herds directed by some invisible shepherd.

Nien's senses could hardly take it in.

Feeling overwrought and literally overrun, it was the inconceivable light cut by the moonlit-skinned people of Preak that threw his mind into an unrecognizable heap.

My race, he thought. So many of them—thousands. *And they look just like me.*

One, a tall man, was approaching Nien amongst the sea of people heading in the opposite direction. Nien suddenly burned with the desire to speak to him. As the man neared, Nien reached out automatically—a passive, welcoming gesture of hello—to touch the man's arm.

The man flinched from Nien's hand and spoke a single word of warning.

Nien didn't understand the word, but its intent was very clear. Dumbly, he said, "Sorry," and stepped back.

The man moved by, but his eyes stayed with Nien briefly, as if making sure Nien was not about to follow him.

Nien made no such move, but his vacant eyes had unknowingly come to rest on an old woman who had begun to spit a string of unintelligible words at him.

Her shouts had the effect of a slap across his face.

Focus! Nien growled at himself. *Find the library.*

Turning off the large street, he dove into an alley, and found himself emerging into another street much narrower than the thoroughfare he'd come in on.

A Quienan-looking man paused near him to look in his bag for something, and Nien spoke to him in the Fultershier, asking if he knew the way to the Library. But the man quickly shut his bag and moved on.

Nien watched him go.

Turning about, his gaze sought the comfort of the sidewalk. When he raised his face again, he found a young woman at an outdoor vendor looking over at him. Obviously, she wanted to sell her wares, and even though Nien had nothing to pay her with hoped she might take pity on him.

Walking up to her booth, Nien introduced himself, and asked if she could direct him to the library.

The woman looked him up and down, to his relief didn't seem too disgusted that he wasn't about to buy anything, and said, "You take Little Cao Street here to Meglinda. Then right, past the Leonna Art House, and keep going till you see the Arc Fountain on your left. Keep right of the fountain to Glenndan Street. From there just keep going like you're heading out of the city—there are a lot of big buildings at that end. If you hit a solid dirt path you've gone too far."

Nien understood not half of what the woman said. He stared at her like a dumb cow.

She shook her head. "That way," she said, pointing.

Nien nodded and, moving off in the direction she'd pointed, had not gone far before stopping again, the only unmoving entity in a vast sea of motion.

If he could not understand the Fultershier better than he had with the woman, what would he do? He did not speak Quienan, nor had there been any books in Rieeve on the subject except for one very small booklet he had accepted from Lant. Most embarrassing of all was that, though he bore the skin colour and characteristics of the Preak, he could not speak their language either.

Perhaps I am in over my head. Maybe this was a big, big mistake.

An unfamiliar emotion had started up inside him, swallowing his mind in a thick, grey cloud—

Panic.

He closed his eyes.

Diving deep inside himself, Nien sought clarity...

Right behind his fear he found it: the persistent curiosity that had always driven him.

It pierced a sunlit hole through the enveloping fog of panic.

No, he told himself. *Now is the time. If not now, never.*

He opened his eyes.

Looking up over the heads of people and the tops of carts and carriages, he spotted a cluster of grand buildings just on the outside of the frenzied commercial area he was now in. At the center of these buildings stood one, taller than the rest. If learning was, as Lant had said, of such great importance to the Quienans, then perhaps this building may be a place of learning—with any luck, the library Lant had spoken of.

His heart pounding, the large building held steadily in his sights, Nien pressed into the crowd and began to make his way toward what he hoped was his destination.

As near and easy to spot as the building had appeared at first, it seemed to grow legs and move away the closer Nien thought he was to getting to it.

Tired, thirsty, anxious, Nien felt despair creeping up again.

Breaking into a narrow alleyway, he worked his way like a hungry rodent through the maze of buildings and streets, hurrying this way and that, weaving through people and diving down alleys until, at last, he scurried through a set of open-faced businesses and emerged on the other side to behold one of the most beautiful sights his eyes had ever seen. Fronted by a long incoming street, a broad sweep of stairs, and a pair of massive columns was the great building. Looking up, Nien recognized one word in the lengthy inscription carved into the stone over the entryway: Kilendatta.

Nien clutched his pack in a barely checked shout of joy: This was indeed, the Cao library.

Leaving the streets, Nien walked up the stairs and through the immense columned entrance. Reaching out with both hands and grasping the large curving handles of two doors twice his height, Nien swung them open—

And stopped.

Endless concourses of books filled his vision, encircling a vista so deep and high Nien laughed spontaneously. Shelves soared over seventy steps above his head, exactly as Lant had said. Ladders led up to a metal railing that wheeled the edifice near its midsection, enabling access of the volumes stored above. The ceiling was braced with arches that culminated at the center in a grand circle. A blending of precious metals and coloured clays adorned the arches creating a swirling fresco of pink berries on light green vines.

Moving deep within the various concourses, Nien began to glance over the books. Unable to read the titles of most of them, he eventually chose one on astronomy in the Fultershier. Intending merely to turn its pages, smell the ink, and continue to look for a book on the Quienan language, Nien caught himself looking up from the book to find that the sun had long set and he was the only one still sitting in the spacious reading area.

Getting up, he slid the book back into its place and walked out of the hall. In the next hall over, he spotted a young woman replacing books into one of the great stretches of shelves. Near as he could tell, she was Quienan, though she could have been a combination of many different races. Nien walked over to her, hoping his luck would be better than it had been out on the streets.

She glanced over her shoulder as he approached. She had pretty features and bright eyes. Her dark blonde hair hung close to her shoulders, and her skin was pale.

"Excuse me," Nien said in the Fultershier.

She looked at him warily.

"Uh, hello," he said. "I guess you work here?"

"Yes," she replied in Fultershier. "Obviously."

Relief flooded Nien—*she knows the Fultershier!*

"It's a beautiful library," Nien said happily. "I love books. I've never seen so many."

She narrowed her eyes at him as if he were strange and continued her work.

Nien fidgeted. Her cold reaction to him was quickly killing the thrill he'd felt over her speaking the Fultershier, but unless he wanted to sleep in the streets tonight…

"Can you help me? I've only come into Quieness this afternoon and, having lost time in a book, it is dark and I've no place to stay. I wonder if you could tell me where I may go to find lodging?"

"There are some short-term lodges—back down in the main shopping district," she replied hastily.

"I, uh…Where?"

"The main—" she started to say in the Fultershier before mumbling something else under her breath in Quienan.

But Nien got the message clear enough: *Good luck—you're on your own.*

Nien's shoulders dropped. He really should have focused. A night alone in the vast reaches of the mountains elicited far less fear in him than the prospect of spending the night on the streets of this immense city…

Into the awkward silence, the girl carefully asked, "Where are you from?"

Looking up, Nien replied: "Rieeve."

She eyed him. "Really?" Her voice was dubious. "You find libraries so fascinating. You have none there?"

Nien shook his head.

"And many Preaks?"

At this, Nien chuckled. "Only one."

She smiled, and hope sprang in Nien's heart.

Seeming to have made her mind up about something, she replaced the last of her books into the shelf. "I know a place you might try—for permanent lodging. Still, that will do you no good tonight."

Nien nodded, accepting his fate that for now, at least, he would be spending a miserable night in the city.

"My name's Necassa Erah, and you?"

"Nien."

Nien met Necassa the following day. She had arranged by some genius with the curator of the library for him to spend the night there—in the library.

Nien had been in heaven.

As the morning light crawled its way in through the ponderous stained glass of the library's sunrising windows, Nien sat across from Necassa at one of the library's ancient tables between two great shelves of books.

"The design of this building is incredible," Nien said, glancing overhead.

Necassa looked up as well. "It is beautiful, isn't it? I forget to look sometimes."

"Your nose is always in the books," Nien said. Though she did not smile, Nien saw a hint of one in her eyes.

"Since you're so into architecture you should see SiQQiy's palaces while you're here."

"Ah yes," Nien replied.

"You've heard of her? Hmm…You know, before you told me your story, I thought you were lying. Rieeve might as well be a mythical creature to Quienans than a real place—and that anyone might actually live there? I've never met anyone who's convinced on that point."

As unfunny as her words were, Nien almost laughed. "I guess we might as well be ghosts," Nien said. "But, believe it or not, a whole race lives there and one of us has, actually, traveled out of it. His name is Lant, and he told me of SiQQiy."

"Well then, if you'd like, we can go out and visit the Palaces sometime."

Nien nodded his agreement and the two saw each other every day as the first turn passed quickly into the second.

Through Necassa, an introduction was made to a widowed man who rented out an apartment above his home. For payment, Nien offered to repair the man's roof and wooden staircase so that the space would be proper for a more permanent resident after Nien left.

Having selected a book on the Quienan language, Nien spent a good portion of the first turn studying it exclusively. Though smatterings of the Fultershier was spoken as well, Quienan was the standard and it seemed most Cao residents, of whatever race, spoke it exclusively.

Other than books on language, there were many more cropping up that Nien simply could not bear parting with. The main problem would be paying for them. As he was earning his rent in repairs, he was keenly aware that he'd need to find a way of acquiring Quienan currency to purchase them before he returned to Rieeve.

With the new language and the quandary of attaining Quienan money on the back of his mind, Nien stood beside another of the large, terribly worn tables in the library, unrolling a large map. Placing a book on each end to prevent it from curling back into its stored position, he leaned over it. Some of the map's details he recognized from the rough sketch Lant had made that day in the Cantfield hut, but the vast and varied array of colour and geographical distinctions in this map were unlike anything he had ever seen.

Nien glanced over the other two continents on the map, and then came back to his own. As he did, his eyes passed briefly over an island, a valley at the top of the map, separated from his continent by a chain of smaller islands. Looking at it, he felt a sudden and very sharp sensation of cold pierce him, as if a river-chilled blade had passed through his midsection.

Drawing away from the map, he reached behind him and pulling his coat from the back of the chair put it on.

"Cold?"

Nien turned to see Necassa. "All of a sudden, yes."

"Spending the whole day in the shadow of all these books can do that. You want to take a walk? We can get out of Cao and go see the Palaces."

Nien's first inclination was to refuse; his time here was limited and the knowledge to be had endless. But the cold persisted, and he realized the help in the offer's timing. "Sounds good."

Thinking to roll and return the map to its place in the great shelves, he could not find the will to touch it, so turning, he followed Necassa through the grand open arch of the library and out into the light of the streets, leaving the map upon the large library table.

Walking side by side, Necassa and Nien followed a short, stone-covered road as it gradually dwindled from Cao city street to open road to cobble-stone path, finally settling into a fairly undeviating hard-packed swath of ground leading out to the horizon.

In the hot season, Nien imagined it to be a very dusty road, but now it was hard and cold.

As they walked, Necassa's sleeve brushed by his. With another brush Nien gently opened his fingers and caught her hand. Neither looked at the other at this small gesture, they just continued to walk, enjoying the sunlight, the feel of their fingers entwined, the firm tread of the hard-packed road beneath their feet.

"How comes Quienan?" Necassa asked in the Fultershier.

"Along," Nien said. "I like it. Do you know why, on my first day in Cao, nobody would talk to me when I spoke in Fultershier to them?"

"On the street?"

Nien nodded.

"Well, because it's weird. You just don't do that. It sets people off."

"Sets them off?"

"Rieeve really is a small place, isn't it?"

No denying that, Nien thought.

"You should have gone into one of the shops—or a restaurant. They would have been more helpful."

As if I could have known, Nien sighed to himself. "While I'm getting your advice on everything: Do you think I could earn some money by repairing the tables and shelves in the library? At least enough to buy a few books to take back with me?"

Necassa thought about it. "I could talk to the curator, Pheal—I've bothered him before about hiring someone to do it."

"Thanks."

Finally nearing the great dome structures of the palaces, Nien was able to begin making out details of the monarchal city.

With Necassa in the lead, the two made their way into the common grounds of the outer domes. Even up close, Nien marveled how the interior design of the domes continued to evolve and expand. It seemed almost… magical. One moment he'd be staring at the ceiling, thinking he'd recognized a pattern, only to discover that the pattern was only a small piece of an even grander motif. He had no idea people could make such things. Necassa had spoken truly—as grand as the library was, it was stark, almost menacing in comparison to the rich warm lines and curves and covered gardens here beneath the palatial domes.

"It's incredible how it changes," Nien remarked. "I've looked at the ceiling of this same dome five times, and each time I notice something I hadn't before."

"Quienans love art. Keep looking, where you think there may be only flowers, for example, you may see…"

Nien peered as closely as he could at the ceiling that ranged well over their heads. "Why it's an image, an outline that I recognize from the heavens."

"The constellation Riqur."

"Riqur? I thought it was called Keda in Quienan."

Necassa laughed. "In the books, yes. But on the streets we call it Riqur. See, the artist that painted this dome named that particular constellation after himself."

"Ah ha," Nien replied.

"Like I said, we take art seriously."

"And your artists take themselves even more seriously."

"Tisquiata. I guess you could say our God is in such expression."

"What did you say?"

"Which?"

"Tis, something."

"Oh. Tisquiata. It's slang. Literally, it means High Art, but it's useful now when speaking about anything that should be obvious in its passion, yet, at times, gets missed."

Unsure whether or not he understood her explanation, Nien turned his gaze back to the ceiling. "Did Empress SiQQiy commission this?"

"No. Most of it was done long ago. You will see each Emperor or Empress' mark in different parts of the palace domes, gardens, or halls."

I wonder what she looks like, Nien thought to himself, as he turned beneath the pendentive of one of the domes. "Have you ever seen her?" he asked.

"Once. She'd come with her personal Guard into Cao. I saw her only briefly as I was walking back to the library from the shopping district. She is extraordinarily beautiful. I admit I was surprised."

"Surprised?"

"That what we hear isn't exaggerated, you know? How beautiful she is, how kind, how strong…I mean her concomitants and advisors have to say that, don't they? But is she *really*?" Necassa shrugged. "Of course I still cannot say whether she is kind or strong, but beautiful? Yes. Her gardens do not outclass her."

Nien continued his slow circle beneath the towering dome above him.

"Do you want to see them?" Necassa said.

"Huh?" Nien replied.

Necassa laughed. "Rieeve is a little, uh, low on visual stimuli?"

"Of this sort, yes."

"Do you like it?"

"Which?" he replied with a smile.

"Quieness."

"Of course."

"Do you think you could get used to Quieness, I mean if you were to stay—for a time?"

Nien looked at Necassa, realizing what she was asking. He did not know what to say. He liked and enjoyed her company and was fairly sure she felt the same—but that she wanted him to stay…

Could I? Could I stay here? Live here? The thought blindsided him. "I don't know, Necassa. At the time I left Rieeve I hadn't planned on it."

She stepped to him, taking his hands in hers. "You can't plan for these kinds of things, you can only know once you're actually there, living it."

Nien looked down into her eyes feeling a strange wave of sickness wash over him.

What would he do? Abandon his life back in Rieeve—the Cant, the school, his family?

Then again, perhaps he was fooling himself, puffed up in the consideration of his own importance in Rieeve. The Cant would go on without him. The school, well, there was no school and the majority of the people would be grateful if that particular effort were to stay permanently by the wayside. Jake would soon be old enough to help father out with the construction projects, and Wing would always keep the fields.

He could stay here with Necassa.

He could take a job in Cao, study in the library and discover everything he'd ever wanted to know. Gone would be the constant struggle against irrational Rieevan norm. He would be free. Free of the burden of attempting change in a place that did not want it. He would be able to live among a great mixing of cultures. Here, in one city, he could learn not only from Quienans but also Legranders, Jayakans, Honj, Majg and—his mind spun—Preaks. For the first time he would be among people who looked like him. For the first time in his life he would have the opportunity to study, to live among others who felt as he did about art, about knowledge, about *life*.

"Well," he finally said, his heart lightening as he thought upon it. "I guess we'll see." He squeezed Necassa's hand and they walked out of the domed edifice.

"So, do you want to see them—SiQQiy's gardens?"

"I'd love too."

Passing back through the dome, Necassa exited through a different archway, and Nien found himself emerging into a dome of hanging gardens.

Necassa dove into a grouping of lustrous vine.

Reaching down from ceiling height, the leaves of the vine stretched nearly as wide as a man's chest and twice that in length. Great droplets of water fell from their pointed tips, cascading down from some indefinable point high overhead.

Squinting, Nien tried to locate Necassa through the droplet waterfall. He was about to call her name when a hand shot out of the vines and pulled him inside.

Plunged into the heart of a warm deluge that drenched him instantly, Nien shook the water from his eyes to find Necassa nose to nose with him. She pecked him on the lips, then made to vanish once more into the arboretic jungle, but Nien was too quick. Reaching out, he caught her by the waist. She turned in his arms and he lifted her up to his chest. Looking down at him, her hair dripping upon his face, Necassa's lips curled back into a primordial smile.

Grinning roguishly, Nien locked his arms under her hips and began to turn. Necassa eyed him wickedly as he began to turn faster. The giant droplets of water sprung from the edges of Necassa's clothing as Nien turned, spinning them into an ever tightening circle, twirling until both their heads fell back and their shouts of laughter vanished into the resounding echo of the waterfall.

CHAPTER 20

I Knew Them

In another place, far distant from the great library of Quieness where Nien had looked over a map of his world that had set a chill upon his skin, sat another hand-drawn map. A mark in the map's corner denoted its origin: *Great Library/Cao/Quieness*

Alone, on a table of deep dark wood, this map was from the same library, but it was not a Quienan table upon which it now lay, nor had it been Quienan hands that had carried it northing to this place—many lengths over land and water—into the heart of a desolate land.

The map itself was a beautiful piece, as much a work of art as a practical guide. Beneath the great body of water that roofed the portrait of the painted world, was a large continent filled with smooth green-coloured indentations representing valleys. About the valleys were course sketches denoting mountain ranges. On the right side of the continent was the largest of the green-coloured indentations, a circle that covered nearly the entire sunsetting portion of the map—Quieness. On the far left were three smaller valleys, separated by some distance from two more valleys situated closer in. At the top of the map was another set of valleys, but each of these had been painted over in a rough, greyish hue. And then, directly in the middle, lying peacefully embedded as a prized jewel at the center of a great confluence of mountain ranges, was one more circle—the tiniest of them all. It was outlined as a perfect oval, the colour of it greener than the rest, as if that space of the map had never been smudged by the oil of a fingerprint. Upon it was written only one word: Rieeve. There were no more details than that. No cities or towns were named; no helpful markers placed.

"What do you know about these smaller valleys?" a subordinate asked, pointing at the valleys near the middle of the map.

"We already have spies here, here, and here," his superior replied. "In all of them—except this one." And then, as if in direct violation of the map's unspoken history, pressed his finger into the tiny green circle at its center. There was a resentment in the gesture, a curling of his superior's voice that the subordinate had not heard before.

The assistant squinted at the word written across the circle. "Rieeve? —Why? Because of its size?"

"Because the people are non-inclusive and the population small. It will be impossible for us to send in a spy."

"I didn't know you knew the peculiarities of these valleys so well."

The leader did not meet his assistant's eyes—he rarely ever did. "I knew a man once," he responded, "from there."

"And this man, was he...?"

"Intelligent. Inquisitive. Strong."

"High praise."

"You may think so."

"But he is only one man."

"Yes, only one."

"Then where to, Supremet?"

"To Jayak. We will see what kind of forces Impreo Takayo can call against us."

"And Rieeve?"

"We will wait—until further information presents itself."

CHAPTER 21

Immortal, Like You

"It's Wing Cawutt," one of the children said.

Wing, on his way to Carly's for the evening meal, had been lost in thought and hadn't heard the group of youngsters playing in the street ahead of him.

"Fa says we should call him Merehr—out of respect," a young girl said standing next to the boy who had first noticed Wing coming up the street.

The children fell into silence as Wing approached them.

"E'te," the girl said. "I'm Lily. I...I saw you once at one of the festivals."

Wing slowed and stopped before them.

All their young eyes looking up and focused on him, the first young boy started to say, "Merehr, I've heard you can answer any question..." but he was interrupted as another boy called out, "I've heard you can't be killed!"

Her large, bright eyes gazing up at Wing in awe, the one who had introduced herself as Lily, said softly, "Is it true? Will you live forever?"

Wing felt a sickening chill sweep like an unwelcome wind through his chest.

One of the boys elbowed Lily and growled: "Of course it's true, and that's why it doesn't matter whether the Ka'ull come here or not, huh?" He looked back up at Wing. "Because as long as you're here, there's nothing they can do."

The temperature dropped. Looking down at the boy, Wing experienced a sudden detachment, as if the boy's eyes were merely small amber pools seen from a great height.

"Is it true," Lily asked, "that we're safe?"

Wing started to speak but could not find his voice. The willingness to completely surrender to whatever he might say was written all over the beautiful little girl's face.

Stepping around her, Wing moved through the rest of the befuddled children and down the street.

In the silence behind him, Wing could feel the trail of the children's eyes with more certainty than the strike of his boot heels against the cobblestone as he passed over the last stretch of road to Carly's house.

On the front steps, Wing knocked upon the door, feeling as if Nien or Joash had accidentally hit him in the head with a roof timber.

"Wing? Come on in!"

Wing gratefully entered the home, pausing just inside to lean against the doorjamb.

Carly's mother, Vay, peered into the room to see if he had actually come in. "Hi," she said with a smile.

Wing pushed himself away from the support of the wall and moved over to her, kissing her on the cheek. "It smells wonderful."

"You," she scoffed, brushing him away sheepishly. "Make yourself comfortable, we're almost ready."

Wing did so, sitting down just as Carly walked in.

"Been here long?" she asked, tossing her long coat across the back of the padded wooden couch.

"Not long," Wing replied, standing again.

Carly pulled off her boots. "What's wrong?" she asked.

Wing looked down into her eyes.

Carly's brow furrowed. "Were you in the Village today?"

Wing shook his head, no.

"Well?"

"It's nothing."

"Do you want to talk?"

Yes, Wing thought.

Rising to her toes, Carly brushed her lips against his face and whispered into his ear, "It's good to see you."

Wing leaned in to kiss her, but the creaking of the opening door negated it. He turned to see Carly's father enter. "Why, Son-Cawutt, it's good to see you. How have you been?"

"Well, Father-Vanut," Wing replied.

Wing saw his eyes shift to Wing's hand where it rested on the low curve of Carly's back. "Better friends than lovers," he warned. "She's a fighter and no cook. You'll starve to death."

"That's fine—I rarely have a mind to eat," Wing said.

Hoath raised his nose into the air and sniffed. "Really?"

"Well, not tonight, of course."

Carly laughed. "Nice save."

Wing tried, but was unable to enjoy the joke.

"Do you want to skip dinner?" Carly asked. "We can take a walk, or..."

"No, let's eat. You must be starving after being with the Cant all day."

"I think we'll only have one or two more training sessions before the Ime break." Stepping closer, Carly placed one of her legs between Wing's and pressed her body against him. "I guess what's bothering you isn't something you can tell me quickly, is it?"

"No," he said.

Standing on her tiptoes, she kissed his face.

Wing appreciated not being pressed and gratefully ran his hand up the curve of her spine. Carly shivered as he lowered his head and brushing his nose against her neck, breathed deeply. Some of the tension began to release from his shoulders—

"Carly! Call your brother and sister, we're ready to eat."

Carly sank in his arms. They shared a sigh.

"Can we just disappear?" Carly whispered.

Wing looked back her, thinking, *Oh, how I wish we could...*

Carly yelled for her little sister and brother and they all emerged into the meal room at once.

"When is the Cant going to take its Ime break?" Hoath asked, spearing a cut of meat.

"In a turn," Carly replied. "I've taken over for Nien till then."

Wing tensed.

"Taken over for Nien?" Hoath asked.

Carly squirmed for a moment. "He's left for Quieness."

Vay dropped her spoon. Carly's siblings gaped at them. But Hoath just nodded. "I'd heard something about that. I thought it was a joke." He looked at Wing. "So it's true?"

"Yes."

"How do you feel about it?"

It took Wing a little too long to reply, "It's not something I would do."

Hoath noted the hesitation. "You don't agree?" It was a loaded question.

"I...He needed to go," Wing said.

The table tensed, wondering if Hoath were going to push Wing into an answer. He did. "So you *don't* agree?"

Wing's eyes studied his plate for a time. "It was not my choice, nor," he added, "should it have been."

Hoath took another bite of food. "It is a bold step." He chewed purposefully. "So, will you be replacing him, then?"

"Replacing him?" Wing asked.

"In the Cant."

As insulting as Hoath's question was to Carly who had just said she'd taken over Cant training in Nien's absence, Wing could not quite believe Hoath's temerity.

"If joining the Cant has not previously been in your plans, might now be the opportune time?" Hoath pressed.

Wing glanced at Carly, but she was busy staring a hole into her father.

"There is much to do before Ime," Wing said slowly. "Both in the fields and here in the Village—"

"So even if my daughter would have to serve as protector to you and your children, and your brother an educator for them, at least you could put a roof over their heads?"

Wing trembled involuntarily. Beside him, he could feel Carly struggling to control her emotions as she said, "Father." Her voice carried a tone of finality.

At the opposite end of the table Vay had stopped eating.

Keir, Carly's younger brother, tapped his utensil against the side of his plate before muttering, "All the people are saying it, Carly." Carly shot him a warning glance; he continued anyway. "Merehr," he said to Wing. "The title is already yours. Everyone's just waiting for you to accept it and join the Cant. They'd even give you Grek Occoju's position on the Council." He glanced around at his family. "I've heard that Grek's said it—that he'd step aside for Wing."

Wing's eyes had come to rest steadfastly on his plate as Carly's baby sister asked quietly, "*Are* you Merehr?"

An even stickier silence crept into the room.

Carly pushed herself away from the table. "If you'll excuse us," she said. Stepping to Wing's side, she leaned down and whispered in his ear.

Wing stood slowly. As Carly took his hand, Wing thanked Vay for the invitation to dinner, nodded to Hoath, and followed Carly out the door.

Carly and Wing walked in silence down a Village row leading out of town and toward the grassy plains that separated the Village from the solitary Cawutt home at the far end.

Wing was withdrawn and appeared physically weakened as Carly released his olive-skinned hand and slipped her arm around his waist. "I'm so sorry," she said.

Wing continued to walk.

A short distance past the Cantfields, Wing stopped and turned to face her. "You need to get back," he said. "You need to eat, and" —he took one of her hands in his and rubbed briefly at the dried mud on her palm— "get cleaned up."

Carly smiled half-heartedly. She wanted to say something to make it all better. She wanted to say sorry a hundred, a thousand times. "Thanks for coming," she said instead. "Thanks for inviting me," Wing replied, but his words were an automatic response, he was already far away from where they stood. Though Carly searched his face for any sign of what she may say, there were no evidences, no hints, and the distance between them was lengthening by the moment.

Wing squeezed her hand, then turned and continued off across the fields.

Carly watched him go until his figure became only a small speck amongst the tall grasses.

If there were no food in their stomachs or roofs over their heads, Carly thought, *how much would it matter whether Wing wielded a sword or not? Whether he sat on the Council?*

As Wing disappeared from her sight, Carly turned back and looked at the Village. She didn't like being inundated with thoughts of politics and prophecies. Both, in her mind, just got in the way of getting on with the business of life. But Wing was inexorably pulled into the heart of both and she was inexorably drawn into his.

Slapping some mud from her pants, she started back toward her house wishing that she and Wing could just be alone, build a house of some sort out at his end of the valley and pretend, pretend, that the only thing they had to worry about was the weather and the Cant's training schedule.

Where Carly's sight had lost him, Wing walked on. Since leaving her he'd had only one clear thought: *I can't feel my feet.*

He'd crossed nearly half the valley when another thought took its place: *Those children. What they were willing to believe…*

He took a breath, but his vocal chords seized upon the air and there came a slight, desperate moan. He locked out the sound. Swallowed.

Nien.

His brother's name threatened the thin hold he had on his throat.

"You were right," Wing said to his absent brother. "It's all falling apart. And I can't do anything about it. I already knew it was, but hearing it from you that day…Yosha. And then you leave. But then," Wing realized, "I didn't give you any reason to stay. I never told you that, as long as there was the two of us, I had hope we'd figure all this out."

A terrible feeling said then what Wing had feared all along, but never, even to himself, been able to speak: *Nien may not come back.*

Wing felt the realization suck the strength from his limbs.

My silence, Wing thought. *The closing of the school. There's nothing for him to come back to—other than the Cant.*

And if it turned out the Cant wasn't enough, Wing wouldn't blame him. Rieeve didn't deserve Nien anyway; he was just too curious, too eager. His voracious appetite for knowledge could not have been contained indefinitely by Rieeve's lack of it, and suddenly Wing felt guilty for wishing Nien home. One of them might as well be doing exactly what they wanted to do, for neither of them had gotten anywhere staying in Rieeve.

Staying. In. Rieeve.

The words hung in his mind like an omen.

What if…? What if the only solution is for me to leave?

It was the choice Rhegal and the one before him, Reeant, had made.

Because, Wing realized, *they were forced to. Because there was no answer. There was no other way.*

Wing stopped walking and stood, a lone figure in a vast stretch of fields.

So, there it is, he thought. *The end that's been in front of me all along. If any of this is ever going to work out, if the people will not look to Lant for direction, then maybe there really is only one solution:*

I'll need to leave Rieeve.

CHAPTER 22

Good Drink, Bad News

Commander Lant tidied up the small wooden desk in the Cantfield hut and, pulling on a long overcoat and favorite hat, stepped out into the fading twilight and began his walk across the Cantfields toward home.

Nearing the space between his home and the tree-lined valley edge he heard: "Psst!"

Stopping, Lant looked behind him into the darkness of the tree line.

"Commander!"

Lant headed toward the trees. Stepping through their leafy border, he found Jason, Master Monteray's nephew, leaning against a tree munching on something.

"Jason!" Lant said with happy surprise. "So good to see you. Have you been waiting long?"

"Not too long."

"You look well," Lant observed.

"I am."

"How was the trip?"

"Quiet."

"And your family?"

"Well and fine. Busy. You know how it goes."

"Certainly. Are you staying a night or two?"

"Just one," Jason said.

"One will have to do, then. Let's go."

Lant slung one of Jason's bags over his shoulder and the two made their way along the valley edge inside the tree line until they were adjacent to Lant's front door.

It was not by chance that Lant had chosen to build his home at the sun-rising edge of the valley, close to the Cantfields and Jhiyak Canyon.

For the most part, Lant made visiting trips to the other valleys himself since a friend coming into Rieeve was required to come and go as quickly and surreptitiously as possible. As overjoyed as Lant was to see Jason, only once in all the revolutions since his return to Rieeve had an unscheduled visit not bode ill; he knew this time would not be the second.

The sun had set and in the dim light it was easy enough for Jason to pose as Pree K until they'd made it indoors—something he'd done before.

"Jason! Bleekla, it's good to see you," Pree K said as his friend walked into the front room behind Lant.

Jason and Pree K embraced and the three set off into the kitchen for drink and food.

"Uncle Monteray really wanted to drop everything and come himself," Jason said. "He practically packed my duffel for me."

"I'll try and forgive him," Lant said.

The three men settled in around the table.

Jason drained a cup of Lant's finest. He then leaned over and pulled a thin, rolled parchment from his duffel. Placing it on the table, he pushed it toward Lant.

This was customary.

Lant and Monteray exchanged letters with each visit. But this time Jason's manner was as tight as the knots securing the parchments. As Lant began to untie them, Jason got up from the table and stepped into the kitchen.

Lant unrolled the familiar parchment, scraped of he and Monteray's last correspondence, and began to read. He read it three times before setting it down.

"What is it?" Pree K asked.

Lant looked at his son. "Monteray received confirmation that the Valley of Tou has been taken by the Ka'ull."

Pree K met his eyes for a cumbrous moment before reaching for his wine.

From the dark kitchen, Jason said, "I was there when the messenger from Quieness came to my uncle's home. The story she told us is enough to make dreams slide into nightmares so terrible you can't tell which is worse: being awake and thinking about it or trying to sleep and dreaming about it. I wandered around for three days afterward like I was lost in a Criyean embarkation ritual." He shook his head. "Awake or asleep, it doesn't really matter—you can't escape it."

Lant and Pree K listened to him quietly.

Jason walked back to the table and sat down. For a time, the three nursed their drinks in silence.

Taking a deep draught, Jason tilted his cup toward Lant. "It's good to be here. You Rieevans have your quirks. Wine, however, is not one of them." He forced a short smile. "For the sake of Legran pride, it's a good thing your people keep to themselves. If word ever got out about Rieevan wine you'd put the Hiona out of business."

Lant pulled himself from the black thread of his thoughts and replied, "Compete with the Hiona? Never." He directed his gaze to Jason's duffel. "You wouldn't have come all this way—?"

Jason tipped a grin. "Have I ever?" He reached down and withdrew two familiar flasks.

Lant and Pree K each took one, uncorking the tops. Taking slow sips, father and son savored the deep maroon liquid before swallowing.

"Flattery is easy when you know you have the best," Pree K said, his voice filling with content.

Jason downed the rest of his Rieevan wine. "Well, a little variety helps."

"Yes it does," Pree K agreed, and the three let heavier thoughts flee as they moved into the front room, settled into a couch and a couple of stuffed chairs, and talked of Monteray, the house, and the latest happenings in the Valley of Legran.

The three had talked into the wee moonsteps of the morning when Lant finally excused himself.

"I need to a get a bit of sleep." He cast a glance at Pree K and Jason. "There's a Council meeting in the morning."

"Are you going to tell them?" Pree K asked.

Lant nodded uneasily before asking Jason, "Will you be leaving before first light or staying on another day?"

"In the morning dark," Jason said.

"You know we would love for you to stay," Lant said.

"And I would. But Uncle Monteray needs me back."

"I understand," Lant said. He looked at Pree K. "Son, in the morning I need you to ride out and speak with Wing. Ask him to come to the Cant hut to meet with me."

The pause between Lant's request and Pree K's answer was long enough for Jason to notice the gravity in it. Though Lant could feel Jason's gaze upon him, he did not look away from Pree K until, at last, Pree K said, "E'te, Father."

The following sunrise caught only fragments of sprinting feet as Pree K lit over the fields like sparks in a strong wind. He'd already said goodbye to Jason, going with him a ways up Jhiyak Canyon before needing to head back to Rieeve in order to fulfill his unpleasant assignment. He ran now, not because he was in a hurry to get to the other side of the valley (part of him would have crawled backwards to avoid the actual arrival), but simply because he loved to run. When he ran, the sun chased him. If there was wind, it turned to have his back. The earth coiled and sprung beneath his feet. It was as if every mechanical effort that went into propelling his body forward was the work of earth and sky itself.

In the midst of this ecstatic whirlwind, the grey smudge in the distance that was Wing and the plow team came at him suddenly and far sooner than he would have expected.

Regretfully breaking his pace, he slowed, and came to an unsteady halt.

Throwing his hands upon his knees, Pree K bathed in the familiar rush of vertigo and adrenaline that gushed out his limbs and gaping mouth, making him shake and pant and smile. In his life, there was nothing like the sweet, sweeping exhaustion that followed a good run.

Carefully, like a first time seaman disembarking from a terrible voyage, he began to make his way toward Wing, the newly overturned rows and furrows doing nothing to help steady his feet.

Pausing, Pree K watched as Wing came to the end of a row. As Wing turned the horses about, Pree K caught a glimpse of his face before Wing had noticed him. Usually impossibly serene when found in the fields, Pree K was startled at the anguish he saw in Wing's concentrated expression. There were dark circles under his eyes and his normally straight, decided gait was almost as wobbly as Pree K's—

It was about the worst thing Pree K could have seen, knowing that the message he'd been sent to deliver would only compound whatever it was that already had Wing looking so misaligned.

"E'te," Pree K called, hailing him.

Wing raised his eyes in surprise. "Son-Pree K, e'te," he called back just as the plow hit a rock, sending it grinding off row. Wing struggled briefly to correct it as Pree K closed the distance between them.

"What brings you way out here?" Wing asked as Pree K came into step beside him.

Pree K had hoped for a bit of small talk, but Wing's question provided too obvious an opening. "The Commander sent me to see if you'd stop by the Cant hut."

An awkward moment passed.

"When?" Wing asked.

"This afternoon, if you will."

"Did he say what for?"

"Not specifically, no."

"I hadn't planned on going into the Village for...a while. Is it urgent?"

Pree K hesitated. "It's...important."

Wing was quiet as he guided the plow through a rough patch. "Alright," he said.

"Thanks," Pree K said, hoping Wing could tell without his having to say how hard posing the question was, how hard it had been for Lant to ask it of him.

"If you'd like," Wing said, "feel free to stop by the house before the trip back. I'm sure Reean would love to see you—and feed you."

Pree K grinned. "I'd be unwise to refuse."

"No doubt," Wing replied.

Wanting but unable to find anything to say to address his concern over Wing's apparent state of distress, Pree K turned and headed out at a jog for the large Cawutt home in the distance.

Back in the Village, Lant was on his way to face his own disquieting event. Unlike his son, he had no inclination to run. He strode down the near-empty streets and entering the Council chamber took his seat to wait for the rest of the Council members to arrive. One of the quiet ones on the Council, Lant normally said very little unless asked. This morning was no different. Tired as he was, it was the news and the price it would exact on the Cawutt family that had his thoughts so deeply internalized that Grek Occoju had to say his name twice before getting his attention.

"Councilman? Commander Lant?"

Lant looked up.

"It appears you have something on your mind," Grek said.

The moment of silence before Lant replied registered heavily amongst the other members.

Lant leaned forward. Beneath the table, his hands were clenched. "I have received confirmation: the Ka'ull have seized the valley of Tou."

The effect of this news on the Council was profoundly worse than the news of the fall of Lou. Lou was the northingmost valley on the continent, it was very far away—it might as well have been another continent entirely. Tou, however. Tou was just on the other side of the Ti-Uki Confluence, the headwaters of the Tu'Lon River just above Rieeve.

As the members' initial reactions vented out into the room, Grek Occoju met Lant's gaze. The two men waited a bit longer for the room to quiet.

—And it did, upon Councilman Moer Ta'leer's saying: "We cannot wait any longer for Son-Cawutt Wing to accept who he is."

Lant and Grek looked in Moer's direction. Lant spoke first. "And what is it you think he'll do? Even if he *is* Merehr, he is only one man!"

"*One* man?" Councilman Brath Vanc said. "I swear, Councilman, it is as if you have never read the Ancient Writings. Merehr's reach far exceeds our feeble mortal attempts to stand against this enemy, if indeed, they have intentions for Rieeve."

"Councilman Vanc is right," Fu Breeal said. "There is no proof that the Ka'ull intend on coming here. It may be they only wanted Lou and Tou. It is possible they will stop there."

Lant felt as if his body were on fire. He wanted to tell them all he knew, how he knew that the Ka'ull would not stop with Lou and Tou, how they were just getting started. How important Rieeve was to them. But the Council and the people were filled with generations of belief that Merehr would call down armies from the sky, perform spontaneous healings, cause earthquakes, reach, even into the otherworlds, to save them all.

The fire in Lant's body spent itself. He suddenly felt like a man twice his age. "You believe in Wing so mightily," he said with deep resignation, "why don't you simply test him, show him to himself? I see no other way to convince him." As soon as the words left his lips, Lant couldn't believe he'd said them.

The sting, however, had little impact as another of the Council members replied in all seriousness: "It's been considered."

Grek Occoju said to Lant, "Will you speak with Wing?"

"I have spoken with him before," Lant replied tiredly.

"Then perhaps you could speak with him again," Grek Occoju suggested.

As Grek said the words, Lant recalled the last conversation he'd had with Nien on the subject: "*This is not easy for any of us,*" he had said. "*And selfishly, I feel it has challenged my friendship with Wing.*"

"*Wing loves and respects you; he always has,*" Nien had said, to which Lant had replied, "*I won't call for him again.*"

Now, here he was. He'd already sent Pree K out to fetch Wing. Before he'd even walked into the Council chamber that morning he'd known it—Wing was the key. The cost would be great, to Lant himself, to Wing and his family, and to Nien. But the cost of not trying to convince Wing was much higher. It could mean all their people.

Merehr. The word sounded in his mind with a weight almost as great as the promise he'd made to Nien—

The promise he'd have to break.

Glancing about at the earnest faces of his fellow Council members, Lant sighed inwardly, and conceded: "I will try and speak with him again."

Lant left the Council chamber and walked slowly toward the Cant hut at the edge of the Cantfields. He was weary. Weary of body but mostly of mind. He had not been long in the Cant hut when he heard a light rap come on the outside of it.

"Come in," he called.

Wing ducked into the hut through the thick leather hide Lant had placed over the door for the cold turns.

Lant looked up at him. It had been so long since he'd spoken with Wing, even as a friend, that seeing him brought a fresh surge of regret and something bordering on shame.

"Wing," he said. "It's good to see you."

"And you, Commander," Wing replied politely—too politely, Lant noticed.

"Have a seat if you'd like," Lant offered.

Wing took the seat.

"Something to drink?" Lant asked.

"No, Commander. Thanks."

Might as well get to it, Lant thought. "Any conversation that begins with: 'I'm sorry to ask you this,' is one I'd rather not have." Wing's eyes drifted to the floor. Lant moved on. "Wing, I, well, this morning I gave news to the Council that the valley of Tou has been captured by the Ka'ull."

Wing's green gaze shot up at him. "Tou?" His query hung in the air. "When?"

"I received a messenger from Master Monteray last night."

Something flashed in Wing's eyes, but the flicker died away quickly and Lant had not time to guess what it might have meant.

"You know that convincing the Council of the need for an armed force was not easy. But now I face an even more difficult situation. Though the Council seems to agree that there may be a need to defend ourselves, it's imperative that they understand no matter how well prepared or armed we are, we could never withstand a force as great as the Ka'ull present. We are a small valley. We need help. And though this is not necessarily good news, we are not the only valley that does.

"Now that the Ka'ull have secured Tou, they will be emboldened, they will attack Majg and Criye and after that Legran and Jayak. They will not stop. But the people will not listen to me." Lant leaned forward, placing his hands upon his desk. "I know how hard this is on you, but I...I'm running out of ways, out of words to awaken the Council to the necessity of an alliance with the other valleys." Lant spread his fingers and pressed his palms against the cool smoothness of the desk. "I'm not asking you to accept historical assumptions. I'm not asking you to claim this prophetic mission.

What I *am* asking is that you at least think about joining the Cant. In such a position they may listen to you on matters of defense—you may be the only one who could convince them that what I say is true."

Wing sat still and stiff and for a time said nothing.

"I know what I ask," Lant said. "I know it is no small thing. But you must understand *why* I ask it."

"I understand, Lant." Slowly, Wing raised his face. "But I cannot."

Through the despair Wing's words wrought in him, Lant stayed with him, remaining open to the possibility that there were reasons Wing had for saying no that Lant had not yet ascertained. "Will you tell me why?"

"False hope," Wing said.

It was as great an opening as Wing had given him in many revolutions.

"Being in the Cant doesn't mean you accept the role of Leader," Lant offered.

"We both know it would mean the same thing."

Lant could not deny it. He knew all about walking fine lines. "It's a possibility, yes."

Wing's eyes fixed upon the table and his voice was so low when he spoke that Lant almost didn't catch what he said— "If it were only just that."

"What, then?" Lant asked carefully. He could see there was a debate going on inside of Wing and he hoped, desperately, that Wing would forge his way through it and divulge the truth of his concern.

"It's, I..." Wing started to say. He stopped. "I wish they would listen to you, Lant. I've tried to tell them…"

Lant's heart hammered. Perhaps this was the moment, at last, that Wing would let him in, reveal his motivations, his reasons. But just as Lant thought Wing might finally part the profound layers of silence between them, Wing got suddenly to his feet and turned to leave.

I've been talking to a ghost, Lant thought, his hope crashing around him. *Did he not hear anything I said?*

With his back to Lant, Wing paused at the hut door. "I do not know the truth of what I am," he said softly, "but that doesn't mean I can live a lie."

Wing slipped through the hut door as if he'd never been there.

As the heavy leather flap fell back into place, Lant felt as if a great hand had wrung the very strength from his heart.

Leaning forward over his desk, Lant buried his face in the palms of his large, weathered hands, and tried to press his eyes into the darkness of his mind.

CHAPTER 23

No Turning Back

The morning sun was bright and cold as Wing worked around the house and barn with the team, pushing snow. Snow levels were not bad and he could have let it be, but he wanted to be outside and keeping the snow cleared out now would help when the heavier storms came.

The sunsteps passed quickly and by early afternoon, Wing and the team had, in places, pushed the snow back to dirt.

"Well," Wing said with a hint of self-amusement, "that should over do it. Let's head in." Hungry, and sure the horses felt the same, Wing released the shift of metal plow and left it behind the barn.

With the long plow reins draped over their backs, the team followed Wing like obedient hounds. Rounding the side of the barn, Wing looked up and stopped dead in his tracks. Beside the house were picketed nearly twenty horses. He recognized a few of them as belonging to Council members.

Wing had not seen such a gathering at his home in—

The blood drained from his face.

—not since he'd been a boy of fourteen revolutions and a delegation of the Rieevan Council and other villagers had come out to speak with Joash and Reean—

About him.

Staring fixedly at the congregation of horses, Wing recalled sitting at the back of the room that night so long ago, listening as the villagers and Council skirted the subject with his parents, asking questions about his behavior, interests, education. Though he feigned ignorance, Wing knew who they thought him to be and he wondered if that were the reason he felt so different, so unlike everyone he knew. Wondered if that was why he just knew things about people, the earth, and even animals that others could neither see nor hear. He'd not thought this ability abnormal, but perhaps it wasn't common. Nevertheless, he'd said nothing, fearing that if he did acknowledge it they would use his confession to trap him into *their* version of what it meant.

So he had held his silence, and as he'd sat at the back of the room, listening, he'd seen in the eyes of the Council members a look that set upon him like a storm, warning him that secrets were the soil from which desperate acts of self-preservation sprang.

In the many revolutions since Wing had tried to hunt out the secrets not only in the Ancient Writings, but also of his own nature and come up entirely empty, without even the slightest validation, direction, or illumination.

In the wake of such a dearth, Wing had watched the warning he'd felt that day coming true—in him, in his family, and in the people who now felt threatened and were becoming fanatical.

Beside the house, one of the Council member's horses bit at another and their brief bout of squeals snapped Wing back to the present.

Turning, he continued on into the barn. The plow team came in behind him and stopped outside their stalls, waiting for him to remove their harnesses. Wing did so by rote, offering an absent-minded clap on their rumps as he poured out some grain and threw in the hay, his thoughts running around the notion of jumping onto one of the other family horses and making for the tree line.

But that would leave his family to face the Council's questions alone, as they had done so very many times before.

Wing stepped to the barn door and looked out at the house.

Nien was gone; the words he'd said when he left rang in Wing's ears: "*Say* something! Say anything!"

As if he were wearing stones for shoes, Wing quietly left the horses and made the longest walk of his life from the barn to the house.

Inside, Reean and Jake were trying to come up with enough mugs and cups to offer their visitors a drink as Joash sat, stone-faced, at the center of them. All eyes shifted to the door as Wing came in. Buying himself a few more seconds, Wing took his long coat off and hung it carefully beside the door. As he turned, "Son-Cawutt Wing," greeted him in a chorus of voices.

He nodded to them collectively, said hello, and moved over to the table. Reean met him, pushing a cup of hot tea into his hand. She looked up into his eyes and he looked back at her and before she could whisper her words of regret, Wing mouthed: "It's all right."

All the chairs from the table were set about the large open living space and as Wing turned around a few stood to offer him theirs. He shook his head and motioned for them to keep their seats. Placing a foot upon the wall that separated the main room from the back bedroom, Wing leaned against it, holding his cup against his stomach. The uncomfortable small talk between Joash, Reean, and their visitors passed over him in a nauseating wave. There was a ringing in his ears and a vacuum in his chest and he almost walked right back out the door.

Sitting near Joash, Grek Occoju said, "It's been a long time since we, as a Council and villagers, have been out to see you and your family."

"It has been," Wing replied.

"I'm sure you can guess," Grek Occoju said, thankfully shutting the door on what could have been another exhausting string of pleasantries, "that we came out to speak with you."

Wing nodded.

"Perhaps Commander Lant has told you that the valley of Tou has also fallen to the Ka'ull..."

Of course, they all knew that Wing knew. They had been the ones to ask Lant to speak with him again.

Wing let it go, let the Council Spokesman continue. "As, it seems, Lant has failed to convince you, we've come to ask you ourselves: The people think you're the one. Is this news of the fall of Tou not sufficient impetus for you to accept your calling? Will you believe in our people as they believe in you?"

Nothing like coming to the point, Wing thought, surprised, shocked, and oddly pleased at Grek's assertiveness.

"What do I have to do?" Wing's eyes were focused on the mug of tea he held against his belly.

"Do?" Councilman Occoju said.

"To convince you that I am not who you think I am?"

Hands worked uncomfortably in laps and short glances were exchanged between the villagers and Council members.

"Why do you think you are not?" Grek Occoju replied.

Though the Council Spokesman's tone was tinged with the voice of a father scolding a child, Wing was surprised at how much longing it contained. Wing knew the present company felt they saw further than he did, saw more in him than he saw in himself. He knew they believed that they understood the Ancient Writings in ways Wing himself had not yet come to, and perhaps they did; he was willing to concede that possibility. Nevertheless, he could not take their word on faith when it overrode all that, to Wing, was incontrovertible proof of the opposite—that he was a farmer, one hounded by garish nightmares, true, but that did not make him special, that only made him troubled.

"If I am," Wing said slowly, "it will only serve our people if I come to it on my own." He looked around the room. "I think it's obvious, after all this time, that we cannot force each other—neither you to disbelieve nor me to believe."

Eyes drifted to the steam rising from their cups. Even Brap Cuiku held his drink in silence.

Slowly, Occoju looked up and met Wing's clarion gaze. "You need not fear our belief in you," he said quietly, "only have faith—in Eosha, in yourself, and in us."

Beneath the weight of Grek's earnestness, Wing felt momentarily diminished.

In painful, awkward moments, the silence passed and the longer it was kept, the stronger its oppressiveness grew. The impulse to give in, to tell them what they wanted to hear resurfaced in Wing. He felt like a child again. A child of fourteen revolutions.

Strangely, he'd felt more confidence as a child that he might be, or could have become, the Leader. But he hadn't had the language as a child to explain why he thought so. Now, as an adult, he had no confidence whatsoever in the idea of a Leader, much less that it might be him. However, as a man, he *did* have the language to explain that.

So, thwarting the impulse to tell them what they wanted to hear, Wing closed his eyes. Burning deep in his gut, he found the fire of his will. He could not surrender to theirs. The cost would be too great.

Steadied in his center, Wing opened his eyes. "You may hate me," he said, "but is that not better than false hope?"

At the word 'hate', Wing saw a Villager's mouth gape in astonishment. When he closed his mouth again there was sadness in his eyes.

"We do not hate you," Grek said solemnly.

"Not now," Wing replied. "But it would come to that if I told you what you wanted to hear, if I said yes, and then did not live up to the paragon. No matter how hard we try, the voice of the many cannot drown out the voice of the one." Wing looked around the room. "I have faith, however, that someday I'll understand how we, as a people, got to this place."

"How *we* got to this place?" one of the Villagers asked; it was not asked softly. "What do *we* have to do with prophecies told anciently? What had we to do with what the Ka'ull have done in the Northing valleys? You speak as if it's our fault."

Wing glanced at the villager. He recognized him but did not know him well. "Perhaps more than we think. Perhaps less. I don't know." Wing paused. "You think I have answers. Truth is, all I have are questions. If you want to know what to do, if you want my counsel on what we should do about the Ka'ull threat, then listen to Lant. He knows more than I—more than any of us. Heed *his* counsel. That is the only answer I have for you."

"But the Ancient Writings say: 'Often the one that knows is not aware of the very thing that chooses. And many things fall away, and some are never found again. Today we stand in certainty, tomorrow in doubt.' Could this passage not be speaking of this very impasse?"

Wing did not reply.

"What do you think it means?" Ne'taan, one of the younger Council members, asked.

"Which part?" Wing replied, his voice heavy.

"Well, what is it exactly, that chooses? And how would one know if something was lost before he ever came to know it, especially if it was never to be found again?"

"Both questions, I imagine, will have answers different to as many individuals as ask them." Wing shrugged. "What did Teqoi have in mind when he wrote it? I suppose only he really knows."

"What do *you* think, then?" Ne'taan asked again.

"I think truth will eventually find truth."

"Such an inscrutable answer," Councilman Cuiku said. "Do you give it merely to avoid conversation?"

"No," Wing said slowly.

Grek interceded. "We do not mean to be combative."

"As long as I do not say what you expect or want me to say, it will seem as if I am purporting elusiveness."

"But do you speak in such a way intentionally? To avoid true understanding?"

Wing's eyes softened, and his shoulders lowered. "No. I speak my truth."

"What does *your* truth have to do with...anything?" Brap Cuiku said.

Wing raised his eyes and looked at Brap. "Because at least I know it is my own."

"But if we cannot understand you, how can we ever come to an understanding?" another of the villagers asked.

"When one is in their mind, the language of the heart cannot be heard, much less understood. The heart must be felt. It is an...experience."

"But we cannot know what is in your heart unless you tell us," Grek Occoju said.

"I *have* told you," Wing replied.

Grek's voice was low. "Sometimes we think you to be blind and deaf—not to see what we see, not to hear what we say to you. To be so read in the Ancient Writings, to be so acquainted with prophecy, and yet so unwilling to…"

"I do not see what you see in them," Wing said quietly. "I am on one road, you are on another; they do not intersect."

"We would like to try."

Wing believed Grek when he said this, and he believed that a few others might feel the same, but the distance was too great. One could not force the crossing.

"I know you believe what you say." Wing's eyes grew distant, seeming to see beyond the room and discomfiting position they were now in. "Perhaps someday, we will find a road upon which we can all travel."

Because right now, Wing thought but could not say, *such a road does not exist in Rieeve, not unless*…An idea formed in Wing's mind. *Not unless there was a way to build a new one.*

Standing there, with all the anxious eyes of the Council members and villagers upon him, Wing suddenly felt light, as if a door in an impenetrable wall had magically appeared.

I've been trying, all this time, to repair the old road, Wing thought. *Maybe that isn't the point…*

When Wing's eyes focused again it was as if he'd come back from some inescapably beautiful land. Grek was looking at him.

"Son-Cawutt?" he asked.

Wing was silent but there must have been something about his expression that had the Council and villagers staring up at him.

Only one seemed to miss what the others were seeing. "Well?" Cuiku asked. "That's it?"

Wing looked at Cuiku. "Yes."

Frustrated, Cuiku pushed his chair back and stood. "You are incorrigible. We will all regret our belief in you."

The room fell impossibly silent. Some were aghast, others embarrassed by Cuiku's harsh words and disrespect, but all remained silent.

Glancing around the room, Wing said, "I can no more account for what you see in the Ancient Writings than for what you see in me. I am not the Leader. More than that, I cannot say. More than that, I could never promise."

As Wing finished, he noticed the Council members and villagers exchanging furtive glances.

Joash stood, Reean began to speak, and Wing realized the meeting was far from over. From up the stairs a villager came down, holding the hand of what looked to be a very sick child.

Ice water flooded Wing's veins. The child's eyes were a terrible yellow, and it appeared he could barely stand.

The child's father led the boy up to Wing.

Wing stepped away from the wall and set his mug down on the Mesko table.

"He's been ill for two turns now. We don't know what's wrong."

"I am not a physician," Wing said, his voice sliding off his tongue like shards of glass across a metal plate.

"That doesn't matter," the villager said. "You, you hear things, know things…won't you please tell us?"

Wing looked down at the boy. The boy did not lift his gaze nor did he speak. Wing felt a deep blackness fill his belly. It felt like death.

"Take him home," Wing said, and without another word moved across the room and out the door.

CHAPTER 24

Furrowing

S potting Wing from a distance, Carly reined in her horse. She had not seen him since before the news of Tou. Since then, she'd heard that Lant had spoken with him and that the entire Council had gone out to speak with him personally, at his home. She'd also heard that they had even asked him to heal a sick child. He had not been into the Village more than twice since Nien had left for Quieness—nearly a season ago.

She regretted that it had taken her so long to go to him.

A cloud passed between their world and the sun, casting a shadow across the fields where Wing walked behind the team and plow, his tall figure bent over the guiding handles. He was always the first one to the fields at the end of Ime. For him, the planting season of Kive was always too short.

Carly continued to watch as he paused at the end of a row and glanced up at the sky. The cloud moved away, and the sun shone upon his face. She saw a faint smile of satisfaction close his eyes. Enjoying his pleasure, she waited a bit more before calling out his name.

Looking around, Wing spotted her and set down the reins to the team.

Carly rode up and dismounted, letting the reins hang free so her mount could wander off and graze. "Hi," she said.

"Hello," Wing replied.

Carly wrapped her arms about his waist. Wing's shirt was warmed by the sun. He smelled like sweat and fresh dirt and horses.

"Bit of sun feels good, doesn't it?" she said.

"It does."

"So, when do you expect Nien?"

"He told mother and fa that he was planning on being back in time for Kive fest." His tone was dispassionate, but in his verdant gaze was a well of doubt and sadness.

"What is it?"

"Nothing."

Carly looked up into his eyes. "He's coming back," she said.

"You don't know how it was between us when he left."

"That's because," Carly said carefully, "you never told me what happened."

"We said...things." Clearly, he still did not want to explain.

Accustomed to letting things go with him, Carly pressed her face into the hollow of his shoulder and breathed deeply, reveling in the feel and flavour of him. Wing went to caress her head but she took his hand and pulled him to the ground.

In rows where Wing had plowed deeply, the black soil was still hard and cold, but where they lay, Wing on his back, Carly on top of him, the surface had begun to soften and warm in the sun.

"I heard about, well, everything." Wing's body stiffened beneath her. "There are few secrets in the Cant," she said.

"There are few secrets anywhere."

"I can't excuse anything the Council does, but please know that I trust Lant with my life. He would never deliberately attempt to—"

Wing cut her off. "I know."

Carly studied Wing's face. She knew the look. It happened before he shut down, shut her out, went deep inside himself and left the world without his voice.

"Wing, please don't disappear. I didn't come to...Just let me say this. I've rehearsed it all the way out here."

Wing looked up at her.

"Whatever decision you make," she said, "I will stand by you. And even if you never tell me your reasons, I've never doubted you."

Looking more disconsolate than he had before she'd spoken, Wing asked: "Why?"

"*Why?*"

"Why would you?"

"Why would I...?"

"Why would you trust me?"

Carly almost laughed. "Are you crazy?" But she could see he was serious.

"Why are you out here? The Village, the Cantfields are that way" —he motioned with his head— "Mien'k and Reel and Teru are there. Everything is there."

Carly placed both her hands on his face. "Not everything."

Wing's chest rose and fell wearily. "Is there anything I am meant to understand?"

Carly traced his shoulders and hair with her eyes. "All that means very little," she said softly, "without you." She hoped Wing could see the depth to which she meant her words, but he had looked away. "I'm sorry. But I had to tell you."

Wing's eyes were shut and he lay distant and closed beneath her.

Reaching down, she pulled free the bottom of his shirt and slid her hand under. Feeling his ribs beneath her fingers, she pushed her hand up over his right nipple, and into the hollow and curve of his shoulder.

As she'd hoped, she felt the rigidness ease from his body and with it the wall between them.

Wing brought his hands up and smoothed her back, curling his fingers into the soft furrow of her spine. Carly went for his belt—

But Wing stopped her. "The horses," he said.

Carly laughed. "I'm sure they won't mind."

CHAPTER 25

Unexpected

N ien retired to the small room he'd acquired in the nearby vicinity of the library. He lay across a short wooden cot, only a couple of small pillows adding comfort to the otherwise dismaying bed.

About the room were many books. There were a few on science and astronomy, one on biology, another on mathematics, as well as a large collection of historical accounts documenting the evolution of nearly every valley on the continent—but none of these were the least bit surprising. These were the subjects he had intended on studying once he got to Quieness. So what *was* surprising were the many philosophical and religious books of every possible discipleship that made up the bulk of the room's untidiness. Upon setting off for Quieness, Nien had imagined religion would be the last subject he would care to research or study. Nevertheless, it seemed these particular books kept popping up, choosing him before he had the chance to convince himself he was uninterested.

The following night in the library, Nien was pondering the oddity of the occurrence when Necassa came up behind him and rested her head upon his shoulder.

"Tired?" Nien asked.

She nodded into his shoulder. "And hungry."

Nien placed a few books back in their shelves and took up his coat. "Let's go then, before I have to carry you to food."

Necassa nodded happily, and they walked together out into the gloaming.

Moving through the streets, now cleared of businessmen and filled with evening diners and shoppers, they stopped into a small, familiar café and sank into hard-meshed chairs. Strings of small candles hung overhead across dark wooden beams, and plant vines grew throughout a thin wall of interwoven fibers creating a bare distinction between inside and outside dining.

Nien had been enthralled by Quienan nightlife from his and Necassa's first outing. It was as if when the sun went down a whole new city was born. Tall lamplights turned down the frantic nature of sunlit streets, encouraging people to wander nightlimned corners where warm shops and warmer diners shone with a welcoming glow. Café's that during the day might not be noted at all now held the seductive blush of a beckoning finger—a promise that inside friends were gathering who were willing to buy you a drink.

"Hello, you two. What will you have tonight?"

Necassa looked up too see Mshavka, a slender woman from Majg whom she'd come to know by frequenting the café, coming toward them.

"That's why we come here—so we don't have to decide," Necassa replied through a yawn.

"You come here no matter what," Mshavka said as Necassa's yawn near stretched her face in two. "Hard work getting smart all day, isn't it? Fit to wear one out, while I wile my life away here—"

"Reading minds," Nien said.

Having visited the café often with Necassa he was aware of Mshavka's special gift. It was more a reading of people than their minds—flashes of their past, of potential, of wishes people held close. The first time Necassa had brought Nien to the diner, she'd pressed Mshavka for what she saw in him. She'd silently scolded Necassa with a look, saying only: *"I see him in Cao City and,"* she'd added almost outside of hearing, *"in the Palaces."*

Well, Nien had thought at the time, *that was fairly obvious.* He was in Cao City all the time and he and Necassa had made more than a few visits to SiQQiy's Palatial City. Though Necassa had felt there was something else, Mshavka never said anything more, sticking with what most considered a waste of her gift: offering food suggestions that matched the mood of the diner.

So, at Nien, Mshavka's eyes narrowed. "You," she said, tapping her finger on her hip, "something new tonight—a leitta mulana, warmed, and a plate of lefendral, not chilled."

Nien chuckled. "Lovely."

She then turned her gaze to Necassa. "And you. Tonight, the same thing you usually get, but more—something slightly stronger than a leitta, chilled, baked kiedel and two—no, three, carmen eggs."

"At least," Necassa replied. "Thanks. You know, you really should be working in the palace where you'd be given a substantial pay raise and your own private residence."

Mshavka cast her eyes about the small café, at the ramshackle structure and dour tapestries. "And miss all this? Never." She winked at them. "Besides, there's plenty intrigue here. I don't need to live at the heart of it."

"Intrigue?" Necassa asked.

"You've not heard?" Mshavka said. "Of course, you two have your noses in books all day—makes me so envious. There are rumours that the Ka'ull have captured the valley of Tou."

As if sucked into a vacuum, the noise of the restaurant suddenly felt out of place, indistinct, like a scratching at the front door when, through the back, someone was emptying the house of its prized possessions.

"It's just a rumour?" Nien asked.

Mshavka gave a look. "In Quieness the definition of rumour is: Dress it down so people don't panic. So far, every rumour about the Ka'ull invasion has been verified—eventually. Working in the palaces..." She laughed mockingly. "I want my peace as long as I can keep it. I'll get your food."

As Mshavka left, Nien's mind leapt to Rieeve without warning. The longing to be home strove inside him so powerfully he felt sick. Had Lant received news? Did he know? Had he told the Council? What was happening? The Council—*Yosha,* Nien thought. What this would bring down on his family. On Wing.

"Nien?" Necassa asked. "Uh, you all right?"

"E'te," he said automatically.

" 'E'te'?"

Nien looked up at her. "Oh, sorry, it's a uh…Nevermind."

"You just took a little walk somewhere else," Necassa said. Eyeing him, her brow furrowed. "It's all right, Nien. Quieness has the biggest military on the continent. No one could stand against SiQQiy in *this* valley. I doubt," she added, "anyone would even try."

Nien tried to look encouraged, but it did not touch his eyes, as he thought, *Rieeve. It's so small. They don't know. They don't know what's happening.*

If the Quienans were worried about the Ka'ull with the size, strength, intelligence, and experience of their military, then the Cant was laughable. Worse, ridiculous.

For the first time, Nien glimpsed the true depth of Lant's desperation as well as the magnitude of his courage—the Commander knew how entirely ineffectual the Cant would be in defending Rieeve. And yet, still, he tried.

"Do you want to go?" Necassa asked, her placation turning into real concern.

Nien looked up at her. "No," he said shaking his head. "It's all right. Let's eat. You're starving."

Unconvinced, Necassa touched his hand.

Nien forced a smile he hoped wasn't entirely fake, and looked for another topic of conversation.

"How long has she been here?" he asked.

"Who?" Necassa asked.

"Mshavka."

"Oh. She came from Majg, mmm, about three full cycles ago, I think."

"Have you ever talked with her about her home?"

Conversing in a motley combination of Quienan and Fultershier, Necassa replied, "A little, yes. But she's never elaborated."

"Do many of them have the ability?"

"I don't know. As a race they may be more attuned to the subtle than the other races I've met—except for the Jayakans. Still, I think Mshavka's special. I've told her that of all the other valleys, Majg would be the first one I'd want to visit, then Jayak."

Nien sat up straighter in his chair. "Why?"

"To see what their native culture is really like."

"Really like?"

"Well, a lot of people come to Cao to start over, to reinvent themselves, leaving their traditional teachings, rituals, even the clothing of their home valleys behind. Those who come for other reasons eventually come to dress and act like Quienans, anyway."

Lost in thought, it took Nien a moment to realize Necassa was looking at him, a shade of worry in her eyes. "Nien?"

He blinked. "Sorry."

"What is it—you've been disappearing a lot tonight."

"Nothing, just…thinking," he started to say, but right then Mshavka returned with their food and the conversation was set aside.

Wishing Mshavka a pleasant evening, Nien and Necassa left the small café and walked down a long promenade that wound its way toward the residential section near the south-sunsetting corner of Cao. The conversation they'd abandoned in favour of food had been returned to and neither had desires for it to end once they'd reached Nien's apartment.

"As much as I disdain theistic belief systems," Necassa said as they climbed the stairs to Nien's room, "there is something about them that has always…intrigued me." Waiting for Nien to unlock the door, she followed him inside. "Though their symbolism may disguise the truth to the point no one could ever understand what they're really trying to say, sometimes I see why it is used, why it can be important."

"It is easy enough to get in the way of a thing," Nien agreed.

Necassa looked around the room at all of Nien's scattered books. " 'Jha dez yonglatt, ne tak sol muun,' " she said.

"What?"

"It's a Jayakan saying," she explained, winking at him. " 'Knowledge in the classroom, wisdom in the world.' Looking at this place, however, I'd amend it to: Knowledge in the library, wisdom in avoiding Nien Cawutt's flat."

"Uh, right," Nien said as he tried to semi-organize the small space—at least enough so they could get to and sit down upon the only piece of furniture in the room: his bed. As Nien cleaned, Necassa pulled a wrapped loaf of sweet bread out of her pocket. Nien looked at it. "Is that from the café?"

"It's for later—Mshavka thought it might be a long night."

Along with his shoulder pack, Nien grabbed up the books from his bed and threw them all into the nearest corner. "You and Mshavka assumed I would have nothing here to eat?"

"Do you?"

Nien narrowed his eyes at her. "*That's* why we went to the café. I forgot that the evening meal for you only starts with dinner."

Necassa laughed. "It's all right. Mshavka understands."

"Understands?"

"I love a good book as much as you, but I also remember to sleep and eat."

Nien sat down on his bed. "It's a good thing I have someone looking after me."

Necassa sat down beside him. Walking her fingers up his chest she grinned at him. "Happy to."

Nien glanced down at her fingers then up at her face. "How am I supposed to talk with you when you do that?"

Necassa ran her finger down the hollow of his throat. "Go ahead and talk," she said.

"You've ruined it now."

"No, no, no," Necassa said, placing her hands dramatically in her lap. "Go ahead. What were you going to say?"

"Cute." He met her eyes and this time the playfulness was gone from her. Something sincere and famished burned in her eyes.

Nien's brow furrowed in question—

His confusion lasted about a fraction of a blink.

Inhaling sharply, Nien shivered as Necassa slid her pale, cold hand beneath his shirt. She ran it up his side as she brushed her lips against his temple. Turning his head, he caught her mouth and kissed her deeply.

Jolting him with the freezing depth of her other hand, Necassa's nails creased his back and as rapidly as if his footing had slipped on a rain-slicked roof, Nien found himself on the other side of her shirt, her skirt, the thin short length of cloth she wore beneath them. By the time Necassa had wrangled him out of his shirt the only thing she still had on were her boots. As she fumbled with his pants, her mouth finding his eyes, face, and neck, Nien's own hands touched her hair, shoulders, back. He couldn't believe how soft she was, how warm. The smell of her skin...

A night breeze blew in through the open window to Nien's small room, cooling their skin as they lay partly beneath the single thin cover of Nien's nearly-as-thin cot.

Necassa's head lay on Nien's shoulder. He breathed deeply, inhaling the scent of her hair that was somehow both sweet and stale—like teeana spilled over a dusty book.

But even as Nien breathed her in, it was strange, he thought, to feel almost burned away.

What have I done?

Necassa loved him—that he knew. And he loved her.

But was it enough?

Was it enough to give up his life back in Rieeve? Was it enough to make him forget his family? The Cant? The school children?

Stirring, Necassa raised her head and looked at him.

The lantern still glowed faintly on the corner table, its pale light falling upon Nien's face. He tried to smile.

Necassa wasn't fooled. "What is it?"

"I'm sorry. I'm sorry." Brushing his hands over the soft skin of her back, he brought his hands up and pressed his palms to his eyes.

Pushing herself up, Necassa sat back on her heels. "But I, I thought..."

"It's my fault," Nien forced.

"Your *fault?*" she said, and her face suddenly set. "Oh..." she muttered.

"No, I..."

With a short cry of embarrassment, Necassa scrambled to her feet, grabbing up her clothes.

"Necassa, no, wait. Let me explain."

She paused.

"It's not that I don't care for you, it's not that."

She slipped her shirt over her head and looked at him. "Then what?"

Nien couldn't find the words he was looking for.

"Don't worry about it," Necassa said. "It's all right, I understand. You like me, but not like that."

"Trust me, that's not it," Nien said. "It's just…"

"—What?"

Nien pushed himself to his feet. Grabbing a sheet, he wrapped and tucked it about his waist. "I…"

Yosha! he swore silently, beginning to prowl the small apartment.

Necassa watched him, her eyes swimming with confusion.

One hand gripping the sheet about his waist in a hold that could have snapped a Mesko branch, Nien said, "It's what you said in the restaurant."

"What I said in the restaurant?"

"About people coming here to reinvent themselves, to start over."

Necassa nodded.

"Well," Nien continued, his voice uncentered, searching, "it made me think. I mean, I thought I came here to learn, to gain knowledge to take back to Rieeve. But…" He paused, as if summoning the courage to speak the thought, not only to Necassa, but mostly to himself. "What if I really came here to escape?"

Wing said it, he thought. *He said I was running away.*

"I find myself here, now, like this—standing naked in a room, trying to decide who I am, who I want to be." He turned and looked at his mostly naked body in the tall, scratched mirror that leaned against the nearby wall. "You said people from other valleys leave their traditions, their religions, even their native clothing behind when they come here." Nien gazed into his mirror image. "I didn't mean to, Necassa, but is that what I have done?"

Necassa looked at him from where she stood near the bed. "Would that be such a bad thing?" she asked.

"Maybe not. But if I have, then where do I go from here?"

Necassa's gaze traveled over his body before she reached toward the foot of the bed to retrieve a shirt that lay there. It was a shirt she had purchased for him in Cao—one that he wore often.

"You might start with the clothes you'd put back on," she said, holding the shirt out to him.

Nien's eyes rested upon the shirt in Necassa's hands. Suddenly it was not the same shirt he'd worn nearly every day since she had given it to him.

Suddenly it meant much more. A great decision now hinged upon that shirt.

If he took it, would there be no going back? Would he no longer be Nien Cawutt? Would he no longer be Rieevan?

Rieevan.

The word denoted his religion as much as his race.

But was he truly Rieevan—in race or in creed?

He stared at the shirt.

What am I?

The question clanged around in his brain.

Heavy, silent moments passed.

It was with conscious effort that Nien finally pulled his eyes from the shirt and looked at Necassa's face. Drawing a breath, he stepped across the room and, taking Necassa's hand in his, sat back down on the bed.

Necassa sat down beside him, both of them staring at the shirt the two of them now held in their hands.

"What does this mean?" Nien asked.

His question only served to deepen the confusion on Necassa's face.

"What if I go back? What if I decide not to stay?"

Necassa flinched. Tears glimmered in her eyes. "But I thought you had decided…" She didn't finish her sentence.

Nien looked up into her eyes. "To stay?" He shook his head. "I don't know. I mean, what about my life—my life back home? My family. What about everything I believe in?"

—Or thought I did? And what if the rumours are true? What if the Ka'ull have taken Tou as well? Am I just going to stay here? Weather the storm in Quieness, the greatest valley on the continent, while Rieeve, Rieeve…

Nien came back to the moment and the young woman on the bed next to him. Reaching out, he touched Necassa's cheek. "And what about this?"

"What about it? We're here, now. You and I."

"But if I go? Then what? Is the time we've spent together enough for you?"

Conflicting emotions swam in her eyes. "I…why do you have to decide all this right now?"

Nien rubbed the shirt between his fingers. "Upon leaving Rieeve I'd planned on returning when the snows broke."

A short sound stopped in Necassa's throat. Her thin, pale hand tightened its grip upon the shirt.

"Why can't you leave it behind?" she asked, her voice frail. "I can't count the times you've expressed how frustrating Rieeve was for you, how intolerant and oppressive. Stay here, Nien. You can study and learn. You could even teach here—teach people who want to learn. No one would judge you here for what you teach."

Everything she said was true, but there was more to Rieeve than his complaints about it and he wondered if he'd ever shared with her the beauty of the valley, how he loved his people and his family.

"You've come so far," Necassa said. "Don't turn back now."

"But what if they were right?" Nien said.

"What if who was right?" Necassa asked.

"My people, they believe that anyone who leaves Rieeve will be corrupted, broken."

Is that what's happened to me? he thought. *Has it happened exactly as they said it would?*

Necassa squinted her eyes at him. "So this is a religious thing?"

Nien paused...*Was it?*

"Would it hold such a bitter taste for you if it was?" he asked.

"So it *is*?"

Nien's mind spun. "It might be."

Necassa snorted in disgust.

Nien's fingers loosened upon the shirt. He barely felt the touch of the fabric beneath his fingertips. " 'I'm walking the path of strangers. My heart bound. My feet turning left and right, straying from...' "

"Straying from what?"

Nien looked at her. The quote from the Ancient Writings finished with: 'straying from the path of holiness,' but Nien couldn't say it. Even though it felt wrong, the thought frightened him.

Necassa leaned close to him. "Don't listen to them," she said softly. "Do you know how hard it was for the Quienans in the beginning? The fight to make a cohesive society out of so many different races and systems of belief?"

Nien looked at her questioningly. "The fight?"

"Against bias," she said, "disguised as religion and passed on like an illness from parents to children. One person's point of view taught as the only true way of the only true God. If the Quienans hadn't fought to break that cycle we'd still be at war with the Grangh and Honj, the Jayakans and Majg would never have come here, and our borders would be as closed as Rieeve's."

Nien's head lowered. Her words rang a painful and familiar chord with him. Those same thoughts and more he'd secretly entertained, the worst of them being: Was the Rieevan way something he believed himself or something he'd simply accepted?

"What can I say to you? I've shared those same feelings. I...I hate it." He paused. "But I have a truth in my own heart, and the thought of being with you and then leaving just feels...wrong. It may be a religious thing, it may be a life thing, maybe they're the same thing; nevertheless..."

"Nevertheless nothing," Necassa bit back. "It comes down to the way you were brought up, to Rieevan dogma."

"That's what parents do, Necassa," Nien said. "They teach their children." And even as the words left his lips, Nien acknowledged how much he loved and hated the Ancient Writings and how he'd spent most of his life trying to reconcile those conflicting emotions.

"—for right or wrong?"

Nien blinked and looked up at her. "What?"

"What if you were born in Legran and your family held a Preak family as slaves, and you were raised with the belief that it was all right—something natural and normal? What if that was a truth you grew up with?"

The golden colour of Nien's eyes deepened. A strange ache set its finger upon him. "I, too, have fought, Necassa, as you Quienans have, but not against everything. I owe more than I could ever repay to my mother and fa—for their love, their teachings, their wisdom."

"What you call love I call indoctrination." She held the shirt up to him. "Who would you be if your parents had left you free to decide—like mine did."

"Necassa," Nien said softly. "Your parents didn't leave you free, they just left you."

Necassa went to speak but stopped. Her lips twisted.

"Necassa," he said, reaching out to touch her.

But she jerked away, her eyes welling with tears—and anger.

"Necassa, I'm so sorry. I didn't think."

How could I have been so naïve? Nien thought, railing on himself. *So blind!*

The look on Necassa's face pierced him through. The void her parents had left her with she'd tried to fill with books, with learning...and with him. For the first time, Nien truly understood her place in the conversation—how deeply his going back to Rieeve would affect her.

Silence filled the room like an entity. Necassa was still, her arms wrapped about her body.

Nien almost reached out to her again. He wanted to take her into his arms. He wanted to erase what he'd said. But as she raised her face and looked at him, Nien knew he'd gone too far. The hurt he'd rendered was too deep.

Necassa got up and, pulling on the rest of her clothes, stepped toward the door.

"Are you coming to the library tomorrow?" she asked, not looking back at him.

"Probably," Nien replied, his voice strained. He got to his feet but could not make them move to her. So he stood in silence, watching as she opened the door and disappeared down the rickety wooden stairs and out into the streets below.

Nien shivered as the door shut, staring briefly at the bronze, oddly shaped door handle before falling back onto his bed. Bringing his arms up to cover his face he found the scent of her hair and his shirt still on his hands. His throat tightened. He shouldn't have told her what troubled him. He'd never intended for the night to end like this, and now this night was possibly the end of their friendship as well.

Behind his closed eyes he saw her face.

Getting up, he looked out the small window over his bed. On the street far below, he caught sight of her. He followed her with his eyes until she vanished into the maze of businesses and tall standing apartments. Lifting his gaze, it was to the distant domes of SiQQiy's palaces that they came, the long dusty road that led there from the heart of Cao glowing like a brilliant silver thread. With heavy heart he watched the silken pink rays of morning creep inch by shimmering inch up and over the brightly coloured domes and gardens of the Palatial City.

He suddenly felt so lost. Necassa had been his guide in this strange new land. She had been his only friend in Quieness. He had made fair acquaintances in a few people but had not taken time from his study to get to know any of them on a personal level except for her. Glancing down at his bed, he spotted the books he'd brought from the library. The words of the Prophet-Poet Eneefa (Wing's favourite writer) came to his mind in a flood:

Abandoned to note
And line
And word
Thrown down from higher worlds
Scratching like a thief
Just a beggar at the door...

For a moment, he wished Rieeve didn't exist at all to create such conflict in him. If Rieeve was not, if his brother and the Commander were not...

Wing, he thought. *Lant.*

He ground his teeth upon their names.

If not for them, he could stay in Quieness, study, learn, be and experience everything he'd ever wanted to but been denied while living in Rieeve. He could even pass through an entire war in this valley and hardly even know anything had happened at all in Lou or Tou. The name, Ka'ull, could pass as no more than a brief collection of letters in a book for him.

But the palaces blurred in his vision and he knew: Rieeve would always be a sore, an annoying ache that he would never be able to shake.

Nien shifted his gaze to the opposite side of the valley, to the great mountains that stood between Quieness and Rieeve. In only a few more turns the mountains would be passable.

He turned away from the window.

As uncomfortable as it would prove to be, and whether he decided to stay or not, there was still much he felt he needed to learn.

Tomorrow, he would be returning to the library.

CHAPTER 26
Old Friends

"Netaia!"

"Mont."

The two men grasped each other. Their embrace was strong, proud, and full. The revolutions had been kind to them, Kate thought as they came into the dining room together all smiles and hearty laughter. Handsome men, they still made a striking team. Kate had often teased her husband that she was the second great love of his life—when her husband and netaia Lant were together they had eyes for no one else.

"So, where have you been?" Monteray asked.

"To see the Old Man."

"How is he?"

"Same."

Monteray chuckled.

"It was good to see Jason—Pree K is always happy to see him, too. Thank you for sending me word on Tou."

The two men locked gazes. "It's coming," Monteray said, speaking both their minds.

"I'm considering drawing up a plan to present to the other valleys."

"A plan?"

"To organize a united force. As the valleys are now, only Quieness stands a chance against the Ka'ull. Jayak—possibly. But we both know, no matter how well trained the Jayakans are, they do not have the sheer numbers the Ka'ull have."

Monteray exhaled slowly. What Lant proposed was an idea so large, so unprecedented in their time that Monteray could hardly imagine how it might be accomplished.

"Thinking small again, are you?"

Lant's eyes squinted at his friend in a very familiar gesture. "I could use your help."

Monteray laughed incredulously. "I wouldn't even know where to begin!"

"Details," Lant answered with a wave of his hand. "What I have in mind right now is just a rough sketch. I'm thinking of beginning with Legran, Jayak, Preak, and Quieness. Eventually, I'd like to include all the valleys."

"Netaia, you know what I know about the valleys."

"No, I don't. You grew up knowing Jayak intimately. In Quieness you were the one that spent time in the Royal Palaces. And Preak—your knowledge of the valley and its people far outweighs my own." Lant's eyes fell and Monteray could feel the weight on his friend's shoulders as if it were his own. "Perhaps in the years since our return we have talked too much about the past, letting the present slip and everything we could be—*should be*—doing about it." Lant looked up and the two studied one another's eyes. "No one in either of our valleys knows more about the Ka'ull than you and I do."

But it's the other side of that coin that worries us the most, Monteray thought, knowing Lant was thinking the exact same thing: That what the Ka'ull knew about the central valleys was because of the two of them—a regret they had carried with them in secret ever since they'd returned to Legran and Rieeve all those revolutions ago.

"What about Rieeve?" Monteray asked. "How are things going with the Council and the Cant?"

"The Cant is coming along much better than I'd hoped; nevertheless, it's much too small to be of any effect without the aide of the other valleys."

"Like Legran."

Lant nodded. "But I've got good leaders—one in particular that I've told you about before."

"Nien?"

"Yes. He's someone you'd appreciate."

"A bit like you, if I remember correctly."

Lant's smile was small, but genuine. "He does not have my failings."

Monteray turned an appraising eye on his friend. "I wonder if your people can take another Lant Ce'Mandu in the form of this leader in your Cant."

Silently appreciating Monteray's suggestion, Lant continued, "And then there's his brother."

"The one your people believe is the Leader referred to in the Ancient Writings."

"Yes. His name is Wing. The Council keeps hounding me in regards to him. Their belief in him as the Leader is strong."

"Of what family are they?"

"Do you remember my mentioning a man by the name of Joash?"

"Of course," Monteray replied. "He was one of the few who did not shun you when you returned to Rieeve."

"That's him. He's a fine man. One of the finest I've ever met. He and his wife were kind to me and Pree K, and though I have no proof of it, I think it was him that helped change not only the Council's mind about me all those revolutions ago, but my own father's as well."

"He must be a man of some weight then, in Rieeve?"

"He's the Mesko Tender—so yes. When he speaks, others listen, including the Council." Monteray could tell Lant was briefly back in Rieeve. "Anyway, what about here? How is your militia?"

"Ragtag," Monteray admitted. "Jason is coming along, though. He has a good head for order, tactics, and diplomacy. Troy Naterey—the current leader of the militia—sees promise in him as well. I have plans to turn the militia into something more like your Cant, but igtakey, netaia, they are a difficult rabble."

Lant laughed affectionately. Rieevans were a very different breed from Legranders. Strict hierarchal observation of detail, discipline, and respect were paramount in a Rieevan's life, and that framework held within the Cant. But Legranders were wild, carefree, and hated to be ruled. The fundamentals of military conduct being such a complete anathema to a Legrander it would take a very special hand to organize a fighting force among them. Looking upon his friend, Lant knew that Monteray had the touch: He had before, and could again get the people of his valley to work together.

"So, to work, then," Monteray said. "Let me retrieve some parchment."

The two men holed-up and worked for days. In her gracious style, Kate kept them fed, urged them to sleep, and scolded them into movement when half a day had passed and they had not so much as leaned away from the writing table.

On Lant's day of departure he left gifts of Rieevan paper, wine, and fine-tipped brushes, hugged and kissed Kate, wished Tei well with her latest boy-crush then walked out to the river with Monteray.

"Thank you, again, for all your help," Lant said.

"It's a start, but you've got a lot to do putting all that in order," Monteray replied, nodding at the rolls of paper and parchment in a long leather case slung around Lant's neck. "The wording of the proposals alone will take turns."

"As always," Lant said, "I am indebted."

Monteray looked upon his truest, trusted, most loved friend. "You come up with an idea that could save all the valleys from a fate such as Lou and Tou have suffered, and thank *me*?" Monteray shook his head in mock castigation. "Typical."

"Well, don't get too enamored. It's just an idea. To work, it will require the right people in every valley to agree to it." Lant paused and met Monteray's eyes—eyes so similar to his own that he felt as if he were looking at himself in a mirror. "I no longer believe you and I alone can take on the world and all of its injustices."

A grin tipped Monteray's handsome mouth. "Do you not, now?" He raised an eyebrow. "That's exactly what you're doing."

"No—I have no such grand thoughts anymore," Lant said, shaking his head. "I'm just trying to protect my small part of it."

And that could save us all, Monteray thought.

"Well, when do we meet again? It has been far too long since I've graced Rieeve with my disagreeable presence."

"And my home has missed it. Once I get some kind of functional proposal drawn up, I'll be sending one of my Cant messengers to you."

"Until the next time, then," Monteray said.

"Until the next time."

They locked hands and forearms. "To us."

"To us."

It was a heady—and to be honest—drunk-induced salute to one another from their long-ago journey together. Though it no longer shot them through with lusty jaunts of bravado it touched upon the deep feelings instilled in memories shared by no else in their lives except the other.

With smiles telling and sad, they embraced, and Monteray stood where they parted, watching as Lant disappeared into the glowing green length of sunlit fields.

CHAPTER 27

Sadness and Serenity

More than once over the next few turns Nien found himself seeking serenity and quiet near the grounds of SiQQiy's palace. Even after so many turns now in the Big Valley, he still wished for a glimpse of her—the idea of a single ruler continuing to pique his curiosity. Marveling at the palace, he found strength in its grandeur and peace in its beauty. He would gaze upon it for long periods, tracing many images, memorizing frame by frame the appearance of it at dawn, dusk, by the light of the stars, against the glimmering glow of a full moon, in shimmering beds of snow crystals. He would miss it—he would miss its comforting presence.

Since that last night in his apartment with Necassa the days had slowly made it evident that he would be going back to Rieeve. As much as he loved the intellectuality of Quieness, he missed the simplicity of Rieeve. As much as he loved the vast halls and buildings of Cao City, he missed the open fields of Rieeve and the nearness of the great mountains. He could not abandon all he had started back there. Though the Council had closed his school, there was still, in the back of his mind, the hope that he might find a way to open it again. And the Cant. If the Cant did not need him, he needed it, and he needed his family. The Preak were an interesting people, but he was not one of them. More than ever he now knew it: His similarity with them was only skin deep.

And then, hovering above and lurking beneath, was the rumour about Tou. Tou was close to Rieeve. Tou was just above the Ti-Uki Confluence. Just above Rieeve.

Regardless of anything else he felt—*Rieeve is where I belong,* he thought, *that is where I need to be. And soon,* he felt. *As soon as the snows break.*

Casting his eyes up toward the Uki mountain range, imagining the small valley that lay on the sunrising side of it, he wondered what was happening with Lant, if he'd received word from Master Monteray. And if he had, what that meant for the Cant and the people. What it meant to his family and to Wing.

Nien purchased a few favourite books to take back with him. He'd finished the work on the apartment and received a grateful thanks from the gentlemanly owner. He did not see Necassa the day of his leaving and thought it fitting—it had been what it was. Though it was difficult to touch at the moment, he knew that someday he would treasure all of their time together: the long walks, especially the talks, the day in the waterfall at the palace, the mornings in the library, and even that last painful night.

On his departing day he passed back through the streets of Cao, loving it, hating it, knowing he would miss it and hoping he would not. The snows had broken and the streets of Cao were already beginning to dry of mud. He left the city behind and began the first long ascent into the Uki mountain range.

He'd summited three separate ridges before pausing to catch his breath. The great valley already lay far below him and on its sunrising edge...

Cao City, he said to himself. How strange it was to look down upon it now and know it so intimately, especially as he recalled the fear and wonder it had set upon him that very first day.

A deep melancholy filled his stomach. It felt as if he was leaving a chunk of himself in the city and he wondered briefly if he would ever see it again and when that might be.

Stuffing his regret and longing aside, Nien turned and continued up the mountain. He had a task ahead of him now that he hoped he was equal to. The snows were still high in the mountains and at some point he'd have to pass through them.

Three days on and the cold mountain weather was putting Nien's outdoor skills to the test. The large patches of deep snow in the higher elevations had him transversing the mountain like a herd animal not quite yet cornered. Braving rough sections at intervals, Nien found that tunneling beneath heavy, low-hanging branches of evergreens offered shelter warm enough that a fire became more of a companion than a necessity. Of greater companionship were the books he'd brought with him. Heavy as they were, he'd not seriously thought once in the arduous going of leaving one behind.

As the third night drew in, Nien picked a handsome stand of tall evergreens and after making a few brief preparations for the night, sat up against one of the heavy tree trunks and laying his head back, rested the book he'd been reading upon his chest and looked up into the night sky.

He suddenly couldn't wait to be home. He couldn't wait to see his mother and father, he couldn't wait to see if Jake had grown or if Fey had any new words she wanted to share with him. And Wing. How much he wanted to talk with Wing. Conversations with his brother could dig up the very earth beneath them or take them past the stars. In Quieness Necassa had been a lifesaver. Their talks had allowed him to explore what he was learning. But she had not shared his background. She had not been able to help put it all into perspective with his past, his present, and what he hoped would be his future. Wing could do that. Wing understood.

Upon the growing twilight rose the first star of night. Bright and brilliant, startling in its early presence above the horizon, Nien gazed at it, wondering if Wing were still out in the fields and wishing he were already home so he could walk out the door to meet him coming in with the horses.

Though Wing had been less open with him in the past few seasons, Nien had never doubted that Wing knew the paths of his thoughts even better than Nien himself did.

So he's probably wondering if I'm even coming back, Nien thought.

"But I am, brother," he said. "I am." And in the comfort of that reassurance Nien rested his eyes once more upon the glowy white rays of the evening star...

Just a few more days.

In Rieeve, beneath a sky spectacularly heavy with stars, Wing struggled for the hundredth time and failed at last to keep his eyes from that shining black overhead sea.

That's appropriate, he thought. *The ocean is up the sky is down, everything's been backwards since Nien left.*

Of course, the family was expecting him anytime—Nien had said he'd be returning once he could make the mountain passes.

The snows had broken, and though there were still great swaths of it in the high mountains, the valley was already warming. Small wild plants and weeds were up and bright green, gleaming even, in the light of the night sky.

But the family did not know how it had been between Wing and Nien before Nien had left. However obvious it was that something had gone wrong, neither Nien before he'd left nor Wing in the time since had said anything about it.

Trapped between the horizons of a flipped world, Wing's emotions swung wildly between elation and anguish. It was already past the Ime-Kive season break. If Nien did not return in time for Kive fest, what would that mean? Were Wing's worst fears true—was Nien not coming back? Every day that passed pressed his mind into a deeper state of anxiety. He carried it into the fields with him. He could feel it acutely in the house at night with the family. He hadn't been able to sleep for well over a turn. Ever since the first sunlight had made an inroad on the snows, ever since the first streams had started waking, crying joyfully, noisily with a fresh surge of bone-chilling water, the last bastion of Wing's respite had fallen.

Staring up at the night, an unexpected moment descended upon him. Spreading his feet, Wing arced his back, let his head fall back, and face up, closed his eyes against the sea. There, he floated. Let his body go. His mind go. Lost himself in the watery realm of sky even as he fell through the empty space of earth.

Out, above Rieeve, hunkered down beneath the branches of a tree, Wing saw Nien. A book was resting against his chest and his eyes, glimmering out from between the branches, were trained up, up, up to a point in the sky.

Wing opened his eyes then, and above him hung a single glowing point—

The evening star.

Wing felt the knot in his chest release into it, felt it anchor him in the world—the part that lay beneath as well as the one that soared above.

Whether the vision was true or not, in that brief, bright instant there was nothing but light against the black.

CHAPTER 28

Welcome Back and Rebuttal

"Jake? Can't be."

Jake whirled to see Nien standing in the doorway. "Nien!" he howled.

Nien dropped his duffel and shoving Jake over to the new Mesko wood table, grabbed his little brother's hand and dropped their elbows.

Jake grinned furiously.

Nien let him wrestle his arm back briefly, then easily pinned him.

"One of these days," Jake said.

"You're closer," Nien admitted. "I've only been gone a season and you've grown four at least."

Jake looked away to hide his pleasure, saying, "Look at Fey. She broke her arm."

"What happened?" Nien asked her.

"A peeiopi pushed me."

Nien chuckled. The egg-laying, nearly flightless birds were hardly creatures of vigorous territorial instincts, but neither were they known for keen eyesight. "Well, I'm sorry," he said.

"Son."

Nien looked up to see Reean.

Moving across the room, she clutched his face in both her hands and held it and kissed it until he could feel her tears wet his cheek.

Behind Reean, Fey looked up at Nien with eyes so shiny and open they threatened to ruin his heart.

Brushing tears from the bottom of her chin, Reean released him and said, "Welcome home."

Nien glanced around at the many not-so-neatly packed bundles. "Looks like festival time."

Suddenly remembering she'd been in the midst of packing, Reean nodded. "Yes. Do you want to go? We can go a day or two late if you want to rest."

"No, I'm fine to go."

A moment of silence fell.

Reean said, "Wing's out in the fields."

Nien's brown eyes glinted. "What a surprise."

Stepping out the door, he spotted Wing far out in the fields, moving along behind the family's plow team.

Hoping to surprise him, Nien set off. A rising euphoria quickened his pace as his feet passed over the sunlit dirt.

Drawing near, Nien could hear Wing singing. It was an old song Reean had sung to them as children—one that not many villagers still knew:

"Tai mai cavana

I fla to veeahl

Ma ta ma ta no'va-hm

A veerta flee-ehn teeana

I pohdre Vasteel a mear hottovonee..."

As Nien walked up behind him, he raised his voice and finished the verse: *"Ma ta ma ta no'va-hi min!"*

Wing stopped with a halting jolt like he'd been shoved between the shoulder blades. The team dragged him forward a few more steps before he got them reined in.

Nien stopped, too.

It seemed to take forever for Wing to secure the plow, drop the reins from his shoulders, and turn around.

Nien could hardly contain the moment of Wing's eyes meeting his. Never had the sight of anyone been so sweet.

"Nien," Wing said.

"Weed Farmer."

Wing smiled. It felt like sunlight on Nien's face.

"Hi," Nien said.

"Hi."

Wing's lip twitched. Nien's hand trembled. Wing made a shrugging motion with his shoulders and Nien met him and the brothers took each other in a bone-crushing hug.

The same height, they met at knees, hips, chests, and chins on shoulders.

Wing laughed and Nien was washed clean in his brother's relief.

"So," Wing said stepping back, "you came back."

"You weren't worried about that were you?" Nien said, his tongue firmly embedded in his cheek.

There was a fall of emotion over Wing's features and Nien wasn't sure if his brother was going to punch him or embrace him again. In the end, he simply shook his head, and asked, "Are you heading into the festival or are you too tired?"

"Tired? Yes. Too tired? No."

Wing didn't manage to hide his disappointment.

"What?" Nien asked. "You aren't going?"

"No."

A depressing bit of silence followed.

"Well," Nien said, "I won't be staying long at the festival. I want to find Lant and I want to get some sleep." He gave Wing a playful shove. "You should get some sleep, too—we've got a lot to talk about."

"I'm sure," Wing said, pleased to hear it. "Here, help me unhitch the horses. I was about to quit for the day anyway."

The brothers released the plow and unhitched the team.

A long-fingered olive-skinned hand took one set of reins, a smooth blue-black hand took the other, and the brothers led off across the fields in the direction of the barn.

Inside the house, Reean glanced out the big window from her last-minute arrangements to see her sons coming in together, walking side by side, the metal riggings of the plow harness reflecting sparks of sunlight as the family horses followed dutifully along behind them. Feeling as if everything were right for the first time in revolutions, she turned back to Fey. "Now, where's your father?" she asked.

Wing and Nien entered the barn to find Joash coming out of the last stall with a bucket of warm milk, leaving the family cow, Jhei, to chew her cud in peace. As he maneuvered the bucket carefully around the stall door, Nien said, "Fa, need some help there?"

"Son!" Joash cried, and nearly spilling the bucket, just managed to set it down before grabbing Nien in a full-bodied hug. "You're finally home!"

"Taking the milk to the festival?"

"It's for Mother-Yiete, she's making some sort of sauce." Nien proffered a lop-sided grin as Joash looked him over. "So how are you? How was the trip?"

"I'm excellent; the trip was no problem. It's good to be home."

"Well, let's get going. We can talk on the way into the Village."

Back in the house, as Wing passed into the back bedroom, Nien stepped up to Reean. "Wing not going to the festival?" he said quietly.

"E'te. It started about the time you left."

"What is it?" he asked.

"Wing hasn't talked about it…"

"But?"

"Your leaving gave the people the opening they were looking for—he was asked if he would be taking your place in the Cant while you were away."

Nien's brow furrowed.

"The children call him 'Merehr' openly. And then a, uh…"

"What?" Nien asked.

"A group of Council members and villagers came out here to talk to him. They…they asked him to heal a sick child." Reean searched Nien's eyes. "He hasn't been into the Village in over a season."

Shades of horror, regret, and sadness played across Nien's face as he glanced across the room through the opening into their bedroom where Wing was helping Jake look for a missing shoe, or so Nien surmised, since Fey stood in the middle of the room with two socks on but only one shoe.

"Their capacity to resent and worship him at the same time is awe-inspiring," Nien said.

Picking up his gear, he hauled it into the bedroom where he hefted it onto his bed.

From Jake's side of the room, Wing said, "If you'd leave them by the door like you're supposed to…"

"I know!" Fey barked angrily.

Nien sat down on Wing's bed. "I'm sorry," he said to Wing's backside.

"About what?" Wing asked off-handedly on his hands and knees, his head all but disappeared as he rooted through the mess under Jake's bed in search of the missing shoe.

"About the position my leaving put you in—with the Cant and the people…"

"It's not your fault, Nien," Wing replied. "Ah ha!" Climbing to his feet, Wing thrust the shoe at Fey. "So," he said to Nien, "we can talk when you get back? I want to know how it was, what it was like, what you learned. And I promise," he added, "I'll listen."

Typical redirection, Nien thought before replying, "I'll hold you to that."

Only a short time later all the family but Wing headed off across the fields.

Inside the house, Wing stood, watching them go through the small back window.

The outskirts of the open fields surrounding Castle Viyer were filling up with families in the process of making camp. Nien looked around at all the activity and smiled. Mid-Kive was a good time. Everything was new, the coldness of Ime giving way to crisp mornings and longer evenings, a hint of warmth in the afternoon breezes. Reean and Joash were quick to set up their selling booth as Nien arranged the family tent behind it before setting off to find Carly and the other members of the Cant.

He didn't make it that far.

"Son-Cawutt Nien, we heard you'd returned."

Nien stopped mid-stride.

Coming up the path were three Council members, one of them Grek Occoju.

"Uh huh," Nien replied warily as everyone exchanged polite greetings.

"And how are you?" Councilman Breeal questioned.

"Very well, thank you."

"You are in a rush?"

Nien nodded. "A little, yes." Though he would have lied to get out of the inevitable catechism, he was anxious to meet up with the members of the Cant, and hopefully, find Commander Lant.

"We were hoping to be able to talk with you," Grek voiced.

Nien knew what was coming.

"We would like to discuss your trip, and," there was a heavy pause, "whether we can allow you to continue in the Cant or be with the people."

Though it had been a concern, Nien had not seriously thought that, upon his return, he would ever be shunned as Lant had been. Such behaviour seemed a thing of the very distant past—and Nien had not been gone nearly as long as Lant had.

"What would you like to know?" Nien said.

"How it went. What you did there."

Nien wondered how he could possibly encapsulate all that he had done, read, learned, and felt in a single reply, or whether he should lie about all of it and say he hated it, never should have left, and ask the Council's permission for going. "That would be difficult," he said.

"You went to study, did you not?"

"Yes. I studied at a great library in their largest city, Cao."

"What did your studies include?"

"Many things."

"For example…?"

"Well, at first I just tried to learn a few words in their language so I could get around. After that I looked into other books on geography and numbers and even a few on military stratagem," he said, trying to steer the conversation away from anything—

"Did you study the beliefs of the Quienans?"

—*religious*.

Nien stifled a groan. "They're not a pious people."

"And this intrigued you?" Breeal asked.

Nien's eyes moved from Grek Occoju to Councilman Breeal. "Intrigued me?"

"Yes, that they lack a broader perspective than that of the temporal," Breeal replied.

"Broader perspective?" Nien asked, incredulous.

"That they lack the teachings of Eosha."

"I wanted to know what they *do* believe in and why," Nien replied.

"But you just said they were not a largely religious people," Brap Cuiku said.

"Not by our terms, no."

"*Our* terms?" Cuiku asked, failing an obvious attempt to keep his tone conciliatory.

"Yes. They have ideas of their own. I wanted to know what they were."

"You were curious," Grek Occoju said.

"I was interested."

"Such *interests* can be dangerous," Cuiku said.

"Dangerous for whom?" Nien replied slowly.

Everyone felt the insinuation flood Brap Cuiku's easily saturated toleration level, but before he had the chance to open his mouth and worsen the matter, Grek said, "We are concerned for the welfare of our people, you, and your family."

Nien dug deep into his reservoir of patience. "I understand your concern."

"Do you?" Fu Breeal said. "I don't think so."

Nien did not look at him.

"Were you tempted to stay?" Grek Occoju asked.

Reflexively, Nien felt his stomach recoil, felt his mind slip into a habitual pattern of employing half-truths to appease them.

And, he thought, *if there was ever a time to lie, it was now, for they could ban me from the Cant, from the people...*

Nien didn't let his mind go any further.

First and foremost, he'd come home for Wing and for the family. Whatever else happened would be secondary misery.

And, Quieness had given him courage.

In Quieness he'd found validation for all the questions he'd been condemned for in Rieeve. He knew, now, that it was no longer him against the world—that there were others out there, *many* others, who shared his passion, his curiosity, his suspicion that things could be *other* than the way he'd been told they had to be.

Straightening his shoulders and raising his eyes, Nien decided that even though the Council was not prepared to hear his truth much less accept it, he would tell them anyway because he was tired of hiding it, tired of pretending to be something he was not.

Let them do then, what they would.

But just as Nien opened his mouth to speak, Fu Breeal raised his hand to greet someone coming up the path.

Glancing over his shoulder, Nien was hit with a wash of relief and irony.

Lant.

"Councilmen," Lant said. He turned to Nien. "You're back. It's good to see you again, Son-Cawutt."

Nien nodded to him.

"We were taking a moment to talk with Son-Cawutt about his trip."

Nien could see that Lant knew perfectly well how it was going.

"I had just asked him if he had been tempted to stay in the Big Valley," Breeal said.

Here we go, Nien thought. *At least Lant's here.*

Nien raised his eyes to Councilman Breeal, and said, "For a brief time, yes."

Breeal and Cuiku shared a pretentious nod of agreement.

"Then why did you come back?" Lant said.

All eyes were upon Nien.

"As I told my family before I left, I went to Quieness not to get away from Rieeve but to bring back to her."

"And in what are we lacking that the Quienans have the ability to fill?"

"Books—for a beginning."

"And you find these books of more value than the Ancient Writings?" Cuiku replied.

"No," Nien replied. "But you—you think other works take away from the Ancient Writings. I think they add to them."

Cuiku said, "What's needful is there in the Ancient Writings. What we don't need are the incorrect or incomplete concepts of another people—however well-intentioned—brought into our valley where our people or our children may be exposed to it."

A familiar wrath unfolded itself inside Nien's heart. "The Quienans may be a very practical people, they may not believe in the Ancient Writings as we do, but I saw much goodness there. I saw great beauty. I became stronger. I became a better person. When the whole is hidden, how can one know what part he has chosen?"

Nien could see that Cuiku burned to say something to this, but the silence of the other three kept his tongue still.

"Until we can meet you with further," Grek Occoju said, "we suggest that you keep your interaction with the people to a minimum." Grek looked at Lant briefly. "Commander, you will be meeting with us after the festival?"

"Of course," Lant said.

With Lant beside him, the two watched the three Council members move off down one of the many footpaths smoothed through the fields of the festival grounds.

"Well," Lant said dryly, "that wasn't the least bit awkward for them."

Nien didn't know whether to vomit from nerves or laugh with relief. "That's it?"

Lant looked at him. "It might be. Unlike when I returned, they had nothing to lose by pretending I didn't exist. You…well, they can't banish you from your family."

Nien understood. "Wing."

Lant nodded, and said with a touch of sarcasm, "Welcome back."

"Yeah, *welcome back*," Nien replied.

"I just got back myself—but they don't ask me anymore where I've been." This, Lant said with a cheerful grin.

"So, *where* have you…?" Nien started to say, but Lant cut him off.

"—Later. Right now, I'm having a small get-together at my house. Members of the Cant are already there, probably destroying it. You might as well come and see."

Nien happily agreed and Lant threw an arm around his shoulders.

The two walked in silence for a few paces, before Nien asked, "In all of your journeys, were you…" Nien paused. "Were you ever tempted to stay?"

Lant's eyes were tracing the deepening shadows cast by the mountains across the valley. After a couple steps, he looked over at Nien and imparted a wistful smile.

The two left the abandoned Village streets and headed into the short stretch of fields between the last row of homes and Lant's home on the northing edge of the Cantfields. From halfway across the clearing they could hear laughter and shouting.

"Wonderful," Lant said, rolling his eyes. "I told you."

The two opened Lant's front door to a gust of hot air.

"Nien!" someone shouted and before Nien could avoid it, Carly had crossed the room, leapt into his arms, and sloshed warm beer from her mug down his back.

Nien just managed to catch her as he stumbled into the house. Lant's spacious front room was filled with Cant members, the smell of fresh brew, and raucous laughter.

Emerging from the floor and walls like inebriated ghosts, Cant members began to leap—or stagger—to their feet, greeting Nien with backslaps, hugs, and roars.

"Welcome back!"—this from Mien'k who, slamming into Nien, gave him a rare hug. "How are you?"

Nien smiled. "Excellent. You?"

"As you can see, very drunk."

Still in Nien's arms, her legs wrapped about his waist, Carly grabbed Nien's face and stared him in the eyes. "You," she said.

Holding her with one arm under her legs, Nien pushed a finger at a small red cut on her cheek. "Shortblade practice?"

Carly bobbed her head to the affirmative, accidentally knocked Nien in the head as she did, and then slurred, "You've got a lot of catching up to do." Slithering to her unsteady feet, she looped her arm through Nien's and dragged him through the maze of people into the kitchen where she poured an enormous amount of the warm brew into a mug. "Shortblade practice isn't the only thing you're behind on." She thrust the mug into his hand.

Nien took the mug, saluted her, and downed half of it.

"We informed Lant," Mien'k said, "that we planned on making a wreck of his home while he was off on his latest mysterious adventure."

Nien looked around at the mess of furniture, food leftovers, and sprawled bodies. "Well done."

Beside him, Carly said, "Look."

Nien looked up. Across the front room, on one of Lant's sofas, sat Wing. He had a drink in his hand and he was smiling. Nien almost dropped his mug. By Wing's reaction, his face must have gone entirely blank.

Carly left the kitchen and, moving over to Wing, sat down beside him and curled into the circle of his arm.

To Nien, Wing held out a fist full of cheese. Nien went to the offering as if he were on the sharp end of a fishing line and took it from Wing's proffering hand.

"Who are you?" Nien asked.

"Shut up and eat the cheese," Wing said.

Carly laughed, Nien bit into the cheese, and all attention turned to Mien'k and Teru tying each other into a drunken wrestling knot on the large rug at the center of the floor.

"You did!" Teru howled. "Wrapped in nothing but denial" —he grunted as Mien'k got an arm over on him— "you stood there, insisting that it got in there all by itself."

"Keep going," Mien'k said with a growl, "and I'll show you exactly how it got in there."

One of their feet caught the edge of the great rug and it began rolling them into a tight, awkward embrace.

"Wonderful," Nien said. "At least somebody's having sex tonight."

Stepping around the writhing rug, Nien made his way back into the kitchen to look for Lant. He found him there, opening a bottle of Hiona wine from Legran. Nien raised an eyebrow in question.

"It's a special occasion. Well, a double special occasion."

"Wing?"

"That's my fault," Lant said with a wink. "I sent Pree K out to tell him."

"Tell him what?"

"That there's something I have to tell the Cant—if they're not too drunk by now to hear me."

Nien glanced out into the front room. "We may have to remind them tomorrow," he said ruefully.

"Come on, then." Grabbing Nien by the shoulder, Lant guided him back into the main room. Clearing his throat loudly, Lant raised his glass. "Everyone!" he called. "We all know why we're here tonight, except for Nien." He looked at Nien. "This isn't just a welcome home party. We've been working on a few things while you were gone." Lant nodded to Pree K.

Pree K came forward and placed a bound package in his father's hands.

"Here," Lant said, handing the package over to Nien. "It's long over-due."

Nien pulled the leather tie free and unfolded the contents. Inside was a leather shoulder mantle meant to be worn over his Cant uniform. Across the right shoulder was engraved the likeness of a shy'teh with a shortblade clenched in its teeth.

Nien couldn't believe it. "The Cant symbol?" he asked, not taking his eyes from it.

"Thought you might recognize it," Lant said.

Nien had worked early on with Lant to create the symbol of a crouching shy'teh holding a blade in its mouth. Elusive and timid, rarely seen and little understood, no other valley regarded the shy'teh as sacred except for the Rieevans—so that part of the symbol was obvious. But the blade. Nien and Lant had juxtaposed the blade into the image as representative of the Cant, as if to say that hidden somewhere inside the timorous shy'teh was a fierceness overlooked and often forgotten.

Seeing it now filled Nien's chest with joy and warmth. It was perfect.

"One more thing," Lant said. "This begins a new tradition in the Cant. This shoulder mantle was made to be worn by my First, the Leader of the Cant."

The room waited for Lant's words to register with Nien.

After a moment, Nien's throat tightened, he started to speak, stopped, and finally laughed with incredulous wonder. The room laughed with him, broke into applause, and everyone raised their glass or mug.

As the room toasted their new Cant Leader, Nien's gaze met Wing's. Wing raised his glass to him; Nien reciprocated.

"Congratulations," Lant said.

"Thank you, Commander."

The two bumped their glasses and as Nien sat down again with the leather shoulder mantle draped across his knees, it didn't matter what fate the Council decided for him tomorrow; tonight was his, here with Lant, Wing and Carly, and his closest friends.

Cradling his mug like a child's face, Nien thought, *Yosha, it's good to be home.*

CHAPTER 29

Revelations

Three days later, the festival ended, Nien made his way home with the family before setting out to look for Wing. He'd not seen him since the night at Lant's and was anxious to finally speak with his brother alone. He found Wing in the fields and for the first time in more than a couple revolutions the two worked the fields together until dark.

"So," Wing asked. "What happened with the Council?"

"So far it's been a real non-event—but they've not had an official meeting until today, so…"

The brothers shrugged at each other.

"Let's eat," Nien said. "Much longer out here and I'll be fighting the team for a chance to gnaw on the bit."

Back in the house the family had already retired so the boys threw together a cold supper and sank to the family room floor.

"It's about time," Nien said, his words muffled through the food in his mouth. Wing's eyes flashed the hint of a question and Nien said, "I've been wanting to talk with you since I left Quieness."

"Just since then?" Wing replied, feigning insult.

Nien indulged the joke with a wry tip of a grin. "I really did miss you—especially at the end. But there's a lot there I'll miss, too. Like the people. One in particular."

"A girl?"

Nien bobbed his head. "Her name is Necassa. She works at the library where I studied. She helped me find a place to stay." He paused. "She didn't just show me her world, she…showed me how to get inside of it."

"Did you love her?"

"E'te, but that would not be the entirety of it, you know? I think my feelings were wrapped too tightly in the whole experience. How genuine could it have been in such circumstances?"

"How did you leave it with her?"

"It was awkward. Sad."

"I'm sorry," Wing said.

"The last time we were together I remember looking down at the street far below me as she walked away. I felt so alone—and I guess that's when I realized that it wasn't her, and it wasn't the city, but that I simply didn't belong there. From my small window I could see all the way out to the Royal Palaces. They're quite a ways out of the city, but you can't miss them. The sight of them was as 'at home' as I felt in Quieness—how weird is that?" Nien paused on the realization. "But that's just where the oddity began. I mean, every day I would see other Preaks. There are hundreds of thousands that live in Cao and yet I felt more alien among them than I did with the Quienans or the Honj. I learned a great deal, but I don't know that I am much the wiser."

"I doubt that."

"No, truly. I'm afraid that little trip of mine landed me squarely back here in your field of expertise."

Wing's eyebrows furrowed. "*My* field? There are no answers grown there, Deviant. Only questions."

"And that's exactly what I need now."

Wing gave him a quizzical look.

"Don't you find it strange how the world works through us and sometimes in spite of us to bring us to a place where we're finally ready to listen?"

Wing was twirling a piece of hair around his finger—a familiar mannerism, something he did whenever he was contemplative. Or worried.

"What?" Nien asked.

"What?"

Nien nodded toward Wing's hand as he wound the piece of hair tighter around his finger.

Wing released his hair.

"You would think the last thing I'd gone to Quieness to study would be works on theology."

"I would have imagined so."

"Well, I ended up studying not only the Ancient Writings there, but the records of nearly every other valley that had something written on their beliefs." Wing locked eyes with him before Nien continued. "I tell you, it was as if these books would follow me around—if I hadn't picked them up, they would have tailed me back to my apartment. What began as some strange cosmic annoyance took over every intent and nearly every thought I had there." Nien took a breath and ran his hand over his head. "Here's the thing, in my reading of them I kept finding common themes and I started to wonder: what if they are all talking about the *same* thing? Maybe I'm hunting out possibilities. Maybe I'm looking for something I only want or need to believe. But if I'm not—doesn't that change everything?"

"Yes," Wing said, his voice soft, full of emotion, "everything. It takes away the very premise of our isolation."

Nien looked his brother over. "You don't seem very surprised by this."

Wing averted his eyes.

"What?" Nien asked.

"I'm just…agreeing."

"Agreeing. So you've thought about this before?"

"Yes."

"That's why it feels like you're patting me on the head."

"No. I'm just…happy."

"Don't drop the reins, Wing. Tell me what you're thinking or you'll make me crazy."

"I'm happy that you know."

"That I know…?"

"That we are all talking about the same thing."

"We?"

"Yes, *we*," Wing replied.

"As in all these religions, all these races—not just you and me," Nien said, trying to clarify.

Wing nodded.

"So you *are* just patting me on the head."

Wing grimaced. "No, Nien…"

"Alright." Nien conceded. "How long have you thought this?"

Wing was silent for a time; he then reached behind him and grabbed his personal copy of the Ancient Writings. Flipping the book open, he turned to a page near the beginning and said, "Here the prophet writes: 'Merehr fled out of his own land from a desolating scourge and sojourned in a strange land. And as I watched I became aware that this was the Leader of Legend that the prophets before me had spoken of.'" He glanced up at Nien. "There are passages like this throughout the Writings that have led us to believe they are talking about the same person."

"*Led* us to believe?" Nien asked. "Isn't it obvious?"

"Then who is this?" And Wing read three more passages, each from a different book of the Poets, each using a different appellation. Wing ticked them off on his fingers after he'd read the verses: "Immortal Promise, Believer, and from the Poet Eneefa—Distant Star."

"Wing, all of those are simply other words for Merehr, the Leader of Legend. After all, those titles are all in the Poets—you know, prophets being *poetic*."

"I know," Wing said. "And what if that's the only reason they were left unchanged? For in every book that is not of the Poets, it reads: Merehr."

"*Unchanged?*" Nien took a breath. "Wing, you *do* know what you're saying?"

Wing looked at him.

"Yosha," Nien swore. "You're saying we, our ancestors, changed the Ancient Writings purposefully?"

"I don't know. Right now, I'm only asking the question. You did say questions were what you were looking for."

Wing's wry grin did nothing to settle Nien's stomach.

"A lot changes with translation of any kind," Nien said, almost stumbling over his words. "And a translation as laborious as the Ancient Writings must have been—?"

"I've taken that into account," Wing said.

"How long has it been since you've suspected?" Nien asked.

"Long time," Wing said. "But more important are the questions behind the question: Excepting the Poets, if the appellations in the rest of the Writings *were* changed—why? Perhaps they saw changing every mention of the Leader to our Rieevan word, Merehr, as simply part of their translation. But if it wasn't that, then why? What noble idea? What dramatic event, good or ill, could have caused them to alter the Writings?"

"Perhaps it was an over-abundant sense of self-righteousness," Nien quipped.

"That's crossed my mind," Wing said. "But if it was so important for our people to believe that the Leader will be of Rieevan blood, then why even include the books of foreign prophets?"

"Well, if foreign valleys believe the Leader will be Rieevan and not one of their own, how could that be disputed?"

"Exactly," Wing said.

Nien laughed out an expletive. "Bleekla, Wing, this is..."

The brothers matched each other's gazes.

"Our questions are dismantling our lives," Nien said quietly.

Wing's eyebrows rose slightly as if to say: *Welcome to the fields my mind plows.*

Shaking his head, Nien said, "Well, none of this will make any difference to the Council. All we have here are feelings and guesswork. Not exactly substantial offerings." In Wing's eyes, Nien could see his own besetment mirrored—and something else. "What is it?"

Wing was quiet, his eyes distant.

Nien waited, trying to be patient.

"The, uh..."

"The dream?"

"The vision, Nien. Real, and worse than any nightmare."

"You've never told me what it is you see," Nien said, his voice still in the faint light emanating from the lantern.

"I think that the Prophet-Poets, more so than the Writers, wrote in poetic verse because there was little other way to describe what they saw and felt. Though their predictions are bloody, combative, and dark—unlike anything I could even imagine—in the vision they are real."

A coldness settled in Nien's gut.

"I saw the destruction, Nien. The devastation they wrote of."

"You saw death? Was it of us? Of our people?"

"Of many people. More than that I cannot tell you." Wing's voice had grown thready. "But what I've seen—is it too late? Can I change that vision? Can it be different? Did I see only one possible outcome—the one the Prophet Writer or Poet themselves saw?" His head bowed. "Every time I reach for these answers, they slip from my grasp. All...all I have is this feeling. I have nothing to validate it." There was a pause, then Wing continued. "As long as our people ignore that the Ancient Writings were written not only by Rieevans but by men and women from other valleys—even far distant valleys—they will never be able to accept that there may be discrepancies in our translation and that some ideas, some thoughts, cannot be translated at all."

"If what you've been saying is remotely true, it's far worse than that—we're basing our whole way of life on a translation that is incomplete or purposefully a lie." Nien's eyes narrowed and looked almost black in the dimming lantern light. "If our people cannot accept that our translation is flawed, they will never be able to believe that the Writings may speak of someone, of a leader, other than Merehr. The basis for our way of life is completely false." Nien could hardly believe what he was saying. "How long have you known all this?" Nien asked.

"Long time." Wing met his brother's eyes with a look as piercing as a white-fired blade.

For more than a few revolutions before he had left for Quieness Nien had felt a distance between himself and his brother, a distance that Wing had placed not only between *them* but also between himself and everyone. Now Wing had crossed that distance back to him and Nien knew he'd stumbled upon the deep and heavy burden that Wing had never been able to share.

Briefly caught up in the disquieting epiphany, Nien suddenly understood the beleaguered dichotomy of his brother's world: Wing was twilight and dusk, sunlight and shadow, warm wood and chilly spring. He *was* what their people needed and nothing like what they were looking for.

How could I have been so blind? Nien thought. *With all of my learning, here with him, I am ignorant.*

"Wing, I...I'm so sorry for what I said when I left for Quieness—about you not saying something, not standing up for yourself."

Nien had expected Wing to cut him off, to quickly say it was all right as he always did.

He was shocked when Wing met his eyes. "Nien, I have tried, so many times, so many ways, to speak to the Council. To *say* something. But they twist my words. They see in them what I don't intend and invent the rest. Until I say exactly what they already want to hear, they will never hear me." Wing took a pained breath. "It could be that on my word they would agree to an alliance with the other valleys, but what if..."

And Nien understood. "They believe Merehr makes the need of the Cant and an alliance with the other valleys irrelevant."

It took only a glance from Wing for Nien to know he'd surmised exactly. "Bleekla—you think their belief in Merehr is that strong?"

"I believe their fear of the other valleys is that strong."

Something deep and real stirred in Nien's chest. "Why is it you never shared any of this with me before?"

"With anyone."

"Why?"

"Because it's pointless to do so unless you know the one you're telling *already* understands."

Nien rolled his eyes in mock exasperation. "*Great.*"

"Now," Wing said. "Will you let *me* apologize?"

Sitting back with a dramatic air, Nien threw his arms over his chest and put his feet up as if accepting a crown from a king. "Alright. I'm ready. Go ahead."

Wing sighed. "What I said about you running away. The truth was, I didn't want you to leave."

Nien looked Wing over. Compassion filled him from belly to brain. He sat up. "I guess I knew that," he said. "I just wanted some peace. I wanted *you* to have some peace while I was gone..."

Wing laughed. "That's your way of trying to *protect* me?" He shook his head. "You really are a bit of an idiot."

Nien grinned like a sheepish child.

"It's good to have you back," Wing said.

With a twinkle in his eye, Nien replied, "For me as well, brother. For me as well." And before either of them could say another word, Nien reached up and, grabbing Wing by the back of the neck, pulled him to the ground. No wrestling had been had in nearly a revolution and despite the late moonstep and sleeping family members, it was long overdue.

CHAPTER 30

Into the Pass

"Jason will be going with the others to defend Jayak Pass."

Call looked up at Monteray. The right sleeve of his uncle's long robe hung empty, reminding Call of the fall his uncle had taken only days before that terminated with cracked ribs and a broken arm. These injuries would keep him from going with the militia.

"I want to go," Call said.

"You're too young. Anyway, the men would never let you," Monteray replied.

"Where's Jason now?"

"Heading into town."

Call ran out his uncle's front door. The length between him and his destination flew by under his feet.

More than a turn ago, merchants traveling from Majg reported that they'd seen movement in the mountains to the southing of their valley. In the past three days, men in town had received word that Ka'ull spies had been found in Jayak. There had also been a few sightings of the dark robed warriors in the lower half of Jayak Pass leading into Legran. Though not terribly organized, the Legran militia had decided to present a force inside the Pass.

All this was running through Call's mind as he approached the large group of Legran militia gathering on the outskirts of town. It didn't take him long to spot his brother at the center of them.

To his brother, Call heard one of the militia say: "The Jayakans will drive them into the Pass and from there right into Legran."

Jason glanced over at Gendt, a farmer by trade, pessimist by nature.

Another militia member, struggling to secure his longbow in the harness at his back, asked, "Has anyone spoken with the Kiutu? If the Jayakans are planning something, maybe we can add our numbers to theirs."

All eyes shifted to Jason.

"Monteray has heard nothing from the Kiutu," Jason said. "The best thing we can do is protect the Pass."

Troy Naterey, a craftsman and leader of the militia, walked through the group of men. A large bow was slung over his back and a short sword swung at his side. "Jason's right. Let's stop talking and get a move on."

The militia moved out.

"Jason! Jason!"

Jason looked behind him.

"It's your little brother," one of the men remarked snidely as Call tried to push his way through the moving line.

Seeing him, Jason managed to extricate himself, ignoring the swearing of the other men whose paths he'd had to cross to get out. "What are you doing?"

"I want to come," Call gasped, catching his breath.

Jason grunted exasperatedly. "You can't come. Why do you always do this? Yiffa, it's embarrassing."

Call's eyes fell. "I'm sorry, I just—I don't want to be left behind."

Jason's demeanor softened. "Listen, someone *needs* to stay behind, take care of things here. It won't be long, not long at all before you'll be going a lot farther than Jayak."

Call looked up into his brother's eyes.

Jason forced a smile. "Be good. Take care of Mom. I'll see you soon."

Call could only watch as Jason turned, and after a quick look back, hurried ahead into the throng of men.

CHAPTER 31

First Battle

Nien stood beside Lant. Before them the leadership group was getting ready, their gear scattered about their feet. It was a couple turns before the Kojko festival and this would be the first full excursion of the new Cant leadership. After officially being appointed Lant's First the night of his return to Rieeve, Nien had appointed six other Cant Leaders: Carly, Mien'k, Shiela, Teru, Reel, and Bredo.

Nien would be leading them up Jhiyak Canyon to the Y where the canyon split one way to Jayak and the other to Legran. They would camp there, at the base of Vilif Pass, before continuing on towards Jayak.

It had not been easy for Commander Lant and Nien to decide on the route. Though things were changing in Legran, that the valley had once enslaved its Preak population meant many Legranders were still leery of the race and would most certainly view a Preak man leading a team of armed men into their valley as a threat. On the other hand, Jayakans saw Rieevans as intellectual inferiors and therefore would not welcome any of the Cant Leaders into their valley, except Nien.

"The whole idea behind this trip," Nien had said to Commander Lant, *"is to scout out routes for future training excursions and to give the new leaders a chance to coalesce. I don't think entering either valley is plausible or necessary at this point. We will admire Jayak from afar and then return home."*

Nien looked up from his thoughts to find Mien'k's eyes upon him; his friend was smiling. Nien nodded to him. This exercise was a christening of sorts and they'd been looking forward to it.

Lant gave them final instructions and a short admonition before turning and thumping Nien on the back. "Take care of each other," he said.

Nien gave the signal to move out.

The sound reached their ears suddenly. The Cant leaders, Nien at the front, stopped, each tilting their head in the direction of a dull clamour.

The small company had camped the first and second evening in the canyon, the third and fourth at Vilif Pass. The fifth night they'd spent in a shallow cove not far from where they were now, following a ridge above the valley of Jayak.

Though none of them had ever heard actual combat, the sound issuing from the valley below was unmistakable.

"That's coming from Jayak—this side," Nien said.

The others looked at Nien.

"A training exercise, maybe?" Teru offered.

Nien didn't want to immediately dismiss Teru's suggestion, but he didn't think so. "Come," he said. "Let's take a look."

Making their way to the top of the ridge, the Cant leaders got their first sight of battle. Breast shields and sword blades flashed in the sun. The tangle of thousands and thousands of men would have made distinguishing sides impossible from atop the ridge—except that something less than half the warriors were dressed in dark robes.

"Ka'ull," Nien breathed softly.

"What?" Shiela and Mien'k asked at the same time.

"Those men," Nien said throatily, "the ones in the dark robes. They're Ka'ull."

"How do you know?" Bredo asked.

"I know," Nien replied. "Lant told me about them." Nien's eyes were fixed on the battle—the eyes of the Cant leadership were fixed on him. "I'm going down there; take a closer look."

"Are you out of your mind?" Bredo blurted.

Nien's eyes flicked to the other leaders as if he'd just remembered they were there. "I will not ask any of you to join me." He turned his sight back toward the valley and the battle. "But I—I have to go down there."

Setting his bedding and food supplies aside, Nien headed down the mountainside. Carly took only a glancing look back at the others as she tossed her own supplies aside and started after him. Mien'k, Shiela, and Teru were immediately behind her. In the end, even the most reluctant of them all, Bredo, followed the rest down the mountain.

The descent passed for Nien in a heart-racing blur. He couldn't believe what he was doing, even what he was seeing, but he could not stop his feet.

At the edge of the valley, in a stand of brush trees, he paused briefly.

Close now, he could see glints of chain armour beneath the dark robes of the Ka'ull as they fought, their sword strikes blunt and powerful. Opposing them, the Jayakans were a splendid sight, their swords bright, their movements fluid and open.

Nien threw a single glance to Carly on his right, Mien'k and Shiela on his left, and then he was stepping out. In a moment so inconceivable that time missed its catch, he drew his sword from its sheath. Brandishing the blade once to assure himself it was real, he met the first metal of an enemy soldier.

Nien thought the crack of their connecting swords must certainly have shattered both sword and bone.

Stunned by the force of it, he stumbled back. His hands burned as if they'd been pressed through fire and his ears rang as though the sole receptacle of a smith's anvil.

But an instant's mental check-in found his sword still whole and his arms continuing to obey his commands. The mere thought-seconds it took for him to take in this information was nearly too much—he only miraculously deflected the Ka'ull's next blow. Stepping back, the Ka'ull rejoined, and came in again. Nien parried the drive before bringing his sword up in a quick half-moon, feeling it move through cloth, then bone.

The Ka'ull lurched away, holding an arm inside the dark robe.

As Nien watched the Ka'ull retreat, a strange, overwhelming sensation flooded his body. Hot and full, he felt sure to drown in the heat of his own rising blood. It felt like nothing he'd ever felt before; it felt like he'd done this all his life. Briefly, the feeling terrified him. The next instant, however, he let the deluge come. It drowned out fear and thought and Nien found that he simply wanted to move; he simply wanted to *engage*...

Not waiting this time for a Ka'ull to come to him, Nien went on the offensive, driving his sword through a Ka'ull who'd only looked in his direction. It took the whole weight of Nien's body to drive the sword in. The Ka'ull fell back, taking Nien's blade with him. Nien readjusted his grip over his sword's pommel and bracing a foot against the Ka'ull's thigh, managed to withdraw his sword in time to avoid toppling over himself.

Bringing his sword back 'round in front of him, Nien's blows now landed with precision. Even the bodies of the fallen did not trip up his feet or thwart his motion as he moved around and over them.

With surprising speed, Nien fought through two more before coming to stand back to back with a Jayakan warrior. Startled, the Jayakan raised his sword to strike—

Luckily, he paused.

Nien started to speak to him when the edge of a dark-robed shoulder appeared behind the Jayakan. Nien's eyes sprung wide, and in a move so fluid one might have thought they'd choreographed it between them, the Jayakan ducked as Nien swung.

A Ka'ull fell in a heap at the Jayakan warrior's feet.

An instant later, the two were swept apart, caught up in the flow of the battle.

But there was very little battle left.

The Cant leaders had come in with the battle-tide already in favour of the Jayakans. Now, with the Ka'ull in full retreat, shouts of men began to fill the air from every corner of the battlefield. The raking of swords diminished as the strange Jayakan shibboleth filled the air.

Nien raised his voice with the rest. The tone sang in his chest, numbed his brain, charged his taut muscles with a healing uplift even as his adrenaline began to bleed down. He felt drugged. Intoxicated. In love.

Like a whisper from the back of a crowded room, it took Nien a moment to recognize the call of his own name.

"Nien!"

Nien turned to see Carly coming up behind him. For some strange reason he noticed blood on her sword, how grey and gooey it looked, but nothing else.

By the time Carly reached his side, however, the tonal intoxication had started to clear. A tired breath escaped him. His arms, now dead weights upon his shoulders, fell to his sides and he dropped his nicked and bloodied sword. Carly leaned upon her own sword, listening as the sound of renewed conflict swept down from a canyon to their left on a rising wind—apparently the fleeing army was being met with battle in that canyon, but by whom Nien nor Carly had time to wonder as the other leaders of the Cant began to stagger their way back into a group.

Nien could see they were utterly drained; he turned to Carly who was still standing beside him. "Do you see everyone?"

"Yes," Carly said, "oh, wait." She turned to the others. "Where's Bredo?"

Reel and Teru began looking around.

"Mien'k, have you seen Bredo?" Reel asked.

Mien'k shook his head. Nien twisted on his feet, scanning the battlefield.

"He was right behind me," Shiela said.

Nien's eyes narrowed as if squinting might bring their missing member into view. "No one remembers seeing him?"

Silence prevailed. Nien felt the awful possibility, like a sickness, pool into his stomach. He was still scanning the outer as well as his own inner landscape, when a Jayakan approached him from behind. Carly caught

Nien's attention and motioned for him to turn around. Coming up behind him, Nien recognized the Jayakan whose life he'd saved. The smaller man bowed to him, and Nien responded in kind.

"Iyak eul flekon."

"I don't understand you," Nien said, responding in the Fultershier.

"We are most grateful to you," the man restated in very uneven Fultershier. "I am Jiap. And you, Preak, are a long way from home. What brings you to Jayak?"

"I am called Nien. These are my men. We are from Rieeve."

The surprise on the man's face was impossible to mistake. He started to speak, then stopped. "Rieeve?"

"I know our people don't travel much, but we would like to. We are soldiers, like you."

The man shook his head, dismayed. "You, Rieevan? I don't think so. Come with me, man of Preak."

"Come? Where?"

"The battle is over. It is time to meet, eat, take a count."

"No, no, I can't. We have lost one of our number."

"We have lost many."

"—No, I don't know if he is dead."

"The scouts will look for him." The man glanced at the other members of the Cant. "And your people can look for him."

Nien refused again. "I cannot. I am the leader of this group, and I am responsible for my men."

"If your man is not dead, then he has been taken. My men will find it out. Now come."

The tone of the man's voice caused Nien to pause.

"You should go," Carly said in Nien's ear.

"But not alone," Mien'k warned. "Carly and I should go with you—at least."

"Well enough," Nien said to Jiap. He then spoke to the rest of the Cant leaders. "Look for Bredo. Search this area—he couldn't have gotten too far in such a short time. We'll be back."

With that Nien, Mien'k, and Carly turned to follow Jiap. But Jiap stopped. Pointing at Mien'k and Carly, he said, "Not them. Not the Rieevans."

"They are my" —Nien paused, trying to find a word the Jayakan would respect— "councilors."

Jiap hesitated, looking upon the other members of the Cant leadership as if they were insects. "Since they fought for us—with *you*—let them come. But only those two."

Nien, Carly, and Mien'k went with Jiap, arriving shortly at a delicate-looking structure. Though quite long, from the outside it did not look tall enough to accommodate even a child's height. But a door, nearly disguised in the side of the building, opened and Nien, Carly, and Mien'k followed Jiap down a smooth ramp. The ramp widened into a large room. Obviously dug into the earth, the room was surprisingly expansive, framed on the opposite side from where they'd entered with a wall of glass windows that looked out into a garden that rivaled SiQQiy's palatial gardens and helped ease any claustrophobia Nien, Carly, and Mien'k might have felt upon entering the building.

Furnishings were minimal, boasting elegant detail. Filling the entire middle section of the room was a large table. Like the building from the ground, the long table sat no more than a hand's width above the floor. Looking at the table, it did not appear that there was anywhere for one's legs to go.

"Sit, please?" Jiap offered, motioning to a row of low, rectangular seats placed alongside the table. The seats had no backs to them and only short silver handles for arms.

Adjusting their swords at their sides, Nien, Carly, and Mien'k situated themselves on three flat cushions finding that the floor beneath the table vanished and they were able to stretch their legs out, their feet coming to rest comfortably on a sunken floor beneath.

They had not been seated long before the hall began to fill with other soldiers. Silken stripes across the breasts of the Jayakan uniforms apparently denoted rank. Nien assumed them to be the leaders of the garrisons that had just fought back the Ka'ull.

Nien also noticed, sitting amongst the Jayakans, two other men. Their dress as well as their physical attributes suggested an earthy, unfussed, but nevertheless menial way of life. As disparate as their presence was amongst the stylized Jayakans, it was the way that one of the two kept looking at Nien that unsettled him. Nien had never felt such a gaze before and did not maintain eye contact with the man for long, choosing instead to direct his attention to the scene through the windows opposite him that framed the long rectangular hall. The garden was filled with trees, exquisite in shape and colour, smooth domed rocks, and various forms of flowering shrubbery.

Briefly, Nien's mind wandered back to a small café in Quieness where Necassa had expressed her wishes to visit Majg and Jayak in order to see their people in their native valleys.

Though exhausted mentally and physically, Nien found himself able to grasp the fantastic reality of the moment.

Jiap left them at the long table and hurried to the far corner of the room where he disappeared through a short door at its end.

"What's going on?" Mien'k asked, his tone thin with apprehension.

"I assume he's going to inform his superior," Nien answered.

A moment later, Jiap reappeared.

Behind him came a man whose height was, at most, diminutive. A fair portion of grey flecked his brief and fairly pointed black beard, but the hair of his head was jet black and cut very short.

The man looked directly at Nien as he entered the room.

Nien forgot to breathe as the man locked eyes with him—eyes without age, onyx black and wise.

Nien nodded to him, but the man made no such motion in return.

"Your presence in our valley is strange, is it not?" the man asked in Jayakan. Jiap translated for Nien.

"It is," Nien said.

"Why, then? And why now?"

Nien hesitated. Obviously, the man suspected them of something...

But what? Of being opportunists? Hiding out in the mountains, waiting for a battle to happen and then quickly joining in order to curry favour?

The truth, however, seemed just as ridiculous.

Well, Nien thought, *I can't think of a lie that would be any better.*

"We," Nien said, motioning behind him to Mien'k and Carly, "are part of the fighting force of Rieeve." He had no desire to give away that they were comprised entirely of the Cant leaders knowing that such information might prove an irresistible target should things take an unexpected turn. "We were on a training excursion in the canyon between our two valleys. We heard the sound of battle and joined the fight, as you have no doubt been informed by your..." Nien paused, "Commander?"

As Jiap translated, Nien felt that the man was studying not only the words Nien had said but if there was truth in them.

On the other side of a few heart-pounding moments, the man seemed satisfied and, turning, went to the head of the table near the door and seated himself. He clapped his hands five times and five men appeared from another door with large platters of food in their arms.

The food was placed down the center of the enormous table and small, round, silver saucers were set before each seat. One double-pronged utensil was provided and the servers disappeared.

Mien'k, Nien, and Carly simply stared at the small silver saucers. Everything had happened so fast that the three felt unhinged, disconnected. Their heads were spinning and dull grey aches had begun to surface behind their eyes.

Beside Nien, Jiap leaned in and said quietly, "You may serve yourself."

Nien nodded his thanks, asking, "Who is that?" referring to the small man who had questioned him and now sat at the head of the table.

Jiap whispered, "He is the Kiutu."

"Kiutu?" Nien said. "That is his title?"

Jiap nodded.

Once everyone had placed only a small portion of food on their plates and filled large bowls with a clear liquid soup, the Kiutu clapped his hands again—this time only once. A young man appeared through the same short door at the far corner of the hall.

"Kicob," he ordered.

Jiap leaned over to Nien. "The men now report on our battle outcome."

One by one around the table, the men abandoned their food momentarily and gave their report. Nien listened carefully as the Kiutu addressed the two men in the rustic leather clothing. They were from Legran and reported that they had lost forty-seven men.

From Legran, Nien thought. No wonder he'd felt so uncomfortable beneath the gaze of the one.

The recital continued until finally reaching Nien. Nien looked to the Kiutu, then at the young man at the Kiutu's side who was apparently recording the reports.

"Were any of your people killed?" the Kiutu asked in Jayakan.

Nien glanced at Jiap for help.

"He is asking how many of your group was wounded or killed," Jiap said.

Nien replied in the Fultershier. "The men that are still with me are fine. However, we are missing one of our number."

As Nien said the words he felt his mind dissociate from both the question he'd been asked and his own answer.

How many of his men had been killed?

Killed?

Today, the Cant leadership, his comrades, his friends had slain men. Taken lives.

And Bredo. Bredo was missing.

The Kiutu thanked him with a look as the rest continued eating. Nien nodded to him and, thinking the Kiutu was done with him, looked back down at his plate. But the Kiutu spoke again, saying one word: "Lant."

Nien, Mien'k, and Carly all looked up. It was the first word Mien'k and Carly had recognized since the meal began.

"You know Lant?" Nien asked, still not sure whether the Kiutu spoke the Fultershier.

"Yes I do," he replied, speaking the Fultershier slowly, perfectly and without accent.

"He's our Commander," Nien replied.

"He is a good man."

Nien noted, out of the corner of his eye, a reaction from the two men of Legran.

"We thank you for your help this day," the Kiutu said before taking a long sip of soup. He then set down his bowl, and after a few words in Jayakan to the others, left the room.

As the rest began to converse among themselves, a few rising to leave, Nien turned again to Jiap. "The Ka'ull. Have you fought them before? How long have they been in this land?"

"This was the first battle. There has only been this one. We have seen them in the woods. Ka'ull spies we found among us—but too late." He looked at Nien. "We drove them back, but they knew where to strike. We are hurt." Jiap glanced to Nien. "Your sword defended me. Thank you."

Nien inclined his head to him—Jiap did likewise then got up to disperse with the others.

"If I may, Jiap," Nien said quickly.

Jiap stopped.

"With whom may I inquire concerning our man who is missing?"

Jiap met Nien's eyes briefly before saying, "He was carried off, taken by the Ka'ull." He then turned and left with the other Jayakan Commanders.

Nien watched Jiap leave, stunned with disbelief, unable to say anything.

Carly nudged Nien with her elbow. "What did he say?"

It took a moment for Nien to reply. "He said that Bredo was taken, carried off by the Ka'ull."

Mien'k and Carly stood numb, their eyes unblinking.

"What do we do?" Carly asked.

"I don't know," Nien said slowly, "but I think we'd better leave here now."

"And go where?"

Nien drew a breath. "To look for Bredo."

Nien, Mien'k, and Carly found the rest of the Cant leaders still moving about the field searching the dead for that one familiar face. Joining them, they continued an exhausting search for their comrade. As nightfall began to crest the mountain ridges and all the dead had been accounted for, Bredo was not among them.

Feeling his despair like a great black hole in his stomach, Nien glanced up toward the canyon where the Ka'ull had made their hasty retreat. Somehow, he knew that Bredo was among them. For what seemed an endless moment, he fought the urge to charge up the canyon in the vain hope that they could rescue their fellow Cant member. But darkness was only a whisper away, and though he felt he might be welcome to stay a night in Jayak, he was not so sure the same would be extended to the rest of the company.

There was only one clear choice: They must return to Rieeve.

Subjugated by the sight and the smell, the Cant leaders walked slowly from the battlefield. A little blood went a long way, and there had been much spilled. Only a few bodies remained, and the Jayakans were already wrapping them in tight white lengths of cloth.

The small group made their way back up the mountain they had descended into Jayak. "We need to go after Bredo," Reel said. "The Jayakans said he was taken and we know which way the Ka'ull went..." His voice trailed off, exhausted but angry.

"We are twelve" —Nien paused— "eleven. What is it you think we can do?"

Reel stood taut. "We can't leave him. We can't abandon him."

Nien leaned into Reel, his short sword swinging at his side. "Don't you think I want to go after him? Don't you think this tears at my guts?" Nien's fists clenched. "But we have to go back. Lant needs to be informed."

"I'd rather report to Lant that we all made it back," Reel replied.

"And I would rather eleven return to Lant than none." Nien rested his burnished gaze upon each of them. "We *know* now. The Ka'ull are not close, they're here! We have our people, *all* of our people to think about. We don't know how long we will have: turns, maybe days only."

Teru turned to Reel. He knew Reel had been closest to Bredo—they had been friends since childhood. He put a hand on his shoulder. Reel's eyes narrowed and it looked as if he was trying not to regurgitate.

"Bredo was our friend, too," Mien'k said, his voice tight, "but Nien's right."

The rest of the leaders stood staring at Nien in silence.

Slowly, with a pain in his heart he could barely fathom, Nien threw his long sword over his shoulder and began to ascend the hill out of Jayak and back toward their discarded gear near the top of the ridge.

The group turned and followed.

By the time they reached their packs, there was little desire to fill their empty stomachs or even bivouac. Setting up a short set of guard-duty shifts, and with nothing more in the way of conversation, they sagged to their tents and blankets.

With his gear strewn about his feet, Nien looked over the camp. Most of them were in a state of shock. He shook his stiff and swollen fingers, aware of the awkward dullness settling over his frame that Lant had once described. Had he the energy, he would have wept away the residue of fear and incredulity that he was feeling.

Ka'ull.

His brain could hardly process the information. The Great Fear—the cause of the dread which filled Rieeve, that drove his people into prophetic frenzy—they had faced, they had wounded, they had even killed. The terror was now flesh and blood, very real, but also killable.

Nien thought he might faint. Sinking to his knees, he vomited.

On his hands and knees, he crawled to his bedroll. Upon it, he lay, but his breath did not ease for a long while, coming to him hard, labored. He'd never even punched another human being before; now, in the impossibly short span of an afternoon, he'd taken the lives of more than a few.

How many had it been? he suddenly wondered.

Cant training practices had made the difference between their keeping or losing their lives. On some level, Nien had always known that no amount of training could ever nudge the truth of what they were learning to do, but he *had* wondered if their skills would ever be put to the test.

Shuddering, Nien felt as if his skin had come alive and begun to crawl, trying to separate itself from the flesh beneath.

Bredo…he thought. *Bredo's gone. I've lost one of us.*

This struck him more painfully than anything. He couldn't believe it, he just…

Sleep doused the fire in his mind and he faded off, a deep sweat layering his body as dreams replaced wakefulness, taking him on a journey into a land where he wished blood was any other colour than red and didn't carry such a wet, malodorous scent.

CHAPTER 32

Tidings

"Who is it?" Monteray called from the kitchen.

"Someone for you!" Call yelled back. He'd been shoving a handful of soft-breaded cheese into his mouth when he'd answered the door and was now trying to wipe it off his hands as well as the doorknob.

Call knew his aunt worried endlessly for his uncle in the construction of their home—and rightfully so. Even with a broken arm and a couple cracked ribs, Monteray had continued the work. Jason had been his main help until leaving with the militia for Jayak. So Call had shown up at his uncle's the following morning to help in any way he could.

Monteray walked through the narrow hallway to the back door. "Yes?" he asked, slapping sawdust from his hand.

"I have a message for you, Master Monteray."

Monteray took the short yellow vellum from the messenger.

Call recognized the messenger as the son of a merchant trader in town, only one of the many men who had gone into the Pass. Without dismissing him, Monteray read, his eyes brushing over the scribbled lettering. Call watched interestedly, wishing he could magically read through the back of the thin yellow parchment.

Upon completion, Monteray asked the messenger, "Has the family been told?"

Call's quick eyes flashed to Monteray. There was something in the tone of his uncle's voice...

The messenger only nodded.

"Thank you. You may leave."

The messenger quickly departed.

Monteray shut the door slowly. "Let's go back into the main room," he said.

Call followed Monteray, feeling as if a small wild animal had suddenly been released inside his chest.

Kate looked up as the two entered the dining area.

"You're scaring me," Call said.

"Have a seat," Monteray said.

Call did so reluctantly. "What is it? Is it about the Pass? Are the men coming back? Is it Jason? Did he get hurt?"

Monteray set the vellum down on the table, taking a seat himself. With a deep breath, he placed his hand upon the letter. "Your brother is dead, Call."

Call opened his mouth, but no words came out.

"Our men came at the Ka'ull from behind while they were already engaged with the Jayakans. The Ka'ull were routed, but we lost forty-seven men. Jason was among those who were killed."

Call's lower lip twisted despite his effort to stop it. "Dead?"

"I'm sorry, Call."

Kate hurried to Call's side, taking his thin shoulders in her arms.

Call gazed numbly at the table's shiny surface and the parchment that lay beneath his uncle's large hand. "Does my mother know?" he asked, silent tears now beginning to course down his cheeks.

"Yes," Monteray replied.

"I should go home," Call said, hoping he could control the unfamiliar frenzy building inside him.

"We're going with you."

But as Kate and Monteray donned their jackets, Call's hold on himself failed. In two steps he'd bolted through the back door, a few strides after that he was sprinting through the fields toward home.

Call slowed just before hitting the front door to his house. His breath shook his rib-thin chest. He swiped at his eyes, opened the door. Inside, his mother sat in a chair in the far corner of the main room—her bent posture needed no explanation. He wanted to sink to his knees in front of her and bury his face in her lap. Instead, he moved across the room and staying on his feet, draped his arms around her shoulders and cradled her head in his belly. He was still holding her when he heard Kate and Monteray step quietly in through the door behind him.

CHAPTER 33

Grim Report

Nien had no mind to urge his mount as it made its way through the light-splashed fields. The sun was setting quickly, casting a multi-coloured blanket across the valley and mountains. Lost, not in thought but rather a wash of emotion that exhausted him, he rode without consideration of time or distance.

He had met with Commander Lant upon entering Rieeve and given his report of all that had happened. Lant had dismissed the rest of the Leaders and spoken with Nien alone—

Nien remembered little of that conversation now.

Habitually quartering his horse in the stable, Nien proceeded on up to the house. He opened the door quietly and was filling his hands with water at the large basin before the family even noticed he was there.

"Nien!" Jake yelped.

Nien splashed his face a few times and, taking back up his gear, moved into the back room. Sitting down on his bed he began to remove his boots.

"Welcome back. How did it go?" Wing said, looking up from where he lay on his own bed, reading.

Nien made no response. Wing was about to ask again when Reean stepped in. "You all right, son?" she asked.

Nien pulled off his other boot. "We went to Jayak," he said.

"You said you would be going that way," Reean offered.

"There was a fight."

"A fight?" Reean asked.

"Yes, we...uh...went into the fight, me and the other Cant leaders."

Silent confusion answered him. Into the bedroom doorway, Joash and Jake appeared.

Nien explained: "The Jayakans were engaged in battle when we arrived upon a ridge overlooking the valley."

"Battling? With whom?" Joash asked.

"Ka'ull," Nien replied.

Reean said nothing. Wing looked at his father and back to Nien.

"The Ka'ull were in Jayak?" Joash repeated, as if hearing his own voice say it would help him comprehend.

"Are they coming here?" Jake said.

"I don't know," Nien said.

"The people of Jayak, were they...?" Joash could not finish his question.

"We fought alongside the Jayakans before the Ka'ull were driven off. We got back only a few sunsteps ago. I've been with Lant since then."

Reean began to look Nien over. "You're not hurt—you weren't wounded in the battle?"

"No, no. I'm fine."

"And the others?" Wing said.

"Bredo was captured and taken."

"Taken?" Reean asked. "Taken where?"

Nien's reply was sharp: "We don't know, mother. He was just taken."

A long silence followed as Reean thought of Bredo's mother and father—their son was gone.

Though annoyed with their questions, Nien felt inexplicably angry that his family had no better queries to make. Didn't they understand the gravity of the situation? Of what he and the other leaders had been through?

But then, how could they? He had been there, and he did not understand.

Nien got to his feet and, squeezing through the crowded bedroom doorway, returned to the washbasin in the main room. Leaning over it, he began to splash his face over and over again. He heard the family come back into the main room, could feel them watching his back in silence. Drying his face, he saw Fey standing in the corner like a doll, her eyes wide and unblinking.

Reean said, "Are you hungry? Would you like something to eat?"

"No. I've no appetite."

Incredible, Nien thought. *The last meal I ate had been in another valley over a battle debriefing, and I hadn't wanted that one either.*

"Are you sure?" Reean said.

In exasperation, Nien sought the room for a look, a word from one of them that would tell him he was not alone, that one of them at least felt the sadness, the incredulity he was feeling.

"Don't any of you get it?" he asked, his voice cutting in its desperation.

Again, the house fell silent. Fey let out a faint whimper. Reean walked over and picked her up.

It's all so unreal, Nien thought. *Should I even be here?*

He'd hoped that in coming home, he could leave the terror behind. Instead, he'd brought it with him.

Joash reached for a lantern. "We can discuss all this tomorrow. I'll turn out the lanterns and let you get some rest."

Nien could not raise his eyes to look at his father. He had wanted them to ask about what he'd been through, yet he did not want to try and explain the unexplainable. He wanted one of them to have the magic words that would cause his pain to go away, all the while having no idea what those words might be. He felt ashamed and lost, and even with his family around him, more alone than he'd ever been.

Without another word, Nien returned to the back room and slumped onto his bed.

The room downstairs fell quiet as Wing extinguished the final lantern.

For some while after Jake had fallen asleep, Nien lay awake in the darkness.

"Wing?"

"Yes?"

"You were asleep?" Nien asked.

"No."

Nien pushed his covers off and got up.

Wing pulled his legs out from beneath his blankets and scooted so that Nien could sit beside him.

"I killed a man, Wing. More than one."

Wing remained silent, waiting for him to continue.

"I, I swung my sword, like I have a thousand times in training, except this time I felt it hit flesh. I felt its sheer power against muscle and bone. I couldn't even see their faces. It was like fighting ghosts. There would be nothing but wind on my blade—and then blood."

Raising his face up at the long wooden beams of their bedroom ceiling, Nien drew a deep breath, forcing back the clear liquid in his nose. "I moved as if only a part of me were real. There was no fear, only motion, disconnected. The real fear came before and then after—after it was all over. We fell as if we were dead upon our bedrolls." Nien shuddered involuntarily. Tears rose to his eyes. He sniffed them back. "I lost one of us. Bredo is gone."

"Bredo was a member of the Cant as well, and a Leader," Wing reminded him quietly.

"Nevertheless, I was the leader of this expedition and he was in my charge. I left him. What if it had been me? Wouldn't I have wanted to know that my friends were looking for me? That they were coming after me? Trying to save me?" Nien's voice faltered.

"He must have known, Nien, that you and the other Leaders were looking for him…"

Nien didn't reply at first. "It's worse than that, Wing; so much worse. Lant said that they probably took Bredo alive—to question him before they killed him." An anguished silence followed. "I…I thought I would be protecting Rieeve. I thought that if I could help the Jayakans stop the Ka'ull in Jayak then they'd never come here. Everyone could stop worrying. Everyone would…"

"Ease up on me?" Wing asked quietly.

Nien's non-reply was answer enough; he continued, "But my action only served to hasten it. I placed all the information the Ka'ull needed and could not have gotten any other way *right* into their hands."

"You don't know, Nien, what it will mean…"

"Lant said the exact same thing. He said not to second-guess myself, but I can't help it…" A shiver ran over his body. "I hate myself, Wing. I hate what I saw, I hate what I did, I…I hate that terrible, awkward bit of metal." He threw his eyes at his Cant sword, lying on the floor near his bed. "I wish I'd never seen it."

His head bent forward again as sobs filled his chest.

Wing let him press against his side, supporting him as he wept, crying silently into the night.

Outside a bivouacked tent lay a body. Still draped about the lifeless shoulders was the leather shoulder mantle emblazoned with the symbol of the Cant. Inside the tent two voices were conversing.

"Rieeve would make the perfect staging ground."

"Yes. That's why it must be taken, and now we know how and when."

"And the people?"

"Inconsequential—obstacles to the goal. What we need is the land."

CHAPTER 34

Fallen On Deaf Ears

"Nien, I'm glad to see you. The Council has called an emergency meeting I have to get to, but we need to talk first."

Nien followed Lant into his hut and took a seat opposite the Commander in a small chair.

Kojko Festival had officially been over the day before. Really, it had been over before it started. Had there not been such a division between Cant member families and unaffiliated villagers, it might have been a festival unlike any other where individual campsites were abandoned in favour of one massive gathering in the center of the fields beneath Castle Viyer, a single large fire blazing at the center. But they were polarized over the loss of Bredo, over first hand accounts of battle, over those that said Wing was their salvation, others arguing that the Cant was the only real solution.

What might have unified them, served only to widen the divide.

Nien had been punished by the Council: not permitted to come to the festival. They'd tried to banish him from the Cant as well, forcing Lant into the position of declaring the Cant a separate entity and not under the jurisdiction of the Council.

It was a decision Lant had been loath to make, and it was far from decided in the minds of the Council.

"I'm waiting no longer," Lant said to Nien, quickly getting to it before he had to go. "Within the next three turns I will be sending out messengers. Premier Messenger Pree K will go to SiQQiy, Empress of Quieness; S'o will go to Impreo Takayo of Jayak; and Jhock I will send to Master Monteray in Legran. I'll be spending the next couple turns with them exclusively. They will deliver my proposal—an introduction and outline of the plan that I have been preparing.

"What I need *you* to do is begin training sessions with the Cant in earnest. The Cant needs to be ready, physically and mentally. Run drills every other day and hold skill practices and maneuvers on the rest. Give them one day to rest. Carly and the others wait for you on the training field. Since Pree K is preparing to leave for Quieness, you and the other leaders will need to notify the body of the Cant."

Lant stood to leave, but Nien didn't move. "Nien?"

"I can't train the Cant," he said.

Lant sat back down. "Why?"

Nien struggled to say the word: "Trust."

"You don't know that the Cant or the other Leaders have lost any in you," Lant said.

But Nien's eyes had gone blank and Lant knew instantly where his First had gone—Lant had been to the edge of the same dark precipice. He knew how ghastly it was, how compelling. He also knew that it offered release, a demonesque vow of liberation from the pain. It was what insanity felt like.

Lant reached across his desk and took Nien's face in his strong, calloused hands. "Nien."

Nien twitched, startled by something only he could see.

Again, Lant said, "Nien."

Nien blinked and his bloodshot eyes focused on Lant's face.

"Good," Lant said. "Good." He hadn't liked the look in Nien's eyes—a look he'd seen before though never in Rieeve.

Nien tried to speak but his tongue cleaved to his palate and Lant reached behind him for water. He pressed the cup of water into Nien's hand. Nien took it and downed it in a gulp.

"You and the other leaders acted like warriors," Lant said as Nien set the cup on the desk. "I would have expected nothing less of you. Perhaps that will be the event that opens the door between Rieeve and Jayak."

He could see that Nien was fully unconvinced.

"Nien," Lant said, his voice steady. "Look at me."

It seemed painful for Nien to focus his eyes.

"No one of our race," Lant said, "for generations, has faced what you faced, has had to make the kinds of decisions you had to make. It would be unhelpful and uninformed to blame yourself."

"So it's that easy," Nien said. "No responsibility, no blame."

"No, with trust."

"Trust?"

"In yourself," Lant replied. "In me. In nature."

"Nature? —*what?*"

"The nature of the world, of life itself, of who you are. Timing and people and place are not random, Nien. Each greets the other with no more happenstance than the raising of a great building."

Nien growled out his incomprehension.

Though Lant did not show it, he welcomed Nien's frustration. Anger was useful at the moment. Anger would keep Nien from returning to the edge.

"Why are the Ka'ull doing this?" Nien asked. "It's not as if they're after human labour or resources. Do they want only blood?"

"Slavery is of ancillary benefit to them, but no, that is not the reason. Resources on the other hand…" Lant paused. "The home of the Ka'ull is a desolate land. They have few natural resources. What is of value is difficult to locate and expensive to extract."

"Then why don't they ask? Why can they not work out trade agreements with other valleys?"

"As they have with us?" Lant said. "All is not as it seems. Though the other valleys are not closed as Rieeve is, they are still closed—they have not traded nor worked with the Ka'ull any more than we have."

"Then we're the bad guys?" Nien asked, his tone dripping venom and tiredness and disconsolation.

"No, Nien. I'm only saying that it is fear for their survival as a race that has driven them to where they are now." Lant's steady features grew heavy. "Their fear is what they want to kill."

"*Their* fear?" Nien said.

Lant understood Nien's dismay. "Most people," Lant said, "are decent at best, indurative at worst. But in the mix are those few who rise above or sink below. The current leader of the Ka'ull is such a person. To him have come the disconsolate, the hardened, the wounded. He fills them with a purpose, a means to justify their hate, their hurt, using it to feed the greed for its satisfaction until the path taken is too long and too hot and turning back seems impossible." For effect, Lant paused. It worked, Nien's eyes focused on his face. "I need you to hear me. The leader of the Ka'ull is a bitter, angry man. His people die in large numbers even as other valleys with rich resources are unwilling to negotiate trade. Desperation has become a way of life for the Ka'ull. Though it may not seem like it, Nien, he sees these attacks on our valleys as the only way to preserve his people."

"He sees attacking and murdering countless others as a way to preserve *his* people? Such an idea makes no—"

"Sense?" Lant said. "It doesn't have to make sense to us, Nien, but it will help us if we understand that it makes sense to *him*."

Clearly, Nien had no idea how to respond. He said instead, "How do you know so much about them?"

Lant's eyes suddenly grew very distant. "That is a long story."

Nien waited.

"I have been in their land," Lant said. "I have known" —he shrugged— "a few."

Another long silence passed.

"I have not spoken of it since returning to Rieeve."

"Does anyone...?"

"No one knows, Nien" —Lant paused— "at least not in Rieeve."

Lant had always thought that, someday, he'd tell Nien about what happened to him all those revolutions ago when he'd left Rieeve. As close as he felt to Nien and his family, it struck him to realize that he still had not told Nien anything about it.

"What was it like?" Nien asked.

"The land of the Ka'ull?"

Nien nodded.

"It was a desolate place—even then."

Again, Nien waited. Lant was grateful to see that Nien's curiosity had not been quelled by the experience in Jayak, nevertheless, now was not the time for stories. Leaning forward over his desk, he looked deeply into Nien's honey-flecked eyes. "I will tell you someday, Nien, but right now, I need you and I need you whole. Will you continue as you have, in training the Cant?"

Nien took a stabilizing breath. It took all of the will Lant knew Nien had in him to say: "We should have known the Ka'ull were on the move. We should have known they were in Jayak."

Lant nodded, grateful for both their sakes that Nien's getting-down-to-business was his answer. "I agree. But the best we can do now is discover the intentions of the other valleys."

"Proof of their support might help us with the people, and with the Council."

"Yes, but we don't have the luxury to wait for that. It's time we tell them," Lant replied.

The two men gazed at each other. A moment of heavy silence passed.

"Will you do it today?" Nien said.

"No. In three turns."

The two men looked at each other—Lant was going to wait to tell the Council after he'd already sent the messengers.

"So it is," Nien said and got up to leave.

Lant stood as well. "You will get through this, Nien. The shock will dissipate with time."

Nien did not look back as he stepped to the hut door. "All I can do is hope you're right."

With the eager faces of his three young Cant Messengers still vivid in his mind, Lant headed for the Council chamber. The three turns since his talk with Nien had already passed. He'd said goodbye to his son, Pree K, last night, to the Cant's two other young messengers, Jhock and S'o, the day before.

In his life, Lant had faced many fears in strange, far away valleys as well as here, in his home valley. He'd faced not only personal terror, but also that directed at him from others in the midst of facing their own. At the moment, however, he was surprised to feel none. Where fear should have been was a hollow. Not a hopeless, vacant hollow, but rather a trusted space. What filled it now, whether change or ruin was beyond his control, for without the Council's knowledge or blessing, he'd acted. And now there was only to face it, holding nothing for his defense but the conviction that he'd chosen as best he could.

"Councilman Lant," Grek Occoju said, welcoming Lant into the council chamber. "As you have called this special session, the floor is yours."

Lant leaned forward a little, pressing his fingertips against the smooth, shiny surface of the room's large conference table. "The last time the Council met, it was to discuss the loss of Son-Velaan Bredo. There is...information regarding his capture that I did not give the Council at that time."

"His *capture*?" Grek Occoju said. "We thought he was killed in the battle."

"He would have been killed by the Ka'ull, but it was not in the battle."

Voices broke here and there around the chamber.

"He *was* captured. But it is not that omission which concerns me. What concerns me, is this: the Ka'ull would have questioned him before they slew him. That is why they took him alive."

This time, only silence filled the room.

Grek spoke. "We do not know what, if anything, he told them."

Lant nodded. "True. But I am assuming the worst: I'm assuming he told them what they wanted to know."

"And what would that have been?" Grek asked.

"Our nature. Our way of life. Our resources. What kind of fighting force or military we have."

"That all seems common enough," Moer Ta'leer said.

"What is 'common' for us is all *they* need to know," Lant replied.

Councilman Fu Breeal knocked his knuckles against the table studiously. "What does this mean, other than the obvious: That we should have disbanded the Cant revolutions ago. The fact that Son-Cawutt Wing has consistently refused to join the Cant should have been a sign to us."

They were heavy words, but the sentiment within the Council had been there from the beginning.

"Just as we should have disallowed Son-Cawutt Nien's position in the Cant as soon as he returned from Quieness," another Councilman said. "Had he not been their leader, none of them would have gone down into a strange valley, much less joined a *battle*."

"The Councilman is right," Brauth Vanc said. "Going to Quieness emboldened Nien beyond sense, desensitized him to the point of rushing headlong into something he had no business being in."

Lant didn't let Brauth finish. "The Cant Leaders did exactly what they've been training to do."

"Foolish, rash boys," Councilman Cuiku spat under his breath.

Lant caught Cuiku's eyes. "Yes," he said, "they joined the battle. Yes, at battle's end Son Velaan-Bredo was not found. But even had they not gone, had Bredo not been taken, there is still this one outstanding problem: We are a small valley. We will not be able to withstand a force such as the Ka'ull represent."

"We have all mourned Son Velaan's loss," Councilman Sk'i Yinut said. "Thankfully, Jayak is far from here."

"Jayak is not so far."

"Far enough."

"Do you know how far Jayak is, truly? I'll tell you: A man can make the trip in less than a turn. An army only a little more."

"The Jayakans are strong. They'll take care of the problem."

"Maybe they could. But it's in the details, gentleman. Son-Cawutt Nien reported that the Ka'ull *retreated*. That is something we need to consider. Perhaps the battle was a test of Jayakan strength. Perhaps the Ka'ull are not yet prepared in this hemisphere to face a foe as formidable as the Jayakans—"

"The Jayakans' strength could mean our downfall."

"How so?" Councilman Ne'taan asked sincerely.

"As an invasion force, the Ka'ull will need a base of operations here, in the midvalleys. If the Jayakans prove too much for their present forces they will choose another valley, a smaller valley, and from there they will organize incursion of the larger."

"Then why not Legran?" Tael Ruke suggested.

"Why not Legran? Why not us? Why not all of us? For it *will be* all of us, eventually, even Quieness. If we're not next, we will follow. It's inevitable."

"Nothing is inevitable," Councilman Breeal replied. "Eosha has entrusted us with His truth and His protection, and we have Wing Merehr."

Lant felt the cold, awesome weight of Breeal's last words. "Wing," he said thickly, "has never said anything to us of these matters."

"He will, when the time is right."

"Perhaps," Councilman Tael Ruke said, "all this happened because we lost faith in Merehr, in the word of the Ancient Writings. We allowed the creation of an army, and sure enough, it has brought nothing but death and discord to us."

"It is not Bredo's death that should worry you, Councilman. I tell you now, we will all die on the sword of misapprehension if we do nothing."

The chill in Lant's voice had the same effect on the room.

Some of the members shifted in their seats. Others rubbed their arms as if to warm themselves.

"It may be that Son-Cawutt Wing is testing our resolve," Fu Breeal said.

"Are the passages in the Ancient Writings concerning the Leader the only ones we should regard?" Lant asked. "Are there no others we honour?" Lant stepped to retrieve the Council chamber's copy of the Ancient Writings. Flipping it open, he read, " 'Be prepared. Prepare your children, your homes, your people...' " Lant laid the book down heartily. " 'Your *people*.' " He looked around the room. "Are we? Do we fool ourselves? Will we do so until it is too late?"

"Your idea of *preparation*, Councilman, is different than ours. You see it as a matter of military strength, we see it as a matter of spiritual fortitude."

"I believe there are many ways to prepare," Lant said. "And right now not one should be overlooked."

Grek Occoju sat forward in his seat. "What is it you are proposing, Councilman?"

Lant took a deep mental breath. "I am proposing that we take into consideration, even vote upon, Rieeve entering into an alliance with the other valleys."

For an instant a dread silence fell—the time it takes for an astonished brain to cognate what the ears had heard—and then ten voices raised at once. The natural acoustics of the Council chamber had never been so exercised. It took Grek standing and calling for quiet to silence them.

As the din settled, Tael Ruke requested to speak.

"Go ahead, Councilman," Grek said.

To Lant, Tael spoke. "Though I wish now that we, as a Council, would have done many things differently, Son-Velaan Bredo is gone and the Cant is here. So, as long as we keep the Cant *here*, I say we allow it to do what it was meant to do: Protect Rieeve."

"You think the Cant, no matter how well-trained and well-armed, can stand against the Ka'ull? You do not know them. You are not aware of their numbers, their strength, nor the depth of their hate." Lant paused. "I have heard members of *this* Council admit that the Cant would not be enough to withstand what is coming."

"I am quite sure your intentions are good, Councilman Lant, but you cannot, out of fear, expect us to break our custom of hundreds of revolutions by forming an alliance with another valley—an action that would see the undoing of not only our way of life, but that of our children and our children's children."

"Fear?" Lant asked incredulously. "Well," he said, almost laughingly, "at least in that much we agree—it *is* fear. Fear of the other valleys that has become a barrier so impenetrable that I doubt even my best desires and the feet of my messengers will be able to cross it!"

"Messengers?" Councilman Moer Ta'leer said.

Lant felt the heat of his next heartbeat. "I have dispatched three messengers to Legran, Jayak, and Quieness. That news is the reason I called this session of the Council."

A consecutive fall of gasps checkered the room.

"With what message?" Grek asked, his voice tight with an edge uncustomary for the ever-composed Spokesman.

"An outline of my own desires and that of the Cant, as well as a request for their support in an effort to unite the valleys."

Three Council members shot to their feet, their arms jerking wildly against their bodies. The rest sat their seats trancelike, as if glued there by some invisible substance.

Breeal, one of the three on their feet, shouted, "People don't change. With you, as with Son-Cawutt Nien, we have made mistake after mistake, offered dispensation, been forgiving, and been repaid every time, like this!"

"It doesn't matter. Without the support of the Council it will never see fruition," Brauth Vanc said imperiously.

"Or do you mean to turn this into a War Council? Is that in your plans, Commander Lant, to establish yourself and your Cant as the government in Rieeve?" Cuiku said.

The council room grew quiet. Though Cuiku had a penchant for abundant paranoia and much less reason, his last words, nevertheless, shocked the room.

The look of disbelief on Lant's face faded quickly. "I sent the messengers from the members of the Cant, doing so as Commander of the Cant."

"Which, until the recent case of Son-Cawutt Nien, was not independent of the Council," Grek said. "Do you now plan to take it one step further? Do you have in mind to supplant the Council with the Cant?"

Lant's shoulders slumped forward over his chest as if Grek's words had pierced the air from his lungs. "Never has it entered my mind to have one replace the other. The Cant exists only to help the people of Rieeve—to serve them. If the people as a whole wish this not to be the case..."

"—it's not that. We have all been in support of the Cant..."

"Until now," Cuiku interjected.

Grek ignored him, continuing, "It was our thought that the existence of the one precluded the necessity of the other—we will not unite with another valley."

Lant sighed. "The Cant is seven-thousand strong. Can you imagine a force of hundreds of thousands? Our entire population is smaller than the number of men in their armies."

Everyone fell quiet. Per protocol, Grek was the first to speak again. "We should have been informed beforehand of the messengers and the message you sent. You have already tried to force a separation of Cant and Council authority over our exclusion of Son-Cawutt Nien. The news you've given us today, this breach of trust, requires your suspension *from* this Council." Grek did not even raise his eyes from the smooth surface of the council room table. "We will discuss this matter further in two days.

"Adjourned."

Nien dragged into the house that night in the same mood he'd found Lant in when he'd stopped by after the Cant training day to see how the Council meeting had gone.

All the family had gone off to bed except for Wing, who sat at the family table, working on his transcription of the Ancient Writings.

"E'te," he said quietly as Nien came in.

Nien grabbed some food off the counter and sat down at the table across from Wing. Wing glanced up from his ledger. "What is it?"

Nien bit off a hunk of bread, holding a piece of cheese in his other hand. "They suspended Lant from the Council."

The writing brush Wing held in his hand tilted absently toward the table. "Why?"

"Because of the messengers he sent to the other valleys."

"I'm sorry," Wing said.

"Lant said it's a small price to pay if even one of the other valleys agrees to an alliance."

Wing placed the brush back in its ink bowl. There was a long silence. "If I joined the Cant, Nien, they might reinstate Lant."

Nien looked up at Wing.

More silence.

"We need his voice on the Council," Wing said.

"They want *you* on the Council, Wing."

Nien noticed it was difficult for Wing to swallow, as if something were burning in his throat. "Whatever it takes."

"What?"

Wing's eyes were fixed on the table. "We're running out of options, Nien. Even if I have to lie, pretend to be..."

"Wing," Nien said, "they expect the Leader to perform *miracles*. Call down armies from heaven or whatever."

Nien could not have described Wing's tone, as he said: "I know."

"No, Wing. No. There's got to be another way."

"There is," Wing said. "I can leave."

The flakes of gold in Nien's brown eyes jumped with sparks of liquid blaze. Throatily, he replied, "No. Don't ever say that. You leave, we all leave."

Judging by Wing's face, Nien's response was not one Wing had considered. "That's..." he seemed to be searching for the right word. "Ridiculous. It's not the family's affair. It isn't your fault or the family's. None of you should—"

"In case you haven't noticed, it isn't your fault either. I'm serious, Wing. You leave, we all leave. You sneak off in the middle of the night, we come find you. There has to be another way."

"There isn't," Wing said.

To Nien, Wing suddenly looked as if he were drowning in fire; nevertheless, Nien would not release him from it. There was no way he would let Wing just vanish as Rhegal had.

"I returned from Quieness," Nien said, his voice pressed thin, "to stand here in Rieeve, with you."

Eye to eye, each a perfect mirror of the other, the brothers sat together in silence, the big roof over their heads like a fortification, the last thing standing between them and the mysterious and terrible future they could not penetrate.

CHAPTER 35

A Boy, a Butler, and a Horse

Pree K entered the streets of the greatest city on their continent, Cao, determined not to spend even one night in it. From above, the city had looked like a swarming of honey-insects in a crosscut of their underground tunnels. Now, not more than a sunstep off the mountain, the streets of the great city had already swallowed him like a half-starved snake.

Pressing his way through the tangle of shops and buildings, he hoped desperately that he would not get turned around and emerge only to find himself having made such an effort in the wrong direction.

But the buildings were enormous, above them he could not see the mountains and so had no reference point for his direction of travel.

Stepping from the street onto a sidewalk fronting a group of small brick-laid shops, Pree K thought to ask a shop owner where he was and how to proceed to the Palaces, when he was met by a blow to the face. The punch sent him sailing off the sidewalk back into the street amidst a string of cursing from above.

"Highnock!" a woman's voice screeched. "Get out here!"

"Old higah," a man spat back.

Shaking his head, eyes watering profusely, Pree K blinked and looked up. Through his blurred vision, he saw a man stepping off the sidewalk toward him.

"Sorry, kid. Here, lemme help you."

Into Pree K's face the man shoved one of his hands; a hand permanently stained with dirt.

Pree K didn't accept it.

"Ah, it ain't nothin'. She's just a little hot tempered," the man said.

Pree K scrambled to his feet and started to back off, holding a hand to his face.

"I ain't gonna hurt ya, boy. I just, well, apparently I got the last plate a hot fiilas ol' Limma Edna had reserved for payin' customers. You know, them seed-grown kind." He looked closer at Pree K. "I ain't got nothin' against you personally, ya see. I mean, we only just met. What's yer name?"

Throughout Pree K's life Lant had spoken in more than a few languages with him, but what this man was speaking resembled nothing like the Fultershier or Quienan.

Muttering a quick "It's no problem" in Quienan, Pree K continued to back away.

"No, ya took a punch for me. That's not something I can overlook. So," he said, licking his fingers, "what can I do for you? Give ya a ride somewhere, maybe?"

"What?"

"Really, lemme do something for you; there must be something 'specially as ya don't look like yer from around here."

This time Pree K understood. "I'm not. I'm trying to get to SiQQiy's palace."

The man's face fairly lit with joy. "Well, my boy, never underestimate the potential of a bad day! You've come to the right man. I was jus' head'n there myself."

Pree K couldn't think of hearing worse news. "No, no it's good, I know the way." He pulled his hand away from his face, checking for blood.

"Don't sound so disappointed. Follow me—quick. Though it takes Highnock the better part of 'n afternoon to come out from behind the counter, he still has a neck big around as my thigh. Best we go."

Though it was probably a bad idea, disoriented as he was now by the punch to the face, Pree K thought his chances of finding his way out of the city and to the Palaces by nightfall were even less than they were before.

Reluctantly, he followed.

Rounding the back of the building, Pree K looked up as a large bay mare jerked her head out of a bag of feed. As two people who are close grow to look like one another so, it seemed, had the big bay mare and the man.

"What're you doin', May?" the man said, swiping the bag away from the horse's nose and giving the girth strap a good yank. "Look now, I can hardly get it wrapped 'round yer fat belly." He tugged on it a few more times. " 's alright, now ya get to run it off." He climbed into the saddle and lent a hand to Pree K. "Get on up, we can be there 'fore ya know it."

This time, Pree K took the hand and swung up.

Just then, the back door to the restaurant opened and a man as big as a house squeezed through it. "Hilloy!" he bellowed. "I'll break you in half!"

Hilloy jumped as if he were about to run. The reaction managed to snap his heels into the mare's bulging sides and she bolted.

Pree K looked back to see the big man take all the run he could after them—about four steps—before coming to a lumbering halt. Heaving, he chucked something—looked to be a rolling pin of some sort—in their direction.

The mare, however, was all but gone and the last glimpse Pree K got of Highnock was of him shouting indistinguishably as he stood in the middle of the back alley, his meaty fists clenched at his sides, looking like a badly placed monument waiting for demolition.

Having made their escape, Hilloy reined the mare down a thin alley that opened up to a thoroughfare crammed with horses and carts.

The jolt of the stocky mare's trot upon the cobbled street felt sure to rattle Pree K's brains right out with the blood still running from his nose. Thankfully, the thoroughfare soon emptied into a long well worn dirt trail. In the distance stood a small city.

SiQQiy's Palaces, Pree K thought with relief as the man urged the mare into a lope that proved far smoother than trotting across cobblestones.

"By the way, ya can call me Hilloy. You?"

"Pree K."

"What's the K for?" Hilloy shouted over the wind now whistling in their ears.

"Nothing, its just K."

"Just K? What's it mean?"

"Kill me," Pree K muttered, sniffing and swallowing a mouthful of blood.

"What?"

"Nothing," Pree K shouted back. "The K doesn't stand for anything!"

"So yer name's Preak?" Hilloy called back. "Ya don't look much like one."

"No," Pree K said with a groan, hoping Hilloy would let it drop.

Before them now, the palace rose majestically and May slowed her pace. Pree K's death-grip on the saddle loosened as his eyes took in the wonder. The rounded domes and towered gates of the small palatial city sat upon a sizeable hill—as hills go—and in the flashing sun Pree K caught sight of armoured guards stationed in an impressive array at the top of every white tower.

Hilloy walked May through a large set of open gates, passing what appeared to be visitor grounds and parks. At the far end sat a section of high wall set with guards at varying intervals. One called out as they approached, "Rider coming!" he called. Then upon closer inspection, said, "Ah, Hilloy. Welcome back." The guard tried not at all to disguise the sneer in his tone.

"They love me here," Hilloy said to Pree K as he guided the bay through the secure gates and into an inner courtyard.

Pree K blinked. The courtyard flourished with tropical plants, trees and flowers. As May walked through the courtyard, Pree K nearly slid off the mare's rear end trying to take it all in. He was still gaping about when Hilloy reined her in before another set of white-gold gates.

"This is where ya get off, Preak. Go on in. SiQQiy should be inside, or there'll be a guard who can take ya to her."

Pree K tore his eyes from the gates long enough to give Hilloy his thanks and swing down from May's broad hindquarters.

"No problem, kid. C'mon old girl, take us home."

Pree K watched him go, wondering if Hilloy wasn't at least a bit insulted by the afternoon's events and finding himself feeling sorry for the old man. As May trotted out of sight, Pree K turned and continued across a short courtyard laid with smooth, flat stone of a silky grey. Brilliant green, delicately leafed trees sided the courtyard up to a set of six steps that terminated at two more large gates, this time of a brilliant gold.

"What's your business?"

Pree K stepped up to the tall guard standing before the gates. Thankfully, the guard spoke clearly and was much easier to understand than Hilloy.

"I am from Rieeve," Pree K answered. "I bear a message from Commander Lant, leader of the Rieevan Cant and traveling companion to Master Monteray of Legran, for the Empress."

The guard eyed him quizzically. "I will need to check your person before entering the palace."

Saying that he carried with him a short sword, Pree K removed the sword and handed it to the guard. The guard took it, looking it over with interest—as a man trained for combat might.

"Why do you carry this?"

"My way was long, through uncertain land," Pree K replied.

"You said you are from Rieeve," the guard said, turning the sword around in his hand. "The workmanship of this blade is curious. A little Jayakan or possibly Criyean." He eyed Pree K a moment, then motioned for him to follow.

Pree K moved slowly behind the guard, his eyes turning upward as he found himself at the entrance to a long hall. Here he paused long enough to turn a full circle, gazing up at the walls and ceiling. Carved out of smooth white stone and set in blocks of ebony, the likeness of birds sat in relief upon the great arches of the hall. The ceiling of the hall was the palest green colour and running down the length of it was a great gilded vine laden with soft pink berries, also in relief. They emerged from the hall and Pree K stumbled, bumping into the guard. The guard pretended not to notice and continued up a steep incline of stairs in front of them. Pree K glanced down at the step over which he had stumbled and saw that it was polished marble rock. Reaching down, he ran his fingers along the cool smoothness of the multi-coloured stone. At the crest of the stairs sat a chair of such immensity that Pree K's brain lost connection with his feet and he fell up the rest of the steps.

That thing could fit three people my size easy, he thought, rubbing a knee as the guard opened and went through a door to the immediate right of the chair.

Pree K stepped in behind the guard and saw a woman standing near a painting on the far end. Set into the bowled center of a thin-legged table on her right was an exquisite little plant with the brightest green leaves Pree K had ever seen, and on the large table before her was spread parchment, paper, and a collection of finely bound books.

SiQQiy.

She was breathtaking. Her skin was a flawless canvas, much like Nien's though more silvery-blue, her hair had the shine of fine Jhedan'ret, and her dark eyes were like polished black stone.

"A messenger, my Lady. He says he is from Rieeve, sent by a Commander Lant, traveling companion to Master Monteray of Legran."

SiQQiy looked up from her work at the guard, then shifted her eyes to Pree K.

Pree K couldn't believe he'd been brought right to the Empress. He'd expected a long wait—possibly days. Obviously Lant and Master Monteray's names meant a great deal more than he had supposed.

"You are from Rieeve?" she asked. The incredulity in her tone was ummistakable. "You came here from there?"

"Yes."

"What is your name?"

"Pree K," he said after a moment, as if he had to think about it.

She smiled at him. Her eyes, like glass, seemed to reflect all the light in the room. Indeed, the look on her face was as if a curtain had been parted to let down a cool rain.

"You are the son of Lant Ce'Mandu?"

Pree K felt like he'd been struck again, but this time by a kinder fist than Limma Edna's. "Yes," he stammered.

The Empress stepped around her table, walked up to him and, standing uncomfortably close, placed both her hands upon his face.

Pree K's throat closed. He felt as if he'd shrunk to half his size. Though he couldn't help but avert his eyes, Pree K noticed a flash of surprise from the guard who had brought him in.

"I knew your father," she said, the deep liquid black of her eyes pulling his gaze back up to hers. "For a time, he was like a father to me, too. My home is honoured to have you here."

She released his face. The heat rose in his cheeks where her slender hands had been. She turned to the two young women standing beside the tall, thin table with the small green plant. "Please prepare the private dining room. Also, warm water and cloth." She looked back at Pree K. "It looks like you had an eventful time getting here."

Pree K glanced down at his shirt. It was stained with blood. "I must look a disaster," he said quickly, apologizing.

"That hardly matters," SiQQiy said. "Though I'm sorry for the welcome. Come, lets clean you up and while we eat you can tell me of your father and the message he sent you here to give me."

As he followed her out, through other doors and winding halls, Pree K felt as if he'd stepped into another story of his life, one that once was or might have been, and though he had no idea how that was so, he suspected the woman walking along before him, gliding like a spirit, knew more about that world and that part of him than he did.

Upon entering the dining room, servants were already scurrying about, guards taking up their places at doors, as SiQQiy's two young female attendants flitted about, one bringing a large bowl of water, the other a bundle of neatly folded cloth. Filled with as much awe as hunger, Pree K tried not to squirm as SiQQiy took up one of the white cloths and cleaned the blood from his face with her own hand.

"So, does your coming here mean Rieeve has opened its doors?"

Pree K almost laughed; he caught himself. "No, Empress. The Rieevan Council doesn't even know that I left. This is all Commander Lant's doing. He sent me here as a member of the Cant. He also sent a messenger to Legran and to Jayak."

"Ah," SiQQiy said, wringing out the white cloth into the bowl. Pree K glanced over and saw his blood spidering out through the clear water. "You are brave." She looked him over. "You have very much of your father in you."

Pree K wasn't sure what, exactly, she meant. He almost felt to remind her that he was adopted, but did not want to come anywhere near an offense, so let it go.

"How long can you stay?" she asked

Pree K didn't know what to say. He hadn't thought about it. "Short enough to not worry the Commander?"

SiQQiy seemed pleased by his answer. "Well," she said, "let's not waste a moment. First, however, we eat."

CHAPTER 36

That Empty Feeling

T he family saw very little of Nien in the following turns. He had begun sleeping in Lant's house in the Village to negate the time-consuming travel between home and the Cantfields. The family missed him. In his absence, a shadow had moved into the house. Wing saw Carly less, too, and when he did she was exhausted, wanting to do little else but sleep.

Pree K, Jhock, and S'o had returned from their long journeys. Ime was drawing in. Soon snow flurries would brighten the valley beneath full moons, adult activity would increase inside the four walls of homes, and child activity would involve stuffy noses and playful objects of snow and ice filling up front yards.

Now that the Vanc home was complete, Joash Cawutt would be trying to complete other smaller housing projects in the Village, Reean and Jake would begin their work of repairing clothing and food preserving, and Wing would be planting rows of winter challak. But this Ime any help Joash, Reean, or Wing might normally have received from Nien was a distant wish, for he was working nearly every day with the Commander and the Cant. A few times Wing would wake in the middle of the night to see a lump in Nien's bed. The family would share a quiet breakfast together, the polite conversation a pale cover for everything each one of them wanted to say but couldn't, and then Nien would be gone again, none of them knowing for how long.

"Commander, the Cant should be given a break—more than a day," Nien said. He was about to give the Cant its schedule for the following turn and had come to the Cant hut to check in with Lant before he did. "I think Ime festival may be what they need."

The last festival, Kojko, had fallen immediately on the heels of the Cant Leadership's return from the battle in Jayak and the loss of Bredo ruining the festival for all their people. Since then, it had not been clear whether or not the Cant would be taking their usual Ime break, or even attending the Ime celebration.

Nien was quiet, waiting for Lant to consider. At last, he said, "I agree with you; let's give them the time off for the festival."

Relieved, Nien saluted Lant and began to leave when Lant stopped him. "Nien," he said, "have them go armed."

Nien couldn't help it, his eyes shot to Lant with a surge of surprise and aversion. Training through the Ime season break had been hard on all of them. Everyone was weary and irritable.

But it was more than that.

None of the Cant members had ever taken their weapons to a festival. In the eyes of the older villagers the sight of a weapon continued to be an anathema.

If the Cant members were meant to participate normally in a normal Rieevan activity, their weapons should not be brought with them.

All this fell through Nien's mind in an instant—and not one word of it left his lips. He trusted Lant. He knew the Commander knew all of this and still his instructions were clear.

Respectfully, Nien nodded and left.

His trudge through the snowy field from the Cant hut to the waiting Cant members felt longer than usual. Taking the Mound where the snowy, wet fields met the mountains, Nien called out: "Cant members!"

One by one they turned to face him.

Nien could see—had been able to see for a while now—the fatigue in their eyes and bodies.

This was not going to be pleasant.

"I know there have been rumours that we may train through the festival, but Commander Lant and I decided today that we will not. Take the festival off and go with your families. Enjoy the time. Rest. Relax. We will meet again after the third day."

The Cant began talking amongst themselves.

That was the easy part, Nien thought. *This is the hard part...*

"We ask, however, that you take your weapons with you."

Happy exchanges over the news of taking the festival off stilled momentarily. Nien waited.

And then, from the back, a low buzz of disbelief and anger began to rise. It surged to the front, carrying with it a single shout that rose above the din: "Enough!"

It took a moment to locate the voice.

"You said you'd changed your minds!" the Cant member called out. "You just said we were going to take the festival off!"

Nien recognized Greal'e. Other men were pushing in around him, urging him on.

"I understand your feelings," Nien said, directing his words into the gathering group. "But we feel it best to be prepared."

"Lant's mad," another Cant member called out. "Making us run all these drills, over and over, all day every day. Forced marches. Barely one day off a turn. And now, taking weapons to the festival? No one will be able to relax during the festival that way—not us, certainly not the people."

Nien began walking down off the Mound toward the group of seething men. Carly moved in beside him joined shortly thereafter by Mien'k and Shiela.

Nien penetrated the outer ring of Cant members to its center where Greal'e stood. "I understand how you feel, but never berate the Commander while I am in earshot."

Greal'e's resolve faltered briefly; however, the crowd at his back imbued his courage. "We've been keeping silent all these turns, but we have families, Nien, and other concerns, businesses that also need our attention. We need to see our families peacefully with no weapons, no reminders of" —he swept his hand across the Cantfield— "all *this*."

Nien missed his own family. He regretted that his father was working twice the sunsteps to handle Villager repair requests and problems that neither he nor Wing were there to help him with. And Jake. Jake was doing all he could, but he was still young and not yet strong enough of body and bone for much of the heavier work that was required.

Nien's silence in the face of Greal'e's words encouraged another member to step forward.

"What about you, First? Will you be going to the festival? The Council banned you from the last one."

"I'll be going," Nien said.

"And the Council?"

"Lant's working on that. Either way, I'll be there."

"Lant," Greal'e snarled. "Maybe the Council was right all along. Maybe a military force has made us all crazy. Maybe Lant *does* want to run the whole show: Leader of the Cant *and* head of the Council. And all this talk about the Ka'ull and the threat they present is merely a ruse, something to push the Council, the people, and us into the fulfillment of one man's personal agenda."

Nien raised his face. Incredulity crashed with indignation in his eyes. "Forget Lant!" The weight of his gaze fell upon them. "Don't *you* feel the darkness closing in? Can't you understand that there may be no more festivals? That there may be no more businesses to run? That there may be members of our families we'll never see again? What is it you think we've been training for?"

Carly had seen both anger and strength in Nien before, like fire beneath a living green mountain, but what she saw in him now was something more than both those things. There seemed to emanate from him something ageless and powerful, an energy that moved through the seething group and drew them into silence.

"If you choose to come to the festival you will do so with your weapons or you will resign your insignias," Nien said throatily. He drew a hot breath. "If I have not, if Lant has not, earned your trust then I have no idea what we've been doing all these revolutions together."

"Trust? *You?* It was because of you that the first Rieevan in generations was killed by violence! Did you think we'd forgotten? You didn't have to go down there; be all heroic. *Join* a battle that wasn't ours! Your arrogance, like Lant's, has put all our people in the middle of this mess."

The rest of the Cant members fell into stillness. Some were embarrassed, others shocked with disbelief, but many agreed, looking up at Nien with a mix of accusation and hope, waiting for his reply.

But Nien said nothing more and as the circle of Cant members watched, the heat drained slowly from his eyes and his features slackened. He suddenly appeared very weary; it seemed even the natural iridescent shade of his skin shunted mute. This shift, subtle as it was on the surface, nevertheless changed the temperature of the field. No sound more than the suck of mud beneath shifting feet stirred the air.

Turning, Nien walked through the silent Cant members and away across the training field.

"Don't walk away!" Greal'e shouted. "An accounting from you on Bredo's loss has never been called for by the members of the Cant! Never been heard!"

"He's right!" someone else called.

A chorus of voices followed. From a sheath there was the sound of a drawing sword.

Carly spun.

Mien'k stepped up from behind her. "Just calm down," he warned, holding up a hand to those moving in to back Greal'e.

"Yck'athay!" Carly yelled, pinpointing the Cant member that had drawn his sword. "Sheathe your sword! Now!"

"They're right, Mien'k," said another member. "Nien's too close to Lant to see it. But you know what they've been putting us through. Ever since the leadership excursion everyone's been crazy, making decisions out of paranoia, not sense."

"You weren't there," Mien'k said, his voice hovering just above menacing. "Nien could have gone down there alone. He didn't order any of us to go with him. We *chose* to go. But what would you know?" Mien'k gave the member a hard shove. "What do any of you know?"

Shiela put a hand on Mien'k's arm; he forced himself to walk away.

"Go home," Carly said. "You heard Nien. We'll attend the festival. We'll go armed. We'll stay alert. If this is not agreeable to some of you, you know where to leave your gear."

Amidst grumbles, chagrined glances, and expressions of sheer bafflement, Carly stood, watching the Cant members gather their accoutrements and disperse.

As the field emptied, Carly bid a silent goodbye to Mien'k and Shiela and took off for Lant's place. If that was where Nien had been heading she hoped to catch him before he got there.

"Nien!" she called. "Hold on!"

Nien kept walking.

Carly came up beside him and caught her breath. "You did the right thing," she said.

Nien shook his head angrily. "No, I didn't."

"Yes, you did."

"I thought the same thing," Nien growled.

"Well, it will be a bit weird, but those that don't understand..."

"I wasn't just talking about taking weapons to the festival."

"Ah," Carly said. "Listen, Nien, Greal'e doesn't speak for all the Cant members, not by a long shot. Until today, I never heard one of them say anything about Bredo or Lant's refusal to discharge you."

"Nevertheless, he has a point, and then I chastise them—tell them to turn in their insignias of all things. There are few enough of us as it is. Greal'e and the others, they're just...tired."

Carly studied Nien's face for a moment before her eyes dropped to her boots. Though the Cant Messengers had returned from Quieness, Jayak, and Legran no one had any idea what the response from the valleys might be, when it might come, or if one would come at all.

A fierce twist of anxiety began to turn Carly's stomach. What was happening out there beyond Rieeve's mountain borders? What was the Empress of Quieness thinking? What was Commander Lant's friend, Monteray, doing? And what about Jayak?

What if the Ka'ull had struck again?

Carly watched Nien walk away.

Turning, she started out at a run for the short corral between the Cant-fields and Lant's house where she'd quartered her horse. Her sword swinging at her side, she dumped her gear near the gate, and throwing the saddle over her mount's back, swung up and spurred him into the barren stretch of fields to the southing.

CHAPTER 37

One Last Time

Carly burst in through the barn door and found Wing arranging sacks of teeana, brevec, and challak in large brown duffels.

"Carly?" he said with surprise.

Carly ran into his arms and buried her face in his chest.

"What's going on?" he asked, dropping the duffel in his hand.

Carly shook, afraid that if she opened her mouth—

"What happened? Are you hurt?"

The tenderness in his voice shattered her fragile restraint. "Things are... things are just, off. Nien gave the Cant some hard news about the festival—it didn't go well, but he wouldn't have done it if there wasn't something going on, something Lant knows. I trust that, I do, but yeefa, you should have seen the other Cant members. They were livid; I thought we were going to have a riot right there on the Cantfields. It was scarier for me than Jayak. It's falling apart. Cant members drawing their swords on one another—can you imagine? Maybe, maybe everybody's right. Maybe this is making all of us insane. Maybe..." She stopped; shook her head. "Don't listen to me."

Wing stepped back so that he could see her face. "What was the news?"

"That they should take their weapons to the festival, no drinking, stay alert."

"Are they going to?" Wing said carefully.

Carly shrugged. "Nien threatened their insignias if they didn't."

Wing didn't reply. Carly didn't care; standing in the shelter of his arms was enough.

"Come on," Wing said, and taking her hand, pulled her up the wooden ladder into the loft of the barn. Passing by the bails of hay, he lay down in a softer bed of straw.

Carly followed, lying out beside him. "Thanks," she said.

Wing held her quietly.

"I haven't felt that before, Wing. Even in Jayak, I mean, as terrible as that was, it felt like I was doing *something*. Leaving the Cantfields today I felt trapped. Like standing in the middle of a house that's falling in—just nothing, nothing I could do. Like it was all too late."

"I understand," Wing said.

Carly emerged from the cover of his arms. "The thing is, we're probably not even an afterthought to the Ka'ull. It'll be the larger valleys that'll face the brunt of this. And Pree K, S'o, and Jhock have returned from Quieness, Jayak, and Legran. If any of those valleys agree to an alliance, then all of our planning and training will be purely academic." She looked hopefully at Wing, but there was a sadness in his eyes and something else she could feel but not put her finger on.

"What is it?"

"Nothing."

Carly touched his cheek, brushing her fingers over his eyes. "Now I've got *you* worried."

Though she had never seen him cry, she saw a shimmer of emotion brought about by what, exactly, she could not tell. Was it something her distress had dredged up in him or something that had already been there?

Running her hand up the smooth skin of his side she kissed him and closed her eyes. Resting her head in the crook of his shoulder, she remembered the way Wing had held her the first time he'd seen her after the Cant had returned from Jayak. He had expressed his fear at that time of losing her. Now, as she lay with him, she wondered—for perhaps the first time— what it would be like to lose *him*.

The thought made her squeeze him tighter.

Wing responded, wrapping his arms completely around her, pressing his face into her hair, hooking her legs with his feet.

Intertwined, their bodies embraced by each other and the cool blonde straw, they fell in touch with the life in each other's bodies—and that alone. The jut of bone, the heat of breath, beat of heart, sticky sweat where flesh met flesh, the tickle of hair on throat and soon this gentle orchestra had them lulled into sleep.

As they lay, dreaming side by side, the silent symphony played on until a short, crisp breeze winding its way through the drafty loft doors touched them with chill.

Carly woke first, and brushing at her blurry eyes, watched as Wing roused. Immersed in the sight of him, Carly traced his face, his hair, his hands with her eyes, but in her heart there persisted a strange ache, a sadness that lingered like heat on a stone after the sun had set.

"I'd better get going," she whispered.

Wing rubbed his face, and getting unsteadily to his feet, offered her his hand.

"I'll skip the festival and we can spend it together," Carly said.

Wing shook his head. "You need to be with your family—you see them even less than you do me."

"I'll see you anyway."

They climbed back down the ladder and went out to where Carly had left her horse. She readjusted the girth strap and swung into the saddle.

Wing looked up at her, meeting her eyes once more before she reined her mount around and galloped off across the fields.

Standing in the doorway of the barn, Wing watched as the light from the afternoon sun caught bright reflections of Carly's hair, causing it to shine like sparks from burning embers.

In the Cawutt kitchen the following day, preparations for the festival were underway. Wing was helping Jake gather up the last of Reean's supplies when Jake said, "I wish you were coming."

Wing secured a long leather lace over the top of a brown duffle bag and glanced at his little brother. "The rest of the family is going," he said, suddenly feeling like a boring older brother unnecessarily stating the obvious. "Besides, you'll be so busy with your friends you won't even notice I'm not there."

"I'll notice," Jake said, his voice sullen. "I always notice."

"There's a lot of tending to be done," Wing tried.

"I know. There always is."

Wing had not been to a festival in more than a revolution, that Jake was now having such a reaction caused Wing to wonder what emotions played in the heart of his little brother. Without offending Jake's manhood, Wing offered as comforting a gesture as he could by cuffing the back of Jake's neck and thumping their foreheads together. This lightened Jake's mood—

But not by much, Wing noted.

"Joash, will you please get Fey's bag, we need to be off," Reean said, walking out of the house.

Wing stood up. "You'll have a good time," he said to Jake.

Jake shuffled toward the door just as Nien stepped in through it, saying, "I think we're all ready to go. I've got the horses saddled." He looked to Wing. "You sure you don't want me to leave one for you? We can pack the extra gear on the back of Ne'lea."

"No, I'll be fine."

"If you're sure."

Wing nodded.

Nien paused. "What is it?"

"It's Jake. Talk with him on the way, will you?"

"Sure. What's wrong?"

"I don't know—he's upset."

"About what?"

"About my not going."

"He's always sad when you don't go."

"I know, but it's worse this time—for some reason."

"Alright. I'll talk to him. He'll be fine." Nien met his brother's eyes. "We'll see you in few days."

"Right."

Reean came quickly back through the family door, knocking the snow off her feet and making one last recon of the house to assure nothing needed for the festival was left behind.

"Goodbye layia. We'll see you soon," Reean said to Wing as she kissed him on the cheek.

Wing picked up Fey and followed Reean and Nien outside.

Joash helped Reean mount. Wing placed Fey in the saddle in front of her.

"Don't overdo yourself out there," Joash advised Wing, flicking his head toward the fields.

Wing nodded to his father and steadied a stirrup for him. Nien and Jake swung onto their own mounts. The family waved as they reined their horses toward the Village in the unseeable distance.

Wing stood silently, watching them go.

CHAPTER 38

Night Carries a Knife

Quiet had begun to spread across the valley as joyful voices, filled with wine, began to lessen and drift off to sleep within the stately main hall of Castle Viyer. Fires burned in the grand fireplaces, their light dancing up against the heady grey-stone walls, filling the room with a red-gold glow.

Settling in with his family, Nien glanced across the hall to where Lant sat, leaning against a wall.

The Commander was awake—alert, Nien noticed.

Nien had taken very little to drink and he'd not seen Lant take any.

Greeted warily and by only a few villagers, Nien had, for the first time, felt like a stranger in Rieeve. Not one Council member had acknowledged him as he'd come in with his family to the festival. The click and clang of armour and swords worn by the majority of the Cant hadn't helped ease the tension felt by those in agreement with the Council that Commander Lant, Nien, and the Cant should not have been in attendance at all. What *was* helping ease the tension, however, was fine Rieevan wine. Though some of the Cant members had refused to come armed, many more than that had not refrained from drinking. The combination of cold outside, warm fire within, and conversation lent perfectly to filled mugs and laughter, which lent to more laughter and more filling of mugs.

Still watching Commander Lant, Nien wondered briefly how he was going to deal with those Cant members who had refused to abide either admonition.

After a bit, the Commander sensed someone looking at him. Raising his eyes, he saw Nien and tipped a smile. Nien smiled back, but it was a gesture he didn't really feel and as Lant redirected his gaze out over the sleeping occupants of the hall, Nien closed his eyes uneasily and wondered if he'd be able to sleep.

As the sound of settling-in began to dissipate in the room, a new one filled the sensitive landscape of Lant's mind. Unnoticed, unheard by anyone else in the Great Hall, it nevertheless tickled the hair on the back of Lant's neck, spiking every intuitive faculty he possessed.

Sitting up straight, Lant stilled his breathing. What he heard was more a dread sense than actual sound—a thin rustling of pant legs and heavy cloaks, a soft swishing that was louder to Lant than the rolling of thunder, as if darkness itself were rubbing up against the living stones of the castle walls.

Ice water poured through his veins and a roiling torrent filled his belly. As the feeling fountained its way up into his chest, he glanced across the room at Nien.

His First had finally fallen asleep.

With a coarse breath, Lant drew all his attention back toward the sound, needing to assure himself he was not delusional.

The dark rustling wave grew inside his mind.

He was not imagining it—

Soon, *very* soon, it would show itself as flesh.

Lant shot to his feet. Bounding across the crowded floor to Nien, he grabbed his First by the leather Cant shoulder mantle he wore, and jerked him upright.

Nien started awake. He looked up to find the Commander standing over him.

"Get up, Nien."

Nien scrambled to his feet, reaching for the sword at his side.

"Get the men up," Lant said.

Nien started with the Cant members nearby, grabbing and shaking them.

From the center of the hall, Lant gave a mighty shout.

Nien's head jerked briefly in Lant's direction. But the people as well as the majority of the Cant members, were groggy, heavy-headed with the finest Rieevan wine—most of them had not even found their feet by the time the massive doors to the Great Hall swung open.

Into the blueish half-light of the Great Hall poured a terrifying flood of dark-clothed beings.

Ka'ull.

The light was so strange, so dream-like that for an instant Nien believed the sight that filled his eyes was only a foul, dark-induced vision. A terrible, breathing, beating nightmare, but a nightmare, nevertheless. The Ka'ull were *out there* somewhere—in Jayak, Lou, and Tou. They were not here. Not in Rieeve. Not in the middle of the night in the Great Hall of Castle Viyer.

Lant shouted again. His cry slapped Nien to his senses and managed to rouse a few more Cant members, but the Ka'ull moved in near silence, the only sound being the ominous brush of their robes as they floated like ghosts over the banded mounds of sleeping families.

Befuddled, disoriented, Cant members fumbled for their weapons in the darkness.

Nien shook Joash and Reean awake. "Get up," he said. "Follow me." There was still a disconnect in his brain, Nien knew, as his eyes moved again to the host of dark figures moving in and out of the shadowed flames of dwindling firelight.

Knowing of a small escape-way, one he had used a time or two while exploring the depths of the castle, Nien began to press his family toward it. Joash followed Nien's lead with Jake, the three of them circling Reean and Fey.

Across the hall from them, Nien glimpsed Carly. She was on her feet, her short, double-edged dagger in her hand as she directed her own family to a set of doors opposite from those through which the enemy was entering—these doors, however, had not been used for a very long time. Rusted and caked with dirt, grown over with root and vine, Nien knew with sickening surety that they would never be able to open them.

Steadily ushering his own family through the tangle of their people— some rising, others still asleep—Nien paused in utter mortification.

Twenty or more of the floating ghosts drew in together and formed a line. Drawing their swords in unison, they raised their hilts high behind their right ears. Slightly longer and thinner than the blades used by the Cant, the Ka'ull swords were curved at the tip.

Those are blades meant for...

Nien never finished his thought.

As one, the line of Ka'ull brought their blades down in a great sweeping arc.

Slashed from clavicles to waists, Nien witnessed every being on the floor beneath that line, die. A scream burst in his belly, but to cry out would draw attention to his escaping family.

Methodically, the line of Ka'ull stepped out two steps, back two steps, and raised their swords again.

This time, they drove in their strikes—

Not one of the inebriated sleepers even stiffened upon the blades that slew them.

Horribly aware that he was buying the life of his family with the lives of his people, Nien heard gasps from other members of the Cant as more lines of Ka'ull formed up, performing the exact same act in the exact same manner, but, like Nien, neither did they leave their own untrained and unarmed families in order to defend the vulnerable sleepers.

Bile burned the back of Nien's throat; his terror struck up against his rage like sharp flint, turning his blood to fire.

Across the room, he heard someone scream. In the shroud of demonic silence, the cry felt as if it had come from another reality. His eyes shot in that direction—

Carly stood over her little brother. He saw her face twist, saw her sword fall, saw a shadow swallow her.

All those that had not already been slain had now woken to the horror at the end of their world. Now, rather than the eerie silence of dying sleepers, there came the short, startled cries of those aware of one quick moment of confusion and pain before being driven back into silence and death.

In almost as orderly a fashion as they'd slain the sleeping, the line of Ka'ull dispatched pods of fleeing families up against walls, in huddles, fighting with bare fists. They struck children into the great fireplaces and without bravado or emotion pressed their swords completely through men who were using their bodies as shields to protect wives, girlfriends, or daughters.

The time purchased in the slain blood of the inebriated and assailable had almost been enough for Nien to get his family to freedom.

Almost.

With everyone else dead or dying, the Ka'ull had turned their attention to the last standing—Cant members and their families. Though the Cant proved more of a problem than expected, the strokes of the Ka'ull soldiers were impossibly systematic. Shorn through rib and leg, Cant members fell in corrugated heaps one after another, their efforts only momentary delays.

Finally, there remained only the Cant leaders that had seen battle in Jayak.

A Ka'ull warrior advanced on Nien and his family. The warrior was soon joined by two more.

Brandishing his sword, Nien shoved Joash and Jake behind him as the first Ka'ull stepped up and struck. Nien parried the strike, but as one of the flanking Ka'ull came at him, Nien was briefly disadvantaged, his range of motion hampered by the close proximity of his family. As he tried to maneuver into a better position, Joash stepped up on his left and met the second Ka'ull with a bone-crunching punch to the face. Reeling away, the Ka'ull's sword missed Nien and glanced Joash across the shoulder. As the Ka'ull fell, Nien saw a great swell of blood bloom upon his father's shirt. The sight quickened Nien toward madness and he charged the two Ka'ull still coming in on them. Driving one through at the belly, he cracked the sword of the other with a lucky strike. As that one staggered back, flourishing the broken half of his sword, Nien bolted forward and pushing his sword into the man's hip, forced him to the floor where he dispatched him.

From both sides of the Great Hall, another influx of Ka'ull flooded in.

Staying close, Nien continued to press against his father, bodily maneuvering him, Reean, Fey, and Jake toward the secret passageway.

At another corner of the room, Lant stood in a wreckage of Ka'ull warriors made possible by a past he had shared with no one in Rieeve but of which the Cant had been the benefactor. Around his feet, four Ka'ull lay dead, and behind him was a trail of lifeless dark robes.

"Netaia!" a male voice roared.

Lant looked up and saw the face of one he knew, a person whose visage brought back poignant and powerful memories from many revolutions past—

"Ketall," Lant said, the name heavy on his lips.

Ketall had been an angry, calculating young man last time Lant had seen him, but he had also been insignificant, really, as Lant himself and Monteray had been at the time. Ketall, however, sought the company of powerful men. Painfully, Lant observed that he'd found it.

"Netaia Lant," the man said in a language that was neither Rieevan nor Fultershier. "How often I have imagined the pleasure of meeting again..."

"I don't know that I'd call this a pleasure," Lant replied in the same language, bringing his sword around to bear.

"You did not exaggerate the beauty of your valley. I shall enjoy living here. A pity that, like you, I cannot abide your people."

A flash of anger and regret lit Lant's eyes. His grip visibly tightened around his sword. "Things change," Lant said, his voice dangerous.

Ketall looked him over. "Clearly." Then he glanced around the Great Hall at the bodies of the dead. "You should not have tried to turn them into something they were never meant to be." He waved his sword over a Cant soldier. "To be a warrior, netaia, is an honour bestowed upon *my* race."

Lant met Ketall's eyes. He did not speak.

"You, however," the big warrior continued. "As much as you are like my people, in one thing, I am like yours—I, too, like my solitude. And after tonight I shall have it."

"I am still standing," Lant pointed out.

"We shall see for how long—" And Ketall struck.

At the opposite side of the Great Hall, Nien and Joash continued the fight for their lives.

Having successfully moved his family to the rear of the Great Hall, Nien risked a glance down and saw what he was hoping to see—a heavy woolen rug. Kicking at it, Nien elbowed his father and pointed. Joash glanced down and saw a set of trap doors. With his foot, Nien flipped open the large metal latch that secured the doors shut. Forming a circle around Reean, Joash motioned for her to open the doors and go through. Reean dropped to her knees and pulled them open.

With racing heart, Nien counted the seconds. Only a few more and his family would be through, they would be safe—

A shout shattered his hopes.

Nien spun. They'd been spotted. Joash looked back at his son—

"Go!" Nien yelled. "Go!"

Anguished, Joash shouted, "No!"

"Go *now*!" Nien cried, and turning, ran pell-mell into the oncoming Ka'ull. Steel blade fell upon steel blade. Nien parried and came back up, struggling to keep his balance upon the blood-slippery surface of the hall's stone floor. The Ka'ull blocked it and made to move in again, but Nien was too quick for him. The man fell on his ass beneath Nien's counter, his sword thumping him in the face. Nien stepped in to finish him, but his sword locked instead with another Ka'ull who'd stepped in around the one who'd fallen. The Ka'ull circled Nien's blade and shoved him back. Nien's blade slid off the Ka'ull's sword but managed to clip the man's arm. By the time Nien came back around the Ka'ull had pitched to the ground and Nien's strike found nothing but air. Where the Ka'ull would have been standing, Nien now had a clear line of sight to the far side of the hall. There, he found Commander Lant. Unexpectedly, the Commander looked up and saw him at the same time; the two locked eyes. And then Nien felt another set of eyes upon him—the gleaming black orbs of the Ka'ull standing opposite Lant. Nien felt the warrior take him in, watched him turn his head back to Lant.

Understanding shot Nien through: Commander Lant and this warrior knew each other—*personally.* Had they not, the Ka'ull warrior would have used Lant's moment of distraction to kill him.

Older than Nien himself but younger than Lant, the Ka'ull warrior was a man of impressive height and build. Dressed in the same leather armour as the other warriors, this Ka'ull's cloak, however, set him apart; it was not made of fabric but of a glossy leather and its hood had been thrown back to reveal a smoothed head tattooed across the back from ear to ear.

He's the leader, Nien thought, *of this Ka'ull Tenkt'tla shock troop. If Lant and I can kill him...*

Glancing back to assure himself that his family had safely made it through the trap doors before moving to join Lant, Nien was hit with a crush of agony so complete thought and feeling vanished.

Joash and Reean lay at the edge of the opening that would have meant life for them. Fey had been torn from Reean's arms and beside her, his body hanging halfway into the darkness of the tunnel, was Jake.

Unable to move, it took Nien's mind an eternity to comprehend what he saw. When it did, a cry of grief tore from his body like muscle seared from bone. Nien rushed toward them—but his foot landed upon the oddly thick hand of one of his murdered people and he fell, his sword hitting the cold stone floor of the hall with a pealing clang. Nien started to scramble to his feet only to find that he had fallen just short of where his father lay.

"Father!" Nien crawled forward and gathered Joash up into his arms.

Joash's eyes fluttered open. "Son."

Nien could see that his father, the Mesko Tender, had stood alone, without a weapon and bare-fisted.

Nien grasped the back of his father's head in his hands. "Fa, Fa..."

Joash's eyes lost their focus.

Nien pressed his head into his father's broad chest as Joash's life slipped away. A sob ripped through Nien's gut and his body convulsed. Joash's body fell heavy in his arms.

Unwilling to let go, Nien slipped from the bloody reality all around him and chased his father into the darkness.

"It is evident you are still the best of this sad people," Ketall said as he and Commander Lant once again locked swords, both men stumbling over the bodies of the dead. The Commander was the only Rieevan in the Great Hall still on his feet. Other than Ketall, all the other Ka'ull had moved away, sweeping out through the castle on the hunt. "And how is our friend Letayin Monteray? Has he, too, retired to his small, perfect valley?" Ketall asked, and then shook his head not waiting for an answer. "The two of you could have been so much more."

Lant met the dark, familiar eyes. "Like butchers?"

Ketall laughed. "Have you always had such a low opinion of me? We were once such good friends."

"You never understood friendship, Ketall. Not really," Lant replied.

It seemed Ketall was momentarily stung, but he recovered quickly. "I will hate to have to kill you."

"It will take more than words to accomplish it," Lant said, and their swords locked.

Through the incomprehensible sound of the dying and the heavy beat of running feet over the stone-laid floor, it was the faint brush of a robe across the back of Nien's leg that brought him back from oblivion and re-engaged his battle brain.

Silently, Nien eased Joash to the floor. Tightening his grip about the blood-grimed hilt of his sword, Nien rose to his feet like a leviathan rising from the depths of a great sea. With exactitude, he swiveled his sword beneath his elbow and drove the Ka'ull through before the man realized how close he'd drifted to a man who, a moment ago, had appeared quite dead.

Nien did not look behind to see the man fall. Lifting his shoulders, he brought his sword around in front of him and grasped it with two hands—

He had only begun.

Blind with tears, blood, and rage, filled with only the barest of animal instincts, Nien rushed the nearest Ka'ull he could see—and split his skull open. The Ka'ull hit the stone floor with a heavy thud, his eyes frozen in dismay.

Only a handful of Ka'ull warriors remained in the hall—besides the one with whom Commander Lant fought. Nien raised his face to see four of them moving in on him.

Something stilled in Nien's chest as he watched them come. Fear fled. Hope vanished. He lifted his sword and waited.

From the first pealing clang, through the twists, the rising blocks and glancing blows, the stumbles over bodies of the dead and the final thrust, Nien felled all four before a single strike found its mark.

With only a flashing comprehension of a fifth Ka'ull, a white light struck Nien's vision from him and dropped him to his knees. When sensation returned, his world had been laid open. Into the fissure in his head flooded a deep exhaustion. It filled then began to sink, dragging him muscle-by-muscle, bone-by-bone through the bottom of the planet, stretching him out till he laid flat and heavy upon the stone floor of the Great Hall.

With the fractured side of his face pressed into the blood-sticky, stone flooring, Nien's vision briefly steadied. The still, rent bodies of Joash, Reean, Fey, and Jake filled his eyes. Beneath him he felt something lift, as if the castle itself were trying to breathe life into him, and he managed to raise his head. But the effort slipped away in a whisper, spilling out through the wound-void in his skull.

Nien's mouth moved but he had no voice.

Wing, he thought. *Run.*

His head lolled back as darkness crept from within and ate away at the light behind his eyes, swallowing him into the unforgiving black.

Ketall stepped away, then came back in.

Again and again their swords clashed, neither gaining the advantage, enervation turning their bones to ash.

Enough. Enough! Lant raged at himself. Ketall was the commander of this force, if he could kill him—

Their two swords struck deafeningly. Ketall countered, but barely. They came together once more, this time falling into each other and stumbling sideways. With their swords and bodies locked in a chimeric embrace, Lant moved to disengage but Ketall had reached down and withdrawn a short dagger. As the two fell apart, Lant gasped and reached for his side. When he withdrew his hand it was covered in blood.

For a moment, Ketall lowered his defenses, certain that his small, thin blade had finally ended their battle. But Lant faked a stagger, and with his sword hand in a tight grip upon the hilt, placed his left palm upon the pommel, turned his right hand over, twisted the blade to his right, and drove the point of it through Ketall's chest.

A surprised look of fear spread briefly across Ketall's face as he sunk back, his knees buckling beneath him. He hit the ground hard and clutched at the leather cross-harness he wore.

"I..." The look of surprise on Ketall's face dropped quickly. "It looks like we both get what we want," Ketall growled out through a throat filling with blood. He almost laughed. "You've killed me, but your people are dead. Your valley, your home is still *mine*." Ketall drew his last breath. "How did I always know it would be *you*."

Lant withdrew his sword, letting Ketall's body slump to the floor like a discarded child's doll.

Surprisingly, the hall was now emptied of Ka'ull. Lant, alone, stood in the Great Hall. Scanning the carnage, he caught sight of his First: Nien lay still as stone, not far from his family.

Ketall's death had been too little too late. The shock force had already done its work.

Fighting back a pain far worse than his wound, Lant sunk to his knees. Pressing a hand against his side, he began to crawl.

CHAPTER 39

All Torn Asunder

Lant staggered out from beneath the castle. The cover of darkness was complete as he made his way through the Village. All was silent except for the howling of the wind.

Falling again and again, Lant continued to pull himself back to his feet. In this miserable way he made it across the Village and to the Cantfield hut at the far edge.

Coated in mud and blood, he dragged himself inside and collapsed into the chair behind his desk. The wound in his side throbbed unmercifully. In an attempt to assuage the pain, he pressed his hand against it. His mouth fell open as he did. He gasped for relief.

Squeezing his eyes shut, they sprung open a breath later as someone entered the hut. Lant started to his feet, surprising the intruder as much as the intruder had startled him.

"Father?"

Lant fell back into his chair, his breath escaping him in a hiss.

"Father!" Pree K rushed around the desk.

Lant reached out with a blood-streaked hand and grasped his son's arm. "Pree K," he breathed. "Son…" His voice was choked with pain but also relief.

Pree K fell to his knees at his father's side. "What's happened to you?"

Lant swallowed and released his grip on Pree K's arm as Pree K began to probe his side to find the source of the blood. Lant winced when Pree K found it. Pulling the shirt aside, Pree K attempted to assess how extensive the injury was in the dark.

"Who did this to you? What's going on!"

Lant pushed his son's hands away from him. The wound was mortal—nothing either of them could do about it.

"Son, there is something I need you to do for me…"

It was only the morning after his family had left for the festival, but being inside the house without his family was claustrophobic and miserable, so Wing had returned to the fields to check on the winter challak and lay out his plans for Kive rotation and planting.

In the predawn moonsteps Wing stood, hands on his hips, his keen eyes seeing the perfect lay of future rows and plants beneath patches of snow. In his palm he held a handful of seeds he'd taken from the barn. They were a mix of winter challak and a hearty brevec, and though he did not expect them to take heart in the cold soil, they were older seeds and would not retain their life force beyond the following revolution, anyway. Bending down, he dug his long fingers into the soil where the snow had melted back. Bringing a handful of the deep black dirt to his nose he breathed deeply of it, loving the taste it left in his mouth.

Arching his back, Wing took a moment to gaze at the mountains. Near the valley floor Kive had begun to creep in, mixing snow with heavy rains. In vibrant contrast, the higher peaks were still white with snow, illuminated surreally by a heavy canopy of cloud. In not too many turns Kive would cover the mountains in a heavy cloak of velvet green, innumerable streams would flow from the high peaks carrying water into the valley and his irrigation channels, watering the young plants. He breathed deeply of the cold, revitalizing air as the lumbering clouds began to move over the sunsetting range, the wind moving into the valley before them.

Wing returned to his knees, pressing a portion of his handful of seeds into the dark soil.

"Wing!"

The cry echoed across the fields.

Wing came to his feet in one swift motion, startled. He'd never heard his name called with such urgency.

His fist unknowingly clenched upon the last of the small seeds; he took a step toward the voice. Unable to discern anything more than a mere shadow on the horizon of fields, he squinted into the pale-grey light bleeding over the cusp of mountains into the valley.

"Wing!" came the cry again.

Wing took another step forward, straining to clarify the source of the call.

Lightning flashed. In the brief glow of heavenly light Wing deciphered the visage.

Pree K?

Pree K vanished briefly before reappearing over the last curve of horizon. As if the wind itself were propelling him, the young man approached at an unnatural rate of speed, his movement almost animalistic.

He arrived at Wing's feet in a heap, as if thrown down by a great, merciless hand.

Wing dropped to a knee, placing a hand upon the young man's back. "Pree K, what in the four winds has happened? What are you doing way out here?"

Pree K's wispy body heaved for air. It took him a couple of breaths before he could raise his head. When he did another flash of lightning lit the features of his face—they were pale as river-washed stone.

"What is it?"

"My father, he...he needs...to see you."

Thunder clapped off Llow Peak.

"What is going on? Are you all right? Is Lant?" Wing returned to his feet, pulling Pree K up with him.

"The Ka'ull," Pree K muttered. There was no strength in his legs, and he leaned against Wing's chest as if it were a wall. "They have taken Castle Viyer."

Wing thought he'd lost Pree K's words in the wind. Taking him by the shoulders, Wing stood him back. "What?"

"Last night, late. Ka'ull. They stormed the castle."

Thunder rumbled through a nearby canyon and a silver-blue surge of lighting struck home against the wooded mountainside. A section of the Mesko canopy exploded in a shower of blood-red flames that cast a resounding echo into the depths of the valley below where Wing and Pree K stood. Both men flinched, turning instinctively toward the great mountain and the brilliant red flames now licking up at the darkening sky. No sooner had the lightning's echo faded than they heard the distant cry of a shy'teh.

Pree K's eyes slowly turned to meet Wing's.

"Where's my family?" Wing said. "Is Nien with Lant? Did they get everyone out?" Wing's voice was tight, upon Pree K's expression he could see that his gaze had the effect of penetrating shards of ice.

Pree K shook his head. "Nien's dead, Wing. Everyone's...dead."

Wing stood motionless. He felt the blood drain from his face, felt his breath catch in his chest, felt the familiar scouring of jagged black demon-claws at the lining of his stomach...

"The Ka'ull, they took the castle in the middle of the night. They, they slaughtered everyone..." Pree K's voice broke.

Wing released Pree K and staggered backward, stumbling over a row of snow and dark soil as if reeling under the blow of a giant fist.

"Our people," he muttered. "The castle!" The cry launched from his gut. "My family!"

Wing started to move—Pree K stepped in his way.

"You must go to my father," Pree K said as he struggled to press him back. "Please."

Wing gulped like he was drowning. "My, my...The castle. I've got to go, I've got to..."

Pree K slapped Wing hard on the face. "No! Listen to me! You need to go to my father—Now!"

Wing's eyes focused. His mouth moved, but no words came out. A breath later he tried again, saying only: "I have no horse."

"Run," Pree K said.

Wing urged his body on. He'd forgotten Pree K's admonition to go to Lant. In the tangle of his mind only one thought reigned: *Castle Viyer.*

Patches of melting snow snatched at his feet as he ran. Even though the sun had now peaked over the Ti Range, the sky remained dark. Heavy storm clouds blotted out the sun making it cold, distant, ineffectual—as if day had come but Rieeve had not been informed of it.

If Wing stopped over the long distance to the castle, he did not remember.

By the time he neared the opposite end of the valley the storm was no longer waiting for later. Hidden behind a veil of wind and blinding rain, Wing could see neither the Village nor the castle. But the many revolutions of traveling the distance between his home and the Village told him he must be getting close.

He pushed on.

Ahead, a window opened in the torrent. Through it, he caught sight of the castle before it was swallowed again in a hail of grey and black.

Taking a painful breath, Wing cried out to himself: *Almost there.* And then to his family: *I'm almost there.*

The next instant he was repelled by something so impenetrable that it was as if he'd been roped from behind and drawn up almost short enough to have found himself on his back.

Just managing to catch his feet, he searched the mottled light for the thing that could have so completely blocked his path and yet be entirely invisible to his rain-swept eyes.

"Wing," he heard a voice say, "I ask you: Turn aside."

It was a man's voice, and even though Wing heard it with his ears, it seemed to enter him deep in his belly.

Whipping his head this way and that, Wing searched the heavy grey sheets of rain for the source of the voice.

He did not search long.

Through the storm's dark curtain, Wing saw a personage appear—one that seemed to stand in a space between worlds.

The wind and rain howled terribly around them, pulling at Wing's hair and soaked white shirt, yet the man who stood before him was completely unaffected, his dusky cloak untouched by the rain, unmoved by the wind. Wing gazed at him through halting vision. He had long black hair and dark olive skin and though Wing had never seen him before, recognized him perfectly. He was Lyrik, his mother's ancestor, the one back to whom Wing himself hailed.

"No," Wing muttered, "my family"—he paused—"*our* family. I must—"

Lyrik raised his hand slightly.

As Wing shrank back, into his mind burst a vision of enormous pits sated with exanimate bodies. The vision tore through Wing's guts. He gasped, staggered, and grabbed his head.

"Go to the castle and you will die," Lyrik said.

Cowed, Wing managed to raise his eyes just enough to stare at the specter with loathing and rage, but both emotions were faint, and he was faint. He could not hold Lyrik's gaze for long.

"It is not yet time, Wing. Go to Lant; he has something for you." Lyrik's eyes were clear but carried a fire's flame.

On his feet but bent, Wing swayed. For an endless beat he couldn't think, couldn't feel, couldn't move. In place of the vision had swelled an all-consuming sense of loss.

Lyrik spoke once more: "You will not be alone." He then dissolved into the sweep of rain from whence he'd come.

Dumbly, Wing turned away from the castle and the death that had awaited him there and clumsily urged his feet ahead again, reining his exhausted body toward the opposite end of the Village and the Cantfield hut.

Outrunning the rain that had come over the mountains from the sunsetting, Wing ducked into the small hut at the edge of the Cantfields. Swiping his wet hair from his face, Wing looked into the dark of the hut and found Lant. The Commander was leaning over an old map, his head in his hands. It took a moment for him to realize Wing was there.

After all his revolutions of travels, trials, and training of Cant members, only the blazing white streaks in Lant's thick head of hair had revealed his age—until now.

Now, Wing saw something in the Commander's eyes he'd never seen before, something plain that had once been only a shadow.

For what seemed an eternity the two gazed at each other.

"Wing, we..." Lant tried to say, but his words were slurred as if said over a very thick tongue. "We haven't got much time."

Wing stepped to him—the Commander was obviously in great pain. "Tell me."

"Everyone was asleep—most were quite drunk. The Cant fought hard, but it was futile. The Ka'ull have secured the castle. They'll now be looking for survivors; it will not take them long. You must get my son and go." With agonizing effort, Lant began to organize the parchment maps and Mesko paper writings upon his desk. "Take these plans with you."

"No! We have to find anyone who's still alive before the Ka'ull do!"

"There is not time, Wing."

"Yes there is, I..."

"No!"

Wing could see that Lant's shout pulled at the life in him.

"Pree K and Jhock are at my home," the Commander said, clutching for air like a fist on the rope of a fleeing stallion. "Go get *them*, and get out."

Wing shook his head. "No, no, there has to be others..."

"If there are, the Ka'ull will find them before you do." Lant's voice was stripped of emotion—it was a statement of fact.

Wing went to protest again, but Lant lunged across his desk and this time his hands found not air, but Wing's soaked shirt. "You have never answered one of my calls to you. You *will* answer this one! Get Pree K and go, while you still can."

Wing shook. The rage in Lant's voice slapped him as no hand could have.

Lant released him and fell back into his chair. "Take these with you." He pushed two rolls of parchment and one of Mesko paper across the desk at Wing. "Take them to Master Monteray in Legran."

Wing gathered up the rolls and stuffed them into his shirt.

Numbed, dumb like an ill-treated beast, he stepped out of the hut into the darkness and headed for Lant's home. He hadn't gone far before a brilliant flash of light lanced across his vision; the glow of flame lit the dark tree line toward which he was running. He spun about. With amorous, reaching arms, he saw fire consuming one of the Village cottages. The fire climbed up into the sky like a great wall of light, beautiful and ghostly.

No thought preceded his next action—he simply took off at a dead run back toward the Village.

Rain licked at Wing's face as he moved, the muddy and uneven ground grasping with thirsty fingers at his booted feet. Only about one and a half furlongs lay between Lant's hut and the first row of homes in the Village.

Wing stopped at the first house in that row to catch his breath. As he stood, breathing desperately, searching ahead, another home caught fire, and then another and another in freakish order, up a row, down a row until the first, second and third rows of homes were burning.

But the rain was preventing the spread of fire from home to home.

In an eerie moment of comprehension, Wing realized that they were having to be lit from within.

In a crouch, he started off again, running along the outside of the first row of burning homes. The heat seared Wing on his left even as rain pelted him from the right—flame and rain racing to battle across his skin. The sensation spun his mind and purged strength from his limbs.

Pained for breath, he was forced to stop. Leaning a moment, his hands on his knees, he raised his shuddering head in the direction of the fires. The newest blazes were traveling back up the fifth row of homes toward the castle. Turning his face into the rain, he took another deep breath and started running again—perhaps he could intercept the arson at the top of the street.

He had made it across the Village and was closing in when he heard a rumble from the castle. Nearly losing his balance in the slick mud and patchy snow, Wing slid to a stop and cast his eyes up toward the great dark image that was Viyer. From its front gates poured a shadowy flood.

Ka'ull.

Though he could see them, he could not hear them. A weird silence ballooned out, pushing into the foul weather before them. A snap of splitting wood cut the air. Wing jerked instinctively in the direction of the sound, glancing back only a second later to find the distance between the Ka'ull and himself closing fast.

Shaking himself, Wing turned back again—he still had a chance to catch the incendiary villain before the last few homes could be lit.

Running low, he rounded the back of the outermost row of homes, the heat from the flames evaporating the rain from his hair and clothing in a matter of footfalls. Only two homes remained that were not yet burning. He urged his body on, his head pulsing from the heat. Behind him he could hear the running feet of many men. They seemed to be racing in the same direction as he, and they were gaining.

Had they seen me? Their intention can't possibly be to capture me. Yet they were pursuing in the same direction he was. *Why?*

Mid-thought Wing stumbled in the mud and fell. The flames from the closest home whipped over his head—the rain in his hair kept his body from catching fire. He glanced behind him. His heart beat once.

Black-lined, the enemy's deep grey cloaks swirled around them like sheets of rain.

Wing clamored to his feet. Another home exploded. Now there was only one house left in the main body of the Village that was not burning—the Vanc home.

Wing fought his way another few lengths—but, too late. Through the roof of the Vanc home spat a ball of fire.

Staggering to a stop, Wing searched wildly in every direction in hopes of seeing the saboteur, but it was hopeless. Not even the light from the flames could catch a shadow in the ensuing darkness of the trees.

Wing's breath sounded in his ears like the pounding hoofs of a thousand horses. All about him the fires raged. The din of splitting wood and roiling flame screamed like thunder against the stormy sky.

Wing turned once more to look behind him and saw that the grey-black shadows were coming to a halt as well.

Enveloped by the deafening roar and consuming heat, Wing did not hear or see one of the shadows until it had emerged upon him.

Standing between the ablaze Vanc home and its burning neighbor, Wing leveled his gaze at the fleshy shadow. He could not see its face or its eyes, but he could feel them.

Ka'ull.

Incredibly, Wing felt no terror. He stood tall, unafraid—the heat and rain, the burnt village had stripped him of it.

Ice water coursed through his veins as an unfamiliar emotion washed over him in a deluge: hatred.

Gazing steadily into the void inside the blackened hood, Wing felt himself moving forward, knowing for the first time an anger that could kill…

But as he moved forward a large chunk of wood, wrested in flame, fell away from the roof of the Vanc home to Wing's right and plummeted through the space between him and the Ka'ull.

Wing jerked his shoulders aside—the blazing timber fell past him. As the timber rolled away and Wing looked back, the dark figure was gone.

For a breath, Wing stood perfectly still, his body a dreamlike visage amidst the reach of flame, sleet of rain, and dark of storm.

"Get away."

Blinking in dismay, the ghostly voice leapt forward in his mind: *"Get away!"*

Turning, Wing sprinted for the black embrace of the tree line.

From within the tree line, the white's of Wing's eyes peered. The Vanc home was cracking and crumbling in a royal bedlam.

The last home his father had built.

Away from the maelstrom of crushing heat and snarling flame, Wing's mind began to clear. As the Vanc home collapsed, he wrenched his thoughts back to what he had to do now. He would pass by the Commander's home one more time. If Pree K had made it back, he would most likely be there. And if he was not there he may have returned to the hut and could be with the Commander even now.

Slipping inside the forest's deep, protective border, Wing dodged to the left and ran. Even in the tangle of trees, snow, and undergrowth Wing moved swiftly and, glancing to his left, saw that he had already passed the last corner of the Village and was nearing Lant's home on the outer edge.

Easing his stride, Wing jogged back toward the edge of the valley and finally stopped. His racing heart stung, burning a hole in his chest. Through the trees he could see Lant's fine home.

It was on fire.

Darting out of the woods, Wing ran toward it, but the flames were overpowering.

Wing slid to a stop. A brief battle ensued: instinct urging him on, despair stoically pointing out the futility of doing so.

Instinct won—at a cost. Each decision to leave behind and continue on stripped a golden thread from his soul.

Into the distance, he squinted and found the dark shadow of Lant's hut. Though Lant had told him to go, Wing could not comprehend leaving him; all he could think was: *How am I going to tell the Commander I couldn't find Pree K? How am I going to tell him the Village is burned?*

Checking the area, Wing started off toward the hut, covering the distance quickly and ducking inside. The Commander was there, his head resting on the table against his arm. A small candle still burned at one corner of the desk.

"Lant?" Wing whispered.

Lant did not reply.

"Lant?" Wing reached out and gently shook Lant's shoulder. The Commander's head lobbed sideways and his hand fell limp from the table. Wing lurched back and fell over a chair.

On the floor where he'd fallen the image of Lant's face, so cold, so wholly devoid of light and life, unraveled what was left of Wing's mind.

With tremulous limbs, Wing grasped at the edge of the desk and managed to pull himself up. Reaching across the desk, he grabbed Lant's still body and began to shake it. "Wake up!"

But the cold, grey body remained disconcertingly resistant to Wing's imploration.

Releasing his grip, Wing stumbled outside, his hands going to his face as he weaved back and forth drunkenly, the muscles in his throat constricting, forcing a strange, guttural sound from his lips.

The storm had begun to sweep up Jhiyak Canyon, cold and cutting upon his back. A blinding pain burst inside his head. His body succumbed and the earth reached up to take him.

Somewhere in the back of Wing's mind a voice told him: *You're suffocating.*

Forging through the inner realms of waking, Wing reached a point of translation and clarity. He *was* suffocating. The rutted ground he'd fallen into had filled with rainwater after his collapse. With a jolt, he brought his hands beneath his shoulders and forced himself up. He inhaled painfully, his lungs blistering.

His head heavy as a timber, Wing pushed himself to his feet and staggered back to Lant's hut. The wind blew in through the hut flap behind him, nearly blowing out the candles' fragile flame as Wing stepped inside one last time.

Taking up a couple blankets, Wing wrapped the Commander's body in them. He then snuffed out the candle, shouldered Lant's body, and made his way through the rain back to the sunrising tree line.

Wing bowed low. He was unable to dig a very deep grave in the rocky mountainside; nevertheless, the Commander's body would be safe and untouched by man, if not by wild animals.

Wing's head dropped. The water dripping from his rain-soaked head fell over the leaves, branches, and snow covering Lant's grave.

He was alone in the darkness.

Powerless and vaguely aware, Wing staggered to a stop and raised his head. Through a break in the tree line he could see his home. For a moment he stood still and with great effort tried to gain a sense of how much time had passed since...since...he'd buried Commander Lant. He must have taken the journey to his home automatically, as he had done a thousand times in his life.

With a pained half-breath he crept out of the tree line and started toward the tall shadow of his home in the distance.

At the door, Wing set a shaking hand to the shiny bronze handle and opened it. The house was quiet. He stepped inside.

"Nien? Mother!" He looked around and called louder: "Father!"

Rushing up the stairs to Joash and Reean's room, he pushed open the door.

Empty.

Clinging to the handrail, he stumbled back down the stairs into the main room where he looked around once more, caught somewhere between disbelief and insensibility.

Walking lastly through the small opening into the back bedroom, Wing glanced around at the three beds that were his, Nien's, and Jake's.

He stared at the empty beds before taking up an armful of heavy clothes. Back in the main room he wrapped food, absently pocketed a bit of flint and spark from the small box at the side of the wood stove, took a long sleeved cloak off a hook near the door, and tucked his transcription of the Ancient Writings into a duffel.

His eyes passing into the emptiness of the house, Wing slowly backed his way to the door, stepped through, and closed it behind him.

CHAPTER 40

Buried Alive

There was heaviness
—and
There was pain.

Something like a mountain pressed down upon him, making it virtually impossible for him to move at all.

Nien blinked his eyes and tried to open them, but something gummy and hard prevented even this simplest of efforts. He tried to raise a hand to wipe at his eyes, but his arms were pinned at odd angles from his body.

Viciously, he rubbed his face against whatever it was that lay on top of him, trying to brush away the goo that had his eyes sealed closed.

He succeeded only in part.

Blinking frantically, he managed to create a small slit through the sticky mess in one eye, but it meant little to him for all was black—

Black like the belly of a cave.

The air he breathed was thick and stifling hot, and it carried with it an odour so repugnant and powerful that his stomach revolted. He gagged. The gagging caused him to need more air—

Air that he was simply unable to get.

Panic seized him.

Madly, he began to heave about, battling to free himself from the hellish weight that buried him. At last, he got one arm free and pushed. The thing he pushed against was soft, it was also hard and cold...like flesh. Like bone.

An arm? Maybe a leg?

Nien felt his mind rupture.

On top of him was no mountain, but the weight of the dead.

CHAPTER 41

Driven to Ground

Reaching the edge of the fields, Wing headed into the Mesko forest. The ground beneath the canopy was wet but free of snow, and so the forest he had moved through so often with his father and Nien rolled past him as he brushed over rocks and deadwood, moving at first with a speed and lightness that alerted not even the shyest of terrestrial creatures. But as the brutal ascent continued and his mind came into his body, he began to falter. Soon his hands were bloody from catching himself each time he fell, his legs and lungs burning from the exertion of the climb.

Impossibly, he kept up the cruel pace until Rieeve had shrunk to less than half its size far below and he'd run himself into oxygen debt.

Quaking spasmodically, Wing landed on his knees and fell over to his side where he lay incoherent, his breath coming in short, harsh rasps, his heart pounding fiercely in his head.

When Wing opened his eyes again he was on his back and the forest had grown dark.

Where am I?

He glanced around. The Mesko forest, yes. He'd run here after leaving the house. Relaxing, he gazed upward. The stars gleamed brightly overhead and through them stretched the milky haze of the Malor-Tuleer galaxy. He sighed heavily. It must have been another nightmare vision. It had to be. But why had he not woken up in his own bed?

And where was Nien?

Dread filled his every organ like a drowning tide—

No. Nien was not here this time.

Not this time.

Scrambling to his feet on the slope, slick with mud and wet rock, he staggered on until he found a large, open root cavern of a giant Mesko. Dropping to his knees, he crawled inside, curled into a ball, pulled his cloak over his head, and for the passing of two nights did not move. He did not hear the scurry of insects, the prowling of animals, or the crack of thunder. For two nights he lay shaking, blessedly dead to thought and feeling.

Only as dawn bled through the giant roots on the third day did Wing finally awaken. He lay still for a time as the dryness of his throat and the pain of thirst registered heavily in his brain. Stiffly, he crawled from within the root cavern to the outside. The sky was cloud-covered in grey. Licking rain droplets from a nearby leaf, he made it to his feet. His walk was a faltering attempt, but the need for water kept him on his feet.

Unsure how long it had taken him, Wing finally crossed paths with a stream. Falling to his stomach, he drank at its side until he felt sick. Rolling onto his back, he clutched his stomach and groaned.

Bad idea.

He thought about finding something to eat, but could not come up with either the energy or the will to do so.

Looking around, he wondered if he'd be able to find his way back to the root cavern. There were other trees with open root structures, but he didn't trust the chances of finding one large enough to hold him that wasn't already occupied by another pitiful creature seeking refuge from the cold.

It took more than a sunstep, but Wing finally relocated the root cavern. Crawling inside, he lay in the darkness dreaming about being with his family again and of how close he'd just come to making that happen…

But the ghostly messenger.

His instructions echoed in Wing's mind: *Go to Lant. He has something for you.* Lant had given him the rolled parchments and papers and told him to take them to Master Monteray of Legran.

Slowly, Wing reached down inside his shirt. The parchments were still there, molded now to his body. Wing unrolled them. All were damp, and Wing remembered that he'd had them tucked in his shirt when he'd collapsed in the rain.

The first in one of the rolls was a sheet of Mesko paper, the ink a bit smeared as if it had been rolled in with the rest before drying completely. At the top, Wing saw his name. His eyes fixed upon it. Squinting in the dim light filtering into the Mesko grotto, Wing began to read:

"Wing. This will be my final call to you—yet this time it is not a call to arms.

Turns ago, I sent Jhock, Pree K, and S'o to three valleys with a brief out-line of a plan—a petition for a uniting of the valleys. My hope had been to prepare a force to protect us in case of an attack. I have failed. The wound I sustained has left this to you and my son. Please take the plans and the map I have drawn up to Master Monteray of Legran. He will know what to do.

Tell my son I love him.

Wing, I do not know what lies ahead of you, but I have some idea what lies within you. Let it guide you now—it will not lead you astray.

These are my last words to you, my plea—not much for one who has lived as long as I, but they are all I can give you.

Wing brushed frustratingly at his eyes, struggling to make out the words.

I do not know what the ancients had in mind, but even though I die dev-astated, I take with me this last hope…

"Merehr."

The word cut a deep groove across Wing's mind. His hand trembled; the letter feathered to the grotto floor.

Though Wing knew painfully little of their continent's geography, a few of Nien's words over the revolutions had actually sunk in: Legran lay to the sunrising, just on the other side of the Ti Range, and he had already traveled a fair distance in that direction—the same way he, Carly, and Nien had often gone in search of the shy'tehn caves.

Closing his eyes, Wing fought a short inner battle: Die now, here, and be with his family. Or go to Legran and deliver the Plan to Master Monteray.

Opening his eyes, looking out into the deep grey of the evening, Wing made a silent vow.

For Lant, he would do this last thing.

With a gnawing hollow in his stomach and an unfathomable vacancy in his chest, Wing wrapped an arm around his head, drew his knees into himself and slept.

With a heart-pounding jerk, Monteray sat up in bed. He was drenched in sweat and he trembled as if he were chilled.

Beside him, Kate woke. "What is it?" she asked, placing her hand upon his back. It was wet and cold. "Are you sick?"

Monteray shook his head. "I...I'm not sure."

"Bad dream?"

Certainly it was that, Monteray thought. *But was it also something more?*

"It's all right," he said. "I'm going to towel off."

Pushing himself off the bed, Monteray left the room and went down the long stairs.

What was that about? he asked himself again, and felt a deep melancholy touch his heart.

Taking a towel, he pressed his face into it and let the breath shudder from his chest. Raising his face, he stepped to the dining-room window that faced the river and the mighty Ti Range flanking its opposite bank.

"What are you protecting me from?" he whispered to the mountain. "What are you sending my way?"

CHAPTER 42
Firebrand of Questions

Snow in the elevation above the Mesko canopy kept Wing in his new home, the large root cavern. During the day, he'd forage about for food and water, hiking out of the Mesko forest to visit sun-soaked boulders, taking in what little warmth they'd gathered from the tender rays of Ime sunlight. Though not exactly warm, nights in the root cavern with a small fire spared him the sharpest edge of Ime's cold. Blocking the entrance with large strips of bark and downfall, he managed to dissuade both wind and creatures from his life-saving den.

A turn passed as Wing waited for the weather to give pause. He would not wait until the rain stopped to move on—it would rain through early Kive—but he would wait long enough to increase his chances of not dying from exposure by spending nights under lesser cover.

Nights within the shelter of the Mesko cavern when he could not sleep were a torture. Unable to stretch his long limbs, a deep aching would set into his joints and his muscles would begin to cramp. At times the pain drove him out into the night where the cold set upon him with equal vengeance.

On the odd nights that his body cooperated, his mind would pick up its relentless firebrand of questions, running itself around in the pursuit and denial of them so furiously that the ruts it created felt inescapable.

Resentfully, Wing wondered which condition he detested more: being sheltered enough that his mind could think, or the cold and exhaustion that finally forced him into oblivious sleep.

Through a break in the makeshift bark door and the cover of canopy, his green gaze spotted a sliver of the night sky.

You knew it was not in me, he said silently. *Everything the Leader is supposed to be I am not—never have been. If there was someone I was supposed to be, why did You not make me equal to the task? Why do I love the feel of earth in my hands rather than the cool blade of a sword?*

Why?

But the sky remained unblinking and reticent, leaving the questions to haunt the back of Wing's mind, affirming his belief that there was no answer, that Eosha had simply turned His back, looked away, and for the life of him, Wing could not comprehend why. Even the incomprehensible act of the Ka'ull came a distant second to this feeling of renunciation.

Next to him, a familiar heavy-bodied spider crept by. It tickled Wing's hand and he looked down. The black hairs on the spider's legs glistened as it crawled through the pale slice of moonlight shining in upon the cavern floor.

"There you are," Wing said.

The spider would have filled the palm of Wing's hand and had proven itself, so far, to be surprisingly sedate. Whether that was because of the cold temperatures or a nonplussed nature, Wing wasn't sure. Whatever the truth was, Wing and the tunnel-dweller had managed to share the root cavern amicably.

"I'd head into your hole," Wing advised. "I'm no good company tonight and it's only going to get colder."

But the spider remained in the bit of pale moonlight, its body hovering just above the ground, the joints of its fuzzy legs jutting up like tiny mountain peaks, its small black claws vanishing into the shadowed valley of its belly.

Irritably, Wing asked, "What?"

The spider still did not move.

"We'll have a problem if you're here after I fall asleep and I get bitten over some sleep-related incident."

The spider scratched the top of its abdomen with a back leg, replaced its foot, and settled in again.

"By all means," Wing said with resignation, "make yourself comfortable."

Glancing around the root cavern, Wing's gaze returned to the spider. There was really nothing else to look at.

After a time, Wing acquiesced to the spider's company. "E'te," he said to it, "here's the plan. As soon as I can, I'm getting on to Legran—deliver Lant's plans to Master Monteray. After that maybe I'll come back, and if you're still around..." Wing's throat closed and the end of his thought passed between him and his diminutive companion in silence: *then at least someone will know where I was, what happened in the end.*

With the spider now swimming in his watery vision, Wing cleared the hitch in his throat. "I've got a mission for you while I'm gone. I'm going to sing a song. You can hold it for me, and just in case I don't make it back, it's important that you remember it because you'll be the last one in this world to hear it."

Wing's once smooth voice sounded impossibly forlorn and small within the knotted amphitheatre of the root cavern as he began to sing:

"I Mesko
A freasente yullalpa
Ma ta ma ta no'va-hm
I fa tendehre a medthre vencentt
Ma ta ma ta no'va-hm
Seeg'ente tepedthre veelan
A leetal's en corashee-on
Ma ta ma ta no'va-hm in"

Wing let the words fade into the thick root and dirt of the Mesko chamber.

The spider had crept away into the dark.

Curling into a ball, his head in the fold of an arm, Wing closed his eyes and somewhere in that supernatural space between waking and dream the fervid beating of the spider's tiny heart was like the softly falling footprints of Fey's running feet, the swelling and shrinking of the tree's great roots was like the sound of Nien's breath as he slept, and the pulse of the earth's deep crust was like his father's voice calling to him from across the fields.

And beyond the heavy cloud cover the stars shone upon a dark log home and a stretch of fields that reached to the edge of a mountain and a single great Mesko tree where a man lay in one hole and a spider in another, and from that hallowed cavern dreams carried over into the land of the dead and for a small moment that which seemed so far away and impossible to grasp was quite real, so heartbreakingly close, in fact, that nothing had happened. The man was not alone in an unfathomable reach of mountains. He was not alone in the world or the last of his race. He had a mother and a father. He had a little brother and a baby sister. He had a home and a warm bed and a brother of iridescent skin colour who was more a part of him than the swell of blood in his veins. And in the morning he would go to the fields where the snows of Ime had begun to melt and the dark soil beckoned, offering its rich black soul to the seeds he held in his hands.

In the morning, everything would be as it once was.

CHAPTER 43

Broken Man

Kate took up the large jug from beside the sink and headed out the back door to the river. The new season was coming, the cold was wearing off, the grasses and flowers were raising their heads and finding their colour. The early evening was uncommonly warm and she smiled a little, glancing up at the mountainous horizon and the lowering sun. She'd almost made it to the river's edge when a dark shadow in the bright green of the grasses caught her eye.

Pausing, she squinted, wondering if what she'd seen had been nothing more than the play of cloud in the slant of evening light.

But her visual search brought no clarity, so, unsatisfied, she set the jug down and moved toward the abstraction. As she drew near the shadow began to solidify, taking on texture, colour. Kate stopped. Lying prone in the thick grass not far from the bank of the river was a man. A Preak man. Moving closer, she saw that his face was bruised and partially swollen, his clothing torn. Blood matted most of his left side.

Kate felt a constriction in her chest—she'd not seen a Preak so ill-treated nor in such a horrible condition since she was a little girl. She made a sweeping search across the fields toward town. They were empty.

Kneeling at his side, she touched his face. It was warm. Placing her cheek next to his lips, she felt a thin brush of air.

Getting to her feet, she hurried back to the house.

"Tei! Tei!"

Tei came down the stairs into the dining area. "What? I was in the middle of something."

"Come with me," Kate said as she grabbed up rags and blankets.

"What's going on?"

"Just come with me."

And the two women ran.

249

Even running, Tei still managed to complain until Kate stopped at a long dark shadow near the riverbank.

"A Preak," Tei said, startled. "Mother, who is he?"

"I don't know." Kate scanned the river and the fields leading into town once more before returning to the man's side.

Tei glanced around as well. "What are you doing?"

"Help me." Kate cast her eyes up to their home in the distance, then at the nearby cabin. "Let's move him into the cabin, it's closer."

"How?"

"Well, if we cannot lift him, we'll have to drag him."

Attempting twice to lift him, they gave up the effort.

"We'll have to pull him over."

"I'm getting all bloody," Tei whined as she reached to take hold of the man's right arm.

"No, don't," Kate quickly said. "Can't you see the shoulder?"

"Well, of course. What's wrong?"

Kate shook her head irritatedly. "Sometimes you're not much help."

"Why are you doing this anyway? Someone could come looking for him. What if he came back for revenge or something? What if he tried to kill somebody in town? What if he deserved this?"

Kate cast her daughter a quick look. "Just help."

After some struggle, the two managed to get the man into the cabin and onto the bed inside.

"Here," Kate said, placing a rag in Tei's hand, "clean that blood away."

Most of the man's visible wounds had scabbed over, the blood dry and hard against his skin. Tei grimaced and reached out with the moist cloth to wipe his face. "Why, he's quite handsome," she said, pausing.

Kate glanced at the man's swollen face. "You can tell?"

Tei shrugged. "Well, I bet he *was*."

"If you *can*, keep your mind on the business at hand." Kate shook her head as her daughter's eyes traced the man's body. "Never mind that. I need some water from the river. And then if you'll go up to the house and get more blankets, rags, a cup and a bowl, and some of your father's clothes—oh, and wood. We need to get a fire going in here."

Tei put the rag down. "Fine. I'll just drag the whole house out here by *myself*."

As Tei huffed out the door, Kate set to removing the torn shirt from the man's shoulders and the bloodied boots from his feet. Looking over the pants and leather leg guards, she wondered if she'd need to cut them away; but rocks and swords, it seemed, had nearly done the job for her—they came off all too easily with minimal jostling to the wounded man.

A few moments later, Tei returned with a bucket of water. "How many trips am I going to have to make?" she asked, setting the heavy bucket down beside Kate.

"Hopefully only one," Kate replied, pulling a blanket across the naked man's genitals. Tei sighed.

"I'll go get the stuff from the house, then."

As the door closed again behind Tei, Kate muttered, "That child."

Rewetting the rag Tei had set down, Kate began to clean the dirt and dried blood from the man's body. Her life with Monteray had taught her a great deal about the nature of fighting, it had also taught her how to care for the wounds it inflicted. With the exception of at least one punch to the face, the rest of his injuries were indicative of those caused by sword combat, the largest of which cut along his left side where it appeared a sword had slid off his ribs. The tattered remnants of a thin strip of cloth had fallen away from this wound as she'd removed his shirt. A jagged section of his scalp was roughly covered in scabs. His left arm below the elbow was a dark purple swell, causing his skin in that area to appear even more iridescent than normal. Kate palpated the area gently, but it was still too swollen to tell how badly it might be broken. Steadying the involuntary shake in her hand, Kate noticed that a poultice of some sort had been applied to the worst of his bruising. Apparently, the man had applied it himself since it was hit and miss across his back. Though the colour and scent was dry and tainted with blood seepage, Kate recognized the combination of plants used to create the poultice.

By the time Tei returned, Kate had cleaned out the contaminated packs and dressed the man's wounds. Asking Tei to leave the clothing and wait outside while she redressed him, Kate clothed him as carefully as she could in a pair of Monteray's pants and loose over shirt. Placing his right arm in a sling and covering him with a few heavy blankets, Kate stepped outside and said, "Let's get dinner ready. Your father will be home anytime."

"You might want to keep it," Kate said.

Monteray stopped shrugging out of his long coat and pulled it back on. "What is it?"

Kate removed her apron and stepped to the back door. "Come with me."

Monteray followed her out.

"You all right?" he asked as they began to walk across the lush, green expanse between the house and the cabin.

"I'm fine, but there's something you should see."

"What?"

"Just wait."

"Where are we going?"

"To the cabin."

"The cabin? What's in the cabin?" Had it not been for the tension in Kate's voice, he might have thought she was surprising him with a small romantic dinner.

At the cabin, Kate stepped ahead of Monteray and opened the door slowly.

Monteray came in quietly behind her, his eyes falling upon a man lying in the cabin bed. He looked him over briefly before glancing questioningly to Kate.

"I found him this evening as I was going for water."

Monteray stepped up beside the bed and lifted one of the bandages. "That's a sword wound."

Kate nodded. "That was my guess."

"Has he been conscious at all since you came upon him?"

"No."

"He's obviously lost a great amount of blood."

"He knows something of caring for wounds—the ones he could reach were bandaged and he'd applied a poultice to the bruising."

"Probably saved his life," Monteray replied off-handedly, his mind occupied.

"I'm most concerned about his head wound. His arm is a mess and there's the bruising across his chest. Oh, and his shoulder looks a little off—a partial dislocation or something."

Monteray shook off the string of thoughts begging for his attention. "You're right about the head wound, but from the age of the scabs, I'd say if it was going to kill him it would have done so by now." Monteray examined the shoulder. "It's not too bad. We can readjust it, but I'll need your help." The break in his right arm was healing well enough but the grip strength in his hand was still not good. "And watch, if he wakes up—"

"Alright, I'll be ready. Just tell me what to do."

With practiced skill and Kate's help, Monteray realigned the shoulder. The man did not wake. That concerned Monteray, but he said nothing. Kate replaced the sling.

"Do you think his other arm is broken?" Kate asked.

Monteray took the man's left arm, turning it slowly, checking the colour in the fingers. "It's a pretty bad contusion."

"What should we do?"

Monteray shrugged. "Wait till he wakes, I suppose."

"What if he doesn't"—Kate paused a hitch—"wake up?"

"Then…" Monteray stopped. "Let's take it as it comes. If he's meant to live, he'll live. You've done all that can be done for now."

On the way back up to the house, Kate said, "Have you heard anything in town? Any ideas of who he is or where he might have come from?"

"I haven't heard anything, but it might be too soon. If there was some sort of incident, I'm sure we'll hear about it, no matter how quiet it's tried to be kept."

The two walked the rest of the way to the house in silence, each lost in their thoughts.

After dinner, Kate gathered together some leftovers. "I'm going to take some food out to the cabin in case he wakes," Kate said as Monteray walked back through the dining area.

"I'll go with you," he said.

"Can I go, too?" Tei asked.

"I don't want him thinking he's the only trader in town," Kate replied. "If you'd finish up here I would appreciate it."

Tei muttered disgustedly.

Filling a container with the remaining meal, the couple stepped out into the cool night air. The sun had just set. Monteray took his wife's hand as they walked. "It's a good thing you did."

"Helping him?"

Monteray nodded.

"I hope it doesn't give you trouble."

Monteray shrugged. "It won't."

"But what if he was the perpetrator?"

"Then we'll deal with that once we know."

Nevertheless, Monteray understood why Kate was worried. Though he had often mediated disagreements not only in Legran but also with other valleys, he knew Kate loathed confrontation and was forever worried about exacerbating sensitive issues. It had not been too long since his and Kate's position on indentured servants had created more than slight rustlings of discontent.

Beside him, Kate took a deep breath.

"You must be tired," Monteray said. Taking the small container of food from her, he moved it to his left hand and took Kate's hand in his right. She leaned into him a little as they walked, and he nuzzled the top of her head with his cheek.

At the cabin, Monteray waited for Kate to go in first in case the man had regained consciousness. A moment later, Kate reappeared at the door. "I don't think he's moved at all," she said.

Together, they checked the wrappings and the shoulder. The shoulder had held in place, and no new blood was present on the binding cloths. These were good signs.

"He needs fluid," Kate said, and taking a clean rag, dipped it into the short jug of water and began to dab at the man's cracked lips.

"Dehydration will be a problem," Monteray agreed, "if he doesn't awaken soon." Glancing aside, Monteray spotted a bundle of clothing near the door. "Are these his clothes?"

Kate nodded. "I forgot to take them up to the house. They need to be cleaned and mended—if possible."

Monteray gazed at them for a time. Upon the leather guard that crossed the left shoulder mantle, Monteray noted a patch engraved with the symbol of a large crouching cat, a knife blade clenched in its teeth.

"Jedan and Lenna. They'd mentioned a Preak—that a Preak had been present at the Jayakan battle debriefing. Curious..."

"What?"

"Oh, nothing. Can I help you there?"

"No, I guess not," Kate replied, sadly.

Monteray forced a wan smile at her. "Don't worry."

Kate nodded, and bundling the moistened rag with the torn clothing, they walked side-by-side back to the house.

Trembling and weak, he lay bathed in his own sweat. Icy water bit into his limbs, searing like white heat through his wounds. He got up, turned, leaned against a tree for support. Cries of terror filled his mind and then silence, a silence so profound that even the blood moving in his ears sounded like thunder. Searching for breath, he found none, his chest aching with the weight, the incredible heaviness of so many bodies pressing down upon him. He plunged ahead through a narrow stream, tripped, fell against stones and flesh-tearing branches. When he managed to get back to his feet, blood coloured the water's clear ripples. Exhausted, filled with pain, he struggled a bit farther before collapsing beside the stream a third time. For a long while, he lay, unaware of the muscle spasms that shook his battered frame. The stream gurgled on and the sun began to fade. A breeze twirled thin, tender branches of overhanging trees. His breathing calmed. His limbs stilled. And then a splash of frigid water caught him across the shoulders. Scrambling to his hands and knees, he gasped as the water—

No, not water.

Blood.

Blood ran down his face, dripped into his eyes...

Nien sat up with a wrenching jerk. His cry of surprise pierced the still cabin air. Heart racing, pain thrumming through his concussed head, he attempted to ascertain where he was, but his senses failed him and all he could feel was a weight upon him, a hot, smothering weight.

He thrashed against it, got his feet turned beneath him, only to fall off the side of a bed.

Unable to rise again, he crawled until he hit the corner of a wall. Curling up there, a guttural moan escaped him as pain seemed to come from everywhere at once. No longer isolated to his specific injuries, it engulfed him like an entity, like a circle: having no beginning and no end.

Slumping, he mercifully lost consciousness.

Kate rapped lightly on the cabin door the following morning. Entering carefully, she glanced at the bed—it was empty. The blankets she'd placed over the man were strewn across the cabin floor. A jolt of fear shot through her before she spotted a huddled figure in the far right corner of the cabin.

Setting aside the goods in her arms, she approached the man and knelt beside him. He was shivering with cold.

"I won't let you crawl into a corner to die," Kate said. "Not after I've gone through so much work to patch you up."

Emaciated as he was, Kate, nevertheless, knew she could never lift him back onto the bed. Gathering up some blankets, she returned to his side. As she placed them over him, he awoke.

"It's all right," she said in the Legrand tongue.

With wild, fevered eyes, he looked up at her.

"Uh, it's all right," Kate repeated, this time in Preak.

Trepidation stiffened the man's frame.

"Help me," Kate said, motioning to the bed.

He looked at the bed, then back at her face. Kate placed her hands beneath his arms and tried to lift him. Managing to get a foot beneath himself, he made it across the room and up onto the bed.

"You've gotten yourself chilled," Kate said, still speaking in the Preak tongue even though the man did not respond to that language any more than he had when she'd spoken in Legrand.

Gathering the blankets now strewn across the floor, she started to place them over him again when he protested, moaning, the look in his eyes feral and dark. Kate glanced down at the heavy blankets.

"All right, not a good idea." She looked him over. "I guess I'm going to have to come up with warmer clothing."

Setting the blankets aside, she sat down beside him and gently began rubbing his arms to warm him. He watched her with a glassy, wondering gaze.

"Now that I've caught you awake," she said, "you need to drink something."

Leaving his side, she stepped to the small round table and retrieved a pitcher of water. Filling a cup, she sat by his side again and raised his head with her hand. The man's lips met the cup's edge and he drank desperately. Kate refilled and he drained the cup twice more.

"That's good," Kate said with relief.

He watched her for a moment in silence before his eyes shut.

Placing the cup and the pitcher by the bed, Kate said, "Now stay put. I'll be back in a bit."

Gathering up a few of the wrappings that had come undone either from being blood-soaked or from his half-conscious trip into the corner of the room, Kate returned to the house. There she retrieved more strips of cloth, extra soup broth, and some thick cold-season clothing Monteray used for outdoor travel.

Back in the cabin, she found the man asleep. Placing the broth on the table, she looked down at the bandages and clothing in her hand. Shaking her head, she decided against redressing his wounds. After what had happened earlier she did not want to risk startling him again. Turning to leave, she noticed beads of sweat forming across his brow and paused. He was twitching, impulses in his arms and legs firing at disconcerting intervals. Taking up a moist rag, Kate pulled the chair over and sat beside him. His eyes were moving rapidly beneath their lids and his throat contracted and released repeatedly.

Stroking his forehead with the rag, Kate spoke quietly to him, "It's going to be all right, you're safe here."

Gazing down at his face, she wished she could think of something more she could do to ease the nightmare that had him gulping impulsively like an undead fish tossed upon a riverbank.

Glancing over her shoulder, her soft eyes lit upon the small riverside window. Walking over, Kate opened the shutter. The night wind blew in through the small window, tracing her back as she returned to the man's side.

Placing her hand upon the man's own hand where it trembled against his chest, she waited, listening to the rustle of swaying grasses, the smooth rumble of the river, and the singing of night bugs. As the moments passed the man's breathing began to calm and his twitching stopped. Reaching forward, Kate placed her thin hand upon his brow—his fevered skin had cooled beneath the wind's gentle embrace.

"Rest easy now," she said. "Whoever you are, you're safe here."

CHAPTER 44

Fevered Memories

L ate morning found Wing cresting the top of Peak Llow. Stopping to catch his breath, he cast his eyes over the magnificent vista stretching out below him. Great swaths of wet, brown ground showed through dwindling lines of snow. The nights were still cold, but not cruel. He had bid the spider farewell and spent his last night in the root cavern two nights ago and was now high in the mountains above the Mesko timberline. Looking over the lofty Mesko canopy, he could see the Uki Range shimmering with rain. He glanced down at the small green valley far below him—

His gaze did not rest there long.

Turning away, he began to run, continuing through another day until the rain and slick, open rock finally drove him beneath a thin, high-altitude tree for reprieve.

Drawing his knees up to his chest, he tucked his face between them and covered his head with his arms in an attempt to block the wind.

Shivering and striving for sleep, it eluded him.

The rain found no reason to stop.

More sunrises followed more nightfalls. Wing had tried—repeatedly—to build some sort of fire to ease the ache of chill upon his body. But he'd not yet been able to find any wood in the rain-drenched forest that was remotely useable.

Stiff in muscle and joint, he continued through another day, the greyness of the heavens a suitable reflection of his listless, lonesome movement beneath them.

Night was again reaching over the mountainous canyons and cliffs when Wing happened upon a large, old tree trunk, having long ago fallen to the ground. Getting to his knees, he peered inside.

Sweet relief flooded him: Dry tinder. Just enough.

It was not a grand fire, but the warmth that emanated from it was unlike any warmth Wing had ever felt.

Though he hadn't remembered doing so, on the night of his escape from Rieeve, he'd obviously grabbed up a bit of flint and spark. While living in the root cavern he'd supplemented them with additional fire-building instruments, but all of it proved useless when he'd been unable to find any dry wood. Happening upon the fallen tree with dry tinder inside felt like more of a triumph than coaxing flame from the union of mineral and metal.

Nursing the tender flames, Wing looked up through the tree tops and out toward the heavens.

Another night, he thought.

He'd never known the kind of darkness that penetrated the mountains at night: the movement of creatures in the ground beneath him, the occasional insect crawling across his skin, the tiny eyes that glimmered in the darkness, watching with a coldness that disturbed what little sleep he got.

Within the tree cavern there had been at least the comfort of being sheltered. Now, he felt naked against the world. Vulnerable to its grandest or smallest whim.

The following morning, Wing gathered up as much of the dry tinder from the fallen tree as he could, bundling it in his extra clothes and stuffing it into the duffel.

Through sunrise and sunset, beneath cloud and rain and the thin silvery cradle of first moon, Wing continued to move.

As the third turn passed away into the fourth, the trauma of his last night in Rieeve and the uncompromising struggle of living in the wild caught up with him. Fevered and chilled, his stomach revolted, rejecting what little he put into it.

Rain and stream water were easy enough to come by and over the past few days he had managed to spear the occasional fish from gathering pools at the base of cliffs, but now, dehydrated from vomiting, his strength expelled, he could only lay sweating, shaking. He desperately needed to make a fire, but doing so was a laborious effort—even when healthy—and one he simply could not manage in his present condition.

So without light, without heat, Wing crawled beneath a short, rocky overhang and with loathing, cast his eyes upon the vast expanse of dark forest that seemed to bend its will against him, intensifying the fragility of which he was already acutely aware.

The night passed into a dark day and by the next nightfall, his condition had deteriorated further still.

Sliding back and forth between delirium and lucidity, Wing's fevered thoughts followed a well-worn path in his mind to places in the past, and for brief moments he felt the sun on his face as he stood in his fields, smelled the sweet fragrance of Reean's fretheral garden, touched Carly's soft skin, saw Nien's smile.

Nien.

His brother's name snatched him from delirium.

Briefly aware of the chills wracking his body, Wing tried to remember Nien's face, the sound of his voice, the anomalous colour of his eyes.

A quixotic, involuntary cry escaped him.

"Nien," he pled. "I won't be long. Not long behind. Wait."

CHAPTER 45

Stranger in a Strange Land

"How is he?" Monteray asked as Kate came in through their bedroom door.

Shivering, Kate climbed quickly into the bed. "He has terrible nightmares. Whatever happened to him, whatever he went through before arriving here..."

There had been no word in town of any repute, not even any gossip that Monteray had heard or been made aware of. Though this was a relief, it did nothing to solve the mystery of the man who lay, hopefully recovering, in their small cabin down by the river.

Monteray adjusted a bed pillow behind his back. "It is likely he is a warrior," he said quietly. "I have my doubts that what happened to him was done in single combat."

"You mean a battle?" Kate looked at him.

"Yes. But there has been no word from any valley of another since Jayak."

"So, what is it?"

"His clothing, that leather shoulder mantle and the symbol on the patch sewn over it—it's Riecvan, of the fighting force that Lant put together."

"The Cant? Why didn't you say so before?"

"I've been thinking on it," Monteray replied.

"And?"

Monteray shook his greying head. "And I've come up with nothing. There are many possibilities, but Rieeve's disassociation negates most of them."

There *was* one possibility, a detail Monteray remembered but which seemed too incredible to consider seriously, so he did not speak it and left off that line of thought. "I'll be going to see Rhusta a little earlier than I'd planned—he might have seen or heard something."

Nien awoke slowly. His head hurt...Everything hurt. He opened his eyes. His surroundings came to him at first in only a blur. After a time, he forced himself to sit up. His left arm and side throbbed. He looked down and saw that his right arm was in a sling.

Glancing across the room, he saw a cup, pitcher, and bowl sitting on a small round table. Like a drunken, boneless man, he managed to make it to the chair beside the table before collapsing. There was water in the cup and some sort of vegetable broth in the bowl. Reaching out of the sling with his right hand, he grasped the cup and downed its contents. He then took up the bowl in his hands—ignoring the utensil beside it—and gulped down the salty broth.

Feeling immediately revived, he looked out the window near the door and saw a beautiful home in the near distance.

Where am I? He closed his eyes. *Legran?* Yes, he remembered coming down the mountain, crossing the river. He was in Legran.

He felt an instant of relief followed by a wave of cold fear that chilled from him the warmth the broth had provided.

Given the shape he was in, had he been wise in coming here? He could not defend himself were someone other than Master Monteray to find him. If that big house happened to be the home of a servant owner, they could tend him till he was well, then expect him to spend the rest of his life paying off the debt.

He would not live like that, but neither could he take another fight—if that's what it came to in order to escape.

Briefly, he contemplated moving on. But the inclination was not one even his half-working brain could realistically consider as weakness forced him back to the bed where sleep took him by the time he'd eased himself down.

The following morning, Kate entered the cabin as she did every day to check on him. Monteray came in behind her. Stepping over to the table, she smiled at seeing that the water and soup were gone. Dragging the chair behind her, she took a seat by his side and began to redress the wounds.

The man woke as she did.

"It's all right," she said in Preak, "don't be alarmed."

He tried to move away from her hand.

"You're safe here. There's no need to worry."

The expression on his face told Kate her words did little to change his mind. Speaking in Legrand, she tried again. Still, his face revealed only confusion and fear. She was about to try the Fultershier, when Monteray said softly, "Try speaking in Rieevan."

Rieevan? Kate thought. She knew a little of the language because of Monteray's friendship with Lant, but why he'd suggest her speaking it to a man of Preak origin was entirely perplexing—

Any other language would have made more sense.

Turning back to the man, she saw that hearing Monteray's voice was stressing his already taxed reserves. "That's my husband," she said in Rieevan.

Something sparked in the man's eyes then vanished so completely that Kate thought she'd imagined it.

Out of ideas, Kate was about to give up when the man asked: "Where am I?" in the Fultershier.

The Fultershier! Kate thought. *Fabulous.* "You're at our home in Legran," she replied, also in the Fultershier.

"How long?"

"We found you three days ago. My name is Kate and that is Monteray, my husband."

"My name is Sep. Thank you for helping..." His words trailed off and his eyes closed.

"Sep?" Kate said.

Monteray stepped over, placing his fingertips upon the man's neck. "He's all right. That can happen in his condition."

"It's disconcerting," Kate replied.

Monteray nodded. "I know. Here, let me help you so we can go and let him sleep."

On the fifth day, Nien stepped out the door of the small cabin. In the close distance stood the magnificent home. Another structure stood to the northing of the house and both, it appeared, were still under various degrees of construction; nevertheless, seeing them now in full view took Nien's breath away—only in Quieness had he seen such remarkable architecture.

"The Monterays," he whispered to himself.

Since the revelation, Nien had stopped running scenarios through his mind concerning what he'd do should things with the owner of the house turn ugly. Now, the obvious thing was simply to tell the Monterays everything—

Except that he didn't want to.

He could hardly believe the sentiment. But there it was. He didn't want to be Nien. He didn't want to remember. He just wanted to be Sep. He could make up a whole new story. What was the point, anyway, in telling the truth now? Perhaps, to warn them, but Monteray already knew of the threat. And he already knew of Lant's Plan.

So there was no reason to tell them the truth.

None at all.

Nien fixed his gaze upon the house and decided.

What mattered most was that he was safe, with people Commander Lant had trusted and loved without reserve.

All I need to do now is give them a reason to let me stay.

The walk to the house seemed an impossibly long distance. Physically, it felt as if there were a slow leak in his strength that continually drained out faster than it filled. His breath came hard and laboured and a throbbing pain curled itself around his joints. Mentally, he'd never felt so...

So unlike myself, he thought.

He also thought that should have scared him. But it didn't. Gone was the relentless drive and the fierce will that had once been softened only by his sociable nature. Now, there was no need of anything. No striving. Rather than create a path, he wanted only to fall in upon one already cut before him.

Reaching the door, Nien paused and leaning against the frame took a moment to gather himself.

He knocked. Pain radiated from his knuckles up into his wrist.

Tei opened the door.

Speaking in the Fultershier, Nien asked, "Are Kate or Monteray in?" He did not meet her eyes.

Tei turned back into the house. "Mother!"

Kate appeared in the doorway behind Tei, wiping her hands down her apron. "Come in, come in," she said.

"Thank you," Nien said.

Kate pulled a chair out from the dining table for him to sit on. "How are you?" she asked.

"Recovering, thanks to you."

Kate sat down in front of him and began checking the wrappings about his chest. She did this with such ease—as if she were his mother and he her flesh and blood—that Nien could only sit, entranced, as she made her inspection.

"There's still a little bleeding," she said. "But I'm impressed. You're a quick healer." She replaced the bandage. "Can I get you something? Are you hungry?"

"No, thank you. I—I actually have something I would like to—"

Kate motioned for him to stop. Looking over her shoulder, she said, "Tei, would you please get us something to drink?"

Across the room, Nien caught sight of the young woman that had answered the door as she hurried into the kitchen from her ill-concealed place near the back of the dining room.

Kate turned back to him. "You were saying?"

Nien glanced at the two short swinging doors through which the young woman had disappeared. "I know it's a lot to ask, especially when you've already done so much..." He paused again.

"Yes?"

"Well, if you could use it, I would ask if I could work—to pay you back for what you've done."

"That's not necessary. You may stay as long as you need."

Caught off guard, Nien muttered, "I would like to work. I realize that sounds a bit irrational by the look of me, but I would feel better if I could do something. I have some skill as a carpenter and builder."

Kate's eyes, as they looked back at him, were so deep and warm that Nien felt some stirring of emotion in the unengaged center of his chest.

"Fine then," she said. "Monteray could use the help, anyway—" it seemed she was about to say something else in explanation but stopped short, saying instead, "I know he's frustrated at the small amount of work he can do on his own without hiring out for help." Kate touched Nien on the knee. "Yes, that would be a very good thing. But what you need to do now is rest."

"Thank you." Nien got to his feet.

"Would you rest here for a while?"

"No, I don't want to intrude. Thank you—again."

Kate helped him to the door. From there, Nien started back to the cabin but made it only partway before a wave of nausea pierced a hole in his knees. He would have sunk to the grass had a steady arm not happened around his waist.

"You should have taken my offer," Kate said meeting Nien's surprised expression with a scoldish tilt of her head.

Back in the cabin, Nien took to the bed with a grateful sigh.

"You may not think so, but you look much better."

"To be honest, I feel quite ruined. Any progress is due to you."

Kate shrugged. "No. You were placed in my field." She patted his knee. "And I'm glad you were."

Her words stopped any reply he might have had.

"I'll bring you some dinner out tonight."

Nien forced a thank you before the sound of the shutting door reached his ears. A lump rose in his throat as silence filled the cabin.

Kate's tenderness. Her caring. It made him think of...

Reean.

Mother.

The names of the rest of his family tumbled through his mind.

Joash, Jake, Fey.

I am Sep, he'd told Kate and Monteray, realizing that along with his name he'd tried to erase his family as well.

Saying their names now twisted his gut like a punishment.

Images of home, of safety, of laughter flashed through his mind—but intermingled with them were the snapshots of frozen stares, great swells of blood, and limbs locked in impossible directions.

Attempting to smother the images from his mind forever, Nien rolled onto his side and pressed his face into the pillow. But the only image that could drive them out was...

Wing.

Like a large, tormented animal, Nien felt everything inside him writhe and strive to banish every image, every feeling, every memory of his brother.

None of them would go.

Nien growled into his pillow, snarling, wanting to cry out his rage. Only the thought of being overheard by Kate as she walked back up to the house kept him from doing so.

With a half-shuddered sob, he slid his chin into his chest and breathed. As he did, the terrible questions he'd held at bay began to scroll through his mind: *Wing, what happened to you? Where are you?*

And the hardest one of all: *Did you make it away?*

Nien uncurled his spine and shoved himself over onto his back.

Staring briefly up at the ceiling, he closed his eyes and with a silent wish that he dared not hold in his hands, whispered, "Brother, if you made it out, if you're out there somewhere, I'm *right* here.

"Find me."

CHAPTER 46
Cabin in the Clearing

Wing awoke to find first moon nearly full in the night sky. A spontaneous sigh of gratitude escaped him for this smallest and most natural gift. He was unsure how much time had passed, but the chills were gone, as well as the fever. His body felt utterly wasted, but the cessation of the symptoms renewed his spirits enough to get him to his feet. From there, he'd sought water.

Before the illness had set upon him, the fear that he was hopelessly lost in the mountains and might never find Legran had gripped him madly, but now apathy had taken over, held in check only by his vow to deliver the Plan to Master Monteray.

Another day trudged on and if for nothing but a change, Wing began to scrape the pulp from the bark of trees to eat as he rested—something he found himself needing to do more and more often.

The past couple nights he'd endeavored to arrange some sort of shelter beneath trees with low hanging branches or ready-made rocky outcroppings, but the hard ground dug into his bones and he forever woke more tired than when he'd lain down. His clothes were ragged and repugnant and he was afraid might soon attract larger creatures than insects while he slept. Worst of all was that the inspiring strength he'd had in his possession only a few short turns ago was nearly spent.

That, too. Take it all, he thought, gazing into a stream where he drank, seeing only the hollowed cheeks and the eyes that looked...

In truth, he recognized nothing about the rippling, distorted image that gazed back at him.

That evening, Wing tried for the first time in many nights to make a fire. Beneath a sparse stand of thin, broad-leafed trees, he found sheddings of nest materials and plenty of dry bark scraps. Mercifully, a spark took quickly and Wing breathed life into it.

Staring into the darkness, Wing leaned forward to feed a handful of branches to his fire and felt the dull edge of something inside his coat press into his ribs. Reaching into the pocket, he withdrew the leather-bound copy of the Ancient Writings he'd been making for himself, and for, he had hoped, his own family. Looking at the book, myriad emotions rose and fell within him as the stars moved slowly overhead and the fire flickered up against overhanging tree boughs. With his long, dark fingers, Wing held it, feeling the leather texture, staring at the feathered, slightly uneven page edges. Then, with a flick of the wrist so fast it was imperceptible between the dance of flame and shadow, he tossed it into the fire.

With a vacant, tired expression, he watched the flames lick over the smooth leather cover.

"You came," Wing said to the disembodied messenger who had stopped him from going into the castle that night. "But you came too late."

By the time the sun had climbed to its highest point the next day, Wing was keeping to the shade of trees, tired and knowing his body had not much left to give.

Managing a walking gait, his breath coming hard as only a long-distance run would have done a few turns earlier, Wing kept on as if in a trance.

Night came slowly across the ridges and peaks, enveloping the sky with a sweet calm. First moon rose high and full, second moon on its tail—a gentle blue glow that glittered across atmospheric reflection.

The return of the moons helped to clear his mind.

"Just me and the crickets," he said to himself. "I guess I'd better find a place for tonight."

Moving ahead a bit more, he stepped out into a small but elegant clearing—and drew up short. On the other side, sat a stout little cabin, its shadow big and beautiful in the night's luminescence.

Wing blinked, not believing his eyes.

A cabin.

He'd never heard that people lived in the mountains.

Unless...

Nien had once said there were tradesmen who lived nomadically, traveling valley to valley. Perhaps this was one of them. But why would a nomad build such a permanent structure?

The structure.

Unsure he could trust his tired, cloudy eyesight, Wing thought the cabin bore a striking resemblance to Rieevan architecture in design, if not materials.

Drawing back into the tree line surrounding the clearing, Wing began to make his way toward the cabin.

Stumbling over clumps of dirt and shrub, Wing stopped again at a short distance. Light from within caused the window shutters to glow and Wing felt that orange light blush inside him as if radiated from a forgotten wish in his mind. Bending down, he scooped up a rock and checking his aim, tossed it at the door. As the rock bounced off the door and tumbled across the deck, Wing folded back into the shadowed edge of the clearing to watch.

An old man, thinning rusty-red beard reaching down from his face, appeared in the doorway. He looked around and then went back inside.

Though he did not look Rieevan (and Wing had no idea what the Legranders looked like), he did not appear dangerous—and he was clearly not Ka'ull.

Exhaustion and pain superseded any further thoughts of wariness; Wing approached the cabin.

Leaning upon the door's wooden frame, he rapped lightly.

On the other side something fell and something banged and this time the old man appeared in the doorway with a worn hardwood stick in his hand. "All right, Jassup, let's get on with it. *One* of us is going to get some sleep tonight."

Jassup? Wing thought. *That's an unfamiliar Rieevan name—wait. Had the man just spoken in Rieevan?*

Pushing himself erect and into the light pouring out of the cabin, Wing's tall frame filled the doorway.

The man started, his scowl briefly vanishing.

An embodiment of the mountains, the old man's face was stony and hard. His hair was like the red-rock of the sunsetting slopes of the Ti Range and his eyes were the colour of a Kojko storm—heavy grey set against the deepest blue. Had Wing not been on the verge of fainting he might have noticed the momentary expression of astonishment that sparked across those stormy eyes...

But Wing could barely stand.

"What is this?"

This time the language was vaguely recognizable as the Fultershier, but after so long with only his own voice for company, the grating tone of the man's accusation astonished Wing's senses. It took an uncomfortably long time to piece together a reply in the strange tongue Nien had tried so often to teach him: "Please, if you would…"

"Go away," came the succinct reply that Wing had no problem translating.

Wing went to speak again, to plead his cause, but his strength failed entirely and sinking to his knees, he collapsed headlong across the door-frame.

For a time the old man did not move, did not speak, his eyes softening as he took in the tall form now lying unconscious in the doorway to his cabin.

"Son of the Mesko Tender," he said at last in a language Wing would have understood intimately had he been conscious. "What brings you way out here?"

Stepping around Wing's prostrate form, he rolled him onto his back, tucked his arms beneath his shoulders and pulled Wing into the cabin. "I thought you were that old wapa again. I was about to knock your head in." He laid Wing in front of the fireplace. "I'm glad I didn't."

Stoking up the fire for light and the heating of water, the old man looked Wing over. His hands and feet were cracked, bleeding and swollen. The back of his shoulders, hips and knees—anywhere bone was thin with flesh—bore heavy bruising. A deep gash in his right arm was oozing with infection, and his eyes and cheeks were sunken and drawn.

The broad shoulders and big bones spoke only reminiscently of a man once strong.

Removing Wing's ruined shirt, the old man cleansed the gash in his arm, splashed and bandaged his feet and hands, and after preparing a poultice, served the rest of Wing's bruised body with it.

Moonsteps later, Wing lay on a bed of blankets in front of the fireplace, his face pale and still, but his body dressed in heavy tear-free clothing and his wounds bound up.

The old man knelt beside him, his mind recalling images of the man who had once filled the emaciated form.

"Not you, too," he said as he pulled a blanket up over Wing's chest. "I know a body can die out there, but I'll wager your problems sit much deeper than anything physical."

With surprising gentleness, the old man pushed a stray black hair away from Wing's face.

"Merehr," he said quietly. "What have they done to you?" He then retreated to his own bed at the other side of the cabin.

CHAPTER 47

Transformation

W ing awoke slowly with the bright early morning rays of sun on his face. He opened his eyes, squinting, and looked around the room trying to collect his thoughts. He vaguely remembered coming upon a cabin, but when—last night? Last night seemed too soon. His body felt heavy, as if he had been asleep for days.

"You'd better get up and get some food 'fore it's cold and I'm gone," a voice said from across the room.

Wing rose stiffly to his elbows and looked over to see a man busily plac-ing bowls of food about a small table. Wing studied him for a moment. The gnarled hands, slumped shoulders, long reddish hair...Yes, these things he recalled. But when the old man looked up, Wing's breath caught. It wasn't the odd, steely-blue colour of the eyes but the way the aged man looked at him—as if he knew him.

"Hurry up, I got work to do," the old man said.

Wing looked down at himself, noticing the shifts of cloth wrapped about his hands and feet. He looked them over and then back across the one-roomed cabin at the old man who was moving about in a hurry as if not noticing him at all.

Wing shrugged—perhaps he was a bit delusional. After all, he had been on the brink of starvation for, well, he had no idea how long.

Getting stiffly to his feet, Wing made his way over to the table, taking in the cabin's effects on his way. Hanging on the walls and lying over chairs were sparse compliments of animal skins and tools, flanking either side of a small window were a set of roughly polished shelves filled with clay jars of foodstuffs, utensils, and cookware, and up against the back wall sat a bed with a small bookshelf at its feet.

This man knows how to live in the mountains, Wing thought as he reached the table and steadied himself against a chair. The feel of the chair under his hands caused Wing to look down.

Mesko wood? Wing thought. He looked the chair over. *And it's nearly perfect. That's not an easy thing to do with Mesko.*

"There you go. Eat up and get movin' on," the old man said pushing a plate toward him. From beneath the pile of food at its center, Wing could see that the plate had been engraved with what looked to be a tree.

"Thank you for taking me in—and for the food," Wing said, still leaning heavily on the back of the chair.

"I've fixed up more wounded animals than you'll see in a lifetime."

Wing wavered for a moment, shocked at his own weakness and wondering what fixing up animals had to do with him—

"Oh," he said, thinking, *Guess I know where I stand with him.*

But it took only the next instant for Wing to decide that he didn't much care as long as the old man could help him reach his goal.

"I need to get to Legran."

"Good luck." The old man looked him over for a moment. "The condition you're in, I'm surprised you made it to the table." With that he headed toward the door, but in a motion that surprised the old man no more than Wing himself, Wing made it to the door first and planted his hand firmly against it. "Will you teach me how to live with the mountains?"

The man squinted up at Wing. "Where'd you come from, anyway?"

Wing felt the muscles in his throat constrict around the word: "Rieeve."

"They don't teach those kinds of things there, Rieevan?"

"No," Wing replied flatly, his words an uncomfortable mixture of Fultershier and Rieevan. "That's why I need you to teach me."

Quiet for a breath, the old man lowered his head and muttered, "Goes to figure. I open my door to someone more than once a revolution and suddenly they're moving in." Straightening his coat he glanced up at Wing. "The name's Rhusta. And it's not about living out here, Rieevan, it's about surviving."

"Maybe, but you don't look like you're starving."

"I'm not." And Rhusta reached for the door again. "Kindly move your hand."

Wing understood Rhusta's words to be a caution, not a question, but he kept his hand where it was.

Rhusta looked up into Wing's face, something in his gaze both portentous and melancholic. "Trust me on this, you should just go back home."

The words entered Wing like a sharp blade. His body bent and his eyes fell to the floor. When he looked back up, behind the fatigue and feverish ache in his eyes bloomed an anger that, even in his weakened state, was surprising in its intensity.

"Teach me," Wing said.

Before him, the old man stood in silence. A heavy silence like rain drenched the room forming riverlets between them. Wing only then realized that he'd spoken in Rieevan and yet the man seemed to have understood.

"I don't wanna waste my time," Rhusta finally said, speaking in the Fultershier.

Wing remained firm. "I promise, you won't."

Rhusta's eyes avoided Wing's as he turned again to the door. "Eat first. You're thinner than a Mesko sapling. I'll be back."

From the doorway, Wing watched the old man's back as he moved off with surprising speed across the clearing and disappeared into the trees.

Wing didn't know how long he'd slept when he woke up to hear Rhusta coming back into the cabin.

Reaching behind the door, Rhusta grabbed a sleeved leather cloak and threw it at Wing. It landed at Wing's feet where he lay by the fireplace.

Wing looked up, his eyes questioning.

"Well, you coming or not?"

Wing got to his feet, painfully pulled on his boots, and followed Rhusta as fast as he could toward a nearby brook. At the brook's edge, Rhusta handed Wing a strip of what looked like the dried entrails of an animal and gave him orders to watch. Taking a long, thick stick in one hand, Rhusta tied the catgut into a notch at the head of the stick. He then dug around in the dirt next to him and came up with a small, jagged bit of bone.

"And if you want, you can even hook one of these little fellows on the end." Producing a worm, he forced it over the point of the bone.

Watching, Wing did the same, then cast his roughly hewn fishing pole into the stream in front of him.

The first four days were spent in much the same way, and Wing was grateful for the rest. Communication with Rhusta was hit and miss, and silence was the order for almost every day, but the long sunsteps in the sun on the bank of the brook warmed Wing's cold, worn body and a steady compliment of food began to renew his strength.

It was somewhere in the third turn as the two sat at the edge of a crystal-clear pool that Wing had the audacity to ask a question: "Do you know the Legrand tongue?"

Rhusta raised an eyebrow at him before looking away into the pool. "Some," he said.

"Will you teach me?"

"That, too?" he growled.

The next day, Wing received his first lesson in arrow making spoken in the language of Legran.

As the two sat side-by-side, carving and shaping the springy wood they'd scouted out for use as shafts, Wing wondered how long Rhusta had lived up here. Part of him wanted to ask—it should have been such a simple question. But it wasn't. Nothing was simple with the old man.

Wing tensed and released his shoulders. He really wanted to leave. If he could learn enough of the Legran language, perhaps Master Monteray would be more willing to converse than the old man.

Wing laughed silently to himself. *Me, wanting to talk.* He glanced up at Rhusta whose head was bent over his work, his gnarled but nimble fingers working the wood with surprising grace. *What you bring out in me,* Wing thought. *The desire for things I'd normally take great pains to shun.*

As time-consuming and difficult as the making of arrows had been, bow-making proved to be of an altogether different complexity. The two spent days just finding the right tree. Once they'd found it, they took the trunk—a span at least Wing's height—and the work really began. By the end of three days, Wing's hands were blistered and his body sore. It was only then that Rhusta thanked Wing for his help, informing him that the wood would make some fine bows in the revolutions to come.

"What?" Wing said.

"The wood's got to season, see," Rhusta said. "So that's why we're going to use these staves here." His eyes glinted. "I traded for them in Legran two seasons ago."

After the many sunsteps, the blistered and bloodied hands, the aching muscles—Wing could only look at him. Clearly, this was what passed as humour for the old man.

But Rhusta's sadistic levity aside, as time progressed and the two men began the work of making glue and drying and fitting sinew to the sea-soned staves from Legran, Wing discovered something unexpected—a feeling that reminded him of the joy he'd once felt working with his father. Even though Rhusta rarely gave spoken direction (Wing had learned quickly to watch and follow), it seemed as if he'd stumbled upon a familiar rhythm with the old man. There were even times when Wing suspected that Rhusta enjoyed his company as well.

With the bows completed and strung, Wing began the next phase of his training by chasing Rhusta all over the hills, hiding behind shrub and tree, waiting and watching.

"It's about stalking," Rhusta had said. "You move well, Rieevan, and you're patient. You just can't be afraid to let that arrow go."

The old man had never yet proffered the remotest compliment, so Wing let it go. Besides, Rhusta was right. Like a sword, the bow and its arrows just felt wrong in Wing's hands. And looking at the fent, watching as it nibbled on the tall blades of mountain grass...well, killing it mid-nibble felt wrong, too.

It also didn't help that whenever he did manage to let an arrow go, his reflex was to close his eyes.

He missed every time.

"Think you could contribute to the evening meal sometime?" Rhusta asked part way through the following turn.

Day had gratefully passed into evening, and as the fire died down to coals and the sun began to fade over the mountainous horizon, Rhusta sat at the side of the fire, belching in gratification at having once again enjoyed a hearty meal. Wing sat a little way off, gazing up toward a distant hillside and a dark stand of solitary trees huddled below the rocky peaks.

"Well?" Rhusta said.

Wing gave him no more than a muted glance.

It was the third night of hunting and Wing was hungry and tired. They'd tracked a large je'der all day, but when the perfect opportunity had come Wing had been unable to shoot the arrow. Rhusta dropped the animal instead. He'd then launched into a demonstration of what could be done with nearly every part of the poor creature: They scooped out and boiled the brains, split the gut, pulled out the entrails, and separated the hide from every possible ligament and sinew. By the time they'd sat down to eat, Wing was exhausted (mentally and physically), and had hardly any appetite left. Rhusta, however, had plowed into the meal like it might be his last and when finally satiated wiped his mouth and, pointing to the pot of boiling brains, said, "The juice from the brain there you use to tan the hide. Once the innards are dry, you use them to string your bow or tie into line for fishing, right?"

Wing had simply nodded. All he'd wanted was to sleep.

Beside him, now, Rhusta obviously thought Wing had not heard his not-so-subtle reprimand and decided to restate it in even less delicate terms: "Won't do you much good to learn all this if you can't, actually, see it through."

To both their surprises, Wing found Rhusta's statement fiendishly amusing. He laughed—a dark hint of a laugh. "Well, that about sums it up."

Rhusta's brow furrowed. "Sums what up?"

There was so much Wing could have said in explanation about all the things he'd not seen through. His study of the Ancient Writings that had uncovered nothing. The repeated offers to join the Cant that he'd turned down. The warning visions that he'd tried, but failed to understand. Even his desire to let the mountains have their way with him had fallen just short.

Fle ke' tey, he thought. *I can't even die right.*

But all this Wing left unsaid and unexplained.

"Well," Rhusta said over Wing's continued silence, "don't wait to eat your own kill. I don't want you dying of starvation."

Wing was sure that was Rhusta's way of being kind, but he didn't bother to stop the only reply that came to mind: "Don't worry that you may succeed where God failed."

Wing felt Rhusta's eyes cut to him, then quickly look away. Unable to tell what impression his response had—whether the old man had felt guilty, amused, or inclined to deride him for self-pity—Wing didn't really care.

If I can retain even half of what he's teaching me, Wing thought, *I'll be able to make it to Legran—finish one thing. After that, it doesn't really matter.*

Beside him, Rhusta gazed into the fire and, like Wing, said nothing.

CHAPTER 48

Surfacing

Wing awoke early one morning near the end of the fourth turn to find the old man already gone. Getting to his feet, he stretched and looked around the cabin wondering what there might be to make a morning meal of.

Walking across the room toward the small wood stove and cupboards beside them, he decided to take the opportunity while Rhusta was gone to look over the cabin wares that resembled the Rieevan style so closely. Rolling a jug slowly in his hand, both admiring and curious, Wing's eye caught a small brown-clad book in the midst of a long row on the second shelf of Rhusta's bookshelf. Setting the jug back in its place, Wing stepped to the bookshelf and pulled out the small brown book. Carefully, he opened its worn pages. There was a bit of scribbled writing in the margins that Wing did not recognize, yet the book and the text itself, he did recognize—it was a copy of the Ancient Writings. And it was in Rieevan.

How did Rhusta get a copy of the Ancient Writings in Rieevan?

Bewildered, Wing went to look in the front of the book where the family name and its history would be written, but caught only a glimpse of a name before he heard Rhusta upon the door of the cabin. Closing the book, he pushed it back between the others and took a few quick steps away from the old wooden shelf.

Rhusta stepped into the cabin, slapping dust off his leggings and hanging up his cloak. Wing greeted him carefully, his pulse racing out a lie against the bored look he was working his face into.

"You hungry?" Rhusta asked as he rounded the small table.

"No, thank you," Wing replied.

"That's different," Rhusta said, sitting down and removing his boots in the chair that sat right next to the bookshelf. Wing glanced sideways at the books, hoping he had not left something out of place that might catch

Rhusta's eye. But even as Wing thought it, he saw Rhusta's eyes flick to the small brown book that Wing had shoved too far into the bookshelf. Rhusta reached up and dug it out with one gnarled finger.

Wing thought he might throw up.

"Can you read?" Rhusta asked, his voice edged by the harsh tone Wing was accustomed to.

"Yes."

"In the Rieevan tongue?"

"Of course," Wing replied slowly.

"Well, here," he said, tossing him the book. "Tell me what you know about that."

Wing missed catching the book and bent to pick it up; he heard Rhusta sigh. Taking the book off the floor, Wing held it in his hands for a moment. Opening it, he looked it over, pretending to discover the contents before closing it again.

Rhusta raised a hand. "Don't. I want to see if you can translate a passage for me," he said, speaking as he usually did, in the Fultershier.

"I'd rather not," Wing said.

"Why not? It might be good for you."

"Good for me?" Wing said, the words spilling out before he could check them. "Maybe for another. I never found a point in it."

"Ah, so you *have* read it." Rhusta gave him a verse number. "Humour me."

A tremor in Wing's hand crinkled the pages as he turned to the verse. For the first time in what seemed like revolutions, he laid eyes again on those all too familiar passages. Sight of his native tongue set a chill to his skin even as it lit something hot in his bones.

Translating into the Fultershier as best he could, Wing began to read, but his voice was weak and the words that passed his lips were barely audible. "And Eosha will send the Leader. With him will come knowledge, light and power. His understanding and mercy will take in all lands and he will be Merehr, the leader of his people..."

Wing closed his eyes as he shut the book.

Rhusta leaned forward in his old wooden chair. "And you believe this, Rieevan?"

Wing shook his head. "No," he mumbled.

"You said 'no'?"

Wing handed the book back to Rhusta. "No. Not anymore."

"Do most Rieevans believe this book?"

Wing felt a cord tighten through the back of his shoulders. *Don't say it,* he thought. *He doesn't deserve to know—he wouldn't care.*

"Well?"

Rhusta's obstinate 'well?' touched off Wing's anger. "They *did*, yes."

"They *did*? Like you, they don't anymore?"

"No," Wing said. "They believed up until the end."

A deathly silence fell inside the room.

"The end?"

Wing slowly raised his eyes. "Death," he said. "They're all dead."

To Wing's own ears, it did not sound like his voice. And the words felt strange, unreal upon his tongue.

But then, he suddenly realized, *I've never said them before. My people are dead, I am the last of my race, and I had no one to tell. Not one human soul to tell—*

Until now.

Wing felt staggered by the truth of it. His anger mounted; anger that the first to know was a gruff old man who would not, for one moment, mourn the loss of an entire world—a culture, a people, a way of life. The old man would not miss the festivals and songs and laughter and nights by fireplaces and warm dinners and sweet, black dirt and snow under moonlight. The old man would not miss Wing's father, the Mesko Tender, the listener of the great trees. He would not miss Reean, the touch of her hands, the smell of her apron. Nor would he miss Carly, the thick curl of her hair, the look in her eye when she wanted to make love. And Nien.

Nien.

Wing felt as if a line of his own sinew was being ripped slowly from the space beneath and between his ribs. Like a dying beast, he felt a roar lurking at the back of his throat. He wanted someone to understand his pain, his loss, his rage. And the only one that could was the old man, for he was the only one present.

Slowly, Wing lifted his gaze.

The anger radiating off him raised the temperature of the room. His eyes shone like the white-hot flame of a swordsmith's forge.

When he'd first arrived at the cabin, he'd been near death. Rhusta's words to him then— 'You should just go back home' —had landed upon Wing with a jolt that he'd not had the strength to support. Now, he was healthy, physically at least, and the pain of that comment had lodged itself deeply into his core, a core like that of a star, one that might birth a galaxy or destroy one.

If the old man greeted his revelation now with his usual disdainful nonchalance, Wing would not suffer the insult, he would see the man dead.

Carefully, Rhusta said, "How?"

"Ka'ull." Wing saw a muscle twitch in Rhusta's cheek. The old man's spontaneous reaction, though minute, was enough to pierce a small hole in the zenith of Wing's rage. Some of the heat began to drain from his eyes, leaving them feeling glassy like fired earthenware and pale as an early Ime morning. "Believe in what you have here," Wing said, his voice a silver thread. "For there's nothing in that book worth interpreting. Not enough wisdom to save even one of those who believed in it so fully."

"But he did save one," Rhusta said cautiously, motioning at Wing with a hand. "You're alive, aren't you?"

The silence in the room was palpable.

"I wasn't saved," Wing said slowly. "I just happened to live. I just happened not to be there."

The old man did not look as if he had anything more to say.

Spent, Wing slipped by Rhusta and into the masquerading half-light cast by the fire at the other side of the cabin.

Early on, Rhusta had insinuated that four turns would be all he could tolerate having him around. Now, only a day of tracking lay between Wing and his continuing on to Legran.

He was happy for it. The grimness of his teacher had been good for him—with the skills he had learned, Wing felt confident he could make it to Legran in better condition than he'd arrived here. But he was also tired of the loneliness. Days spent out of doors with the old man were tolerable, but two men moving about in the silence of the cabin at night with nothing to say to each other was more than awkward, it was a torment, and now that Rhusta knew what had happened in Rieeve, why Wing had left, staying with him would be even more intolerable.

No sound at all came from Rhusta's side of the cabin. Usually, the old man would be snoring by now. Wing glanced over at him—a dim lump of shadow in the firelight.

Four turns here with Rhusta, eight since the night he'd left his home.

Wing shut his eyes to the darkness. Telling Rhusta had brought it all up again. The deep silence of the cabin pressed in on him and he tried for sleep, but like a well-trained boxer, it evaded his every effort, coming back with short jabs and punches, reminding him with every stroke: *You are the last of your race.*

Wing almost laughed. It was the final, cruelest joke that the last of the Rieevan race should be him, someone who looked nothing like his people, who shared not even one attribute that would place him as having been one of them—not the creamy white skin, nor brown hair the colour of Mesko bark, not even in eyes of hazel that changed with the season or the clothes he wore.

As he pictured their faces, he heard their voices in perfect memory:

"What have you seen, Son-Cawutt? Will we be protected?"

"Why won't you tell us? Are we not worthy of it? Are you testing us? Humiliating us!"

"What I am asking is that you at least think about joining the Cant."

"As you know, the people think you're the one. We're here to ask if you will believe in them as they believe in you."

"I've heard you can't be killed!"

"Is it true? Will you live forever?"

Was that why his people were dead? Because he hadn't listened? Because he'd denied them so many times?

Maybe it had nothing to do with the Ka'ull at all. Maybe it had nothing to do with the flaws in the Ancient Writings.

Maybe the only flaw had been in him.

Lant, Wing beseeched silently. *I'm so sorry.* He pressed his palms to his eyes. *I didn't listen to you. I didn't listen to them—*

"Merehr!"

Wing shook his head against the cry, grinding his palms against his face.

"Merehr!"

—A chorus of voices, growing steadily, a reverberating echo carried over mountain on moonlight, thrumming over and over...

"Merehr Merehr Merehr!"

Lurching to his feet, Wing swung out the cabin door and into the night.

At the other side of the room, Rhusta opened his eyes as the cabin door creaked shut. When he closed his eyes again, a sob escaped him. He pounded his face into his threadbare pillow and growled out a coarse torrent of tears.

CHAPTER 49

New Life, Still Hurt

With a bag of tools swinging from each shoulder, Nien made his way around to the sunrising wing of the house. Unlike so many other days, today he did not think about his father or Wing, nor was he reliving the days when the three would separate: Wing and their father heading into the Village for construction work whilst he headed toward the Cantfields. Today he was Sep, the man who had been taken in by a man called Monteray and a woman named Kate, and the sun was up and the gentle wind passing over the river carried a fresh floral scent from its banks. Passing by the doors to the large one-roomed edifice he had never yet entered, he bumped into Monteray.

"Good morning," Monteray said.

"And to you," Nien replied, noting a bundle hanging over Monteray's shoulder. "Traveling?"

"Yes. It's time to go see an old friend." He looked out toward the house. "Thanks for all the work you've done. I hate to leave right now, but—"

"It's fine. What needs to be done in the next little while can be done by one—for the most part."

"If you do need some help, have Kate send for Call. He *can* be useful."

"Will do."

Monteray paused for a moment, seeming to mentally go over what he had in his duffle. Shaking his head he turned back, saying, "I usually forget something." He stopped. "You haven't been inside the Mietan yet, have you?"

"No," Nien replied.

Monteray looked mockishly scandalized. "Well, it's about time you did. Come on in."

Nien unshouldered his burdens and followed Monteray.

Stepping in through the two massive doors, Nien could not help but pause. One large open space, everything about the Mietan fell upon the senses like a seduction. At one end sat a large dais with an unembellished chair, rich in its simplicity. The floor was laid with warm honey-coloured wood, ingrained with symbols that were pleasing to the eye, though none of which Nien recognized. There was in the air the scent and flavour of freshly cut wood, early morning sun, and the discrete tang of metal.

"This...this is a beautiful space."

Monteray turned a full circle, smiling. "I'm partial to it. Kate jokes that I built the house for her and this for me." Monteray led him about, explaining various keepsakes before coming to a section of wall containing a neat collection of various weapons. Reaching up, Monteray took down a long, slender sword. He moved it over his head, sweeping it in a graceful arc before suddenly striking out in two quick movements. The blade cut through the air in silence.

"This is a wonderful weapon," he said, pausing and holding it out in front of him, "one of the finest ever made in Jayak, and a special gift." He looked up at Nien. "You all right?"

Nien stood, knowing what he must look like to Monteray, but unable to make himself disguise the rigidity of his reaction.

Monteray replaced the sword onto its rack. "I guess I'd better get going—oh, wait," he said, and stepping over behind the dais, took up a small knife dressed in an elegant leather sheath. "A gift," he said. "Knew I forgot something."

Nien nodded in silence and followed Monteray back outside.

"Thanks again for all your help. I'll see you in a couple turns."

"Travel well," Nien managed to say, and quickly reshouldering the two bags of tools, disappeared around the corner of the Mietan.

CHAPTER 50

Legendary Ties

D ay broke early to find Rhusta and Wing on this, their last day
together, following a narrow trail above a steep ravine. They had
gone on until about noon when Wing stopped up short. He stood
unusually still, his eyes fixed, his head cocked slightly to one side.

Rhusta looked around to find Wing staring intently at a large overhanging tree.

"We shouldn't be here," Wing said, his voice a whisper.

Rhusta glanced at the tree and heard a low growl emanating from it.

Wing began to slowly back away. Rhusta moved ahead, following
Wing's push. Leaves rustled in the tree and a crack of snapping branches
split the air.

Rhusta was briefly aware of being shoved to the ground as over five
pendtars of black fury hit Wing in the chest, lifting him off his feet and
tossing him backward over the ravine.

Rhusta was scrambling back to his feet in the same moment his knees
hit the trail. He shot to the edge. What he saw halted him in his tracks,
overrode his senses...

Caught in the feral embrace of a shy'teh, Wing was spinning away
beneath him, plummeting down the ravine.

Bound like lovers in a dance of death, Wing and the shy'teh broke through
a swath of rocky boulders, hurtling into a free-slide avalanche of bone-
white scree.

For Wing, time had never moved more swiftly—or so slowly. Grabbing
out, desperate to find something, anything, to hold on to, he fought for his
life. But his reaching only found the rending claws of the shy'teh and the
jagged edges of sharp rock.

I'm going to die, flashed through his mind, just as one of his flailing hands caught hold of something solid.

With a wrenching yank that punched him sideways into the scabrous edges of slivered scree and nearly separated his shoulder, the fall terminated—

But the battle was far from over.

Wing managed to maintain his grip on the gnarled branch of mountain brush that had stopped the fall, but the shy'teh hung on as well—

To Wing.

With one set of great white claws, she dug into Wing's hip. With her other paw, she reached around, hooked his back, and pulled herself up.

Wing howled. Fire exploded in his back as muscle, sinew, and nerve felt sure to be ripped from the frame of his body. Recoiling, Wing tried to get his knees between his belly and hers, but theirs was a wild dance and he lost ground as quickly as he gained it.

Still fighting her with his legs, Wing struck out with his free hand, and managed to curl his fingers into her throat.

A snarl erupted from the shy'teh's barreled chest and she came at him with her teeth. Wing turned his head. She missed his face, and sank her four large fangs into his shoulder. Wing gasped, his own teeth locking around the air gushing out of his chest. Shockingly, his fingers were still dug into the furry mass of her throat, and he clamped down, succeeding in pushing her back.

But he was unable to sustain the mammoth effort for long.

As he felt the strength in his fingers draining out, the cat withdrew her teeth from his shoulder and came at his throat.

This is it, he thought. *Lant, I—*

A whisk of air whistled across his cheek followed by a solid *thwunk*.

The shy'teh jerked. Wing looked up. On top of him, the big cat quivered and her fierce gaze relaxed. Slowly, her claws released, her enormous head rolled to the side, and she began to slide off him. Her ribs caught briefly on his feet, then her front legs rotated over and she was tumbling down the ravine.

Wing couldn't believe it. He looked down. The large black mass that had, a moment before, been the most undefeatable life force he'd ever encountered, now lay at the bottom of the scree field, her body twitching intermittently from after-death reflex, an arrow pulsing in her side.

Wing stared down at her for an incredulous breath before his head fell back.

Upon the steep white field of tenuous rock, Wing found himself engulfed in an impossible silence. He was aware that the limbs of his body were shaking uncontrollably, that his lungs were working terribly hard to gather air. He knew what had happened.

—Somehow, it didn't matter.

All was stillness.

Slinging his bow over his shoulder, Rhusta scrambled through the brush and boulders, working his way to the scree field and Wing.

Coming down behind him, Rhusta made it to Wing's side only to have the scree shift beneath him. Digging in with the toes of his boots, Rhusta managed to stop his slide before he'd gone too far.

With a gulp, Rhusta crawled slowly, carefully, back up to Wing's side and latched onto the same scraggly, but thankfully stubborn, bit of mountain brush that had stopped Wing's fall. Kicking his feet through the scree, he struck dirt and bending over Wing, placed his hand upon Wing's face.

"Wing."

Wing lurched back into consciousness. His eyes were disoriented and terrified. He gasped, scrambling about as if the scree were sliding beneath him again.

"Wing!" Rhusta yelped. "It's all right. I've got you, I've got you!"

Wing either couldn't hear or didn't believe Rhusta's imploration because he continued to claw frantically at the scree in an effort to save himself, pushing out against Rhusta as if the old man were trying to harm him.

"Be still, Wing!" Rhusta shouted in Rieevan. This time Rhusta's voice cut through Wing's delirium and he stopped struggling. "All right," Rhusta said, continuing to talk to him. "Now lie still for a moment. I'm going to take a look."

Rhusta's weathered old hands began to move skillfully over Wing's body, assessing the damage beneath the torn and bloodied clothing. No limbs were misaligned; no bones had broken through the skin. But the rakes and punctures of the long claws had Wing bleeding savagely and Rhusta knew there was no way to tell what internal injuries there might be.

"Everything…everything's going to be fine," Rhusta stammered, tearing the shirt from his own back. "You stay with me and we'll get you back to the cabin." Pulling the shirt into strips, he bound up the two wounds that were bleeding the most profusely. "It's going to be fine, we…we just need to get us out of here. I'll need you to help." Rhusta's throat constricted. *Please,* he begged an unseen source, *please let him be able to walk.*

Climbing out of a scree field would have been a treacherous feat under any circumstance, but as wounded and delirious as Wing was it seemed the odds of Rhusta being able to get them both back to safe ground were beyond consideration.

But there was nothing else to do.

In response to Rhusta's imploration, Wing moved a little, attempting to push himself up in the loose rock, but his knee kept slipping. Rhusta persisted, and Wing finally made it to his hands and knees.

The two began their climb.

Like birds tethered to a frightened fent, they scrambled and slid, plunged ahead, and fell back. Rhusta supported Wing as best he could, striving to keep them in a moving-up direction when the nature of the scree field was to carry them down—and that wasn't the only thing the pair had working against them. Wing's uncoordinated and jerking effort was making the impossible more difficult still.

Nevertheless, Wing's effort swelled Rhusta's heart as he continued to try, doggedly pouring all he had into every excruciating step.

But his body could not forever answer the will of his mind; Wing's knee twisted beneath him. As he hit rock and began to slide, Rhusta managed to maintain a grip on his arm.

Hanging onto Wing's arm, Rhusta reached out for something secure above him.

Step by precarious step, Rhusta succeeded in bringing them out of the scree field and into the belt of boulders below the ridge of the ravine.

Hitting his knees and rolling onto his back, Rhusta could hardly believe what they'd accomplished. The feat set off a tiny, triumphant spark in his heart.

Beside him, Wing lay dragged out, his body liquid, his eyes closed.

"We did it," Rhusta said, but there was not the faintest reaction from Wing. Rhusta pushed himself up and grabbed Wing by the shoulders. "Merehr!" he cried. "Don't you dare!" Pressing an ear against Wing's lips, he felt breath whisper upon his cheek. "Yes. You're still in there. Now, come back, come on, open your eyes. I still need your help." Rhusta slapped Wing's face.

Wing's eyes rolled and his eyelids opened.

"Good," Rhusta said, sighing in relief. "Let's get us out of here. Just put your arm around here."

Reaching down, Rhusta drew Wing's arm around his shoulders and pulled him to his feet.

The air in Wing's lungs escaped in a concussive wave and a terrible rattle sounded in his throat.

Hang on, Rhusta silently implored. *Just hang on…*

Back at the top of the ravine and the game trail upon which they'd been traversing at the time of the attack, Rhusta lowered Wing to the ground again, panting heavily, brushing at the sweat stinging his eyes.

Briefly coherent, Wing muttered, "I'm sorry."

"We'll make it," Rhusta said, his head lowering over Wing as he bore through the spasms of pain burning his joints and lancing his shoulders. "We'll make it. Just stay with me."

But Wing was fading. Rhusta could not get him to open his eyes again or speak.

The trip back to the cabin passed for Wing in fleeting spikes of white pain, sweeping black nausea, and flashes of blue that had nothing to do with the sky overhead.

After that there was only the glow of the fire beside the place on the floor where Rhusta had laid him and the occasional snatches of Rieevan words whispered just beyond his hearing.

For two nights he lay in the throes of a feverish delirium, unaware of Rhusta's fight to preserve his life, of the constant vigil Rhusta kept at his side cleansing the sweat from his body, tending to his wounds, speaking to him in surprisingly soothing tones.

It was sometime during the third night when Wing tried to stand in answer to a familiar voice...

"Come on, Wing. If you don't get up and we don't meet Fa out in the fields, he'll have our hides."

"Nien?"

"Yeah, it's me, let's go."

"Nien, wait. I need help."

"I know, little brother."

Wing took a step toward his brother, but the ground fell away beneath him and he plummeted into a bottomless black.

Rhusta sat up in his chair. Wing had come awake with a short cry and there was a wild, frightened look in his eyes as he searched the darkness.

Rhusta started to his side.

"Nien?" Wing said to him, his voice sounding pale and strange in the darkness. "Brother?"

Rhusta stopped.

Wing shoved clumsily at the blankets covering him. "Carly. I've missed you. Father, we're coming!"

Wing coughed, and Rhusta saw him squint into the darkness at him, as if he were trying to make out who he was.

"Nien?" Wing asked again. "I'm tired, Nien. Really tired. I don't think I can do this."

Rhusta started to answer—but no words came. As he was about to try again, Wing's eyes closed.

Turning, Rhusta stirred the coals in the fireplace and with their soft red glow filling the room, retired to his corner of the cabin.

CHAPTER 51

With You, The Most Trusted Things

A day later and only briefly, Wing came around again, this time to the world of the living. His eyes found Rhusta as the old man sat in his chair, threading a piece of tanned leather.

"Did you find the cub?" Wing asked, his tongue slow in forming the question.

"Cub?" Rhusta replied, leaning forward in his chair. "What cub?"

"The shy'teh's cub."

For a moment, Rhusta wondered how coherent Wing really was.

"By the tree," Wing muttered. "At the base of the tree, under the bushes."

"I saw no cub. Go to sleep now."

"Find it," Wing said, and his eyes closed.

Rhusta lay awake in the darkness as sleep played the elusive hope.

Could Wing be right? he wondered. That the shy'teh had attacked to protect a cub was logical, but had Wing actually seen it?

Rhusta was attuned to the forest, to every space and nuance in the hills and mountains surrounding his home, but he would never expect to be aware of a shy'teh's cub. Seeing an adult shy'teh was an occurrence so rare that most wondered if the big cats were more legend than reality.

Nevertheless...

It seemed Rhusta had only just fallen to sleep when a knock came upon the old cabin door.

Grumbling, Rhusta pushed himself from his bed and stumbled across the room. On the other side of the door gleamed the familiar face of an old friend.

"Rhusta!"

Rhusta blinked a few times before stepping back from the doorway, allowing Monteray to enter.

"How are you?" Monteray asked. "Did I wake you?"

"Actually, yes." Rhusta scrubbed at his eyes. "Come in, come in. Let me wake up and I'll get us something to drink."

Monteray entered, and laying his duffel beside the door, noticed the long stretch of blankets spread out near the fireplace.

"That's the reason the sun's up and I'm still trying to rub the bugs from my eyes," Rhusta said, placing two cups on the table.

"Who is it?"

"Wing Cawutt—Merehr, as my people used to call him."

"That's Wing?"

"You've heard of him?"

"From Lant, yes. He certainly doesn't look Rieevan."

"I know. Neither do I." Looking around, Rhusta swore.

Monteray spotted Rhusta's small black pot and handed it to him.

"Thanks."

"I know I'm earlier than you expected, but—"

"Had another of your premonitions?"

Monteray didn't directly answer, saying instead, "There have been some things happening that I wanted to talk with you about." Glancing at Wing, he added, "Looks like I'm not the only one."

Rhusta grunted in reply.

Monteray watched Rhusta fill the little pot with water and hang it over the rousing fire. "Why did you say your people *used* to call him Merehr?"

Rhusta went to speak, but his voice stalled.

Monteray noticed a tremble in his old friend's hand. A sick feeling like the first drops of a flash flood, trickled into his stomach.

"The Rieevans are dead, Mont," Rhusta said. "Killed by the Ka'ull."

Time stopped. As if a great section of loose cliff rock had shaken free, Monteray felt his heart plunge into a silence so profound he almost forgot to breathe.

"We knew they'd taken Lou." Rhusta said, his voice wavering. "We *knew.*"

"And Tou," Monteray said. He still wasn't sure he could speak. "So this man escaped? The Rieevans are now enslaved as well?"

Rhusta shook his head. "No, Mont."

And Monteray understood: The Ka'ull had no plans to enslave Rieeve. What they wanted was the land. A staging area. Monteray had already suspected this, as Lant had. Still, he could not get himself to think the thought, much less say the words.

Rhusta said them instead: "The Rieevans have been annihilated."

Monteray felt...he didn't know *how* he felt. Emotions spun through him in a crushing kaleidoscope. "Are you sure?"

"Merehr said it. You can believe it."

"When?"

"He's been here nearly five turns. I don't know how long it took him to get this far."

Monteray swallowed, the very air in his lungs felt foreign, deadly. "We waited too long," he breathed. "When the Ka'ull were driven from Jayak we didn't bother to find out where they'd gone."

Or it could have been a completely different force, come down the river and through the pass from Tou. Either way, Monteray thought, running his hands through his thick greying hair, *We didn't bother to find out, and now...*

Monteray froze.

Lant. Lant!

Monteray's eyes shot to Rhusta. "Did Wing say anything of Commander Lant? Have you seen him? He knew what was coming. He would have made it out..."

"No," Rhusta said with great difficulty. "No word of him."

Netaia, Monteray thought. *My dearest friend.*

Of course Lant could have made it out of Rieeve, but Monteray knew with certainty that he hadn't—

Because he knew Lant had chosen to stay.

Overcome, Monteray felt he might slide to the floor, disappear, surrender entirely to the incredulity, the lightning realization of loss that burned his mind and heart...

"Mont," Rhusta said, "pull it together. Wing, there, he needs you."

Monteray strove beneath the elucidation before latching onto Rhusta's words.

He's right, Monteray told himself, *you'll be no good for anything if you don't.* But the only way he could find of doing so was to set aside all thought of Lant—at least for the time being.

Clearing his throat of enough emotion to be able to speak, Monteray said, "In all the time Wing's been here, he's said nothing more? No details. Only what you've told me?"

"That's it." Rhusta's eyes betrayed him. "But I haven't asked him any more—not yet."

"Dear Gods, Rhusta," Monteray said quietly.

"What?"

"You haven't told him?"

A flash of anger and shame twisted Rhusta's face. "No. And don't start—" Rhusta jerked the pot from the fireplace and placed it too roughly on the table.

Monteray's attention returned to rest upon Wing. As he looked at him, a puzzle began to piece itself together in his mind. His mouth gaped. "About seven turns ago," he said, "Kate found a man, a Preak man, out by the river. The thing was, he was dressed in the clothing of the Rieevan Cant and near dead from battle wounds. We took him in, tended to him. He has been working with me on the house and staying in our cabin since that time."

Rhusta listened. After a bit, he said, "Nien Cawutt, his brother" —he pointed to Wing— "was Preak. The only Rieevan of Preak origin I've ever heard of."

"Well, this man wore what I assumed to be the symbol of the Cant's First on his shoulder-mantle." Incredulous, Monteray shook his head. "I suspected...No," he whispered, "*I knew.*"

"It appears," Rhusta said, "that both brothers have attempted to find you since the attack. It makes sense that one succeeded while the other did not."

Monteray raised an eyebrow in question.

"Wing knew his fields only. But Nien...Well, he was uncommonly adventurous for a Rieevan, and knowledgeable. He knew more about our world than any of his people, except for Lant."

"I remember. Lant often spoke of him." Monteray's features were leaden. "But he is not that same man, now." Which might have been an additional factor, Monteray realized, in why he'd questioned his initial hunch about Nien.

Beside him, Rhusta was quiet a beat before replying, "Neither is he."

Both their eyes returned to Wing.

In disbelief, Monteray stared at Wing's long form beneath the blankets.

Incredible, he thought. *In this room, in the blood and body of the man lying on the floor and the man standing beside him resided the mysterious and singular code to a people now extinct.*

"The Rieevans." Monteray's voice was stone laden. "Lant. Pree K. All their people. With such news—how have you managed to keep your identity from him?"

Though Rhusta did not answer, the pain of his silence was plain to see.

"How does something like this happen?" Monteray asked. "Have we been asleep? I am so sorry, my friend…we are too late. Too late with everything."

"I was lost to my people long ago," Rhusta said quietly, "but this young man here…He, he was their hope. It's really been a thing watching him, being around him."

"I can imagine," Monteray said. "We were blessed, Rhusta, that he found his way to you and his brother to me."

Rhusta nodded slowly. "Whoever would have thought all this?"

"Not I," Monteray replied. "Not in three lifetimes." He tilted his head toward Wing. "He's been here four turns you say?"

"A little over five now."

Monteray got up from his seat and walked across the room to Wing. "What happened to him?"

"We were attacked by a shy'teh. They went over a ridge. Between the fall and the big cat he's lucky to be alive."

"A shy'teh attack? Strange. I've never heard of one of the big cats attacking anyone—a good thing, since I don't know how anyone could survive it." Standing over Wing, Monteray looked for clues. "How *did* he? Was it you?"

Rhusta shook his head. "I put her down with an arrow, but it was the fall that saved him. He got in that shape because the cat was trying to save herself."

"Is there something I can do?"

"You can take a look at his leg."

Monteray squatted down and pulled back the blanket from Wing's right leg. It was swollen, purplish-blue in colour. He felt it carefully. "The one bone, lower leg," he said, palpating very slowly. "I can't feel anything that would suggest the bone has separated. No matter how severe the fracture may be, immobilizing it as you have is all we can do. As long as the blood flow isn't interrupted it should heal well enough." Monteray covered Wing's leg again. "You think that he and his brother are the last of the Rieevans—besides yourself?"

Rhusta shrugged. "Hard to say. Seems so."

"If your people also gave him this title of Merehr, then is he not someone who could understand your past? Your heart?"

"My heart died with my past," Rhusta said, something indescribable in his voice. "Looks like his is headed the same direction."

Monteray knew what Rhusta meant and said nothing more about it. For a time, the two friends watched Wing as he lay, far too still and far too silent.

"You said you thought both brothers were trying to find me. So why did Wing come here?"

"He didn't come here," Rhusta replied, "he **ended up** here. He was lost."

"Funny," Monteray said thoughtfully, "that he managed to happen upon a tiny cabin in the southing reaches of the Ti Mountain Range and yet could not find the valley of Legran." Monteray was not surprised to find that Rhusta was avoiding his eyes. "So why me?" he asked.

"Lant—who else? He thought a great deal of the Cawutt brothers. It's no doubt they knew quite a bit about you. Perhaps they saw you as their only hope. I'm planning on sending Wing on to you when he's healed enough to travel. You can do more for him than I can."

"He's a remarkable-looking individual," Monteray said of Wing. "Tall, straight build, striking features. No wonder your people singled him out. What can you tell me about him personally?"

"In Rieeve he liked to be alone. He worked his father's fields. He was very" —it seemed Rhusta was searching for the right words or a way to say them— "connected. Well, connected not so much with people but with…"

"The land?" Monteray asked.

"Well that, too," Rhusta said sharply, obviously frustrated at being unable to adequately describe what he knew. "I don't know, Mont…he saw into things in a way most of us usually don't." Rhusta shrugged off the discomforting exchange. "But that was back then."

Monteray understood. The heart kept no time, recognized no statutes, no frames surrounding events. It held no regard for the dial of the sun. Trauma such as the young Rieevan had been through could press one through a lifetime of change in a single moment.

"I know what he used to be," Rhusta said. "I have no idea what I'll be sending on to you."

"Do you think he has any idea who you are?"

Rhusta shook his head. "No."

"His brother, he's helping me with my home. He's a skilled builder."

"They both are," Rhusta said. "Their father, Joash Cawutt, was the Mesko Tender and an excellent builder, easily the finest in Rieeve."

The conversation was spent there. Rhusta had probably said more since Monteray had come through the door on this trip than in all of Monteray's other visits combined.

Getting up, Rhusta stepped to the door and taking up his leather coat, said, "Let's take a walk. You can help me."

"Help with what?" Monteray asked, reaching for his own coat.

"There's something I need to look for."

A fair hike taken in virtual silence found them at the top of a steep ridge littered with scree.

"What are we doing?" Monteray asked.

"This is where Wing fell; where the shy'teh attacked."

Not exactly an answer, Monteray thought as the two moved along the upper edge of the scree field.

Glancing over the edge, Monteray shivered a little. If this was where Wing had fallen it was a miracle he was still alive, and that Rhusta had made it down to him without sliding to his own death…

Monteray stopped. At the bottom of the field lay a large, twisted shadow: the dead shy'teh.

He was about to say something when Rhusta drew up in order to silence the crunching of rock beneath his feet. Monteray watched as Rhusta knelt down and moved forward on his hands and knees to a short stand of scraggly bush beneath a stand of thin deciduous trees.

Monteray came up behind as Rhusta parted the leaves. Inside lay a mottle of black fur. With a stick, Rhusta poked at the black ball. It did not move. Reaching in, Rhusta pulled the black mass from its shelter. It was a shy'teh cub. Dead. At first glance it appeared to be no more than a few turns old, but upon closer inspection the size of its bones placed the cub's age at nearly a season. It must have been sick for some time.

Rhusta sat back on his heels with a sad sigh, then moving a little way up the hill began to dig. Beside him, Monteray dug in silence. They placed the cub's body in the shallow grave and stood for a time over the mound of rocky soil.

Though Monteray could not put his finger on it, there was a sacred feeling about the place—even though it had seen the death of two rare creatures. Peculiar and affecting, Monteray wondered if Rhusta could better detail the undefined sense of the place, what had happened, and what it might mean. So many ties to Rieeve. The death of a secretive, isolated race. The death of not one, but two shy'teh. And that one of those shy'teh had attacked the man thought by his people to be their holy Leader.

He wondered what Lant would say.

Rhusta and Monteray had nearly made it back to the cabin when Monteray asked, "What made you think the shy'teh that attacked you had a cub?"

Rhusta lifted his gaze. "It was Wing. He knew."

Monteray's brow furrowed. "How?"

Rhusta shrugged a little. "Because he's Wing."

The cabin was quiet. Monteray had fallen asleep in Rhusta's bed as Rhusta sat beside the wood stove in his old chair, reading by firelight.

"Rhusta?"

Rhusta started and looked up from his book. "Rieevan."

"Did you find the cub?" Wing asked.

Glancing nervously at Monteray's sleeping form, Rhusta got up from his chair, and stepping to Wing's side, squatted down beside him. "Yes, Wing. I did."

"Were you in time?"

Rhusta shook his head. "No, I'm sorry. The cub was already dead. I think it had been sick for some time."

Wing squeezed his eyes closed. "I'm sorry," he said. "I'm sorry." And as he turned his head and fell to sleep again, Rhusta knew Wing had not been talking to him.

Rhusta and Monteray passed most of the next few days outdoors, walking, talking, fishing and preparing herbs to lessen pain and encourage healing in Wing's battered body.

On the morning of the fourth day, Monteray gathered his things to leave, for even though Wing's moments of coherency and waking were few, Monteray wanted to respect Rhusta's wish to remain anonymous, a thing that would be difficult to maintain if Wing woke to see Monteray there.

"As soon as he can travel, I'll be sending him on to you." Rhusta forced a short smile, a thing that was not particularly suited to his face. "He's been pretty adamant about getting to Legran all along. I don't imagine it will take much convincing."

Monteray's eyes denoted something of hope and concern as he, too, forced a small smile. "Oh, here, I brought this for you." Digging into his travel bag, Monteray produced the short blade he'd almost forgotten the day he left Legran. "I know how you go through them."

Rhusta took the knife and placed his tough old hand on Monteray's shoulder. "With you, again, are the most precious matters entrusted."

Monteray inclined his head respectfully to Rhusta and, shouldering his duffel, walked away across the long clearing and into the trees.

CHAPTER 52

Alive to Die

A twig snapped beneath his foot. He froze. Glancing about, he sunk slowly to his belly…and listened. Only the sound of the forest filled his ears. With practiced, but tired eyes he scanned the woods— And saw nothing.

Sighing heavily, he rolled onto his back and placed a hand over his racing heart. It was no good today. He was too tired and becoming clumsy. He looked over his shoulder. *How can I return to them with nothing?* All the traps they'd set three days ago he'd found empty today. And the few bushes within half a day's walk that were still bearing edible fruit were becoming depleted. To reach more abundant berry shrubs he would have to travel farther than he cared to, and it would be dark soon. He had little choice but to return. Picking up the five animal skins, heavy with water, he checked the woods once more, and began the slow trek back.

By now, he knew every twist and turn of his cave home. He could navigate it even in the black—and he usually did—at least until he reached the inner chamber. Before entering there he always lit a torch, for no one in that horrible and hallowed place needed surprising.

Holding the torch behind him, he ducked into the room. Pale and silver as moonlight through mist, faces—set with wet glimmering eyes— squinted up at him through drawn hoods and cowling blankets.

He swallowed heavily, and attempting to suppress the burning pain in his heart, set the torch into a holder in the cave wall and let the water skins slide from his shoulders.

"Pree K," a voice said from across the cave.

Pree K nodded to Jhock as his friend stood to help him with the water. He could see in Jhock's eyes how weathered he must have looked—there was more concern there than usual.

"It's all right," Jhock said quietly. "We'll go out together tomorrow. Maybe our luck will change."

Just then a taller young man stepped up to them. "It's my turn to go tomorrow," he said. "The two of you have been going out every day for nearly a turn."

"But your father—"

"Will be served best if the two of you get some rest."

Pree K and Jhock acquiesced in silence. Only En't's father, Grek Occoju, who had once been the Rieevan Council Spokesman, remained of the adult men. He had been sick off and on with fever and cold for two turns now.

The three young men rationed out the water for the night then blew out all but one of the torches and curled up in their tattered blankets.

The anxious and sad faces of En't's little brother and two baby sisters as well as the only other little girl still living, Lily, would not leave Pree K's mind even as he closed his eyes. They hadn't complained or given voice to their hunger and cold tonight—indeed they hadn't for a long time. Even after Lily had lost both her mother and her father, she'd cried only once. Nevertheless, Pree K knew that every day as he, Jhock, or En't left to go out for water or on the hunt for food, the children watched them leave and passed the terrible sunsteps in fear, wondering: Would this be the last time they saw their protectors and providers? Were they leaving now and, like so many of the rest, never coming back?

CHAPTER 53

Obvious Revelation

As the days after Monteray's visit progressed, Wing seemed to slip into the rhythm of the planet and his body began to heal rapidly, its energy threading through daylight into moonlight, rising and falling spherically from sunrise to sunset.

In regular cycles of consciousness and sleep, Wing had begun to eat and his body showed signs of improving strength. Though far from healed, it was not long before he felt the need to get on to the destination he originally had in mind: Legran.

On the eve before his departure, night drew fittingly across the mountains quilting a thin layer of shadows and eventually bedding the world down for rest.

Wing lay in the silent darkness of the cabin—awake—wondering if sleep would come to him tonight.

At some point, however, it must have, for the next thing Wing knew he was being nudged awake by the old man.

"It's time you were up and out of here," Rhusta said without preamble.

Wing opened his eyes and rolled over with an expression of surprise and confusion, wondering what had gotten under Rhusta's skin already this morning.

Getting up slowly and pointedly ignoring the prepared breakfast on the table, Wing threw the new long sleeved cloak he had made for himself over his shoulder, slipped on his tall leather boots, picked up his bow and arrows, and headed out the door.

He had only made it partway across the clearing when a voice rang out—

"Merehr!"

Wing came to a slow stop.

"Son Cawutt-Merehr!"

Beneath a rising sun that had suddenly frozen in its heavenly orbit, Wing turned around.

Just outside the door to the cabin, Rhusta stood, gazing at Wing across the clearing.

Wing had never told Rhusta his surname; but that was the least astonishing thing—

Merehr?

And then Wing recalled a singular feeling, an impression of indefinable familiarity he'd experienced with Rhusta that first morning in the cabin.

Apparently, Wing thought, *I hadn't imagined that.*

Walking forward, Rhusta bridged the gap between them. A few steps away, he stopped. "Wing Merehr."

Wing stood motionless.

"I know your name," the old man said. "I know *you.* Unfortunately, even when one leaves, not everything is left behind." He looked Wing over for a moment. Then speaking in a fluid and reverent tone the melodic language of Rieeve, said: "I was one of them, too, you know. I would read the Ancient Writings as a child and dream of meeting the Leader in the flesh. Then it all went backwards—they thought it was me."

Wing's eyes wavered. He felt stomach ill.

Rhusta continued. "I know you think I could never understand what you felt, what you went through growing up in Rieeve. But I have a pretty good idea."

The two gazed at one another for a lingering moment, and Wing suddenly saw with a clarity so painful and obvious he felt stupid...

"Rhegal," he muttered.

Rhusta met Wing's eyes. " 'Merehr,' " he said softly. "Never has a word been wrought with such hope or such peril. Your heart lifts and sinks with the hearing, doesn't it?"

But Wing could only stare. Here, before him, stood the one who had rejected the prophetic calling of the Leader and fled. Wing had been a child.

"They thought I was everything the Ancient Writings said the Leader should be. Do you know how I repaid their belief?"

Wing's voice came back faint, barely audible, "You disappeared."

Rhusta's eyes narrowed and he nodded. "Yes." A long pause followed. "I don't know if our people were any more right about you than they were about me. And I don't know if you are who you are because of that belief, or for other reasons altogether, but here is what I *do* know..." Rhusta's eyes suddenly shone, leaping with an incandescent light both surprising and intense. "I have seen you in your fields," he said. "I have seen you in the

Mesko forest with your brother and your father. I have seen the care that is in your hands, and I have witnessed moments of pain when you thought no one else could see you. In short," Rhusta said, his voice surprisingly gentle, "watching you has changed my mind about many things I was once unalterably sure of."

Wing had no idea how to reply to such a confession. He, indeed, had no idea how to settle any of it in his mind, so he gazed back at Rhusta in silence, awe-struck and ill-equipped, thinking only, *All those times in the fields in Rieeve when I felt a presence, like I was being watched...It was him.*

"Our people may have failed us," Rhusta said. "Or maybe we failed them. I guess all that is now irrelevant."

Closing the distance between them, Rhusta reached out and—for the first time in Wing's waking moments—Rhusta touched him, placing his rough, aging hand upon Wing's arm.

As rooted as a giant Mesko to the spot where he stood, Wing wavered slightly, unable to speak, hardly able to feel until Rhusta pressed something into his hands. Wing looked down and saw the small brown book of the Ancient Writings Rhusta had kept on his bookshelf. His gaze locked unseeingly upon it as Rhusta handed him two more things: a seasoned stave and one simple length of the green wood they'd cut together.

Rhusta nodded at them and said, "You know how. Take your time. You might need them."

Wing raised his eyes.

"I have not always been what you see here," Rhusta said. "But I have, all these revolutions, let my failure, my own fear and resentment, get the better of me. I have done all I can for you—so I want you away from here. I want you to run, for you have been hurt, and you are angry, and you are frightened, and if you don't re-find your reason for living, you will die, no matter what I've taught you, and all that you are, and all that you're meant to be, will be wasted."

Rhusta's words drained Wing of strength.

Though there had been those who refused to say it, Wing had heard Rhegal's name spoken often throughout his life and on more than one occasion by his own father. For Wing, Rhegal had been a figure, an idea, larger and yet more tragically real than almost any other.

Wing remembered how he had often wondered what the man Rhegal had felt, what he'd gone through, why he'd left. To know, now, that he'd spent nearly seven turns with the man...

There were so many things he could have asked him. So much they could have shared.

Trembling, partly compelled and partly resistant, Wing met the blue-grey gaze of his provider, healer, and guide.

"I...?" Wing stammered. In the word was both a plea and a question.

But Rhegal merely nodded his head and urged him to go.

It felt as if each boot weighed a pendtar as Wing began to back away.

Rhusta backed away as well, watching with silent, smoke-filled eyes.

At last, Wing turned about, and began to run.

Wing ran for a distance far longer than his healing body should have endured but much less than his mind needed to quiet the questions raging inside it. Over rock and root, game trail and gnarled underbrush, Wing's thoughts consumed the path like a man starved until the terrible pain in his leg snapped him back into the reality of that leg's still-healing break.

He came to an abrupt halt and looked about.

Though the sun was not yet growing heavy in the sky, Wing knew he'd be going no further today.

A fire, he thought, and began hunting for firewood, only then did he notice the book he still held in his hand. He looked at it and couldn't believe he'd traveled the better part of a day without even noticing he was holding it.

Later, as evening drew in and the flames of his fire licked up against the darkening sky, Wing opened the duffel Rhegal had provided, and placed the book inside it.

Stretching out onto his back, he gazed up into the darkness. He needed to collect his thoughts, to try and find a place where he could rest easy with them. But the effort was impossible; he'd pressed his body too far. The pain raced up and down the mending bone in his leg, and his head throbbed dully.

Tomorrow. Yes, tomorrow he would wake to find Rhegal a mere imagining and Rhusta exactly who he'd thought he was. There was no way the Rhegal of his childhood could possibly occupy the same body as the man he'd just spent all those turns with...

Sleep embraced Wing mid-contemplation.

Dawn bled through the hills of darkness, its bright rays creasing the lines along Wing's sleeping face. By the time he'd awoken, covered the fire, and repacked his things the shock and confusion of the previous day had slipped into the barred regions of his mind. The goal of reaching Legran came back full and foremost in his thoughts.

Rhusta had given him a hand-drawn map, plotting out the least strenuous route to Legran. Wing had missed the valley in the first place by veering off a direct course to the sunrising and going instead to the south-sunrise. Healthy, it would have taken less than a turn to get back to it, but the break in his leg made such a pace impossible. The terrible wounds in his back and hip where the shy'teh's claws had grappled him were stiff with scabs, and still sore to lie upon.

So each day he traveled as far as his leg permitted, and when the pain became too much he would rest, fish, and bathe in any number of bubbling streams he found along the way.

He now moved through the mountains as if he belonged. Rather than trying to take his life, the mountains had become a friend, offering life without question, without promise of reward or punishment.

A day or two beyond a turn passed as if it were a day. Lying on a bed of tree boughs, Wing watched the stars.

Tomorrow he'd be in Legran.

The notion struck him as fantastical. Rieeve seemed forever ago.

Running a few sentences through his mind in the Legrand language, Wing placed his hands behind his head and watched the insects play around his fire.

"Careful," he admonished them softly. "I understand the attraction, but it'll melt your wings off."

Closing his eyes, he happily let the night come.

Tomorrow, he would at last, reach his goal. Tomorrow, it would be done, and to these mountains he'd return to live whatever remained of his life.

CHAPTER 54

Into Legran

Moving steadily, his eyes trained ahead, Wing followed a well-beaten path down a narrow canyon that emptied into a street of Legran.

Just inside the trees at the mouth of the canyon, Wing paused for a moment to observe and gain his bearings. His heart beat quickly. He took a breath to steady his nerves. He'd never seen another race; he'd never dreamed, as Nien had, that he'd ever visit another valley.

From descriptions given him long ago by Nien and more recently by Rhusta, Legran was a valley only slightly larger than Rieeve and, in general, its native population were smaller than Rieevans and stockier in build, with light eyes and brown hair. It was also a haven for travelers and traders.

Taking a peek in a nearby stream at himself, Wing tucked his hair behind his ears and, with a tilt of his head, appraised the look.

His hair was considerably shorter having been cut by Rhusta sometime after the shy'teh attack. His clothing was rustic and showed some mountain wear. And over his shoulder he had the duffel and the green staves of Legrand make.

I might actually pass for a trader, Wing thought, thinking it funny that he might actually blend in better in this foreign valley than he ever had in his own.

Wing proceeded out of the trees and onto the dirt trail that soon turned into a street of long flat stones. The street grew wider as it made its way into town, breaking off into smaller roads like the branching of a tree. On the main road, the wheels of carts and moveable stands created a steady undercurrent of noise upon which floated a noisy mashing of countless voices. On display in carts and small, open wood-frame shops, Wing took in the colorful array of merchandise for sale: beads and fine linens, animal pelts and fresh meat, pots of clay and wilting vegetables, jewelry and high leather boots, weapons of blade and wood. Most of the traders were dressed in the poorest of materials, clothing that was torn and ragged—as Wing had looked before coming to Rhegal's. But the rest were dressed much like Wing was now, in skins, with what they owned packed on their backs or slung over their shoulders with frayed rope and worn leather straps.

Wing's hope for blessed anonymity soared—until he'd gone about one half-street. From behind booths, shop-owners looked up and stared. Traders and street shoppers paused in their selling and purchasing long enough to watch as he walked passed.

Confused, his heart beginning to race, Wing adjusted the bow and leather quiver against his back and glanced ahead. The many long lines of the open market passed into a section of brief inns and plentiful pubs not too far from where he was.

Perfect, Wing thought. *I need to get out of here and think. Or, I could just turn around and run back into the woods.* That last bit of thought amused him, which, in turn, served to imbue his courage. *What I really need is to find Master Monteray. Just,* he admonished himself, *don't look like you're lost.*

Raising his face, Wing pretended to be bored with the vendors and their wares and began scanning faces, taking them in before they had time to do likewise—but he might as well have been on exhibition. Even those surrounding bartering tables paused and stared openly as he walked by.

Finally nearing the end of the open-market street, Wing's eyes narrowed in on a pub over which hung a large wooden sign that read, "*Hiona,*" in flowing purple letters.

Though he did not know why, the look of the word, the sign, even the general set of the pub's face felt familiar. Safe.

With deep relief, Wing crossed the dusty, stone-laid road, the limp in his leg lending a strange authenticity to the nonchalance he faked.

As he approached the pub, he caught the eyes of a young man leaning casually against the poorly constructed wood-frame building beneath the wooden sign that said "Hiona". The boy was holding a leather-clad journal in one hand and in his other, a writing brush. Something quickened in Wing's chest. Though still a few paces out, Wing thought he recognized the brush to be of Rieevan make. Instantly, his brain argued that he couldn't possibly be sure about that; nevertheless, there was no mistaking the pounding of his heart—

Wing walked straight up to the boy as if it were he that he'd been looking for all along.

"Good morning," Wing said.

The boy's easy manner skipped town. He started to say something only to have his words come out as an ill-collected jumble across his thin lips. He shifted feet nervously and a lock of light hair fell down over his big eyes, their colour reminiscent of a clear Ime day.

Wing smiled ever so slightly and said in well-rehearsed Legrand: "I was wondering if you could direct me to the home of Master Monteray."

The young man's eyes sparked with the clarity of moonlight through fine glass. The apprehension in his features fled. "How did you—Monteray is my uncle! I can take you there if you like."

Wing managed to keep the relief and wonder that lit inside him from showing. "I *would* like—very much."

The boy's face broke into a broad grin of white, uneven teeth, and to the dismay of those gawking from shop fronts, the two walked off together.

A short distance out of town the unlikely pair entered a long stretch of fields. As the green and golden grasses brushed by Wing's boots a familiar calm embraced him. The tension fell out of his shoulders and his heart stilled to a pace that Wing had not thought he would ever experience again.

Glancing at the young man beside him, Wing said, "Since everyone in town believes we know one another so well, you might as well tell me your name."

"It's Call. Who are you?"

"Wing Cawutt."

"You from Criye? You managed to stir up the town."

"Criye?" Wing asked curiously. "No. I'm Rieevan."

"Rieeve?" It was said more from under Call's breath than aloud.

Wing continued to walk.

"Uh, that's the other side of the Ti Range, isn't it?"

"Yes, but it's a lot farther on foot—especially if you get lost."

Call laughed. "I bet." An uncomfortable silence followed. "Rieeve. I uh, I've heard that..."

"Heard?" Wing said, suddenly noticing the existence of something still and deadly residing in the pit of his belly.

"That the Ka'ull are in your valley."

Wing could hardly comprehend the profound understatement of the boy's simple sentence. All he could find to reply with was: "Yes."

Call nodded, his head bowed. "Yeah. I mean, I've heard stuff in town—but it's hard to count on that to be more than gossip. My uncle, though, I trust what he tells me." Oddly, Call wanted to tell the stranger about his brother, Jason, but stopped himself and said instead, "If you don't mind my saying, you don't look very Rieevan—at least not from what I know."

Wing's eyes were distant as he said, "You're right, I don't."

The boy walked silently at his side, but before Wing could think of something else to say, Call stopped and pointed. Wing looked up.

"That's it," Call said. "Right there in front of the river. Just go on up and tell him you saw me in town. I've got to get back to my house. Mum's been expecting me for...a while." He glanced sheepishly at Wing. "I spend more time in town than I should—at least more than *she* thinks I should."

"Understood," Wing said. "And thank you for showing me here."

"No problem. Come back into town sometime and find me, or I'll see you here. I'm out here a lot." Call shifted feet. "I—I'm sorry about what happened to your valley."

Unable to reply to the young man's condolence, Wing said, "When you arrive home I hope you will not find yourself in trouble on my account."

Call shook his head as if to say not to worry and with a quick smile headed back across the fields at a run.

Wing continued on up to the house.

Like his home in Rieeve, this home faced away from the town, yet even from behind the structure was magnificent. It was, in fact, the kind of log home Wing had often imagined building for himself. Stepping up to it, he caressed the wood near a window with the hand of an artist admiring his latest work.

"You recognize craftsmanship when you see it," a man said coming up from behind him.

Wing turned to meet the eyes of a middle-aged man of good height—and forgot where he was. For a confusing instant, Wing was back in the ramshackle hut at the edge of the Cantfields, talking with Commander Lant, looking into his protean gaze and wondering at all the things the Commander knew yet would probably never say.

Slightly embarrassed by the lapse, Wing inclined his head toward the house and said, "That I do. This is one of the finest homes I've ever seen."

The man smiled. Intelligent and strong, Wing realized it wasn't only the man's eyes but also his presence that felt so very much like Commander Lant.

"It's taken more than a few revolutions and at least a few broken bones," the man said, "and it still isn't finished." He chuckled, squinting into the distance. "Was that my nephew I saw running back across the fields?"

Wing nodded. "I met him in town. He was kind enough to show me here."

"He's a good kid. Smart. His father and mother are a bit harangued by him, but it's a thing I think will prove of value. Anyway, the name's Monteray. And you are?"

"Wing, from Rieeve."

For an uncomfortable moment, Wing felt Monteray take him in, not as one would a stranger, but rather as an old friend whom he'd not seen for a long while.

"You've come a ways," Monteray said matter-of-factly.

"I have."

"Well, what is it? I doubt you came all this way to talk about my home—or my nephew."

"I came to fulfill a promise to an old friend of yours."

Monteray's eyes grew thoughtful and then sad before he replied, "From netaia Lant?"

Wing nodded.

Monteray cleared a quiver from his throat before speaking again. "Well then, come, dinner is almost ready. We can eat together and talk after. If you'd like to refresh yourself before the meal, there's a river out back or a wash basin within, whichever you prefer."

"The river, if you don't mind," Wing replied.

"Good. We'll have dinner as soon as you're ready."

Wing nodded in thanks and, following Monteray's direction, headed around toward the front of the house.

In a vaguely numbed state of awe over the many curious cases of familiarity he'd experienced since entering the valley, Wing was unprepared for the vision that filled his eyes.

Stretching out before him was a blanket of grass so tall and velvety he could barely see his boot tops. Amongst the grasses wildflowers of every imaginable colour grew and through them weaved a well-beaten path leading down to a river. The river was not the rushing, rapid water of the mountains, rather, it flowed softly, slowly, the movement of the water barely visible beneath his gaze.

Wing had often thought of mountains as grand, but never a river—until now.

Taking the narrow path through the grass, Wing began to walk downstream. In the near distance beside the river, he noticed a small cabin. Wondering who lived there and whether it belonged to the Monterays, he arrived at the bank, undressed, and slid into the water.

The glassy surface opened to receive him.

As if in the arms of a lover, Wing floated to his back and let the river brush his body with a great warm hand. Backstroking every so often, his eyelids opened and closed dreamily. Immersed in every moment, Wing's breathing steadied and deepened and he unknowingly let the current carry him past the small cabin.

Raising his head as if waking from sleep, he saw just how far down he'd let the gentle current carry him. With reluctance, he decided he'd best swim back and get on up to the house—he didn't want to keep his hosts waiting for too long.

Diving, Wing swam, surfacing near the small cabin, then diving again, and swimming the rest of the way to the spot on the bank where he'd left his clothing.

Carrying his jacket and bow, he padded up to the house in bare feet. The soft grass felt good between his toes, a favorable change from coarse mountain terrain. The door leading into the back of the house from the riverside was open and Wing stepped carefully in.

Monteray looked up from his seat at a large table and welcomed him.

Wing took in the home's interior. There was a high, vaulted ceiling over the entryway and corresponding hall that dipped lower above the dining room in order to, Wing thought, provide a cozier feel. Directly behind the dining area rose a long flight of stairs ascending to what Wing assumed to be upper bedrooms. Two beautifully made rugs—one smooth, one shag—hung adjacent each other high up the tallest walls. The dining table in front of him was set in elegant array with pottery plates, cups of glass, and in the center short arrangements of white and red flowers in square, red vases.

In rare manner, Wing found the home capable of both stateliness and warmth.

"Go ahead and have a seat," Monteray offered. "And this is our daughter, Tei."

A young woman came into the dining area, seating herself directly across from Wing.

Wing looked at her. She appeared to be no more than twenty revolutions. "Nice to meet you."

"And this is Kate, my wife," Monteray said as Kate entered the room through a set of small swinging doors that, Wing imagined, led into the kitchen.

Wing stood and offered to help with the plates in her hands. Kate accepted, smiling at him.

Through the same swinging doors emerged one more person, a man whose arms, like Kate's, were full of serving plates.

Expecting to meet yet another member of the family, Wing was blindsided when Tei said, "That's Sep. He's our servant."

Forgetting until this moment that some Legranders still held Preak as servants, Wing hesitated. How did one greet a servant? Out of the corner of his eye, he caught a disapproving look aimed at Tei from Kate.

What did that mean?

Uneasily, Wing raised his eyes, hoping he could greet someone in the role of servant without being rude to the Monterays or disparaging to the servant.

The concern did not occupy him long. A burst like lightning split his skull—

Nien?

All the air left the room.

The food and stoneware plates Nien carried toppled in a cacophony to the hardwood floor.

Viscerally, Wing was aware of a fall of glances—between Kate and Monteray, from Tei to her mother. And from Nien…

Wing.

Wing heard Nien say his name in his head as if Nien had said it aloud.

Facing one another, neither moved, neither breathed.

Wing's lips parted. Nien dropped to his knees and began gathering up the mess. Wing moved to help; their hands reached for the same piece of broken plate.

In a moment that probed eternity, Wing drank in the glistening tone of the black hand. Its rich textures. The milky white half moons at the bed of its fingernails. He felt Nien doing the same with him and knew they were thinking the same thing—

Impossible…

Their eyes lifted and met. Wing started to speak again, but Nien shook his head and silenced him.

With his arms full of the largest chunks of the serving plates, Nien lurched to his feet and hurried back into the kitchen.

Standing, the room spun around Wing. His legs trembled. Without actually looking, he hobbled backward until he felt something hard bump up against the back of his legs.

He slumped into his chair.

Kate gathered up the remaining bits of shattered serving ware and stepped quietly into the kitchen.

She found Nien inside. He would have been standing perfectly still in the center of the narrow kitchen except that he was shaking.

Pretending that she thought him to be upset over the broken plates, Kate said, "It's no problem. I've been wanting a different set anyway—this gives me the best excuse I can think of."

Taking a gulping breath, Nien muttered something about finding a rag. Kate placed her hand upon his. When Nien turned around, his face looked, indeed, like he had seen a ghost.

"Not to worry," Kate said. "I'll sweep up later. Let's eat."

Kate and Nien returned into the dining room together, Kate taking her seat at the end of the table opposite Monteray, and Nien his customary seat—the one right next to Wing.

Wing stared numbly at his plate. Emotion had turned his guts to jelly; shock immobilized his brain. He was unable to eat or even decipher what he was supposed to do with the food on the plate before him.

Monteray set his utensil aside and spoke to Wing. "You look tired," he said. "We can talk tomorrow if you'd like—after you've gotten some rest."

It took Wing a long time to reply, "Yes. Thank you."

Monteray wiped his mouth. "There is a room upstairs where you may stay."

Wing nodded, but his eyes were vacant.

Kate stood and went to Wing's side. "Come, I'll show you."

Wing got to his feet. Out of the corner of his eye, he looked at Nien. But Nien was not looking at him; his head was downturned over his plate.

Wing followed Kate up the fair length of stairs behind the dining area and into the long hall at the top. Through a door on the right, he stepped into the bedroom that would be his for the night.

Had Wing been capable of noticing, he might have given pause, for the room was exquisite. Across from him two windows faced the river and between them sat a large, raised bed, blanketed with a comforter of pure Jhedan'ret.

Wing had never seen the soft, lustrous material, but Nien had told him of it after his return from Quieness. A polished wood floor felt smooth beneath his bare feet and on the floor beside the bed was another thick shag rug similar to those hanging on the walls in the grand entryway below.

Wing stepped onto the rug. At any other time he might have dug his toes into it, enjoyed the coarse feel of it, but he was awash in a strange concoction of dismay and agony, incredulity and joy, and so took in the sensation only peripherally.

Feeling Kate's hand upon his arm, he looked at her.

"Sleep well," she said.

Wing replied unintelligibly and watched her leave. Turning back toward the bed, he reached out and touched the Jhedan'ret cover. It had a fine caramel luster and felt cool under his touch. He hardly dare lie on it, but there seemed to be nothing else his bruised mind could think to do, so he climbed on up.

He lay for a time, vaguely aware of the dull ache in his leg and trying to think.

How could he possibly sleep?

Nien. Se'te ney Eosha. He's alive…and here in this very house.

They'd called him Sep.

Sep. They'd said Sep. What kind of name was that?

Desire pulled fiercely upon him. There was a thunderous hammering in his chest.

He had to get up. He had to go to him. But Nien's glance had been explicit—

He didn't want to be discovered.

CHAPTER 55

Brothers

As if someone had touched him on the shoulder and spoken his name in order to wake him, Wing opened his eyes.

No one stood by the bed.

Hmm, he thought. *Strange.* And then he thought, *Yosha, I'm so comfortable.* He had a hard time remembering the last time he'd been able to sleep without wood floor or mountain rock digging into his bones.

And then...

He sat straight up. In the bedroom doorway stood a man. The notion flashed through Wing's mind that he was actually awake and the visage that stood before him was the dream.

"Wing," the dream said.

Wing pushed himself off the bed. For a time, he simply stood, staring at the man as if he'd not heard him speak.

As the moments stretched into infinity, Wing said, "Nien?"

Nien nodded, Wing gasped and like the breaking of a tide, the two crossed the room. They met chest to chest, shoulder to shoulder in an embrace that contained enough pressure to mold plating out of raw ore.

Merehr, Nien thought, the word lighting in his brain like a drop of liquid flame. *You made it out. You found me.*

Elation grabbed them up in great crystal wings as the brothers laughed, cried, and shook.

Nien's familiar scent filled Wing and he felt something in his joints melt. "I can't believe it," Wing said. "You're not real. None of this is real..."

Nien stepped back, taking Wing in at arm's length. "Wing! You're alive! I *knew* it."

Tears streamed down Wing's face as he gazed disbelievingly into Nien's eyes. "Seeing you on the floor picking up those plates. Sitting next to you at the table..." Wing paused. "I felt so sick."

Nien gulped. "I know. I'm so sorry."

In silence, the brothers reveled in the sight of each other.

"Come," Wing said at last, motioning to the bed. "Sit."

They sat down together. Nien bounced up and down, running his hand over the Jhedan'ret cover.

"I actually thought I could sleep here and wake up with a clear head," Wing said. "You know, wake up and remember that you were still gone. The reality of that felt easier to handle than the possibility that what I'd seen downstairs had been an illusion."

"I know. I looked right at you and was still not convinced."

Wing asked, "Where do you stay?"

"In a small cabin just down the river. It belongs to the Monterays."

"I saw it," Wing said, an apology in his tone.

"It's not bad," Nien assured. "I like it."

Wing looked him over. "I, I can't believe it," he muttered. "How long have you been here?"

"Nearly ten turns—as far as I can tell."

"Ten turns. And they have no idea who you are?"

Nien shook his head. "I don't think so."

"So, what have you been—"

"—doing?" Nien said. "Helping Monteray with his home."

"Are you their...?" Wing couldn't even finish the sentence.

"Servant? Slave?" Nien replied. "No."

"But their daughter said—"

"That's Tei."

"Then you bring them their food of your own will?"

Nien nodded.

"And you call that...?"

"Being part of a family." Nien paused as the pain registered vividly in Wing's eyes. "They've been very good to me, Wing. I help them, yes, hoping to pay them back for food, for lodging, for...saving my life."

A million more questions were tumbling around inside Wing's head and they all went unsaid except one: "What happened, Nien? Pree K sounded so sure you were dead—that all had been killed."

"I should have been—I very nearly was."

"And the family?"

"I made it out. I saw no one else."

"But you *did* make it. Maybe..."

"No."

"But," Wing insisted.

"No, Wing. The chances are small—so small."

"How can you be sure?"

"I'm sure. It doesn't matter how."

But a familiar wave of desperate hope deafened Wing to Nien's reply—the same he'd felt that night when he'd confronted first Pree K, then the messenger, and lastly Lant. Though a part of Wing begged himself to stop, to ask no more, he could not ignore the return of that long-buried hope.

"It does matter!"

"No, Wing," Nien said, his voice an airy, lifeless counterbalance to Wing's passion. "They are gone."

"Don't tell me that!" Wing reached out and clutched Nien's shirt in his hands. "If you escaped, others had to! Someone. Maybe Jake, maybe Carly..."

"Stop it," Nien muttered.

"All those days in the mountains. I...I thought you were all dead, I thought...But now you're here! You're alive!"

A glint of something terrible flashed in Nien's eyes and he pulled himself out of Wing's grasp.

Startled, Wing released him.

Like a living thing, the nightmare memory of that night took an anxious breath and arched its back. A swift battle ensued as it began to scratch at Nien from the inside even as Nien invoked the denial that had allowed him to survive its presence for so long.

The battle was brief and Nien almost won, but in the end he was powerless to deny Wing the truth.

"I saw them, Wing—our family. They were killed inside the castle walls." As if it were actually happening again, Nien felt hands grasp his ankles, felt a vague awareness of something happening to his body, felt his head crack against cobblestone. "After that, I only remember being dragged, dragged a long way, and then being thrown..."

Nien blinked and looked in Wing's direction, but it wasn't Wing that he saw.

"They threw us all into one huge pit. One huge, stinking, vile pit. I felt their bodies turn from warm to cold all around me. Smothering me. I couldn't breathe, I couldn't see, I couldn't even move. So many of them, pressing down on me, pressing in from all sides. They wouldn't stop—they couldn't. So many of them. They were *so* heavy..."

Wing felt something inside him slip and break.

Nien continued. "So much...blood. It should have dried, but it didn't in the rain, the rain kept making it bleed, it was raining blood, and I couldn't breathe...The uncanny horror of it, the sickening madness of it..."

The words fell from Nien's lips in fragments and coughs until his voice dried in his throat and he was left naked in a flood of memories, images, and feelings that he'd kept safely barred from all his waking moments—

Until now.

For a wraithlike moment, Nien was deathly still. And then the sobs came.

Wing tried desperately to control his mind. Mother, tiny Fey, Jake, his noble father—thrown into an open grave. Not even in his darkest moments, not even when the hand of death had been upon him had he imagined such a thing.

—Imagined

No.

But he *had* seen it—in the vision. He'd seen their people in those visions, he'd known it was them, as well as many others that he did not know—the dead from other valleys, he had supposed.

Wing reached out to Nien, but his trembling hand could not reach far enough. It hung in the air, and then fell back to his side.

I shouldn't have asked, Wing thought. *I should have respected his reluctance to speak of...*

Wing could not even find a word to reference it. None would do.

That night. A terrible night that, with shocking sentience, seemed to bury and then raise itself over and over again.

We'll never be free of it, Wing thought, *never.*

In truth, because of the visions, Wing had not been free of it even before it happened, but at least then he'd held hope, hope that he could find a way to change it. But he hadn't been able to, and his visions had just been recounted to him in detail as horrifying in their reality as the visions had been in the Void.

Beside him Nien had grown silent, like a ghost, as if the core of him had been drawn into the abyss.

"I'm sorry," Wing muttered. "That night, I wanted to find you, I wanted to find our family." Wing couldn't find the strength to explain. Consumed in Nien's pain, he said, "I did not think what answering my question would mean for you."

Wing's voice pulled Nien out of the memory's shadow; its weight lifted and vanished, and Nien found he could breathe again. Raising his head, he met Wing's perfect gaze.

This time, Wing could see his brother and knew that Nien was seeing him as well; nevertheless, Nien's eyes were moist and feverish and Wing felt ripped with longing to make them warm and aurulent again.

"I'm so sorry," Wing whispered again. "I shouldn't have asked."

Nien shook his head. "That you are alive is enough. It is *everything*."

Nien was right. That they were both alive, that they had found each other *was* everything.

Wing took the back of Nien's neck in his hand, pressed his face into his shoulder, and the brothers wept.

CHAPTER 56

Right by Them?

Kate lay awake in bed, Monteray in silence beside her. Each knew the other was not sleeping and that the two brothers were the reason.

During dinner, after Nien had dropped the plates and returned from the kitchen with Kate, she and Monteray had talked with Tei and feigned ignorance, but between themselves husband and wife had been speaking silent volumes:

We knew who they were—had our choice to honour Nien's assumed identity been the best one? Had it, perhaps, been cruel? Should we have prepared them?

Desiring to end the brothers' discomfort as soon as possible, Monteray had suggested that Wing get some rest.

"I can't imagine what it must be like," Kate whispered.

Monteray blinked in the dark as he gazed up at the small, indistinct patterns on the ceiling. "Believing that you might be the very last of your race, only to discover that another survived and that survivor is your own brother—such a revelation is probably not something comprehensible by us."

Kate turned into Monteray's side. He wrapped an arm around her, cupping his big hand around her shoulder.

"They are safe here—as safe as I can keep them."

Kate allowed herself to embrace the comfort his words afforded and they rested in silence for a time before Monteray said, "Wing is expecting that I will talk with him tomorrow, and I will. But I need to find a reason to keep the brothers here for as long as possible."

"You don't think they'll stay? Where else have they to go?"

"The only thing that kept Wing alive after he escaped Rieeve was a promise to Commander Lant. I suspect that once he fulfills this mission of his he will feel no other reason to stay, or even to live."

"But he's with his brother now. Surely that's enough."

"It might be," Monteray admitted, "but their people and their family are not all that they've lost, Kate. Neither of them are the men they once were."

And Wing, Monteray thought but did not say, *I think he blames himself...*

The disappointment and sadness in Kate's eyes caused Monteray to mollify his thoughts. "We'll see," he finally said. "You're probably right— that the brothers have each other back is probably more than enough."

Kate knew that her husband had learned much from Rhegal about Wing and Nien and that he understood their characters as well as one could without actually knowing them. Perhaps that understanding was a natural extension of Monteray's love for Lant and how much the brothers had meant to the Commander.

Laying her head into the curve of Monteray's shoulder, Kate let go of all unknowable considerations. Whatever happened would happen—wishing for a specific outcome would only give her a stomach ache.

CHAPTER 57

If You'll Stay

In the room upstairs, Wing drew a steadying breath and looked Nien over. "I haven't asked how you are. You said the Monterays saved your life."

Nien drew himself up. The shedding of tears had left him weak, but relieved. "I don't remember much of the journey here, but I remember Kate taking care of me."

"I'm surprised that you chose to come here. Monteray aside, it still seems a risky proposition."

Standing, Nien stretched his legs. "I was dying. I know the trip to Jayak would have been less and smarter for me as a Preak, but after what happened I had very few clear thoughts, in fact there was only one: that I had to get to Master Monteray. Once I made it here" —Nien paused— "I just wanted to forget why I'd come."

"So you gave them this name—what was it?"

"Sep."

Wing's eyes narrowed. "I don't understand. They would never have guessed, had you given them your real name, that you were Rieevan."

"But Nien is not a common name for one of my people."

"*My* people?" Wing mouthed.

"The history between our two people is a sordid one."

"Our *two* people?"

"You know what I mean—between the Preak and the Legranders," Nien said tiredly.

Wing felt the urge to vomit. "I've never thought of you as anything other than my brother—not once."

"I am that, and I *am* Rieevan—you know I am. But here it's something different. It would not be a quick telling to explain the events that led to Preak servitude here, but things *are* changing. No Preaks are held as slaves anymore. Most are freed servants, and others—brave enough—are beginning to trade their wares in town again."

Wing was not consoled. "Human reparations."

"You can say so," Nien replied, the weight of it evident in his features.

"Why didn't you just tell them who you are? It's Monteray. Don't you think he'd believe you?"

Nien walked over to the tall open window that looked down upon the river. "I didn't want them to know who I was or where I was from. Not at that time." He gazed out the window, taking in the river, the towering mountains. "My coming here was a good thing, the best thing. I needed a place to recover, a place to" —he hesitated— "hide." Though 'hide' was a terribly pathetic description, it was the most honest word he could think of. "Being here has been a blessing. I have work, a place to sleep, food. Monteray has even offered to pay me."

Wing shook his head miserably.

Nien glanced back and saw Wing's indignation. "You don't understand."

Wing's reply was sharp: "In that you're right."

"Wing, this façade is necessary for the time being. That is the paradigm in which they see the Preak. It's the easiest way."

"It drove a knife through me to see you on the floor—on your knees." Wing flashed an angry glance. "Your school. The Cant. You're a teacher, a warrior!"

Nien met Wing's ire with resignation. "That's what I *was*, Wing." He spread his hands. "Look at me now."

It was not easy for Wing to meet his brother's eyes.

They had known one another, or so Wing had always felt, much longer than a singular lifetime. For Wing, looking at Nien was like seeing the very best part of himself. Now, Wing realized that he had been so caught up in his own questions, in the sadness and sweetness of having Nien back, that he'd failed to see what that night had done to him.

With great unease, Wing did as Nien asked...

It took only a moment to see it—

Nien was undone.

There in his face, in the way he held his body, in his brown eyes that no longer glinted and played in the light that shone upon them; it was all over him. He looked much like Wing himself had when he'd gazed upon his own reflection in the stream after fleeing Rieeve.

"Maybe," Nien said. "People weren't meant to live through such a thing. Maybe..."

Nien couldn't speak the rest of his thought, but Wing knew what he didn't say. He didn't say: *You may see me here, but I really died back there, too.*

The room fell silent as Wing conceded that they were merely beings: alive, breathing in and out, but only existing.

"There are mornings," Nien said quietly, "I'm not sure I have the will to draw breath."

It took Wing a moment, but when he raised his face, he managed to say, "Nor I, brother. Nor I."

Though the night was late, Wing and Nien could not bear to part. Chancing making nuisances of themselves, they stole down the long flight of stairs and out into the night. They walked together toward the small cabin in the distance, enjoying the sound of the river and the feel of each other's company. Once inside the cabin, Nien built up a fire and the two sat down beside it, warming their hands.

After a time, Nien asked, "So, you've grilled me on why I came here. Why did you?"

"Same as you—Lant," Wing replied, gazing into the fire.

"Lant?"

"When Pree K came to find me in the fields…"

"—you said you saw him. So, he made it out."

"No," Wing said. "Lant said he had been at their home. He sent Pree K out to find me."

"You met with Commander Lant, then?"

"I saw him, yes. He wanted me to deliver the plans to Master Monteray."

"Lant made it out of the castle," Nien said softly to himself. "Did he…?"

"He was wounded. By the time I returned to get the plans from him, he'd died."

Nien had assumed Lant had perished in the castle with the rest of their people. Hearing Wing's report made it feel like the Commander had died all over again.

With difficulty, Nien asked, "You have them, then?"

Wing nodded.

A shadow of mixed emotions passed over Nien's face. "Where are they?"

Wing reached into his shirt and drew out the leather-bound rolls of parchment and Mesko paper he had carried for so long. Pausing, he held them in his hands.

Nien cocked his head at him. "What is it?"

"Nothing."

Nien studied the rolled parchment in Wing's hands, reading his brother as he might have the pages.

"Though Lant must have felt as if he failed," Nien said, "his Plan brought us together again."

Emotionally drained, the brothers had fallen to Nien's bed, asleep. Side by side they slept away the rest of the night and far into the following morning.

Wing was the first to awake and he did so as if startled from a bad dream.

"Great," he mumbled.

Nien woke up as Wing began to scramble for the door.

"Monteray's going to wonder what I'm doing out here," Wing said, fighting with a blanket. "If you don't want him to know who you are…"

Nien glanced outside. The sun was well up. "Too late for that," he mumbled. "Just uh, go down to the river. He'll think you got up early for a swim or something."

Wing nodded and clumsily found his way to the door, the blanket trailing behind him.

At the water's edge, Wing sat, trying to regain his bearings and having no luck. Finally, he decided a swim might offer clarity.

He was right.

Gasping as the cold morning water snatched his breath, Wing shook his head, wiped the water from his eyes, and floating to his back, swam a few strokes, turned himself about, and dove. When he resurfaced he was laughing and staring right into the eyes of Monteray's daughter, Tei. Auburn hair fell about her slender shoulders, and her thin blouse was pulled loose, clinging precariously to her small breasts.

Taken by surprise, Wing paddled upright in the water before realizing that he was close enough to the bank to stand. Expecting to have been on the precipice of offense, he glanced down. The water swirled well below the juts of his hipbones, but even had it not, his concern would have been meaningless. Tei stood as she had been, smiling at him, her eyes traveling unabashedly over his body. The fact that his chest was terribly scarred by the shy'teh's claws did little to dissuade her interest. Indeed, the scars seemed to intensify her fascination.

"Good morning," she said.

Wing said nothing.

"I brought you down some clothes," she said, holding out a pair of light brown leggings and beige shirt as if they were an offering.

Wing nodded slowly, his eyes steady, his black hair dripping across his face and back. For a moment, he'd hoped his reserve might dissuade her.

Again, he was mistaken.

"Thank you. I'll get them from the bank in a moment."

"I can dry your back," she offered.

Incredible girl, Wing thought.

"I'll let the sun have the chance," he said.

With a disappointed shrug, Tei set the clothes on the bank and began to walk away—backwards.

Once Tei had finally about-faced, Wing climbed from the river and tried on the new clothes. They felt wonderful, a comforting change from the thick leather hides.

Folding his own clothes, Wing glanced up at the house and stopped short.

Monteray had said he'd hear what Wing had come to Legran to tell him in the morning.

This *was* the following morning.

Finding Nien had eclipsed everything that had passed since leaving Rieeve.

But eclipses were short lived.

Before finding Nien in Legran, the thought of delivering the plans to Master Monteray and then returning to live alone or die in the mountains was the greatest relief Wing had hoped for.

Now there was Nien.

What did that mean? It was everything. But was it enough? In going back to live in the mountains there was the chance that Wing could try to forget who he was, what he'd been, what had happened. He could separate himself and his life into two different lives, two entirely different people.

But if he stayed in Legran with Nien, his brother would be a constant, living reminder of that other man, the man Wing had been in Rieeve.

So that leaves me with only two choices—again, Wing thought. *Stay here and live with my guilt, or run away.*

Wing glanced back at the cabin where he knew his brother lay inside, asleep.

If I stay, Wing thought, *do I tell him the truth?* Wing squeezed his eyes shut.

Keeping his silence and his secret promised agony. The thought of telling Nien, however, was even worse. It would be cruel. His brother had been there that night. He'd fought. He'd tried. He'd tried all his adult life in his work with the Cant to prevent what had happened. He'd done his part; paid such a high price. Nien deserved whatever scrap of peace he could now glean.

Agitated over his mental jargoning, Wing grasped onto the clarity of that one thing: Whether he stayed or left Legran, telling Nien was something he would never do.

Wing started up to the house.

For now, he'd go meet Master Monteray as they'd planned and then...

Then.

He'd make the rest of that decision tomorrow, or...

The next day.

Monteray looked up from the dining table as Wing came in. "You look refreshed," he commented.

"I am. And thank you for the clothes, they fit nicely."

"I'm glad. There are not many men in Legran that could fill them."

Kate and Tei came in and the four dined in relative silence before Monteray asked, "I imagine you may want to rest awhile from your journey?"

Wing looked at him, then at Kate.

"You are welcome to stay with us if you'd like," Kate said, her face so radiant and warm that Wing felt his heart reach out to her as if she were his own mother.

Surprised as much at his emotion as with their offer, Wing said, "Yes, thank you. I would."

"And how are you with a builder's tools?" Monteray asked, a twinkle in his eye.

"I have experience," Wing replied.

"Good. Then I will receive the message you came here to give me. We can meet in the Mietan after breakfast—it's the structure to the northing of the house." Monteray took a long drink from his cup. "I am grateful that you've agreed to stay. The warm turns can pass quickly in Legran, and I'd like to have the roof over the rest of my house before they do."

Walking back to the cabin, Wing stepped inside and pulled the leather-bound roll out from beneath the mattress of Nien's bed before heading to the Mietan. He found Monteray inside the beautiful, one-roomed structure that stood apart from the main house. Weapons of various sorts were arrayed carefully, even elegantly, along the walls. Most were different, but others rather closely resembled those used by the Cant. There were also plaques of metal and wood, their coats blazoned in a strange but beautiful language. Wing made a slow turn in the middle of the room, his feet moving smoothly across the polished wood floor, his eyes directed up toward the ceiling soaring overhead. A circular pane of stained glass fitted the apex of the grand structure, casting a brilliant spectrum of light into the room.

"You like it?" Monteray's voice seemed to emanate from the four corners of the Mietan.

Wing tore his eyes from the ceiling. "Very much. It is perhaps one of the most beautiful rooms I have ever seen."

"Ah...then you have never been to Quieness."

"No, but my brother..." Wing started to say before catching himself. "I never have. But I cannot imagine any edifice there rivaling the likes of this."

"Oh, some do, but even I find this a welcoming place to practice and learn."

Wing figured he was meaning the art of combat for which Lant had said Monteray was renown, but he did not ask.

Monteray walked over to a fine set of stairs that led to a single chair at the top. He sat down on the steps and invited Wing to sit beside him. Wing did so, holding the rolled papers in his hands. Slowly, he handed them to Monteray.

Monteray took the plans and unrolled them. His heart warmed at seeing the familiar handwriting of his truest and oldest friend. Much of what they'd gone over together on what Monteray now knew to have been Lant's last visit to Legran, their last time together, was there on the pages, written in Lant's familiar flowing hand.

"If you don't mind, I will need some time. Please make yourself at home. Perhaps Sep or Kate can show you around."

Wing got to his feet and quietly left.

As the Mietan doors shut behind Wing, Monteray released his hold on the papers, letting them curl back into the scroll they had been in for so long. Taking the roll, he pressed it to his chest.

The tears rose unremittingly in his eyes, and he wept.

CHAPTER 58
Feels Like Home

W ing glanced down from atop the roof to see Nien coming out to join him and Monteray. Nearly three turns had passed and in that time the brothers had spoken very little of Rieeve or of the Plan.

Nien climbed the ladder and came up beside him. Wing looked round and, smilingly, pointed at a splitting log.

Nien grunted. "Not like I need the exercise."

Wing chuckled as Nien retreated back down the ladder.

Night folded upon them before they knew it. Soon thereafter they heard Kate calling them in for dinner.

"Well," Monteray said. "That's it for today."

Gathering their things, the three headed in, neither brother reflecting consciously upon how good, how familiar it felt to be working on a roof-top together, to have at their side a man only a little older than their father had been, to hear a woman's voice calling them in to dinner.

With his arms extended behind him, Wing leaned against a wall of the cabin after dinner, settling into the familiar comfort that was his brother's presence. They talked quietly as Nien sharpened his small whittling knife and Wing rested, sometimes gazing up at the simple cabin roof, sometimes closing his eyes and listening to the sound of the river until a knock came on the door.

Wing opened his eyes.

Nien looked at him and with a curious tip of his head, stepped across the room and opened the door to find Monteray on the other side.

"Mind if I come in?" Monteray asked.

"Of course not," Nien said.

Wing stood uncomfortably, grabbing over a chair from the small table.

"Thank you," Monteray said and sat down. "Am I interrupting?"

"No," the brothers said in unison.

Monteray chuckled. "You know, the way you two get on, one would almost think you're more than friends."

"Well…" Wing started to say. Nien shot him a frigid glance.

Monteray waited.

Wing ran his suddenly sweaty hands down the sides of his pant legs, still looking at Nien. "I suppose there's only one way to tell you."

No, Nien said clearly enough, his eyes locked on Wing. But Wing was going ahead, anyway— "We're brothers."

Monteray's eyes shifted to Nien. "You have no first family?"

In a flood of anger and resignation, Nien swam briefly in Wing's eyes.

Unflinching, Wing held Nien's gaze and just as clearly assured him: *Now is the time.*

With a hitch in his throat, Nien replied, "None that I know of, or even remember. Flashes of my birth mother, that is all. As I am for Wing, Wing is now all that remains of *my* family."

Tension pulsed through the room as Monteray said bravely: "*Nien*. Why have you waited so long to tell me?"

Nien felt shot through. So did Wing.

"You know my name?" Nien said at the same time as Wing said, "You know his real name?"

"I have known for some time who you are."

"Which one of us?" Wing asked.

"You for sure," Monteray said to Wing. "You," he said, looking back at Nien, "I was not certain about at first, though I suspected."

"How?" Nien asked.

Monteray tapped his left shoulder with his right hand. "The clothing you arrived here in had a leather shoulder mantle. Upon it was sewn a symbol. Let's just say, I recognized the style." He grinned and added, "There was also the little detail of you not understanding the Preak language when Kate spoke it to you."

Caught, Nien thought.

"Considering your condition at the time," Monteray continued, "I thought it best to let you take things at your own pace."

"And I thought you were particularly kind considering the shaky sentiment toward my" —Nien paused— "of Preaks, here."

"Yes, *that*. Well, the ideas of Legran are not necessarily my own," Monteray admitted. "Kate and I only desired to keep you safe so that you could rest and heal. Preak, Rieevan, Legrander—what is that to me?"

"We didn't know," Wing offered.

Monteray raised an eyebrow. "Did you not?"

The brothers fell silent.

Monteray was right, of course—they *did* know. From everything Commander Lant had shared with them over the revolutions about Master Monteray there had never been the slightest question regarding Monteray's character and the faith Lant had in him. Wing and Nien's belief in that faith was the reason they'd both come to Legran in the first place. But fear in the beginning had gotten the better of them, overridden their knowledge and trust. Now that they'd discovered the Monterays for themselves, the reasons for going back to the truth seemed insignificant, even foreign—they had become content with what felt like a new life.

"I am sorry," Nien said. "Had I been more myself when I'd first arrived—"

"I know," Monteray replied. "And your wariness has been earned by my people, if not by myself." Monteray left off there, and when he raised his face again there was a gleam in his eye. "Allow me to get to the question I came out here to ask, and now that everything is in the open, it will make the question easier. I have a friend coming to visit and I was wondering if you, Wing, would mind staying in the cabin while she's here."

"Actually, that's been my wish all along, but we were—"

"Keeping up pretenses," Monteray said.

"Yes," Wing said apologetically.

"Very good." Slapping his hands against his knees, Monteray stood. "We can haul out extra furnishings tonight or tomorrow morning."

"Tomorrow will be fine," Wing said.

"Alright, I'll see you two early, then. It's your turn to cook breakfast."

As Monteray opened the door, Wing called after him, "Master Monteray."

Monteray turned back.

"You said you knew that *both* of us were from Rieeve. How did you know that I—?"

Monteray paused, considering. It took only the briefest internal inquiry before he was resolved. "You are acquainted, I believe, with a man who calls himself Rhusta?"

Wing's eyes widened.

"Well, he is an acquaintance of mine through Commander Lant. Customarily, I visit him a couple times a season. On my latest trip you were there."

Wing's jaw gaped.

"You never knew it," Monteray continued, "for I arrived only a couple days after your encounter with the shy'teh. Rhusta told me what happened in Rieeve. And he told me about you. It was then I told him that a warrior of Preak origin, wearing the clothing of the Rieevan Cant, had shown up at my place." Monteray looked to Nien. "That is where your identity was confirmed to me."

"Commander Lant knew Rhusta?" Wing asked. "Is there *anyone* the Commander did not know?"

"I take it Lant never told you."

Wing shook his head.

"I'm not surprised. Rhusta doesn't want anyone knowing about him—where he is, or *that* he is. Commander Lant honoured that. What I have told you Rhusta left to my discretion to tell you."

More than a couple turns were lost to Wing after the shy'teh attack. It was not a surprise that he had no recollection of Monteray's visit. "I...I don't know what to say."

"No need to say anything," Monteray said and, nodding to them, turned again and went out into the night.

The brothers sat in silence after Monteray's departure.

"I need some air," Wing said suddenly.

"I'll join you."

Together, they walked down to the edge of the river. The evening breeze cooled their skin as they sat, looking up at the towering mountains. Nearby, a fish jumped, and the setting sun caught a glint of fluorescent scales.

"By the way," Nien said, wanting to change the subject he knew was on both their minds, "who's Rhusta? And what's so hush hush about him? Lant never said anything to me about him."

"Nien," Wing said, "Rhusta's real name is Rhegal."

Astonished, Nien said, "He's out there? Alive and well? Why didn't you tell me?"

Wing shrugged. "It hadn't come up."

"You don't wait for something like that to 'come up,' you *bring it up*."

"Sorry."

"And you were attacked—by a shy'teh?"

Nien had been stunned the first time he'd seen Wing with his shirt off, but at that moment Wing had been struggling to get out of the cabin before any of the Monterays saw him, and Nien had not brought it up since.

In the gathering gloom, the brothers pondered how much the other had changed. There were the scars upon their bodies. There was the limp in Wing's leg. There were the blankets that always lay at the bottom of Nien's bed, never over him. But mostly there were all the things they could not say, all the questions they wanted to but could not ask.

The sun slipped behind the jutting mountain peak, the brilliant lavender sunset sliding with it, trailing its colour across the ripples in the water.

"Fine, brother," Nien said as the shadows grew long across the river. "We will keep our little secrets."

Wing slapped Nien's leg and together they stood and returned to the cabin.

CHAPTER 59

Call

Work on Monteray's home the following day was warm and relaxing beneath the silvery-blue light of Leer's sun.

Nien and Wing joined Monteray and Kate for lunch before Nien headed back to do some prep-work for tomorrow and Wing left for town to find Call (a thing that had become quite common). Even though the townsfolk were now accustomed to Wing's visits, their curiosity persisted as to why the tall stranger would come into town just to meet up with Monteray's strange young nephew in the Hiona.

"Hey there," Wing said to Call, returning from the bar with their drinks in hand.

Hiona wine, from which the pub got its name, was famous, often the reason travelers from other valleys would stop over in Legran even if they had nothing to trade. It was also the beverage of choice for the odd companionship.

Call looked up at him plaintively.

Wing sat down and slid Call's drink to him. "What is it?"

"I want to go back to Rieeve with you."

Wing almost toppled his glass—"What?" He would have been less shocked had Call suddenly jumped up and slapped him.

"I just...I thought you were. Isn't that why you're here? Why you brought Lant's Plan to uncle Monteray?"

Wing could hardly touch the idea with his mind. What seemed so obvious to young Call had never even occurred to him.

"I, uh..." Wing tried to find some kind of reply—

He couldn't.

Opting out, he redirected the conversation. "I don't understand why you're asking."

"I'm not doing anything here, Wing."

333

"What about your writing there?" Wing said, gesturing to the journal that sat beneath Call's left elbow, the same one Call had been holding the first time Wing had seen him leaning against the wall beneath the Hiona sign.

Call glanced down at it. "Observations and details," he said with a grumble. "I'm tired of recording Legran goings-on." He looked back up at Wing. "I want to help you fight the Ka'ull."

It took a moment for Wing to say, "Where did all this come from?"

"It's not something I just thought of," Call snapped. Wing figured he must have looked rejoined for Call quickly reassembled his approach. "My brother died fighting them, and I thought that's what you've been working on with uncle Monteray—a plan to go back and fight them. I've wanted this for a long time. It's all I can think about, but I can't tell anybody—except you."

"Why not?" Wing asked, trying to understand Call's perspective even as his own mind recoiled at every thought that spilled from Call's lips.

"Because no one hears me. I'm just a kid. It's so frustrating, and I can't tell you how angry it makes me." Such was evident in his face.

Wing leaned forward in his chair. "I did not know about your brother. I am sorry."

Call nodded morosely. "It happened a season ago in Jayak Valley. He was there with the Legran forces protecting Javet, the main pass into our valley, from the Ka'ull."

Call paused and Wing could tell he was waiting for some kind of response. He could also sense that his continued silence was crushing to his young friend. Across from him, Call had dipped his finger into his drink and begun rubbing it along the rim of his glass. The glass was singing hard enough to break.

Wing watched for a moment. Call's eyes were fixed on the glass' smooth edge, his face set and hard.

Wing opted for honesty. "Call, I'm sorry. I don't know what to say."

Thankfully, Wing's confession brought Call's fingertip away from his glass. He licked the Hiona from his finger and said, "You can say you'll let me go back with you."

"Your request," Wing said with as much strength as he could muster, "has caught me by surprise. I have not thought about returning to Rieeve. And I didn't come here to help Monteray with the Plan, I came here, simply, to deliver it."

Now it was Call's turn to be discomposed. "I'm sorry. I assumed you would be going back. I shouldn't have thrown it all on you. It's just…"

"It's *just*?" Wing asked.

Call clenched his glass between his hands. "Well," he said, hesitating. "The thing is—you." Call's gaze slid to the table.

"Me?"

"You're special, Wing. Mysterious. You walk into a room and the whole place comes to a standstill." Call ground his teeth. "And you're so free."

"Free?" Wing found the statement curious.

"Free to be a man! If you **would** talk with them, any one of the towners would listen to you. I know they're all wondering what I could possibly have to say that would interest you. Whereas, here I am, and I'm not taken seriously at all—and I don't fool around! It's only because I'm young. I'm trapped because everybody around here sees me as just a kid."

Another long silence passed as Wing looked down into the deep maroon colour of the hiona, feeling the coolness of the glass between his hands.

"You're not insignificant, Call, and I am no more mysterious than anyone. Your people see me as they do because they don't know me."

"Well, they don't know me either," Call replied.

Without raising his eyes, Wing said, "True."

As the chatter around them continued, Wing found himself drawn into ponderation. He knew how the townspeople saw Call—as an eccentric youth who hung out in town all day, writing in that weird little book of his. Call **was** different, but that Wing understood. Though he did not share the overtness of Call's sociological curiosity, he understood why Call wrote, why he loitered around the pubs and marketplace. He understood the attraction, the need, the paths Call's eccentric and curious mind traveled.

From the other side of the table, Wing could feel Call's eyes searching him hungrily, waiting for him to say more.

"Strength and beauty will always be readily admired," Wing said uneasily. "Be patient. Don't despair that who they see right now is not who you really are. One day they **will** see you. I promise." Wing motioned at the book beneath Call's elbow. "And many more will hear your voice through those words you write."

Call's strained expression softened. "All my life" —his voice cracked with emotion— "I've wanted to know with just a look that I was understood. Jason came close—at least more than anyone else. When he died..."

"He left you without a way to connect the world of your inner life with that of the outer."

Wordless, Call nodded.

Wing sat back from the table then, and even though he noticed Call trying to hide his relieved smile by taking a quick sip of his drink, as Wing raised his own drink to his lips a graveness fell over his features as he thought of Rieeve, of his lost people, wondering at the great disparity between how people see themselves and how they are seen by others and if there might be a way to bridge that gap here, with Call, before it was too late for him as it had been for Wing. Could Call be seen for the gifts he embodied rather than those he did not embrace?

What would this young man's legacy be?

CHAPTER 60

There's Me, Now

His talk with Call was still on Wing's mind that night as he stayed after dinner to help with the dishes before heading out to look for Nien. He found him inside the cabin, lying on the floor, scribbling on some flattened bits of parchment.

"What are you up to?" Wing asked. Upon seeing a thin stack of creamy white pages, he said, "Paper?"

Nien glanced at the sheets lying next to the parchment. "Monteray," he said.

Wing bent down and took up a piece. He ran it through his fingers. "It's Mesko paper," he said carefully.

"Yes."

"Do you think—?"

"That it might have come from Lant?"

Wing nodded.

"How else?"

The brothers shared a look.

Nien held something up in his hand. "Monteray offered this as well."

Wing recognized the Rieevan fine-tipped brush.

"Though terribly generous of him, I gratefully accepted. Parchment is not so much fun to write on—and quills. Never did get a good feel for one."

"So, what are you writing?"

"I'm, uh, trying to put down the high points I remember from Lant's Plan. You carried it for a long time. Did you ever read it?"

"A bit," Wing said.

"Good, help me."

"Not unless you give me the pillow."

337

A pillow hit Wing in the chest. He threw it on the floor in front of him and got down on his belly beside Nien.

"Lant wrote a brief biography of each person he planned on sending a copy to. Here's what I've written down so far: 'Monteray," Nien said, reading over his lines of notes. " 'Born in Legran, traveled early on in his life. Lived in Jayak. Obtained most of his warrior skills there. Traveled into the sunrising after that. Returned in his later revolutions to Legran. Has family there: a sister, two nephews, and one daughter of his own with his wife, Kate. I met him in Jayak when we were both young. He is a wise and a kind man. My dearest friend.' "

The brothers looked at one another wishing—as they had many times back in Rieeve—that they knew more about the adventures the young Monteray and Lant had taken together.

" 'SiQQiy,' " Nien continued, " 'a woman with a vast spirit. Of a Preak mother and Quienan father. She came to the ruling seat of Quieness after the death of her father two revolutions past. She has proved to be a prudent ruler and very capable. Her connection to Monteray is of primary importance in our endeavor.' "

Nien finished up with Impreo Takayo. " 'Impreo Takayo is also a man of good virtue. However, his people have an intolerance toward Rieevans. They see us as a narrow and thus unintelligent race. I have hope that these plans may reveal our desire, or at least a reaffirmation of my own desire, for change. The word of Monteray in this thing may make all the difference. In addition, both the Quienans and the Preak are admired by Takayo's people. If SiQQiy or the Preak agree, it will bode very well for us.' "

Nien stopped reading. Wing was quiet, his chin resting on his arms, his eyes open but focused far off.

"What are you thinking?" Nien said.

Without moving his head, Wing glanced sideways at him. "Worried?"

"Should I be?"

Wing rolled over onto his back, and staring up at the ceiling, said, "Today, when I went into town to find Call, he told me something. He said he wants to go back to Rieeve with us. He wants to fight the Ka'ull."

There was a big, heavy silence.

"Youth," Nien said scoffishly.

"Youth?" Wing said. "What are *you* doing there?"

"Exercising demons," Nien said quickly.

"So, it's never crossed your mind."

"There's nothing to cross. I fought them, Wing. We lost."

"But the Plan..."

"The Plan?"

"Well, Lant..."

Nien looked at Wing as if he'd never seen him before. "What does the Plan have to do with us anymore? Lant's Plan was about protecting Rieeve and the other valleys—not what to do once they'd fallen."

"I get that, and I was as shocked by Call's statement as you obviously are. But he said it—something I've never even once considered—and then I come back here and here you are, wasting Mesko paper writing out bits of Lant's Plan when Monteray has the whole thing up at the house."

Nien growled. That Wing could drag the truth from him, no matter how illuminating, was irritating. "You're not making strides with me, brother, shattering the illusion of my disinterest."

Wing's still eyes met Nien's for a moment, and he laughed. "We're such fools," he said.

Nien snorted. "It's bad enough that I can't be honest with myself, but that it's impossible to lie to you...?"

"So," Wing said, "it's just us. We never have to admit any of this conversation to anyone else."

Nien pushed the pages away so that he had room to stretch out.

"It had never crossed my mind, either, Wing. But now. Well, now, there's you. And there's Monteray." A sigh left his lips that might have masked a quiver in his voice. "The thing is, we don't know what the other valleys think. We don't know what plans they have made. We can be reasonably sure that Jayak intends to do something. But what has that to do with us? Why would any of the valleys help Rieeve?"

"The Mesko, maybe," Wing offered. "We've always had a surplus."

"Possibly."

Wing rolled over to his knees. "The thing is, even if they are willing to help us—and the thought is crazy—what is there to go back to?"

"The land?" Nien offered hopefully. "It is our home." But the bright light of that thought snuffed out as Nien wondered why the people of any valley might risk the loss of men and materials to regain a valley for a race whose people now numbered two.

The brothers sat in silence.

"I haven't thought that we survived in order to retake Rieeve," Wing said. "Maybe the point was the Plan. Maybe the point was to help the *other* valleys." And then, at himself, Wing laughed—a pained, terrible laugh. "Did you hear what I said? 'Help the other valleys.' Help them with what? All I had in me to do, and that was barely done, was deliver the Plan to Monteray. Now that Monteray has it, and you are here..."

"What?" Nien asked.

"Fulfilling my promise to Lant by bringing the Plan here was all I'd hoped for," Wing struggled to say. "After that I'd planned to return to the mountains to—"

"Die?"

Wing met Nien's eyes. "What else is there?"

Nien gazed back at him searchingly. "There's me, now," he said slowly.

Wing's eyes dropped to the floor. Nien had just swung the door wide open to Wing confessing his guilt, telling him the truth. But Wing had promised himself, promised himself that he'd never lay the burden of that truth on Nien. So, he said, "But what good am I, Nien? What can I do? I am not a warrior. I have no great mind for military strategy. You, at least, understand all of this...stuff. I am of no more help to you or to Monteray than I was to our people."

A shift happened in Nien's face, one that pained Wing internally, as he said, "Nor am I." Obviously unable to meet Wing's eyes, Nien rolled over and threw an arm up over his face. "You're right. We have done all that we were meant to do."

Wing stared down at the floor in silent contemplation. "We could go away," he said. "You've always wanted to travel. We could go to a different valley. Start over. Bleekla, I'd fit in anywhere better than I did in Rieeve—so would you."

Nien moved his arm from over his eyes to under his head. "I've had worse thoughts," he admitted. "We could head to the warmer valleys first. Beaches of sand that stretch beyond sight. Sun. No one around but strangers like us. While in Quieness, Necassa told me of the White Sands beaches in southing Quieness that are warm throughout the revolution. Filled with retirees, vagabonds, and tourists neither of us would stand out anymore there than a Quienan in a Cao pub. She even gave me the names of some hallucinogenic herb dealers."

Wing laughed, Nien threw him a grin, but both gestures were half-hearted and the cabin fell into silence.

Night took the day. Inside the cabin, Wing had settled in to sleep on a bed he, Nien, and Monteray had brought out from the house, and Nien had taken up a seat next to the fire when a knock came on the door. Wing glanced across the room at Nien. Nien shrugged, and setting aside the small whittling project he'd been working on, went to the door. On the other side stood Master Monteray.

"Master," Nien said.

"Mind if I come in? Sorry for the late hour."

"Of course not, come in."

Wing sat up on the edge of his bed.

"I'm glad you're both still awake," Monteray said.

The brothers looked to him wonderingly for his manner was heavy. Neither brother had ever seen him so…disconsolate.

They sat for a time, waiting for Monteray to speak.

"I've, uh, I've been reading over the plans," Monteray finally said, his voice breaking a little. He raised his face. It was filled with sorrow. "If there is anything you can tell me about Commander Lant, I would be most grateful."

To Wing and Nien's surprise, he had spoken in Rieevan.

"After Viyer was taken," Wing said, "Lant sent his son, Pree K, to find me—"

"Pree K survived the attack?"

"He wasn't there. Apparently, he'd been at his home with another of the young Cant Messengers. He told me to go to Lant. I left Pree K and met briefly with Lant. He gave me the Plan and asked me to look after his son. After our short exchange, I attempted to find Pree K to no avail. By the time I returned to the Cant hut Commander Lant had died. I buried him in the mountains before my escape." Wing drew a long breath. "He was most fond of you, Master Monteray. It was of you that he spoke lastly and in you that he held the greatest hope for the success of the Plan."

For the first time in their acquaintance, the brothers saw the watery mist of tears in Monteray's eyes. "He was wounded then, in the attack?"

"It was dark in the Cant hut," Wing said. "Though I did not clearly see a wound, I knew he was in pain."

Monteray's eyes grew distant.

Across the room Nien watched Monteray in stillness. In the interest of self-preservation he had re-barricaded the details of that night from the rest of his mind. But the sadness on Monteray's face gave him pause. "In" —his voice failed at first; he tried again— "in the castle. The last time I saw the Commander he was engaged in single combat with what I believe was the leader of that regiment of Ka'ull."

"What?" Monteray said.

"I don't know why, but I remember having the brief impression that Lant knew the Ka'ull he fought—personally. I remember seeing them speak to one another. And their battle, it was not waged with dispatch or indifference. I'd wanted to go to him for I'd thought my family had safely escaped, but they hadn't and…" Nien stopped. "That was the last time I ever saw him. I did not know until finding Wing here in Legran that he had made it out of the castle."

Nien looked away at the fire, but Wing saw Monteray's face. It was clouded, busy in thought. Clearly, Nien's words regarding Commander Lant and the Ka'ull leader held particular meaning.

"Thank you," Monteray finally said and stood to leave.

"Master Monteray, wait," Nien said.

Monteray turned around, seeming to know what Nien was about to say.

"I was wondering what you think of Lant's Plan?" Nien was going to say more, but Monteray turned his face away. Nien waited.

"I don't know if you are aware, but on netaia Lant's last visit here to Legran, he told me of his idea, and for a few days we worked on it together. Once I'd received his messenger with the formal request for Legran's participation in a joint alliance, I'd written up a letter to Impreo Takayo relating my personal feelings and desires regarding the Plan. As a consultant to our forces here in Legran—such as they are—I had intended to send my nephew, Jason, to Jayak with the letter." Monteray paused. "But he was killed in Jayak nearly eleven turns past."

A reflexive sound escaped Nien's throat. Monteray looked at him.

Glancing at Nien, Wing quickly said, "Nien and the leaders of the Rieevan Cant were on a training drill in Jhiyak Canyon on that same day. They fought alongside the Jayakans."

Monteray nodded slowly to Nien. "So you were there. I wondered as much."

"You did?"

"Two of my men reported to me after the battle. There was one detail in their report—one that seemed minor at the time—that a man of Preak had been at the debriefing."

"That was me. I was there with the other leaders of the Cant."

"We lost eighty-nine men that day. I have not as yet attempted to send the message again. I was hoping to send Call, but he is quite young still." Monteray drew himself up a little, seeming to shake off some heavy emotion. "The people of Legran are generally shifty and unconcerned, especially when it comes to the trials of others. Nevertheless, the loss of the eighty-nine has helped to unite them as I've never before seen.

"I will try again to contact Takayo. They are brave, keen warriors, and they know Ka'ull tactics. And there is another possibility in all of this. The friend that I told you is coming should arrive within the turn. She, too, received a messenger from Lant."

"Quieness," Nien said.

Monteray nodded. "Her visits here are normally a time of celebration and relaxation. This time, however, we will be discussing netaia Lant's Plan in depth. We would hope for your input."

The brothers were still for a time. "So you are in favour of the Plan? You think it might actually work?" Nien asked.

"Lant had a heart capacious enough to hold great hope at such a time, and a mind noble enough to conceive a way to achieve it. The idea is a good one.

"But as I'm sure he knew, none of it will be easy. With a little faith, a lot of organization and tactical application, I hope my people can complement the efforts of Jayak and Quieness—if they, too, agree."

The brothers nodded their heads to him, knowing that if anyone could carry weight with the Legranders and Jayakans, it would be Monteray.

"Thank you," Monteray said, "for telling me what you could. I'll see you in the morning."

As the door shut behind Monteray, Wing and Nien sat in the cabin silence, pondering a great many things, among them: What was it that had happened in those revolutions Master Monteray and Commander Lant had been off together? To the brothers' minds it conjured up images of breathtaking adventure and a friendship unassailable.

So why was it that every time either Commander Lant or Master Monteray had ever spoken of that time there was about their faces a shadow, a darkness against the bright light of their legend?

These questions helped drown out the more disconcerting question: Why did they care what Master Monteray or the other valleys thought of the Plan?

What did that have to do with them?

"Monteray!" Wing called the following morning, hurrying out from behind the house with hammers and a bag of nails swinging from the belt around his hips.

Monteray turned.

"If you have a moment," Wing said. "Last night you mentioned a letter you'd written to Takayo and have not yet been able to send. Well, you probably know that I've spent quite a bit of time with Call and I think that sending him on such an errand may be just the right thing" —Wing paused— "for all concerned."

Monteray studied Wing. "Perhaps I should talk with him," he said.

Wing grinned a little, but as Monteray went to continue on his way, Wing stopped him again. "There is something else I've been wanting to ask you about."

"Yes?"

"When I first came into Legran—through town—I, pardon how this may sound, but I thought I might blend in, go unnoticed. But the towns-people seemed wary, even suspicious of me. Do you know why?"

Monteray smiled a little. "It's because you look Criyean."

"Criyean?"

Monteray nodded. "We're used to trading with nearly every race on the continent here in Legran: Jayakans, Grangh, Honj, even the Majg on occasion. But not the Criyeans. Or, rarely."

"Why?"

Monteray exhaled deliberately. "It's a matter of condescension—on their part. Criyeans have little to do with the central valleys."

Feeling now that Monteray's answer had raised more questions than it had answered, Wing nodded to him and the two continued in their different directions.

Wing returned to where he and Nien were working on the house.

"Where'd you go?"

"I had to catch Monteray before he headed into town."

Nien raised an eyebrow at him. "What is it?"

"What do you know about Criye?"

"Criye?" Nien shrugged. "Not much. Even less than I know about Majg. You should ask Monteray. Why?"

"Well, Monteray said I look like I'm from Criye."

Nien squinted at him. "Really?"

Wing nodded.

"Hmm," Nien said, and both in thought, they returned to their work.

Sunsteps later, Nien slapped Wing on the back and announced that he was heading back to the cabin to relax.

"E'te," Wing said. Gathering his gear together, Wing stored it in the house and headed down to the river.

The gentle sound of the water and majestic spectacle of the rising mountains wrapped Wing in a familiar solitude.

Criyean, he thought to himself, soaking in the quiet. *Interesting.*

"You've been here for a while."

Startled, Wing looked around. "Tei," he said, the disappointment in his voice ill disguised.

Tei sat down next to him. "Lovely, isn't it?" she asked.

Not so pretty now as it was a moment ago, Wing thought.

"You're very quiet," she said.

Wing shrugged.

"Do you enjoy working for my father?"

"Very much. He's a good man." Wing's eyes were still directed toward the dwindling light on the horizon.

"I like watching you work. Did you know?"

"No," Wing said shortly.

"I've watched you often. Haven't you noticed?"

"That I've noticed," he answered honestly.

Tei reached up and took a piece of his hair in her hand. "Aren't you lonely out here?"

"No."

"You're alone a lot," she continued, moving her hand around his back before sliding her fingers beneath the cuff of his shirt.

"I *like* being alone," Wing replied.

"Why?" Getting to her knees behind him, Tei moved her hand down his chest, pressing her breasts against his back.

Wing stiffened. Tei brushed her lips against his neck, her breath moist and sweet. Wing pushed himself to his feet. "I've got to get back to the cabin," he said with a short glance down at her. "Have a good night."

Sitting in the grass, Tei watched him go, something sad reflecting in her eyes.

Inside the cabin Nien sat, whittling on a small bit of hardwood. Wing had become familiar with it, as it was the same piece his brother had been working on for some while now. Shutting the door softly behind him, Wing went over to the fire. Warming his hands he watched Nien's skilled fingers work at the deep brown-and crimson-coloured piece of wood. "Do you know what it's going to be?"

Nien moved it fondly in his hands. "Not yet."

The fire crackled and Wing withdrew his outstretched hands.

"So...I saw Tei," Wing said casually, lying down on his bed.

"Yes. We often do." Nien turned the piece of wood around in his hand, examining it. "What brings that up?"

"She came down to the river." Wing twirled an end of hair around his finger. "Has she, well...?"

"Well, what?"

"You know."

"Ah," Nien said. "No. She has the town-Legrander thing going on. With me, I think she's caught somewhere between curiosity and revulsion."

Wing didn't know which part of Nien's statement disturbed him more. "Whatever it is she needs no man can give her."

Nien asked, "What's really on your mind?"

"I know it'll probably sound ungrateful—I mean finding you here, finding you alive, was nothing short of a miracle. It's everything..."

"But?"

"I know I should let it go, but all those nights I spent in the mountains after that night, I wondered if she might have..."

"Carly," Nien said quietly.

"Could she—? I mean, do you think there's any chance?"

"No, I don't think so."

Wing continued to look at him.

Nien felt sick. "Wing, the chaos was overwhelming." Nien paused, his eyes lowered. "No, I did not see her body."

"I understand," Wing said quickly.

"I wish I had something to tell you—anything."

"No, it's fine. Never mind." Wing pulled off his shirt. "I'm going to turn in."

"Good night," Nien said, and even though he tried to return to his carving, his eyes kept wandering to the fire's glowing coals where images of that night flashed before him. Briefly, Nien let himself glance them over, wondering if there might be something that could help him discover whether Carly might have made it out or not. Some clue. But no clear picture was made and his position as observer of the images was drawing thin.

Shaking his head, Nien grabbed up the long metal poker, stirred the coals, and returned to his carving.

CHAPTER 61

Back from the Dead

Work on the roof the following day ended a little before sunset as Wing strode into town to drown his aching muscles in Hiona and perhaps find Call for a little conversation.

Wing entered the Hiona and casually ordered two large glasses. Turning his back to the counter, he glanced about the room in a bored manner, expecting to find Call's clear blue eyes somewhere in the crowd.

From a table in the corner, he did find a pair of eyes upon him, but they were not Call's—

These eyes belonged to a woman.

Her clothes were torn and dusty, her skin darkly tanned. Her hair was long and unkempt, bleached scarlet from the sun. In many ways she looked much like all the other market Legranders in the Hiona.

But she was not Legrander.

Her eyes were fixed on him as she got up from the table at which she sat. Her legs were unsteady, tenuously supporting her very thin frame. She moved around the table and started toward him.

Wing reached back to steady himself against the bar.

As she stepped into the long, narrow path between the bar and the rest of the seating tables, Wing felt the space around him and everything in it, vanish. Though she was painfully emaciated and pitifully worn, nothing had ever appeared to him so beautiful.

Standing now, face to face with him, she stopped. Wing's lips parted.

"Wing," she said softly.

Wing reached out and touched her hair, his throat constricting with emotion, a quiver registering in his hand. For a time he could only stare at her—

"So surprised?" she asked, a faint smile passing across her dry, cracked lips.

347

Wing could only shake his head at her. *Eosha! Carly.*

Reaching out as if for a rope that might drag him from a drowning depth, Wing grabbed her and brought her into his body with both hands, engulfing her in his arms.

Carly clutched at him, but there was very little strength in her.

Supporting her shockingly fragile frame, Wing lifted her and, starting to leave, noticed for the first time that the Hiona had fallen silent, nearly every patron having turned from their casual conversation to take in the deepening mystique surrounding Monteray's guest and the newly-arrived bedraggled female.

Wing moved quickly out of the pub, across the plankboard walkway, and into the fields leading out of town. He had carried her some distance into the wide fielded space between the town and Monteray's home before he paused to rest. Kneeling beside her, Wing cradled her shoulders.

Carly opened her eyes and looked up at him. "You're alive," she said, "you're alive. I knew you would be. I knew it."

Wing blinked back tears, started to speak, stopped. Carly touched his face, her fingers saying far more to his heart than any words. Wing pressed his face into her hand. His shoulders shook.

"I, I'm so sorry, Carly. Had I known that—had Nien been able to give me any hope that you, too, could have…"

Carly gulped. "Nien?"

"He's here, Carly. He's here in Legran."

Carly's sun-darkened features paled, her lips trembled.

Wing's eyes smiled as if to affirm that he'd told her the truth. Carly started to speak again, but the words fell silent from her lips and all she could do was stare up at him as tears trickled down her dirty face.

Wing pressed his face against her and whispered, "Let's go see my brother." He took her back up into his arms and moved on across the grassy plain.

Carly's head rested languidly against Wing's shoulder as he walked. The immensity of her emotions faded away until there was only Wing—the warmth of his body, the smell of his skin, the rhythm of his gait.

The gap between them and the cabin closed quickly, and soon Wing had stepped up to the door.

"Carly?" he said.

After a moment, she raised her head and looked around. Supporting her against his body, Wing set her to her feet, reached for the door handle and pushed the door open.

Nien glanced up from where he sat near the fire. "It's about time—" he started to say.

"I've got a little surprise for you." Wing helped Carly through the door.

Stunned, Nien stood. "Carly?" he said. He looked at Wing. "Carly?"

"You greet a ghost the same way you greet an old friend," Carly said.

Nien took a few faltering steps across the cabin floor, took her from Wing's support, and wrapped her in his arms.

Wing stood silently, taking in the unbelievable—the impossible.

"Nien." Carly looked at him through her hands as she wiped the tears from her face. "You don't look so worse for the wear—not as I must, from the way you two keep looking at me."

Nien's face lit. He coughed and his voice broke.

Another silent tear ran down Carly's cheek. "How did you come by Legran? I was sure that even if you *had* escaped you would not have come here."

"That was my question," Wing said softly, only then realizing... "How long have you been in Legran?"

"Not long. A few turns maybe," Carly replied.

"You spent all these past turns in the mountains?"

"Well, mostly. I lived outside Jayak for a long time. I'd sneak into town at night and get food or anything else I needed, then I'd hide out in different locations during the day."

"Why did you not try to speak with the Kiutu or Jiap?"

"I managed to find Jiap, and he helped me. As soon as I was able, however, I left. His family was kind enough but I could tell it was a strain on them."

Wing's gut tightened. "Carly..."

"It's all right," she said, wavering. Wing caught her as her knees gave way. Carrying her across the room, he laid her down on his bed.

"You need rest, some food, and a hot bath," Wing said. "The order in which they occur is up to you."

"The Monterays will be having dinner soon," Nien said.

"Would you like to go up the house and bathe and eat, or would you rather rest and I bring you some food?" Wing asked, smoothing his hand over her forehead.

"I'd really love a bath," Carly said.

"Alright," Wing said, and getting to his feet stepped to the table only to meet Nien doing what he'd meant to do—pour Carly a cup of water.

Carly drained the water in a breath, then passing her eyes over Wing and Nien slowly shook her head. "It's, it's unbelievable. The two of you. You're both alive." Her eyes strayed to Wing. "I love you," she said. She looked across the room at Nien. "You too, Deviant."

Nien stepped to her side and pressed his lips to her cheek.

"Rest for a bit," Wing said. "Then we'll go up to the house."

"I'll run up right now and tell Kate. Meet me at the back," Nien said to Wing and he ran out the door.

"Monteray, there's someone I'd like you to meet," Wing said.

Monteray looked up from the table.

"This is Carly," Wing said, coming into the room with Carly beside him. "She's from Rieeve. She grew up with me and Nien."

Monteray's smile was almost wicked. "There seems to be some sort of magic worked between our two houses," he said, standing and extending his hand to her. "You are welcome here for as long as you'll stay."

Carly thanked him as Wing held a chair for her. A moment later, Tei came in and sat down—directly across from Carly. Irritated at the ill-fated seating arrangement, Wing introduced the two women. Carly nodded to Tei as Tei smiled sweetly, somehow too sweetly, her eyes shifting to Wing then back to Carly again.

Meanwhile, Nien had headed for the kitchen to find Kate and see if he could help bring out the food.

—It was not Kate, however, that he found.

A woman he had never seen before was standing by the stove and when she turned to see who had come in, Nien left his body.

She was breathtaking.

Her skin was a flawless canvas, much like his own though more silvery-blue. She was tall, and her eyes were like the black wells of space.

She smiled at him.

Her eyes seemed to reflect all the light in the room. Silken thread, beaded with delicate gemstones, held her long black hair at the nape of her neck, and when she looked at him it was with a fiery light that burned him.

He tried only once to introduce himself—and failed completely.

Noting his discomfiture, she said playfully, "Come here often?"

Like the dulcet tones of gently flowing water, her voice sang into his very center, drawing his chest into a hot knot that eclipsed every other sensation. It also caused him to utterly miss the jest. "I do come here often. Can I help?"

"I'd appreciate it," she said, and taking up a heavy pan, held it out to him.

Nien took the pan and then just stood there, as if he had no idea what to do with it.

A gleeful set of crow's feet appeared at the corners of the woman's eyes as she glanced down at the pan before looking back up at him.

"Right," Nien said. Quickly, he turned back through the two swinging doors and into the dining room.

Setting the pan down in the only empty space left on the table, he could feel Wing's questioning gaze upon him but did not look back at him as the woman emerged from the kitchen behind him.

"There's one more introduction that needs to be made," Monteray said. Walking over, he put his arm around the woman like a proud father. "This is—"

Nien had glanced up at her and Monteray caught the look.

"Have you two already met?" Monteray asked.

Nien's lips parted, but no words came out.

Covering for him, the woman said, "Not officially." And again there was that smile.

He felt the knot in his chest burn and tighten.

"Ah," Monteray said. "Well, this is SiQQiy."

Nien caught the surprise in Wing and Carly's faces before closing his eyes in complete embarrassment. Earlier in the afternoon, before Wing had gone into town, Nien had noticed some activity up at the house but hadn't bothered to find out what it was.

Only the arrival of the Empress of Quieness, he thought.

Monteray had told them a friend was coming from Quieness. He had even said that she, this friend, had received a messenger from Lant.

Obviously I passed over the information's full meaning. Yeefa. What had I thought? I knew Commander Lant and Master Monteray knew the Empress.

Perhaps it was a little too incredible—like everything else that had happened since coming to Legran.

I think I'll hide in the cabin for the rest of her stay.

"It is an honour to meet you," Wing said, standing and taking her hand. Carly did likewise. Nien, however, could only cast her a glance of indistinguishable emotion before vanishing back into the kitchen.

From the dining room, Nien heard Call's voice, shout: "Am I late?" as he ran in through the back door.

"No," Nien heard Monteray say. "But if you could cut wooden angles for the house as close as you cut this meal you'd make all of us rich."

"You already are rich," Call replied.

Nien heard chair legs slide across the floor, as Kate said, "Well, all the food's here. Looks like all we're missing is Nien."

Bleekla, Nien thought, as he leaned against the counter at the far side of the kitchen. *Now I've got to go back in there.*

Nevertheless, he bought himself a few more precious seconds alone.

Though he was still having a hard time believing that the Empress of Quieness was, even now, just on the other side of the kitchen's two thin swinging doors, it wasn't so much her or that he hadn't managed to speak an intelligible sentence in front of her that rattled him, but the familiarity she evoked in him, no matter how stupid he felt over the sentiment, fully aware that he was reaching too high.

E'te, he told himself. *It's all right. Probably everybody has that reaction the first time they see her. Perfectly normal.*

Staring down at the counter, he recalled the sight, the feelings of awe he had felt so long ago gazing out the window of his small apartment on the edge of Cao, watching as the setting sun cast silvery rays across the ivory domes of her palaces.

"Nien?"

Startled, Nien turned to see Kate.

"You all right?" she asked.

He nodded quickly. "Uh, yes, I was just—do we have everything?"

"I think so."

Nien tried to pull himself together. "Then let's eat," he said, and avoiding Kate's questioning gaze, pushed open one of the swinging doors for her.

Seating himself next to Carly, Nien dove with feigned enthusiasm into his food, offering very little eye contact and even less conversation as the meal commenced—

Not that anyone in the room noticed.

The Monterays and SiQQiy carried a steady stream of persiflage regarding Quienan intrigue and her trip to Legran as well as Monteray's progress on the house and the latest town nonsense. Even Call was unabashed in the presence of the Empress, interjecting his own thoughts, laughter, and unmediated questions.

Though it seemed to take forever and a day, the pace of the meal at last began to slow as fingers stooped to picking at morsels, and laughter was replaced with contented sighs. There was almost a moment of silence before a sharp clang at Wing's side snapped everyone's attention to Carly; she'd dropped a long two-pronged fork against the edge of her plate. Her hand trembled as she tried to reposition it.

Wing stood and took the back of Carly's chair, saying, "I think this food would serve you best followed by a good night's sleep."

Nien snatched the opportunity to excuse himself as well. "Monteray, Kate, Tei, Call." He let his gaze stray briefly to the Empress. "Nice to have met you."

Back in the cabin, Wing threw back the blankets on his bed and motioned for Carly to get in.

"I can't take your bed," she resisted.

Wing gave her a stern look. "It isn't big enough for two, at least if either of us wants to get any sleep."

"Or if *I* do," Nien said from the other side of the room. "Really, Wing loves the floor."

It took no more prompting; Carly crawled into the bed, asleep before her head reached the pillow.

For a time the brothers stood, quietly watching her.

"I shouldn't be surprised by anything anymore," Nien whispered.

"When I saw her in the Hiona," Wing said, "I almost fainted."

"That she survived is…" Nien paused. "I would have died had I not made it here, had Kate not nursed me back."

Wing looked around at Nien. "So, Deviant?" he said, the corners of his lips turning up.

"What?"

"The Empress?"

Nien averted his eyes. "You're out of your mind."

"Am I? What'd we eat for dinner?"

Nien paused; Wing laughed.

Nien tossed the blankets bunched at the bottom of his bed at Wing. "Goodnight, little brother," he said emphatically.

Wing caught the blankets. "Goodnight."

Nien rolled onto his bed and closed his eyes.

Taking the thick rug from the wall of the cabin, Wing laid it out on the floor, spread the blankets over it, and then knelt down next to his own bed where Carly lay.

There was nothing about her horribly thin frame, ragged scarlet hair, or weathered skin that wasn't more beautiful to him than she had ever been. Though not the same visage he had imagined all those terrible nights after his escape, the sight of this new body that carried the same voice, the same smile, the same eyes of the Carly he had loved in Rieeve seeded his emotions, filling him with an intoxicating flowering of awe.

Shadows from the fire dancing about the cabin caught her face as she moved in her sleep and Wing noticed a long scar that began somewhere in her hair, stretching behind her left ear, and down the outside of her neck.

His heart trembled as he touched his fingertip to it, tracing its length gently to where it ended upon her collarbone.

Leaning down, he pressed his lips to the scar before slipping beneath the blankets and into the fuzzy coarseness of the rug, not quite able to fathom the one that lay only a couple steps away, no longer an impossible dream fragment in his mind, but real, close enough to touch, there to be seen and all he had to do was raise his head a little to see her.

The following day of work on the house was hit and miss as Wing, Nien, and Monteray's minds were all elsewhere.

After dinner, Nien being more than sufficient help with the clearing of the table, Wing excused himself and Carly so that he could take her to the bank of the river in time for the sunset.

They arrived just as the great glowy orb slid behind the mountains, splashing the sky with a hundred vibrant colours from the deepest blood red to the palest blues. Kojko now reigned upon the land and the evening shades were growing darker and richer.

But Wing and Carly took in more of the sunset on one another's faces than over the mountains.

"It's still hard to believe—" Wing started to say.

"That I'm real?"

"Yes."

"Me, too." Carly took one of his hands in hers and caressed it, loving the smoothness of his deep olive skin, tracing a blue-green vein here and there with a light touch of her finger. She could feel Wing watching her as she stroked his hand. Raising her face, he met her eyes and she kissed him deeply, desperately, clinging to him as if he might evaporate.

"You taste of the fields in early Kive," she whispered.

Wing pushed his nose into her hair and breathed deeply. "To be holding you, it's…it's something out of a distant wish, some longing that I could only realize in those moments before sleep."

Carly shivered at his breath upon her neck. "Day and night I imagined you alive. I'd run it through my mind—how you escaped, what you might be doing. It's funny, I guess. I didn't really care if I survived or not—that just didn't matter much. It really only mattered that you did. And so I made it real in my mind." She shook her head. "It's hard to explain."

As if she'd pinched out a candle's flame, Wing drew away from her.

"Wing?"

His features hardened. "*You* thought that?"

His tone nipped Carly's heart, and she realized…

Oh. I might as well have just said: I always did think you were the Leader.

Briefly, she considered trying to cover it by saying that she'd meant to say how it only mattered to *her*—but he had grasped her real meaning.

"Wing, I'm—" She stopped, unable to get herself to say she was sorry even though, for his sake, she wanted to.

Reticent, it appeared Wing was trying to keep his dismay at bay, but his face and eyes had the look of someone who'd just drunk a belly full of soured wine.

"Along with everything else in Rieeve, I thought that reckless idea had died as well," he said.

Carly searched Wing's face, but his eyes were fixed doggedly on the grass between his knees.

Not knowing what she might say, Carly suddenly found herself feeling as helpless and alone with him as she had all those terrible turns in the mountains.

"The people. Rhusta. And now, you," Wing said. Whether he'd said it to himself or to her, Carly couldn't tell. "Only Nien—"

He did not complete his sentence.

Only Nien had never said it, Carly knew he'd meant to say.

Achingly, she said, "I only meant that, maybe, there's a reason."

Flatly, Wing replied, "You and Nien survived."

Carly was about to say that sheer luck, aided by the happy edge of their Cant training were the only reasons she and Nien had lived. But before she could speak the thought, something sparked off in her mind. If she and Nien *had* survived due to something more, what did that mean? Who were *they*? She could see all the reasons why Wing had been miraculously spared, but why she had been?

She had no idea.

Of all our people, why we three? Yosha, she breathed out silently, seeing for the first time how easy it was for her, how easy it had been for their people, to believe in someone else, anyone else but themselves. And that someone else had been Wing.

The understanding rose like an inescapable case of nausea. *I'm so sorry,* she wanted to say, *for not getting it before.*

In echo to her very thoughts, Wing said, "Why anyone should think it only mattered that I lived, I'll never understand. If it *was* Eosha that kept me alive, He has yet to tell me why, and the only conclusion I can come to is that it was to humble me."

Surprised at his words, Carly asked, "*Humble* you? Why?"

"For being arrogant? For trying to understand something I was never meant to understand?"

Carly thought he was referring to the Ancient Writings. "That's not true, Wing."

"Either way," Wing said pointedly, "it doesn't matter. I should have been there. I should have been there with you and Nien and my family. I was a fool."

"Had you been there you would have been killed."

"You were there, and you weren't."

Carly's eyes fell. "Nien and I may or may not have been saved for some reason, but neither of us understand the Ancient Writings, or any of these... mystical possibilities, as you do. Eosha needs you."

"Needs me?" Wing almost laughed. "I think it's pretty obvious He has no use for me or, apparently, for any of us."

"No, Wing," Carly said shaking her head. "No. I'm not saying I know whether our people were right or wrong about you. But Eosha loves you and knows you. The rest is irrelevant."

Wing turned to look at her. "Then why did He not come to our aid?"

Carly could only look at him. She did not know why.

Wing pulled up a handful of grass and turned it to green cud in his fist. "I never joined the Cant," he said, his voice tight. "But I fought. I fought *every* day to make sense of this."

Carly muttered softly, "I know—you did everything you could."

Wing shook his head as if her words landed upon him like killing insects and she did not understand why.

"Everything I could..." Wing said. "Then either I am flawed, or He is flawed. Which do you think is more likely?"

Though she could not say it, hearing such words from him devastated her. Back in Rieeve, the ancient prophecy concerned her no more than the effect it had on the man she loved. But during those long turns after that unthinkable night, alone, hungry, deprived of everything except sunlight and darkness, she, too, had changed. She had begun to pray, and she'd begun to wonder if their people had been right about Wing.

Like the last gasp of a dying hope, she whispered, "Don't regret who you are."

"I don't know *who* I am," Wing said. "Maybe I never did."

CHAPTER 62

They Are the Key

"SiQQiy," Monteray said happily, seeing her appear in the doorway to his and Kate's bedroom.

"Do you mind?" she asked.

"Of course not, come in."

SiQQiy entered the room and sat down on the large bed. "It's so good to be here. Being in this room is like being home. It's how my mother and father's room used to feel—back when they were in it."

"They would be proud of you," he said.

SiQQiy raised her impossibly beautiful face and looked at him. "I've not let it show, but there is a shadow in my heart, and I wish my father were still alive. I don't feel adequate to what lies ahead."

Monteray nodded slowly and placed his arm around her shoulders. "I know."

"As I ever have since his death, I'm grateful to take counsel with you."

"Then let us do so," Monteray said kindly. "How is the situation in Quieness?"

SiQQiy's face grew solemn, and her exquisite features tightened. "The people are going about their lives. The mood that took Cao after the disappearance of our three merchant ships subsided. Rumours of the taking of Lou and Tou flew through Cao City, and also subsided. The people feel Quieness could never come under any real threat. The smaller cities and outlying villages and towns go about their lives as they always have. All in all life seems perfectly normal and safe..."

"But?" Monteray said.

"After the loss of the merchant ships and two of my war galleys, I felt that something terrible was coming, that those seemingly independent acts of piracy were harbingers of something much worse. But I kept such feelings to myself. Now that Lou and Tou have been taken..." SiQQiy paused.

"There are those who stand in wonder at how quickly, how easily those two valleys fell. But I had a feeling, Monteray. I suspected, but did not act soon enough."

Monteray's head bowed. "I share your regret. More than any of us, Commander Lant did the most, acted on his instincts, prepared. He did this even knowing that what he efforted was futile, that his small valley and people could never withstand the Ka'ull."

"And still, I keep my people in the dark," SiQQiy said, her dark gaze on the floor. "Only the men who traveled here with me and a small contingent assigned to my coadjudant know; with only those few have I shared my concern and how close the threat may come."

"No sense in stressing your people over conjecture and speculation. Your messenger and mine will rendezvous at the Tu'Lon Confluence," Monteray said. "Between now and the time of their return, I am planning on sending a messenger to Jayak. Eventually, I will go myself and speak with Jiatak."

"I can send an envoy to Preak."

"Excellent," Monteray said.

"What about the brothers? Now that I've met them, I see why you and Commander Lant thought so much of them."

"They are not ready—not yet. But we have a little time. I have opted for patience with them. If our timing is right, we can perhaps get them back."

SiQQiy knew what Monteray meant. She had seen the shadowy, emotional places warriors and survivors of catastrophic events could go to.

Monteray continued, "If the Ka'ull are using Rieeve as a staging area and base for provisions, outfitting, and ordnance, then cutting off the supply line into Rieeve and seizing those supplies could be decisive, SiQQiy. It could turn the tide of the invasion."

"Then your thoughts bring more urgency to the matter than I had supposed."

"A little, yes. But before such a move is made I feel it imperative that we have the Cawutt brothers with us. Something tells me they are the key."

Like Kate, SiQQiy had learned to trust Master Monteray's intuitions. She nodded her lovely head. "Then I will see if I can set aside the shadow and pass some time here with you as I'd hoped to. Meanwhile, we can write out our endorsements of Lant's Plan to send to the other valleys."

The two sat in silence for a time before SiQQiy said, "Master."

Her voice was soft and fragile, very female in its tone. Gone was SiQQiy, ruler of Quieness and Commander of the largest military on the continent. Sitting beside Monteray now, she was that little girl who'd so often run the palace halls in the middle of the night, looking for him, hoping he could chase away her nightmares. "When messengers arrive at my palace—especially strange ones like the young man from Rieeve—on the heels of dark rumour and missing ships, and all I have to greet them with are old maps and ancient stories of war…"

Monteray placed his hand upon her knee. "We have a little time, SiQQiy," he said, his voice soothing in the blue light of the room. "Let your mind rest. Let your men rest. Let's take this deep breath before the descent into lower things."

CHAPTER 63

Who You Are, Really

"Thank you for your help," SiQQiy said in perfect, unaccented Fultershier as Nien started out the door the following evening after dinner.

Nien stopped and glanced back at her.

Removing her apron, she said, "Would you like to take a walk?"

Nien's face revealed his surprise. Though he'd spent the whole day on the roof wanting to talk with her, he'd not expected *her* to ask him.

"The sun's setting. Wing and I usually go out to the river in the evenings, but he's off somewhere." He motioned with his hand. "If you'd like...?"

"I would." Laying the apron over the back of a chair, she followed him out. Two men of her guard made to follow her. She dismissed them with a signal.

"Perhaps you should—" Nien said.

"I will be safe enough with you," she replied.

Nien almost flinched. *Safe enough with me...*

As the thought clanked around in his brain like a shard of falling glass, he felt SiQQiy at his side and looked up to see that her guards had already disappeared back into the house.

Turning, they walked together into the slanting, misty rays of the sun that shone over the river.

As they made their way through the tall, velvety grasses, Nien wondered at the great oddity that was a Preak-born Rieevan and the Empress of Quieness strolling side by side in the valley of Legran.

Legran, he said silently to himself. A place that had not so long ago enslaved its Preak residents, now refuge for them both.

"I'm sorry about the awkwardness of our introduction," SiQQiy said. "Monteray can be far too generous in his opinion of me."

"I must admit," Nien replied, "even though I knew you were coming, I would not have expected to find the Empress of Quieness in the Monterays' kitchen doing dishes."

"And I would not have expected to see a Rieevan warrior of Preak origin working on their roof." SiQQiy grinned. "The lengths they'll go to get a little help around here."

Nien laughed. "But how do you know what I am?"

SiQQiy nodded as if accepting a challenge. "You have the bearing of a warrior, the mind of a Quienan, and the soul of a Rieevan."

Apparently, she'd thought a bit about it. Nevertheless, if the setting sun had turned to rain and showered about them in hot flame, Nien would have been less impressed.

"Besides, I queried Monteray about you," she added with a wink in her voice. "Forgive me."

A corner of Nien's mouth tipped shrewdly. "Still, your skills are remarkable, for I have never told Master Monteray that I've been to Quieness, unless of course, Wing told him."

"Ah, that..." she said. "Well, the word you used at the dinner table: tisquiata. Only one who has spent time in Cao could have known that." They took a few more sauntering steps before she asked, "And about me. What is it *you* know?"

Nien thought for a moment. "That your father married a Preak woman, that you are the first Empress of Quieness with Preak in her blood, the people love you, and you have the most beautiful gardens in the known world."

SiQQiy tilted her head to him. "You are even more astute than I."

Nien chuckled. "I would love for you to think so, but I cheated, too—I read Commander Lant's individual profiles in the Plan."

"And your Commander included information on my gardens?"

"Not exactly. That I saw for myself."

Arriving at the riverbank, they sat down together, SiQQiy removing her sandals and hanging her feet into the water.

They sat for a long while in silence, watching the sun dip closer to the mountaintop.

"So when did you first visit Quieness?"

"I've only been once, and that was two revolutions ago."

"Would I be safe to assume you liked it?"

Nien nodded. "Very beautiful. It was a lot to take in—at the time."

SiQQiy glanced at him. Nien was looking out over the river.

"I imagine nothing overwhelms you anymore," she said softly.

"Nothing—and everything."

Studying his face for only a moment, she changed the subject. "How did you come to be brought up Rieevan?"

Nien shrugged. "I don't know, other than I was abandoned on the edge of the Cawutts' fields. It was there Joash Cawutt found me. He and his wife raised me as their own. I remember only brief flashes of the time before."

"Monteray said you were Commander Lant's First."

"Commander Lant," Nien said, his voice a blue note. "Yes, I was."

"Monteray and I both loved him dearly." She paused. "I must confess, I recognized who you were when Monteray introduced us."

"Recognized?"

"The name—from Commander Lant's son, Pree K, when he came to Quieness to deliver Lant's proposal."

"I don't believe I was to be mentioned in the message he delivered," Nien said.

"I'm thorough," SiQQiy replied. "Especially when it could involve my people or my armies. I asked him many questions regarding your Cant, its leaders, and Rieeve in general."

"Pree K was a special young man, and gifted."

"I was impressed by him. Our conversation was heavy on my mind when I received a messenger from Monteray requesting that I come earlier than I had intended for this trip." SiQQiy smoothed the hair away from her face. "I try to come as often as I can. That used to be about once a full cycle. Since my father's passing, it's been considerably less."

"I am happy to be here this time," Nien said, wanting, but unable to speak the rest of his thought.

But SiQQiy took his meaning, replying, "I'm happy as well—that you are here at this time."

Nien met her eyes, knowing that had his wish to see her been granted when he'd been in Quieness it would have been from his knees—not that he would have been allowed an audience in any case.

As if reading his mind, SiQQiy said, "The walls that surround me in Quieness are necessary." She kicked her feet in the water. "But when I am here, I am with family. I am simply SiQQiy."

"It's hard to imagine what that would be like."

"You were close with your family, weren't you? I can see it between you and your brother."

In a very Wing-like response, Nien nodded but said nothing.

"I'm so sorry," SiQQiy said quietly. Some moments passed before she spoke again. "Their loss is devastating, but it doesn't have to be in vain."

"No, it *was* in vain," Nien replied, surprised at his honesty. "Good intentions only get one so far. Time ran out on us."

"Because of your Commander and the efforts of yourself and Wing, we may be able to save the rest of the valleys from such a calamity. I believe in the Plan. So does Monteray."

Her words helped as much as any could, but his skin was cold, as if numbed from the heart out and he could not share the strength and determination he saw in her eyes.

Acknowledging her words, Nien nodded his head, hoping his gesture did not appear as hollow as it felt, and as neither of them could find more to say about it, they watched together as the sun closed the day, completing its descent toward the crest of the mountains. The song of the night bugs along the river's edge soon began to fill the air.

Pointing to a canyon far down the river from them, Nien said, "Commander Lant and I conducted training camps in that pass."

SiQQiy's eyes traced the rocky silhouette of Vilif Pass' sloping ridge. "I've often come that way myself. It's beautiful, but...a little ominous."

"It can be," Nien agreed.

"I've watched my guards at times, as well as the soldiers in my armies, wondering how they feel, if perhaps theirs is not the loneliest profession they could have chosen."

"Offers its share of introspection," Nien replied. "On the other hand, I treasured the camaraderie. I was only lonely amongst those who were unfamiliar with the life."

"I imagine you were quite the novelty in Rieeve."

Nien chuckled lightly, a full, welcoming tone that came from deep within him. "A novelty, yes, but not like you. I was accessible."

"I thought Rieevans were leery of outsiders."

"Well, they are, but not for the reasons you might suspect. To us it was a matter of philosophy, not skin colour that determined prejudice. Also," and he laughed sardonically, "racial variance never came up that much in Rieeve—nobody left and no one else wanted to come in."

SiQQiy's smile was brief. "It's all ugly," she said.

Nien nodded his head and let his breath out into the evening. "When I arrived in Legran I did not tell the Monterays who I was. I thought that if I acted the part of a servant it would give them, and me, less trouble than if I told them the truth."

"When Monteray came back to Legran I wondered if problems would arise by my visits, but so far none have. That he's so isolated at this end of the valley has made a difference I think, though I doubt anyone would confront him either way. His reputation is a large one in Legran."

"I have come to see that."

SiQQiy lifted her eyes, as if taking in a larger picture. "Monteray loves Legran. I think there is a part of the randomness, even the low-life of its people that intrigues him. It *is* his homeland, and no matter its faults, will forever be so. Change begins one at a time. Monteray is a good start here."

"I have found him to be everything Lant said he was, and Kate—Kate saved my life."

"Saved your life?"

Nien's eyes traced the river into the distance, possibly to the place he had crossed that day. "I was at my end when I arrived in Legran."

Beside him, he felt a strange quiet come over SiQQiy and briefly thought she was about to reach out and touch him, almost as if his words had pained her personally.

"I had come in the very hope of finding Monteray," Nien continued. "I was grateful when they accepted my offer to work—for the chance to repay what they'd done for me."

SiQQiy looked over her shoulder at the house. "It's been a work in progress for many revolutions now. He's done a beautiful job. None of Quieness is so fine." Turning back toward the river, she withdrew her feet from the water, and sliding back, started to dry them with her sleeve. Nien reached forward, having only his own sleeve to offer, and they both laughed.

Watching as she patted her feet dry in the grass then folded them beneath her, Nien looked over the river, thinking, *Don't do it!* even as his mouth blurted, "You are the most beautiful woman I have ever seen." On the other side of the obligatory awkward moment, he shot her a glance. "I should have said that in Rieevan. Sorry."

"Taking it back?"

"That would hardly be possible."

Amused, SiQQiy said, "You make me feel like a girl in her first-cycle."

"Is that a good thing?"

"Yes," she replied. "And no."

Uncertain which reply to go with, Nien opted out of both and asked, "And what was childhood like for a royal?"

SiQQiy thought about the question. "It was good," she finally said, as if agreeing to the sentiment for the first time. "I was a quiet child. Having no siblings, I was accustomed to playing alone, to being alone, until Master Monteray showed up. He was like the older brother I never had. After he left, I was alone again. And then I became Empress. Since that time, having so much...*need* around me has been an adjustment."

"Did you play 'SiQQiy, Queen of Quieness' as a girl?"

"No. Believe it or not, before I understood what my life was meant to be, I wanted to be a weaver. I dreamt of making quilts in a thousand different colours and textures and then traveling far and wide in a merchant caravan to sell them. My goal was to do this until one hung in every house all over the continent."

"Sounds fairly normal—except for that last part," Nien said. And then a realization dawned on him. "The shag rugs and the other large quilts on the wall and floors in Monteray's house, are they—?"

One of SiQQiy's eyes gleamed beneath a perfectly sculpted eyebrow.

"Well, your dream has made its start," Nien said with a grin. "Commander Lant had one in the front room of his home. It saw lots of use." Through Nien's mind flashed the memory of Teru and Mien'k in a drunken wrestle on that rug the night Lant had given him the leather shoulder mantle with the symbol of the Cant upon it. The replay warmed and scalded Nien's heart in turn. He had to clear his throat of emotion before he continued. "Meanwhile, your reality is probably dreamed of by some little girl in Cao, prancing around in her mother's robe, pretending to be you."

"Probably so," SiQQiy admitted. "And you?"

"Me?"

"Childhood dreams?"

"Other than flying?"

SiQQiy laughed.

"Of course dreams change," Nien said, his eyes taking respite in the gloaming. "The Cant and the school were my ultimate dreams."

"I was told you were a teacher."

"You *are* thorough, aren't you?"

"Hazard of the job, I'm afraid."

"Yes, well, I was—if you could call it that. I had about thirty students for a very short time."

"And you taught...?"

Wondering why the Empress of Quieness would have any interest in what a Rieevan might teach a few young people in a classroom that was no more than a section of field, he said, "I had some books I'd refer to and read from. We would discuss ideas, philosophies, as well as the politics, commerce, history, and beliefs of the other continental valleys. They had so many questions. Questions we never got to answer."

"Why?"

"The Council closed it."

"They closed your school?"

Nien nodded.

"What did you do?"

"I...I ran away to Quieness, actually."

SiQQiy laughed. "Really?"

"I did. I was..." —it felt so wrong, somehow, to say it now, but—"at the time I was suffocating in Rieeve. I was very hungry for learning."

Now, he thought, *there's nothing I've learned that's worth anything.*

Nien glanced back across the river.

"Strange," he said quietly. "I remember now, they asked about death. We'd received word by then of the fall of Lou; it was on everyone's minds. Rieevan children already had a lot of answers to that question, but for some reason they wanted to talk about it. Maybe they thought I would be more honest with them than their parents. Maybe they felt I might have a different view on it since I had read books they'd never seen." Nien swallowed the lump in his throat. "It was almost as if they knew."

"What was it," SiQQiy asked softly, "that Rieevan parents taught their children about death?"

As SiQQiy asked it, Nien remembered Necassa telling him that the Ancient Writings were not taken literally nor studied for spiritual import in Quieness.

"Well," he said, "that death of the physical body is only transitional. That as physical beings we are more importantly beings of spirit."

"Spirit, as in ethereal?"

"As in very real."

There was a twinkle in SiQQiy's tone as she replied, "Really?" Her eyes narrowed then, as if trying to bring a memory into focus. "As a child I remember my mother telling me a story of a little girl who traveled the stars and had such adventures as one could only imagine having in the space between stars. But one day she came to Leer and brought six spicy fiilas and a jug of sweet viatta to an old man who lived alone outside the Quienan palace walls. The thing was, the little girl came before there ever was a palace, or emperors, or a country to rule.

"I didn't understand the story then, I'm not sure I do much more now, but it has always brought me peace."

Nien felt a warmth and tenderness stir inside him. "Do you remember?" he asked.

"Remember?"

"The space between stars."

SiQQiy stared. It took her a moment to reply, "Not anymore. You?"

"At times—with Wing. But no, not like I would like to."

SiQQiy wrapped her arms about herself and glanced up into the sky. "Do you think we were...ourselves? Up there, I mean."

"I think so, or some version thereof."

"That's a good thing, I guess," she said, "since most days I'm all right with being me."

"I imagine," Nien said.

A fish jumped in the river, its opalescent scales flashing against the rippled surface of the water.

Nien was watching the place where the fish had re-immersed when he felt SiQQiy's gaze upon him. Slowly, he turned to look at her. Her eyes were the colour of the shiny black marble he'd seen in the domes of her palaces.

"We Quienans think we're so bright," she said softly, "so advanced in our thinking, and yet with you I feel a sense of wonder that I now realize we have lost."

"Commander Lant once told me that we know everything. That all knowledge is recorded in the planet itself, in the stars, and in us. That discovery is really only *rediscovery.*"

SiQQiy gazed steadily at him. "Who *are* you? Why is all this so...familiar? And why do I feel as if we've had this conversation before?"

"Maybe we have."

"Maybe we have?" She narrowed her eyes at him. "You mean before... this life?" Her words trailed off. Reaching up, she pressed her palm to her forehead as if to alter the course of her thoughts. "Is this your belief or a Rieevan belief?"

Nien shrugged faintly. "A little of both."

SiQQiy's thin eyebrows furrowed together—in worry or in thought, Nien could not tell.

"Though there is nothing taught so specific in Quieness," she said, "I have always wanted to believe that in the chaos there is ultimately a purpose. I don't know if I'm drawn to that belief because it is or because I need it to be so."

Her words caused a volley of thoughts to rise and fall in Nien's own mind—some bringing ecstasy, others torment. "And I...I once thought I knew. Without a doubt." He paused to steady his voice. "And somehow that hurts even more. I don't find peace in it anymore."

SiQQiy reached out and placed her hand upon his. "Nevertheless, I envy you."

Momentarily stopped by her touch, Nien said, "Envy me? Why?" Then in a feeble attempt to lift the gravity, added, "That I can leave my room without bodyguards?"

"There is that, but no," she replied. "That you once trusted in something gives you a serenity, a calmness of soul that I've ever desired yet never found."

Nien had thought himself in the hopeless category beyond even shame. He was wrong. "If only it was with me as you see it. In truth, my lady, I am entirely lost. You mistake surrender for serenity."

Though he did not feel brave enough, SiQQiy's gaze drew his eyes up to hers. It surrendered him entirely to find her taking him in with the sincerest empathy.

"Under such circumstances, who could wonder why?" she said. "The loss of Rieeve was a great blow to Leer. We are all diminished by her loss. All life is a circle, all people are essential to the whole. When one is lost, so are pieces of the rest."

"I once believed that," Nien said, his voice fainter than he'd intended. "But as you say, if life *is* a circle, then I can only hope that those who are left will figure it out before it's too late for them. That the Plan may still be of use to the other valleys is the only thought that gives me any validation for...being alive."

The colours on the horizon had slowly dissipated. Overhead, the gentle blue hosts of the night began to appear in the sky, their faces reflecting in the glassy waters of the river.

"Nien," SiQQiy said. "I want you to understand what I tell you. I know it's too late for your people, but it's not too late for you, for your brother, for Carly, nor for your homeland. The Ka'ull can be driven from Rieeve or they can be killed."

Nien's eyes dropped. "I..." He hesitated. "Empress, I..."

"SiQQiy, please," she said.

"SiQQiy," he said reluctantly. "I don't know if I can. It's not something I'm sure I can do."

And you would not ask me, he thought, *not if you knew me, really. Not if you knew that I lost Bredo, a member of my team, that I handed my own valley over to the entire Ka'ull army, and that my back was turned when they murdered my family.*

"I am not what I once was," he said at last. "I am not the man Pree K told you about. You have met me and not him. For that, I am sorry."

CHAPTER 64

Poet Laureate

"Step aside!"

Anger flickered in the deep-set eyes of the soldier as he stepped aside for the sub-Commander and his assistant. The soldier's long hair was pulled back tight from his face and secured at the base of his neck by a thin piece of worn leather. His hood was drawn up, covering most of his face.

Though much shorter in stature, the sub-Commander growled to his assistant that hurried along behind him. The assistant pushed by the long-haired man, scowling at him. He was still scowling when the sub-Commander stopped abruptly and turned back. The assistant bumped into him.

"Where is your superior?" the sub-Commander said to the soldier.

"In quarters above the main hall," the soldier replied, his voice chalky and low.

The sub-Commander's eyes narrowed. "Throw back your hood."

The soldier slowly pushed back his hood.

"You look unhappy."

The soldier said nothing.

"Well, take comfort. Your superior will be no happier to see me than you are."

The soldier watched the sub-Commander and his assistant go before pulling his hood back up over his head. He trudged on across the compound and to the front doors of the castle to look out across the alien valley. All was quiet. The only sounds in this valley now came from within the castle walls. To his right lay the grey-black carcasses of homes that used to be a civilization.

A grunt escaped him that could have been an angry cry.

Another soldier sat inside the gates to the castle courtyard, stressing a long piece of leather.

"Gren'tel, how's the outside?" Tem'a asked.

The man stopped, his hood still pulled low. "Burnt," he replied.

Tem'a looked up at him. "Yeah, well, I guess they didn't want us moving in."

Gren'tel grunted again. "Not that I would have, anyway."

Tem'a looked him over. "Did you see the Northing sub-Commander come through?"

"Yeah."

Tem'a returned to his strip of leather. "Guess we'll be expecting company."

There had been rumours that the Mat'ta Kell'a, their first and fiercest contingent, was looking to move southing to rest in preparation for the incursion of, well, no one really knew. Would it be Jayak? Preak? Were they actually prepared for the invasion of the most formidable valley on the continent—Quieness?

"The Mat'ta—figures they'd show up here," Gren'tel said, and he moved on, his shoulders slumped as he shuffled off across the courtyard toward the bunks in a large lower hall beneath the northing castle wall.

Tem'a watched him go, hunched beneath his burden of despair and hate.

It was a look Tem'a recognized for he saw it every day: rage barely held in check, fantasies of death (sometimes of the enemy, sometimes of themselves), memories and hopes burned as black as the alien village, dark thoughts passing through their minds in neat, orderly rows like soldiers waiting in line for a meal.

Tem'a had his own dark moments. But he had a reputation for being the carefree one who could, at times, come to someone's philosophical aid. Had he not been a soldier he might have been one of their people's finest poet laureates.

He figured he could be a poet anyway—the war had to end eventually.

He hoped.

After initial training, Tem'a had been assigned to a regiment moving supplies up the Tu'Lon to the Ti-Uki confluence and then overland into the newly captured valley of Rieeve.

He hadn't actually killed anyone yet, and even though he'd seen plenty of carnage in the cleanup of their war ship sunk by a Quieness galley in the Tou Bay inlet, he was still considered a bit of a dandy in the eyes of the "working" soldiers who had seen action in Lou and Tou. But no matter how much they harassed him, he was forever unperturbed and this, it seemed, had impressed the other men on some level.

The unofficial camp psychologist, Tem'a was secretly loved and openly chided, and he took it all in stride.

Dragging the back of his shortblade across the leather strap, he pulled it taught and striated it again.

Turning his mind to home, he thought of Sen't.

Gods of Wind, he thought, *she had been so beautiful.* And the sex. It had just worked—from the very beginning.

He had been her first crush. She had never asked him if she had been his, probably because she'd known how insatiably curious women were about him, a feeling readily reciprocated since he was intensely curious about people in general. His willingness to let people in was irresistible, a trait especially appealing to women who had often responded in kind.

But within every good thing lay a seed of bad: Sen't had felt betrayed because there had been other women he adored, some sexually, some not; his family had felt betrayed because he could not curse his father for leaving; his friends because he questioned the Homeland Cause and the veracity of the invasion—though "invasion" was a word no Ka'ull ever used. The "invasion" was a matter of retribution. Redemption.

Tem'a regretted the wounds he'd caused, but how could he explain his inability to place his wonder, his awe, indeed his love for one being above that of every other?

Condemned outright and often for his thoughts and actions, it had become an idea he frequently pondered: how people could become selfish creatures, putting restrictions on everything, including how, where, and whom to love. Though this could have jaded him, Tem'a still saw people as he saw himself—in layers. He never took an action, a word at face value. He looked deep, seeing the motivations and reasons from which the word or action had sprung. Time and time again, he'd seen a moment of understanding unravel a history of hate. Part of him hoped that by affording it to others he might, someday, be afforded it himself. To his surprise, he'd been offered more of it by the rough, brutal killers he'd been surrounded by since leaving Tech'Kon, than he ever was by his family, friends, or even his mother.

Still working at his strap of leather, Tem'a thought about the soldier with whom he'd just exchanged words. He knew Gren'tel had seen action with another battalion in Lou and Tou. He also knew he'd been turned down for a position in one of the shocktroop units because of unconscionable acts—

And this, Tem'a thought, *coming from the Tenkt'tla troops.*

Glancing up at the sky, he saw clouds beginning to gather at the sunsetting side of the valley and felt their heaviness just as he felt the agitation of the men over the arrival of the Northing sub-Commander.

Tem'a stood and headed toward the castle gateway. Stretching, he glanced up at the mountains surrounding the strange, exceedingly beautiful valley. None of them had ever seen such foliage, such trees. As awe-inspiring as it was to Tem'a, to most of the men it managed only to fuel their rage—such abundance, while in their homeland a stand of thin deciduous trees could equal a blood feud. And then there were the immediate concerns, like the impending arrival of the Mat'ta Kell'a.

He couldn't blame Gren'tel's grim attitude over the thought. But they had all suspected that this valley was where the Mat'ta Kell'a would come to headquarter, and perhaps that was the reason behind the slaughter of the people that had once inhabited this valley rather than their enslavement. Emptying the valley of its natives meant the Mat'ta could rest and prepare for that which lay ahead—a fight far more daunting than that which they'd already won. Tou and Lou and fallen easily for they had been unsuspecting.

That had changed after the Tou Inlet Battle.

With the galley that had destroyed their largest galleon had been two other Quienan ships. These ships had nursed the wounded Quieness galley back down the river—to Jada Post, no doubt.

From that point on everyone knew it would be a whole different war. There would be no more surprise attacks, no easy victories. Soon every valley on the continent would be aware of their presence.

Raising his luminous, unsuspecting eyes, Tem'a looked out over the drying fields. To his right, dark and defeated, lay row upon row of blackened rubble that stretched off toward the mountains on the sunrising side. Not for the first time, Tem'a imagined the lives that had once been lived there. He was pretty sure boys had wrestled in the streets and that blood from one their noses had stained the warm brown cobblestone; that a girl had walked casually past a young man's house, hoping he might finally take notice and think her beautiful; that an elderly woman had walked across the garden behind her house to take food to a neighbor. And he was pretty sure children had been taught by parents that here, in their small secluded valley, they would always be safe and protected.

Life, Tem'a thought. *We bring it, and we take it away.* And somewhere in the back of his mind he wondered whose life he might take, and possibly whose life he might save…

CHAPTER 65

Training

D ays after his long conversation with SiQQiy at the river's edge, Nien found himself lying belly down on the roof of Monteray's house, gazing at the spot near the river where SiQQiy sat, talking and laughing with Carly, Kate, and Tei.

The sound of their voices, the press of the smooth wooden surface beneath his chest, and the view from the top of a roof filled Nien with something he'd never expected to feel again, something he'd felt when bouncing Fey on his knee, arm-wrestling Jake, smelling the woody scent of his father's coat, or listening to the sounds of Reean cooking in the kitchen before dinnertime.

A turn or two that could have been a lifetime passed like this, and every day came a gentle breeze beneath a bright lavender-blue sky.

Mealtime, which had become more of an event than a meal, had been all but cleaned up after that evening as Monteray, Carly, Nien, and Wing headed out to watch the sun set—a family custom. Everyone, including SiQQiy's guards, spent the last sunstep or so of the day on the bank of the river in the fading twilight.

Nien and Carly sat down in the grass by the river, but as Wing went to join them, Monteray said, "Wing, if you will…"

With a curious glance at Nien and Carly, Wing turned to follow him.

Monteray walked a little way off before sitting down. Wing sat beside him, suddenly feeling ill at ease.

"Wing, I hope you'll forgive the boldness of what I'm about to say."

Wing tilted his head a little, waiting.

"We have come to a point," Monteray said. "When I first saw you, when Rhusta told me that you would be coming to find me, I was concerned that once you had delivered netaia Lant's Plan you would have no other reason to stay in Legran. Upon discovering that Nien was indeed your brother, I was sure that would be enough to hold you—and it has." Monteray clasped his hands together; Wing could not tell if the gesture was in thought or concern. "I have seen new life come into you. But that is not all I see. It still seems your faith extends to everyone but yourself. You believe in your brother and in Carly. You have faith in my strength and in SiQQiy's resolve to implement Lant's Plan. In yourself, however, it does not seem you have any faith whatsoever."

"Master Monteray, I..." Wing knew what he was about to say would sound disparaging, but it was honest. "The best thing I could do was deliver Lant's Plan to you; carry out Lant's last wish. He called on me so many times. And every time, I turned him down. I owed him this last thing. More than that...Well, there is no more than that."

Beside Wing, Monteray simply shook his head. He almost laughed. "You don't understand."

Wing's brow furrowed.

"Netaia Lant did not ask you to deliver the Plan to me for the sake of the Plan." Monteray waited till Wing raised his eyes to look at him. "The reason netaia Lant asked you to deliver the Plan was for you—to save *you*."

Wing's mouth went dry.

"It was *your* survival that mattered to him. Delivering the Plan to me was merely a reason." Monteray's voice was kind but intent. "I was not meant to save Rieeve, nor was SiQQiy. Only you can do that. You were saved to do it. We can give you aid. We can give you supplies, men, and arms. But after that is all done, after the Ka'ull are driven from Rieeve, what then, Wing? Can I, can SiQQiy give it back its heart? Can we breathe life into its soil? Can we create a child wherein the blood of a Rieevan may flow? It was in you and Nien that netaia Lant held his greatest hope—not in ideas on a parchment."

Wing sat impossibly still. Monteray guarded the silence, waiting for him to speak.

"You..." Wing felt himself beginning to choke on the words, "are not the first one to tell me that. But everything you think you see, that they thought they saw was wasted on me. I...in Rieeve, I saw things as others didn't, but I don't know what it meant, what good it did." Wing fell silent; with Nien alone had he ever been so open.

"Of that I cannot tell you," Monteray said. "Of that I have little enough understanding. I do know, however, that often we try to wring the truth out of a thing, when, if only we have a little faith and a lot of patience it will give itself freely when the time is right." Monteray patted Wing's knee. "But that is all up to the will and timing of the Gods, I suppose. Until then, we are given time for you to find those answers."

Me? Wing thought. *Had everyone gone mad? Was there something in the water that had found its way over the mountains from Rieeve and into Legran?*

"I feel," Monteray said slowly, as if seeking out his words, "it is that side of your nature which may illuminate the greater purpose behind the dark revolutions to come."

Even more shocking than the words themselves, was that they'd come from Monteray. Inside of Wing, they conjured the same wild sensation that had ripped around in his chest when in the presence of the old Rieevan Council, the one that had always preceded the inclination to run.

This time, however, the inclination was stopped dead by three words: *Nien and Carly.*

They deserved better from him this time, even if it was a lie. They'd paid their price in the castle that night. So, unless he had the courage to leave Legran, there was only one other thing to do: Pretend, this time, to be what they thought him to be.

It took Wing great effort to say, "All that cannot be answered aside, if I am to do this, I will need to know more than how to plow a field; I will need to know how to fight."

"Well, *that*," Monteray said with a smile Wing could see in the incoming dark, "is something I can help you with."

Beside Monteray, Wing returned to sit with Nien and Carly and the rest on the bank of the river. Wing pasted a pleased look on his face, knowing that once everyone parted to their respective sleeping places, he would be telling Nien something neither of them ever thought he would: "It looks like I'm going to be learning the art of combat."

Two days later, beneath the dome of the Mietan, Monteray stood facing Wing. Right arms crossed to right shoulders, Monteray nodded his head to Wing.

"When you bow to another, you honour yourself first, then the other," Monteray said.

Turning, he walked over and from the wall took down a short sword. Sliding it from its sheath, he set the sheath aside.

Wing watched him curiously, wondering if there might be some sort of ritual Monteray was now going to teach him or a lesson familiarizing him with the weapon and its uses.

Instead, Monteray turned, and without even so much as a warning glance, charged straight for him.

Startled, Wing stumbled back, hands flying out to ward the shiny metal thing coming at him.

Monteray dropped the blade away and spun around him. "Do you see?"

Embarrassed, Wing glanced down at his hands. "Uh huh." He'd just tried to use his arms to deflect a sword. Had Monteray been serious, Wing would have been standing there with bloody stumps.

"Lesson number one," Monteray said. "Some instincts will serve you in combat, others not as much."

Again, Monteray came at Wing with the short blade. This time, Wing danced aside, turning a shoulder toward the blade.

"Better," Monteray said.

"But I'm still dead," Wing said.

"Probably," Monteray agreed and he came at Wing again.

This time, Wing pivoted and charged back at Monteray all muscle and shoulder, moving past the blade and right inside the ring of Monteray's arms.

The men hit the Mietan floor; Monteray was laughing.

"That," he said, "*will* serve you!" Monteray got up and took a step back. "Now, do it again."

Wing did so and found himself on the floor. Another lesson learned— tricks usually only worked once.

Monteray waited as Wing climbed back to his feet before spinning around and throwing a left-handed punch at his face. Wing ducked and whirled out of the way, but Monteray caught his arm and completed Wing's circle, bringing Wing's eyes back around to meet his own.

"Efficiency is key. Don't use a big move if a small one will do. Energy travels in circles and in spirals. Notice it once, and you will know what I mean." Monteray spread his arms. "Now, come at me."

Wing did so and found himself on the floor again—a place he was fast becoming used to.

"Let's go over that again."

A couple turns later, late evening found Wing prostrating himself bone-lessly onto the dirt floor of the cabin.

"That seems to be your favorite place," Nien chided, brushing by Wing and approaching the fire with a handful of kindling.

Wing figured Nien got some pleasure in aggravating the flames, especially when they didn't even need the fire most nights.

"How's the shoulder?"

Wing glanced over at the white cloth binding up his shoulder and mumbled, "Monteray does a fine job patching up his victims."

Nien chuckled. "Don't think I'm beyond mercy, Weed Farmer. We'll skip our session tonight." They'd been back at their play-wrestling again.

Carly had suggested that was the reason the Monterays had permanently banished them to the cabin.

Drawing circles in the dirt with a fingertip, Wing replied, "You're a real hero. Thanks a lot." He rolled over and rubbed his hands across his face. "But I'm thinking his offer to train me was a joke—he might really be trying to kill me. I mean, he'll come at me, swinging a sword around, and I'm standing there with air in my hands."

"What do you do with this air?" Nien asked.

Wing shrugged. "Today I waited till he swung, then stepped in behind his sword arm and pinned it against his chest."

"And...?"

"He said it was a good move." Wing shrugged. "We've been doing that same kind of thing for what, two turns now? He's taught me absolutely nothing. He just keeps coming at me with something bright and sharp, and I do whatever I can to *not* die." Wing looked up to find Nien smiling. "What?"

"Think about it, Wing. He *has* taught you. He's taught you something that, well, I thought was unteachable."

Wing's expression said he wasn't following.

"It's a mental attitude, a way of seeing it. Without any training, he's made you prove to yourself that you can fight."

A light smile touched at the edges of Wing's mouth as the realization dawned. "Well...that's pretty great."

Nien laughed.

"Good morning," Monteray said as Wing walked into the Mietan the following morning.

They met with the familiar greeting and then Monteray returned to the sword wall and taking down another short sword, placed the live blade in Wing's hand.

Wing took the hilt, eyeing the weapon with a mix of childlike wonder, aversion, and...

Insight, Monteray thought. It was as if Wing saw everything in the world as a metaphor.

From the first day of working with Wing, Monteray found that he only had to give direction once through a shift of eye or brief physical demonstration and in the next go Wing could implement it: he'd duck or spin, slap Monteray's sword wrist, avoid an arm and roll around his back, or trap an arm. Obviously, he'd had some wrestling experience, but there was more than that. By the end of the first turn Wing had already become incredibly efficient, following the energy as it traveled in circles and spirals, feeling his way through complicated moves as if they were second nature.

In all his time of training students in Legran, Jayak, and Magj, Monteray had never been more impressed with a student—

Until this moment.

Many steps of the sun had passed beneath the glimmering Mietan light deep into Wing's third day of sword work when, at the end of another attack from Monteray that had knocked the sword from Wing's hand, Wing drew out of the circle of combat, and growling under his breath looked at the sword as if he were about to chuck it across the room.

Monteray shook his head. "I know you're frustrated. Wing, look at me."

Wing raised his eyes.

"Knocking your head against a wall takes forever; getting it right is spontaneous. Shift the way you perceive it and the change will happen instantly, without effort. Remember, in the moment you feel it, it will be yours forever. You will reclaim that which you already knew."

Wing was still looking at him, more anger than confusion in his eyes.

Walking over, Monteray picked up Wing's dropped sword, set it aside with his own, and motioned for Wing to sit at the center of the Mietan floor.

Wing did so.

In him, Monteray could see the same thing he'd seen in every student he'd ever had at one time or another: A wish for the training to just be over.

Monteray sat down opposite him, crossing his legs. "Close your eyes."

Wing closed his eyes.

Monteray took a deep breath, releasing it as he relaxed into the posture. "You have a natural feeling in you for energy and its use, extend that into the sword as you do with the tools when we're working on the house."

Wing opened his eyes.

"You didn't think I'd noticed?" Monteray smiled a little. "Close your eyes." Wing closed his eyes again. "Now, wrap the fingers of your left hand under your right wrist."

Wing did so, resting his arms against his thighs.

"Press lightly, just to the outside of the two main tendons running into your hand. Do you feel it?"

Wing concentrated for a moment. "Yes," he replied quietly.

"Good. Now...*feel* it."

The furrow of concentration in Wing's brow slowly relaxed. Monteray watched as Wing allowed himself to be lulled into the quiet realm where nothing existed except him, the steady throb of his pulse, the miracle of blood, life, their world, and the space beyond.

Monteray could feel it himself—

Pulse, Pulse, Pulse...

He saw Wing's frustration drain from him. Saw that his mind had quieted; his breathing still, soft, barely noticeable.

"Wing."

Wing started. Opened his eyes.

"Welcome back," Monteray said.

He waited a moment as Wing's eyes slowly focused on him.

"There are many secrets under the surface," Monteray said kindly. "I believe you've seen them more than most. The same is true, here: Discovery is the power behind the training." Monteray held Wing's gaze for a time. "You once trusted your instincts—do so again. They will not fail you."

Wing looked up at him and behind the glimmering surface of Wing's eyes, Monteray saw tumultuous waves begin to rise, like a churning grey sea beneath emerald skies.

"I know you have doubts," Monteray said. "I know you feel your heart has led you astray, but *my* feelings tell me it has not—nor ever will. There *is* order in the world, Wing. I understand the incredulity my words may evoke in you, but I tell you: The worst thing, even the *very* worst thing, often turns out to be the best thing."

Night had settled over Legran and the Monteray house when Nien stepped cautiously into the Mietan expecting to find Wing and Monteray at the end of their training day; instead, he found only Monteray, standing in the center of the Mietan, a beautifully made sword in his right hand.

Sensing he'd caught the Master in a private moment, Nien started to leave, but as he did Monteray moved the sword in an arc beneath the stained-glass window high above. The light caught the blade's edge and it glinted. Lost in the elegance of the sword and the grace of the hand that moved it, Nien stopped, not taking notice that Monteray was coming toward him, moving backwards in a set of defensive postures.

The dance continued until, at the last moment, Monteray swung around as if blocking a blow from an invisible assailant at his back—

In the path of the blade, Nien had frozen.

Monteray adjusted the sword in time, but Nien felt the air move from the tip of the blade across his face.

"Nien!" Monteray exclaimed, grabbing at his heart.

Nien blinked, coming back from some very dark place. "I'm sorry. I didn't want to interrupt. I was looking for Wing."

"He's gone into town. Probably to meet up with my nephew," Monteray replied, thinking, *I can't believe how close I just came to...*

He looked up to find Nien heading for the Mietan doors. Turning his back as if not to notice Nien's hasty retreat, Monteray said, "Lant often spoke of you. He said you were the best he'd ever trained."

He waited a moment before turning around. Nien had stopped at the Mietan doors.

"If you'd like, you're more than welcome to join Wing and me."

Nien had stopped, but he hadn't turned around.

Monteray set the sword in a long, broad holder against the far wall and walked over to him. Gently, Monteray said: "Nien."

Nien turned and raised his eyes.

"I have some small understanding of what happened to you," Monteray said. "If you will give yourself a chance, you may find that what was once there, is still there."

It took Nien a moment before he managed to say, "I appreciate the idea—the hope—but whenever I think about it, whenever I think of even holding a blade in my hand again, walls close in on me, I smell death, my...my chest...."

Monteray nodded. "Come," he said, and motioned for Nien to follow him. At the stairs to the dais, Monteray sat down and pressed his fingertips together in thought. At his side, Nien sat, his breath uneasy, his eyes fixed on the floor.

"You are an interesting mix, Nien Cawutt. Your strength and courage cannot be doubted. But sensitivity?" Monteray nodded to himself. "That is what makes you great. That is what netaia Lant saw in you. To him, skill with a sword came a distant second to greatness of heart. That you feel as you do would have been of no surprise to Lant, nor is it to me." Monteray laid his hand on Nien's knee. "You are much more than a warrior, Nien. But if you find the strength again, your brother and I would welcome your company in the Mietan, and if our plans succeed the three of you may only have to wield a sword once more in your lifetimes."

Nien felt as he had after the battle of Jayak, when Lant had spoken with him, encouraged him, tried to lead him back to his strength. He appreciated the effort, but still, could not see it. Respectfully, he inclined his head to Monteray and asked his leave.

Back in the cabin, Wing lay awake on his bed as Nien came in.

Walking across the room, Nien sat down on the edge of his bed to remove his boots.

"Nien?"

"Uh huh," Nien answered, he didn't really feel like talking.

Wing drew a quick breath, as if about to ask a question he was afraid to ask. "Do you think you'll join Monteray and me in the Mietan?"

Nien's face was solemn. "Must be a conspiracy."

Wing sat up. "What?"

"I was just out at the Mietan looking for you. Monteray asked me the same thing."

"Oh."

The truth was, he'd been thinking about it, wondering if he could try again.

Just then, Carly came in. "I'd like to train a while with you and Monteray tomorrow afternoon," she said.

She'd already joined them on odd occasions in the past few turns of Wing's training.

"Sure," Wing said. His eyes floated not so surreptitiously to Nien.

Carly noticed. "What?"

"Nien?" Wing said.

Nien groaned. "Alright."

"Alright?" Carly asked.

"Nien's going to join us, too."

"Really?" Her voice was careful but her eyes were dancing.

There was no such enthusiasm in Nien's face. Ever since Wing had agreed to train with Monteray, Nien had felt like they'd been swept up in something none of them had actually chosen. It had just…happened, and he wasn't even sure why. Most confusing of all had been Wing's agreement. That, Nien had still not been able to figure out for there was only one logical reason for Wing to learn the art of combat and that made no sense whatsoever—

Rieeve was lost.

Nien could not imagine regaining Rieeve nor could he fathom fighting in a war for another valley, even Legran, no matter how much he loved the Monterays.

"So," Carly said after a moment, "going back to Rieeve."

There it was, the ghost in the room.

Nien looked at Wing who had sunk into a familiar heavy silence. "Wing?"

After a lingering moment, Wing raised his face and looked at him.

"Want to share?" Nien asked.

"Not really," Wing said.

"How about anyway?" Carly prodded.

Wing looked at both of them, but his eyes returned to the floor when he said, "Why try to regain something Eosha didn't care enough to save in the first place?"

No one could silence a room like Wing. Nien and Carly simply looked at him.

"You asked," Wing said.

CHAPTER 66

Darkness Ascends

"Wing."

Wing turned and looked at Carly across the expanse of the Mietan. He'd been pacing and his hair and body were drenched in sweat. He appeared tall and dark, but it was his face that startled her. Grey and fierce it was, thin and rigid.

What happened? Carly wondered.

Wing had spent the past day or so alone, not even coming up to the house for meals. It was late now and she'd come out to look for him.

"Wing?" she asked carefully.

"Now is not a good time," Wing said, his voice distant, haunted.

The moon shone eerily through the dome of stained glass high above, filling the Mietan with a strange half-light through which Wing ranged, daunting and grey. Bare-chested, the light gleamed across the long, jagged scars that covered his chest and shoulders.

"Wing, please..."

But it seemed he had already forgotten she was there as he returned to pacing, his body flashing against the imperial walls of the Mietan like silvered etching. For the first time, Carly noticed that he held a long sword in his hand.

"What's wrong? Are you hurt?"

Wing's eyes lit upon her. "Go away," he said evenly. His gaze was hard, like pressed metal.

Carly shrank back.

What was going on? she thought.

And then, as if in direct answer to her question, descended a feeling terrible and dark. It cut her off from herself, separated her mind from her body, the space she occupied from the place in which she stood. She

383

might have swum there for a moment or a revolution before a physical jolt reconnected her senses—

She'd bumped up against the Mietan doors.

Her eyes shot across the room. At the far side, Wing appeared then disappeared like a deathly sable ghost, the centrical force of a whirling black vortice. Emanating black light, he shone in reverse, filling the Mietan with a glistening sheen of night.

Whether Wing was enchanted or she herself bewitched, Carly could not tell, but as Wing materialized once more, rather than the apparition, Carly saw instead a tall man walking patiently behind the curved arms of a plow, the crumbly, wet soil churning up at his booted feet, the evening sun causing his hair to shine like coruscating threads of ebony. Though all features of his face were lost to her, Carly heard the heavy beat of his heart in the great openness, felt its throb within the pale pulses of moon and starlight, and she understood:

The emotions that had come over her were not her own, they'd been Wing's.

The realization cleared her mind and set her resolve. Beneath the scars, beneath the towering wall of dark energy, was that man of the fields and he was neither shadow nor blade—

And, Carly thought, *I will not abandon him to either.*

Fixing Wing with her eyes, she walked back toward the center of the Mietan. Her voice was calm but firm as she said: "Don't drop the reins, Wing. Talk to me."

Wing leaned the sword against a wall. Pulling his hair away from his face, he tied it in a knot at the back of his neck and returned to pacing the wide-open floor. Like a caged mountain cat, he passed from moonlight into shadow and back again, the immensity of his grief scratching at the four walls of the Mietan.

Carly waited, hoping she had reached him.

When at last Wing spoke, his voice was throaty, ill constrained and barely recognizable—more the glistening black ghost than the man she knew.

"There is no going back. There is no going back to seed and field and family. There is no going back to mothers, fathers, brothers, sisters, friends. There is only a broken and burned Village and one ancient castle where the slayers of our people sleep on a floor still stained with their blood."

Wrapped in a dark vision only he could see, Carly continued to wait, giving him the time to find his way through it.

"But if we *do* go back," Wing began again, "if we drive the beasts out, we will not be burning Ka'ull homes. We will not be enslaving them or murdering them outright. There can be no justice. There is no replacing all they took.

"But now Legran and Quieness say they'll fight with us. So why do I feel more alone than ever? I can't see Rieeve reborn. All I see are the dead and the barely living. Life is broken. I see long lines of people in chains. I see great pits. All is blood's fire. It's all *wrong*. There is no happiness, no resolution, only more death for that which is irreplaceable."

He paused, whether searching for the words or the will to speak them, Carly could not tell.

"I am wrung," he said. "There is only the land that remains, and" —his throat constricted— "I don't care. I never want to till another row, plant another crop."

His words seared Carly's heart. Wing *was* the soil, the breath, the life in the dirt, of Rieeve itself. She'd always known it, but she'd never seen it so clearly.

"But the Ka'ull," Wing said, forcing himself to continue, "they should die for what they did, shouldn't they? Shouldn't I *want* the satisfaction of seeing terror in a Ka'ull's eyes before I bury a sword in his chest?"

Carly trembled. Wing stood so tall, so magnificent—so terrifying. When he spoke again, Carly thought it might be for the last time.

"What is wrong with me that I don't?"

And then, from out of the floor beneath Wing's feet, Carly noticed a grey smoke begin to rise. In a state of wonder and revulsion, Carly watched it crawl and wrap itself around Wing's ankles like a living thing. Briefly, she wondered where it was coming from—

In the next instant, she understood: Not of its own accord, but by Wing's summon had it come. And not of its own substance was it made, but of Wing's guilt and rage.

In awe, Carly could do nothing but watch as the snaking smoke liquified into a shining black wave. Steadily, it rose, gathering momentum as it twisted itself around Wing's body, climbing about him like a spiral staircase. From its grounding place somewhere in the floor beneath them to its culminating point high above, the black wave shimmered and spun, growing up and out, holding Wing as its center.

Her heart pounding in the cavernous silence of her chest, Carly watched as the cyclonic column continued to spin, slowly swallowing Wing down its swirling black throat. But just as she thought Wing might vanish entirely, the immense column slowed and paused, for a breath neither shrinking nor expanding. And then, ominously, it began to reverse directions.

Carly started back as the wave reached the height of its velocity and came crashing down.

It broke upon the Mietan floor in a starlit wash, flowing out in every direction, bathing her feet in a cascade of caliginous colour.

Turning, Wing grabbed up the sword and threw it. It spun through the air, moonlight glinting off its silvered blade as it revolved end over end before hitting the floor with a resounding clang and sliding to a stop at the far side. Twisting away from it, Wing curled his hands into fists, compressing the dark energy in his palms till it burst from between his fingers in a deathly spray of two black stars.

He howled.

The sound was terrifying and unreal. Carly felt it pull at her own throat.

Struggling, Wing managed a shallow, husky breath. "I don't want to go back," he muttered. Carly could barely hear him; she took a few steps closer. "I want to leave Rieeve" —he coughed, inhaled sharply— "withered, desolate, dry."

In the mystical note of night's light through stained glass, Carly felt Wing's eyes brush hers. "I have no right to ask, but there is you now," he said. "There is Nien. Is that not enough? Can't we just go away and forget it *all*?"

Carly wanted to answer. She felt so inside him at that moment that the voice inside her head cried: *Yes! Of course, yes. Let's just leave. Go away. Leave everything, just start over. Be new people. Different people. Any other people than who we are...*

"I—" she started to say, but in her brief silence, Wing had slipped away. He stood wavering like a great tree in a fierce wind before stumbling backward, tearing at his own chest with his hands as if attempting to rip open an invisible shirt.

Carly tried to go to him, to stop him, but could not get her feet to move.

Wing fell to his knees.

Carly thought she heard a dry sob, but it was only a trick of the wind for Wing was silent, still as carven stone.

Carly tried again to move. This time her feet obeyed as the dark rampart of energy issuing from Wing abated, allowing her entrance.

At his side, she lowered herself to the floor.

Heavy moments prevailed before Wing's weary voice issued out into the darkness: "Nien has said he'll return to Rieeve—that which he fears most he's said he'll face with me." He drew a breath that, to Carly, sounded like the scrape of a hoof file through his lungs. "The only reason he agreed is because he thinks it's what *I* want. But I don't, Carly. I don't. I want to go away. Somewhere far away. Just you, and me, and Nien."

Carly's head lowered. There was nothing else to say, nothing else to do. She found her voice and said, "I am with you. Wherever you go, I am with you."

Wing's eyes were fixed upon the floor. He nodded.

In the deep, languishing silence Carly remained at his side. "Come back to the cabin," she said softly.

Wing shook his head.

"Come back with me," she said again.

He remained silent and sunk a little, as if the very floor beneath him had begun to give way.

"I'll come back soon," he said.

Stroking his cheek with her palm, Carly pushed his hair away from his face and kissed him at the corner of his mouth. She then got to her feet and crossing the long, smooth floor, stepped out through the Mietan doors into the night.

Beneath the stained glass dome of the Mietan, his legs bent beneath him, body curled over, head upon his knees, Wing remained—a sculpted figure in a living painting.

Moonlight through the coloured glass of the Mietan's apex fell upon his naked shoulders. The light ran off his back in a glistening purple flood, illuminating a dark circle around him against the delicate glossy inlay of the wooden floor.

Inside, Wing was burning. Thoughts hammered him, kindling a fiery ache deep in his gut. His quickening inhalations fanned the flame. Scorching its way through him, Wing felt the ropy scars from the claws of the shy'teh begin to burn in hot streaks across his chest and back as if the big cat were there again, tearing at his flesh.

The pain made him tremble. A strange half-cry escaped him. The cry was unintelligible, but that hardly mattered.

His jaw clenched.

Why bare time before me and then close the door? he begged the silence. *What did I do? What more could I have done? Why punish them for my weakness?*

My people. This—the price of devotion.

He lifted his head and his voice shook the Mietan as he roared, "Why!"

His entreaty slashed off the walls of the Mietan, creating an echoic catalyst that cut through him from wall to wall, incising a hole from sternum to backbone.

Twisted by the melee, Wing gasped—

But through the incision, the black strength of his pain found release.

Sagging over, his right shoulder coming to ground, Wing sought the shallowest of breaths...

And was answered in the cool whisper of a breeze pushing its way in from under the two bold doors of the Mietan.

Reaching out, he splayed his fevered palm upon the floor. His long dark fingers caressed the intricate inlay, tracing its swirling path in silence.

E me thelan no' va-nen.

The words echoed in his head like a bitter friend. He drew a quick, sharp breath as the rest of the words came in a flood, rising up from deep inside his throat:

" 'E fe de lebaan'a tuvle

Pesanta telaa

Melaan, I jeik-a' et te luua

Melaan e teh'ta e cansa ma'n

E gret'a tu entar

Ne'lanka uoo e emm'rtal louu

Se meeta ru neta

I me te dona'then

I sc'en ta too

A bonndo' ne

E f'le

E to'ne

Sce'ken te mafa'la

Melaan, e scoka le e do'ur.' "

Carly pressed her hand against her quivering lips as she stood outside the Mietan doors. Since arriving in Legran, the three had become accustomed to the language of Legran as well as the Fultershier. To have heard Wing's lament, to hear him slowly chanting a familiar verse from the Prophet-Poet Eneefa in their native tongue, tore at her heart.

Silently, she mouthed the words with him, wondering as she always had what the Prophet Eneefa must have seen, what he must have felt to have written in such despair:

" 'Why did we forget?

—Was that part of the crime?

To leave devotion out in the cold

—Just a beggar at the door?

Despised and left

—Thrown down from higher worlds

A scant tug on the sleeve

—Forgotten
Abandoned to note
—And line
—And word
Scratching like a thief—
Just a beggar at the door.' "

As Wing's voice faded into the silent expanse of the Mietan, Carly pushed the hair away from her face, and brushing at her eyes, started back to the cabin.

Walking toward the little light that glowed inside the cabin window, Carly glanced up at the night sky—and stopped. Moonlit rays shot down from behind rolling, deep grey clouds. Through them she glimpsed brief handfuls of stars, startling white against the dark. As the clouds moved through space and over mountain, Carly could almost feel the empyreal motion of Leer itself, spinning through the ever-reaching black.

Lost in the sensation, it took a moment for her awareness to shift to a sound carried over the wind-rustled grasses. It was not a sound she'd ever heard before; nevertheless, she recognized it immediately.

Carly looked back over her shoulder at the Mietan.

She'd never heard Wing cry before. To hear it now broke something inside her.

Drenched in opposing inclinations of longing and deference, she wavered briefly, fighting the invisible force drawing her back to him.

Aching moments passed before she turned and continued on to the cabin.

CHAPTER 67

ShadowLand

A few moonsteps had passed when Carly looked up to see Wing step in through the door of the cabin. To her eyes he had no weight, no mass to his lithe frame. It seemed he'd left it all in the Mietan.

He shut the door and though he raised his eyes a little, did not look at her directly. Carly reached out a hand to him. He walked over and sat down on the bed beside her.

"Carly, I," —he stopped, almost as if he'd forgotten what he'd started to say— "I'm sorry I was not there that night. I didn't want to let you down. To let our people down."

"I know, Wing. I know." Reaching out, Carly took his ethereal hand in hers, cradling it like smoke between her own. "And for the record, you've never let me down. Not once. Not in anything." She thought the ghost beside her trembled, but she could not have been sure. "I can't explain why," she continued, "but when I look at the stars, I imagine them whispering answers to your questions, wishing to ease the burden you carry."

Wing raised his face. Carly saw his eyes focus on the shimmering pools of tears in her own.

"If that is so," he replied, "then I am as deaf to them as I am to you."

Saying goodnight to SiQQiy's men and leaving SiQQiy herself up at the house, Nien returned to the cabin.

Opening the door, he moved quickly to the fire to warm his hands before glancing around to see who was there.

Wing sat on the edge of his bed.

Usually the brothers passed a few quiet moonsteps in the cabin at night sharpening tools and patching clothes while they talked.

Tonight something was different. Actually, he'd noticed a slow darkening in Wing for some few days now—ever since they'd talked about returning to Rieeve.

"Wing?"

Wing made no reaction to hearing his name. Nien looked upon him and for the first time in his life hardly knew him. Briefly, Nien thought there might be something wrong with his eyes, for Wing appeared to him more like a ripple on water than flesh.

"What's wrong?" he asked slowly.

Lying over onto his bed, Wing shut his eyes.

Nien's brow furrowed. *What was going on? And where was Carly?*

Glancing back to the door, he wondered if he should go up to the house and find her. Perhaps she knew.

Stirring the fire, Nien stepped back out the door. He hadn't gone far before he saw Carly in the grassy length of riverbank between the house and the cabin. Carly walked up to him, and even in the darkness, Nien could tell that he needn't ask if she knew what was wrong with Wing.

"Were you just in the cabin?" she asked.

"Yes."

"Is he still there?"

"Yes. What's going on? Is he sick?"

"You didn't talk?"

"He would say nothing to me. I don't even know if he knew I was there."

Carly's face grew more troubled. "I'm sorry," she said. "Earlier this evening I found him in the Mietan. When I saw him it felt…"

"—like you were looking at a stranger?"

"More like nothing at all," Carly replied. "What are we going to do?"

"I don't know," Nien said. "If he's not sick, I don't know that there's anything we can do."

"He…" Carly couldn't quite believe the words that formed in her mind. "He's not *alive*, Nien. You should have seen him in the Mietan. There was a moment there that he…he truly frightened me. If we can't reach him— what? I'm afraid I'll wake up in the morning and he'll be gone."

Nien felt as if his heart weighed a pendtar. "I feel the same, Carly. The last few mornings I've woken up relieved to find him still in his bed."

Carly looked ahead to the cabin. Nien did, too.

They were losing Wing. To what, they weren't sure. The only thing that did seem certain was that Wing would never tell them.

Lost for a solution, the two old friends walked on in silence, passing by the cabin once they'd come upon it, unable to convince themselves to go inside.

A few days passed, and though Wing would still go out in the morning to work on the house with Monteray and Nien, there was hardly a word spoken by him and by early afternoon he would disappear and be gone till after dark. The renewed sense of life brought into him since coming to Legran had slipped away and he appeared hollowed out, empty.

As it had been in Rieeve, Wing could bring light to a place or a gathering of people unlike anyone Nien had ever known. The same had been true of Legran. The whole valley seemed to have risen to a new vitality with his coming. Even though he stayed primarily at the Monterays', there was an excitement about him, a buzz surrounding his brief comings and goings into town. The same was true of the Monterays. Nien had seen a livening in not only Tei, but in Monteray and Kate as well since Wing's arrival.

But, as in Rieeve, the opposite was also true—Wing was capable of conjuring dark in the brightest of places. His withdrawal had shut in upon all of them. Beneath every day and every conversation was an underlying silence and sadness, everything and everyone waiting in stasis to see what would happen: Would the terrible storm surrounding Wing break the sky itself or birth a new light unlike any of them had ever seen?

CHAPTER 68
Epiphany

As had become their custom, Nien and SiQQiy left together after
dinner, walking hand in hand along the river, watching the long
grass move beneath their feet.

It had been five days since Nien had talked with his brother.

"I saw Wing this morning, he looked…" SiQQiy hesitated. Nien knew
she, like the rest of them, was experiencing the gloom that had come over
the Monteray house. "In…despair."

"I know."

"Has he spoken to you, yet?"

"No."

Nien knew SiQQiy was being careful with him. "So, still no idea what's
wrong?"

Nien looked up at the dark, shimmering length of river stretching out
before them. "He's alone," he replied after a time.

"All three of you must feel impossibly alone—without your families,
your people."

"It's more than that; I think he blames himself."

"Blames himself?"

"For what happened. For the death of our people."

"How could that have possibly been his fault?"

"Our people thought he was the one, the Leader of Legend."

SiQQiy nodded. "I remember reading that in my studies long ago—of
a Leader who would enlighten his people in a time of devastation. And so
your people believed that the Ka'ull are this devastation from the Northing
spoken of there?"

"*They* did, yes. But Wing? No. He tried, though. He tried to decipher
what the Ancient Writings meant in regards to the Leader and the invasion
from the Northing. He…had visions. Nightmares. He's never told me spe-

cifically about them, but they tortured him. Maybe it was about all this—I don't know."

"In Quieness, we do not take such ancient writings literally. But I can see how your people did."

After a few steps taken in thought, Nien said, "Carly and I lost our people, too, but that Wing blames himself? I don't know how he bears it. Isn't it hard enough, but to carry that as well?" Nien grew distant. "Of the two, what Carly and I went through, versus what he's been through, I think what happened to Wing was worse. He has been more alone than I could ever imagine."

SiQQiy walked along in silence beside him for a time, as if contemplating his explanation. "I'm not sure I fully understand, but something real and fine stirs inside me when I'm with you. Something I'd thought had slipped my grasp forever." She stopped walking. "When I look at you," she said, "I see a depth that I have never seen in any soul. For all your secular learning, you are more like Wing, more of a Rieevan than you will ever be Quienan—or Preak." SiQQiy laughed a little, as if she couldn't believe what she was about to say next. "As a child I remember a voice in my head that would echo the words from books read to me by my mother. You know, fanciful stories full of import and meaning, high morals and beauty prevailing. But soon they became little more than vastly impractical ideas and that little voice learned to stay quiet during days of diplomacy and governance." There was a long break before she added softly, "The other night, I heard that little voice again. It was yours."

SiQQiy's words left Nien bereft of his own.

She let him squirm with it for a moment, then changed the subject. "This Plan that your Commander Lant drew up is...genius. It just might work. But I can tell it makes you uncomfortable."

Nien didn't reply, but he nodded a little.

"I do not want you to worry for me, or for Quieness. You have given me so much, but I believe that will be the least of your influence. Every valley, Quieness included, will be forever indebted to you, to your brother, and to Carly."

"We have no idea if the Plan will work," Nien said.

"No. But we *do* know that without it every valley on our continent will meet the Ka'ull alone until we have all fallen. If the Ka'ull are brave enough to test Jayak, if they are brave enough to take my merchant ships and fire on my galleys, they are bold enough to perpetrate the worst fate for our continent we can imagine."

Nien remained silent.

SiQQiy said softly, "You're troubled."

"I was hoping that if, in all this, Rieeve is liberated that we could offer something," he said. "The Mesko maybe, or…" He paused. "I'm afraid, besides the great trees themselves, the skill to work the wood may be all we *have* to offer."

SiQQiy touched his cheek; there was a wry look on her face as if she were trying not to scoff at him. "*If* the Ka'ull are in Rieeve in force, and *if* the other valleys agree, Rieeve will be our staging ground." She shook her head. "What we may accomplish in Rieeve is pivotal to everything—all because of Lant's Plan, the Plan that you and Wing brought here to Legran. How is it that you can wonder what it is you have to offer?"

Nien understood; nevertheless, he thought her to be making more of it than it was, as a kindness.

"Still," SiQQiy said, "what you said about the Mesko is interesting. I've heard of the great trees. I know they are a fragile species and, obviously, I've seen the great canopy on my travels to and from Legran. Beyond that, I know very little."

"Many hundreds of revolutions ago the Mesko forest had begun to die out. It had dwindled down to even less than half its current size when our people discovered its secret and, with their efforts, the forest was saved, brought back from extinction."

"And this secret was…?"

"Most baby trees of other species receive enough sunlight to mature into adolescence. But not the Mesko. Beneath the great canopy, the saplings do not receive the sunlight they need to survive. It is only in the selective cutting of the big trees that enough saplings are preserved for the next generation. It's like pruning a forest."

"It is a bit disheartening that such a grand tree must die in order for more to live," SiQQiy observed, "but obviously worth the sacrifice."

Nien came to a slow halt as a strange burning sensation began to fill his chest.

'*A bit disheartening that such a grand tree must die in order for more to live—but obviously worth the sacrifice.*'

SiQQiy's words cycled through his mind twice more before he said, "They…they died, but in us many may live again. It sounds crazy, right? I mean, we're talking about people not trees, but maybe we can come back from extinction, too." He looked at SiQQiy. "You're a genius!"

SiQQiy blinked at him. "What?"

"Death means life."

He could see SiQQiy was searching his face for a clue as to what was happening with him.

"There," Nien said, trying to explain, "hidden in the most common, one of the most familiar aspects of my life, was the answer all along. Do you see? We're only three—me, Wing, and Carly. Three very small, insignificant saplings, kept too long out of the sun, damaged, thirsty, but *alive*…"

Spotting a gathering of SiQQiy's guards swimming in the river, Nien called out to them, "Have you seen my brother this evening?"

One of them raised his head out of the water. "No, but I saw him early this afternoon. He was walking downriver."

"Thanks!" He turned back to SiQQiy. "I've got to find Wing. I must tell him!"

SiQQiy gazed at him in confusion, before saying, "There is something you and your brother have to offer our world that will far outweigh the Mesko. Go."

Nien took her face in his hands, kissed her, and took off at a run.

CHAPTER 69

The Time Has Come

Nien had run a fair distance with no sign of Wing. He'd traveled over two bridges: one to cross to the mountain side of the river, and then another further down to bring him back to the valley side. By then twilight had fallen. With darkness coming on, Nien decided to head back. If Wing had doubled back or skirted the valley and gone into town, it was possible he had returned to the cabin by now.

Hopeful but not expectant, Nien entered the cabin on exhausted legs.

To his surprise, Wing sat inside, alone.

Nien wanted to blurt out his excitement, but instead moved quietly to the fire. There were so many things he was bursting to say— "Where's Carly?" he said instead.

"Up at the house with Kate."

"It's uh, good to see you."

Anxiously, Nien searched Wing's face. Wing met his eyes, and Nien was relieved to see his brother again instead of the insubstantial stranger. The sweetness of it washed over him like a clean cascade of water.

"What is it?" Wing asked.

Nien walked over and sat down beside him. "I took a walk with SiQQiy tonight after dinner—"

"I never would have guessed," Wing said. "You look like you just got your sword polished."

Nien slugged Wing in the leg. Having Wing joke with him felt like the dissolution of a season filled with rain. "Yes I do, but no I didn't—it's something else, believe it or not."

Wing waited.

"We were talking, and our conversation led to something…" His voice caught. "It's a whole story, but I guess the short of it is: We have not been forsaken. I know it now as I have never known anything." He pressed his palms to the bed, hoping to steady his tremulous hands. "Our people are dead, but countless lives may be saved through Lant's Plan." He raised his face. "I see something now that I didn't before. Without even knowing I was looking, I have found my answer. This feeling, this realization—my heart aches to have you know."

Nien knew he was attempting to navigate past the long line of barricades he saw in Wing's eyes and it was not unlike moving in unfamiliar territory of rivers and lakes after an Ime storm: Nien had no idea what he'd fall into nor how deep the icy water might be.

It seemed Wing understood Nien's dilemma and decided to relieve him of it—he got up and started to leave.

"Brother," Nien called quietly.

Wing turned back around.

Stepping over to his bed, Nien reached beneath it and withdrew a small leather-bound book. Slowly, he handed it out to Wing. The expected storm of emotions crossed Wing's face. Nien had found it in a pocket sewn into the long leather cloak Wing had been wearing when he'd arrived in Legran. Nien hadn't known whether Wing had forgotten about it or not—either way, Wing had never mentioned it.

Wing took the book from Nien's hand, his face once again an impenetrable mask, and after a brief moment of silent eye contact, walked out.

As the cabin door shut, Nien took off his boots and shirt and lay down on his bed. Squeezing his eyes closed, he released a shuddering breath and though he could not speak it, allowed a prayer, thinly disguised as a wish, to fill his mind.

Wing walked a long way up the river in the silence of the night.

Nien had received his answer. Master Monteray had said that one could carry around knowledge their entire life and never *realize* it.

All it takes is a moment, Monteray had said. *Only a moment.*

That moment had happened for Nien.

Logically, Wing understood that in order for something to live, something else had to die...

But I have died a hundred, a thousand times since that night, Wing thought, *and still nothing can atone for my inaction. Nothing, now, can make any of it right.*

He'd lied to Carly in the Mietan. It wasn't about Rieeve being broken, unredeemable, unreclaimable. And it wasn't about Eosha not caring enough to save their people, either. That was just another way of putting the blame out *there*, even if that was to blame some ethereal god that he, nor anyone else he'd ever known, had ever seen.

It was about—

Me, he thought. *That I would never be able to bear seeing Rieeve again knowing it was my fault. Going back only to fail. Again. Because I still don't understand.*

Near the riverbank, Wing came to a stop. He stood for some time, gazing into the dark emptiness across the river.

His body swayed a little, he stumbled forward, caught himself, sank to the earth.

On his knees, the endless stream of questions that had plagued him all his life surged in his mind, coming from the bottom of a place so deeply scarred that they tore from him like a sword from a wound—

There is no forgiveness, no excuse. I don't know what I'm asking. There is no hope at all, not even in death...

For in death he would find his family, his people, and *there* have to answer to them for what he'd seen, what he'd known, why he'd lied.

A sob escaped his thin lips followed shortly by another and another. Saliva filled his mouth, mucus his nose. His lungs locked up. He buried his face into the river grass.

Overhead, stamped black against the canopy of stars, moved the night, folding around Leer as the planet spun along some invisible line, vaulting through the endless dark conveyor of sound that could not be heard and light that could not be seen.

It could have been days, seasons, or only a moment as the planes of existence shifted. Hidden inside translucent threads, memory as old as life itself rubbed up against the ceiling of life's most ancient longing...

Wing opened his eyes, but instead of seeing dirt and grass, he saw a gaping black maw, endless and impossibly dark. Disbelief pierced him briefly—

The Void.

He'd been there so many times. Every time, he'd fought it, fought it until Nien had arrived, pulled him back. This time, for the first time, he didn't care. He had no fight left. No *will* to fight left.

Surrender poured into him, followed quickly by an overwhelming feeling of resignation—and acceptance.

He slid to the edge.

Wrung of everything, he was at long last willing to let the Void take him. Much better than heaven or hell was the promise of nothing.

Easily, he let the physical world go: the chirp of the night bugs, the brush of the river, the rustling of the wind. Feelings he could no longer hold fell away: hatred, anger, hope.

Lastly, he thought of Nien and Carly. With them, most of all, had his shame become acute; even looking in their eyes had become a punishment. They would be rendered by his death, but he could not live, not one more day, in the unassailable trap of hope and unanswered questions that had birthed the lie he'd once prayed would buy him enough time...

Wing leaned forward a little more and tumbled gratefully into the black.

Inside the cabin, Nien lay in the dark. He'd let the fire die away. On his back in his bed, he gazed at the cabin's simple ceiling, barely able to make out the dark outline of supporting timbers.

Wing.

His brother was out there.

Somewhere in the dark, perhaps beside the river, Wing suffered, and there was nothing he could do about it.

The anger at the helplessness, the injustice of it, welled inside him. He had been there so many times when the darkness had come to take Wing from him.

But not this time.

Closing his eyes, Nien looked for his brother. As withdrawn as Wing had been the past few days, Nien was unsure if he would be able to find him. Perhaps even their bond would be elusive, unresponsive.

Their bond was neither elusive nor unresponsive—

It was nonexistent.

Nien's throat closed. His muscles flexed as if to jerk him off the bed, send him flying out into the night to find Wing.

But he couldn't move.

In his mind, he cried out: *Wing!*

His lips would not move either. He was frozen. Transparent stone.

He's gone, Nien realized. *Wing's gone.*

Wing looked around. If this was hell, it wasn't what he expected. If it was death, it wasn't what he expected either. Maybe this is what the Void looked like now that he'd finally stopped fighting it.

Wing.

"Nien? I...What are you doing here?"

I came to tell you you're being an idiot.

Wing blinked. "What?"

I know what you're thinking.

"You do?"

Yes, Weed Farmer.

"Then you know. You know it's my fault."

Your fault?

"I knew, Nien."

Knew what?

"What was coming. What would happen to our people."

Alright.

"Alright?"

So? We all did. What do you think the Cant was about? Why do you think the people were in such a panic? We all knew.

"No, I mean, I saw it—the destruction. Of Lou. Of Tou. Of Rieeve."

Alright. Then what about Legran? Jayak? Quieness?

Wing blinked again.

If you need to blame someone, blame me.

"You?"

Me.

"Why?"

For what I did in Jayak.

"What you did in Jayak—for fighting?"

For rushing in…

"I don't blame you for that. You were brave. You *acted*."

I acted—rashly. I led a dozen inexperienced men into a battle we had no business being in and lost one of us, giving the Ka'ull the best intel they had on Rieeve. How was your patience worse than my recklessness?

"I didn't just lie to the Council, or to Carly, or to our family. I lied to you, Nien."

And telling any of us the truth—what would that have done?

Wing shook his head miserably. "You don't get it."

What were we going to do had you told us? Move our entire race to another valley? You think they would have gone? And if, by some miracle, we had convinced them to leave Rieeve, what makes you believe they would not have died at the hands of the Ka'ull wherever we ran to, a season, a revolution later?

"I could have left. I should have had the courage to leave."

And that would have accomplished—?

"They would have stopped looking to me, waiting for me. They would have looked to Lant. Believed him. Not fought him—"

Wing.

Wing blinked and before him stood Lant. "Commander?"

I'm here to share your blame as well.

"What?"

You're not the only one who's lied, Wing.

"What?"

Me. I did. It wasn't you, it wasn't Nien. The Ka'ull already knew about Rieeve. They knew about it because of me. I should not have come back after I left, but I did because I was selfish, because I was scared, because of Pree K.

The warrior that led the attack on Castle Viyer—I knew him. At one time, I even called him friend.

The truth is: I should never have left Rieeve.

Wing could only stare.

Wing.

Wing looked up again. "Lyrik?"

The ghostly messenger nodded. *It was my fault.*

Wing could not even react. He just stood.

My father was a beast. I knew it, and I did nothing. In fact, I helped him. I helped him ruin so many people. And I let him do it to Rieeve. I am the reason why Rieeve shut itself off from the world. Had I been stronger, braver, my father would never have come to Rieeve and Rieeve would not have closed itself off from the world and Lant would not have been driven to leave and you would not have been punished by expectations of being something I should have been.

I am at cause in this.

Wing could not speak.

Wing.

This time others joined Nien, Lant, and Lyrik. Wing did not recognize them particularly, but he knew all of them.

As you see, they said as one, *we can all share this blame. You are not alone, but only you can make it right. We are no longer flesh. Go. Make it right. Redeem us all. Turn the tide in Rieeve.*

Had Wing felt his body as flesh, he might have succumbed, dissolved. But there was no physical manifestation to sacrifice. He just...stood.

Now, see. See who you are, said they all.

Into the beckoning Void, Wing's consciousness flew. But where he had expected to find nothingness, he found instead a blinding influx of information, of sensation so immense that it blasted away his mind, scattering him into matter so fine that he passed through the Void itself and found:

Everything

With sight that had nothing to do with his eyes, from a vantage point both intimate and vast, Wing saw the Void tear itself in two. One side spun left, the other spun right. One rose high, the other sunk low, each moving out, creating surface above and beneath itself. He saw the great black giving birth to light. He saw suns born and planets die. He saw fire level a civilization and water raise a continent. Worlds flew past him, riding through an infinite sea of stars that raced to stay ahead. He saw dimensions within dimensions, lives within lives...

He was all of it.

In awe, he wondered: *How can this be?*

In direct and immediate answer, Wing became aware of the driving force behind the great expansion—

Life itself.

A *feeling*, a longing that scorched the core of him, drawing him out so thin that light became impossibly heavy: It was the wanting to be *this* so he could experience *that*.

With sight that could take in every imagining, Wing recognized himself as *this* and from that place saw *that*—

The *that* was shockingly familiar.

It was Nien.

Brother!

Nien gasped. His mind lost its hold on his throbbing muscles; he sprang up in his bed. "Wing!"

His terror dissolved.

In every corner of his mind and heart, Nien found him. In memory, in feeling—Wing was everywhere.

Nien flopped back to his bed. Tears rushed his eyes and ran in hot delicate streams down his temples, slipping into his hair and onto his pillow.

But the wonder was not over.

Though finding Wing at all would have been enough, Nien still wouldn't have imagined the feeling that accompanied it—

Joy and peace, where a moment ago had been only nothing.

Their connection clean and pure, still the truest thing he'd ever felt, now filled with such perfect bliss.

Beside the river lay a body. It might have been dead—in a living kind of way. The heart still beat, the lungs still accepted air, nerves still pulsed with electric waves, but consciousness beyond that of a cell had fled. A thin tendril remained—the physical's lifeline. Just enough. Enough to await a decision. Sustain a choice.

From some distant place, Wing saw blood run out along a smooth stone floor, smelled rent flesh, heard a receding moan.

Taken up from the ground from which it came, he felt the moan transform, rising into a grand chorus of voices, the song they sang unlike any he had ever heard. It rang at the very center of him, his hearing as his sight had become, an entire-being experience beyond individual senses.

Spinning, falling, he saw the faces, heard the voices, felt the joy and pain of countless beings on infinite worlds, none of whom he remembered but all of which he knew…

Wing hit the ground beside the river.

The groan that escaped him on impact died away into the Void.

Enfolding the body that had once been his, he lay slack. It took some time for his senses to return to the plane of Legran, to the sound of the river, to the smell of the sweet wet dirt beneath the grass.

Who am I?

Wing observed as his brain asked the question, but the voice seemed to have little to do with who he actually was.

Who do you want to be? came an answering voice that could have been his own or someone else's. He could not tell.

I don't know.

Who would you choose to be?

The answer surprised him: *Myself.*

Then who are you?

It seemed to take a long time before some part of Wing replied: *Everyone.*

And as the word settled in his mind, Wing felt his awareness shift back to the body that lay prostrate in the tall grasses by the river.

"I…" he muttered, but the words passing over his frail vocal cords caused him to cough.

When the coughing ceased, he mind-whispered, *I'm ready.*

Then it is time, came the answer.

The gap closed.

From somewhere very far but also incredibly close, the translucent tendril thrummed the word: *Merehr.*

Wing tried to raise his head.

What you are has always been enough.

From Wing's core a great yellow flame burst—the fire of a galaxy, spinning 'round a cosmic wheel, now and forever coalescing *One Single Moment.*

Wing inhaled sharply, his eyes rolled back in his head and he vanished once more, this time into fire.

CHAPTER 70

Illumination

The fire had dwindled to smoldering coals by the time Wing reached the cabin.

Nien looked up as Wing came in. Wing's back was to him as he closed the door. When Wing turned around, light from the fireplace illuminated his face. Nien sat up. Wing's eyes shimmered with the remnant of tears but they were also clear—shining reflections in the soft orange light that filled the room.

"Wing, you look…" Nien's eyes flashed something unspeakable and holy. "Can you tell me?"

His leather-shoed feet making only a soft padding sound on the floor, Wing moved toward the glowing coals in the fireplace. In his hand he held the small copy of the Ancient Writings Nien had given him as he'd left the cabin. Opening it to the seventh book, the book of the Prophet-Poet Eneefa, Wing read: "E fe de lebaan'a tuvle…Why did we forget? Despised and left. Thrown down from higher worlds—a scant tug on the sleeve. Forgotten. Abandoned to note. And line. And word. Just a beggar at the door."

Wing gazed down at the book. "I believed this, Nien. Like Eneefa when *he* wrote it, I was lost in a world I thought was real, because, like Eneefa, I had forgotten." Wing looked up from the pages. "But I remember now. We have not been despised nor left. We have not been abandoned to that which we can only sing, or write, or speak. We are not beggars at the door."

Though he was trying, Nien replied, "I'm not following you, Wing."

Wing drew a short breath. "I've just had a set of remarkable conversations."

"With who?" Nien asked.

"Well, with you, and Lant, and someone else I haven't told you about yet."

Nien's expression was an angelic collection of wonder and confusion.

"That night, after Pree K came to me out in the fields and told me to go to Commander Lant, I ran to the castle instead. However, as I neared, a voice, and then a personage as clear and distinct as I see you asked me to stop."

"Who was it?"

"Though I had never seen him before and he offered no name, I knew it was our great ancestor."

"Lyrik?" Nien said.

"Yes."

As told by Reean, Lyrik had been a striking man with deep olive skin and silken black hair. It was to him, alone, that Wing's genetic traits could be attributed.

"What did he say?" Nien asked.

"First, he asked me not to go to the castle. He then told me to go to Commander Lant."

"The Plan?"

Wing nodded.

"Did he say anything else?"

"He said it wasn't yet my time."

Nien looked at him. "Time?"

"To die." Wing met Nien's eyes. "Obviously it wasn't yours, either."

Though Nien did not smile, his voice was as soft and close as the glowing embers of the fire as he asked, "So, what happened? Can you tell me?"

Wing's eyes shone with a crystalline quality so fine that Nien felt pierced to his heart. "He called me Merehr and said that I wouldn't be alone."

It took Nien a beat to find his voice. "Then it *is* you."

"Merehr is a name. Maybe my name. But it is just a name. Our people worshiped the name, Nien, and forgot the truth the name was meant to represent."

"The truth?" Nien asked.

"That everything is one thing."

Wing glanced down at the Ancient Writings in his hand. "These prophets and poets wrote down those experiences that changed their lives, that they thought might open a window to the only heaven there is—the one inside." Wing released a studied breath. "We were the ones who made a religion of it, and by doing so backed ourselves into a corner, setting prerequisite on something that cannot be given or taken away." Wing grinned, almost like a child. "Can you see it, Nien? The Ancient Writings are a collection of words wrapped around a feeling attempting to describe an experience. We forgot that and came to worship the picture those words painted. These errors add up. If we believe that their word is enough for us, then it's a small step to believe that our word must be enough for everyone else."

"It would be like picking one tree in the Mesko forest and trying to prove that it was not only a tree, but the greatest tree, in fact, the *only* tree in the forest," Nien said, feeling his way through what Wing was trying to convey.

"Yes," Wing said. "We lived our lives trying to protect and defend what we thought was the truth, when what *is* true has need of nothing—least of all to be protected or defended."

"If father had taken such a position," Nien said, "if he had loved one of the great trees more than every other, the whole forest would have died. But he knew that even the greatest of the trees must be sacrificed if the new are going to grow, if the whole of the forest is to live."

Wing nodded. "We will rebuild. Rieeve was a grand tree, but it has been cut down. So we will begin again, and this time let's not make the mistake of sacrificing the whole for our own small part of it."

"What I still don't understand is, if you *are* Merehr, are you also the Leader? *Are* they the same?"

Wing's eyes glinted. "The Leader is me. And you. The Leader is in all of us. Merehr is just another name. The truth is something I'd never suspected: that the Poets and Prophets weren't talking about a single person at all, but of the truth that lay within every living thing. They wrote to remind us not only of what we may become, but who we *already* are."

"But as Merehr, you are the Leader," Nien uttered. "You are the other, the one who escaped a desolating scourge to sojourn in a strange land, the one to whom the truth of the writings will be shown" —he paused— "was just shown. Our people were not wrong about you, at least not completely."

Wing lifted his eyes to his brother. "Nien, you escaped the same desolating scourge. You have sojourned in a strange land. And you, too, are beginning to understand." Wing's head bowed for a moment. "At first I was angry, so angry. I spent so many nights in the mountains after that night asking: Why didn't Eosha care enough to save our people? And then the guilt set in. Guilt at having done nothing, guilt over not being enough. Continually asking: Why were the visions given to me when I was not capable of interpreting them, of doing something with them?

"Tonight I learned both questions were wrong. It's not about whether Eosha cares or not. It's about whether *we* care—because we are none other than the God we've been praying to. I once thought I was shown so I could do something to stop it. But, as you pointed out, there was nothing, then, that I could have done."

"Uh, *I* pointed out?"

"The you—there."

"Oh."

"So even though I'm still not sure why I had the nightmare visions, I know this: Life is about more than avoiding death." Wing drew a full, fulfilling breath. "How could I have been so blind? I read this" —Wing motioned to the book in his hand—"everyday for the whole of my life and I did not see it." He looked hard at Nien. "What are we, Nien? Helpless creatures? Castaways? Here to prove ourselves? To be tested and tried? To forever feel less than and unworthy of a God, out there somewhere?" Wing shook his head. "I don't believe it. We took ourselves out of the picture when we *are* the picture. The road we're on is the road *we* laid out in ages past, between star and moon, from breath to breath, to form ourselves as characters of intricate and infinite detail. We create this. Every day, with every feeling, we choose that which we wish to experience and make it so. We are so much more than we think we are. As one, we are all that is, all that ever was, and all that ever will be."

Nien pressed his silvery-blue fingers to his forehead. "I don't understand even half of what you just said, but there's a feeling…How can I explain it when I have no words for it?"

Wing's face was a shade of perfect understanding. Nien's frustration vanished.

"I may not know exactly what I want," Nien said, "but I know now what I don't want—I don't want to live my life on the other end of choices I've made out of fear: Fear of being trapped, fear of not knowing enough, or as you said, never *being* enough." He stood up. "I believe you. Are we going back?"

Wing met his brother's eyes. His smile opened a universe inside of Nien. "No'va-hm in. We will go back."

CHAPTER 71

We Will Go Back

Morning showered its warmth in through the sunrising window of the small cabin as Wing dressed before heading up to the house to find Carly.

Making his way through the dewy wet grass of morning to the house, the toes and tops of his boots were soaked by the time he reached the door.

Tugging his boots off, he left them by the door and climbing the stairs, pushed the door open to the room he'd stayed in his first night in Legran. Inside, on the large, Jhedan'ret covered bed between the two windows, he paused a moment to watch Carly sleep. Pale morning illuminated the white transparent curtains that hung in the windows. Carly's face was smooth and warm, nearly lost in the voluminous pillow.

Wing walked over and sat down next to her on the bed. He'd sat there for a time before she awoke.

Yawning, Carly pushed herself up and looked at him. Her sleepy eyes traced his face in mild misapprehension.

"What happened?" she said.

"Remember when you said that you wondered where the answers lie—if the stars themselves desired to answer my questions?"

She nodded.

"You were right. There is a part of them in us and in that part is the answer to all our questions. As you said, hearing them is the tricky part."

Still waking up, Carly squinted at him as if trying to puzzle out his meaning. "So...what did they say?"

Wing smiled a little. "Much."

"Can you give me the my-horse-just-threw-its-shoe version?"

"Well, that would be: We're going back to Rieeve. We're going to take back our home. I don't know exactly how it will happen, but it will."

Carly gazed at him for a long moment. "There are three of us, Wing."

"I know, but—" His head bowed briefly. "I've only seen glimpses, Carly. But we're here because we are supposed to be here. We are a part of something that is ultimately perfect and absolutely loving. We are a part of it; it is a part of us. And we are never separated, ever."

Carly met his eyes and for Wing, it felt like she was looking at him for the first time. She touched his face. "I've never understood things of this nature," she said. "I've never felt like I needed to. But I believe in you. That is what *I* have always needed to do. So if you say we're going back, and you tell me there's a way three Rieevans can reclaim their home from thousands of Ka'ull, then I believe you.

"When do we go?"

The following day, near the steps that led out of the house toward the river, Monteray sat down greeting SiQQiy, the brothers, Carly, as well as Netalf, Terro Tellah, and Leef Keppik from SiQQiy's personal Guard.

Unfurling a map, Monteray laid it out on the ground before him.

"I am tired of waiting," Monteray announced. "We waited too long for Rieeve—I don't intend to repeat that mistake. Call has agreed to go to Jayak as soon as some arrangements can be made. It is most likely I will be going to Jayak myself sometime soon, but first I will be organizing intelligence out of Legran. If there is movement in the mountains, I want to know about it."

"I will also be sending word out," SiQQiy said. "Leef and Terro will be leaving by riverboat for Preak; by the time I return home I should know what the Preak plan to do. Once in Quieness, I will also begin organizing my troops so that I will be ready once we're apprised of the intentions of the other valleys." SiQQiy's eyes flitted over Wing, Nien, and Carly before her gaze came to rest on Monteray. "We need to know what, exactly, the situation in Rieeve *is*."

"Yes," Monteray agreed. "And we need to know as soon as possible. This will determine how many forces from Quieness, Legran, and Jayak—if Takayo agrees—will be sent."

On the other side of an uncomfortable bit of silence, Wing asked, "Why did they let the people of Lou and Tou live?"

The poignant phrasing of Wing's question was not lost on the small gathering.

"You mean, why did they *not* let your people live?" Monteray said. "Other than being centrally located and naturally fortified, they knew if Rieeve was taken no one would ever know they were there. They could rest, train, and gather without all the men and materials necessary to keep the local population under control."

Though it all made sense, Wing, Nien, and Carly simply needed to hear it from Monteray.

Monteray continued, "And from Rieeve, the heart of our continent, Quieness, Jayak, nor Preak would expect invasion—though we should. It is likely the Ka'ull assumed that we would expect attack through the gap in the ranges, down the Tu'Lon River where the Ka'ull's passage and access to their ships is easiest."

"Then why did they try Jayak? Why did they not come directly into Rieeve?" Nien said.

"My guess is, it's because they would have been going into Rieeve blind—with no idea about the valley or what kind of forces could have been called against them."

Information they didn't have until I gave it to them, Nien thought. *Until I went down, joined the battle in Jayak, lost Bredo...*

"Besides Quieness," Monteray continued, "whose weight comes not only in skill but in great numbers—Jayak is their most formidable opposition. Perhaps they believed if they could take Jayak," Monteray continued, "other valleys would fall more easily. That having failed, they moved on Rieeve instead." Monteray shrugged. "Of course, this is all conjecture."

"If the Ka'ull *are* building up their forces in Rieeve, wouldn't we need to cut that supply line?" Carly said.

Monteray nodded and shifted the map in front of him. "The likely route would be through here, between the ranges. If they could be cut off here, they would suffer." Monteray pointed to a spot northing of Rieeve where the Ti and Uki ranges met before breaking again at the southing end of Tou. "If we cut off supplies and trapped the rest in Rieeve, we'd have them."

"Their advantage would be their undoing."

"While we're at it, we can send a force back up the Tu'Lon and burn their ships," Carly said.

Nien glanced at her; he noticed that Wing had, too.

"Eventually, yes," Monteray replied. "But before that happens we must assure that they are driven out of Lou—and Tou as well. Whether they take their ships back to their own land or die on them, I care not. As long as they never return."

SiQQiy leaned forward, gazing over the map. "I could send a contingent of men through here," she said, and pointed out a large gap near the top of Quieness' sunrising border. "They could drop down and close off the Ti-Uki confluence."

Monteray tapped the map with his finger. "If Takayo goes along with this, a division of his men could meet your contingent from the other side. Each force could work from opposite sides to seal off the notch."

"What do you think the chances are that Takayo will agree?"

Contemplative, Monteray replied, "The Ka'ull have been in his valley. He knows the threat is real. Our disadvantage is the confidence the Jayakans have in their own forces and their reluctance to ally—ever again—with another valley. Our advantage is in Takayo's wisdom..."

"And in his friendship with you and Commander Lant," SiQQiy said. "I can send a contingent to join the Jayakans as well as three or more to Rieeve."

Nien did not meet SiQQiy's eyes, but he knew she had glanced at him. "What about Preak?" Nien asked. "Could the Ka'ull not sail the sunsetting sea line and come at the Preak from the southing—through Zhegata Bay?"

"I've been thinking on that," SiQQiy replied. "This is something Leef and Terro will also be speaking with Neda Ten, the head of Preak's provincial governors, about."

There was a pause in the dialogue and the small group noted Wing and Nien gazing unspeakingly at each other.

Becoming aware of the silence, the brothers looked up to find the eyes of the others upon them.

Wing spoke. "Nien, Carly, and I will return to Rieeve; discover what is happening there."

Monteray said, "I'm not sure of the wisdom in the three of you returning to Rieeve. I will send in spies from my militia."

"It's our valley," Nien said. "We will go."

It was obvious Monteray and SiQQiy wanted to protest: if Wing, Nien, and Carly were caught they would be losing the last three Rieevans on their world. But, of course, Wing, Nien, and Carly already knew this.

"I would offer a small force to go with you for protection," Monteray said. "But until we have armies in place, a small contingent will help you no more than the three of you going in quietly—essentially as spies."

Wing, Nien, and Carly nodded.

"I will be leaving near the end of this short cycle," SiQQiy said. "Depending on the news I receive on the situation in Rieeve, I could have forces there before the first snows."

And then Carly spoke, her tone soft, as if not to give power to the harrowing idea, "Ime," she said in Rieevan, then paused and used the common term for the benefit of the others: "Fon. I wonder where the non-occupying forces of the Ka'ull will spend it?"

The small group was quiet before Monteray spoke. "We will take that as it comes. Until then a plan is in place. You," he said, looking at Wing, Nien, and Carly, "me, and SiQQiy. It is a good start."

The day after their meeting with SiQQiy and Monteray, Nien joined Monteray and Wing in the Mietan.

For the first couple of days, Nien played alone with one of Monteray's swords, simply feeling it, moving it through the air as Monteray and Wing worked together in their own practice.

With one eye, Monteray watched Nien anxiously: Would he find it again? Would it still be there?

By the third day there was no doubt that it was. Nien was strong, centered. There was neither fear nor excitement in his eyes. His strikes were accurate, clean, efficient.

Placing the brothers to spar together, Monteray noticed that Wing's tension and fatigue eased when he practiced with his brother. Wing was moving the sword as he never had with Monteray himself: blocking, striking, staying relaxed, his breathing deep and controlled.

Between training sessions, the three set to projects of war—Monteray to an endeavor he kept from the brothers; the brothers to the collection and construction of heavy leather body armour, knives, and short blades.

Most nights, Wing would return to the cabin to see Nien working, not on the small carving he usually found him musing over, but with awl in hand and drape of leather over knee. There were trips into town to trade for materials, and the smithery burning at all and strange hours, the brothers and Monteray taking turns, all of them picking up a permanent reek of smoke and sweat that even trips to the river and house bath could not extinguish.

And through it all they continued their physical training.

As much as Monteray loved working with the brothers, he enjoyed watching them more. There was poetry in their interaction, grace in every move. Whether sparring free-hand or with weapons, there was not a moment Monteray could remember being more moved by any play, symphony, or opera in the finest halls of Quieness than he was watching the Cawutt brothers as they trained beneath the great arching dome of the Mietan.

CHAPTER 72

Saviour in Despair

The two young men crouched together behind a large tree. They thought they'd heard something move in the woods behind them.

"I can't take much more of this, Jhock," Pree K said quietly.

Jhock's head lowered—he knew. He'd seen nearly every emotion play across Pree K's face in the past turns, but rarely such despair.

From the very beginning Pree K had been their leader. Jhock remembered how, that first horrible night, Pree K had tried to convince them to go to Legran. He told them he knew the way. He confessed that he'd visited Master Monteray with his father on a few occasions. But the elders would have none of it. So Pree K had gotten them out of Rieeve and into the safety of the caves.

As time in the caves had worn on, the adults had deferred to Pree K in every matter—except leaving the caves. And even now that nearly all the adults had disappeared or died, Pree K managed to keep it together, never letting those still alive in the bowels of the mountain see any doubt, any hopelessness; but Jhock heard it in his voice today.

"What else can we do?"

"I don't know," Pree K said with a deep and weary sigh. "But we can't stay in the caves forever."

"They won't leave. Not as long as Grek's alive."

"I know."

Jhock hated that he even had the thought, but there were times, like now, he wished the Council Spokesman would die. Then they could leave, go somewhere—anywhere! Anywhere would be better than the caves.

"We've already held on longer than I ever thought we could," Jhock said.

In his imagination, Jhock tried to find some glimmer of the light he maintained had to be at the end of this dreadful tunnel—for there *would* come an end to the interminable days of darkness and hiding and cold and hunger.

Nothing in life remained forever.

So, maybe, he thought, *the only question that really matters is: Will any of us leave the caves alive? Or, like the adults, will the rest of us die there as well?*

"Let's check the southing trap," Jhock said, hoping to redirect the gloom of his thoughts to tasks. "There's bound to be something in there after that last storm."

Pree K nodded heavily and they moved off into the woods.

The southing trap lay at the top edge of a long scree field. There was shelter beneath the giant trees, and creatures would often make for those holes during heavy storms.

For the first time in five days, there was food in the trap. Problem was, the *food* was still alive.

Pree K and Jhock looked it over from a safe distance. The creature in the trap was not of great size, but it was fierce. Gejn'dy-a bore thick shaggy coats, sharp carnivore teeth, and claws as long as a man's hand on their front feet.

Jhock watched Pree K's hand slip to the smooth sword-hilt at his side.

Pree K carried his father's sword at all times—he'd taken it from the house on that last night before setting his magnificent home to flame—so there would be a fair length of blade between Pree K and the creature, but that didn't mean either of them was looking forward to the confrontation.

"I'll do the distracting, you do the slaying," Jhock said. "Uh, make it quick."

The two young men understood one another and began to make their way toward the creature, which was now staring defiantly up at them with deep black eyes.

Skirting the tree, Jhock came round behind the gejn'dy-a and tossed a rock at it. It scrambled about, facing him, and snarling.

Jhock glanced up; Pree K drew in. Jhock clapped his hands, assuring the animal's attention. The gejn'dy-a growled for a moment, then lunged.

The snare broke.

In a flash, the animal was on Jhock. Jhock screamed. Pree K struck. The sword landed between the animal's shoulder blades, and though the once-perfect blade was now nicked and scarred, it still managed to sever the thick hide and bone of the animal right down to its front legs.

In the scuffle Jhock had lost his footing in the loose rock of the scree field. He slid a fair distance before coming to a stop.

Above him, he heard Pree K gasp and swear as he came down the side of the scree field.

Precariously, Jhock raised his head. Pree K had stopped across from and plunged his sword into the ground, lodging it between rock and root. Pulling a thin length of rope from one of their hunting duffels, Pree K tied it around the hilt before setting out across the shifting surface of rock.

Aching to try and meet him, Jhock forced himself to remain inert knowing that any movement could send the scree spilling away beneath him again.

"How are you?" Pree K asked, his words whispered as if the sound itself might cause the rocks to slide.

"Fine, so far," Jhock answered. They still had to get back to firm ground.

Slowly, Pree K reached out a hand. Just as slowly, Jhock reached out and took it. For a moment the scree held, but as Jhock tried to rise to his knees, it began to move again.

Pree K's hand clenched the rope looped around wrist and fist, and held on as his own feet slid away beneath him.

In a life-saving chain—hand to hand, hand to rope, and rope to sword— the line held. At its end, Pree K and Jhock came to a halting stop.

Crawling now, the boys made their way to the edge of the field and the blessed safety of dirt, tree, and soil.

Pree K lay on his back breathing heavily. Jhock sat beside him, trembling, and holding his left arm with his right hand. When Pree K sat up and looked at him, Jhock saw the fall of despair in Pree K's eyes.

Jhock's heart plummeted.

They had all tried very hard to stay injury-free for the damp and dark of the caves was a hard place in which to heal, and they all had little enough strength for the daily task of survival.

Moving over to him, Pree K separated Jhock's jacket and shirt. There was a deep gash in Jhock's shoulder, starting near the front and reaching around to his back. And just above his wrist, puncture marks from the gejn'dy-a's bite.

"Can you move your arm? Is it broken?" Pree K asked, glancing as he did—as they continually did—into the trees, hoping all the commotion had not attracted attention that could get them and what remained of their people discovered and killed.

Jhock tried to move his arm and succeeded, but with great pain. "I don't think it's broken," he said. "What's wrong?"

"One of the rocks cut you pretty deep. And, the gejn'dy-a got its teeth into you."

Tacitly, the boys looked at one another.

"We'll need to bandage it until we can get back," Pree K quickly said, trying to sound encouraging. "It should be fine."

Jhock nodded, forcing a stoicism he only wished he felt.

Pree K ripped away a portion of his own shirt—the last one, Jhock knew, that he had—and wrapped Jhock's shoulder, circling it around his chest in a brief, makeshift covering for the wound.

Back on their feet, the two reclimbed the slope and packed up the gejn'dy-a for the trip back to the caves.

Following along behind Pree K, Jhock passed over the root and vine-choked ground, ignoring the pain in his arm and back as he concentrated on the moving feet of Pree K, knowing that the hurts he'd just sustained may, finally, be something Pree K could not guide him out of, nor save him from.

CHAPTER 73

Presence of the Ancients

Monteray sat in a tall chair at one end of the Mietan. His training with the Cawutt brothers had come to an end. Soon the Plan would be set in motion. Soon the brothers would be returning to Rieeve.

At the center of the Mietan, Wing and Nien stood facing one another. Nearly thirty steps above them the large stained glass threw refracted sunlight into savory rays of colour across the great hall's floor.

Each brother's hand held a sword: broad steel blades, double-edged and beaten to perfection by Monteray himself. The tangs were wrapped in leather, gilded to the pommel and collar with engraved, folded metal. Three steps long and perfectly balanced, the swords moved as a natural extension of the arm.

"Your training is over," Monteray said, the hall amplifying the depth of his voice. "In my life I have crafted many blades. I see now that all of them were practice for the ones you hold."

Well, that explains his late arrivals and early departures from meals of late, the brothers thought, and as their eyes passed over the swords they saw Monteray in their minds, at work in the smithery—

All that effort, for them. Indeed, everything Monteray had done since they'd arrived had been for them.

"In returning to Rieeve you are taking the first step in what may be a long war to reclaim our continent," Monteray said. "We move upon our world, sometimes like kings, sometimes like beasts, but we are all brothers. The exchange of life should, perhaps, be a matter left alone to a God; nevertheless, here it is before us." He looked them over. "Trust yourselves. Trust each other. What we build here will unveil our new world." Monteray's face was solemn as, with a short raise of his hands, he said, "Begin."

The brothers' eyes left Monteray and came to rest on each other. Formally, they cut and raised their swords. As the honed edges of each broad-steel blade touched, a ray caught fire between them. The fire rushed the blades, flashed at the apex, then leapt to a point of starlight just beneath the Mietan dome.

Monteray's eyes shot up and caught only a glimpse of the star point before it burst with a crack of lightning, flooding the room with a bonding current of energy.

From there, it polarized and leaped from the walls in two opposing currents. One grounded in Wing, the other in Nien, passing along the invisible networks in the fabric of their flesh before diving into the depths of the planet on an errand they did not immediately comprehend.

The conflict began as Wing and Nien parted slowly, both trying to steady their quaking hands as sinew, nerve, and bone streamed residual fire from the current's charge. Mirror images, they each cross stepped to their left, beginning to draw a slow circle around the room.

From his chair upon the raised platform at the Mietan's northing corner, Monteray was taken by how alike they were not only in appearance but also in nature, the way they moved, held their bodies and swords. Flint and spark, sun and moon, they were the two necessary halves of the fire that burned through the Mietan and the tidal pull that threatened to bring its walls in upon them.

Gliding 'round each other like birds of prey, the circle Wing and Nien traced across the floor drew in on itself.

As the circle closed to completion, both drew up on their right—and swung.

Their connecting swords went off like a detonation. The boom pulled back on the energy they'd sent into the depths causing it to re-emerge in a pulse of brilliant blue light that broke like a wave, releasing into the room a cacophony of crying voices.

The wave pressed Monteray up against the back of his chair even as it entered the brothers along the same electrically charged paths through which it had gone to ground.

With crushing clarity, the brothers understood that within the wave of blue light the world of the ancients had found transport into the present.

Moving as if through the deepest of water, Wing and Nien laid blade upon blade. The wave crashed and voices cried:

Who are you!

Wing swung his sword over his head and stepped into Nien. Nien leapt back and blocked.

Do you remember!

The clash and consequent prevalence of ages was addicting. Transported, neither brother found any need to question the fantastical occurrence—it simply was and they simply were.

Nien circled and Wing jabbed. Nien knocked it down. They ringed each other. Nien drove in; Wing met him—another threshing of weight against steel, another wave crashing from beyond, crying:

Will it be different!

As the words echoed in their heads, Nien moved in on Wing the momentum he carried hurling both of them to the floor where, in a web of cyclonic fury, they fought.

Swords clanged wildly against the Mietan floor, nicking the wood and carved inlay. Taut and seasoned muscle pushed forward and retreated back, bone and nerve giving themselves over fully to the energy that moved them, flowed through them, created them.

Somewhere in the nether-reaches of his mind, Monteray wondered at the strangeness and beauty of the brothers so whole-heartedly battling with each other, how the interchange between their blows and bodies could happen in the absence of malice, hate, even the need for there to be a victor.

They were simply…dancing.

In blinding coils of strikes and parries, full-body impacts and twists that carried them into feats of wrestling, the struggle continued until, as if rising from the depths of a sea, the brothers came up upon their knees, each with a sword edge pressed into the throbbing heart-vein of the other's throat.

The voices ceased their desperate cry. With a fading whisper, they breathed across the receding distance: *You are not alone. We are with you.*

And in the heat of Nien and Wing's breath the cry of the ancients died away.

Panting heavily, the veins in their temples throbbing full and heavy, Nien lifted his eyes and looked at Wing. "Brother," he said. "This is finished." Raising his sword, he cried: "Forefathers, loved ones! We will not forget."

Wing placed his own sword flat upon the floor, remembering the darkness that had consumed him the night Carly had found him here. Now, those feelings were merely a memory, like a painting of a stranger, and in their place was a peace, an acceptance so profound and deep that he felt its presence across the face of their planet, reaching out into the great black to their sun and stars, to other countless worlds he could feel and see but not touch.

"Forefathers and loved ones," Wing said. "Many lessons have I learned, but none so great as this: I am what I am, and what I am is what I choose to be. My prayer is that our legacy may be one of understanding, not fear." Wing looked at his brother. There was blood on Nien's neck where Wing's sword blade had touched. Wing smudged the blood clear with a finger. "What is within our power to do, we will do, and perhaps by taking a stand in Rieeve many may be preserved—both those who kill and those who might yet be."

Wing raised his face and closed his eyes. When he looked at Nien again, he said: "Let's go build this new world."

CHAPTER 74

Farewells

"You look tired," SiQQiy said as she and Nien walked out into the night after dinner that evening.

"I am," he said. The fatigue in him made his voice soft and mild.

Monteray had tried to describe to SiQQiy what had happened in the Mietan and had a hard time of it. Thankfully, SiQQiy had understood that words could never adequately fathom such occurrences.

Dinner had been prepared quietly by Wing and Carly and eaten by everyone just as quietly, the usual jocularity that accompanied it absent.

At the river's edge, SiQQiy sat down. Nien got down beside her, his movements stiff. Lying back, he stretched out in the grass.

"So when are you leaving?" she asked.

He looked at her with weary eyes. "Soon."

"You know I wish you would let Monteray and me send in spies of our own...*trained* spies."

He touched her cheek. Pushed a strand of her hair behind her ear. "I know."

Obviously, he was not going to reiterate why he and Wing and Carly would be going anyway.

SiQQiy forced a smile, but her eyes were sad. "Well," she said, "fool-hardy as it is, I suppose you and Monteray are right. No one knows Rieeve as you do; just don't be..."

"Stupid?"

"Brave."

Nien laughed. "Never."

SiQQiy loved his face with her eyes. "A great change is coming. I want to prepare Quieness to receive it. Your people had their isolationism, the Jayakans have pride in their might, we Quienans over-confidence in our size and wealth. It would be prudent for each valley to share its strengths and accept its faults before it's too late for all of us."

Nien nodded deferentially. "I'm not sure what wisdom I've found, but at least I've learned a little about myself. I think doubting the love of someone who truly loves you has caused more hurt than genuine acts of betrayal." He met SiQQiy's eyes in the coming twilight. "My whole life I felt something was missing. I thought I'd traveled to Quieness because I tired of studying religion, but there I found that all life is spiritual, nothing we can see or touch could exist without all of its invisible counterparts. As ashamed as I am for so much that I have done, I've found that, without believing you can be of any use in the world whatsoever, it might just yet show you how mistaken you've been."

The first moon shone its face full of silvery light over the river and a cool breeze blew down from the high snowcapped mountains of the Ti Range.

"You are extraordinary," she said, thinking of all he'd shared with her in their time together in Legran, and realizing that, for all of her learning, she'd never truly learned anything. "It has been an honour coming to know you." SiQQiy clasped his hand in hers and kissed him. "You're cold," she said.

"Really? I was just thinking how warm it's getting."

Caressing his face and neck, SiQQiy pulled back his shirt and pressed her lips into the slant of his shoulder. Wanting to hold him, she placed a leg over him—and caught herself. The last time she'd tried such a thing it had ended badly. Having found Nien asleep in the cabin, she'd come in and gone to playfully straddle him when he'd awoken with a start, pushed her to the floor, and bolted to his feet wild-eyed and terrified.

"I'm sorry. I—" she started to say, but this time Nien stopped her retreat.

Placing his strong hands upon her sides and pulling her up so that he lay beneath her, he whispered, "Perfect. Don't move."

In his face there was no fear and in his eyes only peace.

SiQQiy touched her fingertips to his temples; he was all there was in the world. Nothing she had ever experienced came close to the feeling that burst inside her when she was near him. Palace walls and lush gardens, shining armies and robed ambassadors, priceless art and breathtaking vistas all paled next to the pure pleasure of looking at his face.

"We should get you back to the cabin," she said.

Sadly, Nien acquiesced. "Let me drop you off at the house."

"No. Netalf and Vadet will be waiting for me. They can walk me back."

Nien got to his feet and they walked, arms around each other's waists, across the small expanse between the house and the cabin. At the door he stopped and they stood, leaning into each other.

SiQQiy kissed his cheek, whispering, "Sleep well."

"And you," Nien said.

SiQQiy turned and Netalf and Vadet were there, materializing as it were, out of blades of river grass.

Walking away with them, SiQQiy glanced back once to see Nien still standing in the doorway of the cabin, his silhouette bathed in the warm orange glow of firelight.

Two days later as morning dawned, Wing and Nien walked the short distance to the Mietan in silence. They were leaving today. Last night, over dinner, Monteray had asked them to come to the Mietan in the morning before they set off.

At the two grand doors they paused, looking them over melancholically. Each taking a handle, they opened the doors and stepped into the Mietan together.

At the far end, they saw Monteray. He looked unusually tall standing with his back to the sun, his shadow falling against the towering wall before him.

The brothers proceeded toward him quietly; he seemed to not have heard them enter.

"Monteray," Wing said quietly.

Monteray waved for them to come over to him.

The brothers went forward and as they stepped around to face him they saw in his hands two sheaths of hard smooth leather inlaid, like the hilts of their swords, with engraved polished metal.

"These" —Monteray bounced them gently in his hands— "are yours." He handed the sheaths to each of them.

Wing and Nien looked them over, pausing over inscriptions near the scabbards' throats. The lettering was in Rieevan. The one Wing held read: Weed Farmer. Nien's: The Deviant.

A short smile tipped Monteray's mouth. "I hope you don't mind—I took some liberties."

Tears circled the brothers' eyes like gleaming crescent moons.

Monteray cleared the lump from his throat. "A sword has never been something I've gifted easily, especially ones made with my own hand. To the two of you, however, I have never trusted any blades more."

Reaching out, Monteray touched Nien and Wing on the shoulder. "What you've been through is…unimaginable. But give the world a little time, it may yet reveal that in every hurt is a healer. Hold on to what you have learned. Hold on to each other. It will see you through."

Finding only inadequacy in the words that came to their minds, the brothers each took a knee and bowing, pressed the knuckles of the hand that held their sheath to the floor.

Monteray inclined his head to them as they stood. "I don't know what it is that has, for near the whole of my life, tied my life to Rieeve, but I loved Commander Lant as a brother and I look on the two of you as my own sons."

Nien and Wing met Monteray's eyes. Nien started to speak, as did Wing at the same time.

Monteray chuckled.

"Thank you," Nien said.

"You've been counselor and teacher, new friend and father," Wing added. "Thank you for everything."

Clutching their scabbards, they bid Monteray farewell and walked for the last time out of the Mietan.

Adjusting the long woven strap of a large duffel, Wing turned to Kate and Tei.

"Looks like you're ready," Kate said.

Wing glanced at the duffel on his shoulder and laughed. "Yes, this could get us to Rieeve a couple times."

Kate laughed, too, but there were tears in her eyes. "I'll miss you. I know it's selfish, but I wish you'd stay."

Wing set the duffel down and embraced her. "You and Monteray have given me something I thought I'd never have again—a family."

Kate clasped Wing's hand and kissed his cheek.

Wing's throat tightened briefly with the desire to follow her admonition and just stay—let someone else travel to Rieeve, reconnaissance the valley and get out again.

From behind Kate, Tei stepped forward.

Wing looked warily at her.

"Have a safe journey," she said.

Detecting sincerity in her voice, Wing nodded to her. "Thank you, Tei."

Tei stared at him for an uncomfortable moment. She then turned, and brushing a hand across her face, fled into the house.

"Wing, we're ready!" came Nien's voice. A moment later, he stepped up beside Wing and dropping his duffel, hugged Kate tightly.

"Son," Kate said, as tears filled her eyes and her thin shoulders shook in his arms.

"We'll see you again, soon," Nien said. He looked Kate over. "There are many who do not know the blessing of being loved by their blood family. In my life of adoption I have known such love not only once, but twice."

"Then you had better get going," Kate said, her eyes reddening, "because I don't like having my family scattered all over the continent, and the sooner you leave the sooner you may return." She held out a wrapped bundle and placed it Nien's hands. "You should take this with you."

Nien took the bundle, eyeing it quizzically as he pulled the knotted string free. Inside lay the leather shoulder mantle of the Cant with the symbol of the shy'teh sewn over the left side.

"The rest of your clothes were too damaged to repair," Kate said.

"I'd almost forgotten," Nien said, his voice choked. He looked up at Kate. "Thank you."

As she reached up to touch their faces, Nien and Wing turned their heads and kissed the palms of her hands.

From the back door, SiQQiy emerged with Netalf and Vadet.

"I'll go get Carly," Wing said, and Kate made her own excuse to give SiQQiy and Nien their privacy.

SiQQiy came up and leaned in close to Nien, her foot touching his foot, her knee against his leg, her hands upon his belly. "Send word as soon as you can," she said. "Since no great movement of men or materials have been down the Rieevan side of Hikon Pass in such a great time, we can only estimate how long it will take for my forces to make the journey."

"I will."

"Be careful," she said, cutting to the heart of her highest concern. "Make your reconnaissance of the valley and get out. Come to Quieness. Return with me and my armies."

Nien cupped her hands in his. "When do *you* leave?"

"In a few days."

Nien rested his forehead against hers with a sigh, his shoulders sagging.

SiQQiy's breath touched his cheek. "I know."

Closing the thready gap between them, Nien took her to him.

After a lingering embrace, SiQQiy stepped back, and fixing his golden-flaked gaze whispered, "Not long."

"Not long," Nien replied, and hefting his duffel onto his shoulder, began to move away backwards down the path through the grasses.

Through the shade of tears in her eyes, SiQQiy began to laugh. "You're going to break your neck," she called to him.

Nien flashed her a smile full of teeth and, with a chivalrous nod, turned around to face the path.

In the distance, he spotted Wing walking down toward the river. A bit farther afield he saw Carly coming out of the cabin. Looking back at Wing, Nien paused. The sight of him—the familiar gait, broad shoulders, and black hair—wrought a profound sense of home in Nien's heart. He watched his brother walk to river's edge and stop. Upon river and mountain, Wing's figure cut an impressive image, like the center point in a vast painting. But there was a longing in the way Wing held himself that mirrored Nien's own sorrow at leaving Legran.

Immersing himself in the sight, banking it away like a last meal before a long fast, Nien continued on down to the riverbank. By the time he arrived, Carly was already at Wing's side; they were waiting for him.

Passing by the cabin, Nien and Wing's eyes swept the simple one-roomed timber frame.

They hadn't gone far beyond it before catching sight of a young man standing beside the bridge they intended to cross.

"Call!" Wing said, hailing him. Walking up, he grasped the young man's arms in salutation.

"What would the townspeople say if my best friend left without saying goodbye?"

"I'm glad you came."

"There's something I need to ask you," Call said, glancing nervously at Carly at Nien.

"We'll wait for you on the other side," Nien said to Wing, and he and Carly continued on across the bridge.

Taking in Call's concerned expression, Wing asked, "What is it?"

"I want to come with you," Call said, "but there are some things I've got to take care of first—you know, family stuff."

"Oh," Wing said thoughtfully. He could see in Call's expression the depth to which he wanted to convey his words.

"From the moment you walked up to me your first day in Legran, I knew—" Call hesitated. "I know Jason loved me, but I was always a mystery to him. You...Well, you made me feel not so weird, or at least made me feel that I'm not as weird as I thought I was. It was like there was something I was looking for and something I was meant to do, but what that was or how to get it wasn't clear at all, until you came. I wish there was a way to really thank you..."

Wing searched his own feelings, before saying, "Other than delivering the Plan to your uncle, I had no hopes when I came here—even for the continuation of my own life. Though I never told you, I imagine you had surmised as much by our second meeting."

Call nodded, a corner of his mouth tipping modestly.

"But once here I found not only my old family, but a new one as well. I've never thanked you for *that*."

Call's large, clear-blue eyes shone with affection.

"You are wise beyond your revolutions," Wing said, "yet you've only begun, I think, to know what you're meant to be." Glancing over the narrow bridge and up at the mountains on the other side, Wing drew a breath. "Until then, we both have to straighten things out at home. I am going back for my family, you need to stay with yours until you can feel right about leaving them."

Call nodded. "My brother died fighting the Ka'ull, and I couldn't be there. Now that uncle Monteray seems to have more faith in me, I doubt he'll put up a fight when I tell him I'll be going to Rieeve."

Wing took back up his duffel. "Then I will see you. In the meantime don't lose that little book of yours. There may be some happenings of historical significance here in Legran between now and when we meet again."

Call smiled, nodded to him, and the two friends waved goodbye.

CHAPTER 75

On the Ragged Edge

He'd seen them from a distance—a small scouting party of Ka'ull. He'd seen them before, but that had been many turns ago, in the days immediately following the decimation. Since then, it seemed their searches had slowly tapered off, and though the boys had continued to be extraordinarily careful, they had not seen a Ka'ull patrol in the mountains for nearly a season.

Pree K trembled. He could feel the weight of his father's sword at his side—he had no intention of using it. Emaciated and weak as he was it would be suicide. His only choice was to slip into the woods unnoticed.

Still and silent as a fallen leaf, he crept into the heavy underbrush and lay down. His blood ran thin in his prominent veins as he watched them, his head pounding with the strain as terror drained down like an acid, turning his stomach to fire.

Looking this way and that, two of the men began walking downhill, right toward him.

Pree K's mind swam with scenarios. If they saw him run but did not catch him, would they assume there were others? And if they assumed there were others, would they follow him or suspect that he'd be leading them away and thus look in the opposite direction?

Amongst the myriad possibilities, the one thing Pree K knew for certain was that he'd rather drive himself through with his father's sword than take the chance that they might follow him and discover those still alive in the depth of the caves.

He made his choice.

Laying out his father's long sword in the deep underbrush, Pree K lodged the pommel between a protruding tree root and a rock then pressed its point into his chest.

Gazing down at the dull-silvered blade, Pree K listened to the rustle of Ka'ull feet as they began to move down the ridge toward him. His heart raced. Reaching out, he could just reach the crossguard with his fingertips—at least enough to steady it.

Feeling the tip dip slightly into the hollow beneath his breastbone, Pree K closed his eyes.

Above him the rustling of the Ka'ull's moving feet stopped.

Pree K opened his eyes. He could hear their voices now and they seemed to be discussing something. His breath constricted until he felt light-headed.

Each moment passed, agonizing in its length, until the patrol's discussion ended and the crunch and rustle of moving feet resumed.

Raising his head ever so slightly, Pree K saw the patrol turn and head off to the left of his position. It didn't take long before they'd disappeared over the ridge and the forest had fallen silent again.

Pree K assured himself of their departure before taking a deep, shuddering breath, and releasing his grip on the sword.

A few hundred steps from the caves Pree K lay under a tree—he had lain there for a long time. He had to be sure he had not been followed. That was all that mattered.

Night came and there he still lay, thin and slack, so hungry that the hunger pangs had long ceased. The woods had grown quiet of all but creature activity.

It was just before dawn when Pree K finally began to crawl toward the cave entrance.

He fell into the cave's blessed blackness. There he remained for another long while. There was no movement, no sound but the far-away trickle of water against the stone of the cave walls. Slowly, painfully, he crawled to his feet and made his staggering way in the dark—he had not needed light to find his way in the caves for many turns now.

So quiet was he, in the darkness it took a moment for Jhock and En't to realize that he had returned. Clumsily lighting a long torch, the two younger boys sat and listened as Pree K gave them the news.

"We…we can't leave, not for a while. I…I saw a party, a small party of Ka'ull. I don't know if they were a search party or not. Perhaps it was a simple patrol. Maybe they're expecting reinforcements or searching out supply routes. Either way, it's too dangerous to leave."

"We'll starve," En't said. "We'll die of thirst."

Pree K looked up at En't. "We've got to be very careful. We cannot afford to go out every day anymore. Every two or three is all we can risk."

Jhock sat quietly, listening. He was doing poorly. His wounds had become infected and nothing the boys could do would improve them.

Hammered by his thoughts, Pree K shuddered. Even if he still had the will, he hadn't the strength anymore for going on the hunt for food. The little water that dripped in through the caves would have to do...for a time.

And now, worst of all, Pree K thought, *we cannot leave. If only we'd left turns ago, back when there were more than a handful of us. Back when we were strong enough to travel.*

But now only Grek Occoju and Mother-Yyota were alive of the adults. Pree K and En't were the healthiest of any of them—as if that was saying much. Neither of them had the strength anymore to carry those who were still alive.

Pree K raised his weary face, knowing that their only choice now was to stay—and knowing just as well what that meant for the last of them.

CHAPTER 76

Vision Cry

Choosing a place for camp their first night out, Wing set to building a fire as Nien went off on the pretense of finding some fresh meat for dinner.

As the flames took hold, rising higher and higher into the sky, Wing sat down beside it and stared blankly into the bright orange blaze.

Arranging their sleeping gear, Carly glanced over and noticed Wing looking into the fire, his attention fixed, but not on anything in particular.

Nien returned just then with a small flightless bird in one hand.

"Real shame," he muttered, approaching the campfire. "There's not even a mouthful of meat on this poor creature." He sighed. "I went out there to feel better. Now, not only do I *not* feel better, but worse for having killed the poor thing."

Nien tossed the dead bird into the trees and looked at Carly. With her head, she motioned at Wing. Nien's eyes shifted to his brother.

"How long?" he asked quietly.

"Since just after you left on your bird hunt. You've seen him like this before?"

"Yes. Nothing to do but wait."

And then Wing moved a little. When he raised his face, Nien and Carly were already looking at him.

"What is it?" Nien asked.

"I—I saw a flash of torn robes and blankets. Faces."

"Who?"

"Pree K, others."

Nien's brow furrowed. "In the past, or presently?"

"I don't know." Wing swallowed hard. "I saw darkness. Rock. I felt great despair."

Nien studied Wing's face. Visions were elusive creatures, but Nien had never fully discounted them—especially Wing's.

"You think it means he's alive? Pree K, I mean?" Carly asked.

"I don't know." Wing's eyes saddened. "Wish I did."

The three exchanged uncomfortable glances.

"Hungry?" Carly said quickly.

"Yes," the brothers replied.

Carly dug through the duffel packed by Kate and tossed Wing and Nien strips of dried meat. Conversation was short as they bit and tore off chunks of the spiced meat and tried not to wind themselves too tightly in all the what if's surrounding Wing's venture into space.

As the fire began to die, the three finally crawled into their bedrolls.

In the dark, Carly draped an arm over Wing's belly and asked, "You all right?"

Wing curled his hand around Carly's shoulder. "E'te, I'm fine. Thanks for your patience."

Carly snuggled up against him. "I'm sorry this is so hard on you and Nien—having to leave the Monterays."

Wing pressed his face against Carly's cheek. "Saying goodbye to Kate and Monteray was hard enough, but Nien having to leave SiQQiy as well..."

Carly looked at him for a moment before kissing him. "Why don't you get some sleep?"

Wing closed his eyes, and trying to block the images of the vision, pictured the river in his mind, imagined the coolness of the water against his skin, recalled the fragrance of the flowers and herbs that grew along its bank. And in the few spaceless moments before sleep, not in his mind but with his ears, he heard the river's steady euphony just as it sounded rolling in through the open window of the cabin.

Morning melted through the atmosphere and woke the three with its milky white rays leaking through still tree branches.

Packing the blankets away into the duffels and quickly eating some dried fruit, they were on their way.

The second day of travel passed much like the first: in virtual silence. But as the journey of their feet placed them closer to Rieeve, motion became a healer and their hearts began to follow. On the third day, they were talking again, and by the fourth they'd fallen back into the hearty and familiar rhythm from their past together as inseparable friends.

A turn and a half of steady travel found them making camp below a familiar peak. Wing glanced up at it as the sun set. On the other side of that peak lay the Mesko forest, and below that, Rieeve.

Before the sun had peaked over the edge of their continent the next morning, Nien, Wing, and Carly were on the move.

Wing broke the crest of Llow Peak first. He stepped out upon its rocky summit. Behind him, Nien and Carly came, breathing hard. Together, they directed their eyes downward.

Rieeve.

The wildflowers had begun to die in the fields and the many earthly colours of Kojko covered the scene.

Wing filled his lungs with air, feeling it course through his body, revitalizing his entire being.

Home.

He suddenly wanted to throw himself into the sweet scent of the fields, feel his mother's arms around him, see his father's face reading by the light of the fire. He wanted to see Nien arm wrestle Jake and laugh at the innocent look on Fey's face as she snuck a peeiopi chick into the house.

Gazing out over the breathtaking panorama, Nien was the first to speak. "Shall we?"

Retrieving their duffels, the three began the final descent of their journey.

The Mesko forest lay between them and their family fields, and for Nien and Wing who knew most of the trees by name, the forest rose to meet them in a grand, verdant hug, filling their minds with memories, making it unnecessary to check their way as their feet fell upon the familiar paths they'd trodden with their father since they were children.

With tender smiles and low voices, Nien and Wing greeted many of the great trees as they passed, but there was only one at which Wing paused, saying to Nien and Carly, "Hold on a moment. I want to check on a friend."

Ducking into the familiar root cavern, Wing glanced around at the floor and up at the ceiling, peering into the crags and crevices hoping to spot the furry black spider that had been his companion those first awful turns after his escape. But the cavern was empty and still. His friend had moved on.

"Well, wherever you are," Wing said into the cool darkness of the cavern, "I'll take it from here."

Nien and Carly squinted quizzically at Wing as they continued ahead. Sunsteps later found them passing into the thin section of hardwoods that bordered the valley. It was just inside the tree line that they finally stopped. They had not seen, heard, nor come across any evidence of Ka'ull troops in the mountains; nevertheless, their pulses quickened as they stood now at the very edge of the valley.

Scoping the fields first and finding all still, Wing cried, "Let's go!"

Nien thought sure his little brother had lost his mind as Wing bolted from the tree line and burst into the fields.

Some of the challak he had planted on that dreadful day in early Kive had managed to survive. With incredibly light feet, Wing sprang amongst the stalks and let himself fall, disappearing into their golden embrace.

For a time he lay, panting hard, the challak surrounding him in sweet concealment. He gazed heavenward. Never had he seen the sky so lavender. Here among the challak, here in the fields that would boast teeana in early Kive—Oh, he was home!

Behind him, Nien and Carly entered the fields slowly, cautiously, filled with apprehension. They gazed about as if in a trance, it seeming to them both a dream and a nightmare:

How could they have returned here?

How could they have stayed away so long?

Wing got back to his feet, the smell of seasoned challak rising up into his head and falling down into his lungs. "I'm going to the house," he said.

"Uh, Wing, I don't know. That may not be such a good—"

"Idea? We didn't come all this way to hide inside the tree line."

"No, but a little caution, brother…"

"Maybe we should do some looking around first, Wing. Check the place out," Carly suggested.

Looking them over, Wing smiled gently. "I will go. Watch my back." Running his fingers over the tops of the shafts of challak, he took in Nien's worried face. "I'll be careful."

Nien and Carly watched after Wing as he headed out.

Seeing his home in the distance unleashed a flurry of emotions in Wing's heart.

Don't get caught up, Wing silently reminded himself. *This is not the same place you knew.*

Nearing the house, Wing slowed to a walk, suddenly starting to share Nien and Carly's uneasy feelings. He knew it was probably the emptiness, the darkness of the house that made his stomach flutter, but he drew his sword anyway.

Approaching the family door, he paused and listened.

No sound.

Pushing the door open, he peeked around the corner.

No one.

He stepped through the door.

Inside, all was as he remembered it. Dust had collected on everything from the large dining-room table to the small teapot still sitting next to the old wood stove.

A bit of the tension was just starting to ease out of his shoulders when he heard footfalls behind him. His heart froze; he clutched his sword. The footfalls stopped. Moving silently, he pressed his back to the wall beside the door. Another footfall. Wing drew his sword and unable to wield its length in the doorway brought 'round the blunt, heavy end of the hilt—

The door creaked open. Wing stepped out.

Nien leapt back, accidentally knocked Carly in the face, and yelled, "Wing!"

"Nien!" Wing dropped his hilt. "Don't be sneaking up like that!"

The brothers cast each other reflexive, frigid glances.

"Sorry," Wing said. "Seeing this place so deserted makes me a little jumpy."

Nien turned to Carly who was leaning over her knees, checking her nose for blood.

"You all right?" the brothers asked.

"I'll survive." Carly swiped at her nose again, sniffing to make sure it was still working.

The three stood in silence for a time, looking around the house.

"Well, let's recon fully or none of us will get any sleep tonight," Wing said.

Separating ways, their hands still on their swords, the three moved out through the house.

A short time later, they reconvened in the main room.

"Nothing's been touched as far as I can tell," Carly said.

Nien was walking around the main room as if he were in a gallery.

"It needs some work," Wing said. "A lot of chinking needs to be replaced; it's going to get cold here awful fast. Overall, though, it's not in as bad a shape as I thought it would be." He held something up in his hand. Nien glanced down at it. It was a wooden whistle—the one Fey had gotten at a festival and, to the dismay of the entire family, decided to play all the way home from the Village. Wing had spotted it peeking out from under his bed in what had been his, Nien's, and Jake's room.

Nien smiled a little. Wing bounced the tiny object in his hand for a moment, then slipped it into his pocket.

"We should check out the barn," Nien said.

Carly and Wing followed him out, and the three made their way across the short expanse of thin, browning grass. On the sunsetting side of the barn, they found that all of their domesticated peeiopi were gone, but in their roost a covey of wild hens had taken ownership.

"You're gone for a little while and the whole neighborhood changes," Carly said.

The three looked over the wild hens before stepping into the barn. At the far end stood Jhei, the Cawutts' old milk cow.

Carly looked at the cow incredulously, adding, "Or not."

With tears of joy and disbelief, Wing and Nien patted and rubbed the beast like she was a house pet.

Wing and Nien slept only a few moonsteps that night before awaking to set out for the castle.

"Carly," Wing whispered, shaking her gently, "we're going now. I'm not sure when we'll be back."

Carly sat up bleary-eyed and nodded. "Be careful."

"You, too." Wing kissed her cheek and followed Nien out the door.

The night moonsteps were cool and there was a premonition of early Ime in the air. The brothers ran along side by side, the stars gleaming brightly overhead.

From the many trips across the valley throughout their lives, Nien and Wing knew if they kept up a steady pace they would reach the castle by daylight.

Pausing for a drink in the browning grasses of the valley floor, the brothers glanced up at Peak Llow. The sun would soon be cresting it.

"We're making good time," Wing whispered, water dripping from his lips.

Nien nodded. "Let's see how long we can keep it up. There may be some movement at dawn. From above, on the ridge, we will be able to see most of the inner courtyard and grounds. We should be able to get a good estimate of their numbers—if there are any."

Wing slung the water skin strap over his head and around his shoulder, and they were off again. The brush of cool air against their sweaty skin offered them a needed second wind. By morning, they were lying low in the tree line atop a ridge on the sunsetting side of the castle.

Clearly, they could see that Viyer was occupied. The inner courtyard was filled with supplies. Billets were set up under the colonnade of the inner curtain. The ground of the courtyard was trampled, muddy in spots where barreled water was kept, dry and dusty over the rest.

Remaining in the trees, the brothers watched silently as men began to emerge from within the castle walls and into the bailey. Most of the troops remained within the courtyard, talking amongst themselves and eating.

Only a small group left the castle itself, but they wandered no further than the front gates. From amongst this group an argument arose, the opponents disagreeing so hotly that Nien and Wing could hear their shouting voices from where they hid in the trees.

Scanning the courtyard as well as the towers and open lower compartments, Nien and Wing counted only a few hundred men, but the heavy supplies told a vastly different story. The orderly array of weapons, food and engines of war were enough for at least three Ka'ull battalions. Of course they had no way of knowing how many men were inside the castle walls; nevertheless, it was apparent from the empty watchtowers and casual carousing of the troops that this was merely provision support.

The brothers remained hidden for a bit longer before Wing suggested they continue on along the ridge where it curved behind the castle and back toward the Village.

Staying up the mountain and well within the tree line, the brothers began to move, but they hadn't gone far before Nien stopped. Wing glanced back at him—the blood had drained from his brother's face.

"What is it?" Wing asked in an undertone.

Nien's features were still as quarry stone, and his eyes were fixed upon something in the distance. Wing followed Nien's gaze. There, across the expanse between them and the castle, were two enormous mounds covered in grass taller and thicker, even in its wintering state, than that which covered the valley floor.

A river of ice poured through Wing's veins. He felt his knees weaken as an overwhelming realization emptied out his gut.

How could he have been so ignorant?

It was beneath those two mounds that terrible night had ended for their people. It was there Nien had been thrown, buried alive in one of those pits—

Wing placed a steady hand on Nien's shoulder. Nien flinched.

"Brother..." Wing said. Moving a little, Wing placed himself in Nien's eyeline. Nien's eyes focused on him. "Come," Wing said gently. "Let's move on."

And they did.

Remaining high above the castle, they traversed a shallow canyon and re-emerged, facing the back of Viyer where the Village began.

Pausing, Wing reached out and tugged Nien's shirt, gesturing toward a stand of trees a short distance from the rear of the castle.

Nien looked down and saw a fair herd of horses grazing.

When not taken care of or trimmed, Rieevan horses grew long, thick hair from their knees down to their hooves. The Ka'ull horses they'd seen corralled in the courtyard were sleeker and more robust.

For a moment, the brothers pondered the same thought: *Our horses.*

But, in unspoken agreement, they cast off the thought. No matter how helpful having mounts would be, retaking them would be an act of monumental stupidity, something akin to their having come back to Rieeve at all.

"Before we leave, I'd like to take a look at the Village," Wing said.

"Me, too."

Staying deep inside the tree line, the brothers continued on, staying far above the upper portion of the valley. They'd not gone far before pausing to take in the final devastation of the Village that only Wing had seen the beginning of.

Every single Village home was burnt to ash and cinder. Only a few large, charred logs remained of the Mesko-built homes.

"Nien," Wing said, "can you recall the families that were not there that night?"

Nien shook his head, his mind still pondering the shocking ruin that had once been Melant. "I can't remember, Wing. I've already tried—many times."

"Well," Wing said, "we know that those most agitated over the state of the Council and the Cant might not have come at all. But others could have been absent, too—home with a sick child or something."

Nien nodded. "I know. I've thought of that."

"So what if those that were not in the castle managed to escape before the Ka'ull could find them?"

"But how would they have known to flee?"

Wing thought for a moment, and the thing that had been smoldering in the back of his mind, finally sparked. "The same way I knew," he said. "Pree K."

Nien watched Wing for a moment. His brother's face was a concentrated study.

"The flash I had, our first night out from Legran," Wing said.

"You said you thought you saw Pree K. And something about rock and torn blankets."

"What if what I saw was not in the past, that last night, but since then?"

Even as the words left Wing's lips, Nien's pulse began to race and he knew he and Wing were thinking the same thing—

"The caves," they said together.

It was crazy. But it *was* possible.

"Now we see the path that's laid before us," Nien said.

"Let's follow it," Wing answered.

On their feet, the brothers rounded the back of the Village, dove into the tree line on the far side, passing the Cantfields at a run back toward their house and Carly.

Carly scanned the distance toward the Village for about the hundredth time that afternoon. Lines of worry traced her face, her eyes growing tired of searching for sight of them. Drawing a deep, frustrated breath, she returned to the task at hand as the sun chased two shadows from the trees.

At last!

"Carly!" Wing called with a wave of his hand at seeing her standing next to the barn.

The three met and went inside the house. "You've been busy," Wing said, looking about.

Carly nodded. "I had to do *something*. What took so long?"

"We went 'round the castle and the Village. We saw only a few hundred men, but supplies were heavy. And even though there could be as many as a thousand in the castle, we saw no patrols. It appears to be as Monteray said: To the Ka'ull, Rieeve is secure."

"That's good news at the moment," Carly said.

"There's something more."

Carly met Wing's eyes.

"We think some of the Village families may have survived. We have an idea where they might be."

Carly searched the brothers' faces for less than a heartbeat. "Where?"

"A place you might remember," Wing said.

The following morning the three set out with rope, a small glass jar of oil, a few worn field shirts, and extra water skins.

CHAPTER 77

Life in the Depth

"It's steeper than I remember," Wing said grasping for a handhold on something to support his weight while he swung a leg up over the edge of only one of many massive boulders they were required to scale.

"Farther, too," Carly added, sitting back against a tree just the other side of the same rock.

Nien sat down beside her. "We're older, that's the problem."

"Are we sure they'd come here? I mean, none of our people traveled out here—they never even traveled into the Mesko forest."

"Remember Wing's, uh, black out by the fire just after we'd left Legran? Remember what he said he saw?"

Carly thought a moment. "Oh," she said.

With that, they continued on, Carly refocusing her attention on the climb and wondering how those families, if they *had* gotten out, were able to make this climb not only with children but also in the torrential rainfall of that night.

Surmounting the worst of the boulder field, they fell in upon a thin, familiar ridge. As they filed along the ridge with Wing in the lead, the three silently recalled that day so long ago when above them, on a short outcropping of rock, a shy'teh had sat watching them. It had not been far from that point where Wing had accidentally discovered an entrance to a labyrinth of caves.

Continuing up the path and winding around the edge of another immense shield of rock, they came upon the exact spot where Wing had fallen nearly nine revolutions earlier.

As Nien set to making flambeaux with the oil and shirts, Carly and Wing re-explored the entrance that they knew lay to the right of the hole Wing had fallen into. They found it with less trouble than they'd expected:

the hidden opening between the jagged outcropping, the gentle slope down into the caves.

Nien was first to move through the slit in the rocks; Wing and Carly came behind, peering into the chasm before them to find Nien looking back at them, his face lit by the dancing flame of his torch.

The three walked down the narrow slope and into the large tunnel they'd tried to explore the first time. Along the wall beside them, they noticed a set of engravings—the strange grooves in the rock that Wing had felt with his hand so long ago but been unable to see. Now, they could see that they were indeed carvings—of lone figures, their robed bodies hunched, frozen forever in stone; a reflection of a moment in the lives of their living counterparts.

Raising his flambeau a little, Nien caught sight of another engraving, set apart from the others, of a four-legged creature with pointed ears and a long tail.

Stepping back, the three saw the relief come together as the depiction of a single event. The hunched figures were actually in a row, moving toward the entrance of the caves, each with a hand on the shoulder of the figure in front of them, and in the lead of this lowly procession was the four-legged creature.

Beneath the dancing light of their flambeaux, the astonishing affirmation of legend sunk home—

It was true, their people *had* once sought refuge in these caves and been saved by the great black mountain cat.

Air moving down through the break in the rocks pushed at the flame of the torch Wing held as he turned away from the haunting stone-story. Carly and Nien followed, and they began their journey down into the depths.

With Wing in the lead, the three moved along single file, carefully laying out bits of rope as markers where a tunnel would break off to their left or right.

Moving along the crooked cave walls, the torchlight casting freakish shadows against the damp stone, they made their way in silence. The cold depth of the cave's walls penetrated their bones as the labyrinth wound its way deep into the mountain. The twists and turns seemed never to end.

Wing proceeded with caution. Behind him, Nien said, "It can't go much farther."

But it seemed to.

As fear festered beneath their skin, the three rounded yet another turn, this time coming upon the opening to a chamber on their left. Glancing at one another, the three raised their torches and moved through the opening.

The scene over which their torchlight fell sucked the breath from their lungs and pinned their bodies to the cold cave walls.

In what they thought might be the innermost cave, they found a host of bodies, some partially wrapped in worn blankets, others in nothing at all. The skin over the bones of the dead was taught and greyer than the worn vestiges of their blankets, their eye sockets bare caverns, their hair fragile strands of oil and dust. Most lay in fetal positions, eerily still, frozen in death as they had no doubt passed their last moments of life: hunched against the chill.

Beneath the flickering light of their flambeaux, Nien, Carly, and Wing tried to make sense of it....

But there was no making sense of it.

Though pitifully ragged, the blankets and clothing were distinctly Rie-evan. That aside, not all the bodies had decayed beyond recognition.

These, the last of their people, had escaped the immediate death at the hands of the Ka'ull only to suffer and die in the black belly of a cave.

Firelight from the flambeaux danced freakishly over the bodies, and a suffered cry escaped Carly's throat. Wing pulled her to his side.

Nien turned, and the three backed out of the eerie sanctum, the light from their flambeaux retreating with them, leaving darkness to fall again inside the tomb.

Back in the tunnel, the three stood for a moment, unable to speak, unable to make the decision to simply go back.

It was Wing who finally raised his head and, lifting his flambeau, started back down the way they had come. He'd not gone more than a few steps when he stopped again.

"Nien, lower your flame," he said over his shoulder.

Nien lowered his flambeaux as he and Carly strained to understand what Wing was doing.

"Follow me," Wing said. He glanced back at Nien. "Leave a marker here."

Nien did so as Wing's tall frame led away into the darkness.

With long strides, Wing entered a narrow tunnel branching off to the right of the main tunnel. This smaller tunnel made a sharp turn again to the left, and that was when both Nien and Carly spotted what they assumed Wing had seen: the faint, flickering light of a torch.

Wing went forward, ducking beneath a low overhang before emerging into yet another cavern, this one larger than the last.

Nien and Carly stepped in behind him.

Huddled in blankets and cloaks by the light of a single flambeau were seven beings.

Nien raised his torch as a small face, drawn and pale, surfaced from beneath a sea of blankets. The eyes blinked at him in the torchlight. Nien's hand shook—the light of his flambeau played madly off the cave walls.

Alive!

Glancing about for a place to rest his flambeau, he saw a notch in the cave wall made to accommodate a torch handle. Slipping the torch into the notch, he hurried over and knelt before the blinking figure. It was a young boy.

"It's all right," Nien said softly. "My name's Nien. We're friends—Rieevans. What's your name?"

With large, wet eyes the boy looked up at him, but said nothing. Nien was about to reach out to the boy when he heard a dry voice speak his name. "Nien?"

Nien's head shot up.

Across the room, a man pushed the hood of his cloak away from his face.

"Grek?" Nien said.

"Nien?" the man asked again, his eyes squinting against the additional light from the flambeaux Wing, Nien, and Carly had brought into the cavern.

Nien pushed himself to his feet and hurried over to him. "Yes, it's Nien. Grek?"

The man nodded stiffly.

"Grek!" Nien cried, grabbing the hand the older man offered and clutching it tightly.

"I knew I would live until you came. I knew you would find us."

"You're going to live a long time yet," Nien encouraged.

Grek's old eyes smiled. "Save the young ones. They've been through so much. Save them, Nien. Get them out of here."

Nien nodded. "We will, we will."

Grek coughed and squeezed Nien's hand. "Is Son-Cawutt Wing with you? Has he, too, lived?"

"Yes, yes," Nien replied.

"Good, good boy." Grek's voice grew fainter.

For a moment Grek's grip on Nien's hand was that of steel. It softened then, and released.

Nien stared at the Council Spokesman. Slowly, he reached forward and closed Grek's eyes. When Nien turned about, he found Wing and Carly already looking at him.

Pushing himself back to his feet, Nien joined Wing and Carly as they continued on to the others, tremulously removing blankets and cloaks that hooded faces. To their great relief, they found two young girls and one teenage boy alive, only sleeping.

There remained only one cloaked figure left. Exchanging a slow look with Carly, Wing walked over to it, and crouching down quietly, pushed back the hood.

It was a young man, but so pale and drawn was his face that Wing could not tell at first whether he still lived. Sliding his hand beneath the blanket, Wing pressed his palm to the grim hardness of the boy's rib bone. The movement he felt beneath his hand was slight, and Wing hoped not a trick of his own desire, but hope filled him that there was an exchange of air between the cave's damp oxygen and the boy's painfully thin body.

Wing pulled the hood back over the boy's face, got to his feet and said, "We've got to get them out of here."

"Agreed. Back to the house," Nien said.

"But until we wake them we won't know what shape they're in—if they'll be able to travel far," Carly said. "Or travel at all."

As the three pondered in silence how best to proceed, a resounding clash of metal striking the cave stone shot lightning into their veins.

"*NO!* Ba'curs!"

Before Wing could even place the direction, a glint of steel flashed passed his head; he lurched sideways. As his shoulder hit the cave wall, he was drawing his sword, using the wall to recover his balance and direction, spinning about to face the attacker. But the bearer of the blade stumbled, the sword falling past Wing and grinding along the rock floor of the cave.

Wing managed to terminate the momentum of his counterstrike, and looked up.

The assailant had slumped against the far side of the cave, barely able to support the weight of the sword he held, the silver tip of it wavering a breath above the floor.

In astonishment, Wing said, "Pree K?" and unknowingly stepped out of the shadow cast by one of the torches and into the light of the flame.

On the gaunt, grey features of the attacker's face, comprehension dawned.

"Merehr?" a weak voice said through a shaking laugh. "Wing?"

Joy, like a sweet hot wine, filled Wing's belly. "Yes, Pree K—it is you; it is I."

"Wing."

The sword tumbled from Pree K's grasp as he stepped away from the wall toward Wing.

But the wall had kept Pree K on his feet—

Dropping his own sword, Wing caught Pree K as he collapsed and lowered him to the ground.

Awakened by the clamour, the young man Wing had only hoped was not dead, pushed the hood away from his face and crawled to his feet.

Starting toward Pree K, he saw Wing and stopped short.

"It's all right," Pree K said.

The young man came forward, and glancing warily at Wing, knelt at Pree K's side. "Did you see any of them?"

"No," Pree K said, shaking his head. "Not a sign." With Wing's help, Pree K sat up a little and introduced Wing to Jhock.

"I know," Jhock said. "Wing Merehr."

"Of what family are you?" Wing asked.

"Fen'la."

Behind them another huddled figure moved. With the effort it would have taken a man four times his age, he dragged himself to his feet. After a moment, his eyes cleared and he took in the room.

Wing, Carly, and Nien watched as he shuffled over and knelt beside Jhock.

"Wing, this is En't," Pree K said.

En't looked at Wing. He then spotted Nien standing behind Wing.

"Son-Cawutt Nien," En't said.

"And that is Carly," Wing said.

Carly stood opposite Nien at the other side of the cavern.

"Carly, Uni, the fighter," En't said.

"You are Council Spokesman-Occoju's eldest son, aren't you?" Nien said, feeling a strange constriction in his chest, as if something were slowly pulling a cord that drew his rib cage in upon his lungs.

En't looked up at Nien. "I am." His gaze narrowed a little. Shifting his position, he looked past Nien and his eyes lit upon the still figure in the far corner.

Nien, Carly, and Wing exchanged a short set of glances, but En't spoke before any of them could. "I am now the head of what is left of my family."

The brothers and Carly knew that the Occojus had been a large family. Nien trembled slightly. "Yes. I'm sorry."

En't's hazel eyes revealed only exhaustion, void of feeling. "I have been expecting it." He glanced over his shoulder at one of the smaller, still-sleeping bundles. "She and I alone, are left."

Wing cradled Pree K's head and shoulders in his arms. "We need to get all of you to the house. We can talk there after you get some rest and food in your stomachs."

"Home?" Pree K forced. "Are you crazy?"

"No," Wing replied. "We're leaving this place."

"All of us at once? We'll be spotted," Pree K insisted.

"Not to worry, Pree K. We have not come this far to let even one more of you die in these caves. We're going home." Wing's voice was steady. He looked at Nien and Carly and saw in their eyes the hope that he was right. "Can you walk?" Wing asked.

"Yes." With Wing's help, Pree K got back on his feet. "My father's sword," he said.

Wing, Nien, and Carly looked down at the large blade that lay on the cave floor. Instantly recognizable, seeing Lant's sword was like seeing an old friend.

Wing walked over, picked it up, and tucked it into his sword belt; the sword Master Monteray had made for him he retrieved from the floor as well and slid it into the sheath sitting at his other hip.

Satisfied, Pree K nodded to Wing and turned to help Jhock, but Jhock had even less strength than Pree K. Wing found himself having to steady both of them, noticing as he did the blood stains upon the left sleeve and back of Jhock's cloak.

With fear in his eyes at Wing having noticed the blood, Jhock said quickly, "I...I won't slow you down."

Wing said, "It wouldn't matter, Jhock, if you did. We'll get you back to the house and take care of it."

Jhock's glassy, feverish eyes met Wing's with awesome relief.

Stepping across the cavern, En't picked up his little sister. Nien held the youngest of the children—the boy whose large, wet eyes he'd first seen upon entering the cavern. Wing carried the only other girl in his arms, Lily, and Carly offered Jhock a shoulder.

Nien, Wing, and Carly started toward the cavern opening.

—But the others had stopped.

Turning back, they watched as Pree K, Jhock, and En't looked once more over the cavern.

Only Grek Occoju now remained within the looming silence. A few torn, threadbare blankets lay in desolate heaps here and there. The ashes of past fires scorched the floor.

Bitter Deliverer—their stony shrine.

The young men could not believe they were leaving. For so long they had held hope that they would. And then, just as that hope had died completely from their hearts...

In silence the young men turned round and, raising their eyes to Carly, Wing, and Nien, nodded that were ready to go.

Nien ducked out of the cavern in the lead.

Coming last, Wing watched as Pree K, Jhock, and En't moved slowly before him, flooded with gratitude that they were able to travel under their own power. The thought of having to make the trip more than once tired and worried him.

Looking ahead and away from his thoughts, Wing was surprised to see that they'd nearly arrived at the entrance. The journey back seemed to have taken only half the time of going in.

At the hidden break, Nien placed the torch down, and after placing the boy into Carly's arms, crawled cautiously up through the crevice to make a quick scan of the area.

All was quiet.

Leaning back through the narrow slit in the rock, he retrieved the boy from Carly and helped En't and Wing pass the two young girls through.

One by one En't, Jhock, and Pree K emerged for the last time from the depths.

Smothering the torch in the wet dirt outside the cave, Wing tossed it back down through the cave entrance as a final token.

Turning, he took Lily up in his arms again and started after the others.

CHAPTER 78

Rieeve and Warm Blankets

The sun had begun to set when the small company finally arrived at the tree line. Setting Lily on her feet, Wing edged from the trees to scan the fields. They were clear and quiet, filled only with the familiar chirping of night bugs.

"Let's make our way as far as we can under the cover of trees," Wing said in an undertone. The group retreated back into the woods and wearily followed.

Again Wing crept out of the trees—the house stood directly across from them in the distance.

"Nien," Wing called quietly. Nien appeared by his side, the smallest boy still in his arms. "I'll go ahead and check out the house."

"Be careful," Nien warned.

Wing nodded and moved off.

Nien watched as Wing's dark, crouched figure disappeared into the fields. He could feel the sharp beat of his heart and behind him in the trees the strained breathing of the children. Impressed with their patience and stillness, some huddled together, some standing, Carly and Nien kept close watch on the fields.

And then, out in the black beyond the tree line, something caught Nien's eye, a shadow darker than the night around it, moving swiftly. His breath clenched in his throat and his hand sought the blade at his side.

A moment later, Wing reappeared inside the tree line as if he'd stepped out from behind a curtain. Nien grunted with relief and welcomed him with a clap on the back. "You...You're going to give me heart failure."

"All is quiet," Wing whispered. "Let's go."

The small band moved out across the field.

Once inside their home, Wing got a fire going in the wood stove and then joined Carly and Nien settling in the children. Pree K helped until he dropped next to Lily from exhaustion. After a quick wet-rag bath, En't dried and rewrapped his little sister, Fe, and then fell to sleep beside her.

Wing lifted Pree K to a roll of blankets and getting him out of the pitiful rags he wore for clothes, said, "Nien? Will you grab whatever pants or shirts we have left?"

Moving into the back room, Nien retrieved all the clothing from within the set of drawers that he and Wing had once shared with Jake.

Back in the main room, Nien found Wing inspecting Pree K's right leg. It was terribly bruised and badly swollen.

"What happened there?"

Wing shrugged. "I don't know. I don't even remember seeing him limp."

On the trip down from the caves, Pree K had slipped and taken a handful of vicious thorns. Wing had removed the thorns and bandaged his hands, but he did not think the injury to his leg had occurred then.

Wing glanced around the house. "Teeanacoir."

He found the small jar of ointment in the same cupboard it had always been. Taking a finger full of the salve, Wing worked it as gently as he could into the bruises on Pree K's leg. Pree K groaned but did not fully awake. Not wanting to disturb the boy's sleep any more than he had to, Wing changed the blood-soaked wrappings on his hands and placed a rolled-up blanket beneath his head for a pillow.

Beside Wing, Nien cleaned both the heavy gash in Jhock's shoulder as well as the puncture wounds in his arm before turning to En't and his little sister.

Wing moved to help Nien when Carly called them over to the side of the boy Nien had carried from the caves. Carly had recognized him as Hagen, the baby of the Yyota family who had been neighbors of hers.

"Look," Carly said, pointing to the boy's arm. The limb was cold and stiff, dark grey in colour.

Heart-sickened, the three exchanged worried glances.

"It has no blood supply," Nien said.

"We can try and restore circulation, but the blood may have absent for too long now," Wing said. "We may not be able to save it."

Carly squeezed her eyes shut. Hadn't there been enough?

They watched the boy for a time.

"Let's see what happens tonight," Wing said. "In the mountains Rhegal taught me a little about medicines, preparations that can check infection, ease pain, so on."

Carly and Nien agreed. It was all they could do.

With Carly on last watch, Wing rose before first light. Taking up a small leather bag, he stepped out into the chill morning air. By the time he returned, the children were still sleeping but Nien was awake and Carly was holding Hagen in her arms.

Wing walked over to her. "No change?"

Carly shook her head. "It looks worse."

Wing's face was grave as he took the root he'd gone into the woods for from the small leather bag and set it to boiling.

Once the preparation was done and cooled, Wing gave the water from the boiled root to Carly. She got Hagen to drink most of it and they waited a little longer.

Wing checked his grip on his sword. He never dreamed the first blood to stain the swords Monteray had made for them would be the blood of one of his own people, and a child at that.

Carly and Nien held Hagen's arm down firmly on a block of wood set upon the Mesko table Wing had built for Reean. Carly wrapped one hand around Hagen's eyes. He struggled at first, then lay still.

Wing rechecked his grip and brought his sword down.

His strike was true, the separation clean, instantaneous.

Mercifully, there was little feeling left in the dead limb; nevertheless, the shock and surprise of the blow rent a scream from Hagen that woke the rest, shocking Fe so badly she froze and sending Lily running into the arms of Jhock.

Carly grabbed Hagen to her, pressing him into her chest as Nien quickly bandaged the stump.

As Wing and Nien explained and comforted the others, Carly sat beside the fire, holding Hagen in her arms as he sweated and shook. The phlevian root preparation Wing had made helped as much as anything could; nevertheless, his sleep was fitful, afflicted.

Emotionally drained, Wing cleaned his sword, then replacing it into the sheath sat down on the floor and rested. When he awoke it was late afternoon. The children had all fallen to sleep again and the house was warm with their sleeping bodies and pleasantly dim with all the shutters closed. Nien and Carly were awake, and so the three conversed, only the light from the fire and the occasional popping of wood adding to their whispered conversations.

On the heels of the trauma felt by all over the amputation of Hagen's arm, and the fact that a legion of Ka'ull was camped less than a handful of sunsteps away, it seemed impossible to Wing that he should feel the day to be something rare and perfect. But here with Nien and Carly, the two peo-

ple in the world that meant the most to him, and six sleeping children—
their children—he found himself feeling full beyond bearing.

Complete.

No other work to be done. No needing to be anywhere else. All there
was to do was eat, sleep, talk, and watch.

Near evening, Wing checked the fire and went to Pree K's side. The
young man had changed considerably since Wing had seen him that last
terrible night. His bony shoulders and long legs revealed growth; with
some food it wouldn't take long to get some flesh on them. His once thin,
delicate hands were now taut as talons. His face was creased with lines
belonging to a man three times his age.

If there is a legend to be born from all of this, Wing thought, *it should
be him.*

As a race, those, here in this one room were the last of the Rieevans—
Wing held no illusions on that count. Any blood passed on to children
between them would last no more than a generation. Nevertheless, memory lived longer than blood, and words and music longer still. They would
write new legends, sing new songs, and pass their memories of this time
and these lives to all those that were to come.

Pree K's actions, the tenacity of the six great souls lying upon their family's floor, would endure beyond mortal lines of race.

Adding a bit of fuel to the fire, Wing turned away from Pree K's side
and crawled across the floor to Carly where she lay with Hagen in the fold
of her arms.

"You all right?" he asked.

Carly was looking down at Hagen. They were keeping him drugged
with the phlevian root to help him sleep, but his soft hair was still wet with
the sweat of pain and Carly's face was sad.

"Yeah, I think so." She stroked the boy's head. "It breaks my heart,
Wing, what they've been through. It's not right."

"I know."

"I look in their faces and I want to believe they can start again. I want to
believe that time will heal their wounds, that life can be normal for them
again. But what if they've been through too much to be normal children,
or adults? The task of rebuilding Rieeve may be a simple thing in comparison to rebuilding their lives."

"We can only give them a place to start. They will have to find their own
way from there."

Carly looked up at Wing. "That they survived, I suppose, means they
are here for a reason."

Wing nodded to Hagen. "Want me to hold him for a while?"

"No," Carly said, "he just fell to sleep again."

Adjusting the blanket over Carly's shoulders, Wing pulled another blanket with him and scooted back to lean against one of the sturdy legs of the Mesko table. The turns it had taken him to make the table seemed like an age ago. His mind drifted as he gazed around the room, everything he saw touching off a memory: Jake assuring Reean that it had not been him who encouraged Fey to stand atop an old dung pile filled with angry bees, Joash trying to unclog the drain in the family wash basin, Nien curled up with one of his books—a large piece of the evening's dessert placed carefully between his chest and the hand holding the book.

Across the room one of the children stirred. Wing blinked and came back to the present. He looked over at Lily as she rolled about in her blankets, wrapping herself in a tight cocoon before falling still again.

A whole new set of memories will now be made in this place, he thought.

The blue of night showered in through the open shutters, bathing the children in its calming glow.

To be here like this forever, Wing thought. ***That is a good destiny.***

Glancing up, Wing took in the light from the fire as it played along the high cabin beams overhead before closing his eyes. The next thing he knew Nien was waking him to take second watch.

Carly had watch when the sun came up. The fire had died down and still the log home remained comfortably warm.

Breakfast, Carly thought, glancing around.

Checking the dagger in her boot, she quietly opened the door and headed out to the new wild hen preserve. There were plenty of eggs and she gathered them gratefully. "I'd offer you a pat in thanks but you'd probably try to take my finger."

Back inside, all were still asleep except for Wing. Carly removed her cloak as Wing tiptoed over to her.

"What's this?" he asked.

Carly removed one of the many eggs from within the folds of her cloak.

"Really?" Wing mumbled. "How?"

"The new residents."

"From wild hens?"

Though her eyes were nearly brimming with tears, Carly nodded and smiled. "And this isn't all of them—not by a ways. Now, if you don't mind," she said, and set an old skillet in Wing's hand. "Don't overcook them."

Nien awoke with the pop pop of cooking eggs and the familiar aroma of breakfast at home. Rubbing his eyes, he got up, and finding his way to the large sink, started pumping.

No water came out.

Wing laughed.

Nien glanced at him. "We need to work on that," he said and, dry-rubbing his face, pushed his nose into the air and sniffed. "Eggs?"

Soon the children began to awake. En't was the first to get up, followed soon by Pree K. Over the edges of their blankets, Lily and Fe peered, eyes shining.

Wing motioned them over with his head. "Well, come on. You won't fill your stomachs by staring."

The three eldest boys waited while the younger ones ate before sitting down themselves. They tried to feign interest in Carly, Wing, and Nien's conversation, but they fooled no one. Near starved to death, it was all they could do not to eat the plate once the eggs were gone.

With a short smile, Wing got up from the table and announced that he was off to do some hunting. The wild hens were a blessing, but they'd need more than eggs to feed six half-starved children.

"I can go with you," En't volunteered.

Wing shook his head. "No, you rest. We're going to need all of you in good health; soon."

"Don't worry," Jhock encouraged. "It won't take long."

"I don't doubt it," Wing said.

Pulling on his long leather cloak, Wing took up a duffel from beside the family door. Inside it he placed Joash's knife—the one Joash often spent time sharpening while sitting on the stool next to the door.

Outside, Wing took his favored bow, the first one he had successfully made with Rhusta, and threw it over his shoulder. The fields he had once tended stretched out behind him as he moved off toward the sunsetting tree line, and even with a bow slung across his back and a sword swinging at his side, a familiar sense of preternatural calm assailed him.

The woods were full of animal chatter and the disparate calls of birds. It didn't take long before Wing had picked up on the trail of a fent in the soft ground of oncoming Ime. He followed the trail carefully before spotting the fent in a small splash of sunlight. The young male stood nibbling on grass, his hindquarters protected behind a tree, his front half exposed and partly turned toward Wing.

Placing an arrow and drawing back the bow, Wing let the arrow fly.

It struck true; the fent dropped in a heap.

Wing built a fire and quickly set to work skinning the fent. The sharp blade of his father's knife and his gratitude to the fent and what it meant to the six hungry young people back at the house, made the normally disconcerting job go smoothly, even meditatively.

With the meat cooking, spitted over the fire, Wing searched nearby for edible berries.

Returning with his cloak full of the tiny purplish fruit and finding the meat done, Wing put out the fire, spread the ashes, tore the spit apart and wrapped the venison before placing it in the duffel beneath his cloak.

As he set off back for the house, he remembered imploring Rhusta in naïve desperation to teach him how to live in the mountains. The thought made him smile, happy that he was now making a little good on that promise.

Up at the house, while Nien coerced some flow from the well, Carly worked to repair the damage done to the barn and coop, trying to keep her mind from worrying over what was keeping Wing so long.

"There must have been a terrible storm through here," Carly said to herself, her voice strained as she reached to nail a top board that had come loose on the side of the barn.

"Some help?" Jhock asked, walking over.

"Yes!"

Jhock hurried to steady the board, pressing it firm as Carly pounded the nail home. Just then Pree K came up.

Jhock and Carly could see it all over him—something was wrong.

"What is it?" Carly asked.

"It's Hagen. I think you should come."

Setting aside her tools, Carly shouted for Nien and she and Jhock followed Pree K back up to the house. Inside, En't was sitting in Reean's old rocking chair, holding Hagen. Nien came in just as Carly pulled the blanket back from the stump of Hagen's arm. The deathly green colour was back and had begun to make its way up the rest of his arm toward his shoulder. Lost again in fever, Hagen's small frame twisted and shook.

As Carly, Nien, and the older boys looked down at the arm, it felt as if the green decay was eating its way through the impossibly tenuous threads of their existence.

"We can't continue to whittle away at him," Carly said quietly.

Jhock and Pree K stood silently, their heads lowered, their hands thrust deep into their pockets. En't rocked Hagen, dabbing at the boy's forehead with a moist cloth.

Frustrated and helpless, Carly and Nien continued to stare at the decaying limb as if some answer might spring from it. For all their training this was something they did not know how to fight, and the thought of watching Hagen slowly being consumed was more than either of them could bear.

How was it even possible? Carly wondered. Of their entire race, only nine of them remained. To lose Hagen...

"Where's Wing?" Nien whispered to himself—just as the door opened.

"Boy, you two work quick," Wing said, stepping inside and setting down the duffel. "The barn—" Wing stopped as five sets of eyes lit upon him from across the room.

Removing his cloak, Wing hung it beside the door and walked over to where the small group huddled around the rocking chair.

Jhock and Pree K parted for him, and Wing stepped into the circle, his eyes coming to rest on Hagen's arm. He looked at it for only a moment before shifting his eyes to Nien and Carly. The pain in their faces spoke volumes.

Wing held out his hands and said, "Here."

En't stood, and drawing the blanket back over Hagen's shoulders, handed him to Wing.

Holding Hagen against his chest, Wing stepped out of the circle and walked across the room toward the fireplace.

The others watched from the center of the room.

Near the fireplace, Wing stopped.

Wrung with agony, Hagen's torment caused the blanket he was wrapped in to shiver and jerk unnaturally as if it had taken on life, quivering with a pain of its own.

The room had fallen impossibly still. Uneasily, the younger men exchanged glances—

But Carly and Nien's attention was focused entirely on Wing.

In perfect stillness, Wing stood.

Nothing, Nien thought, *could be that still and yet so...fluid.*

Even as Nien thought this, the air in the room thinned and it seemed as if something new took its place. Or maybe, it was something that had been there all along and he'd just never felt it before...

En't and Pree K stood next to each other, and Lily stood next to Jhock—one hand clutching the hem of his shirt as she peered at Wing from beneath her honey-coloured bangs.

What was happening? Pree K wondered.

No sooner had he wondered then Wing turned and, raising his head, opened his eyes.

Pree K twitched and blinked, feeling as if a spell had been broken, like he'd been on a long journey and forgotten to pack for it.

Wing moved across the room to the cluster of makeshift beds and, kneeling, laid Hagen down on one of them.

Carly, Nien, and the boys gathered around.

There was no sign of the decay anywhere on Hagen's body. The small stump of his arm was a perfect pink colour—the shoulder as well.

Wing covered Hagen up, tucked the blankets in around him, and rose to his feet. Looking over the small, bewildered crowd, Wing smiled a little, his eyes shining like a sunrise reflection upon the surface of a lake.

"Let's eat," he said, and returned to the large duffel he'd left by the door.

Neither Carly nor Nien had ever seen an entire fent disappear so fast—the berries never made it into a bowl.

"I can't believe you did all that up there," Carly said, beginning to clean up. "If Lant had known about all these mountain skills of yours he would have put you in charge of Cant survival training."

Wing took the wet rag from her hand. "I've often wondered what it would take to impress you."

Carly shook her head in dismay. Her eyes softened. "Well, I suppose tracking, killing, preparing, and cooking an entire fent in the mountains is almost as impressive as healing a little boy."

Wing glanced down and met her eyes.

Carly touched his cheek. The very sight of his face, the feel of his skin struck her with such intensity that she felt physically weak. Wrapping her fingers in his shirt she pulled him down and pressed her lips against his neck.

A shiver spun its way up Wing's back. He dropped the wet rag.

"Looks like I'll be finishing up here," Nien said, bending over and picking up the rag. "As if we haven't had enough excitement for one day."

"If you'll excuse us," Wing said, and taking Carly's hand the two disappeared into the house.

Three days had passed and the new family that now lived under the Cawutt roof was getting to know its youngest member as an exuberant, healthy child. Hagen seemed not even to notice that there was less than half an arm on his right side. He was into, on top of, and often hiding behind everything. A constant patrol had been implemented by the older boys, and by the time evenings rolled around everyone was ready for him to go to bed.

At the end of one particularly trying evening, En't and Jhock had fallen to their own bedrolls, blissful in the wake of silence that followed Hagen's descent into sleep.

Checking the windows and doors, Wing noticed Pree K sitting cross-legged on the floor in front of the fire in contemplation. Securing a loose window latch, Wing offered to take first watch. Carly and Nien agreed, settling in for sleep.

"Mind if I interrupt?" Wing asked, his calm tone a conduit for the pale blue light filling the cabin.

Pree K looked up at Wing. "Please," he said.

"Are you all right?"

Pree K was silent for a moment before responding. "Did you see my father before he died?"

"Yes," Wing replied, but his face was unreadable.

"I figured," Pree K replied. "When I found him in the hut, before he sent me to warn those that were in the Village—and to find you—I noticed a deep wound in his side. I tried to help him, but he turned me away, told me to carry out his request as quickly as possible."

"Some of his last words were of you," Wing said. "But what with the burning of the homes and the circumscription of the Ka'ull, I was forced from the Village."

"You were in the Village at the time of the burning?" Pree K asked.

Wing nodded. "I was trying to ascertain where you might have gone after you came to me in the fields, when the fires caught my attention. I ran into the Village hoping to catch the arsonist but failed when the Ka'ull engulfed the burning streets." Pree K's silence brought a profound realization to Wing's mind. "It was you, wasn't it?"

Pree K nodded slowly, only a hint of expression on his face. "They thought they could take everything..."

Wing gazed lovingly upon Pree K's bowed head. *Why hadn't I seen it before?*

"By the time I made it back to the hut, father was gone," Pree K said.

"I buried him," Wing said softly.

Pree K looked at Wing, the first hint of tears welling in the young man's eyes. "Thank you."

Wing nodded.

"Where were those families you helped escape?" Wing asked after a few moments of silence.

"They were hiding in the trees waiting to be led to the caves. Even under the circumstances, it took some doing to convince them."

"How did you know about the caves—I mean, that they were more than legend?"

Pree K's eyes smiled a little. "It's a small valley."

CHAPTER 79

Preparations

The following day, Carly and the young men were busy at work again on the barn.

"Here En't, take this board, will you?" Carly said.

En't took hold of the board, catching sight of Nien and Wing crossing the fields.

"We can try it, Wing," Nien was saying.

"What's the verdict?" Carly asked as they walked up to her.

"Quieness," Nien said.

"But one of the young men needs to be able to make the journey. We three need to stay here."

Carly nodded. Though time was getting on, they would have to be patient for they felt it would be at least another turn before one of the boys could make the long trip. In the meantime, there was much construction that needed to be done—especially for as few of them as there were to do it. Once SiQQiy and her contingents arrived they would need quarters for them and their mounts, as well as shelter for the supplies they would be bringing. They would also need a place to repair weapons and armour. Before, Nien had always had access to Saam's smithery in the Village—he supposed now was as good a time as any to set up one of his own.

Around the table that evening, Wing voiced the need for a messenger to go to Quieness.

"To SiQQiy?" Jhock asked.

Nien nodded. "She is returning to Quieness as we speak. She should arrive there next turn. There is information she needs—from us."

"You need one of us to go," Pree K said.

Wing nodded. He knew all three of the young men would volunteer, but he could see in their faces that they were, in the same moment, hesitant—and he understood why.

"I know you have been through much already, and I know you would not wish to be absent from the ones you've laboured so hard to protect… but this could mean all our lives. Aid from Quieness will be our only hope in regaining the valley."

"Can we think on it for a night?" Pree K asked.

"Of course," Carly answered as she began clearing plates from the table.

Night settled in, and the three older boys returned from their discussion in the fields. Wing built up the fire as the others started to get the children ready for bed. En't moved to help his little sister and Lily into their night clothes when Lily's tender voice reached into the cabin and stopped every other conversation cold: "Why did they have to die?"

En't started to reply, stumbled over his words, and looked beseechingly at Wing.

Getting up from his place by the fire, Wing walked over and sat down beside Lily.

"There are a lot of possible reasons," Wing said, laying his hand on her blonde head. "But I don't think any of them will make you feel any better—at least not tonight."

"Are they with Eosha?" she asked instead.

Wing felt all eyes in the room move to him. Without unlearning most of what they knew, his answer may only serve to confuse them, so he replied simply, "Yes."

"Did Eosha want to be with them more than we do—is that why He took them?"

"I don't think so. I think Eosha knows you miss them."

"Then why couldn't they have stayed? Did they do something wrong? Were they bad?"

Wing felt his gut tighten, wondering if only a Rieevan child could ask such a question. "No, Lily, they weren't bad. It may not help much, but sometimes the death of one means life for many others. Like the fent I've killed—their deaths mean we can eat and live."

"Like the Mesko," En't said softly.

"Exactly," Wing replied.

En't looked down at Lily. "Often, it is one of the oldest or greatest of the trees that is taken down, right?" Lily knew this and she knew why; nevertheless, the sadness in her eyes remained alive and unchanging.

"I know it may not help right now," Wing said, "but even though there are many trees in the Mesko forest, when you're standing next to only one of them, nothing in all the world seems so grand, or so…irreplaceable. But there is a whole forest out there and that one irreplaceable tree is connected to all those other trees. The death of the one nearest you could mean life for many others that you cannot see or that you may never see in your life. The important thing is, whether in life or death, no single tree's importance is diminished."

"But there were so many Ka'ull and there are so few of us."

Wing bowed his head a little. "Yes, but soon we will be many again."

Lily leaned into Wing's side. "I miss them," she whispered.

Wing wrapped his arm around her small, thin body. "I know."

Raising her face, she looked Wing in the eye. "You have to stay now, though. I've told Eosha not to take you—or Nien, or Carly. Alright?"

With effort, Wing replied, "Alright."

Following hugs and blankets tucked under chins, Lily, Fe, and Hagen went to sleep. On his bedroll, Pree K lay, gazing up at the heavy-beamed rafters as Carly, Wing, and Nien talked quietly between themselves. En't sat by the fire braiding a long length of leather into rope. Jhock also sat beside the fire, busy at nothing, only gazing into the soft orange flames.

As the conversation between Carly, Nien, and Wing lagged, Jhock said, "You can still believe that?"

The brothers and Carly looked across the room at him, but it was upon Wing that Jhock's eyes were fixed.

"Believe what?" Wing asked.

Jhock met Wing's eyes, determined to see his question through, even though challenging Wing—*Merehr*—made his heart hammer and a nervous sweat tickle his sides. "About the death of one meaning life for another. I mean, our families weren't fent."

Wing's head hung briefly. "I know," he said gently. "Though you may not understand it now, nothing happens that is not, on some level, an agreement between souls. Would you give your life to protect Lily, or Fe, or Hagen?"

Jhock's gaze briefly brushed Wing's before he looked down at the floor.

"You have already proven that you would," Wing said, "all those turns in the caves."

"But our families. Our people. It's not as if they sacrificed their lives for ours that night when…when they were all in the castle. It's not like they had the choice."

Wing got up and, walking over, sat down beside him. "There's always a choice. We could have chosen generations ago to understand our world, to understand its other races."

"So it's our fault?"

Wing shook his head. "I'm not talking about right and wrong, Jhock. I'm talking about making choices. But making choices that serve life require knowledge of what there is, or might yet be, to choose between. Do you understand?"

Clearly, Jhock did not. There was a great sweeping sadness in his features and anger in his tone as he said, "Nothing you're saying is making any sense."

Wing drew a breath, searching for a different angle. "Based on the information our people had, they chose to remain isolated from the rest of our world. I'm not saying they were wrong, or wicked—I'm saying, given more information, what *else* might they have chosen? I'm saying what might *you* choose, if you had more information?"

Jhock shrugged and sighed as a child might have: unconvinced but conceding. "I don't know, because, well, I don't know anything more than they knew, do I?" Jhock paused.

Wing's eyes glinted as Jhock blinked, and the curve of his lips revealed a dawning comprehension.

"Do you understand now?" Wing asked quietly.

"Maybe," came Jhock's whispered reply.

"Your knowledge has already grown beyond what your parents knew. The risks you took, the risks you were *willing* to take while living in the mountains, proves this." Wing tilted his head at Jhock approvingly. "Love our people—without reserve, without judgment. Don't get caught up in right and wrong, in who or what may be to blame. You cannot answer that for our people; you can only answer that for yourself. What do *you* want? That is the only question that really matters."

Slowly, Jhock nodded, and Wing could see some faraway pain begin to clear from the boy's hazel-green eyes. "You will do this—teach us new things?"

Wing smiled a little. "I will try—and so will others. But trust yourself, Jhock, and yourself alone to choose. There are many paths. Perhaps one I show you will lead to another that I myself have not yet seen. Know that you are free to choose any one you like without punishment, without reproach."

With that, Wing stood, adjusting the sheathed sword about his hips and arched his aching back.

Noting his brother's fatigue, Nien said, "I will keep first watch tonight."

Wing was grateful. As he removed the heavy sword and belted sheath, he felt a hand on his shoulder. Turning, he saw Pree K standing behind him. Upon the young man's cheek was a thin, glimmering mark—the trail of a tear's path.

Wing's brow furrowed in concern.

"I would like to believe," Pree K said, "that the passage to Eosha was crowded on that night."

Wing's eyes softened; he nodded his head.

Pree K continued, "I came to a point in the caves when I wondered why the shy'teh did not come to save us as it had for our people in the legend. And then" —Pree K met Wing's eyes— "you came."

CHAPTER 80

The Clearing

Before dawn the following morning, Nien woke to find Wing kneeling over him. Blearily, he asked: "What is it?"

"Will you come with me?"

Nien rubbed the sleep from his eyes and got to his feet.

"Where are Nien and Wing?" Carly asked as the first sunlight came into the house. Getting up, she went to the large southing window and looked out. The sun was barely up, and the house cast a long shadow toward the sunsetting trees.

"They left together before sunrise," En't said.

"Did they say where they were going or how long they'd be gone?"

"No," En't replied.

Deep in the Mesko forest, in a small clearing beneath the rising sun, Nien stood facing Wing.

Since that night in Legran after Wing had come back from the river and told Nien they would return to Rieeve, there had been so many questions Nien had wanted to ask. As they stood now with time alone together in the familiar Mesko clearing not one of those questions would come to Nien's mind—but they suddenly seemed irrelevant, for somehow every word that Wing spoke was both the question Nien could not ask and the answer he could not fathom.

The last steps of the moons had passed into sunsteps. Weary and overwhelmed, Nien muttered, "Wing, you should write all this down."

Wing's eyes were kind as he said, "I have done so—a little. But be careful of it, Nien. That's what the ancient prophets did and we have lived through what it did to our people. Let this be a little more understanding than you once had. Let it be changing, let it evolve and grow with you. Like the rings of the Mesko—let the next layer expand upon the last. And let it be the same for anyone who asks you to be their teacher. Do not hope their questions will end with the knowledge you give them." Wing reached out and touched Nien's shoulder. "When you need to remember, you will. For now, I'll repeat this: You are the creator and the created, the killer and the killed, the before and the after, the lover and the sinner. Within the contradiction lies the truth of opposition, within opposition lies the truth of life. Between dark and light, between man and woman, between friends and enemies is the truth of oneness. We are everything, working in concert, as opposites. There is nothing and no one we are not."

Nien met his brother's eyes. There was a sensation in his body he'd never felt before, a quality both impossibly light and incredibly heavy. "Wing, I—" He could not finish his sentence.

Wing glanced around them. "Between the sun and the Mesko there is a symbiosis of life, between the Mesko and us another. Our moons pull on the great waters, snows melt and the grasses of the fields grow. There is no thing that is not a part of every other."

The words entered Nien like sunlight and wind; still, he shook his head. "I **know**, but I don't **get** it. And what does this have to do with what we're facing—with the Ka'ull?"

Wing fixed Nien's gaze with his own. "Working in *concert*, Nien, as opposites. There is a symbiosis, a reciprocity between us and the Ka'ull. There is a reason for their actions. Find it and you will end this war."

Grief and glory rent Nien's heart. "*I* will end this war? Wing, I...I don't understand."

"Have a little faith, brother," Wing said gently, almost playfully. "You will."

Nien felt saturated, at the brink of an outgushing that would entirely expel him.

"So many times," Wing said, "you stood as guardian for me. Strong, sure, you brought me back from the black, from the place of my worst fears. A place of complete forgetting. A place where the unreal was all that I perceived as being real. Lonely. Terrifying. It marked the extreme end of opposites. It seems, brother, you are immune to it." A smile lit Wing's face. Tears had begun to stream down Nien's cheeks. "In Legran, that night by the river, I discovered that the Void is what the All That Is has created to experience itself. Encompassing all opposites: above and below, male and female, light and dark, sun and moons. It is to this place that all things come from and to which they return. This life now—you as Rieevan, as Preak, as Nien, as my brother, is but one aspect of many forms. These come and go. Like the earth from which springs life, Wing and Nien are but two trees in the Mesko canopy. When these names are shed, we see again what we *are*—the earth from which the forms grow."

Nien shook his head. "Wing, all these metaphors—you're hurting my head."

Patiently, Wing nodded. "I know. It's because I am trying to explain the unexplainable. Have we ever tried to describe the bond between us?"

Nien understood. "No," he said.

"The truth is you can only know it, but in the moment you do my words will come back to serve you, to validate you—what I'm saying will make sense." Wing raised his hands, palms up. "Do you trust me?"

"Of course."

"That is enough," Wing replied. "Close your eyes."

Nien closed his eyes.

"Remember," Wing said.

Within Nien, Wing's voice struck an unsuspecting chord. Singing out from every seed and root of Nien's body, it flooded his being with song, vanishing every nuance of regret, fear, pain.

There was peace

—and

Nothingness

Clear of everything he'd once used to define himself, Nien found himself.

The expansiveness of it would have shattered his mind had it not been so *familiar*. So...obvious. And he didn't have to go anywhere, do anything. He simply realized he was already there; that a part of him had always been there.

Though it might have been sunsteps, days, or moments that passed in the clearing, Nien would not have trusted himself to say which, but when he again opened his eyes, he saw Wing standing in front of him. His brother had taken on the same quality of translucence he had in Legran, except this time, he was not disappearing into shadow but sunlight, shedding a lambent glow that nearly fooled Nien's eyes into believing him nothing more than a refraction of light.

"I'm," Nien tried to say, "I'm back. As form."

"When I'm with you," Wing said softly, "it is to me a perfect blending of flesh and spirit, dirt and sky, rock and root. I am the beginning, you are the end. Together, we complete our one soul's desire."

The realization struck Nien so profoundly his knees buckled. Even as part of him soared across the great canopy of trees, the rest of him sank to the forest floor.

Wing sank down beside him and locked shoulder to shoulder they wept tears of joy, sadness, dissolution, union, and everything in between.

CHAPTER 81

For as Long as You Choose

Wing and Nien walked into the house one after the other, quietly laying aside their cloaks.

Carly looked up at them from across the room. The brothers radiated an otherworldly glow.

"What happened?" she asked slowly, noticing as she did that Fe and Lily were staring up at them with wide eyes and gaping mouths.

Wing stepped to Carly, and taking her hands in his, said, "It was a good day." He touched her face and looked around the room. "Mind if we all step outside?"

With quizzical looks on their faces, the children filed outside into the starlight.

Unsure his heart could hold much more of one day, a happy tightness filled Nien's throat as Wing took Carly in his arms.

"The old is gone," Wing said, his voice clear and radiant, holding the small group in its peaceful embrace. "I have no wish to bring it back—temporally or spiritually. Our people are gone. I will keep their memory. Their traditions I let die with them." He turned his gaze to Carly. "In this new spirit I say to you: For as long as you choose."

Though it took a beat for everyone to catch Wing's meaning, the tears that had sprung into Carly's eyes caused the children to erupt in laughter and cheer.

Carly's reply was a soft collection of emotion. "For as long as you choose."

Wing looked at Nien. "I wish you'd say something."

Nien shook his head hopelessly at his brother. "Just can't give me any time to prepare something eloquent?" he said.

Wing smiled with his eyes.

Nien cleared his throat. "The only woman brave enough, resourceful enough, to have captured Wing's heart. And the brother I love more than my own life. My two closest friends. I am a very happy man." Reaching up, he placed a hand on each of their faces. "I love you." He then looked at Wing and said, "Have anything else you want to surprise me with today?"

Wing shrugged. "Nah, that should do."

The three of them leaned in, touching foreheads. Around them, the children pressed in close.

Nearly two and a half turns had passed since the caves when Pree K, his bruised leg healed nicely, set out for Quieness. The decision between the boys on who would go had been easy—

Pree K simply told En't and Jhock that it would be him.

Jhock and En't tried to argue, telling Pree K that he'd done enough; it was time for him to rest. But Pree K's logic superseded his friends' sentiment. He had been the Premier Messenger of the Cant and had already been over the route to Quieness. With Ime drawing in and all of their horses captured by the Ka'ull, he was also the fastest on foot. In every consideration, he was the natural choice.

With the food Carly had packed and the water skins Wing had prepared, Pree K donned the pair of leather boots made for him by Nien. To assure Pree K's feet were in good condition for the journey, En't had bravely offered to help break them in.

"All yours, now," En't said, watching as Pree K pulled the boots onto his feet. "And don't worry, my feet should heal in say, three, four turns."

Though En't was speaking playfully, Pree K knew the truth of it—he'd seen his friend's blistered feet.

There remained less than four turns until Ime set in, and as the small gathering looked on at Pree K there was an anxious worry in all their faces.

Nien was the last to say goodbye. His eyes held a very specific kind of longing that Pree K recognized.

"Tell SiQQiy—the Empress..." All the words Nien wanted to say clattered to the bottom of his brain in a jumble.

"I know," Pree K said. "I'll tell her." And he set out across the fields.

Behind Nien, the rest watched until Pree K melted into the woods before turning back to the house and barn and the great deal of work that still needed to be done.

Wing helped with the construction projects throughout the day, but as the night wore on and his turn at watch ended, he sat down at the Cawutt family table and in a new leather-clad binder he'd made, began to write, the table lantern flickering the brush-pen's tiny, dancing shadow across the pages.

"What are you up to?" Carly asked, coming up behind him a few moon-steps later and leaning over his shoulder.

Wing blew on the wet ink of his last sentence. "Just taking a few thoughts for a walk," he said.

Carly squeezed his shoulders. "Well, come on, you need rest and so do they. Come to bed."

Leaving the pages open to dry, Wing pushed himself to his feet and followed her.

The two climbed the stairs together. At the top, Carly opened the door to the bedroom that used to be Joash and Reean's. Wing stepped in behind her and Carly wondered if it was still difficult for him. But Wing moved over to the bed where he removed his sword-belt and boots. He then sat back, and leaning against the engraved Mesko headboard, relaxed.

Carly took up what must have been one of Reean's brushes and hoped she could undo what the past few days of valley wind had done to her hair.

"You're beautiful," Wing said.

Carly turned to look at him. "You're crazy."

"Let me have a go," he said, holding his hand out for the brush.

Carly knelt down on the edge of the bed and crawled toward him. Thumping the brush into his hand, she ran her eyes over his black hair. He'd cut it short and though she thought she'd mourn its loss it was actually quite fetching and infinitely more manageable for him.

Scooching about, Carly settled in between his knees. "Maybe I'll have you cut my hair short, too."

"Whatever you want, but I promise nothing."

"You didn't do such a bad job with yours."

"Yes, well…Why don't we wait and see how the brushing goes?" Wing began to work through the tangles but he hadn't been at the effort long before Carly slumped against his chest.

"It's hard to reach your head like this," Wing said.

Carly sighed her reply.

Wing set the brush down and wrapped his arms around her. They rested in each other for a time, listening to the sounds of the children downstairs.

"That night in the Mietan," Wing said softly, "I don't think I ever thanked you for staying, for not leaving when I…"

When Wing didn't continue, Carly sat up. Turning about, she knelt between his legs. Looking him over as if he were a piece of mystical art, she took a bit of hair from behind his ear and, rubbing it between her fingers, said, "I have had very few moments in my life when I've thought I understood you; that moment in the Mietan was no different." She brushed his temple with the tips of her fingers. "Though I think they wanted to, I guess our people never knew you either—" she paused, "except for Lant, possibly. He knew more about, well, *everything* than he ever let on."

There was a nod of agreement in Wing's eyes.

"When I saw you that day in the Hiona," Carly continued, "I remember wanting you to be Merehr more than anything I'd ever wanted in my whole life—even if it meant I could never have you."

Wing said nothing, only looked at her, a world of emotion wheeling through the far reaches of his eyes.

Pulling her shirt off over her head, Carly dropped it to the floor beside the bed and reaching out, took the top button of Wing's shirt in her fingers and began to unbutton it.

Wing hesitated for a beat, then started at the bottom button and worked his way up to meet her.

Tugging the shirt from Wing's shoulders and down off his arms, Carly dropped it onto the floor next to her own. The scars over his chest and shoulders were something she'd become accustomed to—she almost couldn't remember what he'd looked like before.

However, this time, like the first time, they caused her throat to close with emotion.

Carefully, she laid her hand flat upon his chest, wondering to herself how he could he feel so strong and yet so fragile.

Fragile, she thought.

What a strange word, and then she understood the sentiment: Fragile because she had no idea of the inner-workings of his mind. Fragile, because she'd always felt he might disappear, just vanish into that place she could not see. Fragile, because even though they had been together most their lives, he still felt like smoke in her hands.

Her silence and the curve of her breast drew Wing's hand. "What is it?" he asked softly.

Carly shook her head. For once, she understood why Wing so often chose silence as his only reply—she simply didn't know how to explain her feelings.

Leaning in, Wing pressed his cheek against her breast. The feel of his touch, the smell of his skin, stopped her breath. Placing her hands upon his back, Wing moaned softly as she drew him up, kissing his lips, opening his mouth, caressing the inside of it with her tongue. Putting her weight upon him, she pushed him into the bed. As he sunk beneath her, she traced the lines of his face—the smooth passing of his temples into his black hair, the straight nose, high cheekbones. She kissed both sides of his face, wishing she could pour all the love she felt for him into each one, her body aching with the yearning of it.

The depression of the thick down cover beneath their bodies created a comforting envelope around them. Wing's sure hands sparked fire under her skin. He was patient.

But Carly had no inclination to wait.

With great familiarity and longing, Wing came into her. The intensity of him burned Carly's heart, opening within her far more than a sheath of warm flesh. In pulsations that swallowed time, passion soaked to saturation in the heat of white flame. As it faded to blue rapture, coalescing at last to the steady glowing comfort of embers, Carly buried her face into Wing's shoulder and felt him crying.

Outside their window, Leer's moons passed between cloud and star, the great mountains gleamed in their light, and in the forest the giant trees shivered and sighed as a single snowflake fell like a feather to the valley floor.

CHAPTER 82

Royal Welcome

P ree K stood wearily at the descent into Quieness. His trip had been swift; nevertheless, the turn and four days had been long and lonely. He still had some food left and the shoes had been a lifesaver, but memories of his previous assignment to Quieness came sweeping back and dread filled him at the thought of entering Cao City again.

Great, he muttered.

Yet, on the heels of his aversion, an idea sprang into mind, or rather, a name.

Making his way off the mountain and down into the city, Pree K found his memory serving as he went directly to the part of the city where a familiar bakery and pub sat tucked between a jewelry store and a meat shop. Stepping inside, Pree K scanned the bustling room. He'd looked the place over twice and was about to give up when he spotted the face he was looking for sitting in a corner.

With a smile tugging at the corners of his lips, Pree K accosted the individual where he sat, hunched over a plate of fiilas.

"Did you pay for those?" Pree K demanded.

The man jerked, his thighs thumping the bottom of the table. Feigned innocence that only just masked genuine anger flitted across his blockish face before it burst into a broad smile.

"Preek!" he barked, and bounding to his feet, nearly toppled the table as he grabbed Pree K up in a hug that Pree K thought might snap his ribs. "So good to see you, boy!" Setting him down with a thump, Hilloy said, "Come back for another ride?"

"Yes," Pree K said. "I've traveled all the way over the Uki Mountain Range for a horse ride—May, is it?"

"Well driyar, let's do it! I don't have May, tho—if that doesn't break your heart."

"I'll survive."

"Are you hungry first? I'll even share the fiilas if you want some. Then, you can pay for 'em."

"I'd love some. I'll owe you for the ride anyway."

It felt good to be on his rear and off his feet as Hilloy's new mount—a lusty black and grey gelding—moved over the ground with ample speed.

Once at the palace grounds, Pree K left Hilloy with his gratitude and followed a guard through a set of side gates bordered by a tower wall that rose above him like a bird of prey, majestic and graceful; alert.

It was with a discreet expression of mischief that Pree K noted this was not the way he had been taken to see the Empress on his previous trip; apparently, Nien's name literally opened a different door.

Through a twisting row of columns and corridors, Pree K and the guard arrived at a set of elegant red doors within one of the inner palace domes. Pushing them open, the guard stepped in and said, "The messenger from Rieeve, my lady."

SiQQiy looked up from the map on the table before her and upon seeing Pree K it seemed some of the weariness fled her features.

"Pree K, isn't it?"

"Yes, Empress."

She crossed the floor to him. "You're alive. How blessed is my home that you visit it again. Your story is one, I'm sure, that will become legend." Taken aback by her words, Pree K was relieved when she continued to speak. "I am so sorry about your father. He was a friend to me in my youth, one I, and every valley on this continent, will be indebted to."

Pree K bowed his head to her. "Empress."

"Please, call me SiQQiy," she said. "How is Nien?"

"He is fine, lady. He sends his regret at not being able to come in person." Pree K paused, deciding whether or not to share a more complete thought on the matter. "I believe he is not quite whole without you, that if he could shed his body, his spirit would follow his heart's desire and be here already at your side."

"You are obviously many things, Pree K of Rieeve, but a poet, too?"

Pree K shrugged sheepishly. "I had a long trip to work on that one."

SiQQiy laughed. "So much good news in one day? May I hug you?"

Pree K could only nod as the Empress of Quieness took him in her arms and embraced him. The softness of her breasts and the sweet scent of her skin rattled Pree K's normally fine-tuned senses.

Releasing him, SiQQiy touched his shoulder. "Forgive me, you must be tired after your journey."

"Tired a little, yes."

"Come, sit," she said, motioning to a chair. "Guard, you may leave."

The guard retreated.

"Would you like refreshment—anything?"

Pree K replied that he would and SiQQiy called her two young attendants, each adorned in a single length of shimmering cloth. After only a few words, the girls departed and SiQQiy turned back to Pree K. "What is the situation in Rieeve?"

"According to Wing and Nien, the Ka'ull have, or had at the time I left, no more than a thousand men in Castle Viyer. They believe that if the castle can be taken now it could save much bloodshed later."

"So," SiQQiy said, "they have returned to Legran?"

Pree K paused. "Ah, no. They're still in Rieeve."

SiQQiy started to speak. Stopped. "They're still in Rieeve?"

"Yes, at their home."

SiQQiy's confusion was obvious.

"The Cawutt home is at the other end of the valley," he tried to explain. "The Ka'ull in the castle would not know they were there, unless…"

"Unless they perform reconnaissance."

Pree K nodded. "Unless they do that."

"Stupid," SiQQiy said softly, and Pree K had the impression it was not a word she used often. Snapping her fingers, she summoned two other guards. To one she said, "Please inform Jenta that the messenger from Rieeve has arrived," and to the other, "Ready Granj Two. I will depart with my own entourage and the first contingent of one hundred at first light tomorrow morning."

She's coming? Pree K thought. *Yeefa. Looks like stupid is contagious.*

"We will go via Hikon Pass," SiQQiy said, turning back to Pree K. "It's a more direct route." She pointed to the spot on a map laid out upon her desk.

Briefly stunned that she found him worthy of sharing her plans with, it took Pree K a moment to catch up to what she was saying.

"Two hundred and fifty men of Granj Two," she said, "will leave within three days of my departure via the Nijen Range. They will be followed in like manner, every three days. Companies of two hundred and fifty with supplies will come only through the Nijen Range; if my maps are accurate, there is not sufficient leeway through Hikon Pass for such an assemblage—so we've planned accordingly. Granj One, Three, Four, Six, Eight, Nine and Ten, Eleven, and Twelve will remain here. Granj Seven will hold itself in readiness. Granj Five will continue preparations for the Uki confluence. Once we have word from Monteray concerning Jayak, we will be able to solidify their directive. My Premier, Jenta, and the Cao-based Granj commander will remain here. Weather providing, if a turn of first moon passes, they both have word to send the seventh Granj on to Rieeve." She looked at Pree K, as if awaiting his approval or opinion.

Other than his father's work with the Cant and the Council, Pree K had never seen the inner workings of governance; nevertheless, he was stunned how smoothly SiQQiy had just laid out such massive arrangements.

"I have not been through either the Range or Hikon Pass, but I did take a look at the Pass from high on the mountain. It is narrow, but should be adequate for the smaller contingents. If you have heavy horses, they'd be of use, for though I could not see the bottom of the Pass, the northing ridges are rocky and probably prone to slides." Pree K was about to express his awe over the planning that must have gone into the execution of such a vast compliment of men and materials, when the young girls in their shimmering frocks returned with food and drink.

"You were brave to come all this way unaccompanied," SiQQiy said, pinching off the top of a sweet orange fruit and handing it to him. "You'll like it. Just peel back the leaves." SiQQiy placed another on her own tongue and smiled as the thin skin popped, filling her mouth with nectar. "To have come so far, twice now...You are definitely Commander Lant's son. His Plan is slowly bringing together a force that just might stand a chance against the Ka'ull. We are lucky to have you with us."

Though surprised by her words, Pree K's time in the caves as the leader of the starving, ragtag remnants of his people had distilled in him a bare honesty both strong and sincere.

"If I become even half the man he was, I'll be content," Pree K said.

SiQQiy picked up a glass. "You already are," she said. "Now, let's eat and find you a place to rest before tomorrow's return home."

They talked as they ate and not just of Nien or of war as Pree K had expected. SiQQiy was both curious and knowledgable through a wide array of topics. Nevertheless, at the end of the meal, Pree K offered Nien into the conversation by saying, "I am quite sure Nien will be surprised at your coming to Rieeve. Actually," Pree K amended with a short laugh, "he'll probably think you crazy."

SiQQiy beamed. "As extraordinary as he is, it is still difficult for him to see that what he has to offer is as valuable as what Monteray and I have to offer. But, as the entire night could pass without notice in speaking of him, we had better get some rest."

Pree K readily agreed. Licking their fingers and wiping their mouths, they got up and walked down a long corridor in the palace together.

"It will be another long day for you tomorrow," SiQQiy said.

"Nien asked if it were possible to send along extra horses," Pree K said through a yawn. "All of ours were taken by the Ka'ull."

SiQQiy nodded. "We can and will. Your room is just down this hall and to your right."

"I remember," Pree K said, watching SiQQiy go before continuing on.

At the room, he pushed open the two large doors and stepped inside. It was as he remembered it. There was the amazing story-painting covering the walls and ceiling, the extensive bed, porcelain washbasin, and polished wood floor. A meticulously woven rug covered most of the floor next to the bed, its colour patterns swirling hypnotically to its center.

Pree K wasted little time in bathing—the bed was calling his name.

Tenderly pulling back the covers, Pree K crept into the silken sheets, but as the bed folded in around him on this visit to Quieness, he was surprised to find that the great palace and the elegant covers felt no better than had the log home and the coarse blanket, placed over him by Wing, on his first night back in Rieeve.

CHAPTER 83

One Perfect Moment

Four and a half turns had passed with only light dustings of snow, but a cold had come intensely into the nights and was beginning to creep into the days.

Nien went out early to the barn. Jhei had managed to meet up with a persistent and ornery old bull which had done his part, which meant Jhei had done hers, and the resulting calf, its. Now, Nien had taken up regular milking responsibilities.

The udder warmed his hands in the morning chill as the milk made the familiar spat-spat on the bottom of the bucket.

"I don't relish this before-the-sun-is-up stuff," Nien said.

But the early rising had been good for him—he'd not been sleeping well of late, anyway.

Jhei hadn't bothered to stop eating during the milking and continued on as Nien picked up the bucket and left the barn.

The sun's first rays were beginning to creep over the mountains as Nien walked back toward the house. With his head down—one moment watching his feet, the next staring into the milk bucket—he nearly tripped when a shout from Jhock penetrated his mind's distant wanderings. His head came up. Jhock was pointing.

A company of at least twenty-five men and more horses than he could count were emerging from the sunsetting tree line.

"Quieness," Nien said to himself.

From the company, a rider broke loose and raced toward Nien. It was Pree K.

"Pree K!" Nien called, nearly spilling the milk before remembering he was holding it.

Pree K rode right up to Nien and dismounted before Riki could come to a complete halt. Nien set the milk down and embraced him eagerly. "Pree K Mesko Seed, you're back!"

Pree K laughed aloud. "How good it is to be home!"

"Pree!" Wing called, running from the house.

Pree K turned and ran to meet him, each grasping the other in a back-slapping hug.

Nien gazed out across the fields at the oncoming riders, his eyes fixed on only one of them. That particular rider, it seemed, had spotted him as well.

Speeding away from the caravan, the rider drew up in front of Nien and swung down. Pushing her hood back from her face, she looked upon him and smiled.

"SiQQiy," Nien said, breathing her name as if from the tongue of a ghost.

"Nien."

SiQQiy's entourage rode past the lovers and up into the yard.

Behind the horses and SiQQiy's personal guard came the first contingent of Granj. It didn't take them long to bivouac in the grassy open space between the house and the barn. Others bedded down in a shelter that Nien, Wing, and the boys had built on the sunrising side of the barn during Pree K's absence, while the Hettha—a special unit of sentries and runners—headed down the sunsetting edge of the valley before cutting right into the mountains where they would make their own camp.

By nightfall, a gentle flurry of a storm had layered the valley in a bed of snowy ice crystals and most of the travel-weary had crawled into warm places and drifted off to sleep.

Inside the house, the young men and three little ones were nodding off as well—the wonder and excitement of SiQQiy's arrival having spent them at last. Nien and SiQQiy, too filled with each other and the relating of their time apart to sleep, had gratefully accepted Wing's offer to take first watch.

Standing in the back room of the house—the one he used to share with Nien and Jake—Wing gazed out over the starlit valley. The storm had cleared, leaving the night a glistening sweep of effervescent light. Filled with the sight, he tried to remember how they had gotten from that last terrible night to now, finding that if he didn't concentrate on individual moments it all faded into a kaleidoscope of colour and feeling.

"Wing?"

Startled, Wing turned to find Carly's soft, tired eyes.

"Hello," she whispered.

"Hi."

"You all right?"

"Yes."

Carly touched his face, tracing his cheekbone down to his neck. "When you go to wherever it is you go to think, it intrigues me. I'm sure if I could get a peek it would be quite illuminating."

Wing smiled at her, almost a laugh. "Dreary, more like."

"Doubt that," she said, and wrapping her arms around his waist, hugged him.

Wing leaned into her. "You're not the best help for guard duty."

"So noted." She squeezed him tightly. "Don't worry, I'm done in. I'm going to bed."

Wing bent down and pressed a kiss against the softness of her neck. "Goodnight," he whispered, and watched her disappear into the faint light of the main room.

Turning back, all was quiet outside of the window at which he stood— his window, the one he had spent countless nights by as a youth, watching the lights of the Village homes glittering in the distance.

There had been a majestic silence in those fields beneath the soft glow of stars and moon—the same silence he felt now. It seemed to call from a higher province, speaking in its own particular language.

Across his vision, a pearly silver glimmer caught his eye. Wing blinked. Through the crystalized air, a large bird of prey swept, its wings glistening in the light of the heavens.

Stepping out the back door, Wing was able to catch the rustling sound of its great wings before it faded into night.

What are you doing down so low in the valley? Wing thought. Though he hadn't been able to see it clearly, he thought its wings made too much sound for it to have been a night bird.

"Brother."

Wing turned in the darkness to see Nien coming up behind him. "Is it your watch already?" Wing asked.

Nien nodded, assessing the familiar look in his brother. "Time moves quicker in that other world."

"It does," Wing agreed, his boots crunching softly in a patch of white snow-crystals. "How's SiQQiy?"

"She's good—sleeping now. Eck'theney, Wing. It's good to have her here. I just can't believe she came."

Wing blew a breath into the cold air. "She probably can't believe that you stayed here."

"E'te," Nien replied. "But I thought SiQQiy would have been more..."

"Logical? Practical?"

"*Smart.*"

Wing laughed.

"Of course, compared to all the rest of this, her coming fits right in. I can't think of one thing we've done that couldn't be counted as completely crazy."

"Crazy?" Wing said thoughtfully. "What makes sense to the mind rarely makes sense to the heart. I guess that is not the sort of practicality most are used to."

Though the brothers shared a grin, Nien knew Wing's reply had not been made flippantly. However *seemingly* illogical, each of Wing's choices carried weight—

More than that, Nien thought, amending his description. Wing had simply made the decision to return to Rieeve and the whole continent had turned with him.

Filled with the inexpressible wonder of it, Nien's gaze shifted to the same scene that had been so enrapturing Wing upon his arrival.

"Beautiful," he observed quietly.

"Magic," Wing replied as their sight chased moonlight across the glistening fields.

"Do you remember the night we spent trying to catch that barn owl?" Nien asked.

"Of course. You scared Jhei so bad she wouldn't give milk for two days."

"I miss those times."

The brothers stood in silence, feeling their breath upon the air. The jagged peaks of the Ti and Uki alpine ranges stood straight into the night sky—their silhouettes darker than the night around them.

"Thank you," Wing said, his eyes traveling over the mountaintops and up toward the stars.

"Thank you? For what?"

"For going with me into the Mesko clearing. For…trusting me."

Nien was quiet a moment before replying, "Trust is one thing—understanding quite another."

"But you try," Wing said.

"There were times growing up that I felt I knew you better than you knew yourself. And then there was the rest of the time when it was as if I'd been sharing my whole life with a stranger."

"I *am* sorry about that, Nien."

Nien shook his head. "It's not your fault. I guess I couldn't have known how truly right and completely wrong I was." He smiled gently. "Knowing you has always been humbling, but it's also been my honour. I love you, brother."

Wing snorted. "How am I supposed to top that?"

"At last!" Nien exclaimed dramatically.

Wing laughed, and side by side, the brothers fell into silence, their senses captured by the coolness of the night and the surprising brightness of the valley floor. Overhead, the stars shifted in the sky and the brothers found themselves in a very familiar world—a landscape conjured in their first moments together as children.

Their place.

Secret. Indefinable. Undeniable.

If someone had been watching them from the house, nothing out of the ordinary would have been noted as taking place. Just two men, standing side by side in a field of white under the gleam of heaven. But in artful shifts of energy a great deal was going on above and beneath. At height and depth, earth and sky were assembling here and disassembling there, letting go, gathering in, preparing. And though they were the point to and the point from which the change flowed, its intensity and strength neither burned or admonished them; they existed, rather, in a place of astonishing peace, aware of everything yet attached to nothing.

Over their lives together, Wing and Nien had learned that in their combined field time held no meaning, but even this peripheral awareness was often enough to break the field.

On this occasion, however, it was a shiver of cold upon Nien's skin that centralized his perception and shot him back into the narrow borders of his own flesh. The separation was always distressing—it felt like tearing a hole in some deep inner flesh through which spilled his essence rather than his blood. It twisted his mouth, as if he were silently enduring the painful removal of a splinter. He closed his eyes, and touching on the point of longing around which the pain gathered, gave his body and mind time to readjust. Beside him, he noticed Wing going through the same acclimation, clenching and stretching his fingers, easing the transition, slowly restoring connection to his particular mind and body.

Wordlessly, the brothers turned to one another.

Nien slapped himself, Wing tipped a half-smile at him, and they walked back into the house together.

Taking a seat at the table, Wing picked up a pen with ink-stained fingers.

Nien's eyes lingered briefly on Wing's black hair, wondering what it was his brother was writing, before returning into the back room to take up watch.

Standing at Wing's window, Nien marveled again at what had just taken place, recalling the times it had happened before, treasuring that it happened at all.

CHAPTER 84

So It Begins

The hint of Ime hung cold in the air the following day as Wing went into the mountains on the hunt. Deep in the woods, he'd gone further to the northing and higher than he usually did, bearing in mind that as far out as he went, that far he would have to return with the weight of the kill. As he was about to turn back, head to the southing and try another trail, he caught sight of a mature female fent. Keeping the wind at his face, Wing followed as she entered a deep gorge. He climbed the gorge behind her, stopping when she stopped, waiting for the perfect moment.

Near the top, Wing ducked behind a large rock. He was about to spot the fent when he heard voices. Dropping, he rolled into a thick patch of trees and gnarled bushes. The voices were not coming toward him but passing by atop the ridge, about a stone's throw from where he lay.

Calming his racing heart, he risked a look. A host of battle-ready soldiers were moving in definite array, but casually, unconcerned of being seen.

Wing—the fent entirely forgotten—started at a low crouch. Moving in virtual silence through terribly difficult terrain, he'd pause, listen, then move again. He continued like this until he could no longer hear their voices. He then rose to his full height and took out at a run for the house.

Wing arrived out of breath and exploded through the front door. All eyes in the main room looked up. Carly came to her feet.

"The time is here," Wing said, placing his bow beside the door. "Large contingents of Ka'ull are moving along the upper ridge above the northing gorge. They're headed for Viyer."

"How many?" Nien asked.

"I could see no end to their line." The air in the room closed in like a noose. "I could not see heavy supplies or armaments. It appears this is the invasion force the provisions in Viyer were brought for."

"They're planning on wintering in Rieeve," Nien said, voicing what had been everyone's worst fear since Nien, Wing, and Carly had decided to return to Rieeve.

Wing felt a place inside him grow heavy—

So it had begun. Everything they had trained for, tossed in a nightmarish sweat over, had secretly hoped would come soon and never come at all, was here.

"When can we expect the rest of your second Granj?" Wing asked SiQQiy.

"Two hundred and fifty departed three days after I left. Three days after that, one hundred will depart, and so on. Give the Hikon Pass companies two turns, the Nijen Range contingents a little longer. I also left orders for my Seventh Granj to stand at the ready. If one full rotation of the moon passes without word, they will come in like manner. And" —SiQQiy's eyes moved between Nien, Wing, and Carly— "I left word with the Captain of my first Granj that, in case of the wintering here of Ka'ull forces, I would send word for them to come as well."

"Some reconnaissance of our own will be helpful to confirm the conclusions we're coming to, but it's apparent the forces not in occupation of the upper valleys are planning on doing exactly that—wintering here," Nien said. "We need to get word to Quieness for the remainder of your Seventh Granj to come now and not wait."

"So it is," SiQQiy said. "I will send a messenger to the Captain of my First Granj. The remainder of the Second will come through the Hikon Pass with limited supplies, the Seventh through the Nijen Range with as many provisions as they can carry."

Wing said, "But SiQQiy—Quieness."

Her eyes shifted to Wing. "Seven hundred men each, the Granj are only my smallest, specially-trained forces. In Quieness I have twelve—and that's only the Granj. The larger units: naval and land, fully operational and in reserve, are in Quieness and will stay there. Quieness is well-protected."

The next morning, Omaly—one of SiQQiy's captains and a proven rider—set out for Quieness with a young member of the Hettha on two of the Granj's fastest horses.

Along with a few others, Wing watched them ride out until they vanished into the distant tree line.

Four days after Omaly's departure, the next contingent of SiQQiy's Second Granj arrived in Rieeve.

En route in the mountains, Omaly and the young Hettha made good time, beating the first big storm of Ime as it blew through Quieness, leaving Cao in a veil of white before moving up over the mountains where it gathered strength and announced itself in Rieeve as an unrelenting gale, covering the ground with nearly three steps of ice and snow.

Ime had come with a vengeance.

Inside the Cawutt home, Wing was on guard duty. As he stood at the back window, his gaze left the sleet of horizontal snow outside and came to rest on the sword at his side.

It was not a good time to fight a war, especially against the Ka'ull who could sweep in and wipe them out in an exercise that would be less than a horse tail swatting an insect.

Two days later, a group of ten Ka'ull riders approached the Cawutt home from the far end of Rieeve. Working at the side of the house, Wing was the first of those in what had become the Cawutt Compound to see them.

"Ka'ull!" Wing called out, alerting two of SiQQiy's guards. "A couple furlongs out, northing side!" Spinning around the back of the house, he ran inside. Dousing the fire and shutting the damper to cut smoke from the chimney, Wing cracked open the back door.

The house lay in absolute stillness as the riders approached.

Slowing, the riders came on cautiously, their instincts as soldiers telling them the place was too quiet—

And it was—until twelve of SiQQiy's Granj rode down upon them from the sunsetting tree line.

Reining their horses about in dismay, four Ka'ull had been slashed and dismounted before having drawn their swords.

The men of the Granj let none of the remaining six escape, and in what seemed like a single moment, the first engagement of the nightmare was over.

No one knew what might have given the soldiers from the castle cause to ride to this far end of the valley to reconnoiter. Perhaps it was part of a new set of patrols set up now that regular troops were arriving at the castle, perhaps not. Either way, it would not be long before the ten Ka'ull riders were missed and others sent out to investigate.

On the upside, Nien thought, *we've got ten more horses.*

The snow had turned soft in the late afternoon sun when a guard from the Hettha sped up to the house. Wing stepped out to meet him.

"Netaia Wing, fifty Ka'ull, riding this way fast from the northing."

Wing shaded his face and glanced toward the sun. It had not traveled far in its trek toward the horizon. The Ka'ull were taking no chances.

Forty of SiQQiy's second Granj mounted and took for the tree line.

The bodies of the ten dead Ka'ull had been removed. Nien had seen SiQQiy's soldiers trying to cover and conceal the blood from the first skirmish and his heart had groaned, for no matter their efforts, snow kept a record of all that passed over it and only another storm would quell the spill of red that seemed to be expanding, seeping out in every direction but down like red berry ink spilled over new paper.

And so the snowy slush of a fetid pink hue, torn up ground, and the large presence of the lone Cawutt home caused the new influx of Ka'ull riders to draw in cautiously, their mounts nervous, chewing at their bits and throwing their heads.

A brief signal from their leader had the riders making a uniform split, each taking a side to circle the house.

As they moved through the all-too-silent scene in a parting V, the crack of snapping branches ripped their attention to two separate bands of SiQQiy's soldiers as they charged out from the sunsetting tree line—one to the northing of their position, the other lateral.

Though a few Ka'ull broke for the sunrising edge of the valley, SiQQiy's soldiers routed all of them; nevertheless, no one was breathing easy, for with each minor victory the Ka'ull would become more serious about their investigations—they would not keep losing men in small lots to an unidentified counterforce.

The sun set over the day and settled like a rock in Wing's stomach.

A fire had been built in the house and in the barn, which was serving, for the moment, as barracks. Besides the shelter that had been built while Pree K was in Quieness, another structure had been completed with the help of SiQQiy's soldiers. More barracks were under construction to accommodate the Seventh Granj as well as three secure corrals: two partially covered, one open. Wing hoped they could get all the projects completed before the next storm.

In the meantime, the majority of SiQQiy's Granj had quartered themselves in the fields behind the Cawutt home, and up in the sunsetting tree line was the small camp of the Hettha where they alternated watch and slept, huddling over fires built in the rear of the tents beneath a small hole that opened up into the snow-laden branches of overhanging tree limbs to dissipate any smoke that could otherwise be seen.

Inside the house, Wing had first watch. He was tired, but only in the faint sleepiness that so often accompanies a watch, for there was much to think about. Outside, he saw mounds that could have been snowdrifts but he knew were the bodies of men.

Though it had been a mutual decision on all their parts, still, as it was happening in Rieeve, Wing felt a sense of responsibility for it all, wondering, *Did I start all this? If it were not for my conviction to free Rieeve would SiQQiy and her men be here in the bitter cold of Ime, far from their own homes and loved ones?*

Wing pressed his forehead against the cool side of the window. It helped soothe the burning ache in his mind.

Fully aware of the advantage of Rieeve's location and destroyed civilization he, nevertheless, did not limit SiQQiy or Monteray's intentions of taking a stand in Rieeve to that alone. Irrational, illogical love was its underpinning, and in that vein each soldier of SiQQiy's army was a true volunteer. Wing marveled at the thousands of choices, each as individual as the one to have made it, all leading to this one place, this one time.

"Tonight fear sleeps," Nien said, walking up to stand next to him a moonstep or so later.

Immersed in thought, it took Wing a beat to reply, "Yes, it does."

"Now if it'd take a permanent rest in my heart."

Wing understood, and though he'd often felt the same, he knew that Nien had experienced fewer moments than he of peace like the one they had shared a few nights past.

"It's my watch," Nien said. "You should get some rest."

Glancing once more across the fields, Wing turned, placed a hand on Nien's shoulder, then left the back room for the main room where he went to Carly's side and lay down, hoping he'd be able to take advantage of Nien's suggestion—that sleep would come, that fear would stand down for one more night.

The morning sun had barely caressed the high peaks of the Ti Range when Nien awakened Wing. "Wing, word from the Hettha: Another sixty are coming from the castle."

Before the Ka'ull riders had come within view of the house SiQQiy's men were ready, both at the house as well as those sent into the tree line to back up the Hettha.

Again, the Ka'ull riders were surprised—thirty-five of them had fallen before they had come within three furlongs of the house.

Wing and Nien with twenty others, exploded from behind the house and attacked those that remained from the front.

Engaged on all sides, the Ka'ull began to panic, many of them breaking rank and scattering toward the mountains. Ten soldiers of SiQQiy's Second Granj chased down the deserters.

When it was over, SiQQiy's soldiers reported that two of the Ka'ull had escaped.

All felt the blow.

Suspicion, guesswork, mystery had been on their side—now the Ka'ull would know.

For two days afterward all was still, the tension in camp an alien presence, tangible and suffocating. If more forces did not arrive in Rieeve soon, they would be overrun. Destroyed.

SiQQiy's Seventh Granj was expected any day.

The Ka'ull were expected within sunsteps.

CHAPTER 85

Gift's Origin

Somewhere in the strange land between sleep and wakefulness, Wing thought he heard a rumbling in the ground. A few moments passed before he understood it was not an imaginative spell from his dreams. Opening his eyes he recognized it instantly—the rumble was the trembling of earth beneath the hooves of galloping horses.

A lot of horses.

Rising to his feet and grasping his sword, Wing's long legs brought him to the back window in only a few steps. Off in the distance he could see Ka'ull riders—more than he could count in a glance.

Nien ran in through the back door. "I can't believe it!" he shouted. "They came out of nowhere!"

"Are the men alerted?" Wing shouted.

"Yes!" Nien shouted.

"Help me bolt and lock the doors and shutters!"

Carly and Nien rushed to the other windows, then Nien and Wing ran out to SiQQiy's men in the barracks behind the house.

"Did any of the Hettha get a count?" Wing asked.

The Second Granj Captain reported: "About fifty—what we could see."

"I saw many more than that out my back window," Wing said.

"Wing!"

Wing turned toward the house and saw Carly.

"They're upon the last field," she called.

Men grabbed reins and swung onto mounts.

The children! Wing ran for the house, Nien on his heels.

"Wing, more are coming!" En't yelled as Wing and Nien ran into the house. "A hundred at least!"

491

Lily cried out. Wing picked her up. Holding her in her blanket, he glanced around the room. "Pree K!"

"Here!" came the answer.

"Gather all the children into the corners away from the windows and cover them with blankets and anything else you can find."

Pree K moved, calling to En't: "Help me with this table!"

En't took up the other side of the huge Mesko table. Together, they pulled it across the room, gathering the children beneath its broad back.

"Carly, watch that door!" Wing yelled, stepping to his window.

Looking out, the scene filled him with wondrous terror. The glint of early morning against drawn blades was blinding to the eye. Men were thrashing about; horses were stumbling over bodies and losing their footing in the snow. Shouts of orders and retreat filled the air, underpinned by the wail of the wounded or dying.

And then—to Nien and Wing's amazed eyes—the Ka'ull turned and fled back across the fields, making for the castle.

More quickly than it began, it was over. The silence was profound and sickening.

Twenty of SiQQiy's men had been seriously wounded; forty or more with minor wounds. That left fewer than three hundred and fifty men, to face...

Wing shuddered.

The Ka'ull would empty the castle when news reached them of this, another defeat, and from what? A small rebel force?

As night drew on, the children lay upon their bedrolls—anything but asleep. Carly was sitting with them as Nien came in.

"Where's Wing?" he asked.

"He's out with the men—those of SiQQiy's Granj that were wounded today."

"Oh," Nien said, and in silence he walked over to the washbasin and splashed his face.

A few moonsteps later, the children all finally asleep, Carly got quietly to her feet as Wing came in.

"You look exhausted," she said.

As Wing slowly hung up his cloak, Carly rubbed her hands up his back, massaging deeply. Wing's shoulders relaxed and his chin came to rest on his chest as he mumbled, "You sound a little tired yourself."

"Are you hungry?"

Wing shook his head.

Carly was rolling her knuckles into a knot in his shoulder when SiQQiy came in. She greeted Carly and then cupping Wing's hand between her own, said, "I don't know how you do it, but thank you."

"It's little enough," Wing said.

Stepping out from the back room, Nien said to SiQQiy, "There you are. I was about to head back out to look for you."

"You two take the bedroom upstairs. Carly and I will take first watch," Wing said.

Looking them over, Nien said, "Are you sure, Weed Farmer? It looks like the two of you need it more than us."

Wing shook his head. "Truthfully, I'd rather stay up knowing that when I do go to sleep I can stay there till morning. You'll be doing me a favour."

Nien looked at Carly. "You?"

"I'm fine, really. You two go ahead."

"Thanks," Nien said.

"Goodnight," Wing replied.

After SiQQiy and Nien disappeared upstairs and Wing had blown out the last lantern, Carly joined him at the window in the back bedroom. Resting her head against his arm, she asked, "How do you do it?"

Wing looked over his shoulder at her. "What?"

"Heal."

"Ah," Wing said. "Explaining it is more difficult than doing it."

Carly looked up at him. "Can you try?"

Wing met her eyes then glanced away, his gaze focusing somewhere beyond the window. "It's an understanding. A connection. The soul is free. It *is* freedom, so whatever happens between beings is always in agreement between them at the soul level. This is merely one of those."

"One of *those*?"

"Agreements."

"I don't..." Carly shook her head. "Do you live in another world—one where you can hear these *agreements*?"

"It's there all the time, Carly, like an undercurrent, quietly going about the business of fulfilling the deepest intention you hold for your life. But you can't hear it by listening with your mind. Until you remember that you already know, I've found a great deal of faith is helpful."

"What you're saying seems...I'm sorry, it just sounds really crazy."

"I know." Wing touched his nose to the top of her head and breathed deeply. "With the Cant, weren't there moments when you just acted, you weren't thinking about the moves, they just came, naturally, perfectly, always at the right time?"

Carly felt her mind begin to open. "Yes, actually. Those moments are like…almost like a drug."

"Well, the healing of the men's wounds is a little like that, it just…happens. So, their healing should not be esteemed too highly, nor should their deaths. Remaining in the physical plane is far more difficult than letting it go. Condescending to flesh may be the greatest sacrifice of all."

A wane smile touched Carly's lips. "And I thought I was so close just now to finally understanding what you were talking about."

"I'm not trying to be inscrutable."

"I know," Carly replied. "I know you're trying to answer me."

She looked up into his eyes and as she did, felt him take in the very soul of her. The feeling was exquisite and unnerving and she could not remember a time ever feeling so naked or so loved. "I," she started to say, wondering if she should mention it at all, "I overheard the children—they talk of you as the Leader, the one of Legend. When you're not around they call you Merehr."

Concern clouded Wing's features.

Carly touched his arm. "Does it make you sad?"

"There's been so much going on since we brought the children down from the caves that I've probably let the most important things slip."

"Most important things—?"

Wing shook his head. "Nevermind." He placed his hands upon her shoulders, caressing her face with his eyes. "It's good to share a watch with you, but one of us should get some sleep."

Rising on her toes, Carly touched her lips to his and muttered, "You first."

Reluctantly retiring beside the fire, Wing found sleep elusive. His mind having worked itself deep into a field of worries, he set them aside and decided to meditate. He did not know how long he had been in his meditation when he felt a hand upon his side.

"Wing?"

Wing raised his head and looking over his shoulder saw Carly.

"What's wrong? You're shaking," she said softly.

Wing's eyebrows furrowed, he hadn't noticed. "I'm fine. Maybe a little cold."

Carly knelt down and began rubbing his arms.

"My watch?" he asked.

Carly shook her head. "You looked like you needed the rest. It's Nien's watch."

"Bad girl," Wing said quietly.

"Don't think me heroic, I had an ulterior motive."

Wing steadied his quivering limbs with a deep breath and reached out for her. As she'd covered both their watches, they could now sleep together. Carly lay out beside him, entwining her legs with his.

"Are you sure you're all right?" she asked.

"I'm fine." He could see Carly was unconvinced.

"I find you trembling and you tell me it's nothing?"

Though he ached to tell her, Wing could only look at her.

After a moment of studying his eyes, Carly relented. "Remember all that stuff you said about faith? Hold on. We've not come this far for nothing."

Wing nodded, but was unable to make her believe his sentiment.

"What is it?" she asked.

Wing raised his eyes. There were so many things he wanted to tell her. The regret of it pinched inside him briefly; he embraced it and let it go. All would be made clear soon enough.

"You're right," he said. "The important thing is what we're trying to do here, now. That's what matters."

Still, he could see that he was not fooling her. Concern was all over her features. He regretted doing that to her, that she could read him so well that he could not protect her, but he did not yet know how to explain what he was feeling, what he knew. For lack of any words that might suffice, Wing wrapped his arms about her, tucked his face into her shoulder and wished away all the things he saw, feared, and longed to share.

CHAPTER 86

We'll Keep You Safe

I n the deep of the twilit house, Wing lay in the Void. Since that night on the river when everything had changed, he'd been able to access it at will. Such a thing was easiest at night, in meditation. Riding the waves between worlds, he could take in the infinite paths of river and stream light that stretched across the vast ocean of black space. But during the day when he was needed in the physical world, he'd learned to balance the great emptiness with the world where Carly and the children lived, moving from one to the other and all the spaces in between whenever he chose. It was in this most functional place—a perfect union of everything and nothing—that Wing had come to direct his life.

On this night, however, Wing had let the physical world slip, returning to the emptiness of the Void.

He breathed slowly and deep, aware of the quiver in his lungs and the heavy beat of his heart against his ribs—things that were a part of him and yet not. Sunrise spilled in through a crack in one of the shutters and played about his partially covered chest. Every cell of his body was keenly aware of the calm before the storm. Resting in that peaceful place, he was briefly able to remove himself from the gnawing agony of what was to come.

And then a faraway cry touched the silence. Wing stepped out of the Void and heard the cry again. It sounded like the call of the great mountain bird...

But why would it be visiting the valley again?

And then Nien was at his side and as suddenly as silence breaks at the tip of a whip, Wing was on his feet and moving.

Carly was quick to join them. The three set to strapping on the leather body armour they had started to make in Legran and only recently finished. Tightening a wrist guard, Wing stepped to the window. In the distance, he saw them—Ka'ull—and so great was their number that the

496

length of fields between them and Melant was a moving sea of dark robes and glinting chainmail.

Engulfed by the sight, it was only by sheer force of will that Wing spun from the window in order to secure the door. Running into the main room, the wide, frightened eyes of Lily and Fe grabbed his attention. Sweeping them up in his arms, he carried them to the Mesko table the young men had situated into a corner the day before.

Kneeling before the table, Wing set their feet to the floor.

"Be brave, okay? And stay here. We're going to keep you safe."

Lily and Fe looked up at him.

"We love you. Don't worry," Wing said and touching their cool, smooth faces, motioned them under the table's broad back.

Clutching each other, they crawled to the far corner where the table snugged up against the side of one of the home's strong Mesko wood walls.

Wing returned to the back door and to Nien. By now Ka'ull riders were bearing down upon the house with the fury of a forest fire. The thunder of their galloping hooves caused the timbers of the house to shake.

Wing took a stance next to the door, and pressing his body hard against it, stole a glance around the room. At the other side he found Carly standing against the door leading out to the barn and shelters. Her eyes were already upon him. Their gazes held…

"Wing! They're here!"

Nien's shout took Wing, and he glanced back out the window. He could see them clearly now: the rough edges of their dark cloaks, the long whips of adorned leather that danced from the hilts of their swords, the hot breath from their winded steeds.

Wing looked back at his brother. Their eyes locked and suddenly they were back in the Mietan on that last training day; blue lightning crashing, voices crying from another realm, the hammering of their hearts filling the air like the steady roll of a gong. Wing's bright green eyes lit up like a storm—

This was the time; there would be no other.

In a spontaneous transference of sacred role, Wing touched Nien's mind.

Comprehension blasted a hole in Nien's heart and lit his soul on fire. The sureness of it made him gasp even as he tried to deny it—

"*No!*" tore from his throat, but his shout had not yet faded into the air when En't shouted, "They're upon the door!"

A jolt like that of a bull fell on the door and the brothers were thrown back, nearly knocked from their feet. Beside them, Wing's window shattered beneath the force of a sword hilt, and one of the children cried out.

Wing and Nien recovered and rushed back to the door, forcing it shut.

Again and again the Ka'ull beat against the door. Again and again, Wing and Nien recovered and secured it. But the heavy wood was beginning to crack. Soon there would be nothing to block their path.

With a single look, Wing and Nien abandoned the door. Stepping back, their eyes still on each other, they gave a united shout and charged. They hit the door as one, breaking through the buckling wood with such force that the men on the other side were thrown clear, one falling on the sword of another behind him.

Their cry, the crack of the wooden door, and the brothers' emergence on its other side caused the oncoming Ka'ull soldiers a moment's hesitation—

That was all the time Wing and Nien needed.

From behind the house and the sunsetting tree line, SiQQiy's soldiers had come out to meet the enemy. Soon the horrifying scream of wounded horses and the clash of blade on blade reverberated throughout the encircling mountains. The sky seemed to spin about sickeningly as bodies and blades flashed around and through each other, every man conscious only of his blade and the stinging vibrations each strike sent through his body.

Nien and Wing were quickly separated, traveling out across the field.

Wing did not feel the sword sing in his hand, nor did he feel any more of the fear he'd felt as the Ka'ull had battered down the door to his home. The numbers of Ka'ull versus Quienans was overwhelming. Impossible. But as he'd stepped down off the threshold of the house, new vision had taken over. He saw not only men in flesh, but also the matching counterpoint of their individual light signatures. The sight triggered something inside him and, as instinctually as if he were ducking the swing of a sword or unhitching a plow, Wing called out from the core of him: *Now, brothers!*

With the summons, Wing found himself taking in the valley from a raised vantage point. From every direction, as if walking out from behind veils of weather, warriors emerged—Quienan, Rieevan, and Ka'ull. Varying slightly in definition, they appeared to his eyes much like the platinum signatures of the mortals.

The Ancients, Wing thought.

Alongside the mortals, they began to fill Rieeve, a Ka'ull taking up the side of a Rieevan. A Rieevan the side of a Quienan. A Quienan the side of a Ka'ull. Not against each other or the mortals were they, but rather like wind or sun, their presence profound and unmistakable, without differentiation.

Many passed by Wing, catching his eye in recognition.

Without thought as to how, Wing was able to take them in even as he continued in the world of the mortal, moving the weight of his blade with no more effort than it would have taken to swat at leaves with a stick. In small shifts, as unconscious as blinking, the world remained impossibly fluid, Wing finding that he was able to take in otherwise unfathomable amounts of information effortlessly.

Like three others had before, another Ka'ull drew in upon Wing, brandishing his sword. Wing observed the length of glowing sword come near him and pass by, as if it were spun of pure light not flesh-rendering metal. He then watched the bright blade drop to the ground and its bearer vanish into the panorama of moving colour transversing the valley in ghostly streaks from end to end.

Wing's vision narrowed then, focusing once more within the bounds of the physical world. He gasped, inundated with a hurricane of energy that, in this realm, was both exquisite and excruciating. His temporal senses battered, Wing just only managed to duck beneath a circling sword. The soldier was unable to recover the force he'd put behind the strike and stumbled with it, falling, his body armour making a deep thud as he hit the ground—

But Wing only heard the soldier fall, for looking up, he saw two Ka'ull on horseback coming straight for him and suddenly he was back again, his senses expanding to take in both the world of flesh and spirit.

Since Legran, he'd been able to choose his access to it. Now, his control over it seemed to be growing thin.

Drawing up on his sword, Wing waited...

Beat, Beat, Beat.

Wing watched the two large horses sweeping to his left and right, like yellow phantoms of light moving through water.

At the perfect moment, he sidestepped.

The glowing beasts swam by—there was an exchange of energy as one man tumbled to the ground and the other, growling within the confines of his helmet, went to rein his horse about. But Wing had grabbed onto the saddle's pommel and swung up behind him. With a grunt of dismay, the Ka'ull attempted to knock Wing off only to find that he was already too far off balance himself. He hit the ground hard as Wing moved up into the saddle and, wheeling the horse around, sped back into the fray.

On the sunrising edge of the expanse between their home and what used to be the Village, Nien fought alongside SiQQiy's soldiers—but it was a losing battle. Even though they had managed to drive the Ka'ull away from Nien and Wing's home, they were horribly outnumbered. Like a sea churned from beneath by some invisible subterranean quake, the battle heaved to and fro, profound chaos moving in concert, pushing and retreating until Nien wondered if it were all a dream and at any moment he might wake up at SiQQiy's side in Legran, relieved to be beside her, thankful that those he loved were safe and warm...

But Nien had been here before, and he knew it was no dream. In the dark belly of an ancient castle he had fought this same battle—

And lost.

For a breath Nien's will flagged, and he stumbled, tripping over the body of a dead soldier.

Behind him one of SiQQiy's soldiers blocked a sword and engaged a Ka'ull whose intent had been to slay Nien from behind. Nien shook himself and turned in time to see the Ka'ull fall. SiQQiy's soldier nodded at him and moved ahead.

As adrenaline drove him back into action, Nien realized that, no, this battle was *not* the same.

Ducking beneath a sword, Nien dispatched a Ka'ull with a backward thrust and re-engaged. He had friends now; men from another valley were fighting alongside him. And somewhere in the tumult was his brother. As he strove ahead, he found comfort and resolve in that fact.

Briefly, he touched upon that space inside of him, the one he shared with Wing.

And the answer came—

All is well.

Imbued, Nien found clarity again.

Let's finish this, brother, he sent back, wishing even as he said it that Wing were at his side.

At the southingmost point of the battle, Wing continued to fight. The charger he'd acquired had taken a blow and thrown him. Adrenaline had run its course and liquid will alone kept him on his feet.

His sword nicked and bloodied, Wing parried a strike, came back up and broke his assailant's long double-edged blade. As the end of the sword toppled to the ground, Wing looked up and saw that the dark metal helmet had fallen from the Ka'ull's head. For the first time, Wing saw into the eyes of a Ka'ull. The Ka'ull himself had stopped, his hand still holding the hilt of his broken sword. For an awkward moment the two men stood face to face.

With the heat of their breath brushing the chilled Ime air, Wing looked deep into the man's eyes and asked, "Why are you here?"

Confusion flashed over the Ka'ull's face.

"Why are you here?" Wing said again, speaking in the Fultershier.

A subtle shift in the Ka'ull's face told Wing he understood.

"The belief that has carried you so far away from home," Wing said, "is not whole." Understanding, like the heat felt between lovers, moved out from Wing in a coruscating wave. "Such great hurt. Can it be healed with our deaths? Whatever you believe, whatever you were told, is but one side." Wing looked long on him. "I am sorry for what your people suffer."

And then, from the space between spaces, Wing spoke directly to the Ka'ull's mind—

Tem'a. Be the key.

Tem'a blinked. Amidst the great tumult taking place all around him, he became vaguely aware how suddenly far away it all seemed, as if the space in which he stood existed, somehow, on another plane.

But even as he tried to comprehend, time spun around him and he was back again.

He looked up at the tall Rieevan. He'd never seen such peace, such beauty on the face of a man before.

And then, from across the fields a cry rang out, a cry that somehow rose above all the other shouts of war.

Facing Wing, Tem'a saw, just over the Rieevan's left shoulder, a fellow soldier appear. He recognized him as Gren'tel. The last time they'd spoken was near the castle gates the day the Northing sub-Commander had come into camp.

Spirits of earth, he moaned inside his head. *What do I do?* But it seemed the Rieevan already knew.

Fully aware of the soldier coming up behind him, Wing slowly began to turn. He knew the man. He knew the moment.

No! Tem'a cried—the Rieevan was turning directly into the path of—but he couldn't open his mouth.

A sword drove deep between Wing's ribs.

Wing's own sword raised high and in the upheaval of snow and mud his feet became caught up. His body twisted and Gren'tel's blade slid free.

As if the very motion of the world had stopped, the sights and sounds of battle faded. For an instant and an eternity Wing saw Rieeve as he'd not seen it since his early days in the fields—resplendent, it edges covered in flowering plants of impossible colours, the grass a kind of green that could only be seen with different eyes, the air intoxicatingly fragrant.

Wing blinked and with his mortal eyes saw a flash of feathers and a fine spray of powdery snow from giant wings…

He sagged forward and fell.

Still holding his broken sword, Tem'a watched as Gren'tel, whose sword was covered to the hilt guard in the Rieevan's blood, stepped around Wing's body and began to run.

Dazed, Tem'a bent low and took up his helmet. Before him, Wing lay, his body quaking for a moment, and then falling still.

At the sides of the valley, from the trees in every direction, spilled a deluge of men and horses. A shout went up from the men at the southing end of the valley.

"Quieness!" one of SiQQiy's men called out. "The Seventh Granj is here! And" —the soldier paused— "the forces from Preak!"

Fresh for battle, the new forces charged in. Already in retreat, the dwindling line of Ka'ull was overwhelmed—but the men of the Seventh Granj and contingent of Preak warriors had only begun. They raced on, pursuing the main body of Ka'ull warriors back across the fields.

As her Seventh Granj sped off, SiQQiy saw three break away and ride back toward her. In the lead, she recognized Lead Netalf, on his heels came Leef and Vadet of her personal Guard. Relief flooded her.

"Empress," Netalf said, catching his breath and reining his horse in before her.

"Netalf," she said. "It is so *very* good to see you." She glanced up at Leef and Vadet. "All three of you."

Leef and Vadet bowed to her as another Hettha rode out from the conflict's sunrising flank, his exhausted mount struggling to maintain its master's call for speed.

Spotting SiQQiy, the Hettha shouted breathlessly, "We have word, Empress! Men from Jayak have come." Turning his horse, he pointed. "Look to the sunrising!"

In the far distance could be seen a glittering ocean of bright-coloured clothing and gleaming armour.

As they paused for a moment to watch, another scene fell upon their disbelieving eyes. Though not nearly so grand or ennobled as the first, this one was no less pleasing to their eyes: Coming in behind the army of Jayak were three large batteries of men dressed in rustic coats. They held long spears in their hands and carried bows upon their backs.

"Legran! Legran has come as well!"

A great shout went up from SiQQiy's men as they wheeled their mounts, and with renewed fervor, joined the other Granj battalions and the forces from Preak, driving the Ka'ull back to the opposite end of the valley and into the waiting armies from the sunrising valleys.

Amidst SiQQiy's soldiers Carly had appeared, her sword covered in the blood of a Ka'ull horse whose neck she'd slashed in the effort to dismount its rider.

Her breath coming hard, her eyes scanning the fields, she heard a strange warning cry. Was it the cry of a bird? Human? Had it come from the mountains, the valley, or someplace inside of her? Whirling to hunt out the source, she found that there were no other Ka'ull to engage as they fled in a great wave back toward the opposite end of the valley.

Stunned, she stood, watching them go.

Not knowing why, she made no move to join the fresh troops that had poured out of the surrounding mountains like a flood.

Turning away, she began to pick her way through the terrible wreckage of torn-up ground and cleaved bodies. Very few remained on their feet around her—any that could had already joined the chase.

Haunted by the strange cry, Carly began searching the fields—for what, she didn't know—until she spotted a tall man lying just to the northing of what had been the center of the battlefield.

Dropping her sword, Carly flew across the distance between herself and the man and fell to her knees at his side.

All the sounds of battle had faded from Wing's hearing when he felt knees bump up against his ribcage.

"Wing."

He turned his head as if looking in that direction but saw nothing, only felt the snow cold against his face.

Nevertheless, he knew—

Carly.

"Wing, Wing, ah, se'chna." She took his face in her hands. "You're still in there, you're still here…Look at me."

Wing's eyes slowly focused and he saw her; great wells of tears were forming in her eyes. As she slipped her hand beneath his head, one of her tears fell and splashed upon his cheek and then trickled its way to the corner of his mouth. Her hands were warm on his face. Her tear tasted salty. He longed to touch her. He moved his lips but could not speak.

"Stay with me," she said frantically, "stay with me."

And then the sound of pounding hooves drew near and Wing heard someone dismount.

"It's done," the voice announced. "The Seventh Granj, as well as forces from Preak, Jayak, and Legran are routing them."

They have come, Wing thought. *All of them have come. Together.*

Someone took his hand and said his name.

Wing looked up and saw—

Pree K.

On the periphery of his vision, another voice said, "Pree K, the children are..." The voice stopped abruptly.

Wing knew it as one in the midst of change: *Jhock.*

A hand touched his shoulder and Wing recognized the long-fingered, slender hand of En't.

The boy has a farmer's hands, he thought.

For a breath their grief-stricken voices caused Wing to wonder what he would have to do to comfort them, but he was slipping back and forth too quickly between worlds. It took a great amount of will to remain with one for longer than an instant.

"We need to get him inside," someone said, but as hands began to lift him another set of pounding hoofbeats drew in upon the gathering.

Wing heard the rider dismount.

Nien.

Spattered with blood, Nien's face twisted and he stumbled to his knees.

"Wing?—Wing!" Pushing everyone back except Carly, he began to fumble through Wing's clothing, attempting to get at the wound.

Reaching up, Wing captured Nien's trembling hand.

Nien tried to pull it away. "No, Wing," he said, "e'te. I'm just going to take a look, see how bad..."

Wing's grip tightened and he drew Nien's attention from the wound. Their eyes met. Wing slowly shook his head. "It's alright, Nien."

Nien inhaled sharply. He wanted, needed to protest, but his throat had closed off. Tears flooded his eyes and he blinked angrily, unwilling to lose sight of Wing's face for an instant.

"We thought we should get him inside," someone said, "—but."

Nien turned to see Lead Netalf of SiQQiy's Guard.

Wing's head reeled, his vision failed, and he slipped again from the realm of flesh. All was light. The infinite pressed through a moment. When Wing moved back into time, he'd lost sense of how much time had passed and where he was.

Nien? Where was his brother?

"Nien!"

Squeezing Wing's hand, Nien said, "Wing, I am here."

Following the thin trail of tactile sensation through the hand that held Nien's, Wing stabilized in his body. "The children?" he asked.

"They're safe."

Wing swallowed and nodded, but the relief that washed over him vanished as immediately as it had come—

"MEREHR!"

Like a snow-chilled blade, the pealing clarity of the cry broke upon the hearts and ears of all who heard it.

Nien's head jerked up. Standing not far off, he saw Lily. Her eyes were fixed on Wing. Her small boots were wet with snow. Her fists were clenched.

Her female-child scream had pinched the gathering into silence—

But Wing's reaction to her cry shook Rieeve itself.

Racked by Lily's cry, Wing's back arched.

Beneath Nien and Carly's knees, beneath the feet of those gathered around, the earth began to shift. Armour rattled, startled eyes widened, hands reached out finding only the friend or soldier beside them to cling to.

And at the other end of the valley, Castle Viyer trembled and coughed. A stone slipped here. Another slipped there.

Wing convulsed again.

The valley convulsed with him.

And then the small tremors ceased, giving over to something larger. Like an ocean wave, the valley floor rolled beneath their feet. Those still standing hit their knees. The tremor moved on until reaching the steps of the Cawutt home where it seemed to reach its end, dissipating and sinking back into nothing.

On the opposite side of the valley, the trickling sound of cascading gravel from Castle Viyer filled the air. Then stopped. The great structure paused.

Wing's tall frame seized upon the grievous hole in his chest for an endless moment, then released him.

As Wing came to rest, the ground quieted, those gathered around clamoured back to their feet, and at the northing side of the valley Castle Viyer's mighty stone walls settled, cracked, slid, and with a thunder that shook the mountains collapsed in an avalanche of stone, mortar, and splintering wood.

Up in the Mesko forest the roots of one of the great trees contracted mightily, as if gripping the earth with a giant hand. The earth quivered in its grasp, waiting. When the roots released, the great Mesko split and broke in two. Its sundering report intersected with the rolling boom pushing down the valley from the tumbling walls of Castle Viyer at the point where a veil of warriors stood round a dying farmer.

Still at Wing's side, Nien understood perfectly what had happened, intimately aware of the interplay between Wing and Rieeve. But now, he only saw that his brother lay unmoving. He gasped Wing's name and with both his hands pressed Wing's hand, as if the hand's familiar reality could make true his denial—

"Wing, wait. *Don't*."

With terrible effort, Wing willed himself to speak. "Nien."

"Wing, I'm still here."

Wing coughed and caught his breath. "Ne teka' dey, Nien. They don't remember. Remind them."

"I don't remember, either!" Nien cried, the words tearing from him.

Wing drew upon his connection with Nien, allowing himself, one last time, to embrace the exquisite pain of his body in order to clearly see his brother's face.

As calm rested over Wing, the radiant, inescapable purity of his tone bathed Nien's riving heart: "The clearing in the Mesko forest, Nien. Look!"

Nien found himself back in the Mesko clearing—but it was unlike any-place he had ever seen. It was dazzling. Radiant in colours Nien had never seen before, brighter than a sun and yet it did not hurt his eyes.

"You are always there," Wing said.

Nien blinked and found himself back in the valley; but even it was different now. The season was not Ime but early Kive; however, this Kive was unlike any Nien had ever seen. It was alive, lush. He knelt not in snow and blood but grass soft and tall, so heavy with green he could smell it.

"Just *remember*," Wing said.

Nien looked back down at Wing. His brother lay in tall grass, not snow, but he was still dying. "No, Wing, I don't. I can't hold it. I'll never be able to—"

"It will be enough," Wing said, and his eyes were clear, kind.

Nien drew Wing's hand to his lips, blinked back tears, fixed his eyes upon Wing's face. Wing's eyes held.

It's alright, Nien.

No, Nien cried.

Trust me, Wing said.

I do. But please don't...

Wing shuddered and closed his eyes.

Nien choked on a cry. Something inside him ruptured. In his mouth he tasted blood and tears. Reflexively, he grabbed Wing up in his arms, holding him to his chest in disbelief.

Easily, Wing's head came to rest on Nien's shoulder.

Garroted, suspended, Nien was drowning. Thrusting his face into Wing's shoulder, he felt Wing's chest expand once more, suffusing both of them with indescribable warmth. Though slight, Nien was keenly aware of the last beat of Wing's heart as his energy burst in an unseeable but magnificent flare, pulsing through Nien and out into the space beyond.

From the northing to the southing, from the Mesko forest to the lone-standing Cawutt home the valley burned briefly with incandescent light. It shivered then. Fell still.

Opposite Nien, on Wing's right side, Carly knelt, knees pressed deep into the snow, head down, her hair concealing her face.

From the Cawutt home in the near distance, Fe and Hagen emerged, their feet moving lightly through the snow as they approached the huddled throng. Pree K was the first to notice them. He felt the jolt of adrenaline that shoved his feet forward to stop them, but it was too late. They'd already seen.

The arrival of Fe and Hagen brought Nien's head up. He looked over their tender faces finding himself back in the world of Rieeve as he'd left it: beloved faces consumed in disbelief; snow, cold, mud, blood, bodies.

Bowing over him, Nien carefully laid Wing's head back to the snow. Blood from Wing's wound had spilled down his side and fallen drop by drop to the snow-covered ground. Upon the darkening patch, Nien's eyes briefly focused. Taking an impossible breath, he closed his eyes and with an effort not unlike raising a mountain, got to his feet.

Still as tree trunks, their eyes wide and filled with tears, the children waited for Nien. He approached them slowly. Bending down, he took Hagen up in his arms. The stump of Hagen's arm pressed against Nien's chest as Nien looked down at Fe's wide-eyed gaze.

"Merehr is gone," he said.

Fe moved a little past Nien, staring intently at Wing. En't stepped to his little sister and picked her up.

"Does it hurt?" Hagen asked, his eyes fixed on the wound in Wing's chest.

"No, Hagen, it does not."

And then Lily pressed in through the ring of soldiers. The gathering held their collective breath. Her eyes passed from Wing and turned upon the armor-clad gathering of adult warriors. With indignation and rage, she shouted at them: "We've only just found him. You can't take him!" Receiving only astonished silence in reply, Lily tore her scathing challenge from them and turned it on Wing. "Come back!"

Wing's silence was unendurable.

Rushing forward, she fell at his side and dug her long, child-thin fingers into his shoulder. The ferocity with which she shook Wing's body caused a handful of warriors to look away.

Jhock, the only one of the adults seemingly unafraid of her, or perhaps capable of moving his feet, stepped up and kneeling beside her, took her quivering shoulders into his hands. Slowly, he stood her up and turned her around so that she was facing him.

Surprisingly, she did not fight Jhock as he lifted her into his arms.

From across the fields, through the battlefield, came three figures. All three were dressed in the rustic clothing of Legran: one straight and strong, another slightly bent with long greying hair, and another much younger than the other two, his cheeks flushed with the adrenaline of first battle. Led by the stooped one, they approached the odd and silent gathering.

Lead Netalf and SiQQiy turned at their approach. The look on SiQQiy's face stopped the three men in their tracks.

"SiQQiy?"

She stepped into the arms of the tallest of the three. "Monteray," she breathed.

Call moved forward a little, followed by Rhegal. In the midst of the short circle of men and children lay a tall figure with short black hair.

As if acting upon a silent wish, the crowd closed in around Nien and Carly.

Monteray stepped up to Call's side as Rhegal slowly set aside his old walking stick and removed the bow from his back.

Pree K, En't, and Jhock stood together with the children.

SiQQiy was nearby and at her side, Omaly and Netalf.

White breath from the surrounding company filled the air. Only from Wing's still body could no breath be seen lilting upon the cold light of Ime.

CHAPTER 87

What Lies Beneath Lives Above

Beneath snow, beneath the unbreathing weight of the dead, Rieeve lay in stillness.

At the southing end of the valley the only remnants of battle was that of blood and torn up earth. The stately Cawutt home stood undamaged with the exception of the back door and the small window beside it.

At the northing end of the valley the vestiges of war were far more significant.

Viyer lay in ruins. The earth had opened up and swallowed not only great chunks of the castle but also the two innermost rows of burnt homes in the Village, plunging them like so many dark skeletons into the quake's gaping crevasse.

Those Ka'ull still physically able had run, and been pursued back toward the castle as the arriving troops from Jayak and Legran converged on the burned Village and Viyer. A few hundred had escaped, but more than three fourths of the Ka'ull army lay behind, dead or dying, most killed by the combined armies, others by the shaking of the earth. Those that had survived both these powers and escaped into the northing mountains would not get by the forces from Jayak and Quieness awaiting them in the Ti-Uki Confluence. Supplies, horses, weapons; all but what they had in their hands was left behind—and Nien wanted none of it.

"Whatever the conjoining armies from the other valleys want," he had said, "they can take."

Though most of SiQQiy's forces had already begun arranging their gear and contingents for the trip back to Quieness, a few volunteered to stay behind and help with the rebuilding of Rieeve.

In the silence of the main room in the large Cawutt home, Nien came up behind Rhegal. The children had finally fallen to sleep. Carly lay on the floor among them, SiQQiy sitting with her, cradling her head in her lap.

"If you will," Nien said quietly.

Rhegal followed Nien into the bedroom at the back. There, on the bed in the far corner, lay a long figure, wrapped tightly in teeana-leaf bed sheets.

"Will you help me prepare the body?" Nien asked.

Rhegal nodded his head.

Reaching out, Nien's hand shook as he withdrew the teeana sheet from Wing's face.

Beside him, Rhegal whispered hoarsely, "Yosha," as if the sight of Wing's face had literally taken his breath away. "I bring him in, I patch him up—twice. He'd wanted to die back then; he had everything to live for now." Silence fell briefly. Nien could hear Rhegal's throat working reluctantly. "It was supposed to be me."

Nien glanced at Rhegal. The old man's grey eyes were studying the outline of the man beneath the teeana sheets as if it were a seer stone.

"He came," Rhegal said, and it seemed to Nien that the old man had forgotten he was there. "Merehr finally came. So why am I still here?"

Nien made no reply—Rhegal had not been asking him.

Picking up the end of the length of sheet wrapped about Wing's feet, Nien held it out to Rhegal. The old man cleared his throat, took the wrap, and the two men began their work.

Some time passed in the progression of their solemn task before Rhegal said, "Do you know that I dreamed about meeting him as a child?"

"I think he wondered why you disliked him so," Nien replied, his voice sounding softly in the darkness.

"It was not him I disliked but myself," Rhegal said slowly. "I'd hoped that he'd figured that out."

"He probably did. Most of what he knew he could not tell."

"Those turns in the mountains, when he came to me for help, when he looked to me to be the teacher, I was, in fact, the student. My pride and fear kept me from telling him."

"He would not want you to regret."

Rhegal sighed. "From him, from our people—I've stopped hoping for forgiveness."

Nien was quiet for a moment, before replying, "Only forgive yourself. There is no need for more."

As they finished their preparation, Nien held the end of the new sheet that would cover Wing's face.

This time, it was Rhegal that had to help Nien continue. Wordlessly, he lifted Wing's head, waiting for Nien to make the final wrap.

After another moment, Nien wound and together they tucked the end of the teeana sheet behind Wing's head.

"Take the bed upstairs," Nien said. "I'm going to stay down here for a while."

Rhegal left Nien alone in the room.

Late the following morning, a messenger from one of the Jayakan units arrived at the Cawutt home.

"Commander Cawutt—the bodies," the messenger said tiredly.

Nien nodded heavily, and donning a thick cloak, stepped out the door with the messenger.

In a state far outreaching mere exhaustion, Nien and the Jayakan messenger arrived within sight of what remained of Castle Viyer. There Nien stopped and stood, looking down a seemingly endless line of Ka'ull dead.

Monteray, Netalf, SiQQiy, Rhegal, and the leader of the Jayakan forces had also arrived and come to stand at his side.

"We could dig pits. We could burn them," Oiita, the Jayakan commander, suggested.

It seemed Nien fought some inner battle, as if he were listening not only to the Jayakan Commander but also to a voice no one else could hear.

"Monteray, do you know what the burial rites or rituals of the Ka'ull are?"

"They cremate their dead," Monteray replied. "But there are specific rituals and these I do not know well enough to perform."

Without raising his eyes, Nien said, "Netalf, do we have any captives nearby?"

"Yes."

"Bring one of them here to me."

His eyes still fixed upon the unfathomable sight before him, it took Nien a moment to realize Netalf had returned, leading a Ka'ull soldier along by the elbow, the soldier's arms bound behind him at the wrists.

"Here is one who understands the Fultershier," Netalf said to Nien, "—or at least is willing to speak in it."

Nien looked into the man's eyes and was struck by what he saw there. He'd expected to see pain, hatred, fear. What he saw instead was an intense sadness, entirely devoid of animosity.

"What is your name?" Nien asked.

"Tem'a," the captive answered.

"Your dead," Nien said. "There is a ritual, yes? That you observe in their burial?"

Tem'a nodded. "There is."

"What is it?"

"Under Ka' skies, they burn. To Ka' skies go the dead: life, ash, the dead, to be born again."

"Under *Ka'* skies?" Nien asked.

Tem'a nodded and they understood one another.

Quizzically, SiQQiy and Oiita looked to Nien.

"The burning of their dead must be performed under Ka'ull sky. In their own land," Nien said. He turned back to Tem'a. "You must see that this cannot be accomplished."

Something flashed in Tem'a's eyes. It could have been anger—or desperation. But in the end there was only an undeniable acceptance of what had to be, a soulful cognizance that took Nien off guard and somehow, incredibly, touched him.

This man could have killed Wing, he thought. *And he's Ka'ull.*

So why did he not hate him?

With weariness dragging at Nien's very soul, he said: "We will burn your dead, here, in Rieeve. They will ascend to Rieevan skies, and if they don't find it to their liking then they can make their way to the Northing on their own accord."

For a long moment the Preak-born Rieevan and the soldier of the Ka'ull held one another's gazes. Brown eyes flaked with honey and deep blue eyes of warm Kive rain begged to find understanding in the wreck and stench that filled their senses.

Was this the beginning or the end? Where would both their people go from here?

"I can perform the rituals; I can guide them—if you will permit it," Tem'a said, his voice thin as frost on a blade of grass.

Nien nodded his head to him. "You may perform whatever rituals you need." Nien paused then and glancing over his shoulder toward the far end of the valley imagined the log home and the tall figure wrapped in teeana cloth that lay within. "And I shall attend to mine."

He met Tem'a's eyes once more, and with a deep breath that it pained him to take, turned away and with SiQQiy by his side agreed to meet Monteray, Rhegal, and Netalf back at his home later that evening.

With the wine drunk and the adults dispersing, Nien retreated once again into the back room of the house. He stood alone, facing out the back window toward the Village side of the valley. He'd removed the makeshift shutter, letting the night's cold air and light flow in upon his face and chest. Soon, only the varied breathing patterns of the children sounded from the dark in the main room behind him. He didn't hear Carly come in until she was already at his side.

"Where's SiQQiy?" she asked.

"Asleep," Nien replied.

Carly looked out the window as well. "It's so peaceful now."

Nien agreed silently, asking, "How are the children?"

"They're having a hard time. They don't understand about Wing" —Carly paused— "Merehr. They won't call him Wing. Lily slept on the floor next to the Cove door last night."

Nien glanced over at her. As sheltered space more than a tent was desperately needed, and as Nien could not bear another night in the room with the reminder of what was *not* there, he had carried Wing's body up into the small room opposite the large upstairs bedroom. The little window to the little room was open, the door closed, keeping it as cold as possible. No one had ever used the space much, it being too short and shallow for any grown up to stand up straight in. In their younger revolutions, Nien and Wing, and then Jake and Fey had used the room as a child-lair for dreaming, scheming, star traveling. It was as near and as far and as perfect a place as Nien could think of to rest Wing until tomorrow.

"They don't understand how he could be gone," Carly said. "Especially now. And I...I don't understand either. I don't know if he was or wasn't." In her confession, Nien could hear the humiliation she felt. "I look in their eyes and I'm sure they can see right through me." As if searching for an answer somewhere in the darkness outside the window, Carly said, "How can their faith be greater than mine? When I loved him so much, how could I not have known?"

"I asked him," Nien said sympathetically. "One night in the cabin in Legran, I asked him if he *was* Merehr. He said yes. He also said that I was, that you are—that all of us are."

"Typical," Carly whispered. "Entirely unhelpful."

"Some things are very difficult to unlearn," Nien said. "We, like the children, see the world as this or that: either he was Merehr or he wasn't. But Wing saw everything as both—all one thing. The children heard their parents refer to Wing as Merehr for so long. There were times I wondered myself. But he was also my brother, you know? He had always been there and I believed he always would be. I could never imagine it otherwise." Nien's eyes hunted the landscape outside the window. "I see now that those feelings kept me from asking other, more important questions."

A ponderous silence passed and Nien shook his head as if to dislodge the terrible burden of the realization.

"Yet even Wing saw the prophets and poets of the Writings as people simply trying to describe an indescribable experience. He never liked the idea of one man speaking for Eosha."

"You don't, either," Carly said.

Though Nien had always been more secularly and less ethereally minded than Wing, he found he could not keep the lightest nor the deepest feelings of family and race wholly separate. "I guess not," he said, and drew a shuddering breath. "Did those ancient prophets have husbands, wives, children?" Nien stopped a beat before saying, "Brothers? We hear so little about them. If they were anything like Wing they must have. How could they have kept their hearts from it?"

Carly could only nod.

"I miss him," Nien said.

Carly placed her hand on his arm. Nien placed his hand over hers. She and Wing had been together as husband and wife only a few short turns.

"How can I say how much I hurt when I look at you?" Nien asked.

"I loved him more than I ever thought I could love anyone, but the two of you—you shared the same heart for all your lives." She stroked Nien's face with her fingertips.

Carly's touch thinned the binds of Nien's emotions. "I washed his blood out of my cloak," he said, "as if it had only been from a cut on his knee."

Tears fell silently down Carly's cheeks.

Nien glanced up at the rafters overhead. "He left us with everything he'd ever wanted to give us. There is a roof over our heads, food in our stomachs, and those—" Nien nodded to the three leather-clad books that lay on the large Mesko table. He closed his eyes as a shard of pain shifted in his chest. "He knew," Nien tried to say, his voice so strained he could barely speak. "Did I tell you that? He looked at me before the Ka'ull broke down the back door. I can't tell you how, but he told me in that look. He said goodbye."

"I think he did more than that," Carly said quietly. "I think he knew that you are the one—the one to fix all this. To heal our continent."

To hear the normally pragmatic Carly say the same thing to him as Wing had that day in the Mesko clearing cut Nien off from words.

Useless, pointless words, he thought.

Thus unable to respond, Nien pressed his side against Carly and they stood together staring out Wing's window. And in the room behind them the children lay in slumber and outside the glimmering snow and distant stars seemed to work against the sadness, breathing comfort in their own particular language, as if each star over Rieeve, each snow crystal upon its valley floor, somehow shared Wing's voice—*was* his voice—and for a moment Nien saw the valley again as Wing had shown it to him even as he lay dying.

I know what you're trying to do, Nien thought, *and I appreciate the effort. But right now I want to miss you. More than anything I want you to walk through that door and come stand next to me.*

Right now, I just want you back.

CHAPTER 88

SoulBond

Wing's had been the only grave dug in the cold, hard ground of Ime. Casualties other than the Ka'ull had been carefully wrapped and prepared to be returned to their own lands for burial.

Now, in the midst of the Cawutt fields, a large crowd had gathered. Amongst them were the children and Rhegal, as well as the older boys: Pree K, Call, Jhock, and En't. Monteray was there as well, standing next to SiQQiy and members of her personal Guard.

The air was thin and cold as Carly and Nien stood at the edge of the gently curved mound of freshly packed soil. Carly pulled Wing's long leather coat tight around her body. Her sword belt hung about her waist, but the sword was not in its scabbard.

Nien faced the solemn, longing crowd. He spoke briefly in the Fultershier, but his strength for any sort of formal blessing failed and he simply stopped speaking. It seemed that the blessing, along with nearly every other thing traditionally Rieevan, had vanished.

Turning, at the mound's muddied edges Nien knelt.

In a voice quiet and bereft, Nien buried his fist into the black soil and slipped beyond the presence of the others and into that space inhabited by he and his brother alone.

"You were always a little ahead of me—so I hope you'll forgive me this once for complaining about your timing." Nien gazed down at the mound of deep black dirt and fallen snow. "That day, before the world fell, before we rushed the door together, I knew what it was you did and for the first time I wanted to deny you—but there was no time.

"So now. *Now.* How do I carry this sacred trust? You taught me that we are not alone, but I cannot tell you how alone I feel. What you left to me, what you gave to me, is a gift more than the world, but it doesn't help. I've never felt so lost. I'm stuck here in the dirt."

Carly's body shook with a silent sob as Nien withdrew his hand, black bits of earth clinging upon his black skin as he straightened and raised his face.

With a little more strength, Nien spoke again, and though most of those gathered could understand nothing of Rieevan, the sound of his voice and the melody of the words transcended the barrier and allowed them entrance to the world that Nien had once known only with his brother.

"Wing Merehr. E fle' me te no'va'nen. E te ne fle' ka no-ba'nin. U te'ka de. Ne teka' dey. Fu sche'na de la'nuta feal. Ke lata-na. Uoo fey-lapka dey. Melaan de mee'ta le. Me lanta me do ley. Speeall, schre'na pe low. Tuv'le pu na-te da. Fellan, lee'tan, Melaan..."

Shoving his hand into his pocket, Nien withdrew a small figurine and placed it atop the black dirt. "E te Melaan to'de. Y metta la to-dey."

Nien stood then, took Carly's hand, and as the crowd slowly began to part, Call stepped up to the black mound and took in the delicate carving that lay upon it. It was of two figures, perfectly and meticulously detailed, a striking blend of light and dark wood wound together in a featureless embrace.

Though Call had not seen it thus completed, he recognized the bit of wood that Nien had often carried with him in Legran. Looking down at it, Call felt an influx of words in Rieevan, Legrand, and Fultershier, a yearning to pen everything he could remember of what Nien had said, of everything that had happened since he'd first been approached by a tall, black-haired men outside of the Hiona in Legran.

Over the following busy turns Call wrote as much as he could, even recording the words Nien had said over the grave in Rieevan; nevertheless, it was still some while before he understood the words he had written.

From the Chronicles of Rieeve. Volume I. Revolution 802. Originally recorded in Rieevan by Call of Legran. Supreme Commander Nien Cawutt's farewell to Son Wing-Cawutt Merehr.
(Translation an approximation only)

Revolution 800. Turn 10. Day Seven.

"Wing Merehr. In words unspoken and a time forgotten, come and move over me like fields of silent angels. Like starlight, like white night, younger brother, you are the spirit of this place—before it was and after we will be.

Beneath glowing moon and sun's reflection, Rieevan Soul, I feel you here in a space between. This sacred trust will hold me together—forever. From here to where you are."

Pause for Serenity

"At last!" Kate waved her arms and hurried across the short stretch of grass to the riverside. Monteray came behind her, and the couple met SiQQiy and Nien with open arms, smiles, and Kate's tears.

Between Kate and Nien a few quiet moments passed before Monteray broke the silence, and taking Nien by the arm asked, "So what about my old friend, Rhegal? How is he?"

"He's living in the Village—New Melant," Nien answered. "The children pester him constantly. He purports agitation, but I think he enjoys it."

"And my nephew? Has he put in for honorary Rieevan citizenship?"

Nien smiled. "He may have. At this time he's integral to the rebuilding of the Cant. But I can see him returning someday to Legran. Now that your own forces are coming together, you may want him back sooner."

"I already do. And the two of you? How is your time spent between valleys? Do the Quienans think they have been abandoned by their Empress?"

SiQQiy nodded. "I have to give my full name anymore to get into my own palace."

"I'm sending her back soon," Nien said. "It will do none of us any good if Quieness falls apart."

"And you, Nien," Monteray asked, "what do you intend to do?"

Nien sighed lightly. "Eventually, I would like to turn the Cant over to Pree K and the school to Rhegal…"

"And retire in style to Quienan palace domes?"

SiQQiy touched Nien's face. "I don't know how long he'd be able to cope with such luxurious surroundings, with having every need met."

"I might give it a try for a while." Nien grinned, and then his voice took on a more serious tone. "But there is still much work to be done in Rieeve."

"And I don't imagine it will be too long before the new alliance begins knocking on your door regarding Tou and Lou," Monteray said.

"It weighs on all our minds," Nien admitted. He looked at Monteray. "As head of that alliance, might that be you at my door?"

"Possibly, but only because you passed it up."

Nien bowed his head. "That original decision was made out of sentimentality, not sense. I'm grateful to you for accepting. We each have our work to do."

"And Carly? I understand from Call's last visit that young Jayson-Wing is doing well."

"He is, and walking already. I think Carly may come along on our next visit and bring him to meet you."

Kate was radiant. "It would be wonderful to have a child in the house again."

"Come," Monteray offered with a wave of his hand. "Let's eat."

"Are you sure you don't want me to come with you?"

Nien nodded. "I'm sure. I won't be long." Nien gave her a quick kiss and walked out the door after dinner.

SiQQiy watched him go, knowing where he was going and why he wanted to go alone.

Nien strode through the long grass down to the river. The stars were coming out one by one creating a vast, fine blanket of glimmering reflections, like stones caught in the sunlight of an endless heavenly stream. The breeze off the river rustled the sleeves of his shirt as he stopped at the river's edge. Even in the silence of the night he could barely hear the sound of the water. Reaching inside his shirt, he withdrew a single thin scroll of Mesko paper. He'd found it a few turns after the battle, tucked away in a corner of his brother's transcription ledger. Carefully, he unrolled it. By now he knew every word of it, but carried it with him anyway. Like a mother's song whispered to a sleepy child, he let it play through his mind. He could even hear Wing's voice in his head as he read...

To the children: You have come a long way and have already endured more than most should in a lifetime.

Your hearts are good, the path they lead you on will forever change the future of our world.

Learn all that you can, in everything that you do and in everything that happens to you.

Most importantly, know that you are not alone. Though I cannot tell you that you will never feel alone again, I can only tell you that you are not— nor ever will be.

To Carly: Love is such a strange word. Overused and underrated, it is still what we are left with to try and describe the indescribable.

You told me once that you would always be there, and you have been. You never lost faith.

I have laid my heart in your hands...Thank you.

And Nien.

Emotion gripped Nien's throat.

Oft times I have wondered: In that great expanse of time and space, in those previous worlds, what did I do to be here in this place, at this time, with you as mortal brother?

I want to grow old together. I want to know that in revolutions to come we will sit down together in front of a warm fire. And in that sacred place I will ramble and you will whittle, and we will talk of your star calculations and my harvest season, and our grandchildren will interrupt us, and our wives will scold us...But I will continue to ramble and you will continue to whittle until the fire has dwindled to coals and the moon is high over the Mesko forest.

I love you, my brother, my comrade, evening shade of my soul.

Holding the fragile paper in his hand, Nien stood quietly for a long time, still as the night air. In his mind, he could see that image of Wing, their last day in Legran together, as his brother had stood mirrored against river and mountain. Just as he carried the letter in his long coat, Nien had carried that picture of Wing.

From upriver a cold breeze blew. Shivering, Nien pulled his cloak close and turned back toward the house. Moving up the gentle incline he glanced over his shoulder and felt...

A grin tipped his mouth.

"Don't stay up too late, Weed Farmer," Nien said quietly. "I'm going in."

Nien continued on up to the house, comforted that Wing had not yet made a permanent move to one of those higher worlds.

Just for a little while longer, Nien thought.

He and Monteray could handle preparations for the fortification of the valleys, as well as the liberation of Tou and Lou, but there were many questions Nien had that had nothing to do with the mean practicalities of war, questions that only one person he'd ever known could answer.

Listening to the sound of his feet brushing through the tall grass, a stream of pale light caught his attention. Glancing up, Nien saw that the white, transparent curtains hanging in the window on the second floor of the house were lit by the soft yellow glow of lamplight from within.

Smiling to himself, Nien quickened his pace.

SiQQiy was waiting for him.

THE END

Special thanks—

In the beginning: to Joe Maki who first said to truly be it, you must say it.

All the years in between: my Mom who stayed up all night to type the first version of Merehr twenty two years ago and for all the support since then that only a mother could give. Chad, for effortless understanding (you know where I'd be without it). And to SPA: soul mate, champion, ever-believer and brilliant navigator. Sometimes all you need is one simple thing.

Lately: to Shawn and Lara for letting me live in their minivan. Riley, for letting me whine. Krista, for reading the crap version, repeatedly, which encourages me more than I can say. And Chad and Riley, for last minute edit help—thanks for giving me someone else to blame when it comes out and I find a really annoying typo.

I would also be amiss not to mention the coffee shops and baristas that have graciously housed this itinerant writer over the past three years. There have been many from coast to coast, but steadfastly are those few in SLC, UT—Cocoa Café, Two Creeks Café, and the Blue Star Café, all of whom graciously let me use hours and hours of wifi and table space without ever a grumble or a pass code.

A most heartfelt: Thanks.

Appendix:
Map
Layout
Who's Who and Where They Are
Pronunciation Guide
Complete Come Home (Yullalpa) lyric
Prophet-Poet Eneefa verse

Layout

Leer revolution=416 days
Leer season=17 turns
Leer turn= 8 days
Leer seasons common=Fon (Cool) Nom (Hot) Mof (Warm)
Rieeve seasonal names=Ime (Rest) Kive (Plant) Kojko (Harvest)
Leer direction=Northing (Fou), Southing (Opf), Sunrising (Tuw), Sunsetting (Vuw)
Note: On Leer, the sun rises in the west and sets in the east.

Who's Who and Where They Are

In Rieeve:

The Cawutt Family

Joash and Reean
Wing
Nien
Jake
Fey

Ce'Mandu Family

Commander Lant
Pree K

Cant Leaders
Nien
Carly
Mien'k
Shiela
Teru
Reel
Bredo

Rieevan Council
Spokesman Grek Occoju
Commander Lant
Brauth Vanc
Sk'i Yinut
Fu Breeal (wife-Leeal Breeal)
Moer Ta'leer
Ne'taan
Brap Cuiku
Tael Ruke

Joash Cawutt, the Mesko Tender (honorary member)

Cave Survivors
Pree K Ce'Mandu
Jhock Fen'la
Lily Tren'da
En't Occoju
Fe Occoju
Hagen Yyota

In Legran:

The Monterays
Master Monteray
Kate
Tei

Monteray's Sister's sons
Jason
Call

Troy Naterey—leader of the Legran militia

In The Mountains:
Rhusta/Rhegal

Quieness (Palaces):
Empress SiQQiy
Jenta (SiQQiy's Coadjutant)

SiQQiy's Personal Guard
Lead Guard Netalf
Leef Keppik
Terro Tellah
Vadet Tien
Leit
Hilloy—stable manager at the Royal Palaces

In Cao City
Necassa (Librarian in Great Library, Cao City)
Mshavka (Telepathic waitress, Cao City)

Granj Soldiers (mentioned)
Jerra
Omaly (Rider)

Jayak:
Impreo Takayo

Jiatak, the Kiutu (Minister of affairs to Impreo Takayo)
Jiap (Nien saved his life in the first Jayakan battle against the Ka'ull. Jiap and his family aided Carly after Ime Night)

Ka'ull
Tem'a (soldier with supply regiment, poet, and unofficial camp psychologist)
Ketall (Commander of the Ka'ull Mat'ta and Tenkt'tla-shocktroops)
Gren'tel (soldier with Rieeve occupation forces)

Mentioned:
Lyrik—Reean's great ancestor
Neda Ten—A provincial governor of the valley of Preak

Pronunciation guide
Me •rehr (meh rare)
Ni •en (nee uhn)
Si •QQiy (sigh key)
Ta •ka •yo (tuh kigh oh)
Ka' •ull (kah ool)
Mon •te •ray (mahn tuh ray)
Tem• a (teh mah)

Places
Ri •eeve (rye eave)
Qui •e •ness (key eh nuss)
Jay •ak (jigh ack)
Castle Viy •er (vigh yair)

Yullalpa song
Tai mai cavana
I fla to veeahl
Ma ta ma ta novahm

A veerta flee-ehn teeana
I pohdre Vasteel a mear hottovonee
Ma ta ma ta novahm
I Mesko
A freasente yullalpa
I fa tendehre a medthre vencentt
Ma ta ma ta novahm
Seegente tepedthre veelan
A leetal's en myen-nehl
Ma ta ma ta novahmin

To great mountains
And lavender sky
Come come home
To sweet fields of teeana
To mighty castle and warm cobblestone
Come come home
To Mesko
And fragrant herb
To lonely father and worried mother
Come come home
Follow weary feet
And heart's first prayer
Come come home

Prophet-Poet Eneefa. Ancient Writings. Book Seven.

E fe de lebaan'a tuvle
Melaan y teh'ta e cansa ma'n
Pesanta telaa
Ne'lanka uoo e emm'rtal louu
E gret'a tu entar
I me te dona'then
Se meeta ru neta
I sc'en ta too
Melaan, I jeik-a' et te luua
A bonndo' ne
E f'le
E to'ne

Sce'ken te mafa'la
Melaan, e scoka le e do'ur.

Why did we forget?
—was that part of the crime?
To leave devotion out in the cold
—just a beggar at the door?
Despised and left
—thrown down from higher worlds
A scant tug on the sleeve
—forgotten
Abandoned to note
—And line
—And word
Scratching like a thief
Just a beggar at the door.

He stood in a small valley tucked between two immense mountain ranges, cradled like a loved thing. A Kojko leaf fell from a tree nearby and drifted to his feet. About him there was a stillness, all-encompassing and close, suspended in a world far beyond this one—but quite real.

That was the memory that started all this. It's been an amazing ride slowly remembering them, their world, and trying to write it all down.

SMC

Now that we've met, please feel free to visit me on the website:
www.merehr.com

Lightning Source UK Ltd.
Milton Keynes UK
05 July 2010
156561UK00002B/21/P